MORRIS AUTOMATED INFORMATION NETWORK

0 1029 06430

W9-BZI-482

Parsippany-Troy Hills Library
Main Library
449 Halsey RD
Parsippany NJ 07054
973-887-5150

AUG 0 5 2014

Also by Richard House

BRUISER

UNINVITED

THE KILLS

THE KILLS

SUTLER,
THE MASSIVE,
THE KILL,
AND
THE HIT

RICHARD
HOUSE

PICADOR
———
NEW YORK

This is a work of fiction. All of the characters, organizations,
and events portrayed in this novel are either products of the author's
imagination or are used fictitiously.

THE KILLS. Copyright © 2013 by Richard House. All rights reserved.
Printed in the United States of America. For information, address Picador,
175 Fifth Avenue, New York, N.Y. 10010.

www.picadorusa.com
www.twitter.com/picadorusa • www.facebook.com/picadorusa
picadorbookroom.tumblr.com

Picador® is a U.S. registered trademark and is used by St. Martin's Press
under license from Pan Books Limited.

For book club information, please visit www.facebook.com/picadorbookclub
or e-mail marketing@picadorusa.com.

The Library of Congress Cataloging-in-Publication Data is available upon request.

ISBN 978-1-250-05243-8 (paper over board)
ISBN 978-1-250-05244-5 (e-book)

Picador books may be purchased for educational, business,
or promotional use. For information on bulk purchases, please contact
Macmillan Corporate and Premium Sales Department at 1-800-221-7945,
extension 5442, or write specialmarkets@macmillan.com.

Originally published in Great Britain in e-book formats by Picador,
an imprint of Pan Macmillan, a division of Macmillan Publishers Limited

First U.S. Edition: August 2014

10 9 8 7 6 5 4 3 2 1

For my parents Roy & Pauline House,
my partner Nick Webster,
and to the memory of John Pakosta

CONTENTS

SUTLER

AMRAH CITY

1.1

John Jacob Ford's morning began at 3:03 with a call from Paul Geezler, Advisor to the Division Chief, Europe, for HOSCO International.

Listen. There's a problem and it can't be solved. You need to disappear.

Five hours before Geezler's phone call, Kiprowski came to Ford's cabin and presented him with a Mason jar. Stopped at his door, Ford listened without much interest – until Kiprowski tilted the jar and what Ford had taken to be a nest of beetles unsnagged one from another, and he could see without trouble that these were scorpions, some ruddy-black, some amber, some semi-translucent. Most, except one, with bodies smaller than a quarter. The largest scorpion, black, brittle, almost engineered, took up the entire width of the container from claw-tip to tail.

Unwilling to touch the jar, Ford managed not to recoil. He asked Kiprowski what he wanted and Kiprowski said he didn't rightly know. He'd found them under a tarpaulin close to Burn Pit 5, and while they were dead he didn't trust the other men not to use them for some kind of a joke, Pakosta especially, and he didn't want them winding up in food, in cots, on seats, in pockets – and besides, he said, I thought you'd be interested. They look like toys, he said. Like clockwork toys. And they light up under blacklight. They fluoresce, honest to god. They glow.

Throughout the conversation Kiprowski called Ford *Sutler*, a name still fresh to Ford's ears. Strictly speaking *Sutler* didn't exist. Stephen Lawrence Sutler, the name Ford assumed on his arrival at Camp Liberty, was an alias, an invention set up by his employer, Paul Geezler, to satisfy company policy. *New contracts require new contractors.* Ford understood Sutler to be a useful conceit for Geezler, certainly something more valuable than a quick-fix solution to a sticky contractual arrangement. More useful and more complex than he wanted to know. On occasion Geezler asked for favours, ideas on this and that, news on what was happening at the burn pits or at the government offices.

His six weeks as Sutler were not without interest. While Sutler and Ford were one and the same person, he'd noticed a growing number of differences, most of them small. Sutler, for example, spoke his mind and honoured his word. Ford dissembled, avoided stating definite opinions. Sutler applied himself to his work. Ford just couldn't focus. Sutler endured practical jokes, and given Kiprowski's gift, appeared considerably less queasy about handling venomous insects. Ford was familiar with many small disappointments and failures, but Sutler had no such history and as a consequence felt competent and free.

Ford took the jar into his cabin but couldn't bring himself to throw the contents out, and set it on the floor, far from the bed, shrouded with a T-shirt with a hardback book on top, although he knew the lid to be secure and the scorpions to be dead.

For an hour after Geezler's call Ford sat on his cot while time slipped from him, head in hands as he attempted to reason through Geezler's message.

Listen to me. There's a problem and it can't be solved. You need to disappear. Tomorrow, go to the regional government office as planned and submit the transfer requests as if everything is normal. I've set up four new operation accounts, and opened a junk account. Give the transfer requests and the account numbers for all of the accounts to Howell. Make sure he attaches the four operation accounts to the Massive, and make sure he completes all of the transactions by midday. Then leave. The money in the junk account is yours. Once it's transferred no one but you can touch it. Do not inform Howell about your plans. Do not stay at Southern-CIPA. Do not return to Camp Liberty. If you return you will be arrested. Do not pack your belongings, you are being watched. Make no attempt to contact me. Disappear. Avoid military transport and personnel. The warrant will be issued for you and Howell at noon: I can't guarantee more time. You have nine hours.

Geezler read the numbers out twice, and Ford scribbled them on a sheet of paper rested on his knee: each number eight digits long, four prefaced with HOS/OA, one with HOS/JA. Geezler had him repeat the numbers back to him.

Under these instructions lay an understanding that Ford would follow precisely what was asked of him. This was their agreement. Geezler guaranteed employment under two qualifications, *you go as Sutler; you leave when I say*, and the money, a tidy two hundred thousand, was good enough for him to agree to these terms without question. The warning of arrest alarmed him, although the possibility had occurred to him many times. Geezler's instructions were clear. Proceed as normal. Leave by midday. Tell no one. Make no contact. *Go.*

Ford kept his passport and credit cards (all under his own name) safe in a plastic bag in a slit cut into his mattress. He ran through the possibilities. He could do exactly as Geezler advised, meet with Howell then manufacture an excuse to leave before midday – or, simpler still, leave immediately, take one of the vehicles, fuel up, drive and not stop.

A series of scratches brought his attention back to the room. Tiny and complex, and without any particular location.

As soon as he lifted the T-shirt he could see movement inside the container as one by one the smaller ginger scorpions appeared to revive. With a certain horror he raised the glass to the light and noticed how the smaller scorpions struggled to burrow and hide under the larger bodies, and this seemed strange to him, how something naturally armoured would seek the security of cover.

Listen. There's a problem and it can't be solved. You need to disappear. You have nine hours.

1.2

20:30 at the regional government offices at Amrah City, the Deputy Administrator for Project Finance at Southern-CIPA, Paul Howell, walked through Accounts and told the last late workers to leave. Howell stood at the centre of the office and pointed at the computer screens and said there's a deep-clean scheduled for tonight. Log out, and unplug the terminals. I know, he said, I know. I just heard myself. Tomorrow we'll have an updated system, maybe even something that works. Tomorrow, when you come in, you'll need to change your password.

Howell considered himself a smart and logical man, and he understood that if any of the officers paused to think through the situation it wouldn't make sense. So he stood in the office, chivvied them along, and waited until the last of them were gone. This gesture would cause fresh trouble: a delay in payments to utility workers, a delay in payments to the Oil Ministry, a delay in reports to Baghdad. But in one day, he could be certain, none of this would be his problem.

He sent his officers back to their quarters, knowing there were no bars or facilities within the compound, no place to relax, and that a night off work meant a night without air-con and a night without computers. While most worked late through necessity, others stayed by choice to contact their families back in the US.

Alone, Howell returned to his desk. He shut the blinds, he took out a bottle of malt and poured himself a generous measure. He settled behind his desk, drew a note from his pocket, placed it beside the phone and considered his options – he could shoot himself, he could attempt to disappear, he could destroy the records, he could burn down the office – but knew, in seriousness, that he didn't have that kind of character or commitment. Instead, he waited until the time written down on the paper, then called Paul Geezler, Advisor to the Division Chief, Europe, for HOSCO International.

'I have your note.' Howell spoke softly, as if this were an ordinary discussion. 'There are rumours about who might be the new director. I've heard that David is interested?'

'We need someone in post. He's preparing his bid.'

'You'd move with him?'

'I haven't decided.'

'Everyone knows he depends on you.'

'I haven't decided.' Geezler drew in a long breath. 'We need to speak frankly, Paul. About the border highway. About the transfers. I found the requests – and I wouldn't have questioned them – but the money never arrived. Out of interest, Paul, why Al-Muthanna?'

'Because it's desert. Because no one goes there. There was a one-time project when I arrived, building roads. The project finished two years ago. Right now it looks active, but it's only live on paper.'

Geezler cleared his throat. 'Just out of interest, how close was my estimate?'

'A little low. It's closer to five, five and a half.'

'All from the same accounts?'

'About eighty-five, ninety per cent.'

'And all of it money allocated for HOSCO projects?'

Howell said yes, if anyone was going to build highways through a stretch of desert, it would be HOSCO. 'We had money ready for disbursement to HOSCO accounts sitting without movement. The figures were small in proportion to the overall budget.' These reasons, he knew, came only after the fact. He hadn't deliberately meant to take money, not at first. What started as a modest one-off loan to cover a shortfall quickly became a habit, and once he figured out a ruse, building roads through deserts no one would use, he saw no reason to stop himself. Every day he handed backpacks, suitcases, briefcases, even brown-paper bags packed with cash to ministers, contractors, and project organizers, all of it a legitimate part of his work. Losing a little, allowing a little backward flow to smooth the edge off his own discomfort, seemed natural, easily within bounds.

'How much of this is refundable?'

'None. How did you find out?'

'The transfer requests. Eventually, they're all tracked. There was movement where there shouldn't be movement. Road building is smart. I looked right at it and thought it was ours.'

'How did you know it was me?'

'This could only come from a government office. Only you can authorize transfers over ten. Only you can attach accounts to projects.'

Howell pushed the note away. 'You should know, I can't pay it back.'

Geezler allowed a long pause. 'I'm not looking for you to pay anything back, Paul.' Sounding weary, Geezler said he needed time to think. He'd call back in twenty minutes and make only one offer. Did Howell understand?

Howell said he understood.

'This isn't a negotiation, Paul.'

Twenty minutes later, Paul Geezler called back. In the interim, Howell had attempted to total his spending, but overshot Geezler's estimate and came up with a new and larger figure. He apologized for taking up Geezler's time.

'I'm interested in the Massive, Paul.'

'What do you need to know?'

'I take it the funds are still in place?'

'Something in the region of fifty-plus – but it's barely started. The money hasn't been transferred. The project hasn't moved beyond paper yet. Nothing has been spent. I'm seeing the budget holder in the morning.'

'Stephen Sutler.'

'That's right. You know him?'

Once again Geezler cleared his throat. 'Paul,' he said, 'have you heard the story about the gorilla and the basketball game?'

Howell said he hadn't.

'It's all about a simple bluff. It's from a test. A number of subjects are taken to a basketball game and asked to count the passes. An incentive is offered to sweeten the activity and make it competitive. Halfway through the game a man in a gorilla suit walks onto the court. There's no explanation for this. He stops right in the middle of the court with the game going on around him, beats his chest, then he walks off. None of the players, none of the commentators, nobody in fact gives the gorilla any attention. Do you know how many of the people counting passes notice him?'

'I can't imagine.'

'Less than fifty per cent, Paul. Less than fifty. And do you know how many people raise this in a discussion after the game? How many ask about the gorilla once everything's settled?'

'I don't know.'

'No one. Not one. Because they're too busy trying to get something right. They're anxious, Paul, they want to know if they've done everything they were supposed to. Because, if they can help it, nobody likes to get anything wrong.'

Howell struggled to see how the story applied to him.

'We need to perform something a little different. We don't want the auditors counting passes, we want them to look out for the gorilla. It's very simple. If they look for one thing, if they focus on one task, they won't see what matters. They won't see things *right*. You understand?' Geezler cleared his throat as he came to the point. 'Does anyone else know about the highways?'

'No.'

'That's how we're going to keep it. Everyone is going to be looking for missing money, but no one is going to be looking at those highways. There's no reason to. Now, Paul, I want you to do something very straightforward. Can you change the codes on those transfers you made? Can you make them look like cash payments?'

'I'm not following you?'

'Change your transfers to cash withdrawals against the Massive. Change the codes. Make it look like you supplied Sutler with cash. Can you do that?'

'It's possible, but why that account? This project has a high profile.'

'Monkey, Paul. Think monkey. Change the codes, those codes are yours, no one else will notice. That's the first step. Second – and this is important – I want you to erase all of the personnel information you have on Stephen Sutler, anything non-financial, anything extra-curricular, private emails, anything like that, and when he comes in tomorrow, I want you to follow his instructions and divide the funds marked for his project into four new operational accounts. Sutler has the details for the new accounts. He has it all worked out. Do exactly what he asks. Make those transfers, and make sure the full amount assigned to HOSCO for the Massive leaves your holdings. Divide it however he tells you into the four new accounts: one, two, three, four. Load them up. In addition, he has a secured junk account, and I want you to attach that junk account to your dummy highway project. Fatten it up with two-fifty, let him see the amount. Show him the transfer. That's five accounts, Paul. Four accounts attached to Stephen Sutler, and one to the highways. I want all five of them loaded. Do you understand me?'

Howell said he understood.

'Attach Sutler's junk account to the Saudi border project. Keep it buried. I don't want it found. If you have to route it through other accounts then go ahead and do that. Don't keep any record of these new accounts yourself. You understand? It's important they can't be found. Once this is done, after Sutler has gone, Central-CIPA will catch any irregularities with HOSCO's holdings regarding the Massive. Leave everything to Baghdad.'

Howell said he didn't understand.

'It's simple. All you have to do is delete Sutler's records. Delete all of the information you have about him, and transfer the money into the new accounts. Tomorrow morning, when Sutler makes his visit, you'll do exactly what he asks, which includes making a deposit to a junk account for his personal use. Hide that account with your road-way project. Once you're done just let him leave.'

'But I handle funding and disbursement, they'll know I've had a hand in this. Sutler will tell them he has nothing to do with it.'

'Paul.' Geezler spoke carefully. 'To my knowledge you've helped yourself to four hundred and fifty thousand dollars of HOSCO's money. You've spent this on your family, on visits and vacations you did not need – and you tell me the money is gone. I also understand you have a considerable stockpile of equipment at Camp Liberty, which includes military vehicles and hardware. Whichever way you look at this your work with Southern-CIPA is over. Now, you can try to fix this by yourself, I don't mind, it's up to you. You can continue to move money from one place to another until someone else finds out what you're doing. You can keep on going as you are, Paul, and dig yourself a little deeper. You can hope that no one else is going to check those fraudulent transfer requests or the empty accounts – or – you can let me help you. I'm not saying this won't be painful, but I can offer you a respectable exit. I guarantee. No prosecution. You keep what you've taken, no one will be looking for it, and if everything goes well, you'll see a future in the civil sector, which will keep you as comfortable as you could hope to be. That's my offer. A solution. If you do exactly what I've asked, everyone will be looking for Sutler. You understand? Sutler. And Sutler is going to disappear and no one will find him. Sutler is the monkey in this scenario, Paul. So you need to think carefully about how you're going to manage this. Like I told you, this isn't a negotiation. But I can promise that nobody will see the game while they're looking for Sutler.'

'Does David know about this?'

'Paul, we aren't discussing what the division chief does and does not know. We're discussing the decisions you need to make.'

Howell worked through the night, certain that Geezler was turning this to his advantage, although he couldn't see how. For three hours he sought out and shredded documents and deleted files and correspondence from his computer. He drank while he worked, sensing the night about him and the limits of the compound. No stranger to revising the past, he collated HOSCO employment files, design-build bid sheets and qualification statements, site-reports, and requisition sheets – every scrap relating to Sutler – and document by document he removed the staples, separated the pages, and fed them into the machine. The way the paper jerked into the wheels, the way the information could still be read along the cuts, until the strips started to curl, held his attention. The paper would need to be burned. There were people, in archives, in Europe, who spent their days reconstructing shredded documents, undertaking a tedious archaeology of a culture, reconstituting petty deeds and business piece by piece. Everything here would be sent to the burn pits. Everything here would become smoke and ash.

Done, he called Paul Geezler. 'He's gone. Sutler doesn't exist.'

Geezler's voice sounded ghost-like, distant. 'Did you change the codes?'

'I have.'

'Is there money for him?'

'I'll do that tomorrow.'

'Make sure it happens.'

'And you trust him?'

'He carries no risk. Even if he's caught.'

Howell emptied the waste into a sack marked 'confidential: secure/ burn'. Tied the neck and took the sack to the outer office where it sat with other such sacks. All quiet, unusually so; he walked about the office with a kind of envy rising in him. Tomorrow, at midday, Sutler would walk out of the office and evaporate. It wasn't often a man could make a clean start. Shortly after, Central-CIPA would raise the alarm about the misappropriated funds, and Howell would step back and watch everything unfurl. The next four weeks would be difficult. He would be suspended, without doubt, moved sideways, while every expenditure the authority had authorized would be inspected – but he wouldn't have to pay back the money.

<h2 style="text-align:center">1.3</h2>

The first convoy arrived pre-dawn. A gut-rumble of thirteen trucks packed, brimful, with nine to eleven tons of industrial, medical, and military waste, alongside two supply trucks with food and equipment. The ruckus stirred Ford into action. Inside this early chaos he could distinguish the sing-song voices of the men, the hiss, crank, and slam of gears, of brakes and cab doors. The desert busy with industry as the trucks were dispersed to the burn pits: black rectangular craters into which the waste would be dumped and incinerated. The hot stink of aircraft fuel and scorched rubber overpowered the air and mingled with a deeper faecal stench. No more than four of the five pits burned at the same time, each sending up a roiling column, red at the base and bright with sparks, black fat-thighed legs stomping through a colourless sky. The smoke leaned first then flattened out as an alternate horizon, a skirt-line haze. Everything depended on the wind: the pits being set two to the west, three to the south-west, and two east of the living quarters, nothing more than a straight row of Portakabins that faced the machine shop, a grey-barrelled Quonset hut.

Ford had followed Paul Geezler's advice and packed only two changes of clothes and what money he had into a black backpack. He changed his shoes for boots and left his room with laundry strewn over a chair, with three books and bottled water beside the bed, his papers and drafting equipment on a small table with rulers, pens, protractor, a long roll of paper, a manual of instructions from HOSCO – and on the floor a stack of toilet rolls and the sealed jar of scorpions. He began to consider excuses, reasons to leave: trouble at home, bad news, a failing relative or business, but none seemed credible as everything about Ford spelled out his solitary nature. Ready at the door he watched Gunnersen and Kiprowski unload the two HOSCO supply trucks, which needed to be emptied before the sun hit the wagons and the containers became too hot to work inside. Gunnersen hauled packs of canned and boxed supplies to the tailgate then tossed them down to Kiprowski, his gestures glib and swift however heavy the package. He called out the items as he threw them, wiped his brow, and instructed Kiprowski on where they should go. Samuels, Clark, Pakosta, and Spider still worked the pits, and the trucks returned one at a time, motors droning as they climbed the hill.

Ford decided on Kiprowski as his escort to Southern-CIPA, this being necessary business and Kiprowski being the only man he could trust.

The sun hit at an angle, pink on the huts and the side of the truck, already severe, hot enough to sear, and not yet midsummer. With the vehicles unloaded the men returned from the pits. Clark ran ahead, shrieking with a hoarse cat-call, naked except for his boots, and shot into the sunlight, his thighs and backside covered with HOSCO stickers (*Manufactured in Virginia with Pride*). The men whooped and hollered as Clark, white and skinny with red hair, red arms and a red neck, ran in breakneck circles, kicked back dust, and punched his fists into the air.

With Kiprowski in the seat beside him, Clark and Pakosta in the bucket seats ahead, Ford worked hard to keep his thoughts ordered, but understood nothing more about why he needed to leave Camp Liberty than when Geezler had made the call – and suffered four long hours of *if*s and *what*s and counting down. The promise from Geezler of two hundred thousand, in sterling, seemed unimaginable. Two hundred thousand: enough to climb out of any trouble, enough to pay off a few debts, and then some, just as long as he did exactly what was asked. With this money Ford would settle his conscience and start over. He knew Geezler well, and trusted that some kind of clarity would come as soon as he arrived at the Regional Government Offices: Finance Division, Southern-CIPA. The craft rode up, steep and unsteady, broke through the grey smokeline and levelled out above the haze. Beneath him lay a last glimpse of the burn pits, five hard black oblongs with a sooty trails dusting the desert, the cabins and Quonset already lost to view.

He saw no chance of escape. As they approached Amrah City the craft dropped in stuttered steps to avoid attack – a message came to Ford via the pilot: business at Southern-CIPA would need to be brief. Howell had other appointments. He had time to make the transfers, just about, but any discussion of the project, that over-view he'd asked for, wasn't going to happen today. Kiprowski and Pakosta bickered over a small backpack, some fresh awkwardness breaking between them. He regretted his decision to allow Pakosta and Clark along. He also regretted his decision that they should wear the uniforms Howell had provided. On landing, Kiprowski became so restless that Ford began to wonder if he was somehow involved.

The offices for Southern-CIPA sat in the grounds of a former school in the centre of Amrah City. A perimeter fence and blast wall followed the rough circumference of the playground and nominally protected the offices from the covered market and a row of businesses – although most were empty, the glass shot out of the fronts, the walls blackened in a recent attack, the owners returned to Kuwait and Saudi, some to Iran. The school itself was long gone, firebombed then blasted with rockets until nothing remained but a level lot. The painted outline for a mini-soccer pitch still visible on the concrete slabs.

HOSCO had provided the buildings, the same prefab units as the cabins at Camp Liberty, dropped onto blocks and welded one to the other. Ford didn't like to think about the kind of people who would bomb a school. Burn it down then blow it away. The fact that the new regional government sited their offices on the very same spot seemed ironic and prescient. An invitation. A school smell haunted the new offices, a sourness, not quite the end-of-day musk of unfresh bodies, but some reedy tang that stuck with the place. In meetings he felt this odour creep up on him. The longer the meeting, the more he held his breath, the less he talked.

*

15

Ford unravelled the plans across the Deputy Administrator's desk and took care not to displace the many objects or damage the paper – Howell, with his practised mid-Atlantic accent, loved his tat: the glass pen-holder, the fountain pens, the name plate, the weathered baseball, the photos of his wife, son, and daughter, and more framed on the wall behind the desk (Howell shaking hands with heads of state, Howell beside the few celebrities that paused on their way to Camp Anaconda or from Camp Navistar). Everything set just so. In all of his visits Ford had yet to see the Deputy Administrator sit at the desk. The man liked to pace. He'd heard stories about Howell at Camp Liberty from Pakosta, rumours that didn't match what he knew.

The maps demonstrated Ford's craft as a draughtsman and his serious approach to the project. Howell unrolled the sheets one by one, and muttered 'Ah, our legacy,' a little sarcastically. 'The Massive.'

The plans sketched in soft blue pencil, a pleasing exactness to the lines. Layer one: the existing camp with the huts and burn pits. Layer two: the proposed work quarters and fabrication huts. Layer three: the burn pits dug out and in-filled. Layer four: the basic structures for water, power, sewage. Layer five: the airfield expansion. In a series of twelve overlapping sheets a small compound for remote waste disposal became the basic structure for a new military base and new city.

Howell, owlish, white hair and wire glasses; cool, disinterested, moved around the table and leafed slowly through the plans despite the earlier warning that he would be busy. He muttered a complaint that Ford should not have allowed his men to wear uniform. 'Not here,' he said, 'they only wear these uniforms when they accompany me. They aren't legitimate officers.' Uninterested in a reply, Howell read then raised his hand, indicating that Sutler should wait as he left the office.

Ford waited, first he leaned against the table, then he stood upright with his arms folded. He took in the room. Two iron safes backed against the wall, designed to be built into vaults, they were set instead side by side and took up a quarter of the space. Beside them a row of glass cabinets of sport trophies and more framed photographs. A wall clock mounted opposite the desk. Already eleven o'clock, barely one hour left. He expected Howell to return with the military police. He wondered if they knew his name, and how they might have discovered him. *The warrant will be issued at noon.*

Ten minutes later, Howell came to the door alone and asked if Ford had set up a junk account. 'You've done this already?' The man could not remember. 'And the other accounts, is everything set up?'

'Yes,' Ford appeared surprised.

'You have the details?'

Ford searched through his documents and found the handwritten list of numbers.

'Have you spoken with Paul Geezler about the accounts? You know the restrictions on the operation accounts? I can make the transfers but anything above over twenty-five is automatically flagged to Central-CIPA. Payments or transfers.'

Ford nodded, although he appeared uncertain.

Howell held out his hand for the list of account numbers and transfer amounts. 'One moment.' His mouth tightened in thought. 'Four operations, one junk. How much did Paul agree for the junk account? Two? Or two-five?'

Howell retreated back through the door saying he would make it two-five. Two, or two-five? All a little freakish to be speaking in single numbers and mean not two dollars, but two hundred thousand dollars; not two dollars and fifty cents, but two hundred and fifty thousand dollars. A tidy two-five. Handsome payment for six weeks' work.

Ten minutes later, at exactly eleven-fifteen, Howell returned smiling, pleased with himself. 'I've written the default access codes next to the account numbers. Don't keep the account numbers and the pass codes together. Have you set the security level before? Do you rotate your pass codes?'

Ford said he didn't understand, and Howell winced.

'Unless you set the security your accounts will be vulnerable. This is all the information you need to access them, unless you set an additional line of security.'

Ford thought there was some mischief in Howell's tone. He looked blankly at the numbers. Howell drew his laptop round to show him, and asked Ford to open the HOSCO website and sign in. 'To stop anyone else from gaining access you need to set the security to an appropriate level.'

Ford opened the site, checked into Finance. Howell pointed at the screen.

'Click there – *Privacy*. Enter. Type in the number that starts HOS/JA.

That's your junk account. There at the top. Click *Hide*. Only you can see the account now. Click there for security.'

The screen turned black, then the account number reappeared, and then the balance.

'See. In a minute that zero will change.' They watched the screen, but the figure didn't change. 'Give it a moment.'

Howell checked the account number against Ford's note. 'While we're waiting you can set the security level. You can set up to eight sets of codes to access the account, anything between four and twelve characters.' Howell straightened up. 'I'll leave you to it. If you take too long it will lock you out.'

Ford stared at the screen. Kiprowski waited behind him, and he sensed a hostility toward Howell. At the bottom of the screen a clock ticked down from ninety. Anxious to complete this, Ford set the security at level four, which opened four screens, demanding one new code per screen. Struggling for an idea, Ford used the numbers for the new operational accounts.

Once the codes were entered the screen again turned black, and Ford closed the laptop.

While he waited for Howell, he began to wonder if the money was transferred. If Geezler was as good as his word. He opened the computer again, entered Finance, and checked the Accounts tab. He clicked on the junk account and the first screen appeared. 1 of 4. When he mistyped the site immediately shut down and the screen went blank.

Nervous now, he went to try again, but Howell returned.

'Did you manage?' Howell looked at the laptop screen. 'What are you doing?'

'I set the security level. I typed in a wrong number.'

'How many times?'

'Just the once.'

'You only have three attempts before it locks you out.' Howell straightened up. 'They used to call these hostage accounts. They're designed to be secure. If it locks you out you won't have access. The transfer's been made, so the money will show in the account soon. It's supposed to be instant, but the connections aren't as fast as we'd like – like everything else around here.'

Howell again excused himself and Ford shut the computer down, then folded the paper back into his pocket, aware that if he was going to leave the opportunity was right before him. Two hundred and fifty thousand dollars came close to the fee that Geezler had promised. Dollars not sterling, but close enough to be good enough. He began to sense a design behind Geezler's call, a design which looked to his best interests.

With no sign of Howell returning, Ford turned to Kiprowski and noticed that the boy was sweating, looked ill-at-ease, unwell, his hand to his stomach. Every occupant of Camp Liberty succumbed at some point to flu-like symptoms, chills and shivers and night-sweats, a stomach that cramped and couldn't hold water. Each one of them suffered skin irritations and nose bleeds. Ford blamed the fumes from the burn pits. The men blamed toxic agents, biochemical compounds. He told Kiprowski to sit down, but the boy signalled that he wanted to remain standing, he just needed a moment.

The boy's anxiety increased his own. Still, Howell did not return. Would they arrest him now? Was this all some elaborate delay? Howell appeared to have no awareness of the impending arrest.

Kiprowski leaned back against the second safe and clutched a kitbag to his stomach, his face white and damp.

Ford hooked his backpack over his shoulder – there would be no better opportunity – and walked to the door. A corridor cut between the offices, at one end a wall, at the other an emergency exit. He thought to say something to Kiprowski, but found himself walking before he'd properly considered what to do, knowing that if he used the door an alarm would sound. The pressure of time, a desire to be out, gone from Southern-CIPA, away from smarmy Howell, the baby-sick stink of the offices, from Kiprowski's sweating – everything compounded the fact that he was running out of time. Thirty minutes, less perhaps, now twenty-eight minutes: no time at all. Almost at the door, ready to push the bar, he turned to see Kiprowski running toward him full-pelt, arms beginning to rise to shield his head. And then chaos.

The blast came as a pulse, a punch that knocked Ford off his feet and battered him through the door, throwing him out so fast that he did not know what this was: inside and upright one moment, and in another rolled and shoved, flung pell-mell – the air about him a soup, a welter of heat, of collapsing walls, of plasterboard and ceiling tiles, of powdered glass. The atmosphere, even as it blackened, sparked about him.

He landed on his back, his boots stripped from his feet, his hands and face bloody, his ears raw with shrieks, his body numb, clothes ripped and pecked. With chaos descending he scrambled out of the smoke, deaf to the rapid crack of gunfire.

Listen. There's a problem and it can't be solved.

CUKURCA

2.1

Ford came across the refugee camp in the late afternoon.

In pursuit of a lone mountain goat he stumbled to the peak of a steep embankment with a rock in each hand – breathless, sweaty, light-headed, and above all hungry. Directly under his feet the land swooped down to a city of grey-green tents curved to the crater's smooth incline.

Startled by the view, he stopped at the edge. Two boys with rifles attended a loose herd of goats on the opposite slope. In the camp, bearded men congregated in front of their tents. Women scooped water from the edge of a cloud-bright lake. Black dogs ran feckless along the shore. Smoke rose in wayward strands. For two days he'd been certain he could smell food, and here in rising threads hung the tasty scents of braised meat and some kind of bread. All of this detail, tiny, toy-like, distinct, protected by a natural stone bowl.

He made a divot for himself in the shale at the crater's crest and hunkered down to watch the camp. He couldn't guess how many people the camp housed nor for how long the settlement had been established (the tracks between the tents could be weeks or years old). A dumpsite of barrels and plastic crates, an area set apart for fuel canisters, a separate corral with a water cistern and hand pumps, were evidence of organization, not longevity. After an hour watching armed men and half-wild dogs he decided to avoid the camp. If he came across strangers on the open road it would be another matter, but here in the mountain desert, two days from any village, he looked nothing but suspicious.

He'd slept in the afternoons to avoid the heat, and walked through the night in worn boots and slack clothes across a rising landscape of scree and scrub, a full moon cold on the rock. While he walked he fretted, conflating the bare facts of his flight with notions that did not make sense – so he lost himself to his discomfort, to the alternating heat and cold, to the certain fact of one footfall set before another. He told himself that he was in shock, although he knew this not to be true. In two or three days he would reach Kuzey and the Turkish border, but more immediately he needed water and he needed food.

Uncertain if he was nine or ten days away from Amrah City, he began to draw his route in the dirt. Day one, the flight from the southern desert, Amrah City to Baghdad. Day two, military transport to Balad Ruz, to be taken to a small field hospital where his hands and face were treated for burns and cuts, then back almost the entire way before curving up to Khanaqin and driving east toward Iran to see the faint spill of fire along the horizon. On day three, a free ride on a school bus with steel plates welded to its sides packed with Sorani Kurds shipping to Halabja for work. Then private transport the next morning, by-passing Sulaymaniyah, to Fort Suse with an American engineer – a sturdy man from Butte, Montana, convinced that the Iranians were poisoning their own people and that nothing could contain the toxins, because borders and frontiers, when you think about it, offer no real protection. Ford couldn't disagree, the bandages on his hands and his wandering confirmed it. He managed ad hoc, day by day, progressing from this place to that with the rising doubt that he had made the journey unnecessarily complicated. From here, days four and five, he travelled by taxi to a military checkpoint, then on to Arbil, continuing his northern zigzag with a Jordanian driver who took pity and gave him names of other contacts: a man with a car to sell (although the car turned out to be a '53 trail bike pilfered from an American contractor), and a man at Kuzey who could see him across the border. The days now became confused and Ford scratched out the route: days six and seven, or seven and eight, by motorbike, a painful ride along a dry riverbed toward Sarsil, toward Amedi, where he finally removed the bandages although his hands were still blistered and numb. From here he wasted two whole days heading west instead of north and lost the last of his food to rain. The same rain clogged the bike with mud which later hardened to stone, and forced him to walk through the scrub, complaining at his pure bad luck.

His ambition remained the same. Once he hit Turkey he would head for Cukurca, a small town fifteen miles north of the border. He would find a hotel, a hostel, wait out until he was sure he was secure, then find a bank and transfer the money out of the junk account. He would return to Bonn, give up his apartment, pay his debts, sell what he owned, send the money back to England. Living in a small cabin for six weeks had taught him what he did and did not need. His life would become simple, lived day to day with modest self-sufficiency. He would almost certainly leave Europe. The moment this money was secured he'd leave the Middle East and never return. The attack on Southern-CIPA was a hard lesson, separate from his arrangement with Geezler, that life could change in one instant. In his backpack: two hundred and fifty-three American dollars, one litre of water. Not much of a plan, but a plan nevertheless. Among the flecks of sand Ford found a piece of seashell. He took the shell in one hand and tested his fingers, pressed the shard into the skin to gauge the loss of sensation, and thought that this was improving now the blisters were gone and the cuts were largely healed; although he could not yet feel heat or wet-ness, he could sense pressure. And while he considered how far he was from any ocean, he fell asleep, slipped from one world to another as a man falling backward through a window. In his dream debris flew about him as a tranquil sky turned black. Among the scattering dust: a window joist, paper, his boots flung hard and far, a man diving in a perfect arc, his clothes on fire.

He woke to the sound of approaching aircraft, with pins and needles running from his fingers through his forearm. Above him the sky sang with the drone of engines, a busy vibration of many unseen craft. Too exhausted to walk, he slept curled about a boulder. An hour later he woke again, as a single fighter tore over, and so it continued through the night with troop carriers, bombers, jets laden with menace, passing above the low-lying clouds. In the distance the blistering sound of gunfire, too regular to signal combat. At night these nations spoke in coded rumbles, one to the other, in whispers and threats.

He cowered until daylight and woke sensing that he was alone – the goat, and his ridiculous idea to kill it, gone. Unable to escape the mist that settled about the slope he headed downhill but never seemed free of the mountain or the cloud salted with grit. When the ground levelled he followed a track of compacted stone out of a ravine to emerge in a lowland fen of grasses and marsh and open blue sky. Beside the road, in ditches and clearings, lay abandoned hideouts with military camouflage, stacked sandbags slopped with mud. Above him, strung across the mouth of the gulley, hung a Turkish flag, blood-red, immense.

2.2

A message to call the London office of Gibson & Baker arrived in the early morning, as an email with an attachment, which he picked up on his phone; the subject line marked *URGENT: Call Gibson ASAP*. Parson ignored the request. The word *urgent* worked an irritation in him. A little insulted that the message showed no sensitivity, to how busy he might be, Parson pocketed the phone and started his day. Gibson's desire to have his staff available at any hour needed disciplining, and he wouldn't call. Not immediately.

Later in the morning, out in the desert with a tape measure, a camera, a notebook, Parson clambered up a littered shale bank to reach the road, and remembered the message, and thought that he was foolish not to pay it immediate attention. He should have called London, he should have spoken with Gibson, exactly as he was asked. He returned to the vehicle and finished his notes, marked measure-ments on a diagram of the road – a simple line with a single curve. The road, straight for fifty-three miles, rose on a slight embankment as it turned, then levelled out again and continued through the desert for another thirty-two straight miles. A highway with almost no traffic, and a turn which accounted for a good number of fatalities. Even here, thirty-two miles south of the closest town, the roadside appeared untrustworthy. The siding was indistinct, an embankment of boulders and stones furred with shredded paper and plastic that rattled in the wind. A thick border of potential hazard, which might contain any kind of mess, hide any kind of device.

He took photographs of the tread marks on the road, took shots of the highway, almost of nothing, the sky and land being of equal value, bright and burnt, without particular feature. He braced against the wind to take another photograph of the curve, then returned to the vehicle to write down the details. Seven weeks ago a HOSCO supply truck had missed the turn and careened off the road, blindly launched itself over the drop, a mere three feet: small, but stepped high enough to tip the vehicle to its side before it hit the scree. Pieces from the supply truck could be found without effort, fragments of glass and sections from the frame, rutted aluminium, some pieces of chrome that caught the sun, and as he picked through the debris field Parson re-read the case files. The marks from this incident were hard to distinguish from other marks from other accidents, a history in scorched dirt of drivers falling asleep or just altogether missing the turn and finding themselves, for one moment, mid-air and roadless. HOSCO convoys used the road when security alerts made Highway 80 impassable. Parson never lost sight of the small ironies that made up his work. By seeking a safer route the convoy had come across more predictable enemies – exhaustion, fatigue, inattention – and a translator slumbering in the cabin of the tumbling truck was thrown from the bunk at the back of the cab to the windscreen and broke his neck.

He knew nothing about the translator, Amer Hassan, except that he held a British passport, and had a wife and two children in Darlington, UK. He knew that HOSCO had already terminated the contracts of its American and European drivers and rehired men from Nepal, India, and Sri Lanka. He knew that most of the translators came from Baghdad or the northern cities, and that they would not be able to return home because of their work.

The soldier escorting Parson (one of two, the second behind the vehicle), picked at a hair in his nose, and asked if Parson was ready. Small-talk done between them, Parson nodded and put away his work. He disliked travelling in the HOSCO jeeps, and disliked passing through the small towns. He disliked how men watched, heads turning as the truck drove by, some rooted calculation in their minds. He disliked the trash by the roadside, the dogs, the children who sometimes ran after them, the plumes of roadside fires spiralling into flat blue skies. He disliked the dust, the flies, the heat, the sweat, the way he thought these days of them and us. He disliked how he could be miles from anywhere, cutting through the desert on some unbending road, and how he would still see plastic bags or water bottles, or clothes. He disliked every moment he spent outside the camp compound, but these visits were unavoidable, so he conducted them as precisely as possible, as early in the day as he could arrange.

Back on base in a hut that passed for guest quarters, Parson laid out the case files. An accident. Simple enough, a ranking of 'no culpability' with 'mitigating circumstances', which he trusted HOSCO would translate sympathetically. He sat with a bottle of tepid water. It bothered him to be resolving issues in the field which could be decided in a comfortable office in London that faced the river and the Temple, with plain views of temperate browns and greys, of occasional river traffic and pedestrians, a welcome dullness to the prospect and the work. In London he would argue the matter.

Because he could not receive a signal in his hut, he traced his way to the mess hall, bought another water, and sat under a mural of New York with the Twin Towers restored, an eagle above them, wings outstretched. That the water was cold made him happy. He retrieved Gibson's message. Without doubt the call would mean another delay in his return home, another site visit under police, military, or private guard, another delay in which he spent his days at a hospital, a military barrack, a roadside, speaking through an interpreter, interviewing people who would rather not talk. This call would mean more evenings lost to reports to determine if HOSCO was or was not liable. He opened the attachment and enlarged the image, a headshot from an identity photo, the man's expression slightly bewildered, eyes wide, a little startled, and couldn't help but wonder what had happened to this man. The image set in the past tense. The call passed quickly to Gibson.

'Who am I looking at?'

'His name is Stephen Sutler. He's with HOSCO. Have you kept up with the news?'

'Haven't had a chance. To be honest, I'm closing cases. I'm looking forward to coming home.'

Gibson hesitated, the comment sat without remark. 'The picture you have. He's British, and he's missing. He was at the local government office five days ago when it came under attack and now he's missing.'

'Kidnapped?'

'Doubtful. What do you know about the Massive?'

Parson imagined Gibson in his office, stooped, as he always stooped when he spoke on the phone, voice raised, his accent a little pushed.

'It's a proposal to expand a small military installation in the southern desert. HOSCO won the bid earlier this year. Washington have poured no end of money into the project. Stephen Sutler was HOSCO's man on site, in charge of the initial development, but he's disappeared and no one can find the money.'

'You said he's British?'

'That's almost all we know about him.'

'How much?'

'Well, here's the thing. No one knows exactly. The data was destroyed in the attack. It's being calculated as we speak. We're certainly talking several million dollars.'

Parson allowed a respectful gap before asking why they were involved.

'They want someone to go to Amrah and see the Deputy Administrator at the government office, a man called Paul Howell. He physically managed the money, oversaw the accounts. He's almost certainly involved. It needs to happen soon, though, as soon as possible. Howell has an attorney, and I understand it's all starting to get complicated. They want Sutler found. No one else seems to be getting anywhere. They've also arrested two of the guards, and you'll need to speak with them as well. Ask about Stephen Sutler, see what everyone knows. Oh,' Gibson added, not so much an afterthought as a warning, 'Howell has friends in the State Department. He isn't someone you want to annoy. I doubt he'll come out of this clean, but he's seasoned. Find out what you can about the financial organization. See what's known about Sutler, and leave the rest to the lawyers.'

'You've explained that this isn't what we do?'

'There isn't any choice. HOSCO are our clients and we want to keep them. It's unusual, but it's in the vicinity of what we ordinarily do. They say they aren't liable, that the money was organized by the government office. Anyway, I want to show them that we're available, and that we're happy to help. They need someone immediately, and they'd prefer this person to be British. By the time they find someone else and send him over, Stephen Sutler could be anywhere.'

'So I speak with these men and report back to you.'

'You've misunderstood me. They want you to find him.'

He waited for the flight with the printout in his hands. Two names written on the reverse, *Stephen Sutler, Paul Howell*. The paper folded twice with care. The delay on his return wasn't completely unexpected and when he called his wife she took the news with resignation. In return she gave him little news of her own, and it bothered him that he didn't know her thinking, not to the usual detail.

The proper force of his reassignment struck him mid-flight. A black night with the knowledge of desert and stone waste beneath him, a bad month behind him, and this one fact that he would now have to stay in the country, amid all of this calamity. Beside him sat American soldiers in full kit: tourniquets, boots, helmets, in mottled desert

MARPAT. One replaced plates into pouches. Another – tight mouth, bored – shook with the craft and refused eye contact. Parson looked at the men and wondered how they could tolerate the plain unworkability of the situation. I should not be here, he told himself. I do not want to be here.

Parson arrived at Camp Liberty before sunrise and was taken immediately to collect Sutler's belongings. An hour later, in possession of a single kitbag in a sealed military sack, he boarded the helicopter for Amrah City. The kitbag would go to the team investigating Stephen Sutler's activities, a mix of US Federal Marshals, Iraqi prosecutors, and representatives from the ministries, with a few interested private attorneys. While Parson was officially seconded to this team, he would report directly to Mathew Gibson, who would filter the reports to HOSCO.

Parson focused on the view, unsettled by the craft's sideways pitch he picked out a single Humvee as it cut through the compound in the early light. The camp, marked by water tanks, latrines, a line of Porta-kabins, and a single Quonset hut, lay alongside another unbending road. Back in the desert he could see a number of black oblongs, the burn pits, with lazy smoke trails thinning into ghost vapours. Nothing more than seven black holes and a curve of shacks as provisional as a movie set, its impermanence amplified by the lack of scrub grass, palm groves, or any natural sign of water. A practical logic determined these locations: to protect signals, facilities, borders, supply lines, strategic zones, or some pre-existing feature, but here the logic was lost and the road cut into the desert in a clean unnatural line with the camp and outpost set as nodes on either side – which could, and might as well, sit anywhere along its length. In twelve days this unit would be disassembled and shipped, flat-packed, to Kuwait and Camp Navistar.

He shut his eyes to imagine the unit wiped off the map so that nothing remained except morning light, sunburnt dust, cracked stone. It was easy to imagine it gone, the desert here being ungraded rubble, ridges scorched of colour. Sand filtered into the sky, blurring the land with a pink funk. The flight from Camp Liberty to Amrah City crossed two lines of control: from American to British, from British back to American. The craft descended in a corkscrew, sidling down to avoid attack.

*

Howell's attorney laid out the problem as they walked. *They* – representatives from HOSCO, the military, the New Transitional Assembly, the various Danish, British, and US consulate representatives and their advisers, four internal ministries (which included the National Bank, the Oil Ministry, the Ministry of Industry, and the Ministry for Labour) – wanted Stephen Lawrence Sutler. She counted the authorities on her fingers. 'But instead of Sutler we have Paul Howell and two civilian contractors,' meaning Mathew Clark and Carl Simon Pakosta, the men arrested alongside Howell at Southern-CIPA and charged with impersonating military personnel. 'Which is . . .' she squinted across the asphalt to the hangar, the light about them solid and over-bright, 'useless.'

Parson nodded.

'It's sticky.' The attorney explained the situation in tiny bites. She shifted a collection of bound files under her arms to free her hands, then drew her hair, straight, black, shoulder-length, behind her ear. The heat pushed on Parson's shoulders; the sun sparked sharp across the airfield from chrome on cars and aircraft. He studied the attorney through pinched eyes and thought her younger than he'd first imagined.

'At the moment they can't agree on anything. There's no decision on the presiding authority, so there's no consensus on whether Howell should be handed to civil or military authorities. Right now, until the charges are formalized, the decision is academic, but nobody wants to decide.' She smiled and shook her head. 'If, or when, they make that decision they'll have to decide which military or civil authority takes precedence. It's very sticky.'

They continued their walk; the guard a step ahead, a curve of sweat wetting the small of his back.

'Everything's made a little more complicated because Howell holds dual citizenship with Denmark and the US. He also worked for the State Department, which doesn't make matters easier. Both the military and HOSCO are making a strong case to have him returned to Washington. You understand the complexity?'

Eyes bright, the attorney spoke of patience. None of this was easy or pleasant. Howell was cooperating, while at the very same time he was being stripped of his assets. Each day brought worsening news as his public and private lives were ransacked in the search for the money. 'When the office was destroyed they lost most of their records.'

At the very least he would lose his house in Charlotte, North Carolina, his apartment in Washington, DC. His bank accounts, already frozen, would be cleared. A team of government and civilian lawyers had already divided the claims. 'HOSCO will sue for what they can. The transatlantic flights, the hotels in Damascus, Dubai, London, and every expense relating to these and other such visits during the period of the charges will be clawed back. They're intent on it.' By mid-September Howell's Danish-based properties would be seized. Not that any of this could yet be proved to come from the money they believed he'd extorted. The attorney curled back her hair. Did Parson understand how *unjust* this was? He'd yet to be proven guilty. He'd yet to be formally charged.

Whatever the outcome, Howell's reputation lay in pieces. She said this as an aside and allowed her hand to waver, so-so. She spoke about Howell as if he were a remote element, which Parson found distracting, a quantity they could coolly consider and assay. 'Now Stephen Sutler,' she again curved her hair behind her ear, 'is a whole other matter. We've had sightings in Iran, Bahrain, Sulaymaniyah, Basrah, Kuwait, Damascus, Aden.' Everywhere except the oil-rich wastes of Al-Muthanna and the dusty tracks of Amrah City. A phantom Sutler crawling through the Middle East left open too many possibilities. She pointed in the direction of a hangar. The airfield swam in a humid light. 'Remind me, are you looking for the money or the man?'

'The man.'

'You're from HOSCO?'

'I work for Gibson and Baker. We advise HOSCO on insurance settlements that concern the UK and British citizens.'

'You investigate claims?'

'And we advise on litigation, we investigate fraud.'

'You're part of the clean-up?'

'I'm a public adjuster. There are other people looking for him. I'm here to gather information and because they want my advice.'

'As an adjuster? They've sent a claims adjuster on a manhunt? Can you see why I find this interesting? We're in a country where graduate students run public services, I shouldn't be so surprised. Do you know how much money is missing?'

'I have an idea.'

'Yesterday's estimate hit fifty-three million,' she pronounced the words in pieces, 'dollars.'

'And how did he manage this?'

'No one knows. When you find that out, you find the money. They have no idea.'

'Why have they arrested Paul Howell?'

'Because, like you, he's here.' The attorney nodded and drew in breath. While there could be no doubt about Howell's complicity, it just wasn't possible that Howell could have absconded with fifty-three million dollars, tra-la, like some magic trick. It wasn't logistically possible. It couldn't be achieved. 'The bulk of the money came through his office, so we have to assume that he was involved. Witting or unwitting.' She tucked the files tight under her arm. 'Stephen Lawrence Sutler is a very interesting man. He doesn't appear on company documents. There's no record of him coming into the country. Like you, I've been looking and I've found nothing. HOSCO hired a ghost. Shall we?'

With a signal from the attorney the guard unlocked the door to the hangar.

The interior of the hangar was made out as a makeshift ward, empty of patients but busy with equipment. Green cots, litters, stanchions, and stacked boxes of medical supplies. Some areas appeared to be organized into stations set about black-framed rickshaws to transport the wounded. An American flag hung high above them. Parson couldn't tell if the area was used as a field hospital or for holding patients for transport, and suspected that the function depended on demand.

The attorney walked to a table on which lay a number of files. 'This is everything that survived.' She offered Parson a seat. The guard stood close to the desk.

'Can I see him?'

'I'm sorry?'

'Howell.'

'Howell?' The attorney looked to Parson, at first confused then amused. 'No. He's in Baghdad at Combat Support. You didn't know?' She sat back, took in the long view of the hangar. 'I thought you wanted to see the documents from Southern-CIPA?'

'I came to speak with Howell.'

'Well, he isn't here.' She leaned into the desk and indicated the files. 'Paul Howell was thrown out of the offices when they were hit. He needs surgery.' Of the three people in Howell's office only Sutler, they believed, survived without harm. The boy, Kiprowski, was cut to pieces.

The attorney drew out photographs from a folder. 'This is Paul Howell.'

The man appeared more delicate than Parson had imagined. Recently shaved, the Deputy Administrator wore a smart white shirt and sat upright with his hands flat to the table, angular, poised as if stuffed. His most striking feature, remarked in every report, was his platinum-white hair, which gave him an unreal quality, slightly other-worldly. Howell didn't match Parson's idea of how an embezzler should look; trim and sensitive, with no hint of greed. He could intuit an element of pride in the man's presentation, clean shirt, clean-shaven, a small miracle given the heat.

Parson looked over the images. He couldn't recall the attorney's name. The introduction had passed too quickly, his mind in any case occupied with the strange geography of her office: one desk, hidden away in a field hospital in an aircraft hangar set distant from the base and surrounded by a temporary cordon – a game of Chinese boxes, all of which seemed to intensify the heat. He looked from the attorney to the guard. The attorney spoke in a hushed voice, aware of the current limitations and the presence of the guard. She produced another folder and laid out a loose stack of faxes and newspaper cuttings.

The details of Howell's arrest played across the pages of the *New York Times*, the *Washington Post*, the *Chicago Tribune*, the *Los Angeles Times*. She spread out the papers and turned them for Parson to read. The London *Times, Die Zeitung*, the *Corriere*, ran a photograph of the offices at Southern-CIPA – a building bunkered behind sandbags and razor wire. The *Charlotte Gazette* reported that Howell's family had escaped their homes dressed in sunglasses and wigs and checked into motels along Highway 85, hiding out in the hope that a decent week would staunch the fierce interest now focused on them. Parson looked from one to another and took in the information without reaction. The *New York Times* ran a photograph of pallets of cash, stacked and swathed in plastic, blocks of money rimming the black-ribbed mouth of a Hercules. Paul Howell standing hand on hip with Stephen Sutler beside him, similarly posed, face obscured by shadow. Sutler, the author of this disaster. Stephen Sutler, the vanishing man.

The attorney settled back and looked again to Parson. 'Does this help?'

'It helps.' Parson sat forward. 'Tell me how this worked. How well did Howell know Sutler?'

The attorney shook her head. 'I doubt he knew him at all.' Her voice remained flat and factual.

'But each time Howell transferred, how much?' Parson looked to his notebook. 'Five hundred thousand. Seven hundred thousand. Ten hundred thousand, all in American dollars.'

The attorney levelled her shoulders. A slight aggression leaked into the gesture. 'All by legitimate order. It's all documented. The only interesting feature here is that Sutler chose to receive the money in such small amounts.'

'So a small two hundred thousand?'

'It is small.' The woman paused and cleared her throat. 'How much do you think it would cost to build a new facility in a desert? Imagine? Scale it down, and picture them building one thing, a house, say, what would that take? You have to house the workers, feed them, transport them in and out. Then you have the materials. In principle Sutler commanded a budget of fifty-seven million, which had to be allocated in seven months. Howell had no influence over how he performed this. Camp Liberty was a waste dump for the oil ministry, then for HOSCO, none of this had anything to do with the regional government. Sutler was supposed to design a new facility and prepare the site. I don't see how this could be done in bites of five, seven, ten hundred thousand. His budget covered the basic set-up of the facility, water, power, security, workers' housing. Sutler was one of nearly thirty or so project managers out of the five hundred contractors the regional government dealt with directly, day to day. On top of this they managed payments for all of the ministries based here in the south. Howell dispensed between one and one and a half million dollars per month on wages to each ministry, and all of these payments were made in cash. The monthly operational budget ran into the tens of millions, on top of this were the payments to contractors for reconstruction, not all of them HOSCO projects – schools, power stations, oil facilities, water and sewage, and so on – all approved by Baghdad. Sutler was one of many, and he always collected the money himself.'

'This is documented?'

'We know the dates.' She pointed at the files.

'But other people saw him? Who did he come with?'

'I don't know.' The attorney paused to consider. 'There was the man who was killed in the attack, I've no information on the other occasions.'

'And this was Steven Kiprowski?'

'The boy who died. Stefan. Yes.'

'And Howell always dealt in cash?'

'Yes. The American dollars were kept in Howell's office. But as Sutler was working for HOSCO he had an open card. This wasn't the only expenditure Sutler managed. He had access to accounts back in Washington.'

'Which Howell authorized?'

'Doubtful. And there's no record to show this. I doubt that Howell was a gate-holder for any money held out of the region. Those accounts could be managed online, it would be easy for Sutler to manipulate the accounts, he could have been anywhere to do that.'

'When did he last see Sutler?'

The woman looked up, surprised, and when she spoke her voice curved a little higher. 'He would have given the money directly to Sutler. So that morning.'

'Just before they were hit? Just before the strike?'

'Yes. There wasn't any warning. We have reports from other people in the outer office who say that Howell had just come in to speak with them. It's confused. Everyone in the second office, in accounts, was thrown down. Howell was in the doorway.'

'And Sutler?'

'Everyone assumed he was dead. The blast took everything. Howell's office was obliterated, and the outer office lost almost three walls. One of the guards in the outer office was hit by debris and everyone was concerned about him. You have to understand it was very confusing.'

'And Kiprowski?'

The attorney fell silent for a moment. 'He must have been very close.'

To Parson's surprise the attorney began to smile. 'There's no way of knowing any of this until Sutler tells you himself – he was supposed to prepare for one of the largest engineering projects ever attempted. A new city in the desert, and don't forget, the gateway to the world's largest oil reserve. It was supposed to make up for the failures in Baghdad, Amrah City. This plan was so large, so extraordinary, that no one had their eyes on him. The man is a blankness, a black hole.'

'You're saying we won't find him?'

The attorney thought carefully about the question, and wanting to be honest she said that she just couldn't see it.

2.3

After Cukurca Ford followed the service road that ran parallel to a river (then a fuel line and later a railway line), and throughout the first day he hid from the supply trucks and road tankers, from military craft, all Turkish, all heading east, small flags quivering on the first vehicle.

Now, in Turkey, he was simply John Jacob Ford, engineer – although he guessed it would be wise to keep himself away from the police, the military, away from any kind of official attention, at least until he was well away from the border. Stephen Sutler was gone, he admitted this with a little regret, and understood that he needed to destroy any evidence which would connect him to the name.

Ford couldn't help but fret, until he had the money he wasn't entirely secure. It was possible, even here, that there would be interest in Sutler. He wanted to speak with Geezler and learn more about what had happened, although he knew Geezler would not welcome his call.

At one o'clock on his second day in Turkey, he caught sight of a dun-brown military jeep at a distance of two, maybe three miles. Ford winced into the sun and gave himself four minutes as an estimate. Four minutes. Time enough to form a plan. Salt in his eyes, the taste of zinc in his mouth. He'd trusted himself that once he reached Turkey everything would become easier, but, after an entire morning of silence, only one solitary jeep approached, right where the highway temporarily curved from the protection of the river, the pipeline, the train track. The open plains, gentle and naked, offered no shelter. He could be half a mile off the road and still be seen.

He gave himself three minutes.

The lower right pocket on the front of his backpack held four pieces of identification.

Ford took out the cards and papers. Among the papers he found the list of accounts for the Massive; the list of eight-digit numbers. He couldn't remember putting the list in his pocket after taking it back from Howell – but here it was, safe in his hands. Three chances, he thought, one of them gone. He tucked the paper with his passport into his pocket then set about destroying Sutler's ID. He rubbed the card across a rock and grazed the photo, the name, the magnetic strip, and felt that he was cutting bonds and ties to a project he could not now return to. The jeep could not be seen. Rooks settled close to him. One, three, then five. They approached when he looked down, retreated when he looked up, strange bobbing witnesses. Not ravens, he remembered, but crows with grey breasts and black hoods.

He snapped the cards in half and buried them in the dirt, then squinted at the jeep – lost for the moment in the road's soft dip. He watched it reappear, closer. Two people, jolting in unison, neither in uniform. Better to wave it down than risk another day in full sun with no food, no water; like this could be some ordinary day and some ordinary place to be found walking.

The woman in the passenger seat took off her sunglasses. One hand held her hair in place, fingers split, uncertain, while the other signalled the driver to slow down. When the vehicle drew to a stop beside him the woman dipped forward and stared, busty, cartoonish, head tilted in recognition. She called him Roger. Roger from the *Australian*. Right? Roger? And then a quizzical, 'It *is* you?'

Ford extended his arms, offering himself, innocent.

The woman shook her head. 'Incredible,' she apologized, 'crazy.' She spoke in English to Ford and German to her companion. 'You look like him,' she said. 'I mean it's unreal. How are you here? It's not possible. This area is cut off. The military are all the way to the border.'

The driver began to shove aside the luggage in the back of the jeep. He patted the seat in invitation. As Ford clambered aboard the woman asked if he understood English. Ford said yes, sat down, and found he couldn't stop nodding. He began to explain himself. 'I was heading east. I was following the convoys and they commandeered my vehicle. I've been here for two days. They took my car. Left me in the middle of nowhere. I've been walking but there's no one.' He pointed over his shoulder, then offered his hand realizing that he'd taken up the offer of a ride before the proper introductions. 'Paul Howell,' he regretted the name even as it slipped out of his mouth.

The woman didn't catch the name. What was it? 'Erwell?' She looked hard back down the highway. 'It's impossible for you to be here. The roads have been closed for three days. Entirely closed. Where did you sleep? And food? What about food and water? You have only one bag?'

For the first time Ford realized what a mess he must appear: his trousers worn and dirty, his boots white with dust. Unshaven with sweat sticking his shirt to his shoulders; he stank, he knew this.

'I was supposed to be back this morning. There will be people looking for me. If you drop me at the next town, I can make arrangements from there. Everything I had was in my car.'

The driver and the woman looked at each other, and the man began to drive. Ford leaned into the wind, his eyes half-closed, cat-like. The woman watched Ford in the rear-view mirror and appeared unconvinced by his story. At the driver's suggestion she offered him water and bread. They had nothing else, she said. There was nothing to share. Ford's feet knocked against bottles, soft packets wrapped in a supermarket bag. Cheese, he thought. Meat. Exploring with his boot. They had food.

'What happened to you?' The woman indicated the cuts on his face and hands.

'An accident, not so long ago. A car accident.' He closed his eyes to prevent more questions.

Sleep bore down on him so that he heard only pieces of what she was saying. They were journalists, Susanna Heida and Gerhard Grüner. The three days of one-way traffic meant trouble. 'After Israel,' Heida swept her hand out, 'look, after Egypt, Libya, anything is possible. The Iranians have taken over the western oil-fields and no one has stopped them. The Kurds attempt to declare an independent territory. Everybody wants something. Everything is in collapse. We passed refugees all the way from Semdinli.' She looked to Ford, expecting him to understand. 'The military have closed the villages, blocked the roads. These people are trapped. There have been attacks over the border in both Iran and Iraq. First it was the Shabak and Yizidi, now it's more mainstream Kurd. Iraq is inside out. It's crazy.' To really see what was going on they needed to be in Iraq, she said, but everything, everywhere, was now closed. The borders were impassable.

Ford gave in to the hum of tyres on the tarmac, the hot wind, and slept sitting forward, eyes three-quarter closed.

The journalists stopped at the station forecourt to let Ford clamber out of the jeep. As she said goodbye the woman looked him over again, the calculation clear in her expression that although he wasn't the journalist she'd first mistaken him for, he looked mightily familiar.

'Rowell?' she said. 'Horwell? What was your name?'

A crowd obliterated the open bays in front of the station. The road, monitored by armed soldiers, remained passable. Behind the coach station rose the slim stone minarets and the gold-ribbed dome of a mosque, behind that, five miles north, smoke guttered up from a refinery. An eggy stink clotted the air and stuck in his throat. His thanks came out dry.

Determined to be gone, Ford kept his head down as he straightened the straps on his backpack. With a final hasty goodbye he walked round the back of the vehicle, then slipped immediately into the crowd. His relief at escaping the journalists was tempered with alarm at being back among so many people after a week of near absolute solitude. Even as he entered the crowd he felt separate and distinct, in no way part of them.

Once inside he watched over men's shoulders as the jeep inched out of the forecourt. A bus, however slow and meandering, remained his best option.

He bought a bottle of water, paid with an American dollar, and washed himself over a corner basin in a small mirrorless room. The heat made him dizzy and the water caused the small cuts in his face and hands to begin to spot and bleed. He changed his clothes, found a place to sit at the back of the waiting room and when he settled he caught his reflection in the mirrored side of a soft-drink dispenser. The plastic compressed his face, which appeared in any case longer; his cheekbones so pronounced that it took a short moment to recognize himself. Used to shorter hair, a fatter face, the change fascinated him. With a beard, his skin dark from the sun, abraded and cut, his eyes sharper, a little harrowed, he could pass by people who knew him and be ignored.

While he waited he kept his eye on the soldiers and security guards, the men at the small booths selling halva, cashew nuts, and Coca-Cola, men in couples loitering within the bus station, and the loners stalking the darkened bays. Soldiers armed with rifles minded the entrances. Across the aisle two others slumbered arm in arm, one man's head rested against the other man's shoulder. The floor crammed with civilians who slept head to toe. Men in drab suits with their arms wrapped about their luggage.

Now bored, Ford sat forward with his chin on his hands and decided to steer away from the border and the coast and head further inland. He would find a small hotel, a hostel, a pension. He would keep away from the larger hotels and bars, the cafés that catered to western-ers, the tea houses and public thoroughfares. He would sleep and wait, and while he waited he could be certain that anyone searching for Sutler would push forward and lose momentum.

For most of the evening Ford sat with his head in his hands, mis-erable with the cold. A child slept beside him on a heap of gathered coats while her mother kept watch. These pauses and delays tested his nerve. Wherever there were refugees there would be police and security forces, roadblocks and checks, and they needed to be avoided.

At midnight the electricity failed, and in the darkness broken by the tiny lights of soldiers' cigarettes, he at last felt secure.

In this silence he concerned himself with the attack, and con-sciously dismissed every thought of Kiprowski. At Camp Liberty the threat of such an attack had sat with them through every moment, awake, asleep, so he now felt a kind of deflation, commingled with relief and alarm. Relief that this had happened, it was over: *and what were the chances of it happening a second time?* And alarm at how the event remained unresolved. He couldn't easily dismiss his concern about Kiprowski. *Think of something else now. Wipe him from your mind.* But as he consciously sought less troubling thoughts, his skin prickled in memory of the heat riding over him, bullying him in one hot complex shove, a mess of hands shunting him head over heels so fast and with such force that it stripped the boots off his feet. Surely: if he had survived, then so had Kiprowski. Not thinking of Kiprowski, of course, was thinking of Kiprowski. *There he is, like that man there, or him, or him.*

He missed being Sutler, and halfway through the night believed him-self in transit, heading to, not from the desert of Al-Muthanna and Camp Liberty. The call from Paul Geezler. A five-twenty red-eye from Bonn to Düsseldorf that opened twenty-eight hours of transit flights and slow connections. Geezler wanted him deployed as soon as possi-ble. *Think Vietnam, think Da Nang.* The Massive would transform HOSCO, and Ford, travelling under his own name, slipped into Sutler.

Wide awake, Ford could remember the exact moment he received Geezler's call, and could recall himself, phone in hand, at the window of his small apartment overlooking a street on which nothing moved: the hotel rooms and apartments set above hardware shops, the boutiques and cafés dark and shuttered; the streets leathery wet, the greyness of the view, the ashen un-black sky suggesting a city set on a river.

Up to this point Ford had worked on small schemes, contract by contract: car parks for mini-malls; refits of East German factories; signs for autobahns; ground clearance in Croatia for the Corps of Engineers. All small. Ford knew that Geezler liked him. He knew he had the man's attention. And this was that promised opportunity. *It won't come again. I'm serious. You don't need expertise in business, what you need are people who can do, in one instant, exactly what you ask of them. Are you that man? Are you ready for change?*

The first buses were scheduled to leave at six, all of them heading west or north-west.

The call to prayer came as a dislocated wail amplified through small speakers. Men knelt where they'd slept and bowed in prayer. Women shrank to the sides of the room, minding children, luggage, and themselves. Except for Ford and the soldiers, only one other passenger remained seated, and they looked at each other across the rows of empty benches. The young man, unprepared for the cold, wore open sandals, loose tan shorts, and a navy-blue sweater. He sat with a paperback open on his lap. Occasionally he looked up and scanned the room, his expression dulled by reading, and Ford wondered why such a boy – surely a tourist, a student – would be so close to a war zone.

2.4

Susanna Heida and Gerhard Grüner ate a small breakfast in their room, although neither was hungry. Grüner cut the feta with a pocket knife then sized up the blocks. Bored with him, Heida switched on the television.

The room stank of a zoo-like mustiness. Outside, suitcases and packages lined the stairwell and hallway.

Grüner sat naked at the table and read from his computer screen. A tissue spread out with olives, feta, bruised tomatoes, and bread beside the laptop and an open map of Turkey. Relatives of the hotel staff had paid to have their belongings stored in the empty rooms, and once these rooms had filled up they'd started using the public areas. This was his theory. The hotel would be more secure than their homes, he said, and it was true, the hotel was protected by armed guards. He'd seen this before, in Pakistan, although in Pakistan there was more money and these people had weapons like you wouldn't believe, and bodyguards, ex-SAS, who slept in the corridors. Grüner had a good idea about what was going on.

Heida nodded, conceding to his experience. Crazy. The whole thing. Yes, crazy. There were small fires in the street. People cooking in family groups. People keeping themselves warm, waiting to see what would happen. She switched her attention from the window to the television, clicked through channels and watched the signal jump.

Grüner checked RSS downloads for the current news. 'It looks the same,' he said. 'The border is closed.' He pushed food into his mouth, his attention taken by the computer, the slow download, the erratic link. 'We need to keep moving. They're siphoning gasoline from the cars. The military is running out of fuel. Agri, Van, Hakkari, Siirt, Kurtalan, Mardin.' He plotted an area on the map, point to point. 'The only transport now is north and north-east. These towns are all closed. If we can't get visas by Friday then we're in trouble. We can't go back and we can't go forward. We should have stayed where we were.'

Heida nodded and Grüner nodded back, mouth full. 'There's no news about the visas. There's a message from yesterday saying the border will remain closed.' He glanced up, lips greasy with oil. 'The only flight into Baghdad is from Düsseldorf. That's it. Everything else is military.'

'What about Damascus? If we go to Damascus or to Haleb, maybe there's something from there, a convoy or something?'

'There's nothing. That's it. And anyway, by the time we get there it will be too late.'

Evidence again of Grüner's fatalism. Heida cruised through the channels looking for news. 'Crazy,' she said, 'it's just crazy.' Grüner set the computer aside, stuffed the last of the food into his mouth, and, chewing, reached for her buttocks.

Indifference, this was the word she wanted. This was what she felt about the people outside, about their visas, and about Grüner, especially Grüner, too tall, ungainly, with his fat mouth and busy hands. And there, without warning, appeared the face of the man they'd dropped at the bus station. Heida gasped.

Misreading the signal Grüner pulled her down to his lap. She shoved him away, regained her balance, and pointed to the television. She watched his expression change from hurt to open-jawed amazement.

'It's Howell.' The name came to her, clear and correct. 'He said his name was Howell.' She placed her hand on the screen below Ford's face and pointed out the name Stephen Lawrence Sutler. 'Now we can leave.'

Within moments they were searching for clothes. His scattered carelessly about the floor, hers folded one item on another.

2.5

At the last moment Parson asked if he could interview Pakosta and Clark, the contractors arrested alongside Paul Howell. If possible he wanted to speak with both men at the same time, as one man's memory might prompt the other. He wanted an idea of Sutler's intentions prior to the event. If the man was running with a plan, something set in order, there would be a thread to discover, a trace at the very least.

Parson sat outside a row of uniform grey unit offices while he waited for the response to his request. The security wing, manned by contracted non-combatants, was uncomfortably quiet. The furniture, doors, and partitions marked with stickers: *HOSCO, Hampton Roads, Virginia, USA. Manufactured with Pride.*

Bothered that he knew the facts but couldn't see under the skin of them, he figured through Sutler's last morning. A collection of dockets and transport passes provided no detail about the events of that morning. Within thirty-five minutes of Stephen Lawrence Sutler's arrival at Southern-CIPA, the offices had come under attack, and Sutler had walked from the devastation through a compound heavy with dust and open gunfire, leaving one man in pieces. His flight, from its outset, unnatural, contrary to instinct. Parson couldn't see how any man could so thoroughly vanish unless he was vulnerable, foolish, naive, or halfway gone to start with. People like Sutler rarely managed to disappear unless accident or foul play played some part.

These buildings, provided by HOSCO, were little more than seaside trailers. Flimsy frames and fire-retardant material. Nothing much of anything.

Clark and Pakosta were held under military supervision, dressed in standard orange overalls, and confined to a small, temporary cell. They answered questions about the weekend prior to Sutler's disappearance, and admitted with a little discomfort that Paul Howell, as Deputy Administrator for Project Finance, had paid them to accompany him on a visit to the Royal Palm Hotel in Bahrain. Whenever Howell needed to leave Iraq on his own business he took a group with him, partly for security, and partly to make an impression. Under this simple fact lay the itch of another story. 'Once or twice,' Pakosta explained, 'that's all it was.' On these trips the men were provided with military uniforms. 'As far as we knew this wasn't a problem. He told us to wear them.' There were gifts involved. Watches, whisky, cash.

Parson asked if the civil contractor Stephen Sutler had ever accompanied them on these trips and the men shrugged (although they were not men, but boys aged nineteen and twenty-one). Sutler had attended one or two of these excursions, he came with them to Bahrain, but not Kuwait. Even when he did go he wasn't much of a participant. Clark supposed he was at the bar. Pakosta said he was too involved to care about what Sutler was doing.

Parson changed direction. 'What can you tell me about the Massive?'

'What did we know? We didn't know anything. He had us digging holes, putting up posts, and putting them back up when they blew over. Before Sutler our job was to manage the burn pits and keep the road open for the oil tankers and the convoys. That was our job. That's what we were there for.'

'Then why did you impersonate security?'

'I said, already. I explained. Howell wanted security for his trips. It was good money. He paid in cash. He provided uniforms. He said there wasn't any problem with it.'

Parson turned his attention to Clark. 'What do you know?'

Clark sat upright, hands open in front of him. 'I know there were plans to build a new facility, and we were helping with that. There were plans for a whole city. It didn't make much sense, there's nothing but sand. He was looking at bringing in water, he was blocking out where everything would go.'

Parson returned to his notes. 'You accompanied Stephen Sutler to Southern-CIPA. You were with him on the flight from Camp Liberty to Amrah City. Did he talk about going somewhere else? Did he ever talk about what he would do when he was done in Iraq? Did he say anything about what he planned to do?'

Pakosta shook his head, and Clark said no.

'Did he speak with anyone else?'

'Kiprowski. They spent a lot of time together.' Both men agreed.

'He never spoke about home? Did he ever mention his family? Did he ever mention that he was married?'

Clark tucked his hands under his thighs and sat forward. 'He never spoke about much of anything. Not to me. Maybe to Kiprowski, you'd have to ask him. I don't remember him talking about anything except the project. That's all he was interested in.'

Parson read a list of names. The other men at Camp Liberty with Clark and Pakosta: Hernandez, Watts, Samuels, Gunnersen, Chimeno, Kiprowski. 'That morning at Amrah City, did you see him into the building?'

'We were outside,' Pakosta answered for them both. 'Neither of us went inside.' Pakosta's head tipped sideways, slow and with meaning, and Parson asked himself if this intended threat or irritation – if this indicated that he was lying.

'And Kiprowski? Where did he come from?'

Clark looked to Parson, puzzled by his use of the past tense. 'He's from Chicago. He's from the north side.'

'I meant that morning. Why did Sutler choose Kiprowski? Was there any reason for this?'

A nervous Clark continued shaking his head. Pakosta paused, then answered. 'Maybe he just liked Kiprowski more.'

Parson queried the statement. Exactly what did Pakosta mean?

'He had us digging holes in the sand. The only person who didn't dig was Kiprowski.' Pakosta shrugged. 'Kiprowski ran after him like a dog. When there was real work he always found something else for him. Some other business.'

'And on other occasions?'

'You mean visits to CIPA? That was it. There weren't any other occasions. That was the one time he went to collect money.'

Parson took out a sheet of paper from his notes. 'Howell gave Sutler five hundred thousand, seven hundred thousand, ten hundred. All in cash. All on different days.'

'No.' Clark shook his head vigorously. 'When?'

'July twelfth, nineteenth, twenty-fifth . . .'

'He didn't go more than once or twice before that last time, and that was the only time we were with him. You need to check those dates.'

'There are records of Howell giving him money. On five, six, seven occasions. More.'

Pakosta appeared startled. 'Then Howell is lying. It didn't happen. Sutler went to CIPA with his little plans, a roll of maps, maybe – maybe – three times. He kept coming back complaining that Howell was making him jump through hoops, causing delays. He was waiting on money to bring in materials, to start something, but Howell kept stalling. He never had money.'

'This is what Sutler told you?'

'We saw him. We saw him take the flight. We saw him come back. He had nothing with him but a roll of drawings. He didn't even have a flak vest. Like he landed in the desert with nothing.'

Parson asked Clark to confirm.

'He took a bag, one time. One time only, and that was the last time. The night before he was talking about how big it would need to be. He didn't know if his bag would be big enough, and he was excited about the money because everything was going to start, just like he wanted.'

'How was he paid until then?'

Pakosta shrugged. 'He didn't take any money, there were no other times. Day to day we all managed on credit and account.'

'Did he carry much cash?'

'We were in the desert. Nothing to spend it on. He probably managed the same as us.'

'But you can't be certain that Sutler never took money from Howell.' Parson allowed a short pause, the men appeared confused. 'You know nothing about the money he collected from Southern-CIPA? You can't be certain? After the incident, did you see Sutler leave?'

Again, Pakosta answered first. 'I didn't see anything once he was inside. I was right at the door. Smoking, right by the door. I came out before everything kicked off. I didn't see Sutler. I didn't see Kiprowski.'

Then Clark: 'I was outside with the duty guard. I felt the blast, and right after I heard live fire from the perimeter. After that I don't know. I was on the ground. The blast came from the back, but the shots were close. There was smoke. I had my head covered waiting for incoming.'

'One hit?'

'Mortar.'

'You saw it?'

'Clear as day.' Pakosta lazily scratched his neck. 'You've seen the result? You get to Amrah?'

'Where did it come from? What direction?'

'It came from the factory. From the south.'

'And you saw this? What about you? You saw this, Clark?'

'We both saw it,' Pakosta answered for Clark, 'clear as day.'

Clark sat forward, his hand hesitated close to his mouth. 'I heard it coming. Right from the south. There's a market and some old factories, light industry. Most of those buildings are secured. Most times they drive up and lay down everything they have, but this was just the one. And I guess one was enough.'

'Stephen Sutler, describe his face. His hair? How long?' Parson abruptly stood up. 'Is he taller than me?'

The answer from both came as a shrug. Maybe, said one. Yes, the other. Both unconvinced. Sutler looked British but they couldn't clarify why.

'So about the same height? And build?'

Stockier, they agreed. Maybe. Heavier by ten or fifteen pounds, or twenty even, twenty-five. They couldn't say.

Parson collected his papers and drew out a photocopy of Stephen Sutler's ID, the image enlarged, his face washed of distinguishing features. 'There's nothing more you can tell me about this man? You saw him enter a building surrounded by security forces, from which, it appears, he vanished during an assault. And you had no idea about the money?'

'I swear.'

Pakosta asked if that was it, and Parson said yes, that was all he wanted. With the interview over Pakosta and Clark stood up.

'Why all this interest in Sutler?'

'Because Sutler has disappeared.'

'But what about Kiprowski?'

'Kiprowski hasn't disappeared.'

'You found Kiprowski?'

Parson gave a simple nod. He stopped at the door and waited as it was unlocked.

'What happens now?'

'I don't know.'

As the door drew open Parson placed his cap back on his head. In the centre of the door a single key with a scuffed metal tag in a single keyhole. Parson kept his eyes fixed on the key as the men were escorted from the room.

2.6

An hour out of Kopeckale the coach began to ascend the central plateau. Ford drifted in and out of sleep as the mountains beside the city fell away and the horizon took on a smooth uninterrupted curve. Each time he woke a sense of disconnection veered him back to Amrah City and he returned to the present with a slight pang, a regret that Sutler was done with, and that he would not see the project advance, and that the Massive would develop without him. All of this needed to settle in the past. Ford pressed his forehead to the window and allowed the judder to shake up his thoughts as the land on either side became white, parched, and lunar. Away from the desert the project seemed less about ambition, the pure improbability of building something from nothing, and more about hubris, pride and greed, about the oil, about the minerals, about maintaining presence and influence long after the withdrawal of troops.

Once on the plateau the road became level and the plains gave way to bare fields sectioned by low stone walls. To their right an irrigation ditch ran parallel to the highway, to their left the creosote-caked oil lines; the pipeline irregularly set with field stations, some abandoned, some burned, some scrawled with graffiti, a few transformed into temporary shelters. Ford's eye scuttered along the course and passed over the refugees, figures strung single file in clusters of four or five, seldom more. The driver sounded the horn to drive the vagrants off the road, and they stepped, automatic, onto the margin without gesture or complaint. Heads protected from the sun with cloth or plastic hoods.

Villages set back from the main highway appeared undisturbed by the war; the scars of mortar strikes scored the roadside as rough black craters, as certain truths; a few buildings, remarkably few, pecked with gunshot, fewer still were simple roofless shells – all signs of the earlier insurrection. Signs of the current troubles were limited to the skirting squatter camps of makeshift tents and tarpaulins. Ford watched, indifferent, he would be happier once they were on another route.

The student from the station sat two rows ahead, his feet struck across the aisle, the paperback open on his thigh. The boy's sweater slipped from the overhead rack and one sleeve swung over his scalp, his hair cropped, the skin white, untanned. A horizontal scar, one inch long and lightly raised, tapered to a point above his left ear. On the back of his white T-shirt a logo of a large red star in a red circle. An attendant distributed towels scented with rose water. After the man had passed by, the student dropped the towel under his seat and wiped his hands on his shorts. His arms were lean, muscular, formed through sport.

Mid-morning he woke addled and uncomfortable. Slowly rising to the present, he realized that the coach had stopped and they were at some kind of checkpoint – and there were soldiers mounting the bus.

The military police stood in a line in front of a barrier, the road curved behind them, rising, bare, a tractor and trailer packed with refugees stopped beside the embankment. Passengers assisted each other from the trailer and stood side by side on the hot white scree, sulky and agitated but visibly humble; a few of them held out documents as if offering a petition while the soldiers, regardless, tossed their luggage onto the road. From what Ford could see there was no explicit purpose to the search.

One gruff and baby-faced soldier barked instructions at the coach driver. The driver civilly repeated the soldier's demands and the passengers rose without complaint and began to disembark. The student peered over the headrest, startled, poised a little like a flightless bird.

The passengers began to assemble beside the coach. Their lethargy struck Ford as a sign of assent, a sign that this was not unusual. The student held back, then with a deft stab he tucked a small plastic bag between the seat and the seatback. A guard leaned into the bus and told them, as far as Ford could understand, to get out. The soldier's face became a comedy of infantile demand, plump, sulky.

Off the coach and out of the air conditioning the heat pressed down. Ford rolled up his sleeves and stood with the passengers feeling a wash of heat; everybody squinting at the coach's silver side while the driver sorted through the luggage in the hold. The student waited beside him. The driver, labouring alone, passed Ford the wrong rucksack. The mistake became immediately obvious as soon as he lifted the pack; this rucksack being newer, cleaner, was also heavier than his. The label, a clear plastic star, gave the name *Eric Powell*, and an address in France on one side and in New York on the other. Ford handed the rucksack to the student and returned to the hold to claim his own.

The student waited with him and asked if he understood what was happening. American, he spoke in quick bursts. His accent, East Coast, precise and educated, sounded different to the supple Midwestern drawl Ford was used to. Ford retrieved his bag from a line of luggage, the boy followed and picked out a small metal case then walked back to the line of passengers. He repeated his question and Ford said he didn't know, whatever it was it didn't look out of the ordinary. Ford looked back at the tractor-trailer. Unsupervised, the refugees, mostly women, huddled in a pack as if hiding, luggage loose in the road. The passengers from the coach, mostly men, and most of them smoked, strung out in a line waiting for the patrol to check their papers and belongings. The student set his case close to Ford's feet, looked clearly into his face, and gave a nod, as if Ford had asked for assistance, as if the small silver case were his.

'It's film,' the student said, indicating the case, 'undeveloped sixteen-millimetre film. Shots of landscape. That's all it is. Every time I'm searched they open the camera.' His hands gestured the unspooling of film.

The student stood a distance away with his rucksack, leaving a gap of three or four paces between them. Ford could not see the purpose of it and did not like the boy's assumption that he was sympathetic. Even so, he did not step back.

They waited in line with their backs to the sun as the soldiers inspected the bus. The road cut into an escarpment, a curved chalk wall. In front of them ran the straw-coloured plains of Anatolia. It was good that this was only the Turkish military. If they were British or American he would be nervous – despite the day, the bright sunlight, the broad view of open fields.

One soldier examined the hold and shuffled on his knees through the empty compartment. Above him two soldiers searched the cabin, to check the floor, the seats, and the racks. The coach wavered in the full midday heat. Another soldier, pug-faced, younger than the others, led a muzzled Alsatian between the passengers and their luggage. He held the leash high and tugged the animal between the baskets and suitcases. A compact semi-automatic slung over his shoulder, battered and hand-me-down. The soldier stopped the dog in front of the student and forced the dog's muzzle to the student's backpack. He indicated that the student should open it. To Ford these soldiers were boys. Smug, fresh, untested.

The student crouched and unzipped a side panel to show folded shorts, T-shirts, rolled socks. Tangled inside the main body of the bag lay an assortment of climbing gear: bright-coloured cord, strong steel buckles. The student mimed what they were for, and repeated, *climbing*. It's for *climbing*, until his gestures became cocky, suggesting that the soldier was a little dumb. *Cli-ming. Climbing.* He pointed to the white rockface behind them, then the ropes and steel clips. How obvious did he need to make this?

'You speak any Turkish?' he asked Ford.

The soldier spoke to the boy rapid-fire, aggressive, he snapped the dog to heel and toe-tapped the backpack. The boy became angry, and Ford expected a confrontation.

A shout came from further up the queue. Suddenly nervous, the passengers broke out of line and scattered, and there in the widening gap a slim green snake zippered across the white gravel. The soldiers grouped about it, one flicked a cigarette, another kicked stones and the snake changed direction, twisting in a strange undulation, fast, but not fast enough. A third soldier picked up a rock, a flat white slab, dropped it then laughed. Ford watched the snake wind about itself, its skin a sharp fresh green, the body as thin as his little finger. Head mashed to a crimson stump, its silver underside caught the sun as it rolled into tight coils.

The student asked if it was poisonous.

Ford said he didn't know but thought that colour gave some indication.

The student turned the snake over with his foot. The body twisted about his sandal and he gently shook it off. He looked up at the soldier. 'Why?' he asked. 'Seriously. What was the point?'

The soldier picked up the snake and slung it across the road – and the student swore loud enough to be heard.

'I think he might know that word.'

'They probably hear it enough.'

Ford returned to his backpack, uninterested in the student's disagreement.

The soldiers walked on, attention taken by another vehicle drawing up the highway. The officer in charge slapped the side of the coach to dismiss them; others began to move the barriers and open the road. As a group the passengers picked up their luggage and returned to the coach. Leaving the first group gathered by the tractor-trailer alone. The student returned for his case. Catching up with Ford, the boy offered his hand.

'My name's Eric.'

A wave of cold air blew through the cabin as the coach drew back onto the road.

The student turned about and held up the plastic bag he'd stowed away earlier. A bag of digital memory sticks. 'Two days ago the army raided a village on the border,' he explained. 'They came in trucks. About fourteen of them, and they shipped everyone out. Then helicopters wiped out the village. They used rockets.' He shook the bag and spoke in a low conspiratorial tone. 'They're making all of this happen. None of this is any accident. For days they've been bombing their own border and blaming the Kurds. Every time trouble kicks off in the Middle East they move against the Kurds. Fact.'

When the boy turned back Ford smiled to himself. He should have guessed the boy was doing noble favours, picking other people's fights, working an adventure to take back to his campus, to become someone who has been somewhere and done something.

The stops became less frequent; the villages became smaller and the refugee camps so few that Ford forgot them and imagined himself to be in a country unaffected by war.

In the early afternoon they stopped at a small trading post, a restaurant girdled by a market – a supple chaos of stalls set up in the dust with passengers haggling for produce: fresh dates, dyed pistachios, halva, cigarettes, toys, CDs and DVDs. Young boys sold flags, iced water, sodas, and pastries wet with honey. Smoke blossomed from a row of barbecues and Ford bought two lamb skewers and finished before he could find himself a seat. The attendant who gave out the rosewater and paper towels sat at a separate table, smoking, eyes narrowed on Ford.

Ford wandered through the stalls. Men sold jewellery, bracelets and beaded bangles, small handcrafted pieces. One man punched names into metal dog tags. He set the letters into a punch and imprinted the tags in a small vice. Ford stopped in front of the table and idled through a tray of Zippo lighters. The man spoke to him and he smiled but did not reply.

'American?' the man asked. 'English? You want your name?' The man held up one of the tags to show Ford. The man had a lazy eye, not so acute, but noticeable. He wore a jacket and no shirt. When he looked up the lazy eye shifted with a slight but perceptible twitch, the movement so subtle that Ford found himself watching to catch it. The man waited, all patience. Searching for money, Ford pushed his hands into his pocket and found the note with the account numbers. An idea occurred to him and he held up the note.

'How much,' he asked, 'for only numbers. These numbers.' He opened out the paper and showed it to the man. 'Five tags.' He held up his hand, five wide fingers. 'Five. You can do numbers? How much for five tags?'

The man squinted at the paper then smiled as he looked up and Ford could not be sure that he'd understood. He found a pen on the table and began to write out the numbers to be stamped on each tag. A separate number on each sheet. 'You understand?' He set a tag on the paper. 'This for this.'

The man nodded. Ford continued to write out the numbers and did not notice the student approach.

'I didn't get your name.'

'Sorry?'

'Your name?'

Ford concentrated on the numbers. The boy wanted a name. 'Michael.'

'Michael, not Mike?'

'Right, it's Michael.'

'You're English?'

Ford nodded. He finished writing the last of the numbers and handed them to the man. One account number per tag. The workman held up his hands to indicate that he would be ten minutes.

'That's all? Ten minutes?'

The man nodded and began to set the numbers into the punch.

The student followed Ford back to the restaurant. 'My mother's

English. She still has her accent.' Without asking he set his book on the table and sat opposite. Tucked between the pages a small black notebook. 'Do you know Winchester?'

For the first time Ford noticed that the restaurant sat in a field. The coach had driven off the road and over rough land to reach it. To steer the conversation away from himself he pointed at the book and asked what the boy was reading.

'This? I'm just getting into it. I'm not that far.'

They were talking, he guessed, because the boy felt some common ground between them, something more than the simple coincidence of travel. The silver case, the snake, the confidence about the film, connecting elements, at least for the boy.

'It's making its way round campuses. There's a whole story about it. The guy who wrote it was a student, and he disappeared before the book came out. It's about how these guys, these brothers, copy a murder from another book, a thriller.' He held up the book. 'It's true. They pick someone up from the train station, then cut him up in a basement room, just like the story, then pieces of him are found in the street. It happened in Naples, Italy. There's any number of versions on this story – the original book wasn't published in English till about ten years ago – but the writer, this student, went to Naples and wrote about the people who still lived in the apartment where the murder happened, and then he disappeared. You've not heard about it?'

Ford said no.

'There's a film also. I think it's just out in the States.' The boy grimaced. 'I haven't read the original book yet. The one the brothers copied. But imagine. You write about something like that, a thriller, something gruesome, and someone copies everything you've written for real.'

'What's it called?'

The boy unfolded the cover and held the book up for Ford to read. 'The original book or this? There's a buzz about it online. Anyway, it's huge on campus.'

'So what's it called?'

'The original is called *The Kill*. You're not supposed to say the title or something bad will happen. You disappear.' He nodded toward the coach and grinned. 'I saw you at Kopeckale. You look like you've been in an accident.'

Ford automatically touched his face. 'It isn't anything interesting.'

'So where are you going? Narapi?'

'I haven't decided.'

The boy shied away from the smoke rising from the brazier. 'If you want to stay in Narapi there's a place called the Maison du Rêve. It's good. Nothing fancy. Doesn't have a pool or anything, just two or three rooms around a courtyard. And it's reasonable. I have the address. I'm going through Narapi to do some climbing, but I'll be back by the weekend and this is where I'll be staying.' The boy took out his mobile and while he talked about himself Ford pointedly stood up to go. A copy of the *Herald* stuck out of the boy's bag. 'You want this?' The boy offered the paper. 'There's something in there about what I've been talking about. Something about the movie.'

Ford held up his hand. Thanks but no. There was nothing he cared to see in a newspaper. Nothing he needed to be told. Making his apology he stood up and said he needed to retrieve the dog tags.

Back on the coach he held the dog tags in his fist, a certainty about them that he liked. The metal, thin steel or tin, quickly warmed to his hand. His ran his finger over the ridges, double-checked that the numbers on each were correct, set them in order, then tore the paper into small pieces and let the paper drop to the floor. He threaded the tags onto a small-ball chain which he wore about his neck. The weight of them was reassuring, pleasing, an indication that things were going well. He should email these numbers to himself. Store the numbers where he would not lose them. Better still, he should get online and transfer the money. He wondered if the money was really there, waiting.

The outskirts of Narapi appeared modern, a new road flanked with boxy concrete houses. Wisps of grass sprouted on unfinished walls. The town itself lay in a long hollow interrupted by an oblong flat-topped plug of rock: a bald stone nub.

The student turned and pointed. 'It looks something like a meteor, no?'

Ford asked how far it was to the next town and the boy guessed that Birsim was another hour, maybe only forty-minutes or so. Eager to sleep in a real bed, he decided to stay in Narapi.

As they waited for a place at the terminus Ford asked the student to repeat the name of the hotel. From the back of the coach came singing and clapping. The boy tore a corner from the notebook and wrote down the hotel's number and address, and Ford felt some relief that his journey, for now, was over. The town was far from the border, remote and secure.

'I might see you if you're still there this weekend.' He held up his hand. 'Eric,' he said, 'remember, Eric.'

A child with a bandage at his neck signalled the coach into the bay.

The student watched Ford as the coach pulled away. Ford checked the label on his rucksack, although he could tell from the weight that he was carrying his own. A few saplings planted either side of the square wilted in the late-afternoon sun; their small bay-shaped leaves hung down, crackling in a light wind. As he walked through the town Ford realized that there was no military presence: no Humvees, no road-blocks, no patrols scattered cautiously across the streets. It wasn't that he missed them, but he noticed they were absent. As he walked the dog tags lightly swung against his chest.

2.7

On the Thursday night Anne received two messages. The first, a message on her voicemail, reminded her of a seven o'clock booking at John's in the East Village. *You're late. You've forgotten, haven't you?* Her friend's voice bristled with irritation. Something had happened, she said, and it needed to be talked out. The second message, a text message, came from Anne's son, Eric, who was travelling in Turkey.

Already in a cab heading downtown, Anne did not immediately read the message, Eric used a shorthand she didn't always understand, and her glasses, tucked into the side pocket of her small bag, were temporarily misplaced. Unable to read the text, she stored the message, listened a second time to the voicemail, then, with a small apology, asked the driver how long it would take to get downtown.

The driver shrugged. 'Fifteen, if we're lucky. Maybe twenty? Who knows, right?'

In two days Anne would depart for Rome. She had organized her last week in New York with care, so it irritated her that she would forget this one appointment and took it as something subconscious, a kind of undeliberate/deliberate gesture. More and more, Marian's emergencies coincided with Anne's departures.

She called her friend. 'I'll be with you in ten minutes. I promise.'

'Nowhere is ten minutes away.' Marian didn't disguise her irritation. 'Well, hurry because I've found you somewhere. We're talking Malta. Marsaskala. Town on one side, uninterrupted sea view on the other. You'll love it. An honest-to-god palazzo, totally private, so spacious you'll think you've lived life in a closet. You can have parties, and you can have it as long as you like. This place is an absolute find. A steal. Nobody knows about it. And by the way: big favour, very big. You owe me.'

The taxi took Anne alongside the park. Outside the Met couples walked down the steps, some animated, some arm-in-arm. Lights on in the building for a late opening. One wagon on the sidewalk sold pretzels and knishes. All of this familiar, quaint in a way, but still foreign: the people, the vendors. As the cab changed lanes she felt the phone vibrate in her pocket. Hearing a siren she paused and looked out of the cab and automatically at the sky above the midtown apartments and skyscrapers. Beside her, an acid blackness swam between the last of the trees. The word foreign caught in her head. After finding her glasses she properly read the message from her son: on coach – meet N+M l8r – in ist fri 4 2 wks – call whn u arriv

Anne calculated the time difference, but as the taxi made its way down Broadway she became distracted by the drive. Twelve years in New York City and the streets viewed from a cab still appeared foreign to her. Readable but unstable. The mood of any given street shifted between blocks, a blunt reconfiguration, different each time, brutish and harsh. The streets gave character to the people, she thought, not otherwise. The last time she had drinks with Marian they had disagreed in a sulky, dissatisfied way, and on the taxi ride uptown they had attempted a reconciliation, Marian suggesting that Anne shouldn't be such a tourist all of the time.

It would be Friday morning in Turkey, early, barely dawn. She imagined Eric tired but awake, riding on a bus and heading toward his friends. She'd heard more from him on this trip already, than the entire time he was in Cuba with Mark.

It would be Marian who would tell her about the bombing of the refinery, and how the Turkish government blamed the attack on the PKK and was clearing the villages and settlements close to the border. Marian questioned how Anne could not have seen the news. It was everywhere. For three days. Unavoidable. The region was in chaos. She had meant to call earlier to make sure that she was OK.

'They won't let reporters in. First it was Syria, then they closed their border, and now it's Turkey, all of these refugees, and they've cleared the villages so no one has anywhere to go. These people have come out from Iraq, desperate, and no one wants them. It's what happened with the Armenians, you burn the villages and you keep them moving. Like animals. Herding people like cattle.'

NARAPI

3.1

Ford woke after a fretful sleep, his head muggy with Zolpidem, the sleeping pills he'd taken from Kiprowski at Camp Liberty. It was only natural after two weeks sleeping rough that this – a bed, sheets, a room – would feel so alien and insecure, and that his sleep would be hounded by wakefulness, an awareness of the room, the proximity of things, of temperature, sound, a multitude of disconnected elements. Like most mornings, ideas about the Massive, Southern-CIPA, Howell, Kiprowski, became confused with ideas about returning to Bonn. He dreamed of the wrong people in the wrong places. The idea of reconnecting with his old life – even just to arrange payments for loans, of walking into his small apartment, of returning to John Jacob Ford's dry and ordinary struggles – bore down upon him as a weight he couldn't avoid, a welter of regrets through which he wrestled into his day.

Unsure of the time, he rose without considering that the day belonged to him; habit made him turn out of bed and set his feet on the floor the moment he woke. During the night he'd taken the dog tags off, and kept them secure in his fist, the chain wrapped about his hand. As he looked about the room (a narrow lean-to, simple, little more than a goat pen with a flagstone floor, whitewashed walls, and two low cot-like beds pushed to opposite sides) he thanked his good luck. No coaches today. No crowds. No open roads. Without the pre-occupations of travel Geezler stuck with him, a stream of thought running parallel to his own at equal volume. Geezler. Geezler. So far he had done exactly as he had been asked. Surely he could call him? How serious was he about not being contacted? Ford knew the answer even as he considered the question. He should find an internet café, transfer the money, or at least email the numbers to himself.

On the spare bed he found a well-thumbed guidebook, the pages down-turned to Narapi. It gave little information, saying that the town was nothing more than a transit town with a small hammam, two mosques – almost everything in pairs – two pensions, two large hotels with the only bars, a nightclub of sorts, and a swimming pool. An escarpment crowned by the remains of a fort rose from the centre of the town with tombs carved into its eastern side, barely worth the walk. The guidebook gave no information about this strange geology, except to describe the rock as an inland island.

Beside the door hung a framed print of the Massif du Vercors in the French Alps. Ford took the picture down to use the glass as a mirror. He wet his beard, tweezed the hair between his fingers, and decided not to shave. He washed his face then studied the water, milky with sediment. He changed the water, washed, changed it again, doused his face and neck, the water specked with matter. With a final bowl he lowered his head to take in the musty odour of moss, of rock, a suggestion of subterranean rivers and caverns, a world in opposition to the bright dry landscape and the cold scentless nights of the previous fourteen days. He drained the sink and studied the grit, and wondered if this was plasterboard, pieces of the hut from Amrah City, or shale from sleeping rough? He scratched his fingers through his beard and found small spots, whiteheads, what he'd taken to be ingrown hairs, which when crushed pushed out sharp grains, tiny pieces of dirt, flecks; some white, some black, some translucent. He'd heard about this from the men at Camp Liberty, how in cases of bombings, blasts, suicide attacks, survivors found splinters dug in their skin: pieces of bone, fragments of the weapon, flecks of what they called *environment*. He turned his head to inspect his cheek, now healed but still numb. In the softer skin on his neck and right shoulder he found more small lumps, sensitive peppered specks.

After dressing in clothes he'd washed the night before, the cuffs and collar still damp, Ford stepped into the courtyard to find a woman alone at a picnic table; honeysuckle decked the wall behind her, a small bag on the seat beside her spilled loose sheets of paper. The woman gathered her notes together and told him in a husky voice with a pretty French twist that he had missed breakfast.

She stacked the plates together, a little apologetic. She could ask Mehmet for coffee, but to be honest it wasn't likely there would be any more. Breakfast was a one-shot affair. Four small plates with olive pits and orange rind, a pinch of bread, maybe some oil. Ford wondered if he had missed breakfast or if she had eaten his share. The woman introduced herself. Nathalie. She smiled as they shook hands and squinted into the sun as she looked up. He considered telling her his proper name, but shied away and introduced himself as Tom.

'*Tom*,' she repeated, elongating the name to *Tome*. 'English?'

She was travelling with friends, the three of them touring for the month; except, mercifully, today she was on her own, and how nice it was to have a day to herself. They planned to stop at the Maison du Rêve for a week, perhaps. She didn't know. How long did he intend to stay?

Ford said that he hadn't decided; he might stay a week. He couldn't remember when he'd last spoken with a woman one-to-one, literally couldn't remember, there being no women at Camp Liberty, and none that he could recall at Southern-CIPA.

Nathalie warned him to be prompt about meal times. Water, she said, became scarce in the late morning and was lukewarm at best. As she spoke she gathered her hair in both hands – chestnut-coloured, long and straight – and drew it back in a premeditated gesture.

There was one small problem. Nathalie cleared her voice. 'Has Mehmet said anything, perhaps? No?' She shook her head. 'There's a small mistake.' It was her understanding that they had rented both rooms – there being three people in her party, and only two rooms in the pension at present. 'We booked the rooms before we came. Mehmet must have thought that you were the third person in our group.'

'I think I've met your friend.'

'I don't think so? Where did you come from?'

Ford hesitated. 'South.'

'You came by coach?'

Mehmet had mentioned nothing to Ford about the room and he said so.

Nathalie ran a finger through her hair, her mouth compressed to show that this was awkward. 'It's a room for two people.'

He finally understood what she was asking for. 'I don't mind sharing.'

Delighted, the woman smiled in relief. 'Are you sure it isn't a problem?' This was good then, not the best arrangement, but satisfactory. The third member of her party would arrive tonight or tomorrow morning, she wouldn't know until later. She would explain everything to Mehmet, he needn't worry. Nathalie picked up her shoulder bag and smiled as she drew the zipper shut. 'It's a nice place,' she said, 'the town. It isn't anything special, but it's nice. Very quiet.' Narapi was not without interest. He should visit the fort and the market. It would occupy the morning but not much more.

As she left she warned him not to be late for the evening meal.

Ford followed Nathalie into town, determined to find an internet café. He decided to buy new clothes.

He took the paved road from the bus depot to the mosque, and found the morning air warm but thin – the only indication of the altitude. Tom, he repeated the name, Tom, pleased with the invention. Better Tom than Michael. Too bad he'd told the boy Michael, although, why would he even remember it? If the situation proved too sticky he could move on, although the idea unsettled him. Wasn't this a good place to wait and allow everything to settle? Five days at least, five or six days. The road forked behind the mosque, one tine leading to a small market, the other to a rough track which continued up the escarpment. The road steepened as it turned, flanked on one side by a scrappy rock face, and on the other by a scattered line of garage-like workshops. Ford walked without hurry. Four children followed behind, loosely curious. A man squatted at a doorway, shirtless, skinny, and smoking while he tapped a design into an aluminium bowl held between his feet. The hammer's patter rang light and clear up the escarpment walls. Ford stopped to pick grit from a slit in his boot and noticed that the children also stopped in their tracks. When he turned about they also turned, and when he stared too long they headed back, breaking into a run just before they reached the corner.

At the top of the escarpment the track stopped at a chain-link fence. Ford paused and let his breath even out. A lime-green gecko skittered across the path. The fence bowed beside the road. The stone edge fell steeply away to dry grasses, a drop, a view of pale sky and rooftops. Ford looked down at the workshops as he carefully straddled the fallen fence, unnerved not by the idea that he might fall so much, but by the idea that he might deliberately let go.

He found the fort as decrepit and uninteresting as the guidebook suggested. With over half of the wall collapsed, the hill lay bare, a black slug of rock stripped by the wind. Signs turned about-face warned that the road was unsafe. Broad fissures crazed the stone; cracks which appeared to run the width and depth of the plateau. Close up, the rock appeared to be made of separate upright stacks. Ford stepped delicately across with the same unease he'd felt straddling the fence. A warm updraught blew through the crevices. He crouched and dropped a pebble and listened as it scuttled down, the noise tapering to nothing.

In all directions pale land gave out to pale sky. Scrub farmland cut close about the town. A coach wound slowly through the market to the square. Most of the travellers would only see the terminus and then press on to Birsim. He needed to decide what he would do, when and where he would move on. If things were good now, stable, didn't it make sense to wait, to stay safe? He didn't want to admit that the next steps, the risk of going to a larger town, the risk of transferring the money, were easier to stall for the moment than face. If things were calm, he saw no harm in allowing them to remain calm.

He walked back alongside the workshops. The man turned the bowl over in his hands and looked up with a plain unquestioning expression. They did not talk or exchange greetings.

Without immediate fear of discovery the day fell into order, smooth and easy, and this unruffledness bothered him so that he couldn't determine what he wanted. Twice he decided to have his hair cut, and twice he walked up to the shop and then changed his mind. The clothes he needed, he didn't want, and while there was one shop with a stack of old computers inside, the cafés were too basic, simple rooms with tables and chairs. No internet. No wifi. His lack of purpose leaked into everything about him, so that the market traders, the women shopping, the men at cafés, all seemed idle, disengaged. He returned to the barber shop, sat down before he could change his mind, and told himself not to move. The shop opened on one side to the market and on the other to a boulevard lined with palms and dry bushes, and a slope-roofed building which he first took to be a school, mistaking a parade ground for a schoolyard, a barrack for an assembly hall.

A doorway beside him, doorless, opened to a corridor which led to the hammam. A man scrubbed the tile floor, hosed the walls, returned with towels, ignored the waiting men. Ford watched him in the mirror, preoccupied by his steady labour. Another figure held back in the doorway, and when Ford looked up he saw that this figure was – although it could not be – *Kiprowski*. This certainty came to him with shock and a kind of joy, and when he leaned through the doorway to look into the empty corridor the barber tutted and gently waggled his scissors. In an instant Ford's certainty dissolved. Customers watched with folded arms and pushed their backs into their chairs. It was not Kiprowski, of course, but a desire for familiar company.

Ford faced himself in the barber's mirror and tried to conjure Kiprowski out of the shadow at the soft curve of the doorway, but nothing came to him. Why had he assumed that this stranger or these shadows were Kiprowski when he could not consciously reconstruct the man? When he could barely remember his face?

It was fear, of course, but fear of what, success, that he would return to an ordinary life as Ford, a life in which nothing was at risk, *as if this had never happened*? He missed Sutler, and missed the simple buzz from the deception which ran as an undercurrent to every moment at Camp Liberty. While Sutler had not yet proved himself, he had also never failed. As Sutler he'd given no thought to his return to life as Ford, and made no preparation.

When it came to his turn the barber held up both a razor and a pair of scissors and it took Ford a moment to understand that he was being offered a choice of how his hair should be cut. He looked carefully at the photos taped beside the mirror, and pointed at one and said, there, that one. Like that. He could smell the barber, not unpleasant, a hint of nicotine and talcum. It wasn't Kiprowski he remembered now so much as his absence, a gap in the doorway where no one stood.

While the barber cut his hair Ford watched the soldiers in the barrack yard. Almost midday and the men laboured under the full force of the sun, parading in a tight squad, their skin absorbing light, everything about them soft and unready. He guessed that they had been drafted into service, and while they performed the required manoeuvres he detected a reticence, either uncertainty or reluctance. It would be better if these men were sent home before they caused harm, or before harm came to them.

Ford nursed a fragmentary notion, the image of Howell walking away, of Kiprowski rushing forward the moment before all of the chaos, before the building disassembled and the walls pulsed out. In that moment – before black smoke, white smoke, before the blast came at him as heat but also texture, before it threw him from the building, before his head became busy with pig- and bird-like squeals – in that moment before chaos burst upon them, before all of this, there was Kiprowski, hurtling forward, arms locked to shield his head, his eyes squeezed shut.

*

The barber insisted that Ford remain in his seat, insisted on shaving him. Ford settled back and noticed that the waiting customers looked away with disinterest. When the barber stepped aside, Ford was struck by how different he appeared. Two strangers, side by side, ashen, in a hard sunlight in a bright room. With shorter hair, without the beard, with a skinnier face, he appeared considerably younger. Only his eyes and the way he narrowed them to focus gave any idea of his true age.

He wiped his neck and could not look at the doorway or the mirror. He teetered at the cusp of some understanding – a realization about what had happened at Southern-CIPA. Did Kiprowski know about the explosion? Ford knew he could not depend on this memory, because he remembered very little about it. The fact that Kiprowski appeared to be running the moment before the explosion could be a simple mistake, the events could have been synchronous – Kiprowski running and the smoke blossoming behind him at one and the same moment. He couldn't tease it out: Kiprowski's run, a mere six or seven steps, seemed endless to him, the man running at full pelt toward him as if to hammer him down.

If he could speak with Geezler this would all be different. He wanted to speak with Geezler to figure this out.

At the market he spied Nathalie and caught her off-guard. Surprised, she spoke automatically in French. Ford apologized in English.

Still a little taken aback Nathalie said she hardly recognized him from this morning. 'You look different. Much better. So much nicer.'

Ford stroked his chin. 'I'm a new man,' he said, not quite believing himself.

'Very much so,' she agreed. 'For women it's not so easy. We have to work harder.'

He asked what she was doing, and she told him, half-serious, that the town was too small to become properly lost in, and that she was in the mood to lose herself.

'Are you waiting for your husband?'

Nathalie again appeared confused. With a little laugh she explained that he had this all wrong. 'Martin, no? No, no. They won't be here until later.' The idea returned to her and she laughed again, excusing herself. 'And you? Are you waiting for someone?'

'It's a long story. But no.' Ford explained that he needed someone to help him buy new clothes. 'My luggage,' he said, 'was lost. All gone. I need to change some money also, all I have are dollars.'

'That's better for them, but not so good for you.' Nathalie led him back to a stall beside the barber shop. If he wanted Turkish lire he could change money at one of the banks, although it would be expensive it might be sensible. 'Not everyone will take American money.' She laughed. 'You remind me – when I was a child I was very forgetful, and my parents adored me, they spoiled me and replaced everything I lost with something new or better so I could become even more careless. I never had anything old. I had the idea that one person was collecting my things. Not stealing them but keeping them for me somewhere. This was my excuse. Just imagine all the things you've lost, everything you've mislaid, collected in one room, like at a train station. Safe, all in one place.'

Ford glanced into the barber shop as they passed. The men now talked with ease. He asked if she was serious about the room, the lost property, and she said this was a long time ago. 'I have to admit that I am forgetful now. I have no excuse. I lose things all the time.'

They walked casually from stall to stall. 'Tell me. What do you need?'

'Everything,' he replied. 'A hat. Shirts. Trousers. New clothes for a new man.'

'Really, everything? Sandals?'

'Everything.'

Ford looked over the stall but couldn't see anything he would choose.

'Is there anywhere I can get online here? The internet?'

Nathalie shook her head. 'You must use your phone, or go to Birsim. You can ask in one of the hotels.' She checked her watch. Martin would arrive soon from Ankara and she should return to the Maison du Rêve.

Ford found a hat and inspected himself in a hand mirror. Clean-shaven and with shorter hair his face now appeared angular, crisp. Nathalie held up two shirts. 'Light,' she said, 'but not white.' She spoke in French to the trader then gave Ford a wave. 'You know, I was mistaken about the time. I really should go.'

Ford watched her walk away without hurry. A languid, self-conscious walk. Other men noticed and turned her way as she passed.

3.2

Parson's day began with mixed news. Another message from the London office asking that he contact Gibson: urgent business.

'It's about the Hassan case,' Gibson began, 'the translator who broke his neck in that lorry accident.'

Parson had no trouble recalling the desert road. The tyre marks heading straight. The highway curving west. 'Amer Hassan. What haven't I done?'

'It's your recommendation. HOSCO aren't happy. You asked them to settle.'

'And what did they come back with?'

'No compensation. Final pay only. They are prepared to round up to the whole month.'

'But what about the family? There was no life insurance.'

'They're simply following your findings, you marked the claim "no culpability".'

'With mitigating circumstances, which is why I recommend that they settle. There's more to consider here. It's all in my notes.'

'Well, they've seen your report, and they aren't having any of it.'

'He has a family. He has two children. Their father is dead. They've just arrived in England. His wife doesn't speak English, and she's now without a husband. They live in Darlington, for christsakes.'

'You marked "no culpability". You know how these things go. If the family aren't happy they can contest the claim.'

'With what money? I thought we were supposed to protect them from claims like this. If the family take this to the papers the story won't be good for HOSCO.'

'It's unlikely. I think they've calculated the risks. We're talking about immigrants who don't speak English. HOSCO have made their decision.'

'Remind me why we do business with them?' Parson turned away from the table and sat forward. Realizing that he had embarrassed Gibson, he apologized. About him men in uniform and desert fatigues returned to tables with trays, voices from the kitchen rang sharp and hollow through the commissary. He disliked the smell of fried food, which seemed to thicken and add heat to the air, stick to the floors and tables: fat that reeked of sick.

'I do have one piece of good news.' Gibson passed on to new business. 'Two journalists have spotted Stephen Sutler. And he's in Turkey.'

The journalists insisted on meeting Parson at their motel in Cukurca.

It sat at the intersection of two main roads at the edge of town – one branch east–west, the other aimed north. Without doubt Sutler would have passed this junction, it was the one certain fact Parson knew about him, and if he was attentive he would have seen the motel stuck in the crotch of two roads, surrounded by a shantytown of wind-slapped tents. He would have seen this place.

The meeting struck him as a waste of time. The moment Heida answered the door she became sharp with demands, and he guessed that they had been arguing. Grüner, antsy, bothered, and indifferent, appeared to be sulking. Parson understood that the offer of information came with a condition of some kind, some subterranean demand as yet unexpressed, which threw doubt on anything she might tell him. Heida, edging toward the subject, asked if she could tape the interview. Parson ignored the request and when she set the digital recorder on the table he immediately switched it off.

They all looked at the device.

Grüner complained about the motel. 'The people outside,' he said, 'are different from the people at Kopeckale. It's not so safe. There is only the manager here.'

Parson also felt this tension: this crowd, with fewer women, fewer children, kept separate from the motel by a chain-link fence, had attitude and palpable threat. 'Anyway,' Grüner shook his head, 'I don't see why he would come here?'

'Why not?' Heida disagreed. 'It makes perfect sense. He can pass across the border with the refugees, it's not so hard for him to disappear here. People can come this way without trouble.'

'You saw him in Kopeckale.' Parson drew out a map. 'Stephen Sutler.'

Heida said that they needed to talk first. She looked at Grüner while she spoke to Parson. 'It's simple. We need permits to enter Iraq.'

'I don't know anything about visas.'

'They won't recognize our status. We have proper identification. They are stopping the press from entering the country by requiring working visas. It's crazy. We have a right. A duty. It is impossible to work until we are there.'

Parson didn't understand. There were journalists in Iraq assigned to military units, journalists working with bureaus; every branch of media, every company had people placed in Iraq. 'I don't know anything about this. It's not my area. I don't see what I can do.'

'But you want this man? Yes? You want this person? Yes? Everybody wants to find him. So maybe if you want him you could do something for us? You could help? They won't let us through because the borders are closed. If we want to go to Iraq we have to fly to Frankfurt or Düsseldorf, or maybe Beirut, I don't know, and then we fly to Baghdad, to the American zone, and then, finally, after this, we drive all the way back to the border just to be thirty kilometres away from where we are now. It's crazy. It doesn't make sense.'

Uninterested in repeating himself Parson waited. Heida persisted. Behind her, mounted in a single line, a series of four photographs of small stone churches in deep and lush valleys.

'The people you work for are American? Yes? You work for the same people we called? So maybe if you call these people, speak with the people who sent you, they will do something if they want to know about this man?'

'You want me to call? Who exactly?'

'I don't know, but there must be someone, if this man is so important? Tell them they have to help us.' Heida's voice dipped an octave, becoming more reasonable. 'It's not so much to ask. It's a small thing, very easy.'

'How certain are you this is the same person?'

'It is the same man. No question. The same person. Exactly the same.'

Parson shook his head. It didn't work like this. He wouldn't do it. 'I have no influence. There isn't anything I can do. There isn't anyone to call. There isn't any *they*. I work for an English company based in London. I don't even have a permit myself. There's nothing I can do.'

Grüner appeared to accept the situation. Heida folded her arms.

'Of course there is someone you can call. Someone sent you to us. Someone from the American company called us, I have his name. This man called us two minutes after we contacted them and said that they would send you to speak with us.'

Heida's ideas made no sense. Parson's instructions came directly from Gibson.

'They want to know where this man is now. He is on the news all of the time because of the money he stole. You know, maybe he has the money with him? Maybe we have seen the money? You don't know. Maybe we have information which is useful for you? You didn't even consider what we are asking you. This isn't an ordinary situation and you should pay attention to us. Maybe we should speak with someone else?'

'Who is the man who called you?'

Heida narrowed her eyes. 'His name is Geese . . . Grease . . .'

'Griesel. Paul Griesel, he is from the same company as the man we saw.' Grüner read the name from a sheet of paper.

'I don't know this man.' Parson shrugged.

'He works for H-O-S-C-O.' Grüner spelled out the name, then handed Parson the slip of paper. 'Griesel said he was trying to fix everything.'

Parson stepped out onto the balcony to call Gibson. Nine o'clock in Turkey, it would be seven in England. He looked over the car park to the road, a briny-black night, and felt certain that he would not get a reply. To his surprise Gibson answered before the call went to message.

He explained the situation and said he wouldn't have called except it was urgent.

'It's Geezler. Paul Geezler,' Gibson said. 'And he spoke to them directly? This is interesting. Give me a moment.'

Parson returned in fifteen minutes with an answer.

'I have something.' He tried not to sound surprised and laid a note on the table. 'You need to contact this man. The Americans don't control the border, neither does HOSCO. Who comes and goes is entirely up to the Turkish authorities. But this man can help you.'

Heida leaned forward to read the note. 'Who is he?'

'He works for the Turkish military. You need to speak with him directly. He has your names. He will be expecting to hear from you.'

The woman straightened up. 'This is the truth?'

Parson pointed at the note. 'It's the truth. Call him. He will be in either Ankara or Istanbul.'

'Who gave you this?'

'The people I work for in London contacted the man you spoke with, Paul Geezler, and he came up with this name. He said that this man will help you.'

Heida pushed the note toward Grüner and they spoke briefly in German. Parson stood by while the two disagreed.

'We have two things for you.' She turned the map around and leaned close. 'It was here,' Heida pointed to the map, 'somewhere here on this road. Maybe there. He was walking on his own. We took him to the station in Kopeckale. There were no buses until the morning so he had to stay the night at the terminus. When we found out who he was we went to find him, but he was gone.'

'And did you see where he was going?'

'No,' Grüner interrupted, but they had spoken about a hotel in Istanbul. 'It's for journalists. It's a hostel opposite the big church, Aya Sofya. I think this is where he will go.'

'And how did he appear? In himself?'

Grüner stopped chewing. 'Tired. Not so good. Exhausted I think. His clothes were dirty, you know, and his face was scratched, and he had a tan. His face was, you know, dark. He told us he was on the road for two or three days, but the way he looked, it was longer. I'm sure. He didn't say so much until we told him about the hotel in Istanbul, then he was really interested because he asked questions.'

Parson wrote his number on the map. 'Call me if you remember something else.' He paused, pen in hand. 'You said you had two pieces of information.'

'Yes.' Heida looked to Grüner and narrowed her eyes. 'He had the money with him. He had two big bags. Very big bags, and he sat with his arms about them. I tried to help but he wouldn't let me touch them.'

'Two bags?'

'Two backpacks.'

'And you didn't see what was in them?'

'I didn't see inside, but they were heavy.'

'Tell me, why did you stop for him?'

'Because it was strange. He looked like someone you would see at home. Just someone on the street. This ordinary man in the wrong place. I thought something might have happened to him because of the marks on his face. We had no idea who he was.'

Parson returned to his car. Instead of driving away he slowly circled the parking lot and the one lone vehicle belonging to Heida and Grüner, a military jeep with civilian plates. He drove a full circuit, unwilling to head off, a nagging dissatisfaction with the discussion he couldn't fix. His headlights strafed the motel, the concrete wall, the compound fence, and a row of generators, a bare hill that flattened out to wasteland then the distant sheets of plastic, the slack sides of tents at the refugee camp, low-lying and secretive – then back again to the motel and the neon lights in the eyes of a stray dog. Driving, thinking, he leaned into the curve and began to feel the satisfaction of ideas beginning to stir. It wasn't that the journalists had lied to him, maybe a little, but they had failed to impress upon him some crucial element. Of this he was certain.

He parked beside the jeep and decided to spend the night watching the motel.

Grüner woke him in the morning. A cup in one hand, steam condensing on the window, a sheet of paper in the other.

Parson shuffled upright and squinted at Grüner. The man leaned down, his face grey, unshaven, the sky behind him pale. Still early. 5:34.

'I saw you here, so I brought you a coffee. I have something for you.'

Parson unwound his window. Grüner passed him the cup and the paper, then crouched beside the door with an apologetic expression as if he was sorry for Parson, or embarrassed at what he was doing.

'This is why we picked him up. He looks like this man. Exactly like him. This isn't him,' he repeated, 'but it looks like him. This is why we stopped. This man is our friend and he looks like this man. I've written his name here.' Grüner hesitated. 'You know, what she said about the bags is not true. He had one bag, that's all. I don't think there was anything in it, but I don't know. It was small. I don't know why she told you this. I think she wants a better story. I don't know. I hope you find him.'

'Last night you said he had marks on his face?'

Grüner nodded. 'Scratches. And under his eye one nick.'

Parson handed the image back to Grüner and asked if he had a pen. 'Can you draw those marks? What you remember. Draw them on this face.'

Parson sat with the journalist's printout. Sutler, but not Sutler, with seven lines drawn in blue biro radiating across his right cheek and forehead. He compared the picture with the copy of the HOSCO ID in his file. If this was a dependable likeness then Sutler had lost a great deal of weight and had grown his hair. Locked in this man's expression, he fancied a haunted quality, and arrogance, plenty of arrogance.

He drove to Cukurca and looked for somewhere to eat in the small grey town. Stumpy towers, something like grain silos, stacked either side of the road. Parson drove slowly so that he could look. He would find somewhere to eat first, then call Gibson and see what the plan was. Without more detailed information he assumed that he would be returning to Amrah City. Changing his mind, he smoothly swung the car about and changed direction. First he'd visit the coach station at Kopeckale, he decided, then he'd call Gibson. He could string this out for a week perhaps, chasing ghosts. Why hurry back to reports and cases HOSCO would not want to settle?

3.3

Ford returned to the pension and found Nathalie with her companion Martin. Nathalie lay on the sun-lounger with a book resting on her stomach, the cover folded back, her hair into one long braid, and a smile indicating that everything was in its place. As she made the introduction her arm lazily conducted the formalities (she pronounced his name with slow determination, her voice skipping pitch between syllables):

'*Mar-tan*, Tom. Tom, *Mar-tan*.'

Short and in his late forties, Martin's dark hair and full beard, his round shoulders, hairy forearms and neck, made him faintly baboon-like. He cleaned a pair of heavy-framed glasses with his shirt tail and blinked as if the air was dusty. Preoccupied, he complained about how disorganized everything had become in two short days. Turkey was more difficult than he'd anticipated. Two days of meetings with officials, he tutted, in which 'everybody wanted to speak, but nobody wanted to help. Have you been to Ankara?' he asked Ford, his English almost without accent. 'Everybody talks. They say what you want to hear. Everyone is perfectly polite. But they don't act.'

Ford couldn't imagine the two of them together. Nathalie and Martan. It wasn't a picture to linger over.

'I'm sorry, but you no longer have the room to yourself.' Nathalie turned the book over, ready to read. 'Eric is here. Did you find some clothes?'

Ford held up his bag and excused himself as he stepped into his room.

Propped beside the spare cot lay a black backpack, new and clean. Ford recognized the luggage tag: a clear plastic star. Eric Powell. The student from Kopeckale. He told himself this wasn't anything he couldn't deal with, but the coincidence itself was unsettling.

He changed his clothes and returned the courtyard to find Nathalie alone. Wasps hovered about the table. Behind Nathalie the honeysuckle folded over the edge of the wall, thick and dry, the undersides of the leaves a cold silver – all of this reassuringly familiar. Nathalie fidgeted, nervous of the wasps, every time she moved, even to turn a page, the chair creaked. She set the book aside then sat up and began to inspect her toes.

'Maybe tomorrow I'll come shopping with you again? If you want?'

'You don't like the shirt?'

'No. I like the shirt. Don't you need more?'

Despite this familiarity she was different somehow, less the woman he had met that morning. Ford felt more like an audience, someone she could play to.

He watched her prepare to paint her nails. 'You know this book? You've read this? The author is English, no, American?' She indicated the novel as she cleaned away the old varnish with acetone. Colour bled into the cotton wool. 'There is a lot of interest because someone was killed in the same way.'

Ford remembered his conversation with Eric about how the author had disappeared. 'And you believe it?'

'I don't know. People say bad things about Naples. Always.' Nathalie curled the loaded brush quickly over the nail with one sure stroke. Turning to her right foot, she peered over her sunglasses and asked if he minded. Ford said that he liked the smell.

'But the smell is very bad for you.' As she painted she made a face, mouth curved in concentration, the world focused to this one small act. She continued painting as Eric walked into the courtyard. 'I think you know Eric? He said you saved our film. You know about the project?'

Ford rose to shake the boy's hand. 'Tom.'

'Tom?' The boy caught on the name. He spoke in French to Nathalie and laughed, *what did I tell you?* then in English to Ford to apologize about the room. 'It's all right here? Small but all right. Sorry you have to share.'

Ford passed over the apology and said there was no problem. 'Where did you go?'

'He climbs.' Nathalie indicated that Eric should sit beside her. 'He goes away, he disappears, and he looks for places to climb. He's a little crazy about climbing, and not so safe. He leaves me alone for almost an entire week without any explanation while Martin is in Ankara.'

Eric shrugged and smiled, one hand kneading the other, fingers entwined.

'What's wrong with your hand?'

'Nothing.'

'You told me you didn't climb?' Nathalie stopped, brush poised. 'You said that you were looking.'

'I didn't climb.' Eric turned to answer Ford. 'I was going to, but I didn't have time, and couldn't find anywhere to stay so I came back. Anyway, the climbs here are grade four, the rock's soft.'

'So it's no good?'

'Oh no, it's very good. When it's dry the rock powders so everything falls apart. Then when it rains it turns to clay, so it's pretty slick.'

Nathalie slid the applicator back into the bottle and set the bottle aside, ending the subject. 'I have a question, Tom.' She paused, mid-thought. 'There's something I don't understand. You met Eric in Kopeckale? That's almost at the Iraq border.'

'It's a long a story. It was a mistake. I was supposed to be travelling with someone else. We had a disagreement and I took the first bus out.'

'To Kopeckale?'

'That was the mistake. I had no idea I was heading east. As soon as I realized I decided to return.'

'Did you have an accident?' Nathalie signalled his face.

'No. I walked into a screen door. Glass. It happened a while back, but it's taking time to heal.'

'I might have something.' Nathalie began to search through a make-up bag and after a moment found a small foil tube. 'Here, try this. It's very good.' She set everything aside, sat up, and told Ford to sit forward. 'I did the same thing when I was a girl.' She looked closely at his forehead. 'But this is not so long ago? I ran from the outside, the patio, into a glass door. You see this?' She indicated a small scar on the side of her nose. 'This is the only thing you can see, but it was very bad. I had cuts all over my face and in my hair. Glass is very bad, but it makes a clean cut. You do this twice a day and they will go. It's incredible. It really works.' She mixed the crème in the palm of her hand then smoothed it onto his forehead, then under his right eye. 'When you were in Kopeckale you saw how bad things are?'

Ford said he saw very little. He wasn't sure he understood her question.

'It's very bad there with the refugees. Did you have any trouble getting back? Everywhere is in chaos. The border towns are full with refugees. Did you have any trouble?'

'Trouble?'

'Eric was stuck for two days, there were no coaches.' Nathalie turned his head in her hands and looked for more cuts.

'He arrived at the end of it,' Eric interrupted. 'They resumed normal service, more or less, on the afternoon before he arrived.'

Ford said that he knew very little about what was going on. He'd noticed that there were soldiers, but it was the same at every stop, so he didn't think it was anything out of the ordinary. He hadn't followed the news since he'd left home.

'But it is impossible not to know what is happening? You didn't know? Not even before you came? Surely this is news, even in England?' She nudged Eric to his feet and told him to take the novel back and find a book from her room. Ford watched her give instructions to the boy, and watched the boy obey. 'And your friend? This woman?'

Eric left with the novel and a broad smile.

'My friend? I'm afraid that's unfixable.'

Nathalie sat back, hand clapped to her chest with genuine concern.

'But this is a terrible story. Have you heard anything from her? Is she travelling alone?'

'It isn't quite how it sounds.'

'But is she alone?'

Ford shook his head slowly as if with regret.

'So maybe everything will be all right?'

'It's possible.'

'I hope so, it isn't a good idea to travel so much on your own right now.'

Eric returned from Nathalie's room with two paperbacks. He held up both and she pointed to his right hand. 'That one.'

'You said you came by coach?' Eric handed the book to Ford. 'I thought I saw you in a four-by-four?'

'Sorry?'

'I saw you in a jeep with two people?'

'No. Oh, *that*. They brought me from another town. I was even further east and they brought me back.'

'You should read this.' Now serious, Nathalie pointed at the book. She wiped her hands on a small towel and said that she was done. 'You know, it isn't safe for tourists, not in the east. Read it. It might save your life.'

Accepting the book, Ford said it was a lot to expect.

'You should make sure your friend is all right. You can use my phone,' she offered, 'you should contact her.'

Ford thanked Nathalie for the book and returned to his room, then regretted not taking up her offer. He could use the phone to access the junk account.

Eric smoothed his hand through his hair, shirt buttoned, long trousers, ready for his evening with Nathalie. Ford stood beside him, recently showered, and looked down at his bed deep in thought, trying to decide. If he lay down now that would be the end of the day.

'So it's Tom, right? *Tom*? Thomas.'

'Tom.' Ford nodded and waited for more questions, now anxious. As he leaned forward the dog tags swung out of his T-shirt.

'Tom.' Eric searched under his cot for his shoes. 'You should come with us. She likes you.'

Ford held up the book and decided there was nothing wrong with ending the day. He wanted the boy out of his room. 'I have homework. And I don't have any lire.'

'What do you have?'

'Dollars.'

'I can change some.' Eric took his mobile phone and a roll of Turkish banknotes from his pocket.

'I think I'll stay.'

'I'll see you later, then,' Eric straightened up and paused deliberately, '*Tom*.' A slight pronouncement that Ford felt as sure as a pinch.

Tom. The boy paused at the door then took out his phone and money again and tossed them onto the bed.

'You'll be here, right?'

'I'll be here.'

'If I drink too much I'll only lose them.'

For some reason Eric appeared unwilling to leave. Ford focused on Nathalie's book.

It was not the kind of book he would choose. Chapter after chapter catalogued a government's abuse of its people, photographs detailed a military raid. The army descending on a village with people cowering behind mud walls. Squat shanty-like huts disintegrating in the downdraught of helicopters. Graphs detailed statistics of displaced people and empty villages. Ford browsed, then closed the book. Enough. None of this involved him.

He returned the book to Nathalie and Martin's room. Martin sat at the end of the bed – two cots pulled together – polishing a camera. The lens, detached, lay on a cloth by his thigh. Eric's silver case lay open at his feet, the negative forms for a camera cut into the foam. Martin cleaned the interior of the camera with a can of compressed air. Once he noticed Ford at the door, he waved him into the room.

'You might remember these?' Martin pushed his glasses up to his forehead. 'Sixteen-millimetre. Bolex. Simple. It's more than twenty-two years old. A workhorse. Is that the right word?'

Ford placed the book on the bed, on Nathalie's side. Yes, workhorse was the right word. 'Isn't everything digital these days?'

Martin stopped cleaning. 'It is, but the quality of this is . . . richer.' He smiled and rubbed his thumb and forefinger together. 'We have three cameras. I don't use this so much now. It's from another time.'

Beside the bed, along with papers and notebooks were other books, titles in French and German, photographs on their covers of men in uniform, of rocky terrain, of mountain villages.

Back in his room, Ford lay under the covers fully dressed, because it was cold but also because his forearms were smarting from the sun. Too awake to sleep, he counted out his remaining money. One hundred and twelve dollars in cash. Enough for the room, but little else. He took off the dog tags and read the numbers. He didn't feel confident about going online here. Hadn't he already almost locked the account? And what was the likelihood of surveillance? Would there be some kind of monitoring right now of online activity on HOSCO's website? He told himself not to hurry, to wait until he was in Istanbul. Two hundred and fifty thousand dollars that no one else could touch. He ran his fingers over the raised numbers. The only figure he could recognize was the junk account, the only number preceded by HOS/JA. The figure brought a tweak of guilt. It wasn't that he didn't deserve it. It wasn't stealing exactly, hadn't Geezler promised him as much? *Take the money from the junk account.* Geezler's own words. Help yourself. It's yours. So much for his guaranteed future with HOSCO. So much for being the instrument of change.

He couldn't imagine what was happening at Camp Liberty or Southern-CIPA, and understood when he thought about these places he saw them as they had been, as if they were immune to change.

Eric's book lay on the bed with the phone and Turkish lire. He'd folded newspaper cuttings and a small black notebook into the pages. Ford reached over and picked out the notebook. If the boy kept a diary he wanted to see what he was writing.

He couldn't read the entries, and had to stare at them a while before realizing that the writing was a numeric code. 34425 42 16982 1786 126 74025. Page after page. A simple substitution, numbers and symbols for letters, which he couldn't crack. He read on trying to identify the common numbers, but couldn't decide. These would be the vowels, unless Eric rotated the numbers, changed the key from time to time.

Now curious about him, Ford slipped out of bed. He began to search through Eric's backpack, and found clothes, climbing gear, laundry. The T-shirt with the red star. He checked the side pockets but discovered little of interest: a US passport, tickets, and then traveller's cheques tucked in a plastic wallet. The passport said only that he was twenty-two years old and born in Berkeley, California. The cheques were in dollar amounts, twenties and fifties. Ford counted to one thousand dollars and stopped, guessing he had the same number of cheques uncounted in his hands. He tried unlocking the phone but could not guess the code. Done, he returned everything to the backpack then slipped back into bed.

Eric returned late and drunk and stopped with Nathalie immediately outside the door to talk, hushed and secretive. When he came into the room he whispered to see if Ford was awake.

'Hey,' he whispered. 'Mike. You awake?'

Disturbed to hear the boy use this name, Ford kept himself still, his breathing even and regular.

Eric rolled back on the bed and tugged off his shorts. Stretched out he started laughing. A patch of moonlight lay square across his hips.

'I like you,' he said. 'Mike. You're OK.'

3.4

As Anne came into the hallway her dog ran the length of the apartment to greet her. She set down her bags containing her laptop, papers, and newspaper, and three separate packages of biscotti (a gift for the office, a pack she would keep for the house, and maybe, why not, one as an occasional treat for the dog). She shucked off her shoes and checked the corridor for signs of her husband (the television flicker on the parquet, the faint pepper-sweet whiff of whisky), fretting over her son with increasing unease.

Unable to settle her doubt she stopped at the kitchen counter and called to her husband: was there news about Turkey? Anything recent? No? Had he heard anything more about what was going on? It wasn't only Marian but everyone at the museum from the director down to the preparators: everyone else had a better idea about what was happening in the Middle East. 'Marian knew,' she said, even though she'd waited almost a week to say something. So why didn't they know? Why hadn't they heard? She held up her copy of the *Times*.

Still in the kitchen she asked why they'd let him go. What were they thinking? Seriously? Everyone else was spending the summer in mainland Europe. When he first suggested the idea eight or nine weeks ago there were no reasons against the trip, no doubt, except perhaps money – seven thousand dollars to see him through the summer. Justifying the expense she'd told herself that this would be *good*, this kind of opportunity was *exactly why we sent him to Europe*. Now she couldn't imagine entertaining the idea. In five weeks they had watched a kind of madness spark across the Middle East, self-immolation on a scale which didn't make sense.

Shoes in one hand, glass of wine in the other, Anne approached her husband's study. The dog scampered ahead. I'm serious, she said, what kind of parents are we? The routing of the American Embassy in Libya, protests in Gaza, a riot in Jerusalem, an attack on demonstrators in Tehran, the shootings at Cairo University, acquired a terrible logic. *It all creeps up on you.* Outrages in Israel, the West Bank, and the inevitable reprisals, referenced a common instability and impending collapse. All of this paled against the sudden fire of conflict in the cities of northern Iraq, the destabilizing borders between Syria, Iran, and Turkey. And now this business of unregulated contractors, along with the call for a Senate enquiry. American businesses were being stoned, vandalized, singled out; no one yet hurt, but seriously, wasn't it only a matter of time? She thought of fires, of sparks in strong winds, of cause and reaction, not as someone prone to worry, but as someone who could assay, assess, project; as someone who could understand the wayward world.

'Mark, I'm concerned.' She spoke to the back of her husband's chair, confident that he was listening despite the television: his head cocked slightly, fingers curled round the glass but not gripping.

He turned to speak. 'Today?' he said. 'Nothing new. I came back and watched the news. I looked online.'

'But there have been attacks, a bombing. It's on CNN. The refugees.' Anne stepped into the room, took a smooth sip from her glass.

'An oil refinery near the border. He's no reason to be anywhere near a refinery. It's nothing to worry about. The trouble spots are in the south and the south-east, close to the border. It's all localized. There's nothing happening in Istanbul or in the centre. No one is targeting tourists.'

'I don't know. I don't know. I don't like him being there.'

'I looked.'

'I know.'

'He's your son.'

'What does that mean?'

'It means you *know* him. He's sensible. Call him.'

'I tried.'

'Call him again.'

'I'll try.' Anne said goodnight and headed to the bedroom. On rare occasions she was reminded that Mark was not Eric's father, and that, in fact, before this marriage came a whole other life. On these occasions she asked herself if his calm came from this simple fact – she wouldn't outright call it detachment.

Tired now, she wanted time to herself. She undressed facing her books, a wall lined with monographs and thick-spined catalogues. She preferred her books close, in the bedroom. When she could not sleep she would select one and take it to the lounge and look carefully through the images and choose one painting to examine until she forgot her sleeplessness.

She would write on the flight, because she never slept on an airplane however long the journey, and set on top of her luggage two books that she might need. It was possible that she would not refer to them, but their presence would encourage her to study. It would be better to take them and not use them, rather than leave them and need them. Rome, she told herself. Stop fussing. Think only about Rome.

While the technician worked on her computer Anne waited, first at the door to her study, then in the kitchen, anxious not to appear anxious or too obviously pressured for time.

Tomorrow afternoon she would fly to Rome. She would arrive in the early morning and would need her computer for work. She couldn't remember the technician's name and couldn't find her diary with his card.

When she returned to her study she found him returning discs to their cases. On the screen a counter logged almost full. He was done, he said, as good as. Someone had deleted temporary files containing internet content and had managed to remove an essential operation file. It was easy to do. The man hesitated.

'You said your son used the computer?'

Anne nodded. She used it for work now, but earlier in the summer she had loaned it to Eric and since then it hadn't worked so well.

The man became pensive. He had managed to recover the file and restore the function, but there were pieces of other files recovered also, and they were now stored in a folder on her desktop. He could wipe them if she wanted, but she might want to look. If she needed he could leave the utility disc; a better way to determine which files could be deleted to make more room. From what he could see the hard drive was almost full.

After paying the technician, Anne saw him to the door then quickly returned to her office to check the folder, forgetting her coffee.

The files were numbered and dated. When opened, the screen filled with symbols and rows of zeros, crude decoding of the content. Dates and times repeated themselves, the names of places, cities, along with unintelligible words which she recognized through repetition: *4hotfun, a$$lovr, lucioboner, latino_hole, hotnsingle45, fukU2, 4U69, rut_rod.* Anne scrolled through the document and found pockets of information, half sentences repeated. *Athletic, masculine. Love bigger guys. Can host. Couple interested in third. Short stay, hotel.* Then: *Do u cum whn u r fukd?*

Anne recoiled. Shut the computer. Pushed back the chair. Left the room. Walked busily away.

She sat in the kitchen, set the coffee cup in the sink. She opened the window and let in the noise from Lexington, the cabs and cars, then sat with her back to her office for a whole hour, ignored the telephone, the dog, the work she had to complete, and cast out thoughts as they occurred.

When she roused herself, she washed her face in an attempt to suppress what she now knew – that her son had sought strangers, men, in different cities. He cruised the internet *on her computer* for sex. She avoided her reflection as she stepped back to dry her face, dropped the towel before threading it over the rail, and found herself angry because she didn't want to be the kind of person who would hide in a bathroom and cry into a towel, although she was neither hiding nor crying. She checked her face, almost automatic, but would not look herself in the eye, and was surprised by how red her cheeks were, just the cheeks: a thing that used to happen at school, or at her parents' a long time ago when she was not a mother but a child herself, anger focused on her face in perfect slap-red circles.

U fuck raw?

This discovery could not be undone.

Halfway to her bedroom she decided this could not be ignored – and returned to the computer to check the dates of the files. The information quickly confused her. A number of the meetings were scheduled in New York for the week after his vacation, at a time when she knew that Eric was in France. In the crude half-messages it appeared that contacts were made but the appointments were not kept – a relief to discover. From what she could tell the appointments were with older men, and he was looking for sex, not company. The questions in the messages sparked a warning: did he know how to protect himself, not only from disease, but from people who would use him?

Anne closed the files and worried that she was recording a trail which could be similarly discovered, as if the room itself were suddenly public. She shut down the computer and hurried to the bathroom.

She washed her hands again and called the dog. The dog preferred to sleep on Eric's bed but she didn't like the idea now. She washed her hands a third time and dried them, tempted to search his room. They had talked many times, Eric stating that he did not know what he was, or worse, he didn't know what he wanted, and she recalled with anger her assurance that he had plenty of time to figure everything out, remembering her own confusion at his age. *It takes time. It will get easier. Once you settle, make friends, it will be different. Easier. Give it time.* And when he complained that he was lonely she had asked if there was anyone he could talk with? Someone? Surely? But the only people he spoke with were his tutors. While the conversations had upset her, robbed her of one more certainty, hadn't she supported him? Hadn't she shown understanding? Her consideration, given his actions, appeared laughable. *Tell me anything. Anything at all. Talk to me.*

Anne paused at the threshold of her son's room. There were no souvenirs of his holiday in Cuba with Mark. Not one photograph. Opposite the bed hung a poster of a man climbing bare-handed, bare-chested, inverted under a hood of rock, about and beneath him a limitless ice-blue sky. His fingertips and feet braced the rock, locked, upside-down in the position of an athlete at a starting block. Taped beside it were pictures of Eric climbing, pictures of free-runners, bodies arced, taut, tumbling across skylines, lodged with calligraphic elegance between concrete walls in city streets. In all of their moves, from Berkeley to Richmond to New York, Eric had laid out his room in the same way; having seen it so many times, its orderliness now disturbed her. What other twenty-two-year-old would live so tidily? Would alphabetize his books? Would do, exactly, to the word, everything he said he would do? What she had taken as evidence of sophistication, of sense and good manners, she now saw as symptoms of a disorder. Much like his father, she realized, he wasn't the person she believed him to be. The idea struck her as deeply repugnant.

She resisted the desire to search his room, doubting that there would be more to discover. Its surface, in any case, was too clinical to penetrate.

Returning to her study, Anne hesitated before packing her computer. Enough, she told herself. Stop.

The clock ticked softly, and through the window she could see the traffic on Lexington, a tangential view through the sides of the building, a slice of a busy, wet road. On the mantel beside the clock was a photograph taken over the holidays. In the picture Fed forward, third in a group of five, smiling, the only person aware that the picture was being taken. His focus strayed just above the camera to the person behind it. Taken before he had his hair shorn in an attempt to look older, before he returned to Grenoble; she found it difficult to reconcile the image with the knowledge that during the same holiday he was soliciting strangers, men, for sex. His smile appeared duplicitous, reserved, removed, *much like his father*. Anne looked at her reflection and attempted to untangle how she felt.

Anne woke at four in the morning and could not return to sleep. Her husband slumbered without trouble, his body curled away, back turned. The older they became the less time they spent together, and the less time they spent together the less dissatisfaction they felt toward each other. It was only the points of departure, she thought, they couldn't negotiate. Everything held the same sense of dysfunction: a son who sent messages, city to city, to people he didn't know and didn't intend to meet, an absent father, and a husband who was similarly remote. And how would she account for herself?

She slipped out of bed, chose a book from her shelf, and took it to the living room. The book: a favourite. Images from Correggio, Caravaggio, Titian, Tintoretto. In them she saw distance and cruelty. Bodies pierced, flayed, crucified. A parade of morbid flesh.

3.5

Ford rose first and after a quick shower sat in the courtyard sipping coffee. Nathalie's soap on his hands, sweet and floral. He'd found her washbag on the lintel beside the shower and helped himself to the lotions, not out of perversity or need, but because the scent, jasmine, reminded him of his apartment in Bonn – two small rooms and a featureless kitchenette, nothing much to remember – except, on some nights the neighbour's jasmine inflamed the air, and this scent, more than any other, emptied his head then and now. It surprised him, this nostalgia, for something so bland. How bored he was, *passed by, passed over*, weren't those the words he'd used? He'd bought the apartment on the promise of continued work with HOSCO, but HOSCO provided the meanest contracts, and when they came to an end Geezler had justified: *We can't offer you anything new because you've already worked for us. It's one of those things. Our hands are tied. We can't keep hiring the same contractors for these kinds of contracts. It isn't allowed. The only way I can offer you a new contract is if you open a new account under a new name. You have to register as a new contact. Entirely new: name, address, accounts.* Geezler assured him, *I wouldn't worry, the fact is we do this all the time.*

He tried to remember how Sutler had evolved. Was he simply a way of manoeuvring about a tricky piece of policy? A shared idea developed through discussion? The truth was that Sutler was proposed by Geezler as fully realized idea. Geezler had decided everything. He'd set up the name, the contract. He'd organized the flights. All of it, right out of the blue. *I have something for you, but I need an answer now, yes or no? If you say yes you have to leave immediately.* This would be his one chance. There would be no other opportunity. *They want to build a new city, first as a military base, then as a civilian project. We've bid for the contract and while the announcement isn't official there's little doubt it's ours. We've identified four potential sites. It's safe,* he said, *you'll be in the south, nowhere near Najaf, Nasiriyah, Basrah, or any of those places. In fact, you won't see one Iraqi. No worries about that. We're sending you to the desert. All you have to do is make an initial assessment. We need someone there now. Two hundred and fifty thousand, in and out.*

All this under one provision: *You must become Sutler. We can't give this contract to an existing provider.*

Nathalie showered after him, tiptoed barefoot out of her room. Martin followed and stopped in the courtyard, a cigarette already lit, eyes squinched shut. Disturbed by the sunlight he stood and scratched his head. The food, cutlery, crockery left out with a note from Mehmet saying he would return with the hire-van by quarter to nine and that they should all be ready. Martin studied the breakfast and complained item by item. Dry bread, sweaty cheese, cold milk, no juice. What kind of torture was this?

As Nathalie came out of the shower, her hair bound in a towel, Martin poured her a coffee.

'We're late. It's eight fifteen. We asked for breakfast at seven thirty.' She added sugar to her cup and told Martin that they needed to hurry, and asked in French if Eric was awake yet. 'Is that the last cigarette?'

Irritated, Martin pointed to their room. They had a whole pack of duty-free cigarettes, unopened, less than three metres away. He slumped back to the room to make a point. Ford offered Nathalie a cigarette.

'Don't tell me you speak French?'

'No. You were looking at the packet.'

'Am I really that obvious?' Nathalie leaned forward for a light and held back the towel, revealing a shoulder. 'How can you be amusing so early?' She took a first deep draw. 'What are you doing today?'

'I don't know. I might go to the hammam.'

'No. The hammam is no good. Come with us. Martin is filming. Eric will help him. We've hired a car. It's going to be boring for me and I want some company. You might even find it interesting.' She turned her head to blow smoke past Martin who stood in front of her, a carton of cigarettes in his hands. 'Why not? He can come? You and Eric are going to be busy. I will be bored.'

Mehmet drove with one arm out of the window, abstractly directing the traffic out of their way, while Ford, Nathalie, Martin, and Eric held tight to the seats and vinyl straps, too alarmed to complain. A necklace of fat ebony beads batted the windscreen. Ford spent the hour-long drive with one hand and shoulder keeping the sliding door shut. A sandy breeze buffeted unpleasantly against his face and he momentarily thought of himself as lost, faceless, worn down, his one goal – modest or monumental – to be in less of a fix with each passing day, to be less in flux. To his knowledge this day seemed as stable as the previous day, an improvement already with no visions in barber shops, no awkward introductions, and, so far, no surprises. Staying this comfortable, at least for a while, presented no risk, he could recoup, prepare, ready himself for the next step. The van clipped the verge. Eric tensed into the seat. He listened to headphones as he read the book he'd been reading in Kopeckale, looking up only at the most violent jolts. Newspaper cuttings slipped from the pages, so that he held the book in both hands. Preoccupied, Martin said nothing but appeared to be brewing a complaint.

When they arrived Nathalie took Ford by the arm and said that they would look at the churches. The boys could manage without them. She held her hands out flat. 'Look. See. I'm shaking. I've never been so terrified.' Was Mehmet trying to kill them or was this just something he did for the rush, because there's nothing quite like zooming a group of tourists?

'Zooming?'

'Provoking. Eric's word. Zoom-zoom. Everything becomes a verb.' Nathalie paused to survey the rock face. As they headed to the closest bluff Martin warned them to stay out of shot, and Nathalie waved her hand over her shoulder.

'One hour.'

'I know.' Nathalie pointed at the cliff pocked with holes, stabbed her finger in the air to show where they were heading, 'I know, I know, I know.' She talked as they walked. These churches were the reason she agreed to accompany Martin on this trip. 'When he gets to this point I'm not so interested. I prefer all of the work beforehand – the preparation. At first it's not so bad, but each time it becomes a little more difficult. More fuss. More trouble. I wanted to go to Malta with Eric. I wanted to leave Martin to it.'

Ford remembered the tickets folded inside Eric's passport, a flight from Athens to Luqa. Nathalie continued to talk about the churches. Her university at Grenoble had developed a process to preserve the frescos. 'They are layered one over another. The old painting. A new layer of plaster. A new painting. Whenever they feel like it.' Her hands interwove, indicating layer upon layer. 'They believed the devil would rise from here,' she said. 'I'm serious. They thought he would come up through the cracks in the ground, that there would be an earthquake and he would rise. Dust. Fire. The end of the world. They calculated the day and the hour and built churches to protect themselves. Of course nothing happened. But who knows,' she laughed, 'perhaps they were wrong?'

He liked how she spoke, how her accent re-tuned the words so that they sang a little off-scale. Not unfamiliar but refreshed.

They entered the first church through a short vertical shaft, the steps long since worn away. Nathalie crawled behind Ford and passed her camera ahead. Inside the chamber Ford found an opening and watched as Mehmet unloaded the equipment and Martin and Eric assembled the camera and tripod. The van, the three men, appeared small and inconsequential; the landscape surrounding them unearthly and barren. Ford had not paid attention on the drive and was surprised by the valley's slow swoop and the salt-white peaks, the massive dunce caps worn out of the soft pumice, rising independent from the valley floor. From here he could see more windows and doorways puncturing the rock. Long-abandoned churches and animal pens. Nathalie idly took a photograph as he leaned into the view.

Martin and Eric worked quickly together.

'What are they filming?'

'A documentary. A project. *The Project.*' Nathalie dusted her legs. 'It's a little complicated. Why, what is he doing?'

'I can't tell. How many films has he made?'

'Five.' Nathalie joined Ford to look out over the valley, her hand on his shoulder, her body close. 'One is well known, not seriously well known, not what you would call famous, not really . . . but six years ago he won a big award and some prizes in France, I don't know, maybe it was seven years ago now. Everyone wants him to make something new. It's not so easy today. Six years ago it was easier. It's tough. He's competing with his students.'

'So what is he doing?'

'It's an archive. The project is a collection of interviews. Right now he's interviewing Kurdish leaders. Some are in hiding. Until recently most of them were out of the country in Paris and Berlin, some of them came from Iraq and Iran, but most of them come from the border with Iraq not so far from here. Not far from where you were. The government, the Turks, don't recognize ethnic groups – Kurds, Armenian, Alevi – although this is beginning to change. But everything is unstable again. Everything has become much worse. It isn't an easy project. Some of these people are classed as terrorists, so he has to be careful.'

Ford admitted that he was the wrong person to talk over such matters, he knew little about politics and nothing about documentary film.

Nathalie nodded, maybe it wasn't so bad to know nothing about film, but did he really know nothing about politics?

'How did you meet?'

Nathalie gave an involuntary smile. 'How did we meet? Why do you want to know? We met in Grenoble, at the university. Then, after he met me, when he knew who I was he wanted to interview my father. After that I started to help with his project.'

'So you teach?'

'Not so much. I have research students. I work a little with Martin. These films are part of a broader project.'

'About Kurds?'

'Not only the Kurds. About people in crisis. About belonging. They are testimonies, people speaking for themselves directly to the camera. People speaking about home, about what home is for them. There are groups of interviews, women in Iran, Palestinians who have lost their lands, the Israelis who have occupied them. Algerians living in Grenoble. Nigerians, street-workers in Paris. First and second generation. He has many, many hours of interviews.'

They walked deeper into the church and found the rock carved into columns and alcoves, humble in scale as if people might have been smaller; in places the ground remained rough and heavily fouled. Nathalie explained that the churches had survived because they were used as dovecotes and animal pens and he could easily imagine this, only when he looked up did the church regain its distinction. The ceiling carved as a dome and painted a dusty marine blue and crossed with stars. Beside the entrance full-sized portraits of Old Testament prophets stood shoulder to shoulder, with wild hair and wispy beards, eyes stabbed out, mouths shot with scratches. The lower sections were corroded back to the bare stone. She pointed at the men with beards and laughed. 'Martin, no? So serious.'

'Why did he interview your father?'

'It was part of the project. When he first started he recorded police, magistrates, politicians, people who were involved with immigrants.'

'So why your father?'

'My father was a judge.' Nathalie's voice became dull, lost to the hollows surrounding them. 'I want you to see something.' She led Ford deeper into the church to a wall crossed into quadrants. 'These are miracles from the New Testament.' She pointed at the sections. 'Feeding the five thousand. Water into wine. Casting out devils. And here, walking on water.' At the centre of the painting Ford recognized a familiar white-robed figure, a picture-book Jesus. Painted larger than the other figures, he strode across a troubled sea. Deep umber shadows defined the man's limbs beneath his tunic, his beard and hair. A white plate outlined his head. His fingers, long and delicate, poised in blessing. Behind this figure, the apostles cowered in their boat, small and childlike, their robes streaked blue, hands clasped in prayer. Beside the boat, almost inconsequential, a figure sank in panic, his arms raised, mouth open, waves threatening to overcome him. Nathalie brushed her hand close to the wall. 'The story stops where he's asking for help. It shows everything. The fishermen, the nets, the sea, but it stops at this moment.'

To Ford the man appeared secure. Wedged between waves, neither falling nor drowning. His fear of a different order. Not a horror of expectation, but a horror of what he endured.

'My father was sick for a long time. The interview with Martin happened very late. I haven't watched it. It's difficult, of course.'

'Do you interview people?'

'No. I helped edit – before – but the idea is changed and different. Martin sets up the camera and people speak to it. The films are not edited now. They say what they want. It's very simple and it works well. Sometimes they speak for two minutes. Sometimes twenty. And they say whatever they want. For some people it is a little like a confession. Some are not so good. And some people really show you who they are. It's very intimate. Some have had experiences they've never spoken about. Many have lost families, or homes, or land. Some are in exile. Of course, he's careful about the people he selects and he speaks with them for a long time before he records them, so there's a kind of control, a kind of preparation. It's not so hard because everybody has a story.'

From outside came an impatient pip rousing them back to the present. Nathalie shook her head, impatient herself. 'How long have we been? Five minutes?'

Martin and Mehmet waited in the van. The honks continued as Nathalie and Ford walked back across the scree. Martin pointed at the churches with a petulant stab and Nathalie turned to squint at the cliff-face, then gasped, hand to mouth. My god. Could he see? 'Up there. Right above where we were.'

It took Ford a moment to spot the cause of alarm, until a small movement high on the cliff face softly translated into a figure slung across a crevice in the rock. Eric climbed crablike, sideways and up, drawing himself over breaks and cracks with ease. Today he wore a light blue shirt with the same red star design. Almost at the top he lodged an arm deep into the rock then hung from it, turned and waved, loose and easy, and pointed to the road, signalling that he would meet them there. Nathalie gasped again and looked away.

As they clambered back into the van Martin asked irritably if they could possibly waste any more time.

'I sent him to collect you, and look. Look what he does.'

When they picked Eric up at the road, Nathalie and Martin refused to speak with him.

That evening Nathalie sat with Ford. Martin and Eric took up the table and prepared the next day's schedule.

'It was strange today, thinking about my father.' Nathalie turned the glass beaker to wipe her lipstick from the rim. 'I think about him every day, but there isn't always the opportunity to talk, so it becomes difficult to speak about him. When I was younger my parents did everything for us, my brother and my sister. So I wanted to be able to look after him. I had this idea in my head. I always thought that I would be able to look after him, but it wasn't possible. I told myself that I was busy and that he needed attention from professionals; he needed people who knew what to do. I thought that it was temporary, just for this moment, and there would be time, and if he was in a place where they could care for him he would be – I don't know now – safer? Comfortable? But he was very frightened. I always thought there would be more time, even when I knew this wasn't possible; I thought that there would be a better opportunity, but things don't work out as you imagine. What is awful is that there were always reasons to do one thing and not another, but these reasons disappear. You don't remember them. They just go, and you're left with what you did or didn't do, and this idea that you didn't do enough. The truth isn't always so easy. You can't think yourself back into that place that made everything how it was. I miss him very much.'

Ford could feel Martin's attention. Nathalie leaned forward, the glass clasped between her hands, her voice now private.

'Why don't you ask me questions? You never ask questions. You are always so quiet. Is that what makes you so interesting? A man who listens but never asks questions.'

Ford shrugged in apology.

'See? Do you mind if I ask? The woman you were travelling with, was she your wife?'

'No.'

'But you were married?'

'I was with someone for a while.'

'For how long?'

'Seven years.'

'You don't have children?' Her voice sounded small, without interest in a reply. 'I have a daughter.' She repeated the fact and nodded. 'She lives with her father in Paris.'

They looked, both of them, at a bottle of wine on the paving at their feet, almost gone. Beside it Martin's whisky, a blend not a single malt, which Ford thought telling about the man in some way – cheap or economic – but couldn't decide.

'I buy this wine in Paris.' Nathalie tapped the bottle, fingernail against the neck. 'The same wine. There's a shop run by two men from Algeria. I used to see them every day, but I know nothing about them. Their wine was the same price as the wine from anywhere else, but I always believed I was saving money, because these men know nothing about wine so the prices are too low, so I'm always winning. I told myself that I was always one step ahead.' She stroked her hair behind her ears.

'Do you see your daughter?'

'Yes. She comes to stay with me sometimes. Her name is Elise.'

'And her father?'

'It's not possible to spend time with him.' Nathalie set her shoulders forward, a slight move with a hint of exclusion. 'At first we were not going to be together. I was to going to raise Elise. But after my father died, I don't know, we thought that maybe we should try. It was a mistake. The whole idea. The world for him is very organized. We took two holidays to see if we could be together. The first in Thailand – we booked a hotel at a place called Ban Hai, and took a room on the beach facing the ocean – and it went, you know, it went well, but afterward he wasn't so certain. I thought, maybe, I thought it was possible. It might work. I don't know, so I persuaded him to move in. The next year we booked the same place for our second holiday, but there was a problem with the date, so we changed our minds. Elise was older and we thought we should try a different kind of holiday. Anyway, we changed our minds. Australia was Mathieu's idea. So we found flights into Perth and out of Sydney. Have you been to Australia?'

Ford shook his head.

'You have this idea about how big it is, but you've no real idea just how big until you're there. Mathieu worked out that we could drive three hundred miles a day, which didn't sound so bad. But everything is the same. The same bush. The same trees. The same sky. Whatever direction you head in everything is the same. On the first afternoon we were driving to these mountains. The radio said there was a fire four hundred miles away which didn't sound so bad, until we realized that these mountains weren't mountains, they were smoke from the fire which took up the entire horizon, and we were driving toward it. Mathieu found a campsite and we decided to stop. Another fire had passed through a week before. Everything was reduced to sand, to charcoal. There were no trees, but you could smell the eucalyptus even though the trees were gone. The sky was grey, just smoke, and the sun was red, you could stare right at it, this red circle. That night the fire crossed the highway three hundred miles south, and we woke up to a clear sky and drove onto the Nullarbor Plain, which is this stone desert. Endless.' Nathalie poured herself the last of the wine.

'How was your daughter?'

'Elise? She slept most of the way. At first everything was strange and interesting, but by the second day she just listened to her head-phones and slept. I forgot to say but this was the same time as the tsunami. We came off the Nullarbor when we heard the news. We lis-tened to the radio and it didn't make sense. It didn't touch us until we heard about Thailand, and we realized that if the town of Cham Lek was gone then the hotels at Ban Hai would also be gone. It didn't make sense. We were at this place where the desert stops at the ocean, it just stops, like the end of the world. We found a campsite and Mathieu called home. It sounds stupid now, but no one knew what was going on. They knew we were in Australia but there was this idea that we were also going to Thailand. People were worried for us. We kept saying that we were lucky. We were lucky. Anyhow. Mathieu looked at the tsunami and how we'd changed our plans as a sign. I couldn't see it. And that's when everything, in the end, started to come apart – because I wouldn't see this as a sign.'

Done with speaking, Nathalie set her glass at her feet and excused herself. Ford watched as she walked into her room, a weight upon her, and was surprised when she did not return. Martin and Eric both paused and looked to him and he became uncomfortable.

Ford lay in bed curled on his side. Nathalie's broodiness drew out his own. Their situations unnervingly similar. He turned the dog tags between his fingers one by one.

3.6

Parson sat in the car, parked at the side of the road, door open, one foot firm on the dusty blacktop, the sun falling hard on that leg. A choice ahead of him. A map of Turkey open across his lap, buckled over the steering wheel. Earlier in the morning, after seeing the coach station at Kopeckale and learning the bus routes, he'd circled the main points of exit: Ankara, Izmir, Istanbul, then numerous cities along the long western coast, which meant, clearly, heading west to the coast, or north then west to the cities. The bus routes superimposed on this showed three key towns: Kopeckale, Narapi and Birsim, where the buses offered a choice of north-to-south and east-to-west routes. Three feasible options.

He decided on Birsim but couldn't make himself go. Something about the open plains on either side sucked out his interest. When the call came, he'd been sitting in the one place for over thirty minutes.

The call, from HOSCO, but no one he'd spoken with before, said that they had information about a sighting. Sutler.

Parson pushed the map to the back seat, clear on his directions. He drew in his leg, shut the door, and felt certain as he started up the car, lucky.

3.7

In the morning Ford waited while Eric took a shower. The clap of water sang loose across the courtyard. Nathalie spoke with Eric while he showered. Eric's phone lay on his bed beside his pillow.

'But you should say? You must tell her. I don't understand why you don't want to go? Everything is finished here in two or three days, we can spend a week on the coast before you go. You have to go, she will be disappointed if you don't go.'

He couldn't hear Eric's reply.

'Tell her,' Nathalie insisted. 'Talk to her. If she's in Rome she might prefer to stay. You should let her know that you want to change your mind. She might have other things she would prefer to do?'

Eric returned to the room with a towel wrapped about his waist. He asked Ford how he was, then took off the towel to dry himself. Along the boy's right buttock ran a sour yellow bruise and a trail of parallel scratches. Eric tested the skin, the gesture seemed strangely feminine.

'I slipped.' Eric twisted about, stretched the skin so he could see. 'A dumb mistake. Don't tell Nathalie. She'll only make a fuss.'

Ford straightened his bed. 'I need to get online.' He decided to be forthright. 'Can I use your mobile? I'd like to see if I have any messages.'

'Sure.' Eric picked up his phone, unlocked it, and handed it to Ford. 'The code is 4221. That button for the internet. I think it's charged.' He pressed a small square centred key and demonstrated how to move the cursor.

'Hold a key down to select different letters or numbers.' Eric stood beside him, and left only when he heard Martin complaining to Nathalie outside. *The shower was cold. The breakfast stale. And now they have to wait.*

Ford sat at the edge of his bed, he drew the dog tags over his head and selected the first one. The phone, being small, had a tiny keypad. To avoid making a mistake he used Eric's pen to hit the numbers and unlock the phone. He found the HOSCO website and worried that he could be traced, that his account would be blocked, that, somehow, the moment he signed in, his location would be revealed and everything would be over – and while he knew this was unlikely, he couldn't shake the idea.

As the first security screen loaded the page locked and the cursor would not move. The signal bars faded and Ford held the phone up, then moved about the room to see where the signal was stronger. When he sat down, closer to the door, the bars returned, and the page loaded with the cursor blinking over an empty text box.

The first number from the first dog tag: 42974615.

He entered the first four numbers: 4297 and pressed the keys carefully and watched them appear after a little delay: 4 – 2 – 9 – 7.

He checked the final four numbers from the first dog tag: 4615.

When he pressed 4, the preceding number disappeared. He re-entered 7, then 4, waited for the numbers to appear, and they came up in reverse: 4 – 7.

He balanced the phone on his knee, wiped his hands down his face, picked up the phone and deleted the last two numbers.

Three numbers disappeared.

Ford squinted at the screen: 4 – 2 – 9.

He waited, the numbers stayed in place. He held his breath then typed 7, waited for it to appear, then with particular care pressed 4 (pause) – 2 (pause) – 9 (pause) – 7 (pause).

4 – 2 – 9 – 7 – 4 – 2 – 9 – 7

Catching his mistake before he hit 'enter'. He deleted the entire number and re-entered from the start and watched it appear, correctly, on the small screen.

Finally, satisfied, he moved the cursor to 'enter', then clicked. The screen turned black and returned with a small message set dead centre in white script: SESSION TIMED OUT.

Ford held the phone out at arm's length. He couldn't be sure, did TIMED OUT mean that this was a second unsuccessful attempt, or simply that he'd taken too long?

He sat alone, cancelled the entire screen and allowed the phone to lock. If he had one remaining attempt he would pick the means, the time and place with care. This, he thought, was pure foolishness, a kind of brinkmanship he could not afford. Two chances gone. One remaining.

Later in the morning Ford found Eric alone in the courtyard. He sat reading under a large umbrella, a short-wave radio beside his elbow tuned to the American Forces.

'Martin's gone with Nathalie to buy a carpet. Mehmet's with them. There's a trip this afternoon if you're interested. Birsim. It's a town just north of here. Nathalie will probably ask you.'

'I don't think she'll be too interested.'

Eric thought for a moment. 'You're talking about last night, right?'

'I don't understand what happened. She was talking, and then she went to her room.'

'She does that a lot. I wouldn't worry about it. She told you the story about the tsunami, right?'

At a loss for something to do Ford sat on the wall beside Eric's lounger. 'How's your book?'

'I'm not reading.' He held up a small notebook. 'I wouldn't feel bad about last night. It's what she does. This thing. She talks until she gets upset. It happens a lot, especially when they aren't getting along. You know she gave up her daughter to be with him.'

'Martin? I thought they weren't a couple?'

'They're a couple.'

'How do you know them?'

'He's one of my professors.'

'And you're helping with this film?'

'My options weren't so great. Summer with my mom, or this. Not much choice.'

In an ashtray just under the sunbed, Ford spied what looked like the end of a reefer. Eric asked if he was interested and Ford shrugged yes.

Eric hopped off the bed and disappeared into Martin's room. He returned with a black shaving-bag. 'He won't mind. Anyway, he shouldn't be smoking, he's paranoid enough. We're doing him a favour. He thinks we're being followed. The Turkish Secret Service,' Eric huffed, 'or some Kurdish hit squad. I'm serious. He really believes this stuff. He sees a photo of the Peshmerga in the news and he thinks he's on some hit-list.'

Eric set the cigarette papers across his thigh, opened the small bag, and looked inside. 'He's not sure about you either. Like yesterday, when you were with Nathalie in that cave, he sent me to check up and see what you were doing. *I was spying on you.* Don't worry, he doesn't think you were up to anything, not like that.' He scorched then crumbled the dope into his notebook. Ford again noticed the numbered code the boy used for writing.

'What isn't he sure about?'

'You. Basically. He's suspicious about everything. How we met. About you being in Kopeckale. See, that's the kind of thing that really makes him flinch. He's suspicious. He thinks you're checking up on him. He sends me to check up on you, but he thinks you're the spy.' Eric lifted the papers to his lips. 'They have their theories about you. He doesn't believe the story about your friend. Neither does Nathalie.'

'I don't really follow—'

'You wear those dog tags. Martin thinks you have something to do with the military.'

'Why? Why does he think anyone is following him?'

'Because he doesn't trust *anyone*.' Eric spread out his hands, then whispered conspiratorially, '*Everyone.*' He passed the joint and a lighter to Ford.

Ford lit the joint and slowly drew in breath. The smoke hit the back of his throat, grassy and dry, and he suppressed a cough.

'Yeah. It's a little harsh.' Eric waited to be handed the joint.

Ford held in the smoke then slowly exhaled. 'So what's this?' He pointed at the notebook. 'The numbers. What are the numbers?'

Eric brushed his hand across the pages. 'Here, let me show you. You have something with numbers? Something like a credit card?'

Ford said no and Eric laughed. 'Everyone has a credit card. How about those dog tags?'

Ford ran his finger about his neck and hooked the chain. He drew the tags over his head and handed them to the boy.

Eric turned the dog tags over. 'I thought these things had names and blood groups? You don't have something with a name? What do the numbers stand for? And this? H-O-S slash J-A? What's that?'

'Information I don't want to lose.'

Eric held up the tag for the junk account, counted the numbers then wrote them in his notebook. 'OK, so eight numbers. Drop any duplication as that would make the code nonsense. You could just do it straight A, B, C. So 3 is A, 5 is B, 9 is C, and so on up to twenty-six. But if you really want to keep it private you stop the numbers at nine and use symbols, and you have to draw a key-chart. See? It's not impossible to break, but it would take some work, because you need to know the rationale for the change.'

Ford said it looked too complicated.

Eric quickly explained. 'It's just basic substitution. There are ways of making it tougher. You can pick a word with no repeating letters. Something you aren't going to forget. *Hideout*. What's that? Seven. *A hideout*. Eight.' He wrote in his notebook A-H-I-D-E-O-U-T, a single letter above each number. 'And again, if there's a repetition you skip or substitute a number or a letter, but you use a word as the key. So if you know the key word you can work out the rest of the alphabet. I have a different code for each notebook, a different sequence. You get used to it pretty quickly.' Eric copied the numbers from the other tags, keeping to the sequence. 'It's fairly simple, it wouldn't take anything to crack. But it's enough to stop them reading.'

'Who?'

'Nathalie and Martin. They go through my stuff all the time. It's the only way to keep anything private. Plus it keeps them on their toes. They get paranoid about anything they can't understand. They think everything is about them.'

'Nathalie said you're interviewing terrorists?'

'Terrorists?'

'That's what she said. Terrorists.'

'No, not terrorists.' Eric, already relaxed, began to giggle.

'In the eyes of the Turks?'

'That's a whole different issue.' Eric considered for the moment, the joint poised between fingers. 'The Turks are worse than Martin. They wouldn't like any of this. The whole idea of the project would be a problem. These men are just . . .' He took in a long draw. Ford waited for the end of the sentence. '. . . I don't know, they're just Kurds. And the Turkish Kurds have pretty much lost everything, they've been cleared out of their villages. So yeah, whatever. Terrorists.' Eric slipped lower down the lounger, his knees up, his hand resting on his chest. 'The thing about all of this – I mean what really makes this funny – is that he doesn't have any idea about what's going on. He talks to all of these people, Kurds, Iraqis, Palestinians – he talks to people who have lost everything and he still doesn't have a clue because it's all about him and how stupid he is. The entire project is driven by his stupidity.'

'Martin?'

'Doesn't have a clue—' Eric suddenly froze. 'You hear something? Are they back?'

They both listened and heard nothing.

'We've had our bags searched almost everywhere we've gone. The digital stuff isn't a problem, we can store that stuff as soon as it's taken, more or less, and we've a couple of hard drives, so everything can be backed up. The material we have on film is trickier. He insisted on using film even though it's not practical. There are these shots he wants of the landscape and they have to be taken with film. Each time we go through a security check they expose the film, but he still keeps using it for these landscape shots. I've been back to Kopeckale three times to get the same shots because they keep exposing the film. See what I mean? Stupid or what? The Turks don't like the idea of anyone talking with these people. That's what they don't like. If they had any idea about who we're speaking with we'd all be in trouble. That's probably what will make this project work. Nothing to do with him being a genius or anything, but because he's so fucking stupid—' Eric suddenly sat upright. 'Shit. They're back.'

Nathalie and Martin came into the courtyard before Eric could hide the washbag. Martin walked directly to his room, upright and tight-mouthed.

'What is this?' Nathalie dropped a newspaper on the table with a slap. 'He could hear every word you said. What are you thinking?'

Eric and Ford kept to their room and waited for supper. Eric, flat on his back, scribbled in his notebook and softly swore to himself, leaving Ford contented with the silence.

'What do you think they heard? You think they heard everything?'

'That's what she said.'

'Shit,' he swore slowly. 'Everything? You think he heard everything? I can't remember what I said. He'll be impossible now. I can't wait for this to be done. I'm going to Malta. My mother has found this villa, this old palazzo or something. No one uses it. No one lives there. It's totally isolated. I can stay as long as I like. Free. No neighbours, no nothing. No one will even know I'm there. I can't wait.'

Eric curled up with embarrassment, the newspaper on his lap crackling as he hugged his legs. After a while Ford thought he had gone to sleep, but the boy turned over and offered him the newspaper.

'You should read this.'

Less vexed than earlier, Ford didn't want to move. So, he had one chance left. He only needed to log in once. If that failed, he'd get in contact with Geezler. He'd have no choice.

'That writer.' Eric shook the paper. 'He's really disappeared. Honest to god. He was supposed to be at some conference but didn't show up. This is that book I told you about, where the writer disappeared, I thought it was a publicity stunt, but he's really disappeared. They've reprinted an interview where he talks about the book and the murders.' Eric looked up. 'It's like everyone hates him because he stayed in this palazzo in Naples and wrote about a murder everyone wanted to forget. He basically solved who did it, although he doesn't have their names or anything. *Mr Rabbit and Mr Wolf.*'

'If he solved it then why is he in trouble?'

'Because he's more or less disproved what the police said. It's like these two guys just take a story from a book and then copy it, and everyone who lived in the palazzo at the time just turned a blind eye while it happened.' He looked at Ford as if this were all crazy. 'How insane is that? Nobody wants to know. These two psychopaths copy a murder from a book and everyone is like *OK, that happened, let's all move on now.* You should read it? You really should.'

Ford said he wasn't much of a reader and anyway didn't read thrillers.

'It's nothing like a thriller. It's about a writer who stays in this place in Naples and finds out all of this information. All anyone knows about this murder is that someone has disappeared, he's gone, murdered, and pieces of him start appearing on the street. A tongue. A room with blood all over it. His clothes on some wasteland.'

'And this happened?'

'Right. Yes. That's what I'm saying. Some guy, they don't even know who, was chopped up. Just nasty.' Eric stretched out his legs. 'I'd like to meet him. The writer. I'd like to talk with him because I bet there's stuff he couldn't publish.'

Ford couldn't follow the logic.

Eric looked up from his newspaper, mouth slightly open, halfway through some thought. 'What are you thinking?'

'I'm relaxing.'

'You've got her wrong, you know. Martin's the prize, Nathalie's just some project. Something he's working on.' Eric rolled onto his back. 'Doesn't seem right, does it?' His voice sounded flat as he explained that prior to Nathalie, Martin's taste ran to boys, his students in fact. But that didn't mean that Nathalie wasn't complicated in her own right. Her *partner*, Mathieu, worked at the same university in the same department, and she'd been humiliated by his affairs. Mathieu was the same as Martin, no different, only he picked his entertainment from Nathalie's students, and starting with the research assistants he'd worked his way down to her graduate students – until she confronted him, publicly, at one of his lectures. *Are you fucking my students?* 'It was,' Eric spread his fingers in a small explosion, 'spectacular.' Although he admitted that he hadn't seen it himself and wasn't exactly sure when it had happened.

Ford doubted that these things had ever occurred. He searched for a word – was 'cuckold' specifically masculine? Were women saddled with verbs instead of nouns, with the past-imperfect, the '*was*' and '*used to*' of being cheated, deceived, disappointed. Tired, he wished the boy would let him drowse.

A soft knock came at the door. Nathalie, in a deliberately level voice, asked if she could come in, then edged open the door, anticipating Eric's reply. She stood with her arms folded and leaned into the room, thin-lipped and matronly.

Prepped with new information Ford sat up, expectant, but Eric's information didn't translate to anything that could be read in her gestures and manner. From what he could see she was still angry.

'How is he?'

'I don't know. He has a bad stomach. He's sleeping now. Things have been difficult for him. You know how he is. What have you been talking about?'

'That man. The one in the news. The man who disappeared.'

'The man from Iraq?'

Ford felt his throat constrict. Four simple words. Alarmed by the comment, so sudden and unexpected and so easily presented, he wiped his hands over his face, certain that his expression would expose him.

'We're talking about that writer.' Eric shook his head.

'I don't know who you mean?'

'That writer. The murder. Remember?' Eric's tone bordered on sarcasm.

'That isn't news,' she clucked, 'it's sensation. It's just a story.'

Ignoring her, Eric reached for the paper and asked if Ford was done.

Nathalie looked from the Eric to Ford and back to Eric. 'It doesn't matter. I don't want to interrupt anything.'

Eric folded the newspaper and set it aside.

'What?' For no reason Eric's smile appeared to annoy Nathalie. Relieved that the subject had moved on, Ford watched her unfold her hands with a certain haughtiness he hadn't noticed before, the gesture of someone familiar with humiliation.

'He could be anywhere. That writer. He could be anyone. He could be here.'

'I doubt it.'

'Why not? Think about it. What better place is there? There's all this distraction going off at the border. It's a perfect place to disappear. That's what I'd do.' Eric looked directly at Ford. 'Of course. This makes perfect sense. This is what you're doing.'

'Me?'

'You. You're hiding. You're in trouble. Mystery solved. You aren't travelling. You aren't lost. You're hiding. Laying low. Why don't you tell Martin, he can make a film about you?' Eric lay back, laughing. It was a good joke, wasn't it? Just a great joke.

3.8

Parson waited in his car outside the hotel with a radio on his lap tuned to BFBS. Every morning he listened to the same content, to sentimental dedications from distant families to serving troops, half-touching but also banal. The town names, King's Lynn, Bedford, Maidenhead, Hungerford, sounded invented, overly quaint, although he knew and disliked these towns. Occasionally the simplicity of the messages, the pure-heartedness, say, of a daughter's greeting for her father, made him catch his breath. Tourists walked wide of the row of police vehicles and huddled groups of uniformed men. There were lessons to learn. First among them that he didn't need to be here, and second, he should keep his work with the Turkish police to its barest minimum. Eager to demonstrate their control over the situation they had provided a squad of seven cars, a whole battalion of men, and assured him that this response was occurring at the very same time in Bodrum, in Izmir, at other places with confirmed sightings. Unsure that this was a good idea, he no longer felt lucky and slumped low in the seat. When he ran his finger inside his shirt collar he found the material soft with sweat.

The sun hit fiercer here than inland, hard on the water and stripped to a steely light. He noted the shops beside him, painted white, the restaurants and boutiques, a hairdresser, a clapboard market with signs for cola, ices, thick-crust pizza, burgers, designer clothing; the entire boardwalk appeared over-familiar.

The police lined the balcony of the self-catering hotel and chivvied the guests off the balconies and out of neighbouring suites. Armed militia stopped the traffic from entering the promenade. Tourists hung about the poolside to watch: attention zeroed to Room 42.

The event played out modestly. The door opened to a simple knock to show a man, a giant, dressed in brown plaid shorts and white socks, his gut pushing over his belt. With his hands raised the man filled the doorway – and it was obvious to Parson, even from a distance, that this could not be Sutler: having no hair in the first instance, and being in any case so grossly oversized that imagining him walking through the mountains just didn't work.

Parson came out of the car wanting the whole show over, aware of the hours ahead returning to Kopeckale and the explanation he would have to make to Gibson. No, he waved, then shouted, 'No, no, no, no, no. Stop this. Let the man go.'

Out of the room, shimmying from behind the giant as if dividing from him, appeared two women in swimsuits, both young, then two more, and two more to total six. The man stood with his hands held up, his head hung hangdog, a picture of shame. The police, visibly confused, gathered up the women, and worked the man out of the doorway with their sticks, a little bemused by an event which had every appearance of a magician's act: a fat man sub-dividing into six pretty women. 'Exactly what is this?' Parson asked the man as he approached. 'What is this?'

The calls started as soon as he returned to the car. Expecting Gibson, Parson was surprised to find himself speaking with Paul Geezler. He recognized the name from conversations with Gibson, and thought it strange that the new head of HOSCO operations in the Middle East would bother with a direct call. Not for the first time he sensed a per-spectival shift as his idea of the damage caused by Sutler broadened.

Geezler introduced himself as the man assigned to *pick up the pieces*.

Parson leafed quickly through his papers but could not find his notes on Sutler at HOSCO.

Geezler explained that he had just arrived at Southern-CIPA and was familiarizing himself with everything undone since Howell's arrest, although no one seemed happy to share information with him. 'These days,' he said, 'I talk mostly to myself.'

Southern-CIPA, Geezler hinted, would be disassembled and recon-figured. He was working directly with them, which is how it should have been all along. If HOSCO had kept a tighter eye on the finances, especially the distribution, then it wouldn't have gone so haywire so quickly. 'Independent companies are more responsible when it comes to monitoring. We all know that. That's nothing new. With Southern-CIPA it was always too complicated, all of these processes which were just too much of a mystery,' Geezler explained, weary of it. 'Truth is, we're the victims here, of a government that has no stop checks, and of a system which leaves the financial distribution down to just one man. Where else would you find that? I'm not naive, we need to put our hands up and admit we're vulnerable to any individual who wants to abuse us. Sutler took us for a long ride. I'll admit that. I'll be the first.

There's work to do to make sure this doesn't happen again. But my main duty is to make sure that HOSCO has some place in the reorganization, in whatever comes next, but it looks like the damage is going deep.' Camp Liberty was already dismantled, and even as they spoke, the burn pits were being bulldozed. 'The Massive is over.' Geezler faced a winter of hearings, suits, and litigation. 'Job number one is to make sure we're still a part of whatever develops here, and that we learn some serious lessons. Which is where you come in.'

Parson said it sounded complicated. Stuck on the notion that HOSCO found itself to be a victim.

'I want news on Sutler. I want you to keep me informed on what you're finding.' Could he give him something this morning? Anything? One small thing? Was he *close*? 'As soon as you find him we can start to close this affair.'

Sensing that Geezler would terminate the search if he had no results Parson said he was *close*, as in *closer* but not quite *closing in*. It would be better, he realized, to invent small details than disappoint the man.

'But nothing new?' Geezler spoke in a crisp, self-important tone Parson just didn't like. 'I have a lot of people to satisfy. I need information. You should know I have an announcement to make this morning.'

There was plenty Parson couldn't say. Tourists spread along the coast from Antalya to Bodrum had reporting sightings of Stephen Sutler. The sighting in Marmaris was one such example. After Kopeckale, Sutler had left no direct trail. Dissatisfied, Geezler needled him for news. *He must have something?*

'What level of detail do you want? He was sighted last night at a bar in the Hotel Cettia in Marmaris,' Parson lied, not exactly a lie, but a statement which gave credence to something he knew not to be true. 'It's a confident sighting, but it doesn't look like he took a room. There's a taxi driver who brought him from the hotel back to the coach station. I'm confident I'll find out where he's gone.'

'Confident?'

'There are booking clerks, ticket offices, bus drivers. I'll know when he was at the station and for how long. Finding out where he's going won't be difficult. My guess is he'll steer away from the coast where he's likely to be spotted and find some other way out of the country. But that's a guess. I'll have more concrete information this afternoon. I'll know where he's heading.'

'There are things you should know.' Geezler drew a deep breath. 'We have a report on Howell's office, and we're revising the idea that the attack on Southern-CIPA came from the outside. It looks like Stephen Sutler was the source.'

Parson said he didn't understand, and then the suggestion became clear: somehow Sutler was the cause of the assault. It sounded improbable and went against the evidence. Both Pakosta and Clark had witnessed the attack, and they had both described the mortar arcing down, the impact, the type of blast. They were unequivocal about the source. Howell's evidence concurred. This was an outside attack. 'Pakosta and Clark both saw the mortar. It's in their statements. I don't see why Sutler would do this?'

'All of the accounts and records were kept in Howell's office and they've all been destroyed. Pakosta and Clark are either mistaken or lying.' There was evidence, Geezler explained, that the men at Camp Liberty had accepted money and gifts from Sutler – some of them had received goods, Breitling watches, others the payment of debts. Thanks to Sutler's patronage they lived like kings. According to the evidence the damage to Howell's office came from a device set *inside* the office. 'It looks like Stephen Sutler was responsible.'

'And Paul Howell? What does he say? Has anyone spoken with him?'

'Howell isn't a military man. He wouldn't know a mortar attack from a grenade attack. He sat in the State Department for five years, in an office without windows. He rides a desk. He knows administration not armament.'

Parson found the printout of the Sutler lookalike. He held up the paper and examined the marks drawn by the German journalist, the cut under his right eye, the scratches across his forehead. If Sutler was responsible for the damage to Howell's office, then he was responsible for Kiprowski's death. He waited for Geezler to comment.

'When you find Sutler, you need to inform me directly, and we'll call in the proper authorities to arrest him. You shouldn't approach him. I want to hear from you directly. I spend my day assuring people that this is under control. In three weeks an enquiry opens into the Massive. I want them to know that we're close to some kind of resolve, that we're working together. Better still, I want a result. I want this over.'

Parson didn't want to admit he was nowhere near *close* when it came to anticipating the man's movements: it wasn't that Sutler was unpredictable or impossible to anticipate, he'd simply disappeared as if he'd never been there. Sutler, with one verified sighting in Anatolia, was less substantial than dust, an absolute zero. 'If you want me to continue looking for this man I'll need more information.' Parson felt the responsibilities of his job. 'I have next to nothing from you, no employment file, no details. I have his date of birth but there's no birth registered for a Stephen Lawrence Sutler on that date in the UK. London are checking this, but there's no tax record, no National Insurance, no prior address. I know nothing prior to his arrival in Iraq. I have no idea where you found this man. I need to speak with whoever gave him this contract.'

Geezler promised assistance. 'I have people looking here. It's likely that he came through Iran or Syria on a different passport. If he was working with Howell, then Howell could have prepared this a long time ago as he understands the systems we use. The only way to trace Sutler is through the accounts, and because of the damage to Howell's office we don't have the full record. All we know is that the amounts were transferred by Howell under Sutler's authorization. I'd keep an eye on the banks at the major cities. Istanbul, Ankara. He isn't going to be able to move that money around in a small town, not without being noticed.'

'I have no information about these accounts.' Now Parson felt disadvantaged. 'If he has access to money I doubt he'd stay long in Turkey. He could manage this money online or through another party, no one would know.'

Geezler cleared his throat. 'Would you trust that amount of money to an online transfer? I'd look at the banks, the international banks – Istanbul, Izmir, Ankara.' Geezler's voice became hesitant. 'If Stephen Sutler had one of these accounts he would be aiming to recover that money. Find the money and you find the man.'

Parson spoke with his wife. Her call came immediately after his discussion with Geezler. Her voice, denatured by the connection, suffered stutters, breaks, and hesitations. She wanted to tell him something, and warned him to listen before he made any comment. Would he promise to do that?

'I don't want to stay in Nottingham,' she said. 'I don't, I know I don't. I'd rather be on my own, back at home. There was a bonfire here in Wilford, by the river. A bonfire organized by the Rotary Club. And this man, a resident, threatened a volunteer helping with the car parking.' Was he following? Did this make sense? 'This man threatened the volunteer then returned twenty minutes later to beat him up. At a charity bonfire. In Wilford. It's not the Middle East,' she said, 'it's Wilford, Nottingham. I don't want to be among these people. They complain about a charity bonfire, and right on their doorstep there are children as young as eleven selling drugs along the river. This, they could care less about. This is fine. Children on bicycles selling drugs. Children with dogs, Alsatians, children who hiss at you, who make suggestions of what you might like to do for them as you make your way home.'

Parson let her anger ride, anticipating its conclusion.

'Your sister agrees, I'm better going home. I can't do anything here. I feel useless. I'm waiting. That's what I'm doing. I have three months of waiting. If I need to come back I can come back. I would rather be on my own. I was going to write, but I thought that if you called and I wasn't here that you would worry and I don't want you to worry. I wanted to tell you so you wouldn't worry.' She paused, a beat, as if to prompt him. 'I wanted to tell you because you'd understand.'

'I'll call Gibson. He has contacts with the RAF. He'll send some planes,' Parson replied, 'we'll take Wilford off the map.'

'You promise?'

'I promise. The name will be forgotten. It will be a crime to speak of Wilford. Superstitions will start.'

It took them longer each time to close the conversation.

'Soon,' she said, 'I'm not counting, but stay in Turkey.'

'I'm not sure it's possible. If nothing comes up they'll send me back to Iraq.'

Laura consoled, advised, suggested solutions which would not fit, ideas which illuminated the gulf between how he spent his days and how she spent hers. He couldn't begin to explain.

'Isn't there anyone you can speak with?'

Parson said no. It simply didn't work like that. As long as the claims kept coming from Iraq, Gibson would keep him on site. It was simply cheaper than sending someone from London every time.

You'll think of something, she said, because you have to. 'You'll figure this out. You'll cook something up.' Her voice rang with a clear faith, or this is what he supposed she intended.

Parson promised he would do what he could, and the line clipped short.

He sat in his car, sulky at the prospect of an eight-hour drive back to Kopeckale, his wife's voice lingering with him. The whisky he'd drunk tasted of smoke, of cigarettes. Laura was right. The longer he remained in Turkey the less likely he would return to Iraq – and Gibson would send him back to Iraq the moment the search concluded. As he slipped the printout of Sutler into the folder an idea occurred to him: *If you set a device in an office, if you knew that this was going to explode, you would be running, and you would be running away. You would be running with your back to the explosion. You would not face the blast if you knew it was coming, not without protecting your face. You would not have scratches on your face. It would be unlikely.*

There could be many reasons why Sutler had turned: a door that would not open, an unexpected delay, but surely, he would have protected himself, cringed, shied away? It would only be natural. The simple fact that Sutler had not escaped the building restored his idea that the man was moving by accident, not design. These new ideas did not sit well.

He sat for a long time and considered the situation. HOSCO had refused to settle with the widow of the translator Amer Hassan, and while this was not related, he found that he could not sympathize with their current trouble. It seemed *just* to him that HOSCO would have to struggle, and he no longer liked the idea that he was assisting them. The longer he ran after Sutler the less time he would spend in Iraq. He saw no harm in manufacturing, no, not manufacturing, but *enhancing* evidence. He did this already when he needed to sway a claim one way or another, although he'd failed to do so in the Hassan report. These shifts, these inflections, would depend on tiny *amplifications*, nothing concrete, nothing extravagant, just a matter of small unconfirmed sightings, hotel bookings, taxi rides, travel arrangements, spare and harmless details to keep Geezler off his back while he continued with his search. Geezler also remained a question in his mind, although he could not properly formulate why. The information about the bank accounts, about Sutler being responsible for the attack on Southern-CIPA, about Sutler giving gifts of watches and whisky to the men at Camp Liberty (when Pakosta and Clark had admitted that Howell had provided these gifts), was all conjecture. Too eager to bend the facts to suit a particular reading Geezler sounded like a man trying hard to convince. He probably didn't even know he was doing this.

3.9

Ford waited in the van with Martin, while Nathalie, Eric, and Mehmet ran errands in the market. Martin elected to stay with the equipment and sat with the camera nestled between his legs. Still peevish he leaned out of the window and avoided conversation, pretending he couldn't hear because of the street. Parched, Ford hoped that Nathalie would remember to buy bottled water. She'd made a list but left it on the seat, and he suspected some other agenda behind the trip. Late afternoon and the sun scalded his bare arms.

He began to entertain Eric's ideas that Martin preferred men, or rather boys, or rather his students, and that through some perversity he was attached to Nathalie, who could, in her own manner, be considered peerless. How then, and why, would such a woman satisfy herself with such a man? Whatever Martin's charms, whatever his appeal, Ford couldn't see it.

Martin, lost to his thoughts, tugged at his beard.

Ford redirected his attention to the town.

Larger than Narapi, Birsim's streets span out from a central market. Mehmet had parked facing the main square and left them with a packet of coloured pencils to hand out to children. It was better, he said, to give crayons, but the children wouldn't accept them. Instead they bothered Martin for cash, or took the pencils and poked him with them, then slapped the van's sides when he refused to give them money. Bored, Ford watched a line of mules progress toward them. A whole other order of information: sweaty and exhausted beasts hauling sticks and sacks of concrete with tourist shops on either side; glass windows, white tiled floors, then these animals of bone and pelt tethered one to another, exhausted by the heat. The streets busy. The shops empty. No tourists, not this far east, not this season.

A gentle percussive *ba-boom*, nothing more suggestive than a firework pop, reverberated down the street. Martin perked up, sat forward, and some moments after the stink of scorched rubber overpowered the air. From the far side of the market rose a pall of grey smoke. Martin sniffed and muttered that something was on fire. The smoke, now black, ran thick across the square and clogged the mouth of the street. Wisps of ash – burnt paper, rubber – coiled delicately down upon them.

The crowd immediately became confused. People facing the square collided with people escaping so that the street became impassable. Alarmed by the acrid stink and the unearthly black snow the mules stopped immediately alongside the van. One slumped hard against the door so that the vehicle began to lean. Camera ready, Martin struggled with the door in an attempt to shove the beast aside, but the animal would not budge. Ford clambered into the front seat, wound down the window, and pulled himself out, then up, to the van's roof.

Martin struggled after, and Ford helped him up, his arms streaked with ash. When children attempted to scramble onto the van he pushed them down and they slipped back into the adult crowd. The smoke began to thin, and from their vantage point they could see the source of the fire.

On the far west side of the square smoke pumped through the open windows of a burning bus, the contents of the hold – shoes, clothes, baskets, suitcases, fruit, tatters of paper – spat out across the market. Flames roiled from the undercarriage.

Martin filmed the muddle using Ford as a support, and Ford sighted Eric and Nathalie among the crowd in the square with a pinch of relief. Behind them, a good number of red and black berets of the military police. Bothered by the crowd Nathalie wrapped her arm about Eric's shoulder and Eric directed her forward. Behind them, only just in view, came Mehmet, surrounded by soldiers. When he spotted Ford and Martin on top of the van he began to shout.

Ford drank his share of the coffee, then helped himself to another cup. The bus-burning came as a reminder of the promise he had made in Kopeckale that he would avoid crowds, keep away from public spaces and gatherings, situations which he could not control. Eric finished and then re-started the novel because there were things he didn't follow, he said, things he'd missed, and there wasn't anything else to read but old newspapers. The idea that you could read the chapters in any order appealed to him, even though it wouldn't change anything he already knew. He might go into town. He might try the hammam. He asked Ford if he was interested: you could get proper coffee with hot milk at the barber shop served by a giant ape of a man. There were pastries, honey and almond, yet to be tasted.

Ape. This choice of word, surely a poke at Martin?

Nathalie sat on the bench with her back against the wall, a bowl of olives on her lap. She'd had words with Eric and now they weren't speaking. Her sights fixed on Martin, visibly brewing discontent. Martin picked dough from the bread and rolled it into pellets which he stacked on his plate. None of them were interested in making conversation. Ford couldn't see his place in this. Nathalie moved the bread from Martin's reach, and with a deep intake, a long single breath, she asked if Ford could help settle an issue.

'Tell me, and be honest, I want to know what you think. Was it wrong to take pictures yesterday?'

The discussion which should have been exhausted still had legs.

'Why are you asking him?' Martin spoke in French.

'Do you think it was right to film that bus? Do you think he had any business being there?' She challenged Ford to take her side.

'What difference did it make? There wasn't anything we could do and he had the camera with him.'

'You don't understand,' Nathalie disagreed, 'he didn't do it because he *happened* to have a camera.'

Martin interrupted. What was her problem? Seriously?

'The problem is all about taking pictures like this,' she reached across the table and held her hand flat, close to his face, 'with the camera this close. It's a terrible thing to do, to watch and do nothing. Suppose that somebody was hurt, what would you have done?'

'Nobody was in trouble. I'm not a doctor. I make films. I couldn't have helped even if the situation was different.' Martin reached for his cigarettes.

'But you were filming.'

'You know what goes on here. It wasn't an accident. The fire was deliberate. What do you expect? This is exactly why I came here.' The appearance of one digital camera on the streets of Birsim was a ridiculously small infringement of anyone's liberty. 'I don't see why you have a problem with this?'

'I don't care,' she said, 'but that isn't the issue. You know this. What would you do if your students behaved like this? Anyway, now you have what you wanted.' Nathalie untied her hair and drew it back inside a closed fist, her voice an aside, low and sulky. 'Go see for your-self, now we have someone watching us. Just like you said.'

Martin stood up, a motion left incomplete, his hands dithering on the armrests. He asked what she was talking about.

'There is a man, outside, just as you said, he's been there all morning.'

'What man?'

'Go see for yourself. Your activities have finally brought you to the attention of the police.'

Sulky and wronged, Nathalie stood up, and said pertly that she would see them all later, she was going out. Martin could do as he pleased.

They gathered in Mehmet's small office at the front of the house, Ford, Martin, and Eric, and leaned cautiously into the window for a view of the street. A car, a grey and dusty Peugeot, was parked on the opposite side in a street with no other vehicles. Inside, as Nathalie had said, sat a man, visible in silhouette.

An hour later Ford and Eric checked the street and found the man still outside, waiting. Ford kept an eye on the street and kept up the reports: 'He's still there . . . hasn't moved . . . I think she's right,' while Eric and Martin downloaded the digital film onto separate portable hard drives. When Nathalie returned the man in the car did not dis-guise his interest – he turned to watch as she came to the door, then kept his attention on the house once she was inside.

3.10

Anne sat with her back to the café and gave her order in English.

See, she told herself, *see how well this suits you*. Relaxed, she looked to the hotel and wondered if she should call Eric. She wanted to clear her mind, to have absolutely nothing in her head so that she could approach her work without the framework of other worries or con-cerns. But she worried about speaking with him. She worried that he could somehow divine her thoughts, and guess that she had read his private discussions, this online *banter* with other men. She thought of herself as a bad spy, the world's worst, possessing no cunning, not one ounce. Above her, blinds and shutters clattered open as the hotel rooms were cleaned, sunlight bold on the upper storeys.

The street curved toward the Campo di Fiori – a street busy with scooters. It was disappointing not to have heard from him. If Eric called the conversation would open up as something natural, easy, he would talk about his holiday and they would have a subject to discuss. If she called, it would be her prerogative to steer the discussion, and she had nothing to say – or rather, she knew that whatever she had to say would sound false and he would immediately sense her unease. Disappointed not to have heard from him she checked her mobile for new messages. She called, in any case, and left a message.

'Eric? Eric, it's your mother. I'm in Rome. I've just arrived. I'll try you later this evening.'

Her voice, her tone, she knew, gave away her mind.

3.11

Heida caught her reflection as she came out of the bathroom, and thought to her alarm that she looked uncomfortably like Grüner's wife.

Troubled by the likeness she returned to the mirror. It wasn't one specific detail, more a combination of parts and effect. The colour of her hair, the fact that it appeared so unkempt, and these clothes, admittedly not her favourite (a short skirt, a striped long-sleeve top), made her look exhausted. No, it was something in her stance, some aspect locked in her body that made this comparison true. She turned sideways, and there it was. A soggy downward curve, a stroke of disappointment describing her shoulders, her breasts, her mouth, as if this curve had imposed itself on her overnight.

'Christ.'

'What's the matter?'

'Look what you've done to me.'

Used to not understanding her, Grüner gave a smile intended to show understanding. Heida read this dumb expression as culpable awareness. He knew exactly what he was doing to her. Men always do.

'Don't worry, I'm not pregnant.'

The plan was simple: having contacted the Turkish official who was to help with their visas into Iraq they were to travel, one to Ankara, and one to Istanbul, to be certain to catch the man, as he was, at best, elusive. This slippery subject, always in transit from one city to another, would be caught by one or the other.

'We should have kept the car,' she said, one more point against him.

Heida ran her hand over her stomach. Even when she stood upright, this curve, this gravity, imposed itself on her.

3.12

Eric came into the room as Ford was packing. His decision to leave came to him as a sudden and necessary fact – with the pension being watched he was taking too great a risk. Martin's project placed him square in the eyes of the police, and if the police made any enquiries they would easily discover that the name he had given Mehmet, the name used by Nathalie, Martin and Eric, was different to the name in his passport. If they enquired into this small discrepancy he couldn't be sure what else they might discover. The dog tags, for example, how would he explain those? He needed to make the transfer. He needed to get to Istanbul.

Eric stood over the cot, hands at his side, visibly stung. 'What are you doing?'

'It's time to move on. I'll take the bus to Ankara then try for the Black Sea. If I go now I might catch up with my friend.'

'Friend?'

'Yes.' Ford stood upright, laundry bunched in his hand. 'Amy.' *Amy*? He wasn't good with names. Not off the cuff.

'Amy?'

'The woman I was travelling with.'

'You said she's with someone else now?'

Bothered that he had to explain himself Ford returned to packing. 'It's complicated. I should make the effort.'

Eric nodded slowly, as if he didn't follow, as if other people's situations were always slightly out of his understanding.

Ford checked the small pocket inside his pack, and took off the dog tags and tucked them inside, because the tags, the weight of them, like everything else, was beginning to bother him.

*

Eric accompanied Ford into town. As they came out of the pension the man in the car looked up but didn't move. The sun cut across a clean-shaved chin, a thin mouth, a fat moustache. He remained in the car as they turned off the street to the main road.

Ford gripped the straps of his backpack, ready to sprint if he needed to, but the car did not follow them, and Eric, preoccupied himself, did not appear to notice his anxiety. If the man approached them now at least Ford could run. At the Maison du Rêve he would have been trapped.

With regular coaches to Ankara throughout the day he found he had a choice: one at midday, one at three, and the last at eleven at night; each connecting with a coach to Istanbul. Ford decided on the midday bus, why wait, only to find the service fully booked. Three o'clock? No trouble. Depart later, arrive early in the morning. He'd wait in one of the tea houses in the market square. Eric stayed with him, and they sat under canvas and faced the market.

Eric sought advice.

'I knew what it would be like. No one will work with him.'

'So why did you?'

'A paid holiday. Experience. Extra credit.' He frowned. All of this was well and good, but Martin was a fully subscribed asshole who had managed to isolate himself from his students, fellow academics, from the art establishment. Even so, inexplicably, the project was gaining attention. 'People want to show the work. Museums. Curators. We're going to screen the first section at the Gare du Nord in Paris. Six projections cycling through forty-seven hours of material. Six screens.' He swept out his hands. 'Massive.' Each testimony prefaced with a landscape, each talking head presented in their original language, their own words. Speakers fixed to inverted plastic domes would direct the sound upon the travellers, creating zones where their voices could be heard without interfering with the station's activity – an immense undertaking. There was talk about showing the entire cycle, all five sections, in Grenoble, at Magazin.

Eric continued talking. Ford kept his eye on the market, the stalls, and the three streets that fed into the enclosed square. Police, men in military drab ambled without intent among the traders and shoppers, a muddle of activity. He looked back into the café at the dusty red walls, at the barber shop beside it, the door to the hammam closed – everything so ordinary that he began to relax. Beside their table sat a bulky unlit stove, and the air was busy with the fats of cooking meat, of coffee, of dust. In three hours he would be on his way to Istanbul. The decision to leave felt right and wise.

'You don't get the opportunity to work on material like this. It just doesn't happen.'

Ford only caught snippets: *And when someone is that creative . . . difficult . . . work through it . . . We have history, Martin and me. Anyone on the outside wouldn't . . .* At some point Eric paused as if waiting for an answer, waiting for Ford to disagree or approve.

'Do whatever you think is best.'

The *cay* came to the table in tulip-shaped glasses. Three soldiers took up a table close by, closer than he would have liked. Eric, a little discouraged, continued talking and asked a second time for his advice. Ford, tired of listening, admitted that he'd drifted off.

'I was talking about Malta. You could come. It would be private.'

'Private?'

'She has it booked for two weeks, but there's no one there after those two weeks. I'm thinking of staying for the rest of the break. I don't have to return for another month. It's private, remote.'

'Why would I go to Malta?'

Eric leaned forward and squinted. Pushed off course a second time he appeared hurt.

Ford looked at the boy and began to realize that this wasn't a simple matter. The boy's expression showed him to be wounded, not by some small slight, but by some deeper hurt, something Ford had or had not done.

'You're right. It's not that interesting.' Eric held his breath, as if considering whether or not to speak, ideas collapsing behind that expression, a notion of something solid turning to vapour, and Ford realized that he hadn't been talking about Martin but something else. 'OK. Look, I'm going to go.' He abruptly stood up and said goodbye.

Ford watched Eric walk away, head hung as if heartsick, wounded. What, he asked himself, was that about? On the back of the chair folded over itself, forgotten, lay the boy's sweater.

He paid for the tea, checked his pocket for his ticket, kept his eye on the soldiers, and found himself irritated. Why should he listen, why should he waste his time? Why would this boy expect anything from him? As he stepped out of the café he found Eric at the table, stiff, leaning forward, decisive.

'Who are you?'

'Sorry?'

'Who are you? You're not Tom and you're not Michael, I know, and I'm pretty sure there isn't an Amy.'

Ford could not reply.

'You don't answer when someone calls your name. I just called your name. I just shouted. I was right there.'

'I didn't hear you.'

'I was right there. You never answer to Tom. Even Nathalie's noticed, you don't respond. You didn't hear a word, did you? I *know*. I know who you are.'

'Sorry?'

'I know who you are. I know.' In one swift movement Eric reached for Ford's hand.

Ford veered back, repulsed. Horrified at his action the boy fell into the crowd.

Ford stopped at the café and watched the small road that curved up to the promontory. The sun passed over the market square, but the afternoon remained hot. Eric's sweater lay on the ground, sleeves pointing to the market, and Ford considered how ordinary this was: the market, the café, the afternoon – and so the boy knew who he was? He tried to guess what Eric would do. He wouldn't directly approach the police. This was doubtful. But once he returned to the Maison du Rêve he would talk with Nathalie and Nathalie would automatically talk with Martin. Once loose the idea would prove itself in the history of what he'd said or not said, deeds done or un-done, untranslated facts would slip into place. Everything would suddenly make sense – and if they needed proof it would only take one article, one mention in a newspaper, one news report, one seed. The consequences racked up, one event leading to another. He couldn't judge what their actions would be, that next step. Nathalie with her focused sense of justice would deliberate. She would need facts. She would agonize. Even so, she couldn't be counted on, and she would probably call the authorities. Martin, already paranoid, could not be predicted. Once uncontained the information would spark immediate trouble.

The more he considered it, the worse his situation appeared.

He couldn't gather the connections, couldn't see what had given him away. Alongside this he had insulted the boy, although he didn't know how. Ford understood that his freedom depended on righting this insult, on correcting and persuading him that this idea was fanciful at best, something Martin would create.

Ford waited for Eric to return but the road from the fort remained clear. With three hours to pass he decided to find Eric and see exactly what he knew. He folded Eric's sweater into the top of his backpack, then, with no idea how he would explain himself, he began to walk slowly to the fort.

He did not find Eric at the fort. He stood at the fence at the rough cliff and looked down upon the road, the heat pulsed about him. Crows scattered as he clambered over the fallen barrier. Standing at the edge he traced the track past the workshops and into the market. The thin clatter of a workman's hammer rose in the wind enriched with a faint dry scent of sage. He was certain that Eric had taken the track to the promontory. This was his only exit, but he had not seen him return. He could not have passed without his knowing. Ford looked back over his shoulder at the bald, slick rock and found no one at the fort.

3.13

Eric stumbled as he walked up the path, sore with Tom, sore at himself, knocked back, burning with humiliation.

Even at this moment a part of him remained detached, aware that while he felt low (had he ever felt so miserable?) this whole business was utterly predictable and completely avoidable. Tom was typical of the men he was attracted to (unavailable, remote, almost completely unknowable); he should have seen this coming. Even so, wasn't there something about this that was just plain unfair?

At the top of the promontory he realized that he'd walked himself into a dead end. He'd have to stay and wait until Tom got on his coach as he wasn't about to walk back through the market and face him again. *Seriously, why had he gone back in the first place?* What for? And what was that utter horse-crap he'd come out with, sounding just like Martin? Christ, had he seriously said those things? All that shit about his name? And what was he *thinking* going up to the man and *touching* him like that, right out in public? Seriously? Exactly what did he expect to happen? Wasn't he, come on, seriously, wasn't he the very definition of an idiot?

He switched his satchel from his left to his right shoulder. He'd have to wait for the coach to go, though he wasn't sure of the time, it could be hours, Tom had a choice of coaches, an utter agony to wait up, but at least he would be able to see the coach as it came into the square. He'd probably also see Tom.

Eric turned his back to the town. He didn't want to see him. In fact, if he'd *known* that Tom was leaving, had a little prior warning, he could have prepared himself. He wouldn't have made such an ass of himself.

He saw the man come up the track, and saw with a donkey-kick of recognition that the approaching figure was Tom. No doubt about it.

As Tom clambered over the fence, inching round, Eric sought cover. He followed the edge of the promontory and looked into the cracks to find one in which to lower himself, one with some kind of foothold, one the right width so he could squat at a straddle, brace against the sides and wait it out.

Eric slung his bag behind him and lowered himself into the crevice as Tom rounded the corner, pushed his feet flat to the rock on one side and his shoulders on the other.

His memory of the fall was not of falling or sliding, or of rolling sideways into the cleft, but of being struck by a series of blows so rapid, and of such startling force that the pain came in one obliterating shock, white and sheer, and overwhelming. He'd struck his head, struck it hard, and found himself pinched between the stone walls by his hips and by his chest. While he knew himself to be suspended between two acute planes, he guessed, from the difference in pressure, that he was suspended slightly out of vertical. While he could move his arms, sweep them either side up and down, the cleft proved too narrow for him to bend his elbows and exact enough force to push himself upright. The range of motion for his head was similarly limited, so he could only face left, or look up. His bag, where was his bag with his passport and tickets?

He couldn't guess how far he'd fallen. Thirty feet? Thirty-five? How high was the promontory? One hundred and twenty? A possible further ninety feet below him.

Suspended by pressure on his chest and hips, pinched between the

rock, breathing became hard, a conscious effort, and he found it difficult to draw a deep enough breath to shout.

Eric pressed his fingers one by one to the rock, a thought to each
digit.

1. prioritize to save energy
2. assess damage
3. relieve weight and pressure on chest
4. do not panic
5. in ten days you will be in Malta – OK, depending on new tickets,
a new passport
6. use the force exerted by the rock as a lever – or, maybe not
7. don't think of large gestures, big motions, but incremental im-
provements

He could see daylight, sky, a wide stripe of gorgeous blue, almost
mauve, intense and unspoiled.

8. get laid as soon as you get out of this. Stop sabotaging every
opportunity.

His first seizure came as specks fizzing in a bright sky, and the
realization that this didn't look too good. In the strangeness of what
followed, as his head hammered from side to side, hard and distinct
images came to him: him locked, lying on a floor with Tom on top of
him, the pressure of another body, and while he shook between the
walls he felt the real heat of being held, of strong arms, and a conviction informed by smell, heat, touch that this was Tom.

And 9. What was it? Some question he had to answer yes or no.

3.14

Ford returned through the market. Outside the barber shop he slowed
to a walk and patted his pockets. No cigarettes. He bought a pack and
returned to the terminal admitting to himself that he hadn't liked Eric.
It wasn't indifference he felt now but active dislike. The boy bothered
him, watched him all the time; examined and tested him with all of his
questions, and it was good to admit to this dislike. He considered for a
moment leaving things as they were. He would be long gone before
they could slot anything comprehensible together. But he couldn't be
sure. One word might be enough. One accident. One connection.

After handing over his backpack to the kiosk ready for departure, he sat and faced the square. A single track led up to the fort – he couldn't see anywhere for Eric to hide. The market stalls opened out one to another. However busy, it would be impossible for Eric to pass unnoticed, unless, somehow, he'd doubled back immediately, heading for the hotel and not the fort – although this didn't seem likely.

With no other open option Ford decided to return to the Maison du Rève. If he found Eric he would reason with him, draw these ideas out of his head and persuade him that he was wrong. *I'm not who you think I am. How ridiculous do you think this sounds?* If Eric had figured out his identity it could not have come from anything he had said. His silence might have spiked the boy's curiosity, this was true, but he had given none of them any detail about himself or his life to fuel this realization. He could fix this.

Ford returned to the pension. He turned gingerly into the street. To his relief both the car and the man were gone.

Mehmet allowed Ford into the courtyard. He hadn't seen Martin and Nathalie all afternoon and thought that they were out; he was just leaving himself, but it was no problem if Ford wanted to wait. With the door open to his room Ford was surprised to see his bed already stripped, the sheets and blanket stacked at the end of the bed, military style. The print of the French mountains tilted on the wall. Eric's rucksack lay at the end of the cot, zips open, clothes draped along the towel rail to dry.

He closed the door and made sure it was secure before he searched a second time through Eric's backpack. Among the twists of rope, the steel crampons, he found three identical black notebooks, his toothbrush and razor. Folded in a washcloth in a side pocket he discovered a fat roll of money. The money confused him. He'd found traveller's cheques before, but here was cash. He counted out two thousand American dollars, two thousand exactly. He flicked through the corners of damp twenty-dollar bills, counting up; puzzled that anyone would carry so much money and leave it unsecured. In a washbag he found the traveller's cheques and two more notebooks. For good measure he checked again through the boy's book and found nothing but the newspaper clippings.

He held the book by its spine and scattered the papers free about the bed. He double-checked that the door was secure then returned to the cot. The clippings were folded tidily into small square chits. The articles concerned the novel. Some covered details about the writer's disappearance, some debated issues surrounding what looked to be a murder, although no body was found. Ford skimmed through details: the discovery of body parts (a shopping bag with a severed tongue), a bloody room, clothes cut and dumped on wasteland, a photograph of a mariner's star, and he quickly became confused – were they talking about the plot of the novel or an actual murder? One clipping, an interview with the writer, was annotated and underlined. On the reverse – to his alarm – he discovered a photograph of himself standing beside Paul Howell.

So this is how he knew.

How strange to recognize himself. Strange also to remember the airfield, the aircraft, the delivery of pallets of money packed into thick bricks loaded into orderly stacks – he'd seen this one time, accompanied Howell on Howell's command, and had no idea that they were being photographed. The loading bay stopped with tens of millions of dollars. Howell presented himself with a tight oafish smile, perhaps even a little smug: the man appeared duplicitous even when he was sincere. The photograph wasn't clear. Ford stood in shadow, obscured. The accompanying article gave details of Howell's arrest, the embezzlement of reconstruction funds, and the disappearance of the event's main player – Stephen Lawrence Sutler. Teams of investigators were searching for him in Jordan, Syria, Kuwait, Turkey.

Here was the spark he most feared. Ford's hand began to shake. What he read did not make sense. He flattened the paper onto the cot and re-read the article, this time shaking his head with complete incredulity, stunned to see the name *Stephen Lawrence Sutler* in print, astounded by the charge of theft. *Fifty-three*, he read again, *fifty-three million dollars* of misappropriated funds.

The figure left him giddy. *Fifty-three million*. A mistake, a gross miscalculation. Two hundred and fifty thousand was all that Howell had transferred, money he'd yet to claim from the junk account. *Fifty-three million*? The figure hollowed him out.

I know who you are.

He shoved the clipping into his pocket then began to re-fold the cuttings, a sense of endlessness coming to him, a panic at having to fold each piece of paper two or three times, the minute nature of this action running contrary to the scale of the theft. *Fifty-three million*. Ford scooped up the clippings, cash, and traveller's cheques: details of the article repeated as noise in his head. *Teams of investigators. Deputy*

Administrator Paul Howell arrested. Fifty-three million unaccounted.
He stuffed the papers between the pages of the book, but couldn't see
the point of it. *I know who you are.* Taking one article would change
nothing. Down to his last fifty dollars, his options were more limited
than he'd imagined.

Now sweating he knew that however calm he appeared his agitation would be apparent. He would give himself away. With Eric's
belongings back in place he looked down at the bed. The money. What
was he doing? He needed money, and here was money. Here was
money and traveller's cheques. Four thousand dollars. Enough to see
him clear to Europe. He could head directly to Istanbul as planned,
check into a hotel, use his final opportunity to transfer the money from
the junk account to wherever he wanted.

The decision was already made. He would take the money, *but*, he
told himself, he'd return every cent. Knowing that this was a lie, or at
the very least a great improbability, he took the money and the
cheques out of the bag. He checked the side pockets and found a travel
itinerary with an address. Eric was due to arrive in Malta on the last
day of the month. Ford slipped the paper into his back pocket and told
himself that he would, almost certainly, return the money, regardless
of his situation.

As he stepped into the courtyard he remembered another detail.
The photograph Nathalie had taken at the church. He checked his
watch and wondered if he had enough time to search for her camera.
He knocked cautiously on Nathalie and Martin's door. To his surprise
Nathalie answered, telling Eric that she would be out in a moment.

Nathalie came to the door, eyes narrowed, sleepy. 'Oh, I thought
you were Eric.' Martin huddled on the bed behind her, asleep.

'He's gone. I can't find him.'

Nathalie looked back into the room. She swept her hair from her
brow, still drowsy.

'I'm serious. I think I upset him. I can't find him.'

Nathalie followed him into the room.

'But, everything is here?' Nathalie paused in the doorway, unsure.
'What's the time? He's supposed to be back to help Martin. He's late. I
don't understand why you think he's gone?' Nathalie looked to Ford's
bed. 'Where are your things?'

'I'm leaving. I was just coming to say goodbye.'

'You're going?' She appeared genuinely taken aback – then seeing

Eric's washbag on the bed her attention shifted. She blinked and took a sharp intake of breath. 'This is strange.' Nathalie picked up the wash-bag and looked quickly through it. The money pricked his side through his jacket as she searched.

'I don't understand what's happened. Where is it?' Nathalie spoke in a whisper, she held her hands up, aghast. 'Oh no. He's taken the money. Where is his book?' She straightened up, an idea coming to her. 'Where is his book?'

'You mean this?' Ford held up the novel. 'He said I could take it and read it on the bus.'

'Look between the pages. Is there anything inside?'

Ford held out the book and flicked through it for her to see. The pages slapped together. 'There's nothing here. A few clippings about the writer.'

Nathalie sat on the bed and Ford explained that he had to leave.

'I'm sure he's fine,' he said, trying to sound sincere. 'He said good-bye but he seemed upset. I assumed he would come back here. I thought I would see him.'

Out of the pension Ford walked slowly, believing that the man who had been watching them might still be waiting. He followed a whitewashed wall until it curved into the main road. The moment he rounded the corner he began to run down the street.

At the terminal he asked for his bag. He tucked Eric's novel into the pack, and couldn't decide if the dog tags would be safer in his pocket, or in the bag in the hold. Not knowing which choice would be best he left the tags in the bag and kept the money and the wallet of traveller's cheques in his pocket along with his passport. Just to be sure. After he returned the bag to the attendant, he sat out on the pavement in the kiosk's shade, conscious of every passing vehicle, the quiet curiosity of the other travellers.

Forty minutes later he was surprised to see Nathalie. She walked with her head down, arms swinging purposefully. When she looked up and saw him she broke into a shuffling jog.

'I'm sorry,' she apologized. 'Have you seen him? I'm glad you're still here.'

Slightly out of breath she held her hand to her chest. Eyes now dark. 'He's supposed to go with Martin. They're supposed to be work-ing together this afternoon. It doesn't make sense.'

'I haven't seen him.'

'Before. When you came back. Where was he?' Frustrated, Nathalie stood with one hand at her brow. 'Where did you see him?'

'At one of the tea houses in the market. I think he walked up to the fort.'

'You don't understand. Today is important. It's very strange for him not to be here. Martin can't work without him. Today is important.'

Ford agreed. She was right. He didn't understand.

'He's angry with Martin,' she said, and he took this as an apology. 'He's upset with me. I think he's hiding. It's all my fault.' She asked if he would show her the tea house and Ford said that the bus was coming shortly, but it was in the main square, where he'd bought his shirts, where they'd met, by the barber.

'You have some time.' Nathalie checked her watch. 'The bus won't leave until three.'

Crows circled the promontory and rose on the wind channelled up the rock's steep side. Nathalie shielded her eyes as she walked, worried and angry, increasingly certain that they would not find him. 'This is impossible,' she muttered to herself. 'It's all so stupid. I don't know why they're like this with each other. I don't know why he can't speak with me?'

They walked together about the small market square, then returned to the larger square, making a figure eight, Ford conscious of the time, then agreed to search separately. He would take the old town and check the market, Nathalie the cafés and businesses lining the new square.

He returned to the barber shop and the hammam, the café beside it busy now, and expected to see Eric sat among the men, sulking and hurt. If he saw him he wouldn't approach. *The boy knows everything, he could be with the police right now.*

Twenty minutes later he rejoined Nathalie at the kiosk, privately relieved to see her alone.

'Nothing? No sign. I've looked everywhere. I don't believe this. He can't be here. I've looked everywhere. Nothing. You know, this happens all the time with Martin. Every time he makes a problem. It has to be complicated.'

As the passengers gathered for the Ankara coach, Nathalie hurried to the kiosk. Perhaps he would show himself now? 'It's so stupid,' she said, looking without hope at the other passengers. 'He must have gone.' Convinced that Eric had quit the project, she couldn't understand why he would take the money but leave his clothes, his bag. She looked resentfully toward the Maison du Rève, then curled her hair behind her ear and said that she was sorry that Ford had become part of this. 'It's so stupid. Every day is like this. Can you imagine? Eric is a boy, he's just a boy, and Martin has no idea what he does, the effect he has. It is so stupid. And now he has taken the money.'

Without the money the project could not continue.

A man in a blue uniform asked for tickets. The passengers grouped about him. Too many, Ford thought, for the one coach, and in this he was right. The man handed out numbered notes which were soon gone. Too late to take one, Ford realized he would not make the coach.

'It's too many.' The man removed himself from the arguments sprouting about him. When Ford followed after him and asked about the bus the man shrugged, pushed through to the office, and returned with a new set of numbers for the next coach, due to leave at 23:00.

How typical was this? Ford took a ticket. 32.

Nathalie leaned forward to say goodbye but hesitated, slowly understanding what was happening. 'You can't go?' Relief and hope grew in her smile as she asked him to help. 'I shouldn't ask. I know. It's not your problem. But he likes you. Eric is fond of you, and if he won't speak to me, it's possible he will show himself to you. We could go to Birsim and see if he's there. I promise we'll be back in time for your coach.'

Ford wanted to be gone, for christsakes. He didn't want to find Eric for many obvious reasons. The boy knew who he was, *surely*, he'd stolen his money and traveller's cheques, and insulted him in some way he still couldn't fathom. To add to this both Eric and Nathalie knew that he was heading to Ankara – the police could discover his destination without trouble.

Compliant, Ford returned to the kiosk and asked the attendant if he could change his ticket. The attendant shrugged, confirmed the time of the later coach, and said if he wanted to leave for somewhere else he would need to buy another ticket. Ford collected his bag, smiled through the glass at Nathalie, and signalled that he would only be a moment.

'I still have a seat for the eleven o'clock coach?' The man closed his eyes while he nodded. Ford wanted to be clear about his options.

'I've spoken with Martin.' Nathalie held up her phone. 'Eric hasn't come back. He isn't at the hotel. I just don't know where he is.'

As they returned to the Maison du Rêve, Nathalie said that it was kind of him to help. Ford insisted it wasn't any trouble. The late bus meant that he would arrive in the early morning rather than in the middle of the night. He didn't mind at all.

He waited at the door to the courtyard and felt immeasurable relief that Eric had still not appeared. Neither Eric nor the police.

Nathalie talked with Martin in their room, Ford sat outside and drank the last of the whisky, lightly sweating, his back to the town, the sky beginning to darken. He needed to leave. Make some excuse and get away from Narapi. The boy was still in town, had to be, so if he could persuade Martin and Nathalie to go to Birsim he would be safe.

Martin remained silent as Nathalie repeated the afternoon's events. Stern, arms crossed, Martin asked if Eric had said anything about leaving.

Ford emptied his glass, sucked air through his teeth. 'He didn't say much. He was angry with you but we didn't talk about that.'

'So what did you speak about?' Martin stood in front of Ford, impatient, suspicious.

'He talked about going to Malta. He was looking forward to it.'

Nathalie shook her head. 'No, no.' She spoke in French. 'This doesn't make sense. I spoke with him yesterday and he said that he didn't want to go. Just yesterday. This was the whole point of him coming here, he didn't want to go. He had no interest at all in going to Malta.'

Martin repeated his question. 'Did Eric say anything about leaving?'

'Not in so many words.'

Martin and Nathalie exchanged glances. Nathalie sat beside Ford. She felt sick, she said. 'Perhaps he's right. Perhaps he intends to go to Malta early. It's strange, but maybe it's possible.' He would have to change his ticket. The only place close by where he could change his flight was in Birsim. She turned to Ford. 'This must be what he's doing.' They should go to Birsim. Could Mehmet get a van?

Martin shook his head, stern and unmovable, he didn't want Mehmet to have anything to do with this. Eric had already caused enough trouble. He would take the bus tomorrow morning and search for Eric himself. As far as he was concerned the boy was finished. He could take his money, they would manage some other way.

'How? Tomorrow is too late,' Nathalie insisted, angry now. 'His bag is still here, but not his ticket, and not his passport. I think he's using the money to change his flight. You want to do nothing?'

Ford agreed. If they were going to do anything, then they needed to act immediately. He lifted his bag to his shoulder to prompt them into action.

Ford sat at the front of the car with Mehmet. Nathalie and Martin silent in the back. Dust billowed across the road and they squinted into the cloud with rising dissatisfaction. In the last long light before sunset, a sickly orange hue settled above the horizon.

In Birsim, Nathalie and Martin found the travel office and Ford agreed to check the coach times. Mehmet stayed with the car, and smoked, window down, uninvolved.

The terminus, such as it was, ran alongside the square – a few bays painted into the road and numbered poles mounted on the pavement. A long patch of blackened sand was the only sign that a bus had burned here two days ago. Apart from this the street appeared clean. There were, he thought, altogether too many police. Ford asked for the times of buses out of Birsim; an attendant pointed at a painted board listing the schedule for Narapi, Ankara, Kopeckale. These were the main routes, with only one late departure. Ford checked and double-checked the times and even though he had no choice now but to wait, he felt some reassurance in knowing that a coach was already on its way.

Nathalie and Martin came out of the office visibly frustrated. He guessed their news before he heard it. No one matching Eric's description had made enquiries or bought tickets or attempted to change a flight, either yesterday or today. Plenty of coach tickets had been sold for the coastal resorts, and a few for Ankara/Istanbul, but none, as far as the clerk could recall, were sold to an American. Many of the coaches had already departed. As far as Martin could see, there was little point coming to Birsim, and no point staying without evidence that Eric had even come here in the first place.

They found a tea house and sat silently together. When the *cay* arrived, Ford paid and suggested that they order something to eat, but neither Martin nor Nathalie had any appetite and Martin decided to take a walk by himself. Apologizing, he kissed Nathalie's forehead and said that he needed to think. He would not be long.

'We can take you back to Narapi.'

'Another coach leaves from here. I'm sure I can buy a supplement.'

'But you have a ticket already from Narapi?' Nathalie watched Martin wander away. 'No, we can take you back.' She shook her head and would not hear of any further disagreement. 'The project is almost over, except for this one last interview. But without the money it won't be possible to complete.' It made no sense that Eric would be so selfish. 'We each brought money. As much as we could. Eric's money was to help someone leave the country.' Nathalie looked across the square. 'In exchange for an interview, we give money to help a family leave the country. These are Sunni Kurds living in Alevi villages, and Martin wanted one of these men to speak in his project. It's taken a year to organize this interview.' For the first time, as a conclusion to the series, Martin was to present an entire family, one at a time, each speaking about their experience. 'But without the money the family won't give their consent. Everything's so complicated. It isn't just Martin. Did Eric speak to you? You know that he likes you? You know this?'

Ford cleared his throat. 'Sorry?'

'He likes you, you know. He likes you very much.'

'I think he's hiding.'

Nathalie shook her head, weary, this did not make sense.

'When we parted he—'

'What?'

'It wasn't anything, but he was embarrassed.'

'He said something?'

'No. It was a gesture.'

'A gesture?' Incredulous, Nathalie leaned forward. 'What are you saying? He kissed you?'

'It wasn't quite that.'

'I don't understand. Are you saying he approached you?'

'I was – surprised. I didn't react well. He left. He walked up to the fort. I think he might be hiding.'

Nathalie settled slowly back into her seat, a different scenario beginning to form.

On the journey back, Martin discussed Eric's disappearance. They should check the bus station at Narapi to see if anyone matching Eric's description had tried to leave while they were in Birsim. If not, they needed to consider other options. Unsurprised by Eric's crude farewell to Ford, Martin pictured darker forces and motives at play. It was possible that Eric's disappearance wasn't voluntary. They must consider this. They needed to think carefully about what to do.

Nathalie shut her eyes, exhausted. They should contact Eric's mother, she would be in Malta by now, and see if he had spoken with her about any change in plans. But how would they find her address? Martin sat back and wiped his hands down his face. Nothing about this was easy. He didn't have an address, they would have to wait until the morning to contact the university? Or no, he could call as soon as they returned? None of them were sure about the time difference.

As they drew into Narapi, Ford suggested that Nathalie take a walk to the fort. 'My coach departs in an hour.'

'I'll wait with you.'

'Take a break,' he whispered, 'he'll be back before long.'

Nathalie shook her head. There would be no result from any further search, she was certain. 'You know, maybe this isn't so strange. This is what his father did. When he was a boy his father walked away. He just left.' She convinced herself.

Martin said he'd return with Mehmet to the pension to make his calls, she might as well continue looking if she wanted. Perhaps there would be some news. Nathalie hung her head, unable to make a decision. Ford opened the passenger door to say goodbye and leaned into the car unsure of the most suitable farewell. Nathalie wrapped her arms about him in a lethargic gesture, oddly mismeasured, and patted his shoulder. Maybe he was right and Eric would just return. Ford didn't doubt it, and guessed, privately, that this kind of drama was not rare between them.

As the coach drew away from the square, Ford looked back at the town. His eyes ran along the broken outline of the fortifying walls above the market. None of this mattered, he told himself. It wasn't important.

The coach moved softly, as if through water. Wind struck the bus and Ford imagined the coach winding slowly and steadily away from the town.

3.15

Heida argued with herself for four long hours, persuading herself out of love, or rather, out of the relationship, as she was not in love – clearly not *at this moment*. At Birsim a student took the seat beside her. Pleased to have someone to talk with, Heida began to share what was on her mind. The student appeared keen to listen.

Their problem, Heida began, was that they worked together, day and night. Grüner came with the job. More or less. Theirs was a partnership built on travel, long working nights, deadlines, which encouraged a kind of *intimacy*. The practicalities which destroyed other relationships made theirs viable, regardless of other attachments which she did not mention (Grüner's wife, Heida's long-term partner), so even if their couplings had become distastefully mechanical they were couplings nevertheless, they were something. At the very least Grüner was company. If she broke off the physical side of their relationship she couldn't guarantee that they'd return to their former working relationship. Did this make sense? While they depended on each other for work their physical relationship had corrupted this. It really was that simple.

She couldn't guess Grüner's thinking, never knew, and suspected (kilometre after kilometre, riding through bright dust in a rising landscape, the girl beside her nodding, nodding, nodding) that the threat of an end would make him keen again. Grüner was that kind of a man. Endearingly sentimental when it came to women who despised him.

At the start of hour five Heida had to admit that there were other factors. Maybe her recent indifference had nothing to do with Grüner, because it wasn't just Grüner; everything about her had the same colour, tone, texture, taste. It's like this, she waved her hand at the land – even at night the landscape appeared dusty, endless, flat. Pointless.

'This is how I feel. This.'

The young girl nodded and Heida wondered how much she actually understood.

As the coach came into Ankara the student began to gather her bags. Heida felt relieved that the girl was leaving as she didn't want to think about these things any more. They said their goodbyes a little early and sat silent. The student looked expectantly up the central aisle, and Heida looked out of the window waiting as the coach drew at a crawl into the bay. Light spilled from the pavilion. Heida sat parallel to a man who walked along the pavement keeping pace with the coach, her knees to his shoulders. A slick movement, inside, outside, which she found funny in a small way as she could look down on the man without him being aware.

It wasn't the backpack, so much, but the man's rounded shoulders and his way of walking, dopey, as if medicated, slightly absent. As soon as she saw the man in profile she immediately recognized him: Stephen Lawrence Sutler. Without doubt.

The bus drew slightly ahead. Beardless, shorter hair – shorn in fact – cleaner clothes, almost fashionable. Three-fifty in the morning and she was looking down on Sutler. The man had no idea. He really didn't. She squinted, took a good long look and did not doubt that this was the same man they had picked up a week earlier at the Turkish border. Sutler. *Stephen Lawrence Sutler*.

She followed after the man, feeling conspicuous in sunglasses, her hat pulled low, her hair tucked up. Two in the morning, the air becoming cold, thin, the fine atmosphere of the higher plains.

Sutler dodged through the waiting passengers and wandered into the waiting room, a little dazed by travel, his backpack over his left shoulder. As he approached the men's restroom a soldier called to him, clicked his fingers for attention then pointed at a sign. No packages, no luggage. Sutler could not take his pack into the toilet. The officer shook his head and while Sutler waited, evidently confused, the policeman stopped another man going forward. Beside the doorway lay a loose stack of luggage. Clearly uncomfortable with the demand, but not ready to challenge it, Sutler dropped the pack from his shoulder. Heida turned away as he squatted next to his bag, and she watched his reflection in the long glass windows as he fumbled for a shirt. She waited for him to walk into the restroom, breath held, his bag leaning against the wall; one among a number of packages, bags, and suitcases.

This was too good to miss.

Heida hurried forward, a pantomime of chaos, her own bag heavy in her arms. She gestured at the entrance to the women's restroom and the policeman pointed to the luggage strewn across the floor beside him. Heida dropped her bag right next to Sutler's and turned her body to block the policeman's view.

While at school Heida had stolen clothes from the KaDeWe: skirts, stockings, a good number of fashion tops, and once a pair of shoes, pink pumps that were two sizes too small. When she spoke about this short-lived habit, which lasted only the one summer, she blamed the guards at the store for sparking this urge, for treating her as suspicious and inciting the habit, *as if they had challenged her, taunted her, dared her. It was the 1980s*, she justified herself, *everyone was stealing something. Everybody was on the make. And besides, I wasn't happy.* Chubby and inept, she discovered a natural talent for thievery. And so, as she knelt beside Sutler's bag, the physical memory of this habit ran through her again, a sense of precision, of focus, a quickened heartbeat, the sensation that her hands were too large, a thrill that ran down her neck as she slipped her hand into Sutler's bag.

She was done in a matter of seconds. Both hands at the zip, one inside, deep and digging through clothes, a book or something, discovering an internal pocket at the back. A quick exploratory swipe and she withdrew, zipped up and straightened up, saddled her bag over her shoulder as she walked away, unsure of what was in her hand, but guessing that it was a set of keys.

Heida stood on the concourse, hid behind a pillar, and looked at her hand to find a chain and five military dog tags with no names but a line of numbers on each one. Surely an important find? She rolled the chain into a ball, then slipped it in a side pocket of her own bag. Ahead, the sky began to brighten. An orange horizon reflected rose-red in the tinted pavilion windows. The cold began to seep from the air. She waited for Sutler to come out of the restroom, watched him tuck his old shirt into the bag, then walk, the bag at his side, without any knowledge or suspicion, to join a queue waiting for the Istanbul coach. Once in line he set his bag at his feet and stretched, looked about, a little sleepy perhaps. When he yawned a small shiver ran through him.

A coach drew up at the end of the terminal, signs on the side and in the back window saying *Non-stop: Ankara–Istanbul*. Heida kept her eye on Sutler, and debated what she should do: call the police, have the man arrested, or wait, follow after him, play with him, keep him in her sights? As he came out of the waiting room she slipped back through the doors, and thought to find her camera. How amazing was this? How incredible? The man was on the bus before her camera had charged up, but she took a photo anyway and kept taking photographs. As the coach drew away from the stand she became bolder and stepped out of the crowd and onto the road to photograph.

Satisfied she tucked her camera into the side pocket, along with the dog tags and her wallet and passport. She called Grüner, hoping he was now in Istanbul. He answered on the first ring, and she gave instructions. Sutler was heading toward him, to Istanbul, the bus was direct, no other stops, she would look for a ticket and join him. Grüner should follow Sutler, but on no account should he approach the fugitive. She kept the dog tags to herself, she'd show them to him later as proof of contact. When she jostled back to the waiting room she found a seat and set the bag on her knees, satisfaction burning through her. So, after all of their delay, their trouble in finding visas, the aggravation over every attempt to enter Iraq, finally, a reward. Heida turned the bag about, and found the side pocket open.

In the same way that she had stolen from Sutler, someone had stolen from her. The dog tags, the camera, her wallet, her passport. All gone.

ISTANBUL

4.1

Wide awake, Ford watched as the coach crossed the Bosporus. A grey vapour hung over the water which appeared at first as a limitless field punctured by lights from the opposite bank. A little closer and the rounded backs and shoulders of the distant hills appeared roughened by the city, all in pinpoint detail. The domes, grey, black, dusky, gold-tipped. The spines of minarets, clustered towers, apartment blocks, all backed up the rise to a heavy sky.

It would be killing Geezler, it occurred to him, not to know where he was. Even though he had specifically instructed him not to make contact, it would be Geezler who suffered.

Coaches vied for stands at the terminus; rising from his seat Ford could taste the traffic, taste the fine blue air made sickly and delicate with petrol and seawater. Among the confusion: horses harnessed to small buggies; trams and taxis; vendors with food and souvenir stalls all gathered under the city ramparts. Hawkers waited to hustle the tourists then grouped about the bus as soon as it stopped. Some clapped in welcome, some for attention.

Tired and uncertain, Ford loaded his rucksack over his shoulder then pressed through the crowd, he followed the line of the city walls to a gate. Behind him the remaining passengers picked through their luggage, equally bewildered by the journey, the early morning, the crazy bustle.

The German journalists had mentioned a hotel close by Aya Sofya, and he guessed that there would be other hotels in that area. Now back in a large city he considered it unwise to wander about so obviously when he might be recognized.

At a small tobacconist's he stopped to buy a black baseball cap. With the hat on, the brim pulled low, he felt more secure.

After a long walk he found a hostel in the Sultanahmet district. A flat-roofed building that faced the crouched hulk of Aya Sofya with thirty-two tight rooms and dormitories built around an internal court-yard. Happy to have found a room he lay on the cot and thought that he would sleep without difficulty, but lying down made him wearier and sleep escaped him. Rain struck the tiles of the inner courtyard with a coin-like bounce. He ached from the journey and as he attempted to sleep he began to fret. What if the banks could not transfer the money? What if he made one more mistake while entering the numbers? What if the numbers on the dog tags simply didn't work? What if the money had been intercepted, and the account was empty? And what if they were waiting for him, ready, because, if they knew about the account, then it would be obvious that he'd try to access it from a larger city? If the money had been traced they would have him – but wasn't that the point of a junk account, weren't these transactions secure, confidential, untraceable? Once again Ford had to ask how much he trusted Geezler. It all came down to the simple fact that Geezler had warned him but not Howell. Consequently, he remained free while Howell was in custody. Ford lay still and focused on his breathing. The events of the previous six weeks poised above him, poorly balanced, ready to tumble. The familiar dread of discovery returned to him. He needed to be vigilant and he needed to keep his wits keen. He needed sleep. Now in Istanbul he would find a bank, or better, a computer and transfer the money out of the junk account, and if, for any reason, he had to wait for the transaction to be completed – he would bide his time, consider a new future, and slide through the city alongside every other tourist. He decided to rest, in an hour he would shower, change, get out and find a computer. Once he had secured the money he would find somewhere to hide. Simple, simple, step by step.

In his sleep he returned to Amrah City and tumbled head over heels in bright dust specked with powdered glass. He fell backward side by side with Kiprowski who told him, matter of fact, that neither of them would return home.

He woke in a cold sweat uncertain of the time, troubled by the closeness of the walls, the airlessness, and the double stink of his own sweat and the fusty mildew from the mattress. An ache pushed through his knees and hips.

From other rooms came slight percussive bumps of doors and beds and cupboards, as if everything were loose, and he remembered slowly that he was in Istanbul, travelling again, and that today everything would be fixed as soon as he found a computer. This was all he had to do. Slowly, he told himself, *slowly*, move with caution. He stood on the bed to open the window. Immediately across the street rose the western flank of Aya Sofya. Dark and immense, rain-streaked, the blood-ochre and sissy-pink bulwarks overshadowed the small hostel. Small wonder his dreams were cramped and heavy.

Ford hauled his rucksack onto the bed. He dug his hands deep into the backpack and brought out Eric's sweater. The sweater, tucked down into the side of the bag, was not where he had placed it. He searched the small internal pocket but could not find the dog tags. Not yet worried, he tipped the pack upside down and sorted through his belongings: the laundry, the clothes and sandals he had bought in Narapi, a washbag, a damp and musty towel, and found everything except for the dog tags.

Cramp set in his stomach. Ford doubled up and breathed slowly.

He checked the bag, turned it completely inside out, shook it, checked that everything emptied onto the floor, every fleck and speck of paper. He searched again through the scattered belongings, gathered them onto the bed, then fell to his knees to search the floor under the bed.

Finding nothing he checked the jacket he'd worn the previous day and took out the boy's money and the wallet of traveller's cheques, small receipts for coffees, pastries, lunches, but no dog tags.

As a last measure he searched again through his clothes, through every pocket, every fold, he stood and shook through everything, piece by piece, expecting to hear a rattle, but still could not find the tags.

The dog tags were gone – stolen from his bag.

Without the dog tags he could not access the junk account. Without the numbers he could move neither forward nor backward. This, everything, was useless, all for nothing. Ford sat at the end of the bed and began to strike himself. He struck his face until he could feel nothing but pressure, and in that pressure a kind of concentration, a noise, loud enough to overload his thoughts.

Sense returned with the idea that he should call the pension, speak with Nathalie, ask if she could go to the bus company, enquire for him, complain, make threats if necessary. He couldn't return to Narapi. Not now the boy knew who he was. Without hope of retrieving the dog tags for the junk account and the money it gave access to, he could achieve nothing.

Ford returned to the lobby. The clerk winced as Ford came into the light, and after handing him the phone slipped into his office to return with a damp towel, then settled back to watch the news. Ford dialled the numbers, pressed the towel to the bridge of his nose, a little sore, a little tender, his face reflected red and bruised in the glass beside the board of numbered keys, his eyes watered so he had to squint to see the numbers. No answer. He checked the number with the clerk, dialled again, and again found no answer.

At 15:00 and 15:30 he again called the Maison du Rève.

At 16:00, 17:00, 17:15. No answer and no machine to leave a message.

He sat for an hour, from 18:00 till 19:00, one thought caught and repeating that he was not going anywhere, not now, not back, not forward, not without money. Closer to failure than success, he would have to return to Narapi and face the boy. He had no choice. Ford searched again through the contents of the backpack, through every shirt and trouser pocket.

And then he remembered: Eric had written the numbers down, in their proper order – either in the novel or in one of his notebooks, he couldn't remember. This was all he needed. The account numbers. With this information he could access the junk account. He didn't need the dog tags. He only required the numbers. The theft could be corrected.

Ford leafed through the novel, slowly, page by page, two times, three times, and found nothing. The numbers were in one of Eric's black notebooks. Still, it would be possible to recover this information. If he called Nathalie she could find Eric's notebook and supply him with the account details over the phone.

He settled with the novel on the bed and searched this time for notes written in the boy's coded script. He found an itinerary: Ankara to Athens, Athens to Luqa, and a letter from Eric's mother. She promised to pick him up. They were staying at Marsaskala, a village on the east coast. They would breakfast at Rizzi's. During the day Eric could do as he pleased, buses crisscrossed the island, it couldn't be more convenient, and nothing was more than an hour or so away. By the time he arrived she would be able to set her research aside. She signed the letter *God bless*, and *Mum*. *Mum* not *Mom*, the handwriting ordered, clear, legible, as if she had no character at all. Calmer now, he leafed through the pages a second and third time. Eric had used papers, cuttings, ticket stubs as page markers, but none of them were written on, and he found no clue, not even a fraction of the code from which he might cunningly devise the number for the junk account.

At nine o'clock Ford finally spoke with Mehmet at the Maison du Rève.

'Can I speak with Nathalie? Is she there? Na-ta-lie?'

Mehmet's voice sank to a watery growl. Ford could not hear him clearly.

'I'm calling because there has been a theft. It's important. I need to speak with Nathalie.'

Again, Mehmet's voice swelled and dived. *Something, something,* not possible. *Something.*

'I can't hear you.' Ford dug the heel of his hand to his temple to keep his thoughts sharp, together. 'Could you repeat that? I can't hear you.'

'She isn't here. They are both with the police. The police have taken them.'

'The police have taken who? I can't hear you.'

The line appeared to cut, the signal drop, then, clearly, he could hear the receiver being picked up.

'Hello? Who is this?' Nathalie's voice sounded clear and true.

'It's Tom. Mehmet said that you were arrested?'

'Tom!' She sounded confused, surprised, and he felt his hopes rise. 'Arrested? Why would he say that? Have you heard from Eric? Have you seen him?'

Ford said no, he had no news about Eric.

Nathalie also had no good news. They had returned to the pension to find the police, who'd taken everything: the film, their materials, everything. 'They won't explain why. Martin is with them now. We've heard nothing from Eric. Nothing. When we reported him missing the police came searched the rooms again, although they had everything already. We've asked for a list of everything they've taken. The only things missing are Eric's passport, his money, the tickets. I think he took them with him. I think he's going to Malta.'

'Nathalie, this is important. I've had some things stolen from my luggage. I'm missing the dog tags which have my details. Can you remember? I wore them round my neck? I know that Eric has these numbers. He kept them in his diary. He has the numbers in his note-book.'

'I don't understand?'

'I've lost a set of numbers. Five eight-digit numbers. I need those numbers, and Eric took a note of them.'

'Why would he do that?'

'It was for his code. For his writing. He was showing me his code. It was part of a discussion we were having.'

The line appeared to drop again as Ford waited for Nathalie's reply.

'The police have taken it. They came and they took everything. They have the film, the cameras, the hard drive, everything.' Nathalie paused, confused. 'I don't understand why Eric would have these numbers? I don't understand. The police have confiscated everything, and what belongs to Eric will be given to his family once they're in touch.'

The call ended awkwardly with Ford insisting that Nathalie take an email address. 'When they are sent to his mother. When Eric returns or when you hear from him, whatever happens. I need to know when those notebooks are returned.' He paused, slowed down to make sure that he was making himself absolutely clear. 'Nathalie. This is important. I need you to find his notebook. I need those numbers.' He couldn't be sure that she was listening. Too wrapped up in themselves, he doubted that they would pay attention to another person's emergency. He felt worse now, doomed. The only avenue forward would be to wait for Eric to return. At the very least he knew when the boy would arrive in Malta, although this information also seemed a little useless.

Up on the hotel roof, Ford played through the possibilities. Two ideas occurred to him: that a stranger had stolen the dog tags, although why they wouldn't have taken a number of other items made no sense to him. Alternatively, Eric had rummaged through his luggage at some point, and taken the tags out of spite. Ford looked through Eric's papers and cuttings one last time. He added his own receipts, the ticket stubs, the receipt from the Maison du Rève, evidence of travel, then lit a cigarette and afterward set fire to the pile, carefully burning each item, piece by piece. The ash floated up and began to drift over the street. He knew one sure thing: in six days Eric was due to arrive in Malta. Nathalie had said that Eric's tickets and passport were missing, so it was more than possible that the boy was travelling, and if he was travelling, it stood to reason that he would join his mother in Malta.

4.2

Parson's conversation with Geezler had him worried. Here, the divisional chief of an organization implicated in the embezzlement of fifty-three million dollars had confided in him about privately secured funds held by its project managers. He bought a copy of the *Herald Tribune* and read about the reorganization of Southern-CIPA, and the impending decline of HOSCO. Behind the scenes the divisions were being split and set free from one another. HOSCO was likely to fracture into many smaller independent companies. The report used words referring to war and chaos, bloodletting amid the panic. Parson couldn't think of anything more bloodless than the dissolution of a company, and found the language tired. No blood, no heads, just a lot of missing money.

He sat on the hotel balcony and faced the sea, the distant Greek islands, a faint stacked bank of blue, with a kind of abstract bemusement – if HOSCO broke apart then Gibson & Baker would lose their most lucrative client – and if this break could be felt in London, the situation would mean a keener rupture in Iraq, in Afghanistan, in all of the arenas where HOSCO supported military ventures. He couldn't imagine a more god-awful mess. A world without the middleman upon which everything depended struck him as a truly fearful world. No food, no water, no pay, no cash, no cola, Tang, Rip It, Bawl's, and no Red Bull; nowhere to sleep, nothing to sleep on, nothing to sit on, or sit at; no stores, no spare parts, nothing to drive, no trucks, no tanks, no Humvees, no drivers, no transport, no blast walls, no checkpoints, no protective vests, no bullets, no tourniquets, no doctors, no nurses, no blood, no plasma, no morphine, not one aspirin.

By the time Gibson called, Parson had downed four shots of whisky. Parson sat in his boxer shorts, feeling the sweat work its way down his back, the prickle of a slight wind on his legs. All of this recent immobility: sitting in cars, waiting, had added a few extra pounds.

'You're lucky you're away from this. It's all getting a bit bloody. HOSCO is in pieces.'

He listened as Gibson drew on a cigarette and remembered that the man did not smoke. He let this pass without comment. 'I think you'll be happy with what I've found.'

'You have news?' Gibson sounded sincere.

'I have information. I know that HOSCO encouraged their managers to squirrel money away as a security, just in case something went wrong. It makes sense in a way, but it opens up the possibility that one or more of the project managers might have been less than honest about the budgets. If you look closely you'll find a culture of doctored accounts and bloated budgets. My guess is it's endemic, built into the system. Everyone does it.'

'And you know this how?'

'From the horse's mouth. Directly from Paul Geezler.'

'From Paul Geezler?' Gibson sounded surprised. 'Geezler is a temporary fix. He's an *assistant*, remember, to a division director. When things become clearer they'll move in some of the big guns.'

'He's HOSCO's man in Amrah.'

'For the moment. He's cleaning up, they send in the junior staff when everything is messy.'

Parson disagreed. Geezler, he said, seemed canny. 'Did you find anything about Howell's office?'

'I have a little of the information you asked for, but it isn't much.' Gibson appeared to be reading. 'As far as I can tell there was no autopsy on the man who was killed, and no report has been released as yet on the damage to the office.'

'Photos?'

'None on public record. The demolished sections of the office were replaced almost immediately – as far as I know they were taken to one of the burn pits.'

'So it's gone?'

'All gone. The thinking now is that whatever it was it detonated inside the building. But without the office to examine, and without any official report we aren't going to know. The national bank was destroyed a month before in a similar attack, so even with these suspicions it still looks consistent with insurgent activity.'

Parson followed small passenger ferries leaving the harbour. 'They're blaming Sutler.'

'I'm not surprised. Somebody has to be the poster boy for all of this damage.'

'I want someone to make a mistake.' Parson lifted up the last of the whisky and squinted through the bottle at the horizon, warping the boats and the pleasure craft.

4.3

Grüner rode by coach to the coast, then took a taxi from Izmir to Istanbul. Once in Istanbul he learned that the official recommended by Parson would not be in his office and was possibly en route to a conference in Cairo. Worse: despite an explicit guarantee the man had made no provision for their visas. Expecting similar bad news from Heida, Grüner headed directly to the airport in case he needed to book a flight. This is what they needed to do, get a flight, go anywhere, just out, away, someplace else. At the airport, armed guards monitored the loading bay, the entrances, the public areas; security checks slowed the flow of passengers leaving some areas empty and others over-full. Every flight, arriving, departing, delayed.

Heida's call came earlier than Grüner expected and contained startling news.

'I've seen Sutler, Stephen Sutler. The Englishman. In Ankara. He's on the coach to Istanbul. He changed coaches in Ankara. He'll be there early tomorrow morning.' She first gave details of the coach, then details of the sighting. How remarkable to have spotted him, caught him walking right beside her. How arrogant! Her voice squeaked with delight. Forget the visas, just forget them. This gift, dropped into their laps by Providence herself, was a story of unprecedented scale. They had found Sutler, not once, but *twice*, and he was heading directly to Grüner.

'He's on the coach. He will arrive in nine hours. You must get to the coach station and make sure you are at the Asian terminus not the European terminus,' she warned. 'Take photographs. Follow him. Don't let him see you. Don't call the police. Wait for me before you contact anyone. Just follow and observe. I will be there by the afternoon. I will call. Make no mistakes.

Grüner took a taxi directly to the terminus. He checked the arrival times to make sure the service was running on time, then secured a room in the Hotel Lucerne overlooking the plaza where he could watch Sutler's arrival undisturbed.

He slept for six hours then rose, waited at a window overlooking the city walls and watched the spare flow of traffic, a bare plaza, a scrubby park. He remembered that it snowed in the winter, but couldn't imagine it given the present dust and heat. Not unimaginable so much as improbable. Although he still had two hours he kept on his feet, anxious that if he sat down he would fall asleep and miss it all. As dawn rose over the city he began to disbelieve Heida. How clearly had she seen this man, and for how long? She sounded certain, but then she always sounded certain. The longer he considered the coincidence the less possible it seemed. The man was nondescript, indistinct in his own mind, she could have spotted any number of people who looked like him. This would all be a mistake, without doubt, a misunderstanding.

As Grüner debated the possibilities three coaches drew into the terminus, and right before him, wearing a short-sleeved shirt and light trousers, squinting as he stepped down, came Sutler. The man himself. Grüner looked into his viewfinder, he focused on the coach, moved the camera carefully on its tripod until he had the man in his sights. He tracked after Sutler and continued to take photographs as the man walked alongside the wall – when it occurred to him that the man would soon be lost to the city if he did not hurry after him.

Easy to follow, the Englishman walked slowly and appeared uncertain. He stopped regularly to check street names, to look at signs, as if unclear of his direction. Grüner kept his distance and walked on the opposite side of the street. When the road widened into a boulevard he became more confident and crossed back over to walk behind the man, feeling the distance between them as something with substance.

The walk into the city took an hour. As the hour passed the streets became busier and Sutler began to avoid the main thoroughfares. He stopped to buy a black baseball hat from a street vendor. Once he reached the Heights it became clear that he was searching for a room.

Sutler booked into the Konak Hostel, room nine on the second floor, under the stout bulwarks of Aya Sofya. Grüner took a room on the first floor with a view of the courtyard through which Sutler would have to pass to reach the lobby. Everything looked good.

At midday Grüner received another call from Heida. There were problems, she complained. Her passport, her wallet were stolen. *I have no money.* To add to this the coaches out of Ankara were fully booked, not one spare seat between them, and there was trouble at the airport in Ankara, just as there was trouble in Istanbul. No flights. Nothing. Not one. What was going on? She couldn't believe her bad luck.

Grüner tried not to sound happy. 'I have him. He's here.' He whispered into the phone, aware that the walls were thin, that the hostel was busy with Europeans, some of them German. 'He has paid for two nights. At the moment he's in his room. I don't think he's going anywhere. He hasn't eaten yet. We have him.'

Heida began to cry, and when Grüner asked why, she said that he would mess it up.

'Why?' he asked, astonished. 'How can you say this?'

'Because this is what you do. You make a mess of everything.'

'No.' He tried not to raise his voice. 'How? Why do you do this to me?'

Heida fell into deeper misery, the same stormy, sulky desperation she sank into every time she didn't get her way. Grüner looked at the phone, appalled. 'I don't understand. I'm where you told me to be. I've done everything you said. This is what we've been waiting for. Always. One chance, and then you say this shit to me. I don't know what you want. It's not right. You can't say these things.'

He waited for Heida to compose herself, and pictured her making a show of her misery. An adult slumped on the kerb at the coach station sobbing with frustration – a slightly repugnant image. People would feel sorry for her. Someone would pay for her ticket, find her a seat. One way or another she would get what she wanted. He said goodbye quietly, cancelled the call, then switched off the phone. He would not take it with him when he went out.

4.4

Ford fought against his instinct to hide and forced himself to wander through Eminonu, through the covered markets, the sidewalk crush, and the tight streets that fed the open promenade beside the smog and bustle of the Golden Horn – a crowded quayside, grey and busy with launches, tugs, and ferries.

He walked inland and followed the flow of traffic. The air sweetened by almonds and coffee at an intersection where the streets rose and gave way to warehouses and workshops. Here he found banks, an internet café, and the first of a number of currency kiosks set in an open market selling spice, water-pipes, headscarves, lokum, and old books. *You're going to prison*, he told himself, *you will be caught. Why are you even considering this?* He walked as if browsing, a man with time to investigate the city. To draw attention to himself he bragged at the money changers. He had traveller's cheques, he said, and he needed American dollars. He ambled from one kiosk to another asking at each what the daily limit on any exchange might be and if they could give him a competitive rate. The clerks, each of them, wanted to know how much money he was dealing with as dollars were hard to come by, and Ford said that it was several thousand, he needed to have the cheques cashed today, as a matter of urgency. They listened to him, then waved him away.

Back at the port he found the attention he wanted. In a small kiosk beside a transit booth the clerk quickly became irritated and his gestures drew the interest of a small group of bystanders. On leaving Ford noticed that he had acquired the company of a dour, sweaty man.

When he walked away the man followed.

'Excuse me.' The man hurried after him. Not so different in appearance from Ford, the man wore a casual summer suit which hung loose from his shoulders. English-sounding, he spoke with an accent so schooled and refined that he might not be English at all. 'I couldn't help overhear. These people can't help, and if they could you wouldn't get the best exchange. I know someone who can give you a favourable rate. How much do you require?'

Ford stood among the cars stalled in the midday traffic, the sun directly overhead, a bright heat rebounding from the vehicles. The man led him to the pavement. 'I will take you to someone. Five minutes from here. If you don't like him you can leave. It's not a problem.' Not waiting for Ford's reply the man stepped swiftly into a side street. He caught Ford by his sleeve and asked if he realized that he was being followed. The courier indicated over his shoulder. 'He's beside the bird cages, on the opposite side. A black shirt. Do you know this man?'

They looked cautiously out of the alley to a street thick with people. On the opposite kerb, crouched in a doorway decked with small wire and wood cages, Ford spotted the journalist Grüner. Clear and unmistakable. He winced at the coincidence. *How was this possible?* Grüner made a poor job of hiding. Having lost sight of Ford he dithered at a doorway and stepped in and out of view. Ford carefully scanned the street. If Grüner was here, the other journalist would not be far behind.

'Did you notice anyone else?'

'No. He's alone.'

'When did you see him?'

'He has been following you for a while. When I saw you, I saw him. He isn't so careful.'

Alarmed, Ford began to hurry away, the idea of capture, prison, less abstract than before. The courier followed closely behind.

'Sir, sir! I can help with this also.' The man overtook him and indicated a smaller alley which led back to the main street. He told Ford to follow after him. 'Let him come with us. It will be better if he sees where we are going. It is here, just here.'

The alley opened to a curved avenue of white-fronted workshops. The courier asked Ford to wait and entered a travel agency alone, a shabby shop-front with cardboard taped over the glass door. Above the store hung a sign, *Cossack Travel*, in English and Cyrillic, white figures printed on a bold red ground. Grüner blundered into the street, then stepped back out of view. Inside the shop, lodged in a chair behind a wood desk, sat a fat man in a light summer suit. Both men looked out at Ford and Ford asked himself if he could trust them. The larger man leaned back in his chair and indicated that Ford should come in and signalled him to a seat opposite his desk.

The courier came to the door. 'Please,' aware of Ford's reluctance the man waved him forward, 'this is Afan Zubenko. He is a good man and he will help you.'

The courier spoke to the travel agent in Turkish. The fat man squabbled without interest and became curt and dismissive, his voice rolled from a thick creased neck. The courier leaned over the agent's desk, willow-like, a vagueness to him, and Zubenko waved him away. He closed his eyes as he spoke. 'Come back to me later. Now, go. Go! Go, go, go, go, go.'

As the shop door swung shut, Zubenko turned his attention to Ford. He settled his arms either side on the armrests, palms up, in a gesture of gathering calm. 'I understand that you are interested in changing money. You have traveller's cheques? If you are interested I think I can help you.'

How fat this man was, how sack-like, with a huffing breath, a stomach of stacked lobes and the same exhausted quality to his gestures and expression.

Ford looked back at the street for Grüner. The agent tilted his head and the sun cut a hard line across his baseball cap, his thin ponytail, as he appeared to study him. 'Tell me your business and let me see what I can do.'

'I want to cash some traveller's cheques before I leave tomorrow.'

'And how much do you need to change?'

'Two thousand, in American dollars.'

'American dollars are difficult to find at the moment. You have identification? You have your passport?'

Ford shook his head.

'You have no passport? Or you have no passport with you?'

'With me.'

'Are you sure you want dollars?'

'Yes.'

'And you wish to exchange the whole amount today? Do you have the little dockets as well as the cheques?'

'Yes.'

Zubenko cleared his throat. 'I will buy the cheques at five per cent below their value, but I will pay you for the dockets. Do you understand me?'

Ford took out a plastic wallet containing the cheques, he asked for a pen.

'Please. There is no need to sign them.'

The agent smiled as he passed over the wallet. As he counted through the cheques Ford looked around the office. At the back, in shadow, two young men sat side by side on a box-sprung back seat taken from a car. One older, one younger, almost certainly brothers. The men watched with flat expressions, a little unnerving, one with folded arms who appeared bored, the other picked at his teeth then looked at his fingernail.

Zubenko took out a key attached to his trouser belt by a chain. He unlocked a desk drawer and pulled out a cashbox, the small key pinched between his plump fingers. He spoke in a low voice in Turkish to the two brothers who neither stirred nor answered. Zubenko hissed between his teeth then tutted with dissatisfaction. 'So. You are travelling tomorrow? Did you know that there are problems at the airport? Delays. Security at the airport is very tight.'

Ford admitted that he had yet to make arrangements. He looked at the street, anxious that he could not see Grüner.

'If you were leaving by sea, I could arrange this.' Zubenko pointed at the poster. 'Because, of course, I am a travel agent. Cyprus . . . Rhodes . . . Egypt . . .'

'Malta?' Ford surprised himself with the idea. Malta would work, why not, and it opened possibilities: the boy *might* arrive, it wasn't impossible. At least he knew his travel details, and knew when Eric had planned to meet his mother. Hadn't he also spoken about a villa, a palazzo, a place to stay that was not used? A place he could stay without being discovered. Ford scanned the street for the journalist, uncomfortable that the man could not be seen.

'Malta is a beautiful place, of course. You said that you were departing tomorrow?'

'Tomorrow morning.'

'Tomorrow would be expensive. Can I ask? Is something the matter?'

'I'm being followed. I need some assistance.'

Zubenko continued counting. 'I'm not sure what you are asking.' He laid the notes out in sets of five hundreds. When the counting was complete he made one stack, then counted through again, turning the notes so that they were in order.

'There is a man who has been following me. Can I leave from another door?'

The agent set his hand flat over the money. 'I'm afraid I do not have enough. I need to go to the bank myself. I can change three-quarters of what you need now and a quarter later. Would you meet me this evening, and I will have the remaining money and your tickets?' When he raised his hand he pinched two of the top bills and folded them into his palm. 'Apart from this man who is following you, are you sure there is nothing else I can do? Your passport? You said that you have one? I can't remember?'

'I have a passport.'

Zubenko pushed the money towards Ford, and Ford realized that their business, for the moment, was concluded, and he worried that he would not see the rest of the cash. 'You can leave without trouble. People think that this neighbourhood is not safe. It is perfectly safe. But,' he shrugged a little indifferently, 'you can never be absolutely sure.'

Uncertain of the route, Ford tracked down the hill until he was back at the water. Zubenko's sons followed him out of the agent's then slipped away. He did not doubt that they would soon approach him and take the money, by force if necessary. Why else would Zubenko comment on his neighbourhood? He wondered if they would stab or beat him, or simply demand the money, but he reached the hotel without incident and did not see the men again. Once in his room he checked the street and found it empty.

In the late afternoon Ford woke to a whistle, a low, deliberate call. He stood on the bed to lean out of the window but found the street empty. The whistle came a second time and still he could not pinpoint the source. The German, Grüner, had not followed him back to the hotel, but even so, he could still know where he was staying. Ford began to despair. The more time he spent in Istanbul, the more problems he would make for himself. He stepped off the bed and heard the whistle a third time. He should change his hotel, move, or leave the city.

As he came into the lobby the clerk held out a card. The man would not look directly at Ford, his attention taken by the television on the counter.

The card belonged to the travel agent Afan Zubenko, on the reverse was written a name and a time. *Ciragan. 15:00.* He showed the card to the clerk. The clerk shrugged and stepped back into the office without a word.

He'd lost the money he'd left with Zubenko, no doubt, but he found no grief in this. His plans for cash, for tickets, were much too vague to inspire proper hope. He expected nothing and told himself that whatever money remained should be spent on a ticket to the Black Sea. Go against expectation. Head north to Russia, why not, to some winter state where he could slowly learn the language, teach perhaps, take asylum in a culture so exterior he'd make himself a new man with no echo from the past. His future, without doubt, was shaped in fields of snow.

A hotel, the Ciragan, close by Seraglio Point, overlooked the Bosporus. The straits ran sluggish but sure, slow eddies indicating a change of tide. Ford arrived on time, and found the travel agent already seated at a table, a napkin tucked into his shirt, his shoulders falling in a broad curve so that the man appeared to anchor the room, solid and central.

Laid out in front of him a side tray loaded with plates, sweet treats, small tastes of cakes and pastries, a fork to each saucer.

Afan Zubenko nodded as Ford approached and suggested that he sit down. 'Please,' the agent apologized, 'I know that you are busy.' He stabbed at a piece of cake and twisted it open. He looked at the cake without interest before wiping the fork on his napkin. 'I have your money,' the agent sighed, 'of course, and I have your tickets.'

Zubenko softly tutted under his breath. He raised a fork to another plate and tracked the tines through a small curve of honey seeped from a pastry, his expression one of deep distaste. He looked up at Ford, then down at the saucer. 'Our business this morning has come with a number of obligations.' The man looked again to the pastry. 'There was a man following you. He knows where you are staying, and he has ideas about you,' Zubenko paused, 'and he intends to speak with the police.'

'Where is he?'

'Please.' Zubenko held up the fork. 'You brought him to my business. Do you know if the cheques have been reported missing?'

'I'm sorry?'

'The cheques. The cheques. It is important. Have they been reported missing?'

'No.' Ford answered with certainty, although he had no idea.

'Then this is good.' The cheques, Zubenko explained, would need to work for their money before the police could trace the numbers and put a stop to them.

The agent lifted an envelope from his jacket pocket and slid it along the table. Inside, Ford found the remaining money and passes for travel by boat from Istanbul to Bodrum, to Kos, to Athens, to Malta.

'You will be able to board tonight. The ferry leaves early in the morning. You have a cabin, sadly with no window. If you go tonight you will find that security is not a problem between ten and eleven, these are ferries for people from the islands who bring food, not trouble, and security is less interested in worrying about these people. You might decide to stay in your cabin until the ferry has departed.'

Ford tucked the documents and the itinerary into his pocket.

'Our business this morning was very small.' Zubenko glanced from plate to plate. 'I do not want any inconvenience to come out of this small business. Your cheques are already somewhere else, untraceable to you, untraceable to me, our business is concluded. The problem with the German will also be concluded as soon as you are on the boat. You can leave this city and no one will remember that you were here.' Zubenko leaned forward and spoke clearly and not unkindly. 'Do not think me impolite when I say that I have no interest in hearing from you or meeting you again. Go. Go away. Now. Goodbye.'

Ford rose to leave. Troubled, he asked what would become of the journalist.

Zubenko looked up, his eyes widening, his irritation deepening. 'Nothing,' he said. 'He will come to no harm and he will cause no harm.'

4.5

For a while Grüner could see no purpose to Sutler's wanderings. The man blundered about the old centre but missed the sights. The Hippodrome, the archaeological museum, the Galatea Bridge, the Blue Mosque, the Grand Bazaar, all skirted, unnoticed, unvisited. He waited while the Englishman entered an American Express office but did not change money, from there he was sent elsewhere, to a Western Union, and then a smaller cash booth near the port, and so on, and so on, visiting in total, nine money changers. At the final place, a shop behind the old mercantile quarter, Sutler sat with a man, who appeared, without question, to be the fattest man Grüner had ever seen. When Sutler came out he was accompanied by two men: same mouths, same flat nose, almost certainly brothers, both shorter and younger than Grüner, who behaved like private security – quietly scanning the street as Sutler walked ahead. After a short walk the brothers slipped into a small supermarket and Grüner thought that he was mistaken.

As he passed the supermarket the two men stepped out and blocked his way.

'Can we help you?' The older brother spoke in English.

'I'm sorry.'

The man switched with ease to German. 'We were asking if you need help?'

Sutler walked ahead and looked to become lost among pedestrians.

The brothers smiled at Grüner.

'Thanks, no, I'm fine. Thank you.'

The white of Sutler's shirt became indistinguishable from other white shirts, other shoulders.

'Are you looking for someone? Perhaps there is something that you want?'

'No, I'm fine. Excuse me.' Grüner held up his hands and again attempted to move on. The younger of the two men, who had not yet spoken, stood directly in his way. 'I'm sorry?'

'My brother is learning German. Please. Where are you from?'

'Hamburg,' Grüner replied. 'Are you the police?'

Now uncomfortable, he pushed forward but could not make more than two steps without the men confronting him; a dance in which they remained close but did not touch.

'I like Hamburg. In Hamburg they have a Christmas market. Not as good as the Christmas market in Trier, but a good market, and they have nice museums. Nothing that compares to our museums, of course, but nice and not to be ignored. I think you are looking for someone?' The brothers blocked his way. 'The man you were following? What interest do you have in him?'

'You've made a mistake.' Grüner looked the older brother square in the eye. If it came to trouble he thought that he would be able to handle himself, but he couldn't be certain. 'I'm not looking for anyone. I don't want to buy anything. I am leaving now.' He levelled his hand as a final gesture.

'No.' The older brother shook his head and showed a small silver knife in the flat of his palm. 'You can come with us. Please.'

At the sight of the knife Grüner became completely compliant.

The men escorted Grüner to a cold-storage lock-up at the back of Cossack Travel. The younger brother quizzed the older brother as they strapped Grüner with duct tape to a small office chair. Was it possible, he wanted to know, that the Germans don't have a sense of humour because the subject always comes at the end of the sentence so that everything sounds like a punch line? He asked the same question of Grüner.

Grüner complained that the tape was too tight about his stomach. He attempted to move his ankles, his wrists, he explained that he had money, but the brothers did not appear to listen. 'I have allergies,' he complained, 'it's very serious. To the gum.' He spoke carefully, clearly, made his case without emotion, hopeful that his rational calm would convince them. At school he could hold his breath until he fainted, and he wondered if now would be a good time to pass out.

'See, this is a case in point. This is my point exactly. It was a joke and he didn't understand.'

Undeterred Grüner attempted to speak in Turkish. 'What are you going to do?'

'You speak Turkish?' The older brother looked slightly alarmed.

'I am a journalist,' Grüner answered, still calm. 'I work in the Middle East. I speak four languages. I speak Arabic and I speak a little Hebrew. I speak English and French, and I was following a man because he is wanted by American and British intelligence.'

'But you just said something in Turkish? Is this the language you use to pick up boys?'

The sound of the younger brother zipping duct tape off the roll made it hard for Grüner to hear. Unsure he'd heard correctly, he repeated himself. 'I am a journalist and I have to get back to my hotel. I am following a British man who is wanted by the police and by British and American military intelligence. It is very important that you let me go.'

'You either speak Turkish or you don't.' The man leaned close and whispered in Turkish in Grüner's ear.

'I don't speak Turkish. I am a journalist – and this man should not be allowed to disappear, it is very important that I follow him. You have to let me go. I will pay you.'

'But I heard you speak Turkish.'

'It was a small phrase. I don't really speak – I mean I know a little – but I'm a photographer, a journalist, I don't know much more than a few phrases.'

Done with binding him, the younger brother came to the front and Grüner worried that he would tape over his mouth. 'So you speak a little Turkish?'

Grüner nodded in surrender. 'I speak a little Turkish. I know a few phrases.'

'Enough to pick up boys?'

'Boys? Why are you asking about boys? I was following a man who is wanted by American intelligence.'

The brothers exchanged a glance.

'Yes, you come here, you speak a little Turkish, and you pick up boys with the little Turkish that you can speak.'

Grüner rapidly shook his head, trying to rid the room of the idea. 'I don't pick up boys. I have a wife. I have a girlfriend. They are both women.'

But the man ran to his own chain of logic. 'No, the only reason a German would learn Turkish is so that he can come to the country to pollute the flower of Turkish youth.'

Grüner shook his head more vigorously. 'You aren't listening to me. I've told you what I'm doing here. I am following a man called Stephen Sutler. Look at my camera. Look at the photographs.'

'Is there something wrong with Turkish boys?'

'No!' Grüner rolled his head and began to shout. 'Why have you brought me here? I have to go.' He struggled to free himself but succeeded only in jogging the chair forward.

The brother started laughing. 'I'm making a joke,' he said, still laughing. 'A simple joke! What is it about the Germans and their sense of humour? Should I tell you when I am joking? Maybe I will hold up my hand next time so you know? Hey, here it is, a joke! I am now making a joke!'

Grüner could not be precise on the time. The men left, then returned, but neither would speak with him. After another hour, possibly longer, a woman ambled into the room with tea and a modest lunch. He strained to see if it was still light outside, but the open door gave only a view of a wood-panelled corridor. The woman, old and small, with a thin black headscarf, asked the brothers in Turkish if their guest would like something to eat, and Grüner begged her in German, English, and poorly conjugated Turkish to call the police.

'My wife,' he pleaded, 'my mother will be worried.' In this he sounded sincere.

The woman backed out of the room and the brothers followed after, explaining rapidly that this wasn't anything she should worry about. Hurry, hurry, hurry, they chided as the door swung closed behind them, they would like coffee.

When the younger brother returned he asked Grüner if he liked films. 'When I am studying,' he said, 'I watch two every day. Every day. It is important to educate yourself. Good for your language, but necessary so that you can follow the narrative, learn the tricks for making films because there are rules.'

'Is your brother making you do this? I have money. I can pay you.

You can buy lots of films. DVDs. I have films at my hotel I can give you. I'm telling the truth. I have many, many films. If you let me go, I won't tell anyone. I will give you films. Many films.'

When the older brother returned the younger brother fell back into his thoughts.

'What was he talking about?'

'He doesn't watch films.'

The older brother set his hand on his brother's shoulder as he lowered himself to the floor. They sat side by side. 'He's lying. Everybody likes a good film,' and then to Grüner, 'My brother will one day write many great films. Our tastes are very different.' The man shook his head. 'You must watch films?'

Grüner refused to answer.

'Herzog? Wenders? Fassbinder?' The older brother waited for a reply. The man became animated, he stood up and brushed dust from his trousers. 'I will let you walk out of here now if you can tell me one joke from a Fassbinder movie. One joke. You don't need to make me laugh. One joke and you can walk free.'

Grüner kept his mouth shut and glowered at the man.

'All right. I will give you another opportunity. Do you think my brother is handsome? His mouth, no? Don't you think he has a pretty mouth? I can say without bias that this is a handsome mouth. Perhaps you would like to kiss him?'

With no idea how to answer Grüner closed his eyes and rolled back his head.

The older brother leaned forward with both hands on the armrests. 'I don't know, Mr Journalist. I have tried to like you. Honestly, I have tried, but I don't seem to be able to connect with you. You are a hard man to understand, you know that? I need that knife now.'

4.6

Ford collected his backpack from his room. On his way through the lobby he asked the clerk about the tours along the Bosporus. The clerk, turned to a TV on the counter beside him, cocked his head as Ford asked: How far did they go? How regular? How much did they cost? Did he have any brochures? A leaflet perhaps in his office? He said that he was interested, not for today but maybe tomorrow, if there was something in the morning. He wanted to stay another two nights, and when he came back in the evening he would settle what he owed. There were no leaflets, he said repeating himself, nothing about the trips. The clerk sloped back to his office. It was possible that they had some information somewhere about the trips.

When the clerk returned to the office Ford reached over the counter and opened the desk drawer. He shuffled through the passports until he recognized his own. One eye on the clerk's legs and backside as he leaned into his office and searched for the leaflets.

He slipped the passport into his pocket before the man returned, and waited for the leaflet. On the TV on the back counter he saw the news, a banner tagline on CNN slipped along the frame: *Iraq – enquiry.*

He walked from the hotel to the port as the day finally gave way to night. His stride shortened where the road became steeper, his mood – a certain anxiety about boarding the ferry, about showing his passport and passing through security, about how he would answer if he was challenged – underscored with a hint of optimism, a buzz at leaving Turkey. He liked being on the move, was happy to leave, and felt with this next step a welcome delay in his return to Europe. Malta was a good idea: he would meet Eric, resolve his trouble with the missing account numbers, lie low in a villa, remain undiscovered. Covert. Secure. The decision came to him, clear and true. *I don't need to return to Bonn. Everything I need to do can be done in Malta.* As Sutler, Ford had succeeded in areas he never could have approached as John Jacob Ford. Why return to Bonn – he couldn't properly decide in his future – but why would he return to settle the small debts and rents he owed in his absence, considering the amount money he had coming to him? Why give money to banks and corporations? Hadn't they already accounted for their losses? Hadn't they written him off? Why surrender this advantage? He was skirting Europe, from Istanbul to Malta, it wasn't by coincidence; he could see now that his actions held an instinctive logic.

The ferry sat at the quay as Zubenko had promised, and as he came down the hill overlooking the docks Ford could see that the traffic was light. The ferry's flank overshadowed the quay and arcs of light glanced across the security-booth walls, a small huddle of scuffed white buildings; all a little mournful, as if abandoned. The air by the water reeked of bitter-sweet diesel fumes.

Signs in Turkish and English warned of an increase in security, but he found only two guards, and when he offered his passport and ticket they waved him through without interest. The ease of this disturbed him.

He walked onto the boat without seeing any staff or personnel. On the lower deck he passed behind a solitary cleaner, headphones clapped over her ears as she huffed the machine forward, cleaning the grey linoleum floor and leaving it slick. He found the cabin unlocked and walked into a room of moulded plastic, beige and red, with rounded edges, no window, a draw-down bunk, the air icy from the air conditioning.

In Malta he would find Eric's villa, find Eric, retrieve his money, and revisit the idea that he didn't have to be *Ford*, hadn't Sutler demonstrated this possibility? He could become someone new.

The late summer morning brought rain to Istanbul and he watched the city fall slowly away. He kept his eye on the domes and minarets – a view of steel greys and greens – and felt, despite his pleasure to be leaving, a slight regret. Departures, he told himself, are always melancholic. Passengers crowded the saloons, a few solitary figures lined the wet decks, and cowered under coats and plastic sheeting. The ferry's wake curved back to the port, white, almost fluorescent in the darkening sea. He faced the stern with Europe to his left and Asia to his right, and felt momentarily unstable, an element in constant motion. A tour boat followed them out. The tour guide's voice amplified tinny and clear over the water narrated the view. On the opposite bank lay the palace of the last Sultan. Ahead, the Byzantine fortifications. On top of the hill the Topkapi Palace, beside it Aya Sofya. The first Ottoman Emperor, Mehmet the Second, had looked upon the same rump of hills six hundred years ago. He besieged the city, starved it, then pummelled its tough protective walls with a cannon dragged from the outskirts of Vienna. Such is history.

Ford looked hard across the water as the tour boat fell behind.

In his pocket an open ticket to Bodrum, then Bodrum to Kos, Kos to Athens, Athens to Malta. As per his promise to Zubenko, he would never return to Istanbul, and as the sea-fog enveloped the ferry he could feel himself disappear.

4.7

Parson read of Howell's death in the *International Guardian*. Fifty-seven years old. Heart failure, post-surgery, while undergoing treatment for burns. He also heard from both of the German journalists on the same day. The first call came from Susanna Heida, anxious that she had not heard from the photographer, her partner, Gerhard Grüner.

Heida, a comedy of hyper-disorganization, claimed that she had seen Sutler in Ankara, in broad daylight, two days ago. He'd walked right beside her, la-di-dah, as carefree as you like, no effort to disguise himself. She'd watched him board the coach to Istanbul then immediately called Grüner to let him know when Sutler would arrive. The last she'd heard from Grüner he was at the Konak Hostel. Parson asked Heida why she hadn't contacted him first. Sutler should not be approached. Hadn't he said this? Hadn't he made this perfectly clear?

'But there he was,' she answered, Sutler in Ankara. 'I wasn't looking for him.' This statement, plain as it sounded, came with teeth. How was it that she had seen Sutler twice, yet Parson never seemed to get close to him? 'We had an agreement,' she said. 'You were supposed to help with our visas, you gave us a name of someone who was supposed to help, but this was no good,' because of this she felt no obligation to call him.

Parson didn't believe that she had seen Sutler. The claim was non-sense. No, this was about her not getting the visas for Iraq, nothing else.

Later in the afternoon Parson received a call from the Turkish police that made him change his mind. Gerhard Grüner was in hospital in Istanbul, having broken his leg in a fall. Unlike Heida, Grüner was particular that Parson should know his whereabouts. He had information and wanted to speak as soon as possible.

When the Turkish police checked the Konak Hostel they found no trace of a Stephen Sutler, but plenty of evidence of Gerhard Grüner. The desk clerk stated that Grüner had asked for assistance in procuring the services of a man, or preferably a young boy. He had asked for magazines and places to go. Grüner, it seemed, had been clumsy, and suffered nothing less than he deserved.

Parson took note of the information, but as soon as the call was completed he tore the page out of his notebook. This was nonsense.

It took time to find where the police were holding Afan Zubenko and his sons; because of Grüner's statement the men had been brought into custody, and Parson was having trouble finding out where. When he finally located them at the Central Police Station in Eminonu, he found that the police in Istanbul weren't interested in assisting him. Access to the Zubenkos, he was told, would be impossible. Parson called Gibson to see what muscle he could employ.

Rather than wait for Gibson's reply, Parson met Grüner at the hospital and brought him back to his hotel. The two men stood side by side at the window looking down on the grey parkway before the city walls. Grüner leaned forward on his crutches, one leg bandaged from his knee to his thigh: unbalanced, he veered toward the glass. A scuff ran from his cheek to his temple, pink and sore enough to make Parson cringe.

'This was where you saw him?'

'He came by coach.' Grüner tapped the window. 'Where that stall is, by the wall.'

Parson looked down on the terminus at men selling newspapers and boys with flat baskets of fruit, lokum, sandwiches. Sutler could be among those people right now, he had no way of knowing. While hunting Sutler he'd developed ideas about who the man might be, but he didn't know much. It would be possible to pass Sutler in the street and not know it. In ten days he could have adopted any kind of disguise with minimal effort, although Grüner was emphatic that the man looked exactly like the photograph they were using online and in the US press, the photograph taken from Sutler's ID. Coming to Istanbul was a risk. A risk Sutler could have avoided by veering north of the city and crossing by land to Greece or Bulgaria.

'And where was his hotel?'

Grüner pointed out the Konak and the travel agency on a tourist map. He'd drawn in red the route he'd followed with Sutler. His voice a little slow, lulled with medication.

Within an hour they began to roll over the same information. Grüner's voice became dry, his expression a little glassy. Ready to leave, Parson helped the journalist to a seat. He laid the crutches carefully within reach and asked the man what he would do now. Grüner shrugged and shook a cigarette out of the pack. Lined side by side on the table, a small digital camera, the map, a pencil, and a red sports cap.

'I don't know. Iraq is not possible. Those men took my camera. I don't have the pictures. I have this.' He pointed at the camera. 'It's not as good. Not good enough for work. I have a story now without pictures.'

They looked out at the city to a view of a cold, bright, and cloudless sky. Parson accepted a cigarette. He picked up the camera, turned it over in his hands.

'How did Sutler look?'

'Not so good. His face. He had these bruises, and his nose was big. Swollen.'

Parson drew on his cigarette. 'But describe him.'

'Like before. Thin. Nervous. He has short hair now. English.'

'Does he look like me?'

Grüner looked at Parson and shook his head. 'Not so much. I mean maybe the same shape, more or less, in the face. A little rounder. The hair is much shorter.'

'You need a photo?'

'Of course. Maybe the story runs for a day or so, but with a picture it would be different. It would mean more money. People would take it more seriously. A picture is what everybody wants. I had him in the terminal and outside the hotel. Some in the street.'

'And he doesn't look like me?'

Grüner looked again at Parson and studied him hard. 'Maybe, if you were in the street? It's possible.'

Parson picked up the sports cap as he rose. 'And after this you return to Frankfurt?'

'To Hamburg. They said that I can travel. But I don't know what will happen now.'

Parson shook the journalist's hand and pointed to the window. 'You said you saw him at the buses? Beside the coaches?'

Gibson did not call Parson back. Instead – as he walked among the coaches parked at the terminus, deliberate enough to provide Grüner a good opportunity to photograph him – he received a call from the German consulate. One of their men, Henning Bastian, was interviewing

Afan Zubenko at the Central Police Station and they wanted him to come in.

The tone of the call disturbed Parson. This was not a polite request.

An hour later Parson arrived at the Central Police Station – a long building tagged on to a new apartment complex, with ironwork in front of the lower windows, pale magnolia walls, and bare planters. Informed that Henning Bastian was still interviewing Zubenko, Parson was escorted to one of the interrogation rooms and told to wait.

He sat at a table for an hour in a simple windowless room with the faint odour of fresh paint; two guards at the door, hefty men, both silent, and faintly bothersome, their attention locked on him so surely he began to feel that he had done something wrong.

The feeling deepened with the arrival of the cultural attaché. Bastian: boyish, lanky, thin-faced, dressed in a light grey suit, wiped his hands with a piece of tissue before he sat down. He looked to Parson, then the table, then the three men who had accompanied him, and briskly told them all to sit down, a clipped precision about his instructions. One of the men handed him a black-backed register as the others scurried to fetch chairs.

Bastian looked impatiently about the room. 'Can we start?' He turned his attention to Parson. 'Mr Parson. I am Henning Bastian with the German consulate, and I have been assigned to oversee the claims made by the photographer Gerhard Grüner regarding Stephen Lawrence Sutler.'

Parson jerked his head forward. 'He hasn't made any claims against Sutler, his claims are against Zubenko.'

'I need a little background.' The man closed his eyes and opened them. 'I need a little clarification on why you are involved with Gerhard Grüner, in what capacity you have come to know him.' Once again, the man gave a slow blink. 'I would like to speak with you about your business with the Hospitality and Operational Support Company of Hampton Roads, Virginia.'

Parson intended to say yes, but taken aback by Bastian's formality he couldn't find his voice.

'Mr Parson, please confirm for me that you are working for Gibson and Baker, under instruction from their clients, the Hospitality and Operational Support Company of Hampton Roads, Virginia. I am saying this right? This is correct, no?'

Parson nodded.

'Gibson and Baker are public adjusters based in London? You investigate and assess insurance claims made against your clients? Is that right? You investigate claims and potential suits in order to – what – to advise on risk, on fraud?'

'That's right.'

'And yet HOSCO have you searching for Stephen Lawrence Sutler?' Bastian's hands settled either side of the register.

'They have teams in Iraq, in Kuwait, and other countries—'

Bastian's head gave a single shake, a taut negative. 'HOSCO? No. No they don't.'

'I've been speaking with the new division head in Amrah City, who is coordinating the search.'

Again Bastian gave a short curt shake. 'No. There are a number of agencies searching for Stephen Sutler, but none of these searches are managed or funded by HOSCO. You are the only person employed by HOSCO to search for Stephen Sutler. This is very interesting. Who told you there were other teams?'

'I would check your information.' Parson sat upright and straightened his back.

'I know my information, Mr Parson, and it's just you. There isn't anybody else.' Bastian looked at him, sour and direct. 'Can you tell me how you came to hear about Afan Zubenko?'

'I was contacted by two German journalists who had seen Sutler first in Kopeckale and then in Ankara. One of the journalists—'

'Ah, Gerhard Grüner. The journalist. Tell me, do you believe Gerhard Grüner?'

'I believe he has seen Sutler.'

'You're certain they've seen this man, these journalists?'

'I have no reason to doubt them.'

'Although no one else has seen him they have managed to bump into him twice? That is quite a coincidence. Mr Parson, how is your knowledge of the American Civil War?'

'I'm sorry?'

'Do you read historical fiction? Have you heard of a *sutler*? It's a military term.' Bastian's face pinched with a teacher's concentration. 'A *sutler* is someone who follows the military, they sell provisions, clothes, uniforms, food . . .'

'I'm sorry?'

'Sutler. Sutler. S-U-T-L-E-R. It's from the Dutch. It means someone who does the dirty work.' Again, a pause, but this time a slower blink. 'Tell me, what do you know about Paul Howell?'

'Paul Howell?'

'The Deputy Administrator at Southern-CIPA, Paul Howell, the man who controlled the finances for both government and civilian projects. Paul Howell, the man who came up with Stephen Sutler.'

'Came up?' Parson looked to the men about the room. 'I'm sorry?'

Bastian shunted his chair forward. He spoke carefully, quietly, with certainty. 'There is no Stephen Lawrence Sutler, Mr Parson. There is no trace of this man prior to his arrival at Camp Liberty. Stephen Sutler was invented by Paul Howell. As the man responsible for controlling the distribution of finances to civil contractors, Paul Howell understood exactly how to manipulate the system he was managing. HOSCO hired a man who does not exist.' Bastian looked Parson up and down, an unmistakable evaluation.

'There was a man going by the name of Stephen Sutler at Camp Liberty.'

'But I've told you he doesn't exist.'

'Then I am looking for the man who called himself Stephen Sutler.'

'Perhaps it's possible that Stephen Sutler is a number of people? Mr Parson, can you tell me anything about the current reorganization of HOSCO?'

'I'm looking for Sutler. I know very little about the company.'

'Paul Geezler? What do you know about Paul Geezler?'

'That he works for the division chief in Europe and is now temporarily assigned to the head of operations in southern Iraq.'

'Were you hired by Paul Geezler?'

'No. I was hired because I was completing work here for them. I have only been in contact with him since he took up his new duties.'

'Has it occurred to you that it might be more productive to look at the people who came up with Stephen Sutler rather than the man who is playing him?' Bastian sat back. Mouth pinched. 'Tell me, Mr Parson, did you ever ask yourself why they hired you? You investigate accidents and fraud, and this is very specific work, no? Very particular? And yet they have charged you with a major investigation. Did it occur to you that by hiring you, the company might deliberately prevent the people who understand these things from performing their duties?'

'This is my job.'

'No, Mr Parson. This is my job.'

Parson heard the men behind him snicker.

'My job, Mr Parson. It is my job.'

Rising from his chair, Parson said that he was ready to go. 'I would like to speak with Afan Zubenko.'

Bastian opened his hands. 'There's nothing he can tell you. Zubenko knows nothing. There is nothing to discover here.'

'I would like to speak with him nevertheless.'

Bastian pushed the register forward. 'Be my guest, Mr Parson. There is nothing here.' The man looked over Parson's shoulder. 'Mr Parson, enlighten me, do you think that once you have discovered this man or these people who have been playing Stephen Sutler, that everything will be resolved? Do you think that he has all of that money? All hidden somewhere? All in one account, offshore? Zurich? Nicely waiting for him? Or perhaps he carries it around with him?' Bastian closed his eyes and shook his head. 'You won't find anything here, Mr Parson, and I can guarantee that you won't find Sutler. And when HOSCO cut you loose they will consider the job to be done. Do you understand? They won't look any more. The man will be gone, the money will be gone, and the whole business will be laid to rest.' Bastian leaned forward, something of a smile coming to him. 'Why don't you give your friend in Amrah City a little information? Tell him that you have found Sutler and see what happens. Just to see what they do.'

4.8

The customs boat drew alongside the ferry. The larger ferry bore down upon the smaller launch, the two customs officials stretched out, sometimes reaching, sometimes holding on in their attempts to board.

Ford sat on deck undisturbed, and looked out at the island, Kos: beaches, umbrellas kicked by the wind, stubby palms along the coastal road, white hotel developments tipped back in their compounds, behind them a sharp fin of mountain steep enough to show exposed rock above the olive groves. Almost close enough to swim to, the distance a little deceptive, the sea a little rough and perhaps cold, but blue and clear.

The guards separated once on deck, and demanded that the

passengers show their passports. Ford had already shown his twice – and each time the official had looked without proper regard or interest, Ford knew that they didn't see him, only a white European, middle-aged and undistinguished.

This time the guard flicked through every page in Ford's passport. He flicked back. Stopped at the page which showed a stamp for Iraq, alongside a handwritten date. The guard tipped the passport toward Ford.

'Where is the exit?'

Ford looked at the page.

'What was your purpose for travel?'

'Now? Tourist.'

The man tilted the passport to show it to Ford and pointed to the stamp. An eagle against Arabic script. 'This is the visa with the entry stamp.'

'It's the exit date. That's when I left.'

'And where did you go?'

'I went to Syria.'

The guard turned the pages one by one.

'There is no stamp for Syria. There is no exit stamp for Iraq.'

'I have another passport.'

'Show me.'

'It's out of date, it's with the consulate in the UK. I have two pass-ports for business. It's not uncommon.'

The guard studied Ford's face with undisguised irritation. 'The entry stamp and the exit stamp are always on the same page, in the same passport.' He turned one page and looked closely at the photo. 'What consulate in the UK?'

'London. I meant passport services, the passport office. Where it was issued. You confused me.'

The guard gave a single nod then turned to find his companion.

'Look,' Ford decided on another approach, 'I obviously left because I'm here. If they didn't stamp the passport it isn't my problem.'

'There is no entry and no exit from Syria? Did you go to Syria?'

'I? Of course I went to Syria.'

'And where were you in Syria?'

'Damascus.'

'And they did not stamp your passport. In or out?'

The second guard counted the passengers. He walked by Ford and the guard with a group of people and began to check through their baggage. Once he started the second guard called to the first, asking, Ford guessed, for assistance.

Ford feigned indifference. 'I don't see how this matters.'

The guard closed the passport but still held it in his hand. After a moment he gave it back to Ford, then joined his companion. A history here, Ford thought, of old dislikes, of neighbours who gain pleasure from small provocations, from nursing and enduring small hates.

A woman emptied a basket of fruits: oranges and grapefruit, of newspapers and pots, her face set in a sour pinch. The first official slouched over her, superior, impatient, and allowed himself to smile as the oranges rolled free across the deck.

And so they were allowed to continue. As the boat slipped away the guard turned his head to keep his eye on the boat, and Ford had the feeling that it wasn't the boat that was being watched, but him.

The ferry docked at a pier beside a Crusader castle, a stout stone fort.

Ford changed a little money for euros. Suddenly hungry, he found a row of restaurants lining the portside, tables set in a small grove, branches hung with lights, large-screen TVs out on patios to show the football. Dinner deals, happy hour, laminated pictures of plates of food.

He watched two men arrive on bicycles. They sat close by and drank a beer each, quiet and rested, a sun-glow on their foreheads and arms. He followed them afterward to a pastry shop, watched them choose, and saw himself reflected in the cabinet fronts, as if, instead of two, they were three good friends.

In an afternoon spent waiting between ships he followed these men through the town, and felt himself slowly revive. How ordinary this all appeared. How regular. He imagined himself telling the two men that he was Stephen Sutler, but guessed that they would not recognize this name, or that they would not believe him.

4.9

Afan Zubenko opened the discussion with an apology.

'My son is naive but he is not stupid. This man approaches him in the street and speaks to him, and my son is unaware that this is a dangerous man. A deviant. Personally,' he said, 'I say live and let live. But if one of these men makes an advance to my son or both of my sons, it is their business what they do . . .' He shrugged. 'To be honest, it isn't an issue which gives me any trouble. Cossack males are known to follow deviancy only in very rare cases, prison perhaps, and there are maybe one or two stories in our entire history that have the whiff of such deviancy. It is doubtful that you could find a full-blooded Cossack who would voluntarily take part in any such activity, as the girl, so to speak. The receiver. I cannot think of one example myself, not one case which involves a full-blooded Cossack. Historically, this is a weakness of the Greeks, the Italians, and of course your own people, who are particularly fond of this vice.'

'Gerhard Grüner has made a report stating that he was bound to a chair and thrown down a flight of steps.'

'None of this is true. We have no steps.'

'These are serious claims. He has a broken leg and cuts to his shoulder and head. There has also been damage to his property.'

'It has nothing to do with us. My sons did not touch him.'

The report from the hospital concurred. Grüner had not been beaten. He had escaped from the storeroom still strapped to the chair, a sight variously described as curious, very wrong, unnatural, like watching a dog run on its hind legs – he appeared to throw himself down the steps in a kind of apoplectic seizure.

'The police are waiting to take your business apart.'

'The police,' Zubenko indicated the guard at the door, 'are not interested in me or my sons.'

'That might be, but there are a good number of people who are interested in Stephen Sutler, and they will examine every transaction, every piece of paper.'

Zubenko gave a short huff but remained silent.

'What was he here for?'

'I've told you, he had designs upon my son.'

'Not the journalist. Stephen Sutler.'

'I do not know that name.'

'I'm curious about why you would do this for a person you don't know?'

Zubenko seemed to sense Parson's exhaustion and echoed his weariness. 'Whatever I say you will search in any case, and you will find whatever you will find. Because this is what you want to do.'

'I want to find the man you were photographed with. His name is Stephen Sutler. I don't understand why would you risk anything for this man?'

'Show me these photographs.'

Zubenko asked Parson for a cigarette. Parson took out his cigarettes and looked to the guard, who appeared so sleepy, so disengaged, they both could have walked free.

'Bastian will cause you a great deal of trouble.' Parson offered the packet, and Zubenko's hand flicked quickly, dismissively at the guard.

'Bastian? I have never heard of this man before today. He tells me that he is a cultural attaché. I tell him my sons like films, they go to museums, they like the art galleries, if he is a cultural attaché he should be speaking with my sons, I do not know him. I have not met him before. I have no dealings with a cultural attaché.'

'He says that you know nothing.'

'He says the same of you.' Zubenko leaned forward for a light then took in a small breath. 'Perhaps I don't know so much. There are always conspiracies. But what do I know?'

Parson set the register on the table and began to leaf through. 'Why did the police confiscate this?' The information, from what he could see, appeared two years out of date.

'Because they had to take something. Much like you, they cannot be seen to leave a building empty-handed.'

Parson idled through the pages and found bookings for trips, a small map at the front, everything long out of date.

'My doctor,' Zubenko continued, 'allows me to smoke. He is irresponsible when he thinks that he is being realistic. If he demanded that I follow a more rigorous regimen I would do exactly as he asks.' He drew in a long breath and held the smoke for the moment. 'Between you and me, I have no objection to what you are doing. In three or four hours it will probably be over. The problems you are concerned with are happening a long way from here. The Americans are unhappy and they want a man who has stolen from them, and for this everyone will make a lot of trouble for themselves. A lot of trouble for you.'

There were, Zubenko became wistful, plenty of witnesses who would testify that the German had thrown himself down the steps like a crazy man. His two sons were educated men, trained in Germany and treated like Turks, so there were any number of reasons why they might feel disinclined to be courteous to a German journalist, although, personally, he could not imagine his sons being so rude.

Zubenko turned his attention to his register. His forefinger rested on the map.

'What are you telling me? Malta? Is that what you are saying. He has gone to Malta?'

Zubenko gave a quick glance at the guard then looked hard at Parson and impatiently tapped the page. 'I am not, personally, telling you anything.'

Parson waited for a call from Gibson. He stood at the window and looked out on a tiled courtyard at two cats. One on a stone seat, the other in a dry flowerbed stretched out in prickly disregard.

When Parson answered he gave his news in one clean breath: 'I've found him. Sutler is in Malta.'

Gibson rushed him through the details. Parson described his meeting with Bastian.

'People aren't interested in Sutler any more. It's gone so much further than that. Does it make any difference if HOSCO did or didn't send other people on his trail?'

'They send one man to look for a man who has stolen fifty-three million?'

'That's how it looked when it started. At the time no one had any idea it was this big. They have a team in Syria, they have a team in Iraq. I have it on good authority.'

'From HOSCO?'

'On good authority.' Gibson's voice rang with boredom.

'What if Bastian is right, and Sutler is nothing more than a distraction?'

'I don't see the point.'

'But that's the point. All of this money is missing and no one's interested in who did it or why. The entire budget for the Massive has disappeared. HOSCO is losing most of its government contracts. The company is being split into smaller units. Bastian is right. Sutler is a distraction. I don't think they want to find him, not HOSCO, and not Washington. I don't think they're looking for any particular answer for any of this.'

'You have to think about the bigger picture. This is about individuals who aren't comfortable with their association with the entire thing.

People who supported the idea from the start. It's looking very embarrassing. Not only for HOSCO. There are people who backed the Massive who would rather it was all allowed to die down. HOSCO might be in pieces but these people want to survive.' Gibson drew in breath. The technology transformed his voice to a powdery whine. 'I need you back in Iraq. If the Americans aren't happy it doesn't matter. Time to pass this on. We've done everything they've asked.' Gibson continued to explain himself in headmasterly terms, allowing no break, no opportunity for interruption, no avenue for disagreement. When the monologue stopped Parson found himself listening to static.

And so they expected him to return to Iraq.

Smarting from his discussions with Bastian then Gibson, Parson found a kiosk on the Heights overlooking the strait and sat with his back to the city. Talking to Gibson was a mistake, the man, isolated, knew only what others told him, and now because of this Parson had cancelled himself out of the investigation. Bastian's assessment wasn't wrong, no one was interested in Sutler any more, and by locating the man he'd completed his job. *Tell them you've found him and see what happens.*

A late-afternoon fuzz settled between the hills as fog returned to the city from the sea. In front of him, attached to the side of a building, ran a row of billboards set to face the train track. In one image, an advert for a phone company, a smiling woman threw back her head, laughing perhaps; a tag line ran beneath her asking: . . . *where are your friends tonight?*

Parson turned to face the city. None of this sat right. A disjointed view, a city made of parts and pieces, of apartments, offices, mosques, immediately behind him a church with minarets. What could he be certain about? Exactly what did he know? He knew that HOSCO, having suffered so many blows, could not afford further speculation or humiliation. The disintegration of the company was in process, not quite begun. No one wanted to hear about Sutler.

A new gesture needed to be struck.

He decided to speak with Geezler, blow a little smoke and see if he could revitalize his interest in Sutler. Quite how he would manage this he couldn't imagine.

After three fortifying beers he called Paul Geezler directly. 'I have him,' he said. 'Sutler. He's headed to Malta.'

The response from Geezler sounded unenthusiastic, and Parson guessed that he had spoken with Gibson, that the matter was concluded. 'We'll take it from here.'

'I think I know who he is. I know his name isn't Sutler.'

Geezler said he hadn't heard properly and Parson repeated the information.

'His name isn't Sutler. Do you know what a sutler is?'

'So, what is his name?'

Parson hadn't thought this through. He pinched the bridge of his nose to concentrate. 'We should be looking at other employees. Maybe the reason we can't find anything about Sutler in the UK is that he doesn't live in the UK. Maybe he's never worked there? Maybe he works somewhere else? Maybe he's one of your employees from another region? You have people in Amman, Saudi, Afghanistan. We should be looking elsewhere, London is a distraction.'

'Do you have any idea how many people we hire in Europe alone?'

'Why Europe?'

'Or Saudi. Or Kuwait.'

On a note beside his glass Parson had written '*Paul Geezler*' and circled it twice. He needed a different kind of lever, this wasn't going to work.

'Do you know Sutler's name?'

'I know what his name means. I know this is a game. I know it's not his real name.'

'So, again, you have nothing for me?'

Parson turned the paper over and felt a sting: every time he spoke with Geezler the man asserted himself, humiliated him in small, indirect ways: through his exactness, through his precision, as if Parson would never surprise him, as if Parson would always fail to produce a result.

An idea came to him with absolute clarity, born from a moment of spite. 'He's using your name.'

Geezler's hesitation suggested new possibilities. 'I don't understand. You know his name or you don't know his name?'

'His name is Paul Geezler. This is the name he's using?'

Again Geezler hesitated. 'I don't understand what you're saying. How is he using my name?'

'I'm sorry, this line is really bad. I can't hear you. You keep dropping out.'

Parson cancelled the call, placed the phone on the bar, and then settled his head against the counter. What game was he playing?

His phone immediately began to ring. He watched it vibrate across the counter. The barman, wiping glasses, approached him and he signalled for another beer.

Parson answered the call when the phone began to ring a second time. He wiped his hand across his forehead. 'Sorry, I couldn't find a signal.'

He heard Geezler draw a long breath. 'Tell me what you know.'

'I know that Sutler has used your name for his hotel and travel bookings. Some of his reservations are booked under your name. Why would he do that?'

'I don't know,' Geezler answered. 'I have no idea.'

'He's also starting to spend money. He booked a room in your name in Istanbul. There is a room booked in Valletta in the same hotel chain, in the same name. Why would he use your name?' Parson looked about the bar for details, for any information which would help. 'It looks deliberate. It's not a common name. There are other interests searching for him now. American and British. Sutler has to know this is happening, and he's deliberately using your name. He's spending money. He's making a point. I don't think he's running any more.'

'And this changes what?'

Parson played a hunch. 'If you knew him it would change a great deal.' He waited, but Geezler didn't reply. 'If he ever worked for you?' He waited again, still no answer. 'Paul, consider. How many men have you worked with in your years at HOSCO? It could be someone you worked with a long time ago. Someone who is trying to confuse the picture by drawing your name in? How troublesome would it be if this turns out to be someone you have worked with, someone you know? I want to go to Malta.'

Geezler answered immediately. 'You're certain he's in Malta?'

'Positive. And I can't do anything unless I'm there.'

Geezler said that he'd be in touch. 'We can't have him stamping up dust. You understand? No complications.'

'You want him found?'

Once again Geezler paused.

'Is this question serious?'

'Completely.'

'It's true,' he said. 'If he shows up now then everything is in question again. The damage is done. It might be better that he remains undiscovered.'

'Send me and we will discover who he is, and if necessary, he will remain unknown.'

'What are you saying?'

'I'm saying I can clean up whatever noise, whatever mess, he makes.'

The call from Gibson came almost immediately. In a crisp voice he changed his instruction.

'I've heard from Paul Geezler, he wants you to go to Malta. Go there directly. HOSCO are prepared to set more money aside for you to find Sutler, a fund to ensure that he stays out of the picture. Don't allow him to cause further embarrassment. If you find him you will need to negotiate with him, find out what he is doing and what his intentions are.'

Parson returned to his hotel and booked his flight online and a hotel in Valletta, then for good measure he booked a room for Sutler at Le Meridien, Balluta Bay, under the name Paul Geezler. He sang Geezler's name as he typed.

VALLETTA

5.1

Anne walked through the three rooms that made up the apartment, dissatisfied with the arrangement. This was not the villa she had imagined, and definitely not what was promised – a separate, remote, and spacious palazzo. Instead she had a shared house on the edge of the village, with nine small apartments each rented out and an empty pool. Eric's bed, a folding cot shunted under the windows, didn't appear solid enough and looked like an animal trap, with springs and wires ready to snap shut. He wouldn't complain even if it gave him backache, not immediately. She would hear about it in years to come at some holiday meal. *That room in Malta*, he'd say. *That awful bed. Can you remember?* And then some story. She couldn't remember if he still smoked, another one of his deceptions. If he did he could stand on the balcony and smoke and she wouldn't need to know. The balcony gave him privacy. He'd like the room, but hate the bed. She had to remind herself of his age, that there were boundaries not to cross, information she did not want to know. She thought of him as someone who switched on and off, a boy who logged into accounts and identities, someone who could choose when to be her son: as if this were an account into which he could or could not log into. Weren't there boundaries also for her, didn't he need to know this also? It occurred to her with sudden dread that he might – as he had at home – seek out men.

Shabby, unkempt, and cramped, wasn't this his assessment of the hotels and *casas particulares* Eric had stayed at in Cuba with her husband? Anne wondered why she had thought that this arrangement would work, of how much easier it would be if she simply hadn't arranged the holiday. She looked at the cot and couldn't see her son, an adult, sleeping in it, but the cot came standard in these kinds of apartments, which was better suited anyway for a couple, rather than a mother and her adult son.

The prospect wasn't quite desperate. Its best feature, a view over Marsaskala, the village, and the bay, would please him. For the last three mornings she'd sat out and watched the view change, watched how the light reverberated through the room carrying colour so that the room and the view seemed continuous. Even in autumn the sun came through with a clear brightness and the water remained an intense blue, almost unreal, and she could feel the colour as she looked at it, the fulsome blue of a deep sea, nocturnal and without limit. Anne regretted not renting an apartment with an extra room for him, knowing that Eric would prefer privacy over a nice view, if he still smoked he would resent having to sneak out for a cigarette. The shutters which could halve the room weren't substantial enough for him, for her. She'd lie in bed fretting over the cot, knowing that what troubled her was not the bed, not his discomfort, not the issue about him smoking.

Catching her reflection she pressed out a smile and closed her hand about the keys. She should not over-plan. If he wanted to do nothing, he could do nothing, but if he wanted, if he was in the mood, she would show him around Valletta and around some of the island. It would take a little time, she told herself, to learn how to *be* about him, to regain that ease. On the weekend they could take a boat and stay on Gozo. Despite the promise of a few trips the notion they would spend time together no longer seemed as ideal as it had on previous visits.

It was strange not to have heard from him. No text messages, no calls, and no email. Strange as it was it fitted with this new understanding. The new Eric, post-computer. Ready to leave, she called her husband and checked herself more carefully as she spoke. Her eyes were a little red from reading, from squinting at the manuscripts in the archives, considering for too many hours an evasive, slanted script. Her hair was also beginning to frizz, however short she had it cut the heat and the rain made it too active.

'You'll talk to Eric?'

'He hasn't called. He doesn't call me, he emails. You know this. If I hear from him I'll pass the message along.'

'But when you speak with him you'll not forget to ask about the flight?'

'If he calls I'll make sure I ask.'

'You'll forget.'

'I won't forget. I'm writing it down. If he calls I'll tell him his mother is worried about the flight.'

'I'm not worried about the flight. I'm worried that he'll miss the flight. I'm worried that he has made other plans. It's a different thing.'

There were ways in which her husband irritated her: how he talked without paying proper attention; his assumption that he understood her better than she understood herself; how he appeared never to doubt himself.

Leaning into the mirror she ran a finger over her lips and again looked into her eyes, the same weary blue as the evening light on the walls, a bruise, blue leaning toward violet.

5.2

Ford sat in the bar nursing a sweet local brandy. He watched three men labour up the street arm in arm, shirts undone, drunk and roaring at the rain. When they passed by the window they raised their fists and cheered in companionship for no reason he could see. British or German, he couldn't be sure. Ford checked his watch, leafed through a two-day-old *Herald Tribune*, and felt another grain of aggravation. An irritation had plagued him recently, a sense of many things shimmering, sliding along the periphery. It was the city, he supposed, the drama of tight hills, steep streets, the hint of some satisfaction waiting at the peak, just out of view, when what he needed – an idea, a solution, a single sensible reason not to go to the airport – remained far from his grasp.

Nothing in the paper interested him. The war figured in its pages without mention of HOSCO, Geezler, Howell, or the Massive, and no Kiprowski. Never news about Kiprowski. Space given instead to roadside bombs, Shia and Sunni assassinations, multiple attacks at police stations and oil refineries, a suicide bombing at an employment office. He read about the UN stalled in making any practical decision on the occupied oil-fields. The trials of former heads of state. As reassuring as this should have been, the absence of any reference to fifty-three million missing dollars increased his anxiety – the absence of news about HOSCO he regarded as suspicious. Ford folded the paper and drank up. He checked Eric's agenda, the flight would land in two hours and he needed to find a taxi.

Among the options lay the possibility that Eric had already arrived. He played this through but couldn't escape the image of a bright airport lounge, of glass doors, of an emerging group, then Eric, backpack on shoulder, lagging behind. The boy would be there, he was absolutely certain. His mother also. Ford needed to pick her out first, whatever else he intended to do. His choices were limited: confront the boy and risk exposure, or hold back and follow them to their villa and risk losing them, risk causing alarm. Other possibilities suggested themselves. Eric could arrive with the police, or the police might already be waiting and it would all be over. The notebook could be lost or stolen, the page torn out, scrawled over, the number erased. He couldn't quite picture what would happen once the boy came into the arrivals area, but he trusted that an explanation forced by the situation would flow from him. Would he be able to approach the boy, walk right up before the mother had a chance? Nothing he imagined would work.

Rain broke hard upon the street, overflowing the gutters and blacking the road with a smooth lacquer. Over the past four days he'd spent the morning searching for Eric's mother, calling accommodation brokers and agents in Valletta, Floriana, and Sliema and asking about villas. The afternoons he spent at the cafés and pavilions the beaches on the west and north sides of the island, sheltering from the weather and watching tourists, not enjoying the humidity. The only Powells on the island were British, a family from Wolverhampton booked into the Hotel Intercontinental in St Paul's Bay. A chubby family of five in matching white shorts and caps. The father bullied his family with his moods, he swapped plates with the youngest son when he refused to eat and finished his food with mixed elements of spite and silence. The daughter chewed with her mouth open, and he thought them crass until he realized that the girl had some kind of disability and needed to be told, prompted, and reminded. The realization stung – how could he not have noticed? Ford regretted not taking the exact address of the villa or the village. Such were the consequences of not planning ahead.

He didn't spend his whole day fretting. There were moments of distraction. Valletta surprised him with its café-life, old cars, walls and doorways pasted with election posters. A quieter city than Istanbul, of handsome honey-coloured stone, buildings with long ornate windows, small enclosed balconies, wood shutters, gloss-painted doors. All a little secretive.

The brandy furred his teeth, clung to his breath. Couples dressed for the opera sheltered in doorways, hailing and hurrying to taxis.

The idea came to him fully formed. He would pay the taxi driver to come into the terminal, he would identify the boy to the taxi driver, and the man would hand Eric a note saying something simple, a number to call. I'm going, he told himself as he finished his drink. Going. I'm ready. I'm going. Going.

The plan faltered as soon as Ford sat in the cab. The driver, thickset and doughty, couldn't understand a word he said. When he gestured *airport, airplane, aircraft*, his hand rising, fingers spread, he noticed the hearing aid in the man's right ear. *Lu-qa*. Ford sat in silence as the cab drew around a fountain against the flow of buses. It wouldn't work, even if he could explain what he wanted, because this broody man would draw attention to himself. No, he decided instead to call the airport courtesy phone, leave a message for Eric to contact him. He wouldn't need to give details. Just some message. If he could think of one.

Once at the airport it occurred to him to stay in the cab and return to the city. An understanding coming to him of how strange this was, of how, on some slender possibility he'd crossed the Mediterranean, point to point, when he really should have returned to Narapi, sought out Eric's notebook for himself. But fear of HOSCO, fear of the police, and a desire to push on had sent him island to island, to a bright strip of road alongside an arrival hall.

Stumped by indecision, he paid the driver and waited for the change. Rain drummed hard on the cab. The man half-turned in his seat and took a good long look.

Inside the terminal, Ford hung back beside the rental booths and cash machines. He kept his eye on the police. Three lonesome security guards. Two at the entrance, one, a free wheel, walked a length between the bureaux de change and the Hertz booth. Each of these men short, black-haired, weighty. He measured himself against them and realized that with very little effort they could catch him if they needed.

The flight, marked as landed, topped the message board. Ford watched the first passengers waddle through customs in a sudden huddle. He watched the backs of the waiting families and greeters and noticed how they steadily pressed forward each time the glass doors parted. Most of the passengers arrived in pairs and once through the gate they either scanned the crowd or walked purposefully on, burdened with luggage. He waited to see who would come forward at each arrival and had the feeling that these selections were random, as if these people did not know each other at all, as if this were a job in which some people were employed to arrive and others employed to greet. To stop himself fidgeting Ford crossed his fingers in his pocket.

Eric Powell did not appear.

Family groups welcomed friends and relatives, held them close, hugged and kissed with closed eyes and compressed smiles. Fewer arrivals now, and still Ford kept his eye on the greeters. If he could not identify Eric's mother he would miss his only opportunity. No older single women stood out, so he walked to the back of the hall and stood by the automatic doors with an impatient eye on the arrivals. The security guards came together, chatted briefly, parted. A stubborn indolence locked in their movements.

Within half an hour the last fussing groups trooped out of the building and the taxi drivers returned to their cars, which left one lone woman in thin summer slacks and sandals, waiting with her back to a rental counter. Her hair a little flat from the rain, her shoulders damp. Her arms tightly crossed. The security guards stayed fixed to their positions.

The woman strained for a glimpse about the barrier. Ford held his breath. This woman, crisp, slight, dressed out of season, self-aware, a kind of quote about her ash-blonde hair clipped straight at her shoulder: the image of a professional who has to work at appearing casual. He wouldn't have guessed that this was Eric's mother, although the connection, now drawn, could be seen. A face too gaunt, too white, too proper: Northern European, while Eric appeared southern. Latin, perhaps Spanish.

She stood on tiptoe each time the automatic doors parted. She walked the length of the arrivals hall, past the clean line of desks to a solitary attendant closing the airline booth. She spoke with the attendant and appeared distant at first, then irritated. He could hear her questions repeat through the hall. *Was it possible that someone might still be in the baggage area? Or the toilets? Was there any way of checking?* Without a satisfactory answer she returned to the gate.

The announcement board began to clear. Air Malta, Libyan Arab, Lufthansa. The flights from Tunis, Bari, Zurich, and Tripoli disappeared in a neat clatter as the slates slapped blank. Ford stood under the board, head upturned, giddy at the idea that this was it, he'd found the boy's mother but not the boy.

That Eric hadn't appeared wasn't exactly a surprise. For the boy to walk through customs bag in hand would be too simple a solution. Too occupied to properly consider this, the fact hung before him undigested. No Eric: no money.

The woman waited close by the gate. She asked the security guards if there were people still to come through. The men shook their heads and directed her back to the airline desk. As she returned through the hall she brushed her hair back, self-conscious now, a little brusque.

Ford followed behind and when the woman stopped at the desk he stood slightly behind and slightly to the side, as if waiting in line, close enough to listen. His only interest now was to locate the villa.

The woman gave a tight smile to the clerk. 'Would you check to see if someone was on the flight?' English, yes, but American also. The slightest lilt. She'd noticed Ford, half-turned, was that for him?

The attendant gestured at the computer and explained that she'd shut down the system but couldn't in any case give information about the flight.

'I understand. But I'm asking about my son. You can look, can't you, for my son? The passenger list? It can't be complicated.'

The attendant looked at her, cold. A girl, hard-faced, eyeliner etched fine along the lower lid. It wasn't a matter of simplicity, she explained. She simply didn't have the information.

'My son's name is Eric Powell. My name is Anne Powell. I have my passport. Check under Henderson. Eric Henderson. He might be travelling under his father's name.' The idea clearly aggravated her. She pinched the brow of her nose, summoned patience. 'No. I bought the ticket. It's Powell. He should be under Eric Powell. Has everyone come through from the baggage area? Could you check? They obviously won't allow me through.'

Ford gave no visible reaction to the name.

The attendant, stiff in every gesture, said she would return.

'It's Powell,' Anne repeated. 'Eric Powell.'

Anne Powell waited at the desk, one arm on the counter. She turned to Ford with an expression of fixed irritation, and they looked at each other without remark, her eye catching on the small cut under his eye.

'I'm sorry – are you waiting?'

When the attendant reappeared through the automatic doors, Anne immediately forgot her aggravation at Ford and walked toward her, brisk and clipped. Ford followed after, then asked the attendant himself if everyone had come off the flight. 'I'm also waiting,' he explained.

'I'm sorry?' Anne stopped and appeared puzzled. 'But do you have information about my son?'

Ford tipped his head to the side and blinked. What was she asking?

'Do you work for the airline? Do you know if my son was on the flight?'

'No,' Ford replied. 'I don't work for the airline.'

'Then can't you wait?'

Stung, Ford stepped back.

Anne turned to the attendant. 'Did you find anything? Was he on the flight?'

The attendant gave a sympathetic frown as she explained that she had asked someone to check the arrivals area and the baggage-claim area, but there was no one there, and no one either in the facilities, the toilets. The manifest did not show her son on the flight. 'I'm sorry,' she said. 'I'm really sorry, but there's nothing we can do.'

The security guards hovered close by with folded arms.

Anne Powell stiffened. 'What do you mean, he wasn't on the flight? Are you certain?'

The attendant apologized and slowly repeated that there was no one travelling under the name of Eric Powell. No such name on the manifest. It happens all the time.

Ford asked if *everyone* was off the flight and the attendant patiently repeated the information. 'Sir, everyone has come through.' The halls and lounges were all clear.

The guards grouped closer.

'I don't understand. What are you saying? Was he taken off the flight? Would you know if he had changed his booking?'

The attendant explained that it would be impossible for her to know what Anne was asking for, not without a booking reference, and this information couldn't be retrieved right now. She would have to wait until the morning. She could either come to the airport or go to their offices in Valletta. Irritated, Anne turned smartly about and walked to the exit. The guards separated. The slap of her sandals clacked through the hall.

Ford followed quickly after and came purposefully out of the terminal to find Anne Powell with a mobile phone in her hand: if she was speaking with Eric he wanted to hear. Instead of speaking, she snapped the phone shut and signalled a cab.

The woman hesitated before she opened the door, as if she sensed him, Ford couldn't be sure, but some doubt caused a momentary pause. When she sat in the cab she closed her eyes, and Ford saw her mouth the name of the village, the name he had read in her letter: *Marsaskala*. She leaned forward, the cab window opened, and she repeated the name to the driver, a hint of anxiety over her pronunciation. *Marsaskala*.

He watched the cab round away from the terminal and repeated *Marsaskala, Marsaskala*, into the night.

The next morning Ford set up post in a café opposite the airline office. He sat in the shade cast by a statue of Queen Victoria, obstinate, pig-faced, the grey stone flecked white. He watched the streets, the offices, the surrounding shops with a sharp eye, alert to every change. The sun slowly crossed the square. Anne Powell did not show.

Ford revised his plan. He would go to Marsaskala and find a similar café where he would wait. The waiter brought him a newspaper which he scanned quickly for news of Howell, HOSCO, and again found nothing.

5.3

The rain stopped in the late afternoon, the sky broke in one moment from grey to a mellow blue. On his way from his hotel to the bus terminal Parson browsed through a small market. He took with him a baseball cap he'd bought in Istanbul, and bought a plain short-sleeved shirt, a pair of Oakley-style sunglasses he thought he might keep afterward, but chose them mostly because he thought *this* or *that* suited his idea of Sutler. In front of the mirror he asked himself how a man who'd stolen fifty-three million might dress. This shirt, that shirt? These sandals, those flip-flops? He found himself distracted by the buses rounding the fountain with their white roofs and sunny yellow sides, as if these were familiar to him, part of a memory – or were strangely some kind of a joke, too small and toy-like to take seriously. *Laura would like this*, he told himself. *This would be her thing.* Finally, everything ready, he was satisfied that with the hat, shirt, sunglasses, he looked nothing like himself. As there were no photos of Sutler, this would have to do.

He took the bus to Msida then walked along the marina, the sunlight beginning to dry the pavement. He liked the view across the inlet, the watchtowers at the bastion walls, the water flat in the bay, silver and alive, the boats, their ropes slapping at masts, and how lazy this appeared, picture-perfect: there wasn't anything he didn't like. He began to prepare for Sutler's departure, thinking all the time what a great game this was, and under the name *Paul Geezler* he upgraded the room he'd reserved at Le Meridien to a suite, then booked a passage, second-class, from Valletta to Palermo and on to Naples. If he was to negotiate Sutler's silence, then he would first need to find the man, and this could take some time. Sutler, under Geezler's name, would travel at night to Sicily, and slowly roam the small Italian islands on his way to Naples. He asked for the booking information to be passed to the hotel and gave a fake credit-card number, knowing that this would be reported first to the hotel, then to the police. He couldn't gauge the amount of fuss he should stir: how much trouble would a man who'd stolen fifty-three million dollars make? He couldn't guess. Just as he had no real knowledge of what fifty-three million dollars would look like, or what, in any real sense, fifty-three million dollars actually meant in any meaningful way. What, for example, would that be in yachts? Fifty yachts? Thirty? Twenty? Every yacht in the harbour? How much did these things cost? It wasn't that he didn't care, but imagining the harbour without thirty or fifty yachts made little difference to him and would barely alter the view. Busy or empty the harbour would appear just as picturesque.

A kind of melancholy grew in him as he walked along the promenade. It troubled him to realize how so much money could mean so little.

While most of the boats were occupied, only one appeared occupied, with a couple on board, who were preparing for the evening: *L'Olympia, Bordeaux*, stately white and blue, held herself politely in the water.

On a first pass Parson saw through to the saloon. A woman in the lower cabin, dressed in a long cream-white dress, prepared for her evening. Above, on deck, a man in slacks, similarly presentable, busied himself tying ropes, securing blue hoods over white seats, a cloth in his hand, an impatience about him. Two worlds in one view. The man on deck, in public. The woman alone, studying herself, hand roving down her stomach, shifting from side-view to three-quarter to make up her mind. Sunlight softly breached the port windows and bounced off the water, the water, untroubled, stirred with a soft lick and a lap.

Parson found shade and sat on the wall so that when the man straightened up he would look across the promenade and see Parson, or rather, not Parson but Paul Geezler, or rather, not Geezler, but Stephen Sutler as Paul Geezler. For this to work they would need a name, Sutler or Geezler. Either would work.

When the couple came off the boat Parson stood up, brushed pastry flakes from the front of his shirt, and swore loud enough to get the man's attention.

He followed them along the promenade's curve. As they walked the couple admired the boats massed about the slat-wood piers before the Sailing Club. He allowed them to move ahead certain that he had fixed himself as an event in their minds.

Once the couple entered the restaurant bar of the Msida Sailing Club he decided to return to his hotel.

Parson reserved a table under Geezler's name at the Hotel Blass Grand – why be subtle now? If Sutler had money, this would be the time to spend it. He leaned over the counter as he made the booking, spelled out the name, insisted that the clerk repeated it, and gave him a tip for pronouncing it right. After roughing it in Iraq and Turkey, the luxury of the Blass Grand would be impossible to resist, and Parson wanted the idea put out that Sutler was beginning to spend his money. The hotel sat on the harbour edge, elegant in the day, but splendid at night with strings of light reflecting in the bay from the terrace, the city appearing as an extension of the hotel, as wings opening out, honey yellows and gold.

The next afternoon Parson returned in the same clothes to the Msida Sailing Club restaurant and bar, and was the only client for the first hour. When a group of women came breezily off the promenade, he assumed that they were tourists and noticed that some of them were dressed alike. He watched out of idleness as they took two tables by the windows, and realized that the women were in pairs because they were twins, not all identical, but still, twins. He counted as more came off the promenade, seven couples now, eight couples and more, all of them women, and this time their likenesses being very close: not only their faces and build, but the clothes and hairstyles were matched without flaw. Parson welcomed the diversion. He no longer wanted to think of Sutler, the whole situation having occupied him continuously for so long that the idea just tired him out.

The group of women grew, split, spread to five tables, then six: women from different cultures, some Asian, most European-looking, and different age groups, but all of them paired. By eight o'clock Parson was beginning to sober up again. The day was working in waves, dry and wet. He moved tables to sit closer to the massed twins who now gathered around a stage – a platform with a small sequinned arch that famed a handsome view of the old city. The bold fortress walls, a stone ribbon outlining the bay. With no guarantee that the couple from *L'Olympia* would show up, he began to consider another plan.

Soon, with every table occupied, the room became loud. The twins largely kept in their pairs, American and English voices rising above the humdrum. Some of the women sang along with the music and the small glass-walled room took on the air of a private party.

'What's happening?' he asked the couple closest to him. Sisters dressed in white blouses and ice-blue cardigans, their eyes the same intense blue. The women did not understand, could not hear him. One leaned closer with a smile, suddenly intimate.

'Is this a conference?'

The woman nodded enthusiastically. Her sister sipped her beer, cool and untaken with him, looking at him as if measuring him up.

'For how long. How many days?'

'Today,' the first sister answered and smiled. 'Tomorrow we go.'

Parson also nodded. He couldn't guess from her accent where they were from, but was happy that she could understand him, happy to keep the conversation small.

'To Malta.' He offered up his beer.

The women nodded politely, again with smiles, then understanding that he was proposing a toast they raised their glasses with him.

The first woman leaned forward and indicating the room with one finger she said something that he couldn't hear, then sat back and nodded again as music began to play. The women turned to the stage.

On the stage two other twins, smart and severe in evening dress, began to sing. Microphone in hand, they leaned shyly forward to read from a monitor. The first few bars played too loud, soon quelled, so that their voices could be heard, sweet and fresh, and Parson thought that this was something of great beauty. Delicate and shy, their voices seeped across the room, singing easily of love and loss to the cheers of their friends and a synthetic beat – and while they looked similar, moved with the same gestures, sang with similar voices, it was the slight mismatches which kept his attention: one hand slightly out of time, one word sung a little faster, or clipped a little short.

The sentiment woke in him a longing. And where were his friends? A serious question: where was his room of people ready, rowdy, happy for him? Where were these people after all his years of labour, the constant moving, the broken associations, and the endless starts? Parson sang along, the table sang along, the women looking one to the other as if one common thought passed between them.

The couple from the boat sat at the bar. Heads turned to the small stage. The woman smiled, her hand to her chest, amused. She pointed to the group and leaned toward her husband, who turned and looked about the room, a realization coming slowly to him.

Parson asked if the table needed more beer. The women said no with generous smiles and Parson struck his heart in mock hurt.

'It might be my birthday,' he said. 'I might be very insulted. I can't celebrate alone.'

But the women still said no, no thank you.

He stepped up to the bar, and took a position beside the woman from the *L'Olympia*, and a smile passed between them at the strangeness of the circumstances. 'Have you ever seen anything like this?' he asked. 'There's a conference. Twins. I've never seen anything like it.'

The couple looked to each other before including Parson, a quick check between them.

'I know you,' he said. 'I know your boat.'

The woman leaned back, her husband leaned forward, hands folded on the bar. Parson ordered drinks for the table.

'You're French?' Parson offered his hand to the husband. 'You have a beautiful boat. I was looking at her earlier. Did you sail from Bordeaux by yourself?'

With an element of pride the man admitted that they had.

They spoke for a brief while, the wife remaining silent, the husband reticent but polite, his English a little reserved. Parson learned that they had come from Sicily, and before that they'd hopped along the coast of Spain. In one month they would complete the loop and return to Gibraltar, unless they decided to go to Sardinia, where the boat would be handed to another crew to bring back to Bordeaux. 'I don't want this to be work. I work hard enough.'

Parson offered to shake the man's hand. 'I understand,' he said almost with a wink. 'Paul. Paul Geezler, and you?'

The man introduced his wife, Pamela, and himself, Paul.

'Another Paul!' Parson laughed. 'What's the chances? Sounds nicer in French, of course.'

They talked business. Paul about exporting, Parson about working as a manager for one of the world's largest hospitality providers, although, he said, 'it's the worst kind of business right now.'

Parson ordered the couple another bottle of wine, mostly to bring himself back to the script he'd decided – *what he needed to say.* 'This is good. I mean it's good we've met,' he said. 'Because I'm thinking about making a similar journey myself. I'm serious.' He started to laugh. 'I've always wanted to sail, but I don't have any experience. So what does a man need to do if he wants to go to Spain or Sicily . . .' He allowed the idea to float as a possibility. 'I was hoping someone would take me on as crew, train me, or let me just outright pay. I'm serious. This isn't about money. Maybe you know someone who'd be interested? Maybe you should think about it yourselves? I'm completely serious. Take me to Spain. Why not? Or maybe you know someone? Let me tell you where I'm staying.' He wrote the details down for Le Meridien, and noticed their expressions change from blank refusal to curiosity. 'Think about it. See if you know anyone. I work hard. I'm like you. I want experience. I'll give you my name again.' He wrote out the name in capitals, P A U L G E E Z L E R. 'Nobody ever spells that right. You should hear the names I've been called.'

Back on the promenade Parson sought out *L'Olympia.* Light shone from the lower cabin. A bottle with glasses stood on deck. A plan for the late evening. A small rope cordoned off the walkway and he felt the exclusion of that one thin line. He couldn't judge if he'd done enough, or too much.

5.4

Anne waited for word from her husband. She calculated the time difference and counted the hours, working the shift between Malta and Turkey and New York. She thought to go to the airport but decided against this and felt herself constrained by the apartment, the view of the bay spoiled now, irrelevant. Eric wasn't answering his calls, *couldn't* or *wouldn't* she had to ask herself; her husband also was playing shy, and she left messages for both of them, alternating calls; at turns angry, self-mocking, bemused, confounded. What does this mean, she asked herself, this disrespect from her husband and her son? What exactly was going on here?

She spoke with Mark in the afternoon and instantly forgot her irritation. 'I thought this might happen,' she said. 'Didn't I warn you? I had an idea. I knew. He didn't call, and he usually calls. He calls me from the airport when he's going somewhere.' She closed her eyes for a fraction of a second, a tell-tale flutter. '*Usually*. He usually calls me when he is going somewhere.'

'What are we supposed to do? How long are we supposed to wait? Do we report this? Is there a required period?'

His questions suggested that she would know the procedures and she waited for him to ask outright: *What did you do last time?*

'Why don't you ask? Why don't you ask me? Do you think this is deliberate?'

'I think it's a mistake. I think this can be explained. I don't need to ask you that.'

'But his father? What if this is deliberate?'

'He's never done anything like this before. There will be a simple explanation.'

Her husband's attempt to soothe only increased her alarm. 'You're right,' she said, 'I'm being stupid. It's just one day. One day. I think we can wait. Allow him to contact us before we jump to any conclusions. I called the airline and they said he hasn't changed the ticket. But this isn't unusual. Do you know how many people miss their flights each day? It's in the thousands. They regularly over-sell because this is not unusual.' Anne pressed the receiver hard to her ear. 'He'll like it when he gets here. And the view.' She hesitated, not wanting to speak at all, but hating the silence. 'This happens all of the time. There was someone else at the airport waiting for someone who wasn't on the flight. This happens all the time.'

They agreed to wait one more day, and when she hung up Anne felt the weight of the next day already upon her and decided she could not sit in the apartment.

The phone rang as soon as she set it down. Her husband's voice sounded unexpectedly close: 'The university, they've tried to call me at work. I have a message asking me to call back at eleven, that's four hours. I'll contact you as soon as I know what this is about.'

The news had to be repeated. She couldn't understand the logic: why would he receive a message about her son through her son's university? When the core of the information struck her – *there is a problem* – she hung up.

Anne left the apartment knowing that if she hesitated she would change her mind, and the hours would pass at a painful drag and she would frustrate herself. She kept the phone in her hand, and checked that the signal was still active, and that the batteries were still charged. Immediately on the street she had no idea what to do with herself and thought that if she needed to return home to New York, or possibly someplace else, she should stay near the apartment. Stopped in the entrance, a small marble-faced hallway, she debated what to do and decided not to pack until she knew that she had to. Such a gesture would show a lack of faith and pre-empt any information the university had to tell them. She followed a path toward the village and the port, the church below strung with bare white bulbs that outlined the windows, the entrance, the single tower, and illuminated the square. But all this prettiness soured in her eye and she suddenly resented being alone. How perfect this could otherwise have been. Around her the fields were divided into small landholdings, too tiny to be of practical use. As she came to the portside she found a crowd gathered facing the darkening sea.

Firecrackers had sounded off all evening, giving the night an uneasy edge. Anne caught the first salvo as a reflection in the windows of the houses and bars along the front, a bright cascade, quickly fading to a supple reverberating pop. Again and again fireworks sparked across the harbour, skewing the sea and sky in a strange perspective. When one display ended another began further along the coast, and when that ended another started closer still behind them. Rockets fired over the church and spangled wide above their heads; the crowd leaned back to follow the sparks and showers above them, the light flattening the upturned faces.

She held the phone against her chest and felt it ringing.

'He's missing.' Her husband's voice came clear above the crackle of fireworks. 'Eric hasn't been seen for five days. His tutors called from Turkey. The last they saw of him he was at their hotel. This is five days ago. They've reported this to the police. At the moment they don't know anything. There's no reason to believe that anything bad has happened. It doesn't look like he's in trouble.'

'Five days?'

'He left his bags at the hotel but he has his mobile and his passport with him, and he has money. I think they thought he was going to come back.'

'Why didn't they contact the police immediately?'

'I don't know.'

She felt sick, she said, and sat with her back to the church. It was unlike Eric to do anything without telling anyone where he was going. It wasn't like him to disappear. He knew better than that. He wouldn't do this deliberately. He wouldn't just disappear. He wouldn't. It was too easy to imagine something going wrong. Some trouble. Some accident. The wrong place at the wrong time. Too easy to picture.

5.5

A long evening spent in Marsaskala. Ford avoided the small crowd of families, mostly villagers, people in any case who appeared to know each other. When the display began he found a bar beside the church and retreated to the counter, beer in hand. Unsettled by the noise – the gunshot clatter and sudden bangs and light firing through the square – he kept himself separate, irritated at his reaction, but the noise, each time, drove into him.

She almost saw him, would have seen him if she had looked up, but with a phone in her hand Anne Powell turned her back to the firework display, and kept her head down as if struggling to hear the person she was speaking with. Ford concentrated on the woman and thought she might be wearing the same clothes as the previous night, and looked, again, presentable, smart, cosmopolitan. This, in any case, was certainly how he saw her. Done talking, Anne Powell walked away, in the same manner as the previous night, focused, a little angry, he couldn't tell, but she cut directly through the tail of the crowd and headed up the street away from the town.

He left his beer on the counter and followed after, cringing at the expectation of more noise; finding it less easy to push through the crowd he plugged his fingers into his ears and shoved his way through. Another display started up, rockets whistled over their heads, cut out, and exploded above the narrow street. The fireworks pulsed with a stuttered delay, the thump echoed off the walls and amplified in his chest. Away from the crowd it was just her and him, the rockets' shrieks, and a steep climb. She walked without paying attention to anything around her, oblivious to the sound and the night sky burning about them. At the top of the steps she turned right, walked on, faster now, then began to run so that he thought that he had spooked her, that she had somehow sensed him behind her. Encouraged that she was head-ing away from the village Ford followed after. The villa would stand by itself, abandoned, a little decrepit. One floor or a suite would be in decent enough repair for occupation, but the remainder would be in ruins.

Anne Powell did not slow her pace until she reached a building set on its own, large and stern, sheer-sided. Up on the roof, occasionally illuminated, a number of the residents watched the display.

Eric had exaggerated or was mistaken. The villa was not aban-doned. It wasn't isolated. Neither was it private, but busy and occupied. This clearly wasn't the hideaway the boy had promised.

Ford waited for lights to come on in one of the apartments, then counted the floors: one, two, three. At the entrance he studied the list of occupants. Ca' Floridiana. Third Floor. Suite 5.

Disappointed, he walked along a black road, relieved to have his back to the display, more relieved when it finished and the night sank into more regulated noise: cicadas, the beat of an approaching car, the blank unquiet night. He asked himself what would he do as Sutler? Sutler would return in the morning, reassess his options, adjust to the circumstance. Ford would give up, surrender to circumstance. Sutler would persist.

5.6

The consul's assistant kept her waiting. Anne sat beside his desk in an office subdivided by small temporary walls, feeling a little more confident, allowing the language of the office – a bank-like odour and finish: sensible furnishings, beech-wood veneer, blue carpet squares – to convince her that business was accomplished here: at these desks, on these phones, problems were approached and pragmatically addressed. In such an environment the answers would come as a simple yes or no. Anne sat bolt upright with her arms folded, reassured by the openness and order.

On the desk, weighted by a folder, were a series of faxes and printed documents from an email account.

The assistant arrived out of breath. His shirt, crisp and white and tight; his tie, fat, red, and out of style. Not much to like, and a little too young, it occurred to her that she was saddled with a junior clerk. He made his apologies sound like an aside.

'So, this is our man. Eric Powell.' He pushed the file aside and picked up the papers, reading as he spoke. 'We don't think we have anything to worry over at this point. We have information from the Turkish authorities. They have been helpful, although there's nothing much they can tell us at this point. They are in contact with the people he was travelling with. Has your husband heard anything?'

Anne nodded. 'The university contacted him yesterday. This is how we heard.'

'So you have no news today? Nothing direct for how many days?'

'Five.'

'You heard from him five days ago?'

'No. I heard from him last week, I think last week, perhaps the weekend before. Before I left New York.'

'And is he regularly in contact – in other situations?'

'He's a student, so . . .' Anne hesitated, not wanting to give the wrong idea. 'This is very different, he was supposed to join me. According to the airline he hasn't tried to change his ticket, he just didn't make the flight. He usually, he always calls me before he comes home, or when we meet up.'

'Sometimes people don't realize the trouble they cause.'

She couldn't place the man's accent. Not southern, and not identifiably urban. She could never place the East Coast accents.

'In most cases these are simple matters. At this point there's nothing to signal that we should be alarmed. No previous misdemeanours, no offences. We'll find him in some hotel, I don't doubt. He's young, looking for adventure. He might have met someone. I'm absolutely sure.' The idea bloomed promisingly between them. With the help of Eric's companions the man was confident that they would track him down. He didn't doubt that they would soon hear from him. 'But just in case, here's what we do—' The assistant began to describe the usual checks and procedures. They were keeping an eye on the hospitals and clinics. The embassy in Istanbul would distribute a description of her son, and they would check anything that came up from such a search. In these situations they would know immediately if he was arrested or if he was in an accident. 'It happens, very rarely, but it happens. People end up in hospital without identification. It would be rare for someone his age to disappear without provocation, and from what we have here there's nothing to worry about. There's no history of drug use, no family problems. Is he most likely to contact you or his father? Mark?'

Anne corrected the officer. Mark was not Eric's father. The man apologized, still smooth – almost utterly disengaged.

'I should be doing something.'

'Until you hear otherwise you have to assume that everything is all right, and that this is, one way or another, his choice. That is, until we know something which otherwise changes the situation.'

She called her husband from the street and found that speaking increased her anger.

'They have nothing. Nothing. They aren't doing anything. The man is retarded. He's a child. They employ children who speak about themselves in the plural, who talk about procedures, about what could be done without doing anything. He talks about nothing. He said nothing. We have to *wait*. They won't do anything until more time has passed. Do nothing other than what we're already doing. He thinks he's having an *adventure*.'

'Did he say this?'

'It's what he thinks.'

'It's possible. He might have met some girl.'

Anne could not reply. The idea made her wretched. She hadn't liked hearing this from the consulate, and she didn't like hearing it from her husband. She caught her reflection and felt suddenly vulnerable speaking in the street about matters which were private. But it wouldn't be *some girl*, would it? It wouldn't be something so straightforward. It was possible that he was continuing with the behaviour he had started at home: contacting men, speaking with them over the internet. It was possible. And if he was doing this, then what other possible opportunities, and what activities were there for a young man seeking company? This potential terrified her. Nothing could be worse. Anne immediately changed the subject. 'I didn't mention that he was a climber. I should have said something.'

She satisfied herself with the idea that he was somewhere remote, with a new group of friends, people who shared the same passion. He would be climbing somewhere. Almost certainly. Somewhere remote. 'I'll come back. There's another flight on Thursday, I'll go to the airport and see if he's there. But I'll come back. I'm done with my work in any case.'

Anne made her excuses and promised to call later. As she cancelled the call she found herself alone.

5.7

Ford returned to Ca' Floridiana early in the morning in the hope that he would see Anne leave and he could risk a closer look at the property. The road that swung about the villa appeared less dramatic in the daylight, the village of Marsaskala smaller, the houses strapped to the bay-side road all faced the sea. Now that the rain had stopped, the sun regained its heat and grew fierce enough to draw scents off the blacktop, the sides of houses, the tin that covered shacks and shop fronts. A burnt fuzz of scorched straw hung in the air. Ford waited two hours. Certain that Anne was not home he counted people coming in and out, and realized it was, as he had found on the previous night, too busy. People would want to know his business. Ford returned to the village and sat out his afternoon, feeling the opportunity slide away from him. Why, exactly, had he come here? He felt distant enough now, even secure; his concerns began to shift to other matters – what he should do, where he should move on to, how he could earn money?

Without the dog tags, without Eric and his notebooks, he needed to refigure his plans. While he was free, he was also penniless.

The sun encouraged a kind of laziness, and he half expected to bump into Anne, to find her in one of the cafés or walking beside the port browsing the smaller shops. The longer he sat, the less he wanted to do. Money in any case was short. He had enough for food, and if he didn't pay for his hotel he'd have enough for a flight. He'd paid for the first night in cash and the manager, pleased to see him stay, happily allowed the nights to accrue.

He found a small café-bar on the waterfront and bought himself a beer. The café offered free internet, and lost for what to do he sat at the terminal, knees just sliding under the table, and typed in names.

'*Eric Powell*' brought almost nothing: a comic-book enthusiast, a sculptor, Myspace and Facebook pages for high-school students, a video of a boy taunting a dog. '*Eric Powell +Turkey*' returned photographs for Thanksgiving, some jokes about food poisoning. He searched for '*Anne Powell*' and found information on an exhibition in Rome, lecturers at minor US universities – nothing of interest. For '*Paul Geezler*' he found more substantial information, pages of reports from the *New York Times*, the *Washington Post*, the *Financial Times*, all linked to HOSCO. In separate reports he found that Geezler was supervising the break-up of HOSCO in southern Iraq, and that he would head a new company managing private construction and supply.

He bought himself a second beer, picked and scanned through pages, and learned that Geezler was returning to Washington to report on the decommissioning of HOSCO, its devolution into smaller companies. On an image search he found photographs of Kiprowski, a head shot accompanying a report on contractors in Iraq. On a first read it made little sense. Here, Kiprowski, looking not quite like himself – Ford couldn't recall him smiling, at least not so unguardedly – and underneath a tagline noting his death from an insurgent attack on Southern-CIPA at Amrah City.

Kiprowski killed in a mortar attack on Southern-CIPA.

A memorial to be held at St Jerome's in Rogers Park, Illinois, attended by his parents, his brothers, his sister.

He'd asked Kiprowski to come to Southern-CIPA after he'd changed his mind about Clark and Pakosta. He wanted Kiprowski because Kiprowski kept himself to himself; because Kiprowski could be asked to do something and he would automatically attend to the task;

because Kiprowski was easier company; because if Ford was caught leaving the compound, deviating from their usual routine, Kiprowski would not raise any alarm.

Kiprowski had run after him the moment before the mortar strike. The boy came running out of Howell's office with Ford steps away from the door. The boy had run, hammering down the corridor, teeth gritted, arms beginning to rise – and in that final moment he'd closed his eyes *as if he knew*.

For Ford the moment before the explosion stuck with him in clear definition. Kiprowski running with his eyes closed, sprinting hard, then everything in pieces, the corridor, the air, the ground suddenly liquid, dense with matter. Flung outward, thrown by the blast, Ford had landed on his back, winded, but was on his feet by instinct, and had run out of the dust to the perimeter fence. He couldn't see, he couldn't hear anything but a shrill mechanical jabber. He didn't ache until he arrived at Balad Ruz two days later, when his hands had begun to burn and his back had seized up. He felt like he'd been beaten, kicked, but knew, even so, that nothing serious had happened. The blast had knocked them out of the building, small enough to damage an office, but nothing of substance. His assumption to this point was that Kiprowski, two steps behind, was fine, because he was fine.

Ford drank through the afternoon, he read through the articles, clicking back through his history, refreshing his searches, checking repeatedly on Geezler, and finding in every report mentions of Southern-CIPA and the Massive. Geezler: responsible for reorganizing HOSCO contracts in southern Iraq. Geezler: negotiating on behalf of the company, apologizing for the disarray. Geezler: the only company representative ready to step up to the mark. Geezler: apologizing and accepting that HOSCO was *entirely responsible for the hiring of its personnel, but that questions about the mismanagement and misappropriation of government funding should be directed at the appropriate governing bodies*. Geezler: admitting that the money was gone. Geezler: recovering part of the funding; first twelve million, then five, then another thirteen. Geezler quoted: *the company can no longer continue to operate along these lines without accepting responsibility*. Geezler: HOSCO operations must be redistributed, the company must be reorganized, restructured, rebuilt, *trust needs now to be earned*. Geezler: architect and director of a new company, CONPORT, taking over the support contracts for US military in southern Iraq. Geezler: the man of the moment.

He drank. He paid for the beers one by one to keep a check on his money, each time leaving a small tip. In the late afternoon he asked for a telephone, *international*, and the barman pointed him to a corner store where he spent the last of his money on a phone card.

It took a while to find the company number. Geezler's extension he could remember: an easy rhythmic 6363. He could not remember the direct number for the company, nor the man's private number, and could not find the line for the government offices at Southern-CIPA – it occurring to him too late that there was no number because Southern-CIPA no longer existed.

Central-CIPA government operations in Baghdad were split across divisions. Dealings with HOSCO, with outsourcing, with contractors, were managed across administrative departments contract by contract.

He felt them stalling, evading, every person he spoke with, and down to his last five minutes he cancelled the call then dialled the number for HOSCO at Hampton Roads, Virginia, and found himself routed to an answering service who recommended that he call Geezler directly at Southern-CIPA, although they had no number. *Don't you know*, he said, *don't you pay attention to the news?*

He redialled, a last attempt, went directly to message and found that he had nothing to say.

'Paul. Paul, I just want to know how this happened. I want to know if this was planned. If you worked this all out right from the start. I want to know if you organized this down to the last detail, had me sent me out there with this idea, so that step by step you'd end up at the top of the heap. I just want to know. What came first, Paul? Was it Sutler? How long did you have the idea for Sutler? Or was this something more haphazard? Someday, Paul, I hope we have a conversation about how this all came to happen.'

5.8

In his first weeks in Iraq, Parson had spent some of his time in barracks. In the evenings they watched DVDs in the mess hall, war films, thrillers, and when a man was shot or stabbed or otherwise killed they shouted *die* until he died, and then they cheered. They would play the scene over, with some smartarse making a mockery of it right before the screen. The same death, the same keen pain on the recruit's face, and as he folded to the floor the room rose in uproar to applaud. They watched men die and quoted these deaths, walked into rooms with a stagger, hand to heart, hand to guts. Like the phrases they repeated to each other, like the nicknames they were given, these copycat deaths became part of the language.

Through his last night in Malta, Parson dreamed of endless endings. Falling, shooting, stabbing, suffocating: actions stopped before a final result. He woke and returned to these dreams, these quotes of other deaths, and woke again laughing at their absurdities.

Today he would call Geezler, let him know that Sutler was heading to Palermo, returning to mainland Europe. He was close now, *closer*. So close they walked practically side by side.

The last news on Sutler would not come for a while – not until he'd marked a trail through Italy, the south of France – names span in Parson's mind: Corsica, Sardinia, Slovenia, Croatia – places he was keen to visit: Sutler would be busy before his final confrontation. At some point, this Sutler would learn about Parson, and Parson would negotiate a settlement with Sutler before the man disappeared permanently. He couldn't decide how obvious to make this ending. There needed to be some back door, some possibility of a sequel because the real Sutler might show up, in which case Parson would have to admit to a certain ineptitude. *I was working on my own. Following my own nose. I did what I could.* But by then, really – three months, one year – what would it matter? It was equally possible that the real Sutler would simply evaporate, just disappear into some white fog on some white landscape. But thanks to Sutler, Parson had hoisted himself out of the Middle East: no longer the available man on the ground.

Parson called his wife: *Laura, listen. You pack. You put together what you need. You make arrangements for your mother with your sister. Leave as soon as you can. Find a cheap flight to Naples. You don't need to think. You only need to say yes.*

He held the phone away from him, hand over the receiver, high above his head so that he would not, for one moment, hear her reply, so that he would not feel disappointment in her excuses, her hesitation, or her refusal, so that he would not need to offer encouragement or rebuttal. And so he waited, marking the time it would take for her to come round or reject the idea.

With the phone high above his head he let her thoughts spill out above him, thinking, for the moment, that this might be possible, and that what might be possible at this point would be good enough. And with that idea satisfaction burned through him.

NEW YORK / KOBLENZ

6.1

The idea that she should speak to a private investigator came from her friends, the ones facing divorce, bankruptcy, or abandonment by husbands and partners, and for a while, being reluctant to enter this damaged world, she resisted the suggestion. But within two months of returning to New York, Anne realized that the various embassies and agencies were coming up with nothing and were starting to avoid her calls: the search, which was never a proper search, had no impetus and no direction. Hiring a private investigator became the most logical, and necessary, next step. She arranged an appointment with a Manhattan firm, Colson Burns, who came recommended as the best of the best; the most professional, the most discreet, and the most thorough, although this came at a high price.

The company agreed to undertake an initial assessment before they took on the case, a good number of missing-person cases were handed over to federal or state agencies, they warned, as they often involved prosecutable offences which came to light through their investigations. She needed to understand this – if they found anything illegal they would always hand the information to the appropriate authorities. It would also, possibly, draw up information about her son she might ordinarily choose not to know. Anne said that this was not an issue. She didn't mind what they discovered, as long as they found him.

On her first visit to the company, the offices, being so deliberately against type, confirmed the rightness of the decision. Airy, bright, on the forty-third floor overlooking Fifth.

She arrived exactly at the time the meeting was to start and found herself uplifted by the bright lobby, polished concrete walls, and a series of drawings by Cy Twombly mounted along the corridors, strange investigations themselves, fine pencil lines irritating white fields, words or fragments of words suggesting logic, or sense to be made.

She was interviewed by a woman, Marcellyn, who would collect everything they needed for their *primary assessment*. Dressed formally in light pinstripe suit, lawyer-like, pale, she made listening a hard

213

physical fact, her face and body set in concentration. Like visiting a doctor. The woman's attentiveness made Anne question herself.

She told the woman facts about her son that she had not yet expressed out loud. She spoke about the computer, the recovered files, her son's attempts to contact men, and her fears about these men. Marcellyn listened, nodded, and waited for Anne to break before picking up her pen, uncapping it, and writing herself a note. This rhythm continued through the interview. She would listen, and then she would write.

'And this was your computer?'

'Yes.'

'And you have deleted these files?'

'Yes. I think so.'

'But you have the computer and we could examine the hard drive?'

'Yes.'

The woman laid one hand on her notes. She had an outline, she said, which was a good start. She would contact the university lecturers and collect their testimonies, their outlines, but what she wanted to do now was draw out a timeline. Anne's timeline. Marcellyn drew her pen elegantly through the air. 'It helps to understand the sequence,' she said, 'from each perspective. It really does.'

Anne looked to the windows. The building seemed to give a giddy shift to the side, a view of sky, an unbroken grey, unfathomable. Aircraft level to her view.

In the months since her return from Europe not one person had asked for a simple recounting of what had happened, a simple step-by-step, not even Mark. Everyone already settled into their own idea, she could see it even before they spoke.

'Take your time, Mrs Powell.' The woman sat, tuned, attentive, the entire room an apparatus to focus and collect thought.

6.2

The businessman picked Ford up at Aachen service station and offered to take him south.

Rolf Ebershalder spoke at length about his country. Germany has no soul, he said. What was ripped apart is not bound together but lost.

The younger generation have inherited a place that is strange even to them. How can they know what Germany is if it is always under question?

The businessman explained that he was heading to Boppard, a small town beside the Rhine close to Koblenz. Ford was welcome, but there was nothing in the town except a fine hotel overlooking the river. Quite something. But nothing much of anything if you didn't have business there, and didn't care for history, unless you wanted to buy wine or brandy or local crafts. He asked if Ford could drive, then found a lay-by so they could swap seats.

'I drive all day. I have five people, I need more, but the taxes,' he shook his head, 'Europe is expensive, so I work and work.'

The businessman slumped back in the seat and gave directions. The road wound through the woods, beside bare green trunks, the ground copper with leaves. Rolf pointed out the hunters' hides and said he had a good story about wolves.

The hotel sat on a stone bank and commanded a view of the river. Ford parked in front of the hotel and Rolf asked him to remain in the car.

'I could use a driver tomorrow,' he said. 'There's a group of us, if you like I can arrange for you to stay in the hotel.'

That night Ford dreamed again of Kiprowski: the boy leapt forward through the dust and mayhem, not thrown so much, as taking a long lithe pounce.

6.3

The emails began shortly after her return to New York and continued through the early winter; monologues, which, at first, Anne did not answer as it seemed to her a final discussion. The beginning of a conclusion she would not welcome and did not want. Nathalie informed Anne about the briefest details of her own return, of how she had initially taken up new work at the university, but her interest in research, in teaching had diminished. 'These people are remote,' she wrote in a complaint about her colleagues. 'They know nothing about the world. Not one thing.' She imagined herself elsewhere, in London,

Los Angeles, or New Mexico, where she would wait for news, start a new life. She could not decide.

She wrote: *I heard from Martin a month ago. I knew he would be returning soon, but I didn't want to see him. He has surrendered his position at the university and now works in seclusion because he fears for his life. I don't know if you know, but he is continuing with the film – this is the reason for my writing. He intends to finish the films and to have them exhibited. I'm not sure what I think. He believes that Eric was kidnapped because of his project, although, of all the ideas about what has happened, this seems the craziest. Now he regrets ever having Eric involved. Although it is too late for this decision or such a discussion.*

The Turkish authorities still have our materials, they say that they are to be released soon, but this has been promised for many months. The arrangement is that everything will be returned to the university.

She wrote: *For the whole year before the trip Martin was in contact with an organization who work with the Kurds in Eastern Turkey and Northern Iraq. He met the group in Paris many years ago, and promised that he would do something to help with their cause. While this was only a small part of what we were doing, it became the most important part. I wanted you to know that Eric was involved in helping people come to Europe. He was helping people to make a new start, perhaps saving people's lives. I want you to think of him in this way. The work we were doing, this part of the project, could only happen if we were allowed to speak with certain people. Martin arranged for us to bring money into the country, and this money was used for the families to come to Europe. Some were in need of medical attention, and others, families, had been separated for a long time. When I think of this I think that Martin is right to continue, and that this is something Eric would have wanted to see. But everything is in pieces. I'm not sure what can be salvaged.*

She wrote: *I know nothing about the things you have asked. If he was climbing then why did he leave his equipment? There is so much that I don't understand. He would go on his own to these places. I made him promise that he would not climb, but I know that he climbed. I am certain. But I think if something had happened to him as you say then he would have been found. He had no transport, so he could only go to the places that were close, and the police checked these. It is unlikely that he would have gone to a place that wasn't already in use, a place with other climbers. I don't know what to suggest.*

She wrote: *I have spoken with Martin who has been in contact with the investigators you have hired. I have also made a statement to them. On the day that Eric disappeared the pension was being watched. Martin believes that this was the police. He thinks that they have taken Eric, because everything was taken from the room when we came back from Birsim. First Eric disappears, and when they go looking for him the police confiscate all of our belongings, all of our equipment for the project. There is hope that interest in Martin's project will put pressure on the authorities in Turkey, who have not helped, and continue to be difficult.*

She wrote: *I have a theory about travel, that if I keep myself on the move I will finally find him. I see the same faces at airports and train stations, the same people in coffee houses and cafés, the same people are on the move, and there is an inevitability that, if he is moving, then we will connect through this motion. It is inevitable. I hear him sometimes, I see him often when I am boarding a train, or when I am tired, I see someone who has elements taken from him. I see these pieces that are taken and adapted by other people.*

She wrote: *Everyone believes that there are plots. Everyone believes one or another theory. That he was kidnapped, taken as a hostage, so that he is innocent and we are guilty. Everyone believes that we are involved and that we know where he is, and there is some ransom to be paid and that we are hiding something, because it is impossible for someone to disappear so completely. They have found Eric's traveller's cheques, and it is possible that he was in Izmir.*

She wrote: *Our film has been returned. Eric's notebooks are among the last of the pieces to come back from the police. Everything is here. The people you have hired came to collect them yesterday. At last we can move forward. Perhaps there is something in his notebooks which will help us.*

*

217

Anne spent her days in the apartment. She explained to her husband that it was easier to work at home. There were politics at the museum she would rather avoid, and as long as she completed her research and met her editor's deadline then no one worried about where she actually worked.

Her mornings followed a pattern. On a good day she would contact Marcellyn at Colson Burns and work through the information they provided. Much could be accomplished from her home computer: checks and queries, messages sent. She could call and hassle the consulates in Istanbul and Ankara. She would feel herself surmounting the problem. On a bad day she curled on her son's bed, inactive, unable to move. On a very bad day she would take the room apart, carefully re-explore every drawer, every item, every moveable speck. She would take the posters down from the wall and return them with particular care to their exact place. Recently there were many more *very bad days* than *bad days*, and more *bad days* than days she could tolerate.

The habit established itself. As soon as Mark left in the morning she steeled herself to her tasks: started up her computer, set out her books, opened up the files, drew out the images of *The Betrayal*, and *Portrait of a Knight*, ready across her desk. Then – force of habit – she would walk to Eric's bedroom, and lose her day.

The last message from Nathalie knocked this schedule aside in one swoop.

Nathalie wrote: *I am glad for your letter. He wanted to see you. I know because we spoke about this, and he was looking forward to coming to Malta – of this there is no question. Of the Englishman Tom we have heard nothing. And I have held back a small piece of information from you, which, given the concerns you raise in your letter, might help settle your mind.*

Tom was at the pension for a short time. Three nights only, I think, and he shared a room with Eric, and Eric became fond of him. I thought this was only a small thing, nothing more, but it is possible that this was something more important for Eric? I don't think this affection was returned. It was just a start, but what this means I can't say. On the day that Eric disappeared Tom helped to look for him. Tom said that Eric had approached him and made it clear how he felt – when they came to say goodbye Eric tried to kiss Tom – and Tom was embarrassed. He was uncomfortable about this, I think it seemed strange to him because Eric had known him for only a few days and because he did not feel the same way.

I have found one picture, which is enclosed.

Anne opened the attached image and found a photograph of a man, taken three-quarter profile, almost in silhouette, light spangling about him, furring the image. She studied the photograph with care, and thought the man familiar, but not familiar enough to place. He wasn't a friend or an associate, she had a good eye for faces, but someone she had met or seen more casually. Recent, yes, but not so recent. Her instinct made her dislike the man – so this was the kind of man her son sought out, the type he talked with, online, on this very computer. She read Nathalie's message and tried to keep herself composed. He'd met the man in a coach station and later attempted to kiss him in a market, in public, in a small town in Turkey. This gesture seemed both rash and delicate, too tender and impetuous for a boy who solicited sex, advertised himself in online forums, spoke frankly about his experience. The pure naivety of falling so quickly for a stranger struck her as a sign of inexperience. The kiss was a truer sign of who he was, and it hurt to think that it had been refused. He deserved to feel loved, as everybody is deserving of love.

With a print of the photograph she returned to Eric's bedroom and set it on the bedside table. Curled up, hands to her chest, she told herself to sleep, and in this sleep she would figure out who this person was, or who he reminded her of; the connection would come to her as soon as she set her mind elsewhere. But the image remained locked and became immoveable. The figure stopped tantalizingly . . .

Anne called her husband, then cancelled the call as the dial tone sounded. She contacted Colson Burns and told them to expect a message with an attachment.

She spent her afternoon, and many afternoons afterward, examining the image, scanned every pixel to interpret the data, to draw out information: but returned only to the basic fact of a man, English, perhaps forty years old, thin-faced, short hair, sharp features, drawn, dark against the focused light.

6.4

To save money Ford slept in the cars he delivered rather than stay in the roadside motels. He returned receipts to Rolf Ebershalder, who never queried the expenses, and seemed happy that Ford took his work seriously and did not complain about the hours or the lost weekends. Ford, living hand to mouth, told himself that he was lucky, but understood that Rolf could terminate their arrangement at any point.

At Aachen services Ford pulled into the car park and began to make himself comfortable. He reclined the seat, tuned the radio, and took out the mobile phone Ebershalder had given him so that he would be more available on the road. Intrigued, he checked through the functions and games, and attempted to connect with the internet. With a small satisfaction he found himself online, a satisfaction which failed when he realized that he had nothing to check or search out – except for the one email account. He'd scored a line beneath HOSCO and Geezler, a temporary decision.

Doubtful that the account would still be available after such a long time, the password being the same as the account name, it opened on first attempt to thirty-seven messages, fourteen marked urgent from a man called Colson Burns, which he immediately deleted. Among the remaining messages were eight from *Nathalie_SD*, the subject lines reading: *Tom; Tom Please Open; Nathalie from Narapi; Turkey; message regarding Eric Powell.*

He read the messages in order. The first, an apology, said that she had passed his details to an investigative team hired by Eric's mother. *They want to speak with you. I have given them your details, told them everything I can remember. I hope this is OK?*

In the second message Nathalie gave details about the search for Eric: *The Turkish authorities still have our equipment, the cameras, the lenses, the tripods, all worth a small fortune. I think they mean to punish us. Everything else is in the hands of investigators hired by Eric's mother. They talk to us regularly, and ask for this detail or that detail, which gives us an idea of what they are thinking, but nothing real. They say that they have not heard from you? Are you there? Are these messages getting through? They look at what they have, examine an idea, and then discard it. They take up with another idea, and so on. On and on.*

Perhaps when you speak with them you will remember some small thing, something which helps them. For now they go endlessly over the same material. Nothing new is discovered. They take trips to Narapi, to Birsim, to Kopeckale and find nothing. Eric's diaries caused a great deal of interest, but once they broke the code they found nothing unusual, and they began to believe that his explanation of everything he was doing was another kind of code for something else. But still, even now, they have discovered nothing.

I write to Eric's mother. I cannot imagine what she is going through. I think that these letters must be an irritation to her, but I cannot stop myself from writing – and I do not want to.

I do not believe that he is alive. I do not. Is this terrible to write? It is impossible to say. But I cannot see how someone living can become so silent.

And you also do not write. I have no one to talk to. Martin will lose his work, this is certain. The university cannot get rid of me. My father gave money to the department, my chair is secure, so I have been offered a sabbatical which I will take. Returning to Grenoble is too painful.

My hope is that he has written to you, that Eric has something to say which he can only confide to you, and while we worry about him you understand, or know, somehow, what he is doing. How he is. You must write. You have no curiosity?

Her final message contained a suggestion that they meet: *I write in the hope that you will receive this. Eric's belongings will be returned to the university so that his mother can collect them. The investigators are returning from Turkey and they will leave everything here for his mother. His dormitory also is to be cleared and offered to another student. They cannot keep it. I know that you wished to see his diary, that there was something in them of concern to you. The situation is not so easy between me and the university, but I still have some friends, and I could arrange for you to see these notebooks if you want. If it is possible for you to visit I could arrange for you to have access. Let me know. I will not trouble you again. Nathalie.*

Under her name in smaller text ran an address and a contact number.

*

221

Ford retrieved the messages from Colson Burns, and read of their interest in meeting him, and their interest in allowing him access to Eric's papers if he could consent to an interview. There was a window of opportunity between their arrival in Grenoble and Anne Powell's departure. Everything, most likely, would then be taken back to New York.

The small car shivered as trucks passed on the slip-road, gathering speed for the autobahn. Ford watched traffic come and go in the long lot beside the motorway services, a kind of game, a possible pattern: one arriving, one leaving; two arriving, one leaving, as if some strategy was being played out, some binding intelligence to their movement. He had no money. Ebershalder paid him cash, gave him a pre-paid swipe card for fuel, and repaid in cash his train journeys. Not unlike the cars he was watching there also appeared to be some pattern behind his movements, when in fact there was none: this was motion which only sustained itself. He wasn't going anywhere, not unless he called Nathalie and took up her offer to see Eric's notebooks.

6.5

The report from Colson Burns told her nothing that she didn't know. The man in the photograph remained unplaceable. The irony of it wasn't lost on her: this is what I do, she complained, I study, I examine, I look for likeness, for similarities, in images, this is easy. I find one man in two paintings painted three centuries ago, this is easy, this I can do.

Despite her efforts the man remained unknown to her.

At Colson Burns the enquiry focused on two men from the Maison du Rêve. The first and most suspicious, a man believed to be working for the police who was monitoring the pension, and second, the traveller Eric had met at Kopeckale. A man called *Tom*. Tom's replies to Nathalie's emails came from different locations. The IP addresses confirmed that they originated in Germany, but never from the same location. 'The man is travelling in Germany' appeared to be as much as they could say, information included in the content of the messages. Information which was interesting because there was nothing else to focus on. The man had not replied to Colson Burns' requests, which told her that he had nothing to say.

From December 13: *Nathalie, I'm sorry for all of this trouble. The way things are I doubt I'll be able to come to the university. Is there any way that you could copy or somehow find the information I need in Eric's diaries. I could reimburse you, or pay someone to do this? Tom.*

From December 19: *I can't. I'm travelling. I can't say where I'll be next week. There are five numbers, one begins with the letters HOS/JA: followed by eight digits. He wrote this in the back page of one of his notebooks. As I remember there's a codeword, something like HOMELESS, A. Cheers, Tom.*

From December 22: *Let me know when the material arrives. Tom.*

From January 14: *I can make February, this is the soonest. Will you be there? Sincerely, Tom.* Except for one mention she found no mention of Eric, but found nothing out of the ordinary in this. He met her son by accident, shared a room, and until Eric had attempted to kiss him, he had no knowledge about his affection for him. His expression, one brief mention, was at least sincere. *I hope he returns soon, I can't imagine how difficult this must be for his family. Regards, Tom.*

Anne sat up in bed and couldn't settle into Eric's book; the stories, she found, were scattered and repugnant. No reason, no solution offered. Mark refused to read, refused to talk through the details of the investigation.

'Why don't you read this?'

'You know why.'

'No, I don't. I can't imagine why you would be indifferent.'

Mark hefted onto his side, propped his head in his hand. He took the book from her hands and folded over the pages, deliberately losing her place. 'Exercise the inner critic,' he said.

'And I'm supposed to know what that means?'

'It means you need to listen to yourself.'

'I listen. All the time. It's you who ignores what's happening.'

'No. You don't hear yourself. You tut. Four times a page. You complain in small ways. You move like you have cramp. You read this because you think it's something you should do.'

Anne removed her glasses. 'I do?' She swept the novel from the bed. 'I don't want this in my head.'

'What do you want?'

The question, so obvious, hurt when she considered it. How could he ask something so profoundly stupid?

'There are things,' she said, 'that you don't know about Eric.'

'What things?'

'It's nothing.' Knowing he would not insist on a proper answer, Anne turned to her side, her habit now of ending conversations with a hard refusal.

GRENOBLE

7.1

The train leaned into the curve of a slate-blue lake, a bank of mountains surrounded them, and as they glided almost without sound into a tunnel the view snapped to Ford's reflection. He looked, he thought, too thin. Weight gone from his face, his hair, grown back with more grey. A young couple in matching anoraks sat across the aisle, legs splayed, both wearing shorts, a fact that didn't make sense, this being February, there being snow outside. They looked foolish, a little plump, thick ruddy thighs as round as ham hocks. The girl wore an iron brace on her leg, and her suitcase was too heavy for her to lift. While boarding the train a long line of people had bottlenecked behind her, when Ford offered help she had thanked him in German, making a point of her partner's uselessness.

Out of the tunnel the carriage became brighter. The falling snow obliterated the mountain that rose directly from the tracks in simple white plates, fields sloping up, broken with black outcrops. The train's slick motion, more serpentine than mechanical, unsettled him. Anxious about his decision to come to Grenoble, he consoled himself that this was for one day only. By the weekend he would return to Koblenz and explain his absence to Rolf. On Monday he would transfer the money from the junk account. He imagined two scenarios: one in which he stayed for a period and continued delivering cars until he was certain that everything was OK; in the other he was immediately elsewhere, gone, although he could not specify where this *elsewhere* might be. Before any of this he would have to explain to Nathalie why he had not contacted Colson Burns, but could not figure a suitable excuse.

The young couple opened a pack of sandwiches and the stink of vinegar hit his stomach, and he wished that the journey was over, wished that he was in his hotel, asleep, with everything done.

Despite the snowstorm the train arrived on time. As arranged, Nathalie's brother Stéphane met Ford at the station; polite, he bowed and swept back his hair as he straightened up, then offered to take the backpack. Confused by this formality Ford held on to the pack and made the mistake of answering in French. Full of apologies Stéphane explained that Nathalie would not arrive until the following afternoon. The snow had caused problems with trains and flights out of Paris, but it was only a matter of a short delay. He would take him to the university instead, tomorrow, as arranged. Hopefully Nathalie would be able to meet them later in the day. Eric's belongings were in an office on campus, and Ford would be able to spend a little time with them. The man spoke quietly, as if this were all underhand. The university, he said, knew nothing of his visit, but Nathalie had many friends who were guaranteed to be discreet.

Tired, Ford asked to be taken directly to his hotel.

'But you're staying with me? Nathalie arranged this.'

'I have a hotel booked. I'm afraid I've paid.' Ford looked as apologetic as he could manage. He wanted to keep this brief, in and out, everything done quickly.

Nathalie's brother wouldn't leave after he'd dropped him at the hotel. The man was too attentive, and while Ford made excuses for his tiredness, Stéphane paid no attention to his yawning, his reminder of the time.

Happy to be finally alone, Ford lay on his bed. The blue floral wallpaper extended up the wall and onto the ceiling. The fidgety pattern matched perfectly so he could not find the seam. The bed was too soft and the room too warm, and it reeked of perfume, old-fashioned, rose geranium. He recalled other hotel rooms, times when he didn't have to mind the expense.

He checked the street, and half-expected to find Stéphane outside, still dithering, but the street was empty, silenced by the snow, the bulk of the view taken up by an office building.

As he undressed, Ford settled his mind over the small changes to the following day: Nathalie's delay was no inconvenience, he didn't know what he would say to her in any case. After he had seen the notebooks he would leave as quickly as he could. Most of what needed to be done would be managed ad hoc, on the spot. The circumstances themselves were so foreign – in every sense – that it disturbed him, although he could not explain why. Closer now to success than failure he decided he needed a drink, more than that, tonight he would rather drink than sleep.

*

Ford sat at the bar in his hotel on a smooth leatherette stool. The bar was nothing more than a padded banquette and a small shuttered counter, a row of optics bolted to the wall, not a bar so much as a rec-room, the same room used for breakfast. He drank the only malt they had, drank half the bottle, taking it in steady measures, using the whisky to work through the expectations for the following day, a certain anti-climax to find himself close to what he wanted. While he liked the idea that no one would join him, he regretted not going out to a bar. Although he didn't want company, he wouldn't have minded the presence of others, a distraction from his own thoughts. He reconsidered the idea when a young man in a business suit came into the room. The man also appeared unhappy at the coincidence, took the seat beside him with a small apology and waited for the desk clerk to come through from the lobby to serve him.

Ford bought the man a whisky, which they talked about, both admired, stated their preferences. An American with a name of two first names, Mark Mathews or Mathew Marks, said that he was in town for business, and after an appreciable silence Mark Mathews / Mathew Marks asked Ford if he was also in town for business.

'That's right.' Ford straightened his back and sipped his whisky.

The man looked hard at Ford, a weakness to his posture, he shook his head as if to shift an idea.

Ford raised the glass to his lips, and spoke softly over the rim. 'I know what you're thinking. You spend all day driving, or flying, or flying and driving, or sitting on some train, and you find yourself in a town you don't know and you want a quiet drink with company, but not small talk.'

The man shrugged and ducked his head. 'I won't disturb you, but small talk is fine with me.'

Ford set his glass at the bar, and pushed it back with two fingers. 'There's a parasite, a very common parasite – I don't know how I know this – in every situation it becomes something different. First, it starts as something that resembles an egg, and it gets eaten by a snail, but there's something about this parasite that makes the snail sick, so it regurgitates the parasite along with this fluid which, as it happens, is highly attractive to ants. So these ants eat whatever it is that the snail has left, and with it the parasite. The parasite then changes into something different inside the ant, only instead of making the host sick, this time, it does something to the ant's brain, and remember, this is a simple single-cell organism which can't survive on its own. But what it does is it makes the ant behave differently, and when it becomes night instead of returning to the nest as it would ordinarily want to, instead of going down, looking for safety, instead of looking for its nest, underground, it has this urge to go up. Up. As high as it can go. In most cases this is only going to be a blade of grass, because most of these ants, in this instance, live in fields. So these ants, in the evening, have this urge to climb instead of hide. This is where the ant gets eaten by a sheep, because sheep prefer to graze in the evening, and the ant is right on top of that blade of grass. And this is where the parasite comes into its own because the sheep is the parasite's pre-ferred host, sheep are the target, and once it's inside the sheep it begins to thrive, and it changes again. It becomes something new and it begins to divide and for a while there is a kind of equilibrium: the parasite helps with the sheep's digestion, and the sheep provides a happy home, until, inevitably, the parasite over-populates the intes-tine, which prevents digestion, stops everything from working, and is just a bad, bad, situation. When there are too many of them the sheep gets sick, and the parasite, sensing this, changes again, but this time, it becomes exactly what it was at the beginning, so that when the host dies or otherwise evacuates the parasite, and snails come to feast on the sheep, or on the sheep's waste, the whole process can start over.' Ford paused, and looked directly at the businessman. 'I know. You have to ask yourself if this is true. You have to ask, how is it that something without a brain can be so cunning, so in control, that's what you have to ask. Because most things with a brain just, somehow, don't have that wherewithal. Unless you understand that intelligence isn't what mat-ters here, that behaviour, not intellect, is what commands this little parasite, and behaviour, in this instance, is entirely reactive. So all that this parasite is doing is reacting to a situation. That's all.'

He stood up, feeling the whisky in his legs and stomach, and the room to be a little too warm. 'The man who told me this story works for a man who is fat. He's just fat. He's big. And he works for this com-pany, which is successful beyond belief, and it was built out of a whole bunch of smaller businesses which were brought together, over many years, to become the top of their field. But. Rather than settle with being in the middle of something big, what he did was he, the man who worked for this fat man, broke this company into pieces, or, maybe he just knocked off one piece – but he hid some money, a lot of money – to do this, and then, once everything had blown over, once that company was in pieces, or once he got the piece he wanted, he found that money, and everyone liked him so much that instead of being one man lost among other men, rather than settling in the middle, he became the only man at the top. You see this? You see how this works? That's proactive, that's being proactive.'

As he walked to the door he heard the businessman ask his name, and for one moment, before dismissing the idea, he thought to answer *Stephen Lawrence Sutler*, just for the hell of it. After so much caution, what harm could it do?

'What are you doing in Grenoble?'

Ford shrugged. 'Someone is missing. They think I have information about where he is, they think I know what has happened to him but I don't. I honestly wish I did. I'm here to collect some information for myself and then I'm leaving.' He ran his hand through the air, sawing up, free.

7.2

Stéphane arrived early and sat with Ford as he finished his breakfast. The hotel's comfort was increased by knowledge of the snow outside. Stéphane sat without speaking in a thick coat that seemed to hold cold about it. Ford thought that he was wrong about the man, he wasn't inept at all but shy, he stuttered slightly, blinked, shut his eyes when he spoke, and found English uncomfortable, as if his thoughts did not quite lend themselves to this language. He passed Ford a leaflet and suggested that they both go. Martin's exhibition was open, and it was very close. They could visit Magazin before the university. It would be on their way.

The exhibition centre, a refurbished factory with a large glass roof, a flat front, and broad hangar doors, was located at the edge of the city in an old industrial estate. Ford came into the building through a small metal door. The word 'Magazin' ran in a signature pale blue across the entire front. Inside, incongruous with the arcane industrial iron and glass building, sat an immense white cube, bigger than a house, with one curtained wall. Through this – and it took Ford's eyes a moment to adjust – was what he took to be a cinema, although there were no seats and one wall, being larger than any screen he had seen before, held a massive, pulsing and shifting digital image. An image so immense that the people standing inside the cube appeared irrelevant, diminished; mites in an upturned box.

Overawed by the scale, Ford looked up. Hands crossed the screen, red fingers of spangled light, before the blur clarified to a close shot of scrubland, or rocks and sand: a rock face. The image twisted in and out of focus, showing a sinew, white then pink, the sky, the rock face, a strange beat to the pace, slowed down and almost soundless: the entire space brightened and plunged into darkness as light swelled from the screen. When the picture came into focus it showed the wide bowl of a dusty valley, and Ford felt a pang of recognition. The shot held for a brief moment, and Ford could recognize Mehmet's van, and stopped some distance before it two figures: Nathalie, himself. Breathing filled the space, intimate, laboured, drawing down the air and calling upon the people watching to breathe in time. Not one word spoken, but Eric's breath, husky, edged with tone, just about to speak, a hesitation between thoughts. And there, bright for one moment, the camera turned to show the boy himself, his hand wedged into the rock face, hanging by one arm and smiling – dark eyes, jet black; a generous mouth – another hesitation, a half-smile held and lost.

His first sense that he was running to a plan outside of any agreement he might have made came as they returned to Stéphane's car, and Stéphane mentioned that Eric's mother, Anne Powell, was in Grenoble collecting her son's belongings from the university. The statement, which was supposed to sound casual, came out of Stéphane's mouth as a brittle and predetermined fact. Nothing casual about it.

'She would like to meet you.'

And how interesting would that be? How dangerous? Already seated and belted, Ford could see the trap, and guessed that they had no idea what they had set up. Anne Powell would recognize him from Malta, without doubt, and there would be no rational way to explain this coincidence. For a mother missing her son she would see only plots and intrigue. This simply couldn't happen.

'Will she be at the university? Now?'

Stéphane half-turned. He didn't think so, but his explanation sounded untruthful. 'I heard from her yesterday, she's staying at

Nathalie's in Lyon. She has a car to collect. I think she's in town tonight, but I can organize something for you.'

'Tonight?'

'Yes. Tonight.' The man nodded to himself. 'I think so?'

They discussed times and suitable restaurants, Ford knew he would be long gone. As soon as he had the information from the notebooks he would leave.

It wasn't until he came into the room that he realized he'd been tricked. Stéphane's slowness that morning, his suggestion that they visit Magazin, was calculated to bring him to the university at a specific time.

On the table, set deliberately in view, laid side by side, were six of Eric's small black notebooks. Behind the table sat two investigators from Colson Burns who rose immediately, hands offered in introduction, beside them two vacant seats. One of the men was the man from the bar, Mark Mathews, and he offered his hand a little apologetically, admitting that yes, it was quite a coincidence that they were staying at the same hotel.

'I didn't see you at breakfast.'

The man flushed and admitted it was a long night. Ford doubted that any of this was coincidental.

Once the men had introduced themselves they suggested that they wait. They were hoping that someone else would join them.

After an awkward wait they started. Whoever else was coming would arrive later, if Ford didn't mind the interruption. The men apologized, and seemed a little uneasy, fidgeting with their jackets and hands. First, there was the question of his name: in Eric's notebook he was first referred to as Michael, not Tom? It is Tom?

Ford nodded, 'Tom Michael.' He held Mark Mathews' eye then smiled.

Mark Mathews said, 'Oh,' simply, and returned Ford's smile, 'I see,' and drew a pen across something he'd written. 'Do you have any form of identification?'

Ford titled his head and said that his passport was back at the hotel.

'A driver's licence?'

'Hotel.'

A poor performer under stress, Ford was surprised to find that he had the situation in hand. As a man who actively disliked the pressure of small negotiations and interviews, he decided upon presenting the facts, and presented them in their simplicity, starting with the coach station at Kopeckale. These people wanted answers, he told himself, plain statements, they did not want questions or doubts.

He gave a brief description of his first encounter with the boy, and allowed the investigators to interrupt. When he answered questions he made sure that he appeared thoughtful, and made allowances for interpretation. Between them the group explored the inconsistencies that rose between the three versions: Nathalie, Martin, and Ford.

'He stayed on the coach, and said nothing about where he'd been. I later saw bruises and scratches down his side when he was changing, and he asked me to keep quiet because Nathalie wasn't comfortable with him climbing on his own. He said he'd made a promise to her.'

About Martin: 'Nathalie told me about the project, and Eric let me know some of the tensions. I think his interest in the project was sincere. Martin was clearly his tutor, and Eric worked for him, as you'd expect. I didn't see anything that looked otherwise. In private, I think he wasn't impressed by Martin, he didn't have much respect for him. I think he found Martin hard work. They bickered in the way that people bicker when they've spent too much time together.'

About Eric's interest in him: 'I didn't have any idea. The last time we spoke, as I've said, I was waiting for a bus and I wasn't paying much attention, and he was annoyed with me. I really didn't catch what he was talking about. He was looking forward to leaving, but it didn't sound like he had an immediate plan. I think he was going to meet his mother. We had a couple of drinks, just tea, then he left, he seemed frustrated, but nothing out of the ordinary. When I paid the bill he came back, and that's when he approached me. It wasn't much, but I wasn't expecting it. I think it was obvious that I was surprised and that I wasn't interested.'

'This is when he kissed you?'

'That's a misunderstanding. He didn't kiss me. I'm not sure what it was, but he stepped close. He had one hand on my hand. It wasn't like a formal goodbye. It was intimate. I was surprised. It was strange, he just quickly stepped up to me. I think it was just a moment where he forgot himself. I don't know what it was, but we were both embarrassed. It happened out in the open, in the market. The misunderstanding came when I was speaking with Nathalie.'

About the notebooks: 'He told me that he had a code for writing in his diary. I'm not sure what it was, but he showed me how the code worked, and took down some numbers of mine from an account number. My luggage was interfered with on the way to Istanbul, I had some things stolen and I lost those numbers. Which is why I contacted Nathalie. I assumed he'd turn up. That his disappearance wasn't anything significant.'

Ford managed to keep his attention away from the notebooks.

When the conversation turned to his own affairs he tried to maintain his command, but immediately began to feel uncomfortable.

Mathews was curious about what he'd said last night, about a friend? A business?

'I deliver cars for a company based in Koblenz. I used to have my own company, but that ended a while ago. It ended badly – business debts.'

'You were specific about a company breaking up.'

Ford sighed, a little manufactured perhaps, but not ingenuous. 'I don't like to go over this. I lost my business. I was made bankrupt, which caused – do I have to go over this? My partner took control. It was a long time ago – and sometimes, when I drink, it doesn't seem so distant.'

The men's expressions remained fixed, and Ford could not tell if they saw through him, or saw instead a man disappointed in business, in life. Someone so used to failure that he wore it with resignation.

7.3

Before collecting Eric's belongings, Anne met with the Dean of Undergraduate Studies. He appreciated her visit, he said. He *appreciated* how difficult this must be. The man spoke in a clearly prepared monologue: the tutor that her son was travelling with has been disciplined, he is no longer teaching, and his companion would also not be invited to return to the faculty to teach. The announcement of this decision lay in the hands of the disciplinary board, and these things usually took their time: but they would not return. It was hard to understand how such a thing could happen, and he felt deep regret that this had occurred.

'Eric is old enough to make his decisions. I know that. When he asked about the trip, it wasn't to ask permission. It was something he wanted to do.'

The dean appeared uncomfortable. 'So you will visit the project? You will go to Magazin?'

Anne shook her head and lightly whispered, 'No.'

The dean looked to the door and held a question to himself. 'I'm glad,' he said, beginning to rise, 'that we were able to meet.'

She wasn't sure that she wanted to take the boxes. Now, more than before, it seemed pointless. Who would wear these clothes? Who would listen to this music?

His bedroom looked out at the mountains, the tiny detail of so many trees foregrounded by snow, the chair lift, the stanchions, and the long bunker-like restaurant at the top. She had seen photographs of this view, perhaps from a postcard he'd sent her, when in the summer it was greener, or greyer. Had he even seen it with snow? She imagined he would have kept his room similar to his room at home: ordered, smart, the poster of a climber on the wall, the course books lined in alphabetical order. She imagined that having to share a room would have been an agony. The boy whose room it was now stood beside the door and looked down at the carpet, and she was grateful that he looked nothing like her son. She found it hard not to look at the bed, unmade, the quilt drawn over the mess of sheets. Eric would have kept everything in place. The room had a shiftless disorder, although it was not untidy; something hurried about its appearance. He would have kept it in better order.

Uncertain how to leave the room she wished the boy well with his studies, and the boy, breathless, nodded as she spoke. 'This is strange,' she apologized. 'I don't mean this to be so strange. I'm so sorry.'

Four students walked with her to load up the car, and she felt ridiculous following after them, redundant.

After clearing the dormitory Anne drove to Lyon. The two men from Colson Burns would be completing their interview, and she agreed to wait at Nathalie's apartment on the understanding that they would call her as soon as they had any information.

Nathalie had set aside a bottle of wine with a few of Eric's belongings, a book, some photographs and DVDs, along with a note saying that Anne should make herself comfortable, and that the DVDs contained small videos of Eric taken from the trip. Most of the photographs were of Nathalie and Eric, pictures from restaurants, a photo of

Eric standing with bags, distracted; Nathalie featured in each photo, hugging him in some, or sitting beside him and leaning into him so that their company looked easy and companionable. Anne felt a pang at how beautiful Nathalie appeared in these photographs, and felt a great sense of waste. She imagined scenarios, situations of how Eric might be living, of where he might be spending his days, but could not believe them.

She settled in front of the TV with a glass of wine and played through the DVDs one by one, pausing and freezing the image, replaying to catch his voice. She returned to one specific sequence of Eric setting up a camera, a bright blur of sunlight then darkness while his hand twisted the lens, and suddenly his face as he stared directly into the camera. So serious, so focused. Anne caught the image and sat close to the screen to assess his expression, scanning back and forward and back to measure how happy he was. This was important. She wanted the film to tell her that he was happy, and she examined the footage until she found a smile. He was talking with someone off camera, a conversation lost to the wind, when his expression suddenly brightened – and there, at that moment, she could see that he was happy, and she imagined that he was talking with Nathalie, but along with the smile came one word, spoiled by the wind, but clearly one short word. *Tom.* She replayed the moment. The smile, then one word: Tom. It was Tom. Without doubt. He was smiling at Tom. She replayed the image, frame by frame, and watched how this smile burst from him, how he couldn't help himself. She recognized him in these images, not only though the simple surfaces and sounds, but as someone who was deeply familiar to her, known and loved, as if this was something she had forgotten. She recognized his complicated expressions, his swift shifts of mood, how his mind always, just always, seemed busy, so that worlds of thought could be operating all in one instant, you would never know – and she realized, while watching his reaction to this man, that after finding the computer files she had thought of him as someone different, and she had allowed this knowledge to change him into someone she did not understand. In this footage, she found the same person she had always known, that smile, so instant, so given, and so familiar, wasn't that just like him? It was always funny how seriously he took himself, how you could ask him a question and see him think, how you could watch him consider the possible answers. And didn't he always break away with a smile? She could recall this trait from his childhood, how he could never make a choice, how he always pondered as if the idea of making any choice was just too difficult, and then, decision made, he would laugh.

She replayed the footage in real time and reacquainted herself with her son.

She exhausted herself examining the DVDs and decided to return to Grenoble that night. Although the weather remained foul with a storm pushing from the mountains into the plains, she was determined to make the journey.

In the car she could smell Eric's clothes, musty, unaired; the cardboard boxes gave off an odour of something long forgotten, ignored. The stink of stored clothes soured her stomach. Her first husband had left the house with the clothes he was wearing, money, and nothing else. A year later she had cleared away his belongings, a task which took almost no time, as there were no photographs, few keepsakes, only bundles of clothes, as if he had deliberately lived provisionally, spent his life waiting to disengage. This, she understood, was different: despite Eric's love for order, he'd left too much behind, too many pieces – she drove carefully, a little hesitant, intimidated by the traffic, and realized that she wanted this over. She wanted the investigation to stop. She wanted an end, some kind of mercy. The entire enquiry was built on an idea about her son that she no longer wanted to consider.

At nine thirty the promised storm broke and snow began to fall, wet and heavy, mesmerizing as it zipped over the windscreen, the wind picking white whorls in a black sky. Anne drew off the motorway and waited for the call from Colson Burns. She waited on the hard shoulder, hazard lights blinking, the snow quickly thickening and limiting her view. The car shuddered as traffic passed on the motorway. When the call came it brought only disappointment.

'There's nothing,' they said. 'He admits to being in Narapi, but his information adds nothing new. He delivers cars for a dealership in Koblenz. He was helpful but this gives us nothing. We showed him the notebooks, and he apologized for not being able to meet you; he's leaving early tomorrow morning. We're checking his information now, but much of what he says tallies with what we already know.'

Anne had trouble starting the car. The engine turned, slow and cold, resistant, and when it finally started it gave a feeble tremble. As the traffic passed the wind seemed to batter harder, rocking the car, and she could not see clearly enough to turn back onto the motorway. She drove along the hard shoulder at a timid pace, but the traffic would neither slow nor make room for her to merge into the lane. Where the hard shoulder ended at roadworks and a bridge she stopped the car, alarmed that she was trapped, she could not now move forward, and was locked into place by the passing traffic. She spoke out loud, leaned her head against the steering wheel, hands gripped either side, whispering, *I-don't-know-what-to-do, I-don't-know-what-to-do. Somebody, tell me what to do.* She thought to abandon the car, thinking it better to brave the weather than wait to be hit.

She called her husband. Woke him, and managed, until she heard his voice, to keep herself calm and then immediately began to cry. She heard him panic, tried to draw herself in, then quickly explained her situation. 'I'm trapped on the hard shoulder. I can't turn. I'm stuck. I don't think they can see me. I don't know what to do.'

She listened to his voice, how he came out of sleep, worried for her, advised her to stay with the car, to keep calm, to stay on the phone. 'Wait,' he said, 'and the traffic will clear. Keep talking to me.'

Why had she come alone? Why had she insisted on this trip? What had seemed important, a necessary step, she understood to be completely beside the point. She had told strangers facts about her son, facts she had not spoken over with her husband. Facts which had seemed huge, transformative, which were now a small part of a larger picture.

'I want this to stop,' she said. 'I can't do this. I can't. I don't want them to investigate him any more. It's too soon. It's all too soon. It's too fast. I want them to stop. I want this to stop. I want you to call them. I want you to ask them to stop.' Colson Burns were the wrong people, the wrong approach. What had they achieved? What had they discovered? What was their purpose except to regurgitate the same facts, strike the same bruise, insist day after day on her son's absence? I want this over. I want this to stop. I want to talk with you about Eric.

7.4

Late in the evening, Anne received a second call from Mark Mathews telling her to come directly to the Hotel Lux. He gave directions, and told her the room number. She readied herself for the discussion.

Mark Mathews waited for her in the lobby. He stood as she came through the door, and with an air of intimate care he guided her through to the guest lounge. He had news, he said, she should sit down.

Anne took a chair at one of the small tables and asked if he had spoken with her husband. The man paused and said no.

'Tell me what you have, but there is something we need to discuss,' she said, collected now, determined that this was the right decision. Heat from a small radiator hit her legs and she changed her position so that she faced the man, appeared ready for news, although, in truth, she wanted to tell him that she'd had enough. She'd practised on the way in, refining the words: *You've done excellent work. Thank you. I'm very grateful for everything that you've done. But I don't feel that this is helping. I'm sorry,* she would say, *I think this is too soon. I want you to stop what you are doing. Immediately. I do not want this to continue.*

Mathews passed over a small device and a pair of headphones and told her to listen, his voice low, but containing excitement.

'Listen to this,' he said, 'we have a development. He's speaking about himself.'

Anne took the earphones and looked at the investigator as she listened, uncertain about what she was hearing. Ford's voice sounded as part of the texture of the room, coherent, calm, measured, not quite rambling, the alcohol unlocked stories which came not quite free enough, elliptic, busy with potential.

She took out the ear-buds, uncertain about what she had heard. 'I don't know what this means? Did he know he was being recorded? He sounds drunk.'

Mathews shook his head. 'We have informed the police. My partner is with them now. The name he's given us doesn't check out. There is no Tom Michael or Thomas Michaels. He isn't who he says he is. The numbers, his travelling in Turkey. We gave the police photographs and a copy of the interview earlier this evening—' He drew a folded sheet of paper out of his pocket. 'What do you know about this man?'

Anne found herself blinking. Uncomfortable. 'I don't understand what this has to do with finding Eric. He said he didn't know anything.'

Mark Mathews flattened the paper on the table. 'There are other issues here. He isn't the man he says he is. We can't allow this to pass. We have an obligation to confirm what he has told us.' He asked her to look at the photograph. 'Do you know who this man is?'

Anne looked at the image, a printout of an ID, a man looking slightly stupid, a little lost.

'I don't know who this is. Is it him? I don't know?'

Mathews sat upright, unable to suppress a smile. 'We're not entirely sure, but the scars on his face, his travelling close to the border in eastern Turkey, it's *suspicious*. At the very least.'

Anne shook her head, caught up in his words. How easy it was to deliver. *We can't allow this to pass*, as if she also agreed, as if this decision was something she would naturally follow. 'I don't know who this is. What does this have to do with my son? Is he responsible for what has happened to Eric? Does he know where my son is?'

Mark Mathews shook his head. 'Mrs Powell? Anne—'

She pushed the photocopy away and struggled to remain calm. 'Please. Explain to me what this has to do with my son. What does this change? Will this get us closer to finding my son?'

Mathews' face began to redden.

'You told me that he had no news, he knew nothing. You told me that he has nothing to do with Eric. He said this on your recording. Has this changed?'

'We have to check, these are our procedures. He might not have been forthright. It's taken three months to get an interview with him. The only reason he's here is to look at your son's notebooks. He might be exactly the kind of man we're concerned about. He might have other information about Eric. He might not have told the truth.'

'Might? So you doubt what he told you about my son? What are you saying? Are you saying he has or he has not told you the truth?'

Mathews stood up. 'I have to be honest. I don't know. This is looking like something separate. As a witness he's looking unreliable at this moment, but until we have more information it's impossible to say. If he's lying about who he is, then he might be lying about the information he has.'

Anne closed her eyes and asked carefully. 'Does this change anything he told you earlier today?'

'What he told us sounds about right. It confirms everything we already know.'

'But you have suspicions?'

'About his name. I think he was lying about his name, and he has refused to show us any identification.'

'But in regard to Eric?'

Mathews' phone began to ring and he stepped back to answer. While he spoke he looked to Anne. 'Room nine,' he nodded, 'I'll wait.' When he cancelled the call he said that the police were coming. The matter was completely out of their hands.

Anne asked for the phone in the lobby, and called room nine. She spoke quickly and left no room for interruption. Done, she thanked the clerk, and turned to her purse to find a set of car keys. As she breathed out she felt a contraction of something more than breath, a keening sense that she was culpable for a mistake which she wanted to correct.

7.5

'*Please listen to me.* My name is Anne Powell. I am Eric Powell's mother. You spoke today with investigators from Colson Burns, a company I hired to help find my son. I have to warn you that your discussions with them have been recorded, and that they have approached the police. I'm sorry if this is going to cause you trouble. This isn't what I wanted. I have a car, outside, I will take you wherever you need to go. I think the police are coming now. I think they are on their way.'

Ford took the notes he had taken during his meeting with the investigators. He checked the numbers on the paper, then thought to write the number elsewhere, on his hand, but realized he didn't have time. He tucked the paper into his pocket determined not to lose them a second time. Passport. Wallet. Numbers.

Leaving his backpack in the room he came quickly down the stairs and out of the hotel to the street, numbers repeating in his head. His left hand thrust in his pocket on the slip of paper – everything else left behind. The snow had begun to fall in rougher bouts, and he drew a scarf over his mouth, pulled the hat lower, and squinted into the scurry. The storm brought snow and silence to the city. On a side street cut directly up from the hotel he caught a double flash, headlights from a stationary car, and made it across the road only moments before the first police car rounded the corner, soon joined by a second vehicle.

Anne hunched forward, hands braced on the steering wheel. She resisted flashing the headlights a second time as the man came toward the car, as the police were now directly in front of the hotel.

Ford sat quickly in the passenger seat, and she told him to hunch down and stay down. She slowly backed away, the headlights dim. The lights from the two police vehicles wheeled across the front of the hotel in bright loops of red and white. Anne spoke nervously, half-aware of what she was saying: they should leave, she wasn't sure how, she didn't know the city. Keep down, she said, keep down. Once they were out of the city she would take him to a railway station, an airport – anywhere he wanted – and then, when she realized that he had nothing with him, she stopped talking, startled that this was all he had, the clothes he was wearing, while the car was over-packed with her son's belongings.

She drove slowly, an agony. Came to the river and needed to decide a direction. Ford asked if he could sit upright now, and Anne looked up and down the road for police cars, but said no. No. No traffic on the street now. The snow began to fall thicker, obliterated the distance, seeped colour from the night, so they seemed to be enclosed in a bright and intimate world. Simply a car, busy with packages and bundles. A man slumped forward, his hands gripped over the back of his head.

'I have his clothes,' she said. 'Eric's clothes. I don't know if they will fit you. It might be worth looking through to see what you can use.' How vulnerable this man seemed to her, crouched in a car, entirely dependent. 'I feel that I owe you. I can't say why exactly.' And this was not true. She understood exactly what she wanted to express: gratitude that her son had met him, and that it did not matter whether these feelings were reciprocated. She was happy that Eric had felt, what, love? It didn't have to be love. She suspected it was small, a wayward attachment, one of the intensities of travel, of being loose in the world. She would settle for something lesser, it just needed to be something akin to love. She wanted to explain this, because what matters, what counts, isn't how well you are loved, but how able you are to give love. Wherever he is, whatever has happened, she can be certain of this.

There was one place she could think of to go. A small village, La Berarde, up in the mountains. A mountain hut above the village, she was not sure how far. La Berarde wasn't much, just a hostel for climbers and student groups, closed in the winter. She was pretty certain about this.

'I'll take you to a place in the mountains.' She heard herself speaking, and felt surprised at how orderly she sounded. Rational. 'There is a climbing hut. They should have provisions. Beds. I'm sure. I'm sure there will be something. I can find you there in the morning. I can bring you clothes that will fit. Tomorrow, I can take you somewhere else. I think they will be watching the stations and the airport.'

According to Eric the Glacier du Chardon was a desolate place and one of his favourites. There were some climbs there, good ones, climbs that were complex and testing. She had a box of his climbing gear, and she had wanted to drive to La Berarde, to leave his things there, the CDs, the books, the climbing apparatus. She felt good about this decision. If he came back. If. He would understand the decision. This felt right. She would go there. Leave him. Later they would regroup, figure out what needed to be done. She would help this man out of trouble.

Ford said thank you, and once they were in the suburbs she told him that he could sit upright.

They drove through empty villages. Houses of grey and black flint. The road two simple black tracks in a thread of white. She talked sporadically. Let ideas come to her. It was a shame not to have come here with Eric when it would have been busier. She knew that climbing was important to him, and wished she'd shared that with him a little more. Shown more interest. There isn't much to La Berarde. One climbing hut. She was insistent about this. The climbing hut.

Anne drove in silence. The road followed the river, veered from one bank to the other across small iron and stone bridges poised above vast gullies. The sides of the gorge rose steeply beside them, banked with fir trees, thinning out to rock and snow, below them it fell to steep shorn rock, black chasms, and white rapids. She switched off the radio and said that she knew that her son was not coming back. Was it bad to say so? She was certain. Everything was against him being alive.

The next moment she was equally certain that he was alive. You hear these stories about people, who for no reason start a new life. Define an entirely new path. There's no logic to it, but everything old has to be discarded. Some people can't settle, it just isn't in them. They just aren't attached to the world. They can't see the damage they cause. Some people. It isn't deliberate. They just can't see it.

'I don't mean you,' she said. 'I'm sorry, I really don't. I mean Eric. I think he can do that sometimes. Just drop everything and start from nothing. School. University. The move to New York. Each time it was a reinvention.' She turned to Ford, who looked ahead, the dim light from the dashboard soft on his face, a scar under his eye. 'I'm just not ready. You know. It's too soon.' She whispered to herself. 'I think you understand?'

She wiped her face, her sweater curled over the heel of her hand. 'I'll go back,' she decided. 'I'll find out what's happening. I'll come back in the morning. I'll bring food and coffee. I'll come back tomorrow.'

He found the climbing hut further up the road, beyond where the ploughs had stopped, so the path became deep and uncertain, hard to follow, and difficult to stride through. He saw the car idle, red lights blooming on the snow, the exhaust funnelling thin and low, before it slipped quietly out of view.

He pushed through the door, looked back down the path but could not see the road, and could not see any suggestion of the car. The night now entirely silent. *Some people*, she'd said, *I think you understand.* Despite her explanation, he knew that she was talking about him.

The building, a strong black stone house, similar to the houses in the village, stood as a block on a steep ridge below the stark walls of the gorge; the valley extending before it in a soft white swoop.

Some people.

The door wasn't locked, but the building was cold, entirely without heat. There were five rooms upstairs, in the first three the beds were stripped down to the wire springs. In the last two he found mattresses and thin blankets. There was nothing to burn in the kitchen, and in the communal rooms the windows, jammed open, tipped snow over the slate lintel and onto the floors. A smaller drift had settled in the fireplace. He found no food, no water, only an old travelling alarm clock and a torch with one battery that clattered about inside when it was lifted up. There were blankets, thick, army grey, and rubber wellingtons stuck upside down on pegs on the walls.

He prepared to sleep. Took off his socks and laid them out beside him. He lay on the mattress, curled into himself. His feet, his hands, quickly lost sensation, and his thoughts began to run scattershot over the same ideas:

She isn't coming back.

She's changed her mind about helping.

She's bringing the police.

THE KILLS

She's bringing the investigators.
She knows who I am.
She believes I am responsible for the disappearance of her son.
She has abandoned me.
This is a punishment.
She wants me to disappear.

The snow continued through the night, so that it did not become dark, and the room held a faint luminescence. He considered what he should do. The road would be lost now, buried. If he had climbing boots he would have better hopes of making his way forward. She wasn't coming back. His only hope now would be to walk out of the mountains.

In the morning the storm had worsened, and the flakes thickened, so that the house appeared to crouch under the weight of the snow. His hands and feet remained numb and his thinking seemed disjointed, inarticulate.

Grey rock rose close and steep on either side of the path, and although it was cold Ford began to sweat. The path ascended through a narrow pass, over small bridges, packs of ice which spanned a rivulet so blue it appeared thick with dye. Ahead of him, perhaps four or five hundred feet from the house, the valley opened to a bowl, snow-covered and rutted in broken folds, and stained with dirt: a mammoth's skin. Far below the skyline brightened along the horizon, and he imagined the streets of a vast city laid out in the plain, the dark curve of a river cutting through. In this city he would not be Sutler, he would not be Ford, but someone entirely new.

The cold, so bitter, sharpened everything to the present, and tempted him further into the snow. He shed his jacket and determined that he would walk for as long as he could manage, out and down from the mountain, into a field of white.

THE MASSIVE

MEAT

By the time he arrived at the Pioneer Residential Home in Normal, Illinois, Luis Francesco Hernandez (Santo) had discarded his full family name and much of his past. Throughout his final seven years at the home he never spoke about his family, his business, the time he spent with Rem Gunnersen at the burn pits in Camp Liberty, or his participation in two killings. Only once, in direct answer to a question, did Luis Hernandez admit that when he was thirty-two he had abducted a man from his home, drugged him with a horse tranquillizer, and abandoned him in a secure room without food and water. While he couldn't be certain he'd caused the man's death, he didn't doubt that this had been achieved.

For thirty-six years Luis suffered from psoriasis and crescent-shaped sores at his elbows and the base of his scalp which sometimes bled and set an irritation deep into his bones – about which he never complained. In the year before he died he lost his sight and became so absent that when residents spoke with him they expected no reply. The staff washed and dressed him, fed and managed him from room to room; in the afternoons they sat him in the parlour, where he leaned toward the window, his face turned to and following the sun. Everyone noticed in that last fall less and less response.

Luis died quietly, watched over by another resident, Dorothy Salinas, who'd known him from the day he arrived. And while Salinas could be counted as a friend, she knew little about him – except that he'd spent time in Montreal, and slept rough for a period before returning to the Midwest, where, eventually, he set up a smallholding in Lansing, to which he devoted the majority of his working life. In the month prior to his move to Normal, Luis signed his house and business over to his sons, who in turn sold up as soon as they could then moved their families out of state and did not stay in contact. Luis had no complaints. Only once did he open up and mention that a long time ago he'd followed a course of action he shouldn't have, and she supposed that Canada was the way he worked this out, and that isolation helped compress this problem to a manageable size.

While preparing his body the funeral home found a tattoo on his right shoulder, an eagle with a standard emblazoned with the word 'Santo'.

Luis's family, his two sons with their wives and five children, drove from Florida in a shabby three-day convoy. On the morning of the funeral, under a clean winter sky, the attendants hid in the parking lot between the fat-backed pickups and smoked dope, and they were soon joined by Luis's younger son, Rick, who spoke without emotion about his father. Luis, by his report, was a man who would not settle, a man agitated at life, deliberately at odds with everything about him. He'd lived with his father just long enough, then fled like his brother before him, because you can only spend so much time with a man who always seems to be in another room or another town, just someplace else. Although he knew that his father had spent time in the Middle East, he wasn't sure in which country – the subject never came up. There were no stories, no accounts of service, nothing to help him admire the old man. The attendants shared their marijuana and dug their boots into the gravel as they listened. After two deep tokes Rick glanced back at the figures outside the funeral home and said that he should get going, yep, they were off already; then, to their embarrassment, he began to cry. He wiped his eyes with the heels of his hands and said that he didn't understand why he was crying because he didn't, no, he never had loved the old man. It wasn't either that he hated him. Luis was difficult to be with, difficult to like, difficult to love. And when you're young aren't you supposed to be unconditionally loved, just loved without having to earn or deserve it? Rick looked across the parking lot for an answer, and found a colourless prospect of tract houses, a scuffed sky, low-slung telegraph cables. When they drove away, he said, that would be it, *finito*: no reason to return. The attendants shifted back on their heels and said, yeah, they supposed it went something like that.

Luis Francesco Hernandez was buried without the family in attendance.

Before Luis, by eighteen years, came Clark, who'd had most of his tongue cut out and his voice box removed. Mathew Clark died unattended in a private room at the BVM Hospice in Albany. Allergic to penicillin, his throat sealed and he choked. A simple clerical error. Five minutes' inattention. His funeral at the St Eustace Crematorium was small but attended by people who expected a more miserable demise, and were now faced with something sudden and inexplicable.

Clark's daughter, Elizabeth, eulogized her father as an uncomplicated man, and passed over the details of his absences, how he would up and go without incitement, and how as a child she was convinced he had another family somewhere, another more fulfilling life. She did not speak about the cancer, about the lesions that peppered the soft skin on the back of his hands, his lower arms, his neck, behind his knees, and about how he often struggled for breath. Not many knew, she said, that her father was an artist. In Clark's hands she tucked a photograph of herself taken when she was five: a small girl standing beside her mother on the banks of the placid Hudson. Her mother's hand raised uncertainly to steady her hair or wave, clouds running wild in the sky behind them. She remembered that it snowed later that day, and there was something wonderful about how the photograph appeared so summery, when it was in fact her first memory of winter, her first remembered Thanksgiving. The photo was sent to him in Kuwait, or was it Iraq: the corners blunt and creased, where the sun of that hard country, whichever it was, had bleached the colour to milky whites and yellows.

Before Clark came Watts, who at forty-seven was struck by the downtown bus at a crossing in Kansas City: heading from the Holiday Inn to his car, Watts had his mind on a bottle of bourbon.

At Watts' funeral his wife, Lara, confided to a work colleague that he wasn't as likeable as everyone made out. Throughout the service she whispered bad stories about him. How, before the christening of their only child she discovered him leaning over the crib calling the baby a cunt. He'd kept it up for an hour, she said, a revolting rapid-fire *cunt-cunt-cunt-cunt-cunt*. Even as she told this story she knew, hand on heart, that he had uttered *can't – can't – can't* in a whisper so low she'd had to kneel beside him to hear. He was sick when he came back, she said, and she was sick herself, had lost a child, carried it in her dead, and later, despite the birth of their son, their marriage had similarly perished. They lived in a small two-room apartment in Missoula, and his depression, his inactivity, had poisoned their lives. But some things you have to set in the past and leave well alone. He had lived his life and she had lived hers, each without regret. As a man of habit his infidelities ran to a timetable. And he was hung, she said, my god how he was hung. Looking back through the chapel she scanned the crowd and was grateful that the woman he was with on the day he died had the sense not to attend the service, and the better sense to clear away the foil, the glass tubes, the pellets of resin from both the hotel room and the car before the police came. A man with one lung who smoked. How dumb, she said, seriously, how stupid is that? The box of para-phernalia was left on her doorstep two days later, minus the drugs, as a hint that everything should be allowed to lie where it landed. The bus company sent flowers to the house. She had to buy a suit, the only one to her memory he'd ever worn, although secretly she harboured a desire to bury him in a novelty costume. Watts had once told her she had a wide and flat mouth: the mouth of a frog. He wasn't saying she wasn't pretty, especially her hazel eyes, so complex they sometimes appeared to be struck with gold. Her chestnut hair, her pale New Eng-land skin, gifts from her ancestors, but, my god, everything lower than her nose came right out of a cartoon. After he said such things he'd laugh a little as if it were only a tiny mischief, nothing of consequence. It wasn't that Iraq changed him: he was always duplicitous, always cold, but he'd come back believing that she did not and would never understand him, although he could never say this directly. His behav-iour wasn't due to any syndrome, PTSD, or a result of his work at the burn pits. No, he was wilful, cruel, contemptful even before his depar-ture. The only syndrome Watts suffered was asshole syndrome. As the curtains closed about the coffin, the sound of the rollers overwhelmed the music, she watched with a steady eye and whispered *can't, can't, can't.*

Before Watts came Samuels, whose body was not discovered, and whose death went unrecorded. Two days before Christmas, Samuels bought a car with cash and a fake ID and drove from Illinois to Louisiana, joining Highway 10 at Baton Rouge. The last people he spoke with were a young couple from his hometown, Topeka, Kansas, he found loitering at the entrance to the services. For a moment he believed that they were summoning the courage to rob the diner, and when he realized that they were hesitating because they had no money, he gave them all the change he had, everything from his pockets, and they tried not to stare at the eczema on his arms, at how he shed his skin in fish-like scales. The coincidence of meeting a young couple from his hometown confirmed the rightness of what he was doing, and with the simple gesture of handing over a fistful of coins he felt that he was handing something on. Samuels, who was always short of breath, sat in his car and thought about how perfect this was, of how endings naturally meet beginnings, then got right back out and returned to the restaurant where he sat with the couple and spoke for an hour, uninterrupted, about the work at Camp Liberty in the southern desert of Al-Muthanna. He spoke at length about a member of their unit, Steven Kiprowski, and how you know you should stop something but you don't, and you know, even as you do nothing, that this will corrode through you, ruin your life. Unbothered about the proper sequence of events, or whether he was or was not making sense, he told his story in full. Thirty minutes after he was done talking he turned off the highway and tipped the car into a swamp, the small doubt occurring to him that this would not be easy.

Four days after the mud had taken him, the upturned car was swept free and marooned on a high tide on the banks under the raised span of the highway. A storm hauled his body out into the Gulf, and Samuels came closer to what he wanted: to become unaccountably small, to disappear, dissipate, to become less than dust.

Pakosta shot himself in the elevator at the UC Santa Barbara Hospital. With his back against the mirror siding he faced the doors and placed the shotgun under his chin, certain that the damage would obliterate his face. His previous attempt, an overdose of whisky and diet and sleeping pills, caused nothing worse than diarrhoea and a restful sleep, and when he revived he blamed his actions on the weather. It wasn't easy being poor in Santa Barbara, he said, and it wasn't easy once the weather straightened out to have one day so similar to another. A handsome man with an open face, the nurses felt the tragedy deeply, unaware that Pakosta was a violent drunk who daily harangued the students and college types taking coffee outside the Flat Earth Café on Main Street with strange obscenities. This man would defecate on doorsteps and harass veterans at the town's shelter: there was little to recommend him, little that remained decent. Like Samuels he suffered from a skin condition, a red blush at his throat which often coincided with a shortness of breath and the feeling that he was under deep water, separate from the world. Carl Pakosta disliked communists, Californians, and Mexicans, and believed that his neighbour, a schoolteacher and former union organizer from Oaxaca, had deliberately poisoned his dog, when he knew the responsibility for the animal's death was his own. His body was cremated at the expense of the city of Santa Barbara. His ashes were scattered by a volunteer in the Garden of Remembrance because of an error that marked him in city records as a veteran.

Pakosta was missed by the regulars at the Flat Earth Café, and by the tour guides on the whale-watching boats who were used to his bullying rants, and how he'd stand at the pier and disabuse the tourists, asking what, seriously, what did they expect to see out there? You take pictures, he said, pictures. You can't *eat* the whales. In Pakosta's last months, time folded over itself and he forgot to eat, began to slip from his routine, and the comings and goings of day-trippers, the simple matter of people departing, became unbearable for him. On his last day he ran after the boats and shouted that the sea would swallow them and they would vanish as if they had never been born.

Rem Gunnersen lived long enough to celebrate his second wedding at St Lawrence's on Lunt Avenue on Chicago's Northside. For that one day he assured his guests that he was comfortable and grateful that they had come to witness him rectifying an earlier mistake: his separation from his first wife, Cathy, which he was now correcting by re-marrying her, and making her, simultaneously, his first and second wife. Shrunken, unable to eat solid food, he insisted that everything that could be done had been done many times already. It was now a matter of keeping one stride ahead with his medication, of keeping comfortable. The weekend after the wedding Rem's lung collapsed, and following directions downloaded from the internet his wife administered the morphine she had stored in preparation and sat with him as he faded.

Before his funeral, conducted in the same church, the doctor gave general answers about the source of Rem's cancer, and while he could not be absolute he agreed that Rem had sickened after his return from Europe, two years after his time in Iraq, and never properly picked up.

Rem's guests returned to the church, sat in the same small groups, wore the same suits, and learned how, when exchanging vows, Rem had whispered that he was sorry, that life just cheats you, robs time from you right at the moment you find yourself to be truly content. His daughter, Elsa, presented the eulogy, and refused to find comfort. Rem

Gunnersen was a good man who had suffered for no reason. Through all of their troubles, despite all of their years apart, neither Cathy nor Elsa had imagined life completely without him. I want to know why, she asked. I want to know what all of this is for.

Rem had come into money in his last year through the sale of land and the settlement of a dispute, and he had decided, with Cathy's agreement, that the money would be entrusted to a Quaker fund to support veterans returning from combat.

Rem Gunnersen's wake was held in his house on the night before the funeral. As per his instructions, Cathy opened the casket and undressed him, and he was buried naked in a coffin of compressed cardboard, along with a handwritten note stating that while he'd tried his level best to protect the people under his care, some had come to harm, and while he could not rectify these mistakes he asked to be received with forgiveness.

Chimeno (Spider) returned to Iraq nine months after his time at Camp Liberty and was killed in a direct strike. His remains were flown back to Fort Dover, repatriated, and taken directly to his hometown, Peoria, Illinois, to his parents' farm. The attack occurred in daylight and was the first killing that year. As the helicopter cleared the bulk of the abandoned Ministry of Oil in Amrah City the pilot turned to Spider to say that one day all this would be automatic. An ops team on the other side of the world would feed in every known piece of information about a suspect, every god-damned thing, their taste in women, shoes, the side of the bed they slept on, and predictions would be made about where this person would most likely be at any given time. They'd know, before it even occurred to the target, where they wanted to go that day. With this information they would take out insurgents without ever being present. No armies. Computers and drones. They'd show it on the news, like they showed the Scuds in Libya dropping onto bunkers, targets braced with digital sights. Unseen, inside the building, lay a simple IED; triggered by the 'copter's down-thrust it blew a funnel of debris between the floors.

On the day of his funeral the Department of Defense released a video of the incident. After it was hit, the helicopter, an HH-60, spun into the side of the building to fold into the concrete honeycomb with a cold familiarity, pieces of it ricocheting out and down.

*

THE KILLS

Steven (christened Stefan) Kiprowski was the first of the group to die at the government offices in Amrah City.

Kiprowski, Chimeno, Pakosta, Samuels, Watts, Clark, and Hernandez were Rem Gunnersen's men for six weeks; known as Unit 7, the men were handpicked to work at the burn pits at Camp Liberty in the southern desert of Al-Muthanna.

TWO CITIES

A year after the events at Camp Liberty, while Rem Gunnersen was living in Europe (Halsteren, Amsterdam, and afterward Bruges), he was asked in a casual discussion to describe two bad days. They didn't have to be the worst days he'd ever had, just two stinkers. It's a game, the man, a Norwegian, said. If your story's worse than mine, I'll buy the next drink.

While the men did not know each other, they'd passed the day in a canal-side bar drinking shots and chatting with ease, and a game, whatever the premise, would add purpose to the late afternoon.

Rem had two stories in mind before he'd properly considered the idea. When he did consider it, he realized that he'd chosen these days not because they were his worst, but because they worked as parentheses either side of a year he wished to set behind him.

On the first bad day (story one), his dog, Nut, a dirty white insecure Staffordshire bull terrier, went missing.

On the second (story two), a man he'd worked with kidnapped another man, then drove halfway across the country with him in the boot of his car.

The thing is, Rem explained, he'd almost certainly kidnapped the wrong man.

If the Norwegian had asked for one story Rem would have chosen the first.

Nut slept in the same room as Rem and his wife. The dog suffered gas (no diet would cure it), and being timid the creature didn't like surprises. He ignored other dogs; was never heard to bark or growl; sat between people as they talked and appeared to understand their conversations.

Rem loved the routine. The early walks, the late walks. The lakefront at Rogers Park dusted with mist. How Nut waited to be told to run. How the dog loved water. How, every year, he rediscovered ice. Nut doted on Rem and Cathy, walked jauntily in their company, shone with affection, would lean against a door if he was shut out of a room, *just to be close.*

Nut disappeared before Rem left for Iraq, and Rem later realized that if the dog hadn't vanished, he would have stayed in Illinois. Nuts' needs and routines set a perimeter they never questioned; without that perimeter, their horizons automatically broadened.

☆

Rem set his morning in order. First the Robinsons, then the Rosens, the Colemans, then Matt.

He found Martin Robinson on the driveway of his home in Lake Forest. The man leaving, car pointed downhill, the weather turning from indeterminate drizzle to a harder, full-on rain. Rem ran from his car with his jacket pulled over his head and leaned through the passenger window, and Robinson pushed Rem's head back and kept his hand out for the money.

As the car drove away Rem looked back to the house. He never envied people money, seldom felt bruised at others' entitlement and excess, even now, handing over cash on a broad driveway curved to give a last long view of the lake, the landscaped garden, treeless until the incline, the flat-roofed house, the lap pool, the edge of a Chihuly chandelier, those slab windows reflecting a sombre two-tone view. Grey lake. Grey sky. These people didn't need money, not in the same way Rem needed money.

The cleaners along these lake-front houses arrived in vans labelled *Maintenance Technician*. The trash collectors – *Waste Managers*. Decorators – *Design Consultants*.

Two thousand. Four thousand. Five thousand.

Twenty minutes later Rem met with Martin and Samantha Rosen in their house with its Tudor frontage. Said he wouldn't come in because he was wet, and thought it kind when Samantha Rosen returned with a towel, asked if he wanted a coffee, and behaved with less embarrassment than her husband. Rem left the money on the kitchen counter, and didn't look at the package as he sipped the coffee and calculated the cost of the appliances. Those cabinets are engineered and hand-crafted, you can't slam the doors, even if you kick them they slide home with a sigh.

It wasn't green they'd wanted but *chartreuse*. Rem wasn't a house-painter, but an *interior decorator*. The money he brought wasn't anything other than *satisfaction, under the circumstances*.

At the Colemans', Rem spoke with a housekeeper who said that Marie Coleman had just left, and Rem wondered what was going on. They have these people in their houses, coming and going, and yet they figured the problem came from some sticky decorator. Cathy had a point, he shouldn't be so easy to ride. A Yorkshire terrier, small even for the breed, scuttled for the door, and the housekeeper held it back with her foot and called it *Lucy*. Andy Coleman – nicknamed 'turd-cutter' by either Matt or Mike for his tight mouth and pudgy cheeks – worked for the Lake View office of the Chief of Police. A portrait of the man and wife, black-and-white head shots, mounted on the wood panelling.

Rem held on to the money; while he didn't want to return, he didn't trust leaving an envelope containing this much cash. The Colemans held the deepest grievance. *The ring was an heirloom piece*. The housekeeper recognized the logo on Rem's car and told him: You need to speak with the Stahls.

Before he reached Chicago, Rem received two calls from Andy Coleman. Both abusive. The first call nothing but an indignant sulk: 'You said you'd be here. We gave you a specific time. We had an agreement.'

The second message was less constrained and the man shouted. 'How would you feel if someone broke into your home? How would that feel, Gunnersen? Hey? You tell me? How about I come to your home and take something of yours? How will that feel?'

Rem wanted to tell him to go to his apartment, no worries, help himself to whatever he wanted. Instead he managed to sound reasonable, even made himself smile so his voice would carry some colour.

'Sorry to miss you. There's a misunderstanding. I came by earlier but you weren't there. I didn't want to leave anything as the house didn't look secure. Let me know when you're about. I can come back tomorrow. Mornings aren't a problem.'

The last visit promised to be the most difficult, and Rem waited a long time in the car, and smoked despite his sore throat. *You need to speak to the Stahls*. The point of the exercise already undermined. If Rem was paying people to keep their mouths shut he wouldn't need to speak with the Stahls, because the Stahls wouldn't know. Just as some slack-mouthed housekeeper shouldn't know either.

Nobody but the Robinsons and the Rosens had any business with him. These were the people named by Matt. The only two. The Colemans were included for containment.

Cissie let him in, wrong-footed him with a kiss on the cheek, said breezily that Matt was in the back and how about a coffee? Rem couldn't calculate if this was bravado, because they'd known each other for so long – was she supposed to answer the door in sackcloth? Weep? Cower? What did he expect? She hadn't done anything wrong. Even so, her cheeriness made him sore.

No such breeziness from Matt. Sequestered on a dark internal porch, Matt wiped his hands down his legs but didn't offer to shake hands. His expression fixed in a gawp, a slap-red rash ran up his neck. He moved in slow counterpoise to Rem, a greasy movement, distrustful to the core.

Rem laid out the papers for the loan agreement, the book of payment slips, a separate sheet listing the names and amounts he'd paid. Payments that counted into thousands of dollars. He outlined them one at a time, but didn't mention the Stahls.

While Rem spoke Matt hastily gathered the papers and looked to the door, and Rem guessed that Cissie knew nothing, had no idea.

When he asked, Matt drew a small in-breath that sounded like incredulity, perhaps even scorn. 'I'll pay every cent back. As long as I have work I can pay you.'

Rem closed his eyes, quarried for an explanation.

'There isn't any work. No one wants to hire us, Matt. We're done.' Rem let the fact sit before venturing. 'I have to explain the situation to Mike and the others. I have to find reasons why.' Rem stood, hands to his knees, a simple, pneumatic movement. 'You pay in each month. That's all you need to do. We don't need to be in contact otherwise.'

Cissie busied herself in the kitchen as he left. No coffee being made, instead it looked like a supper of pasta and eggs and ham and sour cream. Rem had left his cigarettes on the table, had set them down when he'd taken out the papers. He didn't want to return for them, didn't want them at all.

Rem arrived home to find the lobby unlocked, the mail picked up, which meant that Cathy was home – although she never left the door open, this was his habit, and his problem when people came in and fouled in the hallway. At the top of the stairs he found the outer, heavy warehouse door, metal-sheathed, open. The second apartment door also open. No welcoming dog. No Cathy either.

He searched the neighbourhood with the leash wrapped about his knuckles, hopeful at every corner and block-long view that Nut would be there, shivering – because this is what he did when he was lost, he shivered, he cowered, he whimpered. This was Coleman's doing. No doubt. Rem couldn't imagine anything more provocative than breaking into a house and letting a dog out on the street.

☆

Unlike Kuwait City, Amrah City had no central business zone, and only one building higher than four storeys, the Ministry of Oil, a honey-coloured, hive-like building of twenty-five storeys, which could be seen some distance from the city. Rem looked for similarities to other cities, but three factors – the vast plane of squat oblong houses, the pounding heat, and how disturbingly vacant the city appeared – dominated any familiar elements.

Amrah City Section Base (aka: ACSB, The Station) lay four miles from the Regional Government Office, Southern-CIPA. Pinched between Shi'a and Sunni districts, the former light-industrial complex had once housed a packing plant, a cannery, a coach station, and an ice factory. The buildings wore scars from the conflict, and there was evidence that the Palace Guard had used the complex as a garrison. The compound was barely adequate in scale and location, and housed nearly twelve hundred non-Iraqi foreign nationals, Fobbits, who bedded down in stacked container units – alongside a further fifteen hundred Americans and other allies, although this number declined by the day. The recent increase in security breaches made the post less attractive for contractors who had no military experience. Protected by a fortified outer wall, Section Base housed a cinema, a sports hall, stores, and a PX, and in the courtyard a row of cabins, referred to as 'the ovens'. The electricity seldom ran longer than four hours, so the compound rang to the thrum of generators.

The job fell short of expectation on the first day. Rem, assigned to Unit 409, was told that he couldn't stay inside the compound, as ACSB was classified as *home territory*. If he wanted the Strategic Placement Bonus he'd have to leave the compound every day.

Rem built walls to repel and redirect blasts: walls to stop cars, mortars, rockets, objects propelled with great force and speed; walls to stopper windows, doorways, shop-fronts either side of the new highways; walls to segregate Sunni from Shi'a. The project involved the fortification of the north, south, and western routes into the city – routes which cut the city into separate zones.

For the first week the crews worked a night shift (four nights on, one off), and laboured under arc-lamps in vacant neighbourhoods which reminded Rem of the Southside of Chicago. On the midday news, by satellite, he saw the ramps he'd built, the road divisions and blast walls, the routes broad enough to carry troops and convoys. Unlike Baghdad, Amrah City would have no Blue or Red Zones. If the old city didn't work they would sweep it aside and build a new one in its place. The neighbourhoods straddling the main routes were razed in a one-block strip either side of the highway. Houses, hotels, and businesses were demolished, along with every facility, school, surgery, or market which might house any kind of crowd, and Rem became used to seeing the city through a pale haze of dust.

They worked at night, as if in a fever, to the clatter of gunshot and the glow of street fires. The cleared space beside the road buzzed with itchy expectation, and Rem wondered what had happened to the people who'd lived in these districts and how much of the dilapidation was new. He worked in a crew with a security escort of ex-soldiers and ex-marines, American in the large part, but also Australian and Danish, independent security outfits with repurposed Humvees front and back, apprehensive boys dressed in full protective gear, who wouldn't hold any position for very long, anxiousness riven through them.

Eight nights in, a woman stumbled over the debris between the generators and spotlights. Rem rode on the back of a roller, an eye on the trash that spilled into the street, the broken stone, the dirt road. He saw the woman, dressed in a black abaya and niqab, dust rising about her, turning as if surprised, unsure of the next expected move. With shouting and a mighty clack of armament security established a perimeter about the woman and shouted instructions in English and crude Arabic. Rem saw men running, some toward, but most away, throwing themselves over the barrier they were building.

And nothing happened.

'They use children. They use women. They use crazy people, retards, the deaf and the dumb. They make bombs in their homes and strap them to the mentally infirm then detonate them by remote. They slaughter their own people. There's no logic.'

The man driving the roller, unit leader Luis Hernandez, from Minnesota, known as Santo, spoke as if he was an authority, as if these were established facts.

'They hate us. They hate life. They'll kill everyone to show it.'

Rem didn't want to agree, but the woman was crazy, without doubt, and she'd been shoved out as a threat, even when she was not primed.

The next night the bombing started in earnest. A length of wall along Jalla Road taken out, along with a number of the new watchtowers, concrete perforated by EFPs. The exposed rebar, the scattered blocks and punctured walls became a kind of signature, Rem's image of the city. Two supply trucks returning from the airport were assaulted, the drivers dragged into the street and cut to pieces; the incident posted online before the news reached ACSB. To add to the slow accumulation of deaths (highest among them the foreign nationals from Nepal, Pakistan, and India) came specific assaults against the units working on the new highways. The incidents quickly became continuous and seemed organized. Work stopped, and while they waited out the trouble Rem spent his quiet hours playing cards with Santo, and won every hand.

At the end of Rem's second week 'the ovens' came under attack. Shielded by the PX the cabins had always seemed secure, but on this night the mortars made determined arcs, as if magnetically drawn to their tin sides and roofs. In the first volley two cabins were obliterated and six damaged, fragments of debris pierced the PX. In the second, one hut took a direct hit, killing two men from Unit 89, and wounding three. Rem watched the team of men clean up. They wore the same green overalls, the same protective gear, and moved with practised care bagging what they found.

The PX, the most secure building in the compound, became Rem's second home. During the day he stored his sleeping roll in a locker with a bust hinge. He changed clothes every other day, started buying sweatshirts from Stores to avoid using the laundry which was sited right beside the inner blast wall. Since the attack most of Unit 409 used the showers beside the PX in any case. Rem made sure he didn't present a problem. He slept in the commissary during the day, hunched over a table, alongside the Indian and Nepalese truckers.

Santo began to take his meals with Rem and when Rem asked why he wasn't as familiar with the other men, Santo shrugged. 'I'm unit manager.' He held up a small sheaf of papers. 'I hold grave responsibilities their young minds cannot comprehend.'

Rem asked what the papers were.

'The rotas. I'm deputized to post the work rotas. On a noticeboard.'

'It's a skill.'

'I decide the colour of the pin. Exactly where the paper goes. The hour they're posted.' Santo smiled. 'You know the trouble you cause? They talk about you all the time. They want you to return to your quarters but they think you're a little crazy.'

'How so?'

'Look at you. Nobody wants to mess with a big guy. Everybody's afraid of you.'

Rem asked how much of this mattered.

'I'm just saying. Nobody wants to fuck with you. That's all.'

Santo liked to run his hand back over his head, the palm flat and one or two fingers bent to scratch his scalp, which he generally kept shaved, so the noise, for such a small gesture sounded loud. Rem thought of this gesture as something urban, partly because he knew that Santo came from Minneapolis, and partly because the Latino boys, with their shoulders burned with tattoos and their various styles of goatee, appeared more urban than rural. He couldn't picture Santo outside of a city.

'I'm short. People fuck with me all the time. Like Fatboy, they hit on me like Fatboy there. Difference is, they do this only one time.' Santo pointed to Fatboy, a weedy nineteen-year-old, a mouse. Stunted in pre-pubescence, the man/boy ate burgers, fried meat, drank power drinks, never slept, suffered from bad skin, and remained rake-thin. Fatboy liked to smile, a smile which showed small and weak teeth. He never disagreed or bad-mouthed anyone, no matter how unpleasant the exchange. Rem hadn't seen him angry, despite the abuse he had to tolerate, and because of this he admired the boy. Fatboy managed supplies for the PX. He lived to supply and delivered on every request (Cheetos, Oreos, Chipotle dip, Mega-Moca-Latte-Mix, Vegemite, DVDs,

Blu-Rays even, CDs, and, according to rumour, porn of any variety). Fatboy navigated with ease around HOSCO's complex systems. And best of all, he let Rem sleep wherever he wanted.

As a consequence, Rem drew Fatboy into their breaks and lunchtimes, invited the boy to sit with them when he played cards with Santo before their night shift. And while Santo rarely spoke to the boy he didn't appear to mind his company, especially when Fatboy brought chips and Cheetos, dips and sometimes fries.

Santo smiled every time he spoke about the money he was making. 'In thirty days the pay becomes unreal. Now I'm in *extra*-overtime. I'm printing money. Soon it will have my face on it.'

Santo liked to smoke home-grown smuggled by the convoy security. He liked the day to slip from him, he liked to feel easy, so if anything happened he'd be in the best shape to take it, because bad news shouldn't be taken straight. 'I have this idea.' He leaned toward Rem, his breath sweet and grassy. 'You know. Something *you* should do, because you're a big white man and they won't say no to a big white man. The idea? We work on the teams that go in after the attacks. We volunteer.'

'We volunteer? This is your idea?'

'It's a good idea. You've no idea how much they pay. By the time they go in everything's over. It's meat, it's not even people, what's left over.'

Rem didn't like it, but Santo persisted. 'You put together a team. They want people just like you. Big white people who do things.'

Rem wouldn't consider it. He'd seen enough devastation from a distance, and had trouble forgetting the cabins obliterated by the attack, the stink of scorched blood and fat, his fear over what had happened to the men inside.

The shifts altered once the buildings had been cleared either side of the new routes: so they began to work during the day. Every night, after Santo returned to the cabins, Rem spread out his mat and lay under a table in the cafeteria and knew he would not sleep. Santo's idea stuck under his skin. *Them and us.* They blew up markets, employment queues, clinics, schools, colleges, funerals, any protest or procession. They bombed exit routes, corridors, roadways, targeted surgeries, emergency vehicles, so that there could be no escape. And when this was done *they* went to the hospitals and blew up the

arriving ambulances, the waiting rooms, targeting relatives, the doctors and nurses. How many times did Rem, Santo, and the crew of
Unit 409 listen to the attacks then wait for the follow-up blasts? Rem
had no language for this, but understood that he was part of the
dynamic. However separate Santo and the others might regard themselves, Rem at least admitted that he was, in some way, connected.

Three in the morning Rem woke to see Fatboy stacking candy bars into
the vending machines. A slight nervous energy ran through the boy, his
feet jiggered as he unloaded the boxes.

Rem watched him walk away, arms full of snacks and cardboard
flats, and told himself he wanted company. He followed Fatboy
through the complex, a small channel of light marked a corridor to an
exit, a set of folding doors. He found his cigarettes in his pocket, caught
up, and offered the boy a smoke.

'Can't sleep?'

'Don't seem to need it.' Fatboy looked at the sky, at a yellow
horizon edged by shadowy palms and the distant square hulks of
buildings. He pointed at the cabins with boards secured behind the
windows to prevent blast damage. 'Like a face,' he said. 'See? Eyes?
Mouth?'

Rem looked back to the PX, worried about the light from the
corridor.

Fatboy's thoughts were often disconnected and Rem became used
to the chaotic switches: 'What's the most people you ever saw?'

Rem said he didn't know.

'The most people – in one moment. Right in front of you? Face to
face?'

Rem wasn't sure, and Fatboy led him back through the PX, past the
Stores, the commissary, the humming fridges; the canteen seeming
longer in the half-darkness, its recesses deeper. The boy leaned against
the door before he pushed. 'Tell me how many you think there are.'

The door opened to a series of interlinked spaces – a loading dock,
a parking lot, the remnants of a boulevard – one large area bordered
on two sides by blast walls, and along the far side, by low-rise prefab
buildings. Lamps mounted on the buildings cast an acid wash over
the compound. To Rem's amazement the ground was covered with
sleeping bodies.

Fatboy leaned against the door to keep it open. 'Wild, right? TCNs. Third-country nationals. They run the facilities. Everything.'

From their feet to the far perimeter slept the drivers, shelf-stackers, cleaners, sales clerks, barbers – he couldn't account for the numbers.

'They don't have anywhere to sleep?'

'Most do. There's an area behind with shipping containers. They're modified for sleeping, each container holds around nine men. They're mounted one on top of the other. Not everyone's working. Some are going home, others are being shipped out, or transferred. If you aren't working, you aren't assigned quarters. You ever seen anything so wild?'

'I don't see how this is any safer?'

'The containers get hot. A while back some of them were burned out. After that most people started sleeping like this. It's better to be outside, especially when there's trouble.'

From what Rem could see the bodies were male, men sleeping side by side, fitted together, on and under vehicles, lodged crazily, puzzle-like, head to toe, with little space between them. Most slept in thin T-shirts, trousers, with rags or paper or newspaper over their heads and faces. Rem couldn't absorb the detail, so that group immediately at his feet stood in for the many laid out before him.

Rem and Fatboy began to spend their nights together.

Fatboy's habit would be to smoke, pause, then ask a question, as if there was something on his mind.

'You ever pray?'

Rem answered no.

'Your parents alive?'

Rem shook his head but didn't answer. He finished one cigarette, lit another.

'My mom lives in Michigan. Doesn't do much but eat.'

There were times when Rem thought the boy wasn't right, that somewhere along the spectrum of normal and crazy Fatboy pulled up short. When he noticed how poorly the boy looked after himself he took on duty of care and presented him with food, fruit, nuts, things he thought would be good, and sat with him as he ate. Fatboy, for his part, began to open up.

'There're these marsh Arabs. They live east of here between the Tigris and the Euphrates, and they build these huts out of reeds on these stilts. Real small. And there's one big hut, this place where everyone meets. You just go in and you ask anything you want to ask, like, where are all the fish, and someone will tell you. Or you go there because you're troubled, or you want an answer to something, and someone always has an answer. Someone always knows what you're supposed to do.'

Rem thought the boy was homesick, but not for home. 'You've seen these people?'

'I will do. Some day.' Suddenly the boy choked up, and Rem wondered, if he ever made it to this place, this raised hut set above the marsh, what question he would ask.

'You have someone at home?' the boy asked.

Rem said yes, he had someone. 'My wife comes from Texas,' he explained. 'A place called Seeley.'

'Same as the mattress?'

'Same as the mattress. I think she's happy to be out of there, but I think she misses Texas.'

'You think you did the right thing coming here?'

Rem shrugged. 'My mother had these ideas. She'd say something like: everything you do puts you one step forward. Some things are better not known.'

'You wish you hadn't come?'

Rem looked up and took in the sky, blank because of the light-spill from the compound. Fatboy came from a small town himself. He never could have imagined these things or such a place. This wasn't their home.

☆

The idea that Rem Gunnersen should take employment away from home came from his wife, Cathy, because, she said, *she needed a vacation.*

Cathy Gunnersen's realization came to her after her sister's wedding. This being no special night and no special occasion, except Rem had started drinking at midday as a party of one and left a full beer in the utility room right on top of the washer, so when the spin-cycle kicked on, the can tipped over and the beer saturated the laundered clothes. She found him splayed across the couch, feet on the armrest, heels digging a groove, with another beer gripped between finger and thumb, jiggling to some rhythm or some other agitation. Cathy wanted to know was wrong with the first beer. Hey? And the second? What was wrong with that? Come on? An open can on the kitchen counter, another in the fridge, another beside the couch – she could map his afternoon. Did he have any clue how much he was drinking? Seriously, was anyone keeping track? It wasn't the drinking that bothered her, no, what angered her was the idea of *him* drinking while *she* worked. And why, could he please explain, was the dog out in the hall?

'Listen to me,' she said. 'Listen. I need a vacation. OK? I – need – a – break.'

Rem understood the distinction: her disagreement wasn't about the event, per se, it was about the timing. And hadn't he felt wrong-headed all day? Besides, it wasn't about the beer, it wasn't about getting drunk, but some continuing aggravation set against him: a bad curve to the day of nothing being in place, of everything beginning to prickle. Another Gunnersen self-detonation

'You – Rem Gunnersen – need – to – work.'

Cathy Gunnersen could wrastle a problem until it became unbearable. Formerly these situations were managed with sex. Rem would just unbuckle and they'd have at each other. These days, right now, that possibility was spoiled by her habit of closing conversations with a monumental sulk, which demonstrated nothing but disappointment. Most times she walked off in less and less of an act.

'Get over this,' she said. 'Start over.'

Rem held his tongue. It's always the people who don't have to start over who speak like this.

The wedding party had ended badly. It wasn't that Rem disliked his sister-in-law's partner – a fashion buyer for a high street chain Rem could never remember – he just couldn't stop needling the man (*Don't worry, you'll always be her first husband*). In return the groom preened at the news from Cathy about Rem's business *not doing so well*. Everything was headshakingly 'too bad'. But times were tough for everyone, right? At least Rem still had a business, right? However diminished. And he could always go back – where was it now – to I-raq, Afghanistan, Kuwait, wherever it was he'd gone that first time, and earn some more? Right?

Cathy wouldn't hear of it.

Rem's speech, volunteered without request, included a joke about men who design women's clothes and another about sodomy. *A couple, newly-wed, come into the doctor's office, and after a thorough examination the doctor finds the woman to be a virgin, despite her husband's claim that he 'puts it to her' every night . . .*

Cathy repeated Rem's jokes to Maggie at work. She specified the targets, punch by punch, the blows levelled at the groom's faith, his occupation, his sexual prowess (about which, she had to admit, her sister never expressed enthusiasm). It wasn't embarrassment or humiliation she'd felt as Rem slowly pumped his hips in demonstration: this crudity, these dim thrusts meant nothing. Cathy drew a picture of Rem looming acute over a long table loaded with plates and glasses and lit candles, a table dressed with flowers and napkins, with creams and fleshy pinks – and this she found inexcusable. Rem, top heavy, ox-like, boxy, overburdened, ready to topple, slake off and hammer down like some great hunk of glacial ice. It was this: his pure force, his size against the delicacy of the table which she found humiliating, and how the entire room remained silent for the duration of his speech, listening to his Continental English, aching for him to hit the deck and take out the cake.

As it happened, Cathy was the one to fall over. Not one drop of drink in her, she flopped to the floor. Couldn't remember catching a heel in the carpet, but one moment upright, the next, prone, knees spread, and a feeling afterward of indigestion, a low-grade bellyache stuck to the gut that lasted too long.

Rem slept with his head on one arm, the other tucked under the pillow. Cathy spoke to the back of his head. The vacation became a simple matter. She didn't want to go anywhere, she wanted to stay home, in any case she couldn't leave, not with her work. They could spare her, sure, but her last break had resulted in Maggie receiving the promotion to shift-supervisor – and wasn't that the start of everything going wrong? No, this vacation would come under a different arrangement. Rem, who wasn't doing much except a whole lot of moping around, would have to find a *real* job that paid *real* money, and send the money back. He could use this time to consider his drinking, his attitude, his habit of grinding people down, of riding someone's back until they were just plain tired of carrying him. Better than sun beds, a Mexican beach, an ocean of mojitos, this vacation would cost her no effort and no expense. Which is exactly what made it perfect.

Rem sat up and turned on the light – which improved nothing.

Cathy drew herself to her elbows. Looked about ready to say something she'd been saving.

'This isn't a discussion.' As Rem left the room he felt it drag after him. Nut followed in a sympathetic sulk.

Maybe going someplace else was a good idea. He looked out the window at Clark. A subterranean night, yellow and dim. The changing stoplights. The lack of traffic. The taqueria, open and empty.

Nut settled half-on, half-off the rug, raised his head and huffed. A heaviness to the sound that Rem could appreciate.

Cathy's stubborn disconnection outlasted any other bad mood, and through the weekend it became obvious that things weren't going to settle in their usual way. Rem knew when to stay clear, and Cathy took on double shifts at the Happy Shopper, took anything extra that Maggie could offer.

Cathy blamed Rem for the dog. He never locked the doors. Never checked they were locked. Despite Rem's claims, she didn't find it strange, just sad, and didn't blame a third party for the dog's disappearance. Once again, this all came down to Rem.

'The doors, Rem. See for yourself. They aren't forced.'

Rem kept the payment to the Colemans to himself, along with his certainty that Nut's disappearance was related. He took a two-day job refurbishing a dentist's office at 5 North Wabash, and for two days lost himself to the sticky swipe of a roller, to the soft spray of white emulsion, the thrum of the El as the trains scudded the corners on the raised tracks. While he painted he boiled with plans of revenge. He spoke with Mike, who said he'd be up for anything, if Rem could devise a workable plan. Rem realized that neither of them were graced with SEAL-like stealth or had any kind of smarts for housebreaking. He couldn't see them storming the Coleman compound, then roving SWAT-like through the apartment to find the dog, expose the Colemans, then *fuck them up*. Mike's ideas involved juvenile desecrations, urinating on beds, crapping on dinner plates, and they agreed that in all likelihood Coleman had driven the dog someplace and just let him loose.

He abandoned himself to the dream of being elsewhere. Cathy's idea of a vacation wasn't so extreme. With the business on hold he could return to Holland, spend time with his brothers, maybe even go back to his family's roots and see his sister in Norway. While he was away he could canvass for work, reimagine the business, and return with energy. His enthusiasm soon failed him. Could he even call Halsteren home after so many years away? And did he really want to go back now that his mother was dead? And would this really be the best time to set the business aside? Aren't you supposed to work through the tough periods? Persist?

At the end of the second day Rem found himself disinclined to return home: hours festering over stale possibilities had fed a bad mood. He understood Cathy's proposal for what it was – a failure on multiple fronts. Home. Business. Wife. Work.

Unwilling to drink at the Wabash Inn where he might meet people he knew, he chose the cubby-hole bar at the Palmer House Hotel.

Rem sat with his back to the counter and looked over an area divided into zones by arrangements of furniture and potted palms. He lost an hour to watching men in suits amble from the elevators to the lobby to the bar with unengaged distraction – then realized, just as he was watching the businessmen, that one man, seated in an arm-chair close to the bar, was watching him.

The man – smart, trim, black hair, white skin as if he never spent time outdoors – watched Rem, unabashed. Dressed in a smarter suit, with smarter shoes, a trimmer haircut, the man appeared separate from the other businessmen gathered in the lobby. *You come to a town, any town, you stay in a hotel, you do business. This could be any week of the year.*

Rem decided to go, toasted the businessman and drank down the beer. The man turned his head to the side, glanced at leisure along the bar, then back at Rem, and Rem wondered if he was missing something. He couldn't suppose what the other man was thinking, and thought the exchange so blank that it bore a hint of hostility.

The man stood and came up to the bar, and while he didn't face Rem, it was clear, by the way he spoke and the turn of his shoulder that he was being addressed.

'One of my favourite novels opens on a street in New York. The main character thinks he's being followed, so he slips into a bar to lose him, and this man follows right after. Another?'

The businessman watched the last foam spitline slide down Rem's empty glass. *Did he want another drink?* Hooded eyes. Dark lashes. A man so carefully presented that he might be playing himself. His accent, Southern, not a drawl so much as an affectation, pronounced and aware.

'Another?'

Rem said he would, though he shouldn't. The businessman nodded. 'Same. I'm supposed to meet with people.' He signalled to the waiter for two more beers. '*Business*. They talk figures. Statistics. Money.' He took a twenty from his wallet and folded it around his forefinger.

'You were talking about a book?'

The man drew a quick breath. 'He thinks he's being followed. It's a great moment, because he's right, he is being followed, although he's wrong about the reason.' The businessman leaned against the bar, all smooth friendliness, a light turned on. 'It's just. Well, it's just very strong, how he thinks he's being followed because he's done something, and he thinks he's been found out – and, you know, you never find out what that trouble was, the reason for him being so anxious. You never learn. Instead this man offers him a job. He wants him to go someplace and find someone because he's mistaken this man for someone else. So both men are mistaken. It's a really nice place to start.'

Rem looked to the elevator. The doors opened to an empty cab. 'I never read.'

The man smiled at Rem's accent. 'You sound British,' he said, 'but I'm guessing you're not. I'm hearing something else?'

'Scandinavian. Raised in the Netherlands. Norwegian father. Dutch mother.' Rem spoke as if giving evidence. Nearly four years in his early twenties working ad-hoc jobs in London had fixed his accent, and once in a while it struck him, came to his ears at a wrong angle, and he'd wonder at the foreignness of his speech, of the assumptions people made, the unintended deceit of belonging to one place but sounding like another.

'Family?'

'Wife.' Rem raised his glass. 'From Texas. You?'

'Pittsburgh, then North Carolina, then Virginia, now Europe. You don't look like you're here for the expo?'

Rem said no and set his glass on the counter. No he was not.

'You look preoccupied.'

'I do?'

'You do. So tell me, what do you do for work?'

'I have my own business, house painting, decorating, but . . .' Rem opened his hands, showed them to be empty.

'It's like that?'

'Most definitely.' Rem sucked in air, slow and deliberate. 'I'm think-ing of letting everyone go. Putting it aside and waiting out whatever we're going through.' He looked at the man. 'To be honest, I don't know.'

'How many people do you have?'

'Three full time. Seven part – or casual – depending on the job.'

'Small. I don't know if that makes it easier or harder. And this means what? You'll go self-employed?'

'Natural step.'

'Self-employed, you'd be looking at, annual?'

Rem shrugged, stretched his back against the bar; he had no idea. 'Twenty-seven?'

The man gave a laugh as if this was a good joke. Twenty-seven, now that was funny.

'I meant twenty-seven is what I owe.'

The businessman hesitated, absorbed the statement, then offered, 'Twenty-seven isn't so bad. If it's fixed.'

'If you have work.' Rem explained himself in a low voice, keen not to be overheard. 'Twenty-seven. That's what I owe in wages and loans, debt I've taken on.'

The man drew a wallet then a business card out of his pocket. His suit, tailored, black, a little feminine with a sharp-blue lining, behind or ahead of the times, Rem couldn't tell. *Paul Geezler, Advisor to the Division Chief, Europe, HOSCO International.* Rem shook the man's hand and repeated his name. Geezler. German?

'Pennsylvania Dutch. If you're serious about looking for work,' Paul Geezler took back the card and wrote a booth number on the back, 'take a look at the expo. If this doesn't interest you there are others recruiting, and they'll be looking for people with skills.' He pointed to Rem's paint-specked hands. 'They're looking for anyone who'll take on a challenge. People who don't mind a little hardship as long as the money is good. And the money is good.'

Rem couldn't help but smile. 'Where's the work?'

'Dubai, less and less. Now it's Kuwait. Kuwait and Iraq.'

'I can't do that.'

'You'll clear your debt.'

'That's how I raised the start-up money: Kuwait, worked on the hotels.'

'Construction?'

'Six weeks. Fitting, finishing, painting. They kept building. You could watch them go up. Fourteen new builds in six weeks.' Rem raised his hand and tower blocks grew around them. 'Every one a hotel.'

The businessman nodded. Rem referred to the card, the memory of those six weeks caught with him.

And when was Kuwait? Before the surge or after? He couldn't remember. He could hardly say he'd seen Kuwait, just views from hotel rooms in which buildings grew faster than flowers. It wasn't even six full weeks on site, closer really to five. Five short weeks with a team of men, one from St Louis, one from Cedar Rapids, and two Brits from Dev-un, that's how they pronounced it, Dev-*uhn*, all particular and resentful, not Dev-*on*, the way it's spelled. For five or six weeks the men barely spoke and worked in high-rise high-class hotels, progressing floor by floor, and paid in cash by the completed unit. Money rained down. Tax-free. Divine.

Paul Geezler nodded, brisk and dismissive. 'There's a good number of possibilities.' He became distracted as four men, all suited, came out from the elevator and drifted across their line of view. Paul Geezler fixed on them the same attention he'd fastened earlier on Rem.

'You know them?'

'I know him.' Geezler gave a nod to the man in the middle of the group. 'In six months his company won't exist.'

'You know this?'

'Intimately. It's a volatile world.'

'And you?' Rem asked.

'It would take something to shake us. Something newsworthy. Monumental. Can I ask about your business? Can I ask what the problem was?'

'Sorry?'

'The problem. With your business.'

Rem straightened his back. 'There isn't any problem, except there isn't any business. People stopped calling.'

'I ask, because people ordinarily tell you why things haven't worked out. You gave no explanation.'

'It's a small business. People stopped calling.' He changed the subject. 'You're serious about having work?'

Paul Geezler turned to face Rem, to make sure he had his attention. 'If you have a moment I'll tell you what we do.'

Both men looked at the full beer glasses set beside the taps, and Rem, imagining Cathy's complaint, had the notion he should return home. Paul Geezler, of HOSCO International, pushed the beer toward him.

'I'm giving a presentation tomorrow.' Geezler looked at his beer. 'An overview. Sixty-eight per cent of our business is now based in the Middle East. Last year it was forty-two. Even for us that's exceptional growth.' The man paused as if this fact might impress Rem. 'We oversee large-scale development projects. The majority are military contracts, although that's not exclusive. We handle contracts for building, and we provide maintenance and operational support, but the bulk of our work comes from supply. Eastern Europe, Indonesia, West Africa, Central America. Now it's the Middle East.' Geezler cleared his throat. 'We supply transport, drivers, security, accommodation, food, clothing, entertainment. In the past nine years we've built everything from schools to refineries, banks, police stations, prisons, sewers. We have a lot of experience, Mr Gunnersen. There isn't an aspect we don't manage. If you take a shower it will be in one of our booths, with water and soap we supply and deliver. You'll dry yourself with one of our towels.' Geezler drew in breath. 'I've been looking forward to steak tonight. If you'll join me, I'd like to make you a business proposal.'

Rem deliberately made no gesture.

'You have plenty of time to finish your beer.'

They sat at a table in the dining room. A recessed glass ceiling high above reminded Rem of a cruise ship, a room so creamy and vast their voices sounded thin. Along one wall ran a mural of a woodland, a steamy forest clearing with near-naked Indians and deer, strafing sunlight, a kind of overreaching nobility to the scale, everything pitched at the same grand status, animal and man.

'I was recently in New Hampshire.' Geezler looked to the mural. 'Have you been to New Hampshire, Mr Gunnersen?'

Rem said that he hadn't.

'They have woods in New Hampshire, old forests. You think of these as wild places, these habitats, as something unique. After a while everything looks the same and you come to realize that it's all managed. Very little is what you'd call natural. They plant and cut and replant, redirect streams, build dams, lakes, fire ponds. What appears old isn't old at all. Everywhere you go looks the same. Even the animals. Everything is controlled. Anything excessive is eliminated.'

Geezler waited as the meal was delivered.

'Our problem is we're too big. The only way to manage diversity on this scale is to treat everything the same. We don't think we do, but we do. The way we handle meat is essentially the way we handle electricity, oil, transport, information, manpower. Source. Deliver. Maintain. Resource. If we have a demand for hamburger in Balad, then we buy land and we raise cattle in Wyoming, because, long-term, it's cost-effective. We go deep, Mr Gunnersen. New-growth forests in New Hampshire will provide lumber for construction, for paper, pallets, crates, and packaging. If we need water, we filtrate it ourselves. If we need to clear mines in Kuwait or Kosovo, we buy into the manufacturer of the sweepers, and hire and train the labour force ourselves. We'll own an interest in the company that fabricates the body armour, and an interest in the company that produces the fibre for the armour. We bring the same approach to everything we do. It's how we work. First it was about supply, about making connections, but now we have interests everywhere you can imagine. And there are issues with this, of course. At some point it becomes difficult to distinguish between what's ours and what's someone else's. Does that make sense?

'Do you have children?'

Rem shook his head.

'For the first four months they can't tell the difference between their own mouths and their mother's teat. That's how it is with us. We don't know our limits. We started in minerals a long time ago. Then oil. And we just grew, we kept saying yes. Eighty-five years on and there's probably only four people in the entire company who properly understand the scope of what we do. We live in departments where we make our work appear mysterious. The problem is structural.'

Paul Geezler lifted coverings from the platters and satisfied himself with what he saw.

'I like how they do this. Speaks of another time.' He smiled. 'Think about that wood, Mr Gunnersen.' Geezler leaned forward. 'The reason everything works in forestry is because they knew what they were doing when they started. They understood the job. They set up a business knowing their parameters, and they created the world in which they operate. You know what they did with the existing woods? They cut them down. They started from scratch. We didn't. We started out doing one thing and we've ended up doing everything. I'm not saying we're greedy. I'm saying we're promiscuous. The Middle East is raising lots of questions for us. People like what we provide, maybe they even like what we represent – more than they'd admit. But they don't like us. That's the issue. It's animal, Mr Gunnersen. Instinctive. We make ourselves too available. That's the scope of our problem. This is what it comes down to. We operate in other people's territories. Territories we do not control.'

Geezler moved his steak to the centre of his plate. He gripped his knife, pen-like, held the meat in place with his fork, then cut the meat into equal sections. Done, he laid down the knife.

'I'm not sure what we do about this. It might be something that can't be addressed. I don't know if it's too *global*. For everything to work properly you need good foundations, which means building the territory from scratch. Cut down the old wood. Plant a new forest. Start over. But, like I said, we live in departments.

'I can do something about more local issues. And for that I need people who can be my ears and eyes. I can't do this myself.' He stuck a piece of meat with his fork, lifted it to check that it was cooked to his liking. 'I want to look at how we do things – I want to know our day-to-day workings in specific, intimate detail. I want to see how our services work, and at what temperature. Understand what's lacking. What we're getting wrong.' He looked square across the table. 'I need to know how we do business. Does this interest you?'

Rem cut into the steak Geezler had ordered for him. Rarer than he liked, salted and seared, the meat had a good rich taste, but as he chewed he felt a vague wave of disgust at the texture, at how the meat gave, uncooked, easily to his bite.

'It doesn't matter that you don't know our procedures. It's probably better not to know. All I need is someone to interact with our operations and report back. How does this sound, Mr Gunnersen?'

Rem said he wasn't sure what he was being asked, and for a moment Geezler appeared disappointed, as if Rem had missed the point of the discussion, just hadn't appreciated the general thrust.

'I'm not asking you to do anything other than observe. That's all I'm asking.' Geezler set his fork beside his knife.

Rem stood at the front of the carriage and watched the train lights skid along the rails. A friendly comfort to the bump and jostle of the first carriage on the last train. Two calls on his mobile, one from Jay, the other from Mike, both asking for news on Matt as neither had heard from him in over a week, but really asking after money. As he looked out at the city he thought of Nut, lost or stolen.

He considered Geezler's proposal and found no argument against it. Go to a trade fair on Navy Pier, wander about, speak with the handlers and exhibitors, then report back in the evening on how it went. Just return with his impressions. Five hundred dollars.

He rehearsed the conversation with Cathy, played through how he would introduce Geezler, and how he would ridicule the man's dull concerns and intensities, *that entire ramble about his work, that fuzz and fuss about woods and forests*. Even as he rehearsed this he winced, slightly superstitious about laughing at the man.

☆

The story as Santo tells it goes something like this: He's a unit manager, in Amrah, four nights on, one night off, which is how and where he first met Gunnersen. He's used to the heat, but this was something else. Insanely fierce. And the wind, when it picked up, carried a dry scent of desert, burnt land, a thousand-plus miles of waterless Arabian plains and rock. He started as part of a team that cleared the roadside trash, which is burned on the spot or bundled into skips to be taken to one of the burn pits, and worked his way up. Work isn't anything he has to *like* exactly, but *endure*. Even now the work bothers him in ways he can't describe. Too much junk, too much dust, broken concrete, stuffed shopping bags, too much crap to properly know what's being hidden. These buildings, he shakes his head. They clear them out, knock them down, and then build these superhighways right through them. A superhighway crashing right through some medieval sun-scorched slum. He splays his hands to describe the scene. Broken furniture, mattresses, you name it, TVs you'd sort of expect, but fax machines (who uses those?), PCs, game consoles, office furniture, beds even, you name it, all out on the roadside, doorways opening to unpaved roads. There's no need to mention the water bottles. Always, everywhere, those ribbed plastic bottles.

He says things that aren't entirely true: *You smell what's there. You get a nose for trouble. You learn the difference between someone running because they're frightened and someone running because they're the root cause of trouble. You get a nose for these things. You get to know the people you work with. You get close.*

Fatboy wants to buy DVDs. He's wearing one of the armoured vests supplied by HOSCO. He's ready and he begs, literally begs, to be brought along. As soon as he's in the vehicle he's asking these stupid questions, the way he does. The boy can nag. He wants to know about the vests, how good they are, how effective. Like if you were shot in the chest would the vest protect you? How about the stomach? At what range? All of these questions none of them can answer. Then it becomes obvious that Fatboy has a gun with him. Something no one's happy about, because the regulations are clear about contractors carrying guns, or rather *not* carrying guns, even though they can buy them easily enough, or sell or trade them on when they leave, because contractors are dying daily out here and the law is against them when it explicitly states that they Can't Legitimately Protect Themselves. Guns aren't allowed for non-combatants. No, no, no. On account of the gun and the questions, they change their minds about taking Fatboy with them and leave him in the vehicle, mulling, and tell him they'll bring the DVDs right back, whatever's new, whatever they don't think he has, and plan to speak with him later about the handgun and about how he needs to behave if he wants more of these trips. Behave and Shut the Fuck Up. The point is made and the men walk off, and leave another guy, Samuels, for company, no one thinking that the weapon might be loaded or what kind of damage one bullet might make in the confines of a metal bucket like a Humvee. Barely into the market, Santo and his accompanying guard hear a contained report. A shot. Unmistakable. Back in the Humvee Samuels has blood specking his face, arms, shirt, and he's freaking out, he's screaming like he's the one who's hurt. And Fatboy has shot himself in the gut, although this isn't so easy to work out at this particular moment. It's an unbelievable thing, the interior of the truck is a canning-factory mess, sticky, black and red, just nasty, and Fatboy is crumpled like some strings have been cut; hands are sopped to his elbows and worst of all his face, his expression, like he doesn't believe it, like this can't be happening.

Santo will tell this story to the men at Camp Liberty who are curious about Rem, because they want to know who they're working for and why he keeps so much to himself, and Santo seems to have an idea.

Rem won't go to visit the boy before he's shipped out, there's a two-hour opportunity in which he makes himself scarce. Fatboy wants to see him, but Rem won't visit and won't say his goodbyes. He doesn't do much other than look like he's going to cry every time Fatboy's name comes up, this ox of a man, brought low over this wounded skinny boy.

It's like this thing comes at you, and you don't even know it, and you've no idea what it's going to do to you. Santo can't explain himself. He wants to find meaning in this, but knows there's a limit to what can be taken from such an event. The story is simple and not so rare, and he doesn't do much at the end of telling it but shake his head. Fatboy. Stupid Fatboy. No harm to anyone but himself.

☆

Wednesday. Up before Cathy, Rem took an early walk to the lake, a habit now in case Nut might be at the shoreline, then returned only to skulk out the house again and head downtown with a half-planned notion, *two birds, one stone.* He left without explanation. No tall tales about Paul Geezler or shared jokes about the man's manner or his work. No hint on what he would be doing today. Just a plan to attend the expo, report back as requested (although he still wasn't sure what the man wanted) and earn in one day what had taken three weeks in the previous month. Plus, if he returned with brochures and information it might be enough to quieten Cathy. *Two birds.* Prospects for the early summer weren't looking good. At some point he'd need to speak more formally with Mike and Jay and the others about putting the business on hold. He might have to explain about Matt.

Riding the train, Rem made a decision about Coleman.

Posters along Grand advertised tickets for the expo at twenty-five dollars. A crisp wind blew from the shore, cold and without aroma. Wagons and trailers for a film production blocked the sheltered roadway under Lake Shore Drive, and Rem picked a route between the idling vehicles, the gathered onlookers, expecting to be challenged. The city stopped at the pier, an abrupt wall of glass towers behind him, ahead a clean rolling blue that stopped the running argument in his head.

His phone trilled in his pocket: *Coleman – 1 voice.*

Rem found the entrance to the expo through a fixed fairground, a hotdog and souvenir stand right beside the stairway. As soon as he'd mounted the steps he realized that he was out of place. Dressed in jeans and trainers and a hooded top, he cut a scruffy figure, a slouch among men in pressed suits, military uniforms, and military fatigues. Men with heads shorn to express discipline.

The exhibition space, a long glass-topped gallery sectioned by two parallel aisles of open booths, stretched the length of the pier. In each booth the company names and logos were stencilled large across the walls, every one of the small kiosks dressed with carpets, counters, and tables, little sets busy with leaflets and brochures. And why hadn't he worn his suit?

Rem had a list from Geezler of the HOSCO partners, the subdivisions, and the subsidiaries. The companies he needed to check out.

He took the job seriously, and strolled through the booths as if to satisfy a particular interest. The booths close to the entrance were wonderlands of massed hardware, of all imaginable kinds of armament: machined, bright, mysterious. In the first booth, and the first business on his list, Proteck Inc., he found a display of jackets and helmets, whole body suits opened layer by layer, some with ceramic plates, others reinforced with micro chainmail padded with a webbed lining and a fine downy insulation. The more expensive jackets fitted with sweat-wicking undershirts and optional protection flaps for the neck and crotch (like necks and crotches weren't essential), easy-release binds and fasteners, and a guarantee that a personalized suit could be fabricated and shipped to any unit, worldwide, within twenty-one days. These suits, wall-mounted dissections, all impressively clean. Grey and black and busy with pockets.

Rem's phone trilled again and again, another message from Coleman. He deleted both messages then turned the phone to silent.

The more serious equipment came further up the central aisle – handguns and rifles, semi-automatic and fully automatic, hardware monitored by security guards. The guns, presented on Perspex mounts, pointed to a hoarding-sized poster of a desert populated by sneaky blacked-out turbaned figures with targets marked over their chests and heads. Rem knew next to nothing about guns, they simply didn't figure in his imagination; but being the kind of man who prefers the engine and not the car, the machined parts held a certain fascination. New, clean, oiled. Untouched. He examined the barrels, the sights, the disassembled trigger mechanisms, the hollowed-out carbon stocks, as if he understood the language.

His phone vibrated against his thigh.

Coleman – 1 message, 2 voice.

At Parkway CI Technologies (third on Geezler's list of subsidiaries) he found a display of landmines and devices – ETPs, IEDs. On the wall ran a client list of diplomats and businesses, recognizable global brands, sports teams, with a small under-scored by-line as *suppliers of expertise* to entertainment and production companies. As in the first booth, the combinations of hard technology and recognizable detritus (spent shells and casings, gas canisters, detergent boxes, computer monitors packed with dummy explosives) were opened out for display and marked 'genuine'.

Mike SMS: I'm getting calls from Coleman.

As Rem bent down a rep approached, talking, and Rem slowly straightened up. He hadn't bargained on talking.

Mike SMS: He's saying you won't answer his calls?

Rem held up his hand to stop any discussion, and continued looking. The man stepped back and asked which service Rem was with, and as Rem didn't understand the question the man flatly added that there was nothing for him here.

Mike SMS: What do you want me to tell him?

Rem headed back to the aisle.

A sign, 'Employment Services', hung in the centre of the walkway, and the booths separated out to a border area marked 'Food Court'.

In this area the reps dipped anxiously into the aisles, a stickiness to their movements, an anxiety that someone might slip by. As he passed a group of men, each with a coffee, he overheard advice: 'Set an exit strategy.' 'They don't own you.'

Rem checked his phone. Three further voice messages from Cathy. He'd wait till later to explain himself. He could imagine the confusion if he told her he was looking at guns.

When he checked the messages from Mike he had to sit down.

'I'm getting questions from Coleman about where you are and why you aren't answering his calls. He's threatening all kinds of things.' Mike spoke quickly. 'He's called two or three times an hour. If he comes round . . . I don't know. I just don't want any trouble.'

Rem looked up the aisle at the guns and displays of weaponry. Grenades. Rifles. Semi-automatics. A three-quarter model of a heat-seeking missile.

*

Rem returned to the Palmer House Hotel to find Paul Geezler waiting. They sat in the main reception, both in high-backed armchairs. For the second time that day he had the notion that he was on stage, that behind the vast lobby walls were banks of seating, an audience eager to witness a humiliation.

Geezler, smooth and smart in a different suit, his hair neatly parted, comb-tracked. A newspaper across his lap with an image Rem couldn't quite see – was it a hunter on one knee, or something more benign, a man by a road, a farmer? Geezler sat with his elbows on the armrests, hands clasped, ready to listen. He asked Rem about his visit to the fair.

Rem decided to be honest.

'I'm the wrong man. I don't know anything about these things – to be honest – it isn't that I'm not interested, I just don't have the knowledge. This isn't what I do. I'm not the man for what you want.'

Geezler gave small considered nods, and appeared to agree. 'You're right. I'm using you in the wrong way.'

'Don't get me wrong. I appreciate what you're doing, but I'm not the person you need.' Rem was beginning to rise, when Geezler held up his hand.

'I'm serious about wanting to know how we work. I have a better idea of how to use you. We work with employment agencies. Why don't you go to one of the recruitment drives and report back to me?'

'Again, it's a "thank you", but I don't have the expertise.'

'You don't need expertise. Submit an application, show up at the recruitment event, attend the presentations and processing, and we have a discussion afterward about how it all went. That's all it is. You only have to look like someone who's looking for work.'

This was something Rem could manage. The phone rang again in his pocket, he stood up, offered his hand to Geezler, and apologized.

'Maybe some other time.'

Geezler reached into his pocket and drew out his wallet. Rem said he couldn't accept the money. Not in good conscience.

'Think it over. If you're interested, call me.' Geezler insisted on a final drink, looked alone simply because he'd asked, so Rem agreed. After he'd placed the order, he asked Rem if there was anything wrong.

'You look different from yesterday. I'd say you look a little harassed.'

Rem said he probably needed to go.

Geezler rose with him. 'Out of interest, was I right about there being some kind of trouble?' Geezler's interest appeared genuine. 'I'm curious, that's all this is.' He settled back into his seat and looked to the bar, to the deeper lounge, as if placing people, calculating proximities. 'Sit down. Talk to me. Let me know what the problem is, make it hypothetical if you need. I might be able to help.'

Rem thought for a moment, it would be good to lay out the situation, hear it from his own mouth. Rem zippered his thumb across his mouth. 'We had some *issues*.'

'Issues?'

'Trouble.'

Geezler shifted in his seat. 'Related to hiring or performance?'

'Hiring.'

Geezler gave a broad smile. Satisfied. As if he knew it.

'One of the men stole from the houses we were painting.'

'Recently?'

'Recent enough.'

'Houses?'

'Two. That I know.'

Geezler nodded in encouragement.

'You paid them?'

'Two I knew about, a third I had to go with. I didn't want the rumour spreading. I wanted to keep my business.' Did he need to explain this?

'How did you find out?'

'We weren't getting referrals. People stopped calling. So I knew something was wrong.'

'Why did you pay?'

'Everything depends on reputation. If it ever went to court we'd be finished. As it is we're almost finished. I have loans I can't service, and wages.'

'And no one called the police?'

'Nobody wanted to involve their insurers.'

Geezler took in the information for a moment, then looked directly at Rem and said he appreciated what Rem had just told him. It took spine to be that direct. People around him barely spoke so plainly. He remembered the debt and said he could help. That is, if Rem wanted his help.

*

Rem returned with the money. Cash. He set it on the table to see how it would look. Four fifties – what he was comfortable accepting, given his poor performance. Geezler had wanted to press more on him, had offered it as *security* for the next occasion, which Rem decided not to take up.

Cathy wasn't home, and probably wouldn't return for another couple of hours. Rem looked at the notes on the table and understood that it wouldn't have made much difference to Geezler how much he'd paid. The only person it made any difference to was Rem, and right now the qualms he'd had about accepting money for a shoddy piece of work seemed beside the point. Two hundred dollars was better than nothing, but in reality, given their need, two hundred dollars wouldn't make much difference.

Three new messages on the home phone, seven stored. John first then Jay. *Mike said you might have something coming up? Let me know.*

Rem scooped the cash off the table.

His phone vibrated in his pocket.

Maggie – 1 new message. Coleman – 3 new messages. Mike – 2 new messages.

Cathy had collapsed at work, mid-aisle at the Happy Shopper. Looked like a spell had been cast and she was felled, instantly asleep.

'She'll have bruises.' Maggie spoke in a droll voice as if there was a punchline. They hadn't called an ambulance because Cathy had come to, clear-headed, and said something about not eating, about stress, about how she wasn't sleeping well.

'We gave her tea, tea with sugar.' Maggie called Rem 'the Brit', and enjoyed how the reference irritated him. The story had a coda. She wasn't done. 'It happened again, at four o'clock.'

The second time could have been serious. Cathy keeled over on the kerb. Outside, smoking, taking a quick five-minute break, and she'd done the darnedest thing, lurched forward like she'd been shot and launched herself into the road. Out before she hit the ground. Lordy. She didn't even raise a hand to protect herself. Not a mark on her. Nothing broken either.

This time they'd called an ambulance but Cathy had refused to go.

'We called you. I called. Cathy called.'

'I was downtown, working.'

'At least you're here this time. I'll drive her back.'

'Take Ashland. Clark and Western will be busy.'

In the background, Cathy complained. 'I can drive.'

'You want a word?'

'Look.' Cathy's voice came extra-loud. 'They said it was low blood pressure. I didn't eat this morning. That's all it was.'

'Maggie said it happened twice?'

'Low blood pressure.'

Maggie, now in the background, added, 'I didn't eat last night, but I'm not passing out.' Her voice obscured by Cathy's shushing.

Cathy had fallen at the wedding and this sounded like the same thing. She'd picked herself up immediately. Or was it immediate? Hadn't he noticed a pause? Hadn't the thought occurred to him that she was embarrassed, ashamed to have fallen, and just wanted to lie there, let everything get along without her? Add to this the fact that she clearly wasn't herself lately.

Through the door and home Cathy hurried directly to the bathroom, leaving Rem with Maggie. Maggie winced when she saw him, winced again while he clumsily said thanks, with the expectation that she would leave.

'I've been with her all day, and you want me to leave before the good part?' Maggie drew hard on her cigarette and squinted through the smoke. 'She needs a friend. Someone on her side.'

Rem dug his hands into his pockets and found Geezler's business card and cash.

'You really want me to go?'

'No. Stay. Tell me what happened.' Rem minded that he didn't sound sincere. He could never pitch himself right for Maggie.

'She won't shut up about money.' Maggie took out another cigarette and counted through the remaining pack before looking at Rem. 'At least you're here.' She held the cigarette just free from her mouth.

Cathy stood at the bathroom door, arms folded, 'Maggie, don't start.'

'I'm just saying.' Maggie shrugged. 'That's all. The last time Rem was in Kuwait, or something. What do I know?'

'This isn't—' Cathy tightened her arms. 'It's not the same thing. I didn't have any breakfast. I've not eaten.'

'She wouldn't go. They wanted to take her to Cook County.'

'It's not the same thing,' Cathy protested. 'Fainting isn't a sign.'

Maggie narrowed her eyes. 'Isn't a *good* sign either.'

'What did the medic say? You saw a medic?'

'I said. There were two medics. One of them took my blood pressure. I've explained this already.'

'But what did they say about the blood pressure?'

'That it was low. High or low, that's all anyone ever says about blood pressure.'

Maggie rolled her eyes, folded her arms to mimic Cathy. 'How do you know this isn't the same thing?'

Cathy turned back, defiant, walked to the kitchen. 'Because that was my thyroid. It's not the same thing.'

'Tell her,' Maggie nudged Rem. 'She has to get this checked out.'

Cathy answered so quietly she had to repeat herself. 'Enough. All right? Enough.'

Maggie began to ask more questions, and Cathy returned to the bathroom and locked the door.

Once Maggie was gone, Cathy came out of the bathroom and told Rem to sit down.

'I checked the messages from work. Seven messages from Andrew Coleman. What's going on? Have you heard them?'

Rem automatically answered no.

'Is he asking for money? Why is he calling, Rem? He doesn't even make sense. Listen to it.'

'No.'

'Are you paying the Colemans?'

Rem wouldn't answer.

'Jesus Christ, Rem. Why? They'll all want money. Who won't you pay?'

'There won't be any more.'

'Rem, you haven't done anything for the Colemans in, what, two years? At least? Why?'

'They're missing a ring.'

'Since when?' She rubbed her forehead to tease out an idea. 'He works for the police.'

'He's not in the police. He works for the office for the Chief of Police.'

Cathy found herself a seat.

'I haven't given them the money yet.'

'But you've arranged it. You've agreed it. Why is he calling?'

'I was late paying him. I still have the money. I'll call him. I'll settle this.'

Before she walked to the bedroom he thought she paused, something too small to properly register as a pause, but a tiny measurement of doubt, and he realized that she hadn't asked how much he was paying Coleman.

Flush with Geezler's money, Rem took Cathy to the movies. This being their habit, at least once a month, to agree on a movie, Cathy's preference being the Music Box, or at a push the Art Institute or MCA. For Rem, any Cineplex would do, with comfortable seats, surround sound, and a responsive crowd.

The film was Cathy's choice, but more to Rem's taste. She sat stiff throughout, resistant to the violence, didn't see how it was possible, the entire plot.

The movie was *fact*, Rem pointed out, based in an honest actual event, a piece of uncontested history.

'It's not the facts, Rem. It's the whole flavour of the thing. OK, so it happened. But how did it happen?' It wasn't the event she doubted, but how the event was demonstrated. They – the screenwriters, the actors, the director, whoever – had taken something real and made it implausible.

'People don't disappear like that.' Cathy wouldn't let this go. How could a young American, worldly, white, male, be abducted from a train station *in broad daylight*? This was Italy, supposedly, where everyone makes it their business to know everyone else's business. How could this be possible? Come on, not without *one single person* noticing. At the very least? The whole thing struck her as highly improbable. It wasn't the film, so much, as the idea that people could disappear. It didn't matter how loved they were, how vital, how dynamic. They could just vanish.

'And why? Was that ever explained?'

'The book.'

'I don't buy it. Imagine, you're given a job stapling plastic to a wall in a basement room, and you never ask yourself why? What might this room be used for? Come on? You never ask? It just wouldn't happen like that. And the names? Please. *Mr Wolf.*'

Rem only knew things in retrospect. Only in hindsight when

motives and meanings became apparent. In this regard film was the perfect media: with the answer laid out at the end.

☆

Rem took it as his responsibility to clear out Fatboy's room. Following Rem's example Fatboy had moved from his assigned quarters and taken residence in a store closet in the corridor between the commissary and the PX. Rem didn't like the idea of anyone messing with Fatboy's possessions, and decided it was his duty to box everything up, ready to ship back to his family. The boy had mentioned a mother in Michigan, but no one else, although Rem had fashioned the idea that Fatboy came from a large family and couldn't shake the notion. He saw Fatboy as the runt among many brothers and sisters and imagined that there were other versions, none of them quite so skinny or fragile.

The clean-out started one evening when other options were exhausted: he couldn't face another game of poker with Santo, and didn't want to watch another DVD, where the disc more likely than not would be corrupted. To avoid the other men in his unit he quietly roamed the PX, did the rounds of the food stalls, the vending machines, but couldn't occupy himself. As he came out of the commissary and headed toward the showers he had to pass Fatboy's closet.

The room: windowless and strewn with trash, the heat compacted the stench (Fatboy's stink of sweat and sweet nutmeg). Shelving units on three of the four walls were stacked with boxes, TV monitors, radios, wholesale packages of candy, out-of-date chips, jars of chip-dip in flats of twenty-four. Fatboy lived like a shut-in; everything within reach of a makeshift bed, a modest single black mat laid across the floor with barely enough room to stretch out, a radio kept inches from his ear. How could he stand the heat? Under the bottom shelf Rem found clothes, laundry, stiff and stuffed away with things he didn't want to see, some magazines and balled-up socks. The boy's taste ran scatter-shot: small Asian girls, breasty hipster blondes in cowgirl outfits. Rem couldn't imagine Fatboy with a woman, partly because he was so young, but mostly because Fatboy appeared innocent. He could be coy when the other men spoke of sex.

He worked with the door closed. Head throbbing when he stood up. He drank a warm Red Bull, the fizz hurt his throat, leaked through him, and he immediately began to sweat. He recognized this sweetness as the cause of the stink in the room: what he'd assumed to be the smell of the boy was only the smell of the drink.

On the bottom shelf Rem found a black folder with a notebook and a collection of loose paper. At first he thought that Fatboy had kept a diary and determined to burn this, because it was hard enough thinking about him, wondering if he had or had not ever loved anyone – and knowing, if he survived, that these injuries would blight his life.

Rem settled with his back to the door and began to leaf through the notebook. It looked like junk, just lists and scribbles, many of the pages swollen as if once wet. Fatboy had scrawled crosses on page after page; some plain, some three-dimensional with ornamentation as if wrought from iron. The notebook reminded Rem of a book of tattoo designs, demonstrating different varieties of the same thing. Loose rows and columns of crosses. On other sheets he found lists of names, possibly three to four hundred with a good number of repetitions, some from the military, but most of them contractors listed by their units. While he recognized some of the names, he couldn't figure out what linked them. He found Santo, alongside Clark and Samuels, two other men working with Unit 409. Next to these names were the same simple crosses. Others – Watts, Pakosta, Chimeno – were annotated with a cross in a circle, others with an ornate cross with spiral arms. One, drawn in negative, in a black circle, appeared against names which had been crossed out: ~~Forester~~, ~~Marks~~, ~~Bell~~.

For no good reason he'd thought of Fatboy as a Quaker. Rem liked to think of him equal to his peers, dressed in plain clothes, humble, sat alongside his brethren, waiting until the spirit singled him out. Instead the boy appeared a more common-or-garden evangelical Christian, born again, though that didn't tally with what he knew. Didn't those born-agains proselytize? Didn't they hunt people, hound after their souls? Didn't they pester God into every corner, bend every conversation? If Fatboy was a born-again he'd kept his counsel: Rem couldn't see God in any kind of detail here, not the faintest trace, and thought the idea laughable. So what kind of God-fearer was Fatboy? Some youth holed up in a storage room who saved souls by writing names and scrawling crosses? Fatboy collected names not souls.

Rem took over the room. He packed Fatboy's belongings and made sure they were returned to his mother. Night after night when he could not sleep he read repeatedly through Fatboy's lists, but knew that he would never understand why the boy had collected them.

His missed Fatboy's banter.

'If you had a special power,' Fatboy had asked, 'what would it be?' The power of flight, or X-ray vision, the ability to transform into a wolf, to swim like a dolphin?

Santo huffed. He already had a special power. 'Invisible.' He looked for a place to spit. 'True. I'm invisible. The only time people see me is when they want something. Blame. I exist to shoulder other people's shit.'

Rem said he wouldn't want anything special. No. According to his wife, he needed the simple gift of instant hindsight, so it wouldn't be hindsight at all. There probably wasn't even a word for what he needed, but he knew there wasn't one single day he didn't need to go back and fix something.

'I'm off-pitch,' he said, 'that's what she calls it.'

'Not a problem, bro.' Santo leaned forward, let out a fine stream of spit. 'I blow my nose, I get blood. The air. It's *dry*.'

Fatboy wanted everything. Let's face it. What's the point of just one thing? You'd need super-strength, super-speed, heightened senses, the whole bag of superpowers – and flight. One lone power wouldn't cut it.

'And what would you do with all that?' The idea vexed Santo. He looked up, took in the hot white sky. 'I mean, what's the point? You get to do all this shit, but what for? There's always stuff you can't do. My sister, she sees angels. All over the place. Angels with wings. Every-where. Her cat died and she still sees it. Follows her around. Why? She thinks she's gifted. What use is this to her?' He shook his head. 'Noth-ing. She still works minimum wage. Still married to a creep. Still unhappy.'

Fatboy said he'd been reading, and found some differences. 'We have people who do things. Fly, climb buildings, all that. Here they have *things* that do stuff. Carpets. Lamps. Bottles. Magic *stuff*.'

'The Arab is superstitious.' Santo shook his head. 'They ever cut my head off, they even try, I'm telling them they're cursed. Their family, their neighbours, everything they touch. Fucked up for ten thousand years. Their sperm will have no tails, their children will be retards, their women frigid. Their water poisoned. The wheat will die in the field. Locusts. Fat-assed locusts in their millions. That's my superpower. Fear and doubt. They even touch my head I'll curse them, and everything that happens, everything bad, big and small, is down to me. I'm giving them *doubt*. That's my superpower. *Doubt.'*

Fatboy liked the idea. In all those stories, the ones where you get three wishes, they never work out. Not even once. There's always some trick. Better to do it like Santo, and live for ever because they can't *fix* you, can't get you straight. Even when you're gone they don't know who you are so they have to keep rolling the idea over and over. He liked it. Santo was on to something.

'Just claim something you haven't done. Famine. War. Disease. Say it's yours and they'll make you a saint.' Santo pointed at the ovens, he'd promised them rum, proper Cuban rum. No joke. Security from Anaconda could bring you anything. Only if they even got caught *thinking* about alcohol they'd lose their jobs and entitlements. Better to drink it in his hut.

☆

The package from Geezler arrived on a Friday. Rem hid it from Cathy and took it with him to the library. He sat at the back by the magazine stacks with a view of the door and the computers beside him.

Geezler had filled in much of the form, and with it came a simple note asking Rem to complete the sections he'd marked and make sure he signed in three places, and to call once it was in the mail. As far as Rem could see it wasn't much of anything. Geezler had him marked down for manual work in Region 3: Bahrain, Iraq, Jordan, Kuwait, Oman, Saudi, Syria, Turkey, UAE, Yemen. He did exactly as he was asked, dropped the package in the mail on his way home, and called Geezler.

'So you'll do this?'

'It's on its way.'

'I need one favour. I need what we're doing to remain between us. Just us. No one else. If other people find out it won't work.'

Rem couldn't see any problem with this.

'So, we're agreed. Complete deniability. No one else knows. Not anyone you meet in the interview, none of the candidates, no relatives, no family, not even your wife.'

'I have to tell my wife.'

'You can't. As part of the clearance procedure they'll want to con-firm details, they'll call you at home – what if she answers?'

'I'll tell her.'

'It's a risk.'

'She'll understand.'

Geezler paused. 'It's too much of a risk. If they have any idea we're sending people to check on them it isn't going to work. To be honest, you're no use to me otherwise.'

Rem considered hanging up. He could tell Cathy and not tell Geezler that she knew. 'OK.'

'OK?'

'OK.'

'Don't tell her and think it will work out. She can't know. Are we agreed?'

Rem hesitated and then agreed.

He wanted to know when he would hear, and Geezler assured him that they turned these things around quickly.

After the call, Rem began to wonder what he'd agreed to, and what difference it would make if Cathy did or didn't know.

Rem walked up Clark and was struck by how solid the street appeared, how this was, he couldn't think of any other word, except, *natural*. As if today was how the neighbourhood should always be seen, that every other season the street would be out of perspective. For example: walking now, the budding afternoon, the late-spring air, the buses, the fried meat scent from the taquerias, the split cartons and crates beside the supermercado. All of this seemed right, in place. Ordinary. He couldn't imagine the same street three months earlier, grey with old snow, rutted with ice, cars shifting forward and sideways, the sidewalk limited to one narrow path, figures disguised under jackets and coats, and hunched under the assault of a brutal wind, the windows at the eateries greased with condensation. He couldn't imagine himself either with his dog, because this was the route they took from the lake, each morning, each night. He couldn't picture the dog, and had to work hard to resurrect him. Rem looked about as if to fix the street, the corner, Clark and Lunt, in memory. *One day I won't live here. This will all be lost.*

Just over a week after submitting his application Rem received a package from Headspring Training offering an interview at a choice of venues: the Welcome Inn outside Knoxville, Tennessee, or the Best Western close by O'Hare.

Curious about the pack, Cathy asked what was going on. Was this some agency? Had he registered for work? Did this have anything to do with their loans? Rem shuffled through the papers, which asked for insurance details, health, and next of kin.

'Is this a job? *Induction*. That sounds a lot like work?' Cathy took the papers out of his hands. Sat down as she read, assumed a slow bending stoop, her expression becoming tighter. 'What is this?' she asked, serious, confused. 'I don't understand. Why do they want details about your health? These are questions about your family, about diseases? I don't understand. She read on. 'What's Headspring? Who are these people?'

Rem said he didn't know, he'd sent an application to Manpower Recruitment who managed civil-engineering contracts, so he had no idea about these Headspring people.

'Engineering? So this is work?' She sounded surprised. Rem didn't like this reaction. 'You found work? Where?'

'It's a recruitment agency.'

'I don't know that I like the idea of you working on construction sites.' Cathy turned the papers over. 'It says region three. What does that mean?'

'Region three means places like Saudi.'

'Saudi?'

'Like Saudi.'

'*Like* Saudi? Where else is *like* Saudi?' She gave a short laugh. 'I don't know what that means.'

'Like the Middle East. Like Jordan. Syria. Dubai. Like Iraq.'

It took a while to penetrate. Iraq. He could have counted the seconds.

'Iraq?' She spoke as if absorbing some mighty concept. 'Iraq?' And then she appeared to disassemble, her hands descending to her lap, her shoulders, her face even, taking on weight. When she did speak, her voice came considered and final. 'I'm not doing this again.'

'It isn't the same. I'm not going anywhere.'

'Rem, when I said somewhere else, I meant Iowa or Indiana, or maybe, I don't know, someplace *like* California, but Iraq?' A small pry cut through her voice. 'Iraq? Rem? You paint rooms. In houses. In hotels.' She held the papers to her chest and shook her head, and her expression became so sorrowful, so lost. This wasn't going to happen again. Kuwait had been bad enough. Iraq was out of the question.

After some moments she softly asked if he had signed anything. 'You have to call. You have to tell them there's been a mistake.'

Rem leaned forward, set his hands on her knees to reassure her. 'It's information,' he said, 'that's all. Something I found. I sent off an application and they sent this back. It's nothing.'

'This isn't nothing.' Cathy held up the papers. 'This doesn't just *happen*. You've already applied. I don't understand why we're talking about this.' She twisted free of his grasp then set the papers carefully on the table. 'You've done this deliberately.'

Cathy left the room and Rem considered how to clarify his arrangement with Geezler without breaking his word. Cathy returned from the bedroom with more papers.

'You see these. This is on top of what we owe. You understand? You need a job, Rem. Something that has healthcare. Insurance. A job. A stable job. *Here.*' She shook the papers at him before dropping them on the table. Bills for scans, blood tests, X-rays. 'That's what we owe, and they haven't even got started. We don't qualify for anything, Rem, we don't get assistance. No one else is going to look after these. Do you understand the problem? How is this going to work if you go to Iraq?'

Rem separated his papers from the pile on the table. 'It isn't what you think. I'm not going to work in Iraq. It isn't what you think.'

'When is it ever about what I think, Rem? It has to be something more complicated, doesn't it? It's always something else with you. That is an application for a job. It's in your name.'

Rem straightened the papers on his knee. Let her do this, leave her alone. Explain some other time.

When Cathy returned from work that evening she took a cup of hot water with her to bed, and complained of a migraine, her mood too dangerous to confront.

Rem called Geezler and explained about Cathy. He wanted to tell her, he said. This past month hasn't been easy. She needs to know. She hasn't been well. This isn't helping.

'You're not going anywhere except O'Hare,' Geezler soothed. 'You go to the induction. You call me. We speak, and then you explain everything to her.'

'She made a point about the application being real, being in my name.'

Geezler appeared to give this some thought. 'You're right. We should have used another name. You're still going?'

'I'm still going.'

'I'd like to send you to the training camp in Austin. I could use you out in the field.'

The idea had its own logic.

'You know I can't do that.'

'I know. I'd pay a bonus. A straight fifty, no questions. However you wanted it. Fifty thousand on top of anything you earn. No tax. No questions.'

'You're talking Austin?'

'Two for Austin but fifty for both Austin and Iraq.'

'Nice numbers, but not possible.'

'I wish it was. She already thinks you're going.'

'I can't.'

'Think about Austin then. Will you do that?'

'I know I can't do it.'

'One week at the training camp.' Geezler backed off. 'It's just a thought,' he said, 'it would be useful.'

They agreed to speak after the induction.

☆

On the last day in May, Unit 409 were sent to Jalla Road to lay the final section of blacktop. On this night, the people who had lived in the neighbourhood gathered at a squatter camp in an archaeological park bordering the highway. It wasn't that their tents and campfires hadn't been noticed, but everyone assumed that these people were part of the influx of refugees from Basrah, Nasiriyah, even Baghdad. A mistake with serious consequences. The highway, nearly complete, with its steep walls, was little more than a deep concrete trench. As the long convoy of vehicles approached, none of the crew of Unit 409 noticed the refugees beginning to congregate on the walls above them. By the time they did notice, and stop, the angry former residents, raised above the convoy, were able to pelt them with stones and bottles loaded with gasoline.

The crews, expecting back-up, withstood the first barrage. A second wave brought a hail of bottles which burst into fire on impact.

They watched the front vehicles burn, their companions scuttle from one vehicle to the next seeking refuge. When security did not show the convoy steadily reversed down the unpaved highway and abandoned the stricken vehicles. As they retreated, the bolder citizens came down the concrete banks as a wave. Rem watched the mob fill the roadway. As the contractors made their way back to ACSB they passed the security forces, a pack of armoured trucks with helicopters riding overhead. The zone behind them strafed with streams of tear gas.

The next morning the highway was blasted to pieces. IEDs planted every twenty metres uprooted hanks of concrete, pitched holes, spoiled a road which had never been used.

☆

Rem arrived an hour early for the sessions at the Premier Suite, and sat in the parking lot facing the white front of the motel. A few cars on either side. Cathy's '*don't commit*' hung with him, and he regretted not explaining the situation to her. 'Why are you even going? What are you trying to prove?'

In a beige VW parked beside him sat a man who appeared to be speaking to his fist, a white wire ran from his ear.

Rem gathered his papers, locked his car and paused for a final smoke. The man in the VW wound down his window and asked Rem if he was here for the Headspring event. The induction.

'Which company are you with? Manpower?'

Rem nodded.

'Manpower. Roads, right? Highways and byways.' The man gave a thoughtful nod. 'That makes sense. Civil work? You're not security, then?'

Rem shook his head. The man stepped out of his car and still appeared small.

'Pendleton, Manpower, RamCo, ReServe, Outcome. Headspring recruits for them all. They're all the same, in any case. You've heard of HOSCO?' This wasn't a question so much as an assumption, the opening of a conversation.

The man looked up as Rem shook his head.

'HOSCO. Look them up. They run everything. Most of these companies are subsidiaries, but HOSCO run the show. They're the people you'll work for. You're serious?'

'Serious?'

'About going?' The man answered his own question as he locked his car. 'Serious enough to come, I guess. Serious enough to find out.'

In the first session they were given nametags, offered coffee and an over-large platter of mini-Danish. Rem counted thirty people, exclusively men, the majority Black and Hispanic, and they sat facing a roll-down screen, silent while an introductory video titled 'Amrah City – New City' played and replayed. Rem watched as a decrepit city of low-rise buildings of dead whites and tawny browns, with blank dusty skies, was digitally transformed with new roads and highways, a river, then, rising from the ground, office buildings, libraries, schools, a museum, an entirely new administrative centre surrounded by flags and trees under a slick blue sky. No people, he noticed, not one placed in there. This, he guessed, was the project the man in the VW had described. *Regeneration For The Next Generation.* The title faded out. Re-build. Re-generate.

After the video a man of about Rem's age delivered a short introduction. He clasped his hands as he spoke, thanked everyone for coming and said that this was the final round of the post-application, pre-selection process, then introduced himself as Steve.

'Today, we go through our final screening procedures – nothing to worry about.' He pointed at the screen. 'We want you to have an idea of the scale of the project. Forget what you've heard, or read, or anything you've been told. This is a whole new situation. You'll be involved in rebuilding. Helping to finish what we've started out there. Amrah City is the hub. Government. Business. Communications. Industry.' While he spoke he looked slowly through the seated rows, man to man, and when he stopped he gave a little hesitation as if expecting applause.

Steve asked if there were questions, and one man struck up his hand and said he didn't get it. 'Are we working for the military or the government?'

Steve nodded through the question, then said he understood and that this raised a good point. 'When you are out in the field you are a contractor. A private individual. You're working for yourself. Except, we provide the opportunity for you to work. We'll go more into this later.'

After the introduction they formed four queues in the foyer, A–F, G–L, M–S, T–Z, where they showed their papers and documents to a couple at a desk, after which, with everything satisfied, they returned to the seminar room. Rem noticed fewer people returning, and was joined by the man he'd spoken with in the parking lot. A sticker, *hello, my name is – Rob*, on his shirt pocket. They shook hands.

'Did you show references?'

'Do we need to?'

'You'd think? This is an employment agency, right, and they don't ask for references? You think they don't have enough people to build their own roads out there?' Rob kept his eye on the door. 'Have you spoken with any of these guys?'

Rem said no.

'Security is usually ex-military. Who knows who these people are?' His voice low, he asked Rem questions while men were called out for their medical evaluations.

Rem wondered if the man was part of the recruitment process, a spy to vet the candidates they were unsure about, and with this doubt he became less confident about answering his questions. Was he working for the company, or for a rival? You have to consider these possibilities.

When the assistants called the candidates for interview, Rem noticed that Rob became quiet.

Rem took off his shirt, wondered how far he should go with this, gave blood anyway, breathed in and out when he was asked, answered questions about his general health which made him laugh, and then, behind a screen, produced a urine sample and made sure he filled the container to the top although he had been asked not to. He signed a form certifying that he'd never been convicted of a felony and faced no ongoing charges. When he returned to the seminar room he noticed that Rob was gone, along with half of the applicants. Eight men remaining. After a small wait he was asked back to another seminar room where a formal offer was made. On the wall hung a row of prints, scenes of windmills, fields, and waterways.

Rem allowed the man to talk. If he signed the contract he'd be working with HOSCO: the Hospitality and Operational Support Company of Hampton Roads, Virginia – just as Rob had said. Steve explained that HOSCO managed civil contracts in Europe, Africa, and across the Middle East, but they were hiring now for southern Iraq in a last bid to complete contracts within Amrah City. Rem also needed to understand that while these projects were nominally classified as *civil*, they were, in fact outsourced *military* projects: meaning that they were open to private business, and that those private businesses enjoyed military protection.

Rem fought against the urge to explain himself, the pure fun of stating that he was already working for HOSCO.

In Amrah City, Steve promised, you won't see one local. Not one. It couldn't be safer. Plus (not that you'll need it), you have the entire US Marine Corps looking out for you. Posters behind Steve showed men beside diggers, smiling, shaking hands with men in desert MARPAT, a ziggurat in the background, a long low-lying adobe village; or men seated during a work-break at some stumpy oasis surrounded by skinny dogs, handsome strays with dark almond-shaped eyes; or (Rem's favourite), an employee in a flak jacket playing soccer on wasteland with a scattered group of boys. '*HOSCO: Building Communities One Project at a Time,*' the sky a clear wondrous blue, suggesting worthy effort and reward. Naive? Sure, but so what, at least they appeared sincere.

And how did the money sound to him? The first figure presented didn't look impressive, but the advisor added up overtime, what he called 'strategic placement bonus' and a 'completion of work bonus', then explained the allowance for meals and reimbursement for any work-related accommodation. 'This is covered while you're at Amrah. We have a complex close by the government compound, with housing, stores, a PX, a commissary, a fully-equipped gym. And remember, there's no tax. They can't take a dime.'

As an idea Rem could see its appeal. The man continued. There were two kinds of insurance, one for life, one for catastrophic trauma.

'You won't need it, but it's there. And supposing, and I mean supposing, something were to go wrong, we'd ship you to Germany and bring you back home. No questions. No trouble. You get the same cutting-edge medical attention as the military. It covers your family back here if you or they have to be provided for. Tell me,' he asked, 'where you could make this kind of money, *every month*. No tax. Not one cent.'

The man asked how good it sounded now, and Rem, understanding that the figure represented his potential monthly earning, not his yearly gross, admitted that it was starting to sound very, very good. Kuwait had paid well, except the agency had subtracted a sizeable monthly fee. This guaranteed considerably more.

When Rem said he'd like to think about it, the man sucked in his breath and placed his hand flat on the papers.

'Sure,' he cleared his throat, 'of course you do. You can't take a decision like this lightly. You need to consider it, think it through. I understand. I can hold this offer for a week. Think about it, talk it over, do whatever you need to do. If it takes more than a week I won't be able to offer the same package. We have quotas, and once those are full we won't be hiring any more. This is our final drive, there aren't so many places. I'm offering the last of what we have. It's a favourable package. If you need a week, take a week. I'll hold it for you. I can't promise any longer.'

Rem took up the pen, but said that he could not sign without speaking first with his wife.

The man pushed the papers forward.

'It's four months,' he said, 'you'll be back before anyone knows you're gone.'

Rem folded the contract into his back pocket as he came out of the building, the shift in temperature, from crisp air-conditioning to the humid outdoors, made him hold his breath. As he unlocked his car door he noticed Rob sat on the barrier across the parking lot, an attitude about him, a deliberate wait. A man smoking with intent, thin legs stretched out, looking like the slightest gust would push him over.

'You didn't sign anything, did you?'

Rem again wanted to explain what he was doing – just the once.

'I didn't sign.'

'No? Not yet, but you will. You'll go home and think it over. You'll think about the money until it sounds so good you can't see the harm in it. Be careful, though. Take a good look at these people before you agree to anything.'

Rem didn't have the heart to explain how he'd done this before, as good as. What could be the difference? A complex in Amrah City? A hotel in Kuwait City? Two contained environments.

Three security guards came out of the building and waited under the awning, arms folded. 'This is public property,' Rob shouted across the road. 'I have every right to be here.'

The men watched but kept their place.

'They think they know me. I'm not a journalist,' he said, 'I'm an interested citizen.'

The two men sat outside the Intercontinental bar on a balcony over-looking the highway. Rem watched the cars and cabs turn off for the terminals, the hive-like hum of the highway, the hotels, the concrete spill of the parking lot and the approach to the airport, he felt part of a larger vista – the wind carried breadth and distance, a scope of land running right the way to Nebraska, Wyoming, the idea of a prairie holding a sense of potential, of unknowing. He let his eye hop over the billboards running alongside the airport approach – hotels, airlines, credit bureaus – as Rob paid for the drinks.

Six weeks with a fifty-thousand-dollar bonus from Geezler.

No tax.

'I'm not saying the money isn't good. They get kids direct from high school, promise them three, four times as much as the military, then whisk them out, and what for? You know how many contractors have been killed this year?' Rob stabbed out his cigarette. 'You don't want to know. The equipment is substandard, nothing can cope with the heat or the sand. They say they'll provide protection; the military won't touch the gear they use. And the place you'll be staying – they can't protect you, whatever they say. Security is a joke. I tell you this for free. If you go, stay clear of the military. Have nothing to do with them, they're leaving, they don't care what happens next. It's only HOSCO that won't admit it's over. Avoid Iraqis whenever possible. Don't go there to make friends. Get in. Get out. Better still, get a job managing food services, or something so remote no one knows you're there. Have nothing to do with guns or any kind of munitions. At the moment Amrah City's nice and quiet, but it won't last long. All this talk of rebuilding? They've poured millions into reconstruction, to satisfy agreements that no longer stand. It's about taking one more bite out of that apple before they dump the barrel. Nothing is being done right. The whole thing's failed. The idea that they can rebuild a dying city right at the edge of the desert is a dumb idea cooked up in Washington where they don't know anything about Amrah or the Arab mentality. Fact is, no one can control the districts, they think they have one place settled, and then the next day they're right back where they started.' He lit another cigarette. 'You signed, didn't you. I know it. You haven't said a word.'

In the air, still, that sense of space. Rem held up his glass and closed his eyes.

Fifty thousand dollars, in hand, plus wages, no tax, every cent he earned. Money for his business. Money for their debt. Money for Cathy's medical. Plenty of money.

He called Geezler. Read from his notes, and broke the day down, hour by hour. He repeated Rob's concerns verbatim. Allowed himself a little joke when speaking about Steve, but had to admit, in the final analysis, that the man didn't seem to know his subject.

'There was pressure,' he said, 'and it was confusing. I've had an easier time buying a car. They come across as desperate.'

Geezler became most interested when Rem began to talk about the contracts. 'They follow a script,' he admitted, 'how did it sound?'

'Unclear. They could stick to the information. Give a few hard facts. Even with the contract it just was hard to follow.'

'You've done a good job. I'd like to use you more. I really would.'

'Would you offer more than fifty?'

'You're considering this?'

'More than fifty?'

'Fifty is my discretionary limit. But you're considering this?'

'I can't say I'm not tempted.'

'I'm guessing that you've already decided.'

☆

The men from Unit 409 were called to a meeting. One of HOSCO's division directors, a man from Hampton Roads, Virginia, intended to visit Amrah and wanted to meet one of the teams in situ. He'd spend an hour at the compound, inspect the site, and most likely be accompanied by a photographer. Rem sat next to Santo and wondered what, actually, was the reason for the visit.

'This isn't to honour us,' Santo shook his head, 'this is PR. You've seen the news? The protection. The vehicles. The body armour. It's all sub-substandard. Might as well be wearing targets. He's here because of Fatboy getting shot through one of their shitty vests. Some lawyer smelling trouble has made them do this.'

Rem sat back, Fatboy's notebook in his hand.

'What are you doing with that?'

'You've seen this before?'

Santo looked Rem in the eye. 'Depends.'

'On what?' Rem scoffed, this was absurd. He'd either seen it or he hadn't.

'I've seen it.'

'The names?'

Santo gave a shrug as a yes.

'You've seen the names?' Rem opened the notebook on his lap. 'Then you know what all these crosses are about?'

Santo took the book. 'Fatboy was keeping a slate.'

'Betting? I don't follow. On what?'

'On who was going to get hit. Fifty per contractor. One hundred if they worked internal with military or security. Two hundred if they worked over the line. Hit. Maim. Kill. There's *hit*, which is just hit, nothing more, maybe something superficial, anything that heals or is non-essential. Accident or deliberate, doesn't matter. Loss of anything smaller than a hand, fingers as such, ear, nose, anything they can reconstruct classifies as a hit. Then *maim*, pretty obvious, no? Non-replaceable damage, loss of limb, use of limbs, sight, dick, you name it. Then there's *kill*. Kill speaks for itself. See, he marked the odds with crosses.' Santo flicked through the book. 'It's a shame about what happened, because it was just getting started. I mean it's been going for a while, but it was just getting *properly* started. These guys,' he pointed out the names on the first page, 'they're small. They never go out. Waste of time. This place would have to take a direct hit to get money on them. The big money is on these guys. You pay two hundred to start, because they're more exposed. Anyone working over the line is more vulnerable, so naturally you pay more. See here: Pakosta, Watts, Chimeno, these are the prime candidates. They work in transport, security, and comms. They go out every day.'

'You knew about this?'

'Sure. I knew about it.'

'So these crosses?'

'That means the first bid was two hundred. Every bet after that would have gone up by fifty.'

Disappointed in Fatboy, Rem didn't want to push. 'How do you know about this?'

'It was mostly the military. *Was*. They were the people who started it. The MODS were betting on which contractor would go first. It worked in two ways, if someone was killed, you'd get the whole pot. Half if they were medevaced out. The slate was wiped clean with every hit. Fatboy took the basic idea and turned it into an art. He had this notion that if you bet on a string of kills, four or five in a sequence, you'd be solid.'

'Meaning?'

'We're talking a lot of money here.'

'How much?'

'Pick a number. That book isn't even old. This was Fatboy's scholarship fund.'

'Did anyone get hit?'

'Plenty.' Santo scanned through the pages, then opened the book at a page where the names had been scratched out, then another, then another. 'See. And here.'

'And how did you know about this?'

'Rem,' Santo hit his chest in mock grief, 'man, *everybody* knows about this. I knew about it, and I'm on the list. I worked at one of the FOBs before this, and I knew about it then. Hernandez, right there, that's me.'

'Why aren't I included? We do the same work?'

Santo folded his arms. 'He wouldn't accept a bet on you. Wouldn't hear of it.'

Rem looked to the book: Hernandez, Samuels, Clark, Watts, Pakosta, Chimeno.

☆

Cathy didn't understand, and had a look about her like she wasn't ready to make the effort. What was this? The whole thing? *Geezler*? What kind of a name was that anyway? What kind of scheme? Was this a hoax?

Rem tried his best to explain. It was good money. That's what it was. Money for those medical bills for a start. Money to help pay their debts. Money they couldn't hope to make otherwise.

Cathy looked at him, astounded. 'My God. You've made up your mind haven't you? You're going?'

Rem struggled to stay calm. 'It's a training camp. It's where everyone goes before they're shipped out.'

'You'll die.'

'He wants to know how it works.'

'And who is this man?' Cathy summoned anger from the air.

'He's the head of the parent company.' Rem knew this not to be true, but the fact that Geezler could be undertaking this kind of enquiry meant that he was placed high in the company.

'You don't know what you're doing. You don't know what they're asking. This isn't a solution.'

'Yes, it is. You just don't want it.' Rem's answer came with a nasty calm.

'Call him,' she answered. 'Go. See if I care.'

Rem picked up the phone, walked to the bedroom to find Geezler's business card in his jeans. When he returned to the kitchen Cathy half-stood, half-leaned against the kitchen table. Eyes small and black.

'Do it.'

'It's six weeks.' Rem drew a chair back from the table, sat down, made his actions certain, definitive. 'In six weeks we can have everything paid for. I don't see much of a choice. I don't see a lot of options.'

Cathy narrowed her eyes and hung her head. Call him. She said. Call him. Get it over with.

☆

Santo wouldn't answer Rem's questions about Fatboy's book. He didn't outright refuse, just became weary, rolled his eyes, his patience with this almost out. If it was running, Rem reasoned, up until he was shot, then what had happened with the money?

Santo had no idea. 'How should I know? You knew him. He wasn't normal. He didn't do things like everyone else.'

'You said people paid in hundreds of dollars each a week. So there had to be money?'

'It wasn't all cash. Not hard cash. There aren't exactly many banks round here. He kept a tab. That's – the – reason – for – the – book.' Santo dropped his head, exhausted. 'That book.' Santo tried to explain. 'It's like everything else here. It doesn't work how you think. Let's say I won, all right. Let's say I bet two hundred on a top kill, and I won. Then I might get some money upfront from Fatboy, a little money, but the rest would be owed to me from the other people who'd laid bets. So other people who had unsuccessful bets would have to pay. Understand? Far as I know no one ever paid out. It was like a rolling debt. If I won,

311

then anyone who'd placed a bet owed me, and it was carried on like that, week after week. Likewise.'

'But there was still money. Five dollars. Ten dollars. A million dollars. I'm telling you there wasn't a cent in his room. He left with nothing. I packed everything up for him.'

Santo finally appeared to understand. 'Well, there had to be some.'

Rem found Samuels in the commissary. Since Fatboy's *accident* Samuels had refused to go over the line and was in forfeit of his Strategic Placement Bonus. Samuels haunted the commissary, sat at tables with coffee nested between his hands, his skin growing whiter under the stark overheads, the lack of natural light.

Rem bought them both coffees and slid into the booth. Samuels, as insubstantial as Fatboy himself, cringed at the memory, and never spoke of the incident.

'Did he have anything with him?'

Samuels pinched his mouth and shook his head. Rem thought his eyes looked glassy, not like a drinker, but fearful, rabbit-like.

'He didn't have a bag, a hold-all? He wasn't carrying anything?'

'He had the gun. That's about all I remember.'

Rem looked up the hall. They could be in a school. The linoleum floor, the tiled ceiling, the sameshit double-glass fire doors. Cream-coloured walls. This could be Idaho, Iowa, Illinois, not Iraq.

'He had nothing. He had a gun. He didn't know how to hold it. I'm lucky it didn't go off in my face. He shouldn't have had that gun. He had no business being there.'

Rem thanked Samuels, and when Samuels asked him why he was asking, Rem shrugged. He didn't rightly know, not really. Just had this notion that Fatboy had a bag of some kind, something he might have carried with him.

Samuels shut his eyes and softly shook his head. 'Everyone wants to know where the money is.'

'The money?'

Samuels gave Rem a long *come on, be serious* look. 'Everyone wants to know about the money from the club.'

Just as Rem walked off, Samuels called him back. 'On the seat. You're right. A sportsbag. Singapore Airlines. That logo. Singapore. That's what he had. I don't think there was ever any money. I'm sure there never was any cash.' Samuels talked and moved as a man disturbed from slumber. 'It was all promises. Credit notes. IOUs. That's all it was about. Winning. You promised money, and kept going, hoping for a perfect run.'

Rem couldn't see what Fatboy would get out of it.

'When people left they owed him. Fatboy was building a future. People who owed him favours. People who could help him out one day. It wasn't about money, never was.'

Rem thanked Samuels again, and Samuels asked if Rem knew Fatboy's name. 'William. At home he went by Billy.'

Rem returned to Fatboy's room, settled on the mat, and found himself sweating before he'd opened the notebook. Knowing someone's name took away their mystery. He wondered who Billy was, back home with his family and his mother. Another timid boy. One among others, undistinguished. Plain William, borrowed from uncles and grandfathers.

He slept through much of the afternoon and woke to find email from Cathy on his cell: *Call me. It's about Matt.*

☆

For all but his last night Cathy slept separately and avoided talking with him, until, in a final capitulation she slipped, silently, under the covers beside him.

He'd taken a flight from the Netherlands via Austin the year before they married, spent time at immigration being questioned about his visa, about how many trips he'd made by officials for the Department of Homeland Security who didn't quite understand that Schiphol Airport served the whole of the Netherlands. Rem insisted that his family came from a small village swallowed by Bergen op Zoom where people strived to live undistinguished lives, hold moderate values, the kind of people who knew their neighbours, rarely visited the city, and feared God with a powerful superstition, and he wondered, while he insisted on this distinction, why he had to attach himself to a place he hadn't lived in for over twenty years, to people he'd worked hard to leave. He didn't understand Halsteren when he was a child, and he held no attachment to it as an adult. His family simply lived there, and year by year, there were less of them. Nevertheless, Halsteren remained in his passport as his place of birth. For immigration these distinctions meant nothing. As a big man with a casual lope, they took him as a type. They detained Rem for four hours in an eight-by-nine space defined by six rolling screens he could have pushed aside. They left him alone, in this temporary space, not even a room, and he expected the man to return, passport in hand, to escort him to departure. He wasn't sure how it would work, but he couldn't see himself reaching Chicago. He missed his connecting flight and had to sleep in the terminal with the threat that these men could return, pick him out and pack him off, just as they pleased. The whole experience was so unpleasant it resolved him to marriage, although neither of them wanted to marry. The visas gave limited security. He understood that he might have chosen Chicago as his home, but Chicago had not chosen him.

On his return to Austin the same dread set upon him. He couldn't imagine the next step and half-hoped for a call from Cathy telling him to come home, this was ridiculous, just come right back.

At the carousel a different certainty struck him. He watched bags tumble down the baggage claim and realized he'd gone too far.

On the first night Cathy went early to bed, took a mug of hot water with her, her glasses, a book, a thriller she'd bought for this specific night, switched the TV on, quiet and low, as if this was normal, or better: as if this was something long anticipated, a treat she was determined to enjoy. She settled naturally on her side of the bed, rested her glasses and the book on her stomach and wondered what she should do next. She wasn't exactly sure what she wanted, and looked about the room and wondered how it had come to be furnished in this way, not through any one decision, but through a gradual accumulation: a dresser from her mother, the built-in wardrobe Rem had salvaged and fronted with mirror. The TV, large, flat-screen, paid on credit they hadn't yet settled. She watched her reflection. The light from the TV picked out the rounded shapes of her feet, her knees, her stomach and breasts, all softened by the quilt, her face shone a little greasy, and she was alarmed at how surprised she looked, as if it wasn't Rem that was missing, but part of her body.

He wouldn't call, she guessed, so she sent an SMS, typed a hug and a kiss at the end of the message, and thought this hypocritical but necessary, then turned to her side so she wouldn't have to watch herself.

He'd come back, she didn't doubt, he didn't like Austin in any case. He'd be back in two days, four, tops.

She decided to sound perky. Practical. She'd call, if he didn't answer she'd leave a message.

When the home phone rang she looked at it in surprise.

'Hello? Rem?'

'My cell's flat. I'm calling from the dormitory, plugged-in. They've given us rooms. You know those movies where the parents take their daughter to college? It looks nothing like that. What are you doing?'

'I'm in bed.'

'I woke you?'

'No. It's early. I thought I might read.'

'The people I'm with . . .'

'I was going to ask.'

'. . . are from the Philippines. No one speaks English too well. We haven't been fed. They brought us from the airport, told us we could-n't leave. They'll pick us up at seven tomorrow. I'm not sure what they're going to do with us. There's one row of showers, two toilets – don't ask – and a snack machine. There's a rumour that we don't get paid until we're actually in Iraq.'

She thought to tell him not to do this, to walk out, face whatever trouble came their way because of it, but to come right back. They could pay the company back for the flight, somehow make everything right with Geezler, move on and forget this. She didn't know how, but they would figure this out.

'What are you reading?'

'I don't know. I haven't started.'

'I'll leave you to it.'

Cathy kept the phone to her ear long after Rem had hung up. The only decision she wanted to make was whether she would take West-ern or Lake Shore Drive to work the next morning.

She read the last chapter of her book because she didn't want to start something that would end badly.

☆

Immediately after speaking with Cathy, Rem called Geezler, to let him know about the arrival, the chaos of the place, and sound off a little about the squalid lodgings.

Mid-ring he changed his mind. Intuition told him that this wouldn't be the worst of it. Geezler didn't need to hear every detail. He should concentrate on what mattered, essentials, not make reports day by day, but digest the experience first.

His phone rang before he could pocket it. Geezler on an unlisted number.

'You wanted to speak?'

'I thought better of it.' In truth Rem had lost the mood.

Geezler said he'd take anything Rem had to offer. 'The whole point is to hear your take. You understand? That's why you're going. I want your perspective.'

Rem started again on his day. 'I'm in a room with nine men from Fiji and the Philippines, who think they're heading to Dubai. Their contracts say Balad. They don't know where they're going. They don't have their passports. This can't be legal.'

Once again Geezler listened and was ready with questions, and on occasion, an explanation.

'These people are in transit. Technically, they aren't in the country. We've had trouble before. If they have their passports they disappear.'

Rem wouldn't drop the subject. 'Benigno. Beni. He's thirty-seven, he looks like he's fifty. He has a fourteen-page contract busy with small print. Only four out of nine in my room can read English, and everyone is going to Iraq and they don't know it. How can they not know?'

Geezler promised to look into Beni's case, and asked Rem to find the names of the other men. Although, he said, his arena was Europe, which limited him in certain regards. It wasn't *if* he could do anything, but *when*.

'I don't want to play my hand too early. I'm operating in someone else's territory. There might be a more apposite time for me to be involved.' To be honest, he said, he hadn't anticipated so many issues, certainly none as serious as this. He asked Rem to keep an eye on Beni. 'Let me know when he receives his deployment date. I can intervene at that point without making undue trouble. Make sure you have his full name.'

Rem accepted the situation. Geezler at least was listening, he paid attention. Rem understood the constraint under which he worked. Geezler had set up the whole operation, had sent Rem into the field to discover these problems. While Geezler hadn't said as much, he guessed that he'd put his job on the line. If discovered Rem would lose nothing. Geezler stood to lose plenty.

He took another quick look at the facilities before turning in, and what he saw depressed him. It wasn't so much the lack of cleanliness as the smell and disarray of too many men in too small a space. Everyone was to be woken at five, a schedule laid out the order for showers and breakfast.

Unused to sharing a room with men, Rem slept uneasily.

The first four days in Austin passed quickly, on each day the information changed, the briefings became longer, repetitive. First they were heading to Iraq via Dubai, then Bahrain, possibly Düsseldorf, then definitely Bahrain. Once in Bahrain they would be held in a hotel close to the airport while they were processed, which could take anything up to a week because the parent company, HOSCO, needed to figure out exactly where they were needed.

Geezler called on the sixth day to notify Rem that a placement had been confirmed and transit was organized for the next morning. Geezler wished him luck, and Rem said that he was ready. Rem called Cathy with the news.

'You don't have to do this. If you don't go you won't be letting anyone down.'

'It's six weeks.'

'You don't have to go.'

'Six weeks. We'll owe nothing. Tell me what you want.'

'And what difference would it make, Rem?'

The fact, unspoken, lay clear before them, if she asked him not to go, he would not go.

☆

On his last afternoon in Chicago, Rem visited Mike in his house on Ravenswood.

Mike's wife opened the door, looked less than pleased to see him. 'When are you taking that dog back?'

Rem said it wouldn't be with them much longer.

'It's cruel,' she said, blame in her voice, 'it's not right keeping something in a cage like that. And I don't like lying to Cathy.'

'I'll deal with it.'

As she walked away she muttered, *Make sure you do*, then told him that Mike was waiting in the back.

The houses on Ravenswood lay close to the tracks. Trees sheltered the yards and darkened the stoops and porches, and while he used to enjoy this – shade in the summer for beer and end-of-day business – it struck him now as oppressive.

He found Mike sat at a table. Geezler had settled an advance of three thousand, enough to pay the most urgent outstanding medical bill and give Mike a little of what he owed.

Mike stood up, squeezed past the table and asked Rem if he wanted a beer.

Rem spoke while Mike was out of the room. Easier to talk without facing him, to speak with a little pep and verve, to make the news sound inconsequential.

'I found work. It's a short job, but it means I'll be able to settle everything.'

'Short?'

'Six weeks, guaranteed bonus. No tax, so I can settle with you when I get back.'

Mike stopped at the door, a beer in each hand.

'No tax, so that's abroad, right?'

Rem nodded. Mike's head made a slight jolt. 'Is this what I think it is? Because you don't have to do that.'

'It's a lot of money. In six weeks I can clear everything I owe.'

Mike set both beers on the table. 'Rem, if this is Iraq, I mean, we can all wait. What's done is done. You don't have to do this. Don't go on my behalf.' He scratched the back of his head. 'You should have just cut us loose. That's what you should have done. You have this whole thing mixed up. Other businesses fail. It's not your fault. As soon as you didn't have the jobs you should have let us go.'

Mike popped the cans open, slid one across to Rem.

'And then there's Matt. I don't see why you helped him out. I don't see it. You go to Iraq and what does he do? You haven't saved anything. The end result – I really hate to say – is what? What does Cathy say?'

'She doesn't like it.'

Rem took out the money and set it beside Mike's beer. Mike looked at it and repeated, 'This just makes me feel bad. I don't want to hold you to anything.'

'I promised I'd pay you.'

Mike picked up the money, note by note. 'I can't refuse this. You know that. But I don't like being in this position, Rem. I think I should take this and we should call it quits. You've done what you can.'

'I said I'd pay. And I'll pay.'

'You just have to give it up. Sometimes you just have to say *enough*.' Mike shook his head.

'It isn't as bad as it sounds. Won't be much different than Kuwait.'

'It isn't just about going, Rem, you know that. It's leaving here. Leaving Cathy. You two always mess up when you're apart. You know that.'

'It's not the same.'

'She was sick, and you were away. You think she doesn't remember that?'

As the light failed, the house became unfamiliar, through all the years Rem had visited it had never seemed so drab.

They spoke in conditional terms about events that were already decided.

'We might move.' Mike looked to the kitchen, to indicate the choice wasn't his. 'Be closer to her sister in Cicero. It isn't just the money. The neighbourhood's changing. On one side the rents are going up, on the other, it's turning into a place you don't want to be.'

'When might this happen?'

Mike pointed to flats of cardboard stacked alongside the wall, boxes, ready to be made up.

'That soon?'

'Soon.'

Rem looked hard at the table's edge. He cleared his throat. 'About the dog.'

On the porch, in a cage – nothing more than a rabbit hutch – set on a workbench, a small Yorkshire terrier curled on a folded blanket. Rem bent forward, cooed, *Lucy, Lucy,* and the dog came up, licked his fingertips through the mesh.

'It has to go back.'

'She's fond of it now.'

'It's not right, though.'

'Eye for an eye.'

'I can't be certain.' The thing is, he explained, you can take all of the facts, mix them around, give them to five people, and you'd have five different versions about what's going on. Things get so mixed up, you just can't tell the truth any more.

☆

Rem wouldn't hear the news until the next morning. Not until Cathy returned from the hospital.

'How do I get hold of you?' she asked. 'Calling your cell is going to cost a fortune.'

Rem suggested they keep the mobile strictly for emergencies. They could record messages, video or sound, on their phones and upload them. Cathy asked how.

'Use the library. It's free. They have a stack of computers. Send emails, use the Yahoo account.'

'Are you serious?'

'It's only six weeks. It's not that much hassle.'

And here they were, spending money talking about talking.

'Keep the phone for emergencies. I can pick up messages just as long as there's a signal. But keep it to emergencies, OK?'

'That's the thing.' Cathy's voice became hesitant. 'I've news and it's bad.'

A call had come from Mike, and at first she couldn't understand what he was saying, but he wanted her to check out Channel 5 or Fox, it was on both *right now*, then get in contact with Rem, because Matt had done something so unbelievable he couldn't credit it, couldn't begin to express how profoundly disturbing it was: he just couldn't comprehend what he was seeing.

This is the kind of stunt people used to do on LSD.

Matt had been caught in action by a news team, who just happened to be coming up Lake Shore Drive right at the moment he appeared. The newscaster advised viewer discretion, because, despite the hazy picture quality, you could see a good amount of unpleasant detail. Matt had opened his wrists with a box-cutter, walked with a woozy stride across six lanes of rush-hour traffic in what looked like wet red jeans, then tipped himself off the flyway to land on his back on the grass, one unholy mess. Unlucky in everything.

'Can't even kill himself.' Mike's voice stopped down to an incredulous whisper.

Cathy watched, stood up, sat down, hands to mouth, as Matt tipped over the balustrade, a full head-over-heels dummy-drop, slam on his back.

She wanted a drink. Needed something in her hands. Ducked toward the TV to make sure that she was seeing this right. Matt. That *was* Matt? Right? Their Matt? Former neighbour/friend/Rem's employee, *Matty*, the man who threw the party when they came back from New Orleans? She watched him amble – what else could you call it – across the expressway, through the fierce downdraught of a police helicopter, just outright saunter across Lake Shore Drive, off his box, to topple ragdoll over the far parapet.

The grass rippled about him, the ground velvet, soft as an undulating sea.

Two helicopters now. Three. One to medevac him to Northwestern, two to monitor. The traffic backed up from Fullerton to Loyola. People were sending images from their cellphones to the network. Matt seen from a passenger seat. Matt taken from the back of a bus. Matt, definitely Matt, curving by a driver, blank-eyed, to disappear, head first, arms at his side, with a heavy inevitability, the man in the car shouting, not even using language, just a bellyful of awe and shock.

Cathy went to the bedroom, dreamy-voiced, like this could be normal, talked out loud, as if the dog was there, or Rem. 'I'm calling Cissy.' You watch a former friend (your husband's one-time *best friend*, for what, fifteen years?), a deeply compromised person who has caused you unending trouble, someone you hope you might forgive (one day), perform a sloppy *unsuccessful* exit on prime time and you decide to call his wife, as if for a chat.

Matt's wife and Cathy had history, and while Matt's thievery unspooled in a long and ugly fall, Cathy had insisted, at least to Rem, on their friendship.

Cathy couldn't make the call but sat at the edge of the bed, head in her hands. She couldn't sit, couldn't stand, found it impossible not to move, spoke briefly with Mike a second time then paced the hall with the phone saying, *Jesus, oh Jesus Christ*, as Mike's voice began to break.

Then: a touch of relief as Cathy understood that there wasn't honestly any other narrative Matt Cavanaugh would decide for himself.

*

Cathy sat beside the bed, simply because being low, close to the ground was a comfort. She called Cissie *because she wanted to do something*, and learned that Matt was at Northwestern, downtown.

Once on the El, Cathy began to seethe. Why did she have to be so reliable?

She called Maggie to tease out her anger. 'I tried calling Rem. They're nine hours ahead so it's, what, three in the morning already? He never answers. It's pointless calling.' She stared hard at the tracks, and focused her aggression on the apartments beside Wilson. 'I don't know what to do. This whole thing has been chaos.' She couldn't answer questions about Matt and looked at the apartments, the ornate cornices and balconies, and wondered if they were supposed to look Spanish or Italian, like haciendas or palazzos. Who knows how anyone is going to react? There's never any telling. She could barely anticipate her own reaction to any situation at any given moment. Cathy rolled her eyes, tipped back her head. 'You know what I resent? I resent being on my own with all of this.'

She loved the curve before Sheridan, how the track veered left after the cemetery into a tight corner. The design of it pleased her as did the effect, the loveliness of your bodyweight tipping because you just can't help it. Even now, in this circumstance, she couldn't ignore the curve and how her shoulders pressed against the side of the carriage, how the standing passengers jostled to stay upright.

Only family. A regulation Cathy felt thankful for, a mercy not to face the man. No police, no journalists. A shiny corridor slick with light. A smell she could barely stomach. Cissie beside a noticeboard, hands squeezing out grief.

Cissie couldn't look her in the eye as she explained that Matt was essentially stapled to a board to hold his spine in position. We're through the worst, she said, the two halves of her face in disagreement: pure haggard shock in her eyes and a fleetingly sociable smile she could just about keep steady. 'It's very kind of you.'

Cathy wanted to ask *why*, but couldn't find the heart.

Cissie pecked randomly at facts, and it was clear that she didn't understand the full picture either. She asked after Rem, asked if they had spoken, and Cathy answered no, not yet. Hadn't Rem told Matt he didn't want to see him again? *I don't care if you're on fire, you don't call me. You stay away.*

Cathy asked if anyone else had come and immediately regretted the question. Cissie froze, clenched, terrified at the idea. Then, steadily, the tension dropped, her hands and shoulders relaxed, because, what else could happen, really – what else could now go wrong? She didn't know what to hope for, she said. She didn't know what to think, and Cathy replied that no one *blamed* Matt. Not now. What had happened was all in the past, and they needed to think about the future.

Cissie's expression laid open her heart. Everything rested on the word *blame*. She didn't understand.

'What he did,' and now Cathy had to spell it out.

It seemed, at least to Cathy, that this blunder – at the very least – illuminated with a terrible clarity what must otherwise have been an intolerable situation. Cissie had no idea.

Cathy came out of the hospital in a hurried half-run, as if heading for a train or a ride. She slowed at the kerb and walked toward Michigan Avenue, relieved to be outside, the image of Cissie's slow realization stuck with her. She stopped by a group of smokers close by the stock doors to Neiman Marcus, checked her pockets for keys as an excuse to pause. One of the smokers asked if she'd come from the hospital and Cathy nodded.

'That bad?'

She couldn't think how it could be any worse, couldn't bear to see her reflection in the store windows, thought that she was inhuman.

When she did speak with Rem she managed to keep her patience while he told her what to do. His voice in any case was filtered, unreal, so she might be talking via a third party, or a stranger, some abstracted Rem-like idea. She didn't like telling him news that she had already processed, and found he didn't absorb the basic facts quickly enough.

'It didn't have to go this far.' She didn't mean to say this, especially now when anything she could say would sing with too much purpose.

He wasn't responsible, he said. It wasn't his fault.

Rem wasn't prepared. He took it in for a moment, she could hear this in his pause. He never could keep up in any kind of confrontation. Coming back from the movies that last time they'd argued, and Rem, unwilling to stick with it, had changed seats, moved along the carriage, and left her to feel the solidity of the houses speeding away from them, the flat roads, the weight and volume of the city.

She understood that the discussion wasn't going to go further. A second piece of news, she decided, she'd save for another call. This was about Nut, and Rem would need a little more time to process this.

According to Cissie, Matt had come to see Rem the day that Rem came over to see him – if that made any sense. Rem had made some plan, but Matt wasn't sure if they were supposed to meet at Clark Street, or if Rem was going to come over to theirs. Around ten o'clock Matt had walked up Lunt to Clark, and found the doors unlocked. At first he thought Rem had just slipped out, was probably in the store downstairs or something. Anyway, Rem hadn't come back, so he must have left in a hurry without locking the doors. He must have been pre-occupied. What happened – somehow, Cissie didn't know how – but Matt had let the dog out. It was his fault. It wasn't deliberate.

'He didn't tell me at first. Waited a couple of days. I think he thought you'd find him. But he felt bad about it. I'm really, really sorry.'

☆

On the day Rem heard the news about Matt Cavanaugh, Fatboy's replacement, Stefan Kiprowski, arrived at the section base. Seconded from Food Services at Southern-CIPA, the regional government agency, the post was intended to be temporary. Geezler hadn't lied: HOSCO ran everything, food, water, sleep, employment. Kiprowski reminded him of someone. Not because of his height, and not because he was thin. He couldn't place the reference.

Rem loved the complexities. Each morning when they returned to ACSB he sat with Santo in the commissary. They drank coffee while they watched the TCNs gather and prepare for their drives.

'You can always tell where they're going.' Santo nodded at the drivers. 'The smilers are southbound, Kuwait. The shitters are heading north,' he deepened his voice, 'to a land of desolation,' then more sweetly, 'bye, boys. Say bye-bye.'

Santo offered to refill the coffees so he could hum 'One Headlight' as he passed by the drivers. When he returned he told Rem he looked happy. 'Happi*er*, I should say. Don't get me wrong.'

'I might stay here.'

'Here? Iraq?'

'Safer. I just heard news.'

'Home?'

Rem nodded.

'Thing is. You aren't there. You're here. Can't do one thing about it. It's win–win.'

Rem began to explain about Matt's walk across Lake Shore Drive: how cars hadn't hit him and how he'd survived a tumble over a parapet, and something like a fifteen-foot drop. 'Didn't even hold out his hands to save himself.'

'I saw that,' Santo cooed. 'The jumper. You know him?' He sat back, hands on his thighs, impressed.

Rem gave a slow nod.

'I heard they opened him up and found everything pushed up.' Santo heaved his hand from his chest to his throat. 'They had to take it all out and put it back in the right place. He had shit coming out of his ears you wouldn't want coming out of your ass. Can you believe that? Some people die falling off a chair. Man, you know him?' Santo shook his head in disbelief. 'Why would a person do that?'

Rem said he couldn't believe it himself. Some things are beyond imagining.

Santo, seeing the conversation heading in a bad direction, pointed out the new manager. 'Speaking of Chicago. He's from your town.'

Rem looked across the commissary at the tall thin boy, still couldn't place him, but doubted that they knew each other from Chicago. More robust than Fatboy: corn-fed and wholesome. 'Looks lost.'

'Talking of dumb-assed, you hear what KCP did to him yesterday?'

'KCP?'

'Transport. They hear this new guy is coming in from Southern-CIPA, which is right on the other side of Amrah. He's here three hours and he has to go back for one last duty. This is a journey you can't make without security, without armoured cars, guns, SWAT teams, nuclear devices. So he goes to Transport, places his request, says he has to get to CIPA, as soon as. They take a dislike to this guy, because, well, I don't know, they just don't like him. So they give him the brush-off and tell him to come back in an hour. So, he's back in an hour, and the office is closed, and there's a sign saying come back in another hour. These guys are just messing with him.' Santo took in a deep breath. 'An hour later he's at the counter, and there's a new sign saying "back in five", only they aren't back in five. So he calls them, tells him he has to be back at Southern-CIPA in two hours for a function. He's supposed to be laying on the food for this function. Cutting sandwiches. Making coffee. He goes away. He comes back a third time. Still nobody there, this time the sign says, "vehicle in loading dock". He goes to the loading dock and there's nothing there except a fat-assed BFV. A tank. And just for good measure they've leant a bicycle against it with a dishwalla and one of those headscarf turbans. You know what he does?'

'This already didn't happen.'

'You know what he does? He dresses up. He puts that shit on, he dresses like a fratboy heading to a hazing. He takes the bike, and he cycles all the way to Southern-CIPA.'

'It's not true.'

'It's true. Fact! Jalla Road. Ask him. Ask him how he got to the tea-party at Southern-CIPA yesterday. Ask him.' Santo shook his head. 'What is it with Chicago these days? Is there some kind of crazy in the water? I'm putting money on him for a kill.'

Rem looked across the room. The boy checked items on a clipboard. Something about the turn of his head, not directly down, but tilted, gave Rem the reference he couldn't place. Nut. The boy looked like his dog.

☆

Matt survived two strokes in his first week in hospital, and suffered a blood infection in the second, which temporarily turned his skin yellow, but responded immediately to treatment. He held on. This is what they told themselves: Cathy, Cissie, the attending medics. Matt was holding on with superhuman determination. The doctors ordered scans and tests, amazed that he demonstrated any brain function at all given the damage caused by his fall. They depended a good deal on the word *instinct*.

Cathy came to the hospital when she could, and kept in touch with Cissie by phone on the days she could not visit.

Cissie's quiet unnerved her. She ran her day to a bare routine of arriving and departing, picked the same seat, sat in the same attentive poise, wrung her hands and waited. On the phone Cissie had nothing to say, and in her stillness Cathy saw a kind of madness.

The news that Matt had been transferred to Kansas City came as a relief.

☆

The arrival of the Division Chief signalled another change in HOSCO: a potential reshuffle of directors and deputies assigned to the regions. No one could put a name or a face to the Division Chief for the Middle East, or could find such a man on the company website – that the position might be vacant meant little to the men of Unit 409 who were bothered only by the disruption that accompanied any such visit or site inspection. Since the assault on Jalla Road resentment had begun to grow and the Iraqi Ministry for Infrastructure and Sanitation had become more diligent. Permits for clearances and demolitions were stalled. Rem guessed that the delay depended on the right amount of money hitting the right person or the right clan before they would be able to continue with their work. This, he thought, would be the real motivation behind the visit. He doubted it had anything to do with Fatboy and substandard equipment.

Still, curious enough to show up, Rem accompanied Santo to the meeting.

The commissary was sectioned off with small rope barriers to mark out a rough rectangle. Men from the unit sat on either side of the tables interested in the boxes stacked alongside the vending machines. Two of the tables were marked with a 'reserved' sign.

The Division Chief arrived with a posse of bureaucrats: uniformly dressed in white shirts, chinos, buckskin boots.

'Jesus Christ,' Santo whispered, 'would you look at that. The Banana Republic hive mind. They sleep in one big bed, swap clothes. Have interchangeable limbs. They have no genitals.'

Rem watched the group approach, the Division Chief concealed by the huddle, then, as the deputies spread out, revealed. Large in every sense, he wore a white linen suit and carried a light-blue handkerchief with which he mopped his forehead. Disproportionate, tall, and so overweight that walking appeared cumbersome. The man swung his arms, breathed through his mouth, had a sprightly edge, and seemed, at least to Rem, uncommonly alert.

Santo swore under his breath. A chuckle stirred through the unit, then the men fell unusually silent.

The Division Chief was introduced by the section head, Mark Summers, who appeared decorous beside the chief.

Santo complained that he hadn't heard the Division Chief's name, and the answer came back, whispered down the row: Mann, David Mann. Division Chief for Europe.

'What happened to the last guy? The one for the Middle East?' Santo asked in a voice that was not so quiet. 'You think he ate him?' The men looked back and considered the possibility.

Summers stood beside the boxes and began to speak. His shirt was wet at the armpits, his hair matted. The boxes contained new protective jackets.

'These,' he said, struggling out one of the black flak vests, 'are what we're offering all ground personnel. Gratis. You can take these now.' He opened the vest, spoke about the new neck guards, the crotch-bib.

'What did I tell you?' Santo nudged Rem. 'I must be psychic. They'll take pictures now, and this goes in the company magazine. Gets sent to the newspapers.'

To Summers' embarrassment the men stopped in their seats. Rem kept his eye on Mann and was surprised that he did not intervene, but appeared, instead, to study the men.

Summers, quieter, squeakier, said that the men could sign for the jackets at the PX. 'One each,' he said. 'One.'

Rem hung around the visiting party as Summers and Mann were shown 'the ovens'. He overheard Summers ask if he could see the men's quarters, and the mistake stuck with Rem, not because of its irony, but for the lack of understanding. Neither Summers nor Mann had visited a live compound before. They couldn't have. The accommodation was no different from HOSCO's usual provision: inadequate for a combat zone. As European Division Chief, David Mann could be forgiven. Summers had just never left his office.

Rem followed with his arms folded.

That evening Rem found Paul Geezler in the commissary. Paul Geezler. In Iraq. Amrah City.

Rem picked a soda from self-service and stood at a distance. Geezler wore a blue shirt with HOSCO sewn in white along the right breast pocket, a plate of pasta-bake in front of him.

Aware that he was being watched, Geezler looked up. 'Gunnersen.'

'What are you doing here?'

'I'm with the Division Chief. One day. In. Out.' Geezler indicated the seat opposite him. 'Join me. I was hoping to speak with you.'

Geezler shifted his tray to make room, asked Rem if he was eating. 'I haven't heard much from you lately?'

The air-conditioner focused a fine stream between Rem's shoulders.

Geezler spoke of his business, a tour to Singapore then Indonesia. 'Denpasar. They insist, even now, on a face.' He gave a resigned shrug. 'You like it here? It's a sincere question. Do you like your work?'

'It's complicated.'

'Have you thought about staying?'

Rem couldn't help but laugh.

'You've been useful.'

'There hasn't been much happening.'

'I have what I asked for.'

'I want to get through this without trouble. I had a friend—'

'The boy who shot himself.' Geezler nodded as if considering a personal sorrow. He paused, set down his fork. 'I don't think we're using you to your full advantage. I'm thinking you're in the wrong place.'

'I have two weeks.'

'Hear me out. What if I could offer you something uncomplicated? How would that sound?' Geezler's eyes were a perfect blue, disarming in a man. 'People are frightened of you. Did you know that?'

Rem shrugged. 'I want to go home. There are things happening, I should be home.'

'Maybe you want something safer?'

'Safer is good. Home is better.'

'How is that business of yours? Can you go home and start that up again? Will the money be enough?'

Rem looked at the man and focused on not giving a response.

'I need a manager. Have you heard of Al-Muthanna?'

'It's the desert. In the south.'

'Remind me what you earn?'

Rem held up his fingers.

Geezler nodded again. 'What if you earned that in one month?'

'Total?'

'Total. No tax, as per.' Geezler held up his hands and looked at them. 'You'll need to decide quickly.' He asked for a napkin. 'I see you as a manager. What do you know about the burn pits?'

Rem pushed a pack of towelettes across the table.

'Tell me. What have you heard?'

Rem shook his head.

'Everything we've brought here needs to be taken away. What can't be taken away needs to be burned. We have four sites. Camp Bravo, up north. SB Alpha and Camp Victor, both central. And Camp Liberty, south-west. Every one except Camp Liberty is manned. I need a manager to assemble a team. No more than seven men. You'll be your own man. It's secure, remote, and absolutely safe. HOSCO have set up the pits, the systems, the deliveries and sites are independent.'

'How long?'

'Two months. It's hard to tell. Until we close them down.'

Rem reflected for a moment. Kiprowski in a paper hat, a white bib, tall and lanky, waited behind a counter, head forward, arms behind his back, bored.

'You can pick whoever you want.'

'You need an answer now?'

'I leave in three hours,' Geezler checked his watch, 'but let me know by the end of play tomorrow. I won't ask anything else of you.'

It took Rem an hour to find Santo down in Transport watching the TCNs being dispatched. 'Makes me feel bad watching them go like that. You ever seen those convoys?'

Rem said he hadn't and followed Santo across the central quad.

'I have a proposal. There's a man here from HOSCO and he's asked me to put together a team. Seven men to go down to Al-Muthanna. They need a team. He's asked me, but I think I could persuade him to take you if it's something you're interested in?'

'Why would I want to go? Things are working fine here.'

'It's double the money.'

'Where is this again?'

They waited by the entrance to the transport dock. Three rows of vehicles, the noise shuddering through the garage, the fumes rising. Santo pointed out a mechanic who stood among the security and drivers as they decided on a running order. Santo waved the man over. 'This is Pakosta, he's been here longer than me.' Pakosta wiped his hands on a rag as he came to them. Confident and fresh, he shook Rem's hand as they were introduced.

'Should have stayed here,' he said to Santo. 'Had a fight. No one wants to ride in the first set.'

'It's that bad?'

Pakosta shrugged. 'The problem is how they drive. People fall asleep. Lose the road. They won't slow down or stop. I'm sick of picking dogs out of fenders. Last week one ran through a herd of goats. Refused to stop. They think if they stop then they're dead. Most are high on chaw anyway.' Pakosta pinched the bridge of his nose. 'They wear adult diapers. Honest to god. Like monkeys. Don't even stop to shit. You don't want to go inside those cabins after a long haul.'

Santo asked Pakosta when he was done, and Pakosta said he was looking for an extension. 'You mean here, right? You're asking when am I done here?'

'You heard of Camp Liberty?'

Pakosta looked up in the air in thought. 'Which one?'

'South-east. Al-Muthanna. On the way to Kuwait.'

Pakosta nodded, he knew it. 'Camp Crapper? Off Highway 80 someways? I've been there on a recovery. It's not occupied. Why?'

'He's putting a team together.'

'For?'

'A short job, managing the burn pits.'

'They need people for that?'

'The pay is good.'

'They dump stuff and set fire to it. Why do they need people?'

Rem said he didn't know, and Santo asked if it mattered. Pakosta said he guessed it didn't. Santo asked a second time if he was interested, and Pakosta answered that he'd sooner just wait in Amrah and see what came up.

Ready to leave, Rem began to make his excuses. Pakosta rolled up his sleeve.

'You see this. Here.' He held up his arm to show a fresh scratch, a short thick line, as thick as a finger. 'Nearly died last night.' Santo and Rem looked at the scar.

'What is that?'

'We were recovering a vehicle on North Jalla. We just got it hitched and someone took a shot.'

'Is that a graze? You saying it just missed you?' Santo leaned in to look closer.

'They shot out the bulb from the headlight. Burned right through.' He turned his arms so he could look.

331

Santo disagreed. 'Doesn't count. No one's getting rich off a miss.'
As they walked away Rem and Santo were silent.

Imagine you could do something undeniably, unquestionably good. That dropped into your hands was the opportunity to achieve One Good Thing.

Imagine a man stumbling across a motorway, blind, out of his mind, and you beside him, guiding, making those split-second choices.

Let's say it's only temporary. Let's say it's in your power to grant someone a reprieve. You can snatch them away, and offer a short respite. And maybe what's coming might become less of a certainty?

Rem slept, woke, slept again, revived the same dream of scooping people from highways, buildings, cars – elemental dreams with floods and fires. Dreams of stress not salvation. The last hours of the night he slept heavily and decided on a plan. These men in Fatboy's book were lined up, dead certainties while they remained at ACSB.

LIBERTY

The story as Watts tells it goes something like this: it's his third time in Iraq, he's working directly with Southern-CIPA on comms across the entire South-Central region – we're talking basic communications, because everything digital and terrestrial has been looted, bombed, looted. Not one hub or exchange has survived intact. They haven't come close to re-establishing the basic services available fifteen years ago, it's that backward. (Watts sits in a folding chair. Magisterial. Elbows on knees, thick forearms, a broad forehead, and explains himself in a voice Rem would describe as Midwestern, grained, husky, rangy.) What you have to understand, he says, is the mentality of the Iraqi versus the mentality of the average Westerner. An Iraqi, for example, can't be relied on to innovate. You can't give an Iraqi a job and expect it to be done; these guys have been trained over decades to do nothing. This isn't your average Arab. You have to give explicit instructions and tell them step by step what you want and exactly how it's going to happen, and even then you have to supervise. Why? Because these people don't *improvise*. They have to be told. Free food and regular government handouts have made them lazy and unambitious. It's all clan-like, top-down, *individual responsibility* just isn't in the picture. Alongside this, there's the talent of the Iraqi to completely fuck up anything that might look like progress. Which brings him to Rule Number 1: if something can be dismantled *it will disappear*. He's seen whole substations stripped in one evening.

So anyway, the story: they're scrambling to establish basic communications, with the mightily reduced aim of refitting a minimal seven out of the seventy-nine exchanges and substations. That's seven. Count them. Seven. Less than nine per cent of the number they've been paid to complete. Alongside this his team is also responsible for the main communications router for the company – that's HOSCO, remember – so every speck of information, every byte, comes through his small four-man team, and they get to hear *everything*. Every blip of information the parent company is telling its subsidiaries, and every anxious twitch those subsidiaries are feeding on to their project managers, everything but everything is filtered through this team. *And let me tell you, it's chaos.* So, early one morning, HOSCO's network goes wild. A message from one of the division directors announces that a statement will be made in Washington that very morning and the content of this announcement is to be passed, immediately, to all senior staff. According to this director, the statement they are waiting for is a follow-up to a statement made by the President himself, in which, while touring southern Iraq, he inadvertently blabbed out information on a project that was not intended to be made public. At. This. Point. This *statement* has slipped out so far ahead of schedule it threatens to kill the project unless they act quickly. You follow? Washington is now obliged to dump a fuckton of money upon said project, and unless HOSCO is ready for this shit-shower of money, they'll miss out altogether on the mother of all projects. The story, Watts says, is a classic.

First though comes the story about the trip.

The commander-in-chief's visit has been scheduled for a long time. The visit is little more than a fly-'n'-stop, a series of parsed hand-waves at relevant outposts along the Iraq–Kuwait border. Things aren't right in Washington, and what was a planned pre-exit howdy to the remaining teams has become politically toxic.

Picture this: Air Force One, accompanied by small fighter jets prowling wing-tip to wing-tip, wasps cutting through a blue hood of sky toward a copper horizon, a jagged edge of what might be mountains but is in fact the smoke of burning refineries. The mission is important. Everyone agrees that there are few usable photographs of the commander-in-chief alongside his forces because he has the bad habit of looking bored while speaking with people he does not know.

At Camp Navistar the commander-in-chief and team decamp to a fleet of helicopters to be flown direct to the 0-9 at Camp Hope. In readiness the base has long been secured and emptied of all non-nationals, but right at the last minute the media-unfriendly wounding of four Iraqi civilians outside the compound makes the stop at Camp Hope *ill-advised*. Instead, the commander-in-chief will make his announcement on changes to the Third Iraq Key Strategic Plan at the next nearest manned station, Provision Camp Liberty on Route 567 in South-West District 2 near Amrah City. The change, mid-transit, makes it necessary to gather a great deal of information en route.

Down on the ground, a Colonel Pritzker, is the first to learn that the commander-in-chief has come to Iraq to announce a new development in strategy and now intends to visit Camp Liberty. That day. In fact, within minutes.

Pritzker is suspicious: there are radio shows that do this kind of thing, and he can taste the end of his career. First off, he's never heard of a *provision camp* before, and he has no idea who is in residence at Camp Liberty. Camp Liberty, to his memory, is a lowly set of HOSCO cabins, a star-like arrangement of burn pits, and a vacant squatter camp.

The colonel's advice is passed back to the team, and after some discussion the secretary gets back to Pritzker and says, great, we're going to run with this. It's a go. And it finally occurs to Pritzker that this really is the President, and that Air Force One is, as he speaks, winging its way across the Arabian Desert to its imminent arrival at an empty set of burn pits. His final word, the only thing that occurs to him, is to ask the secretary if he knows what a provision camp is. Has he ever heard this term before? The secretary is a little preoccupied because there are other items to concern him now, but the question stops him. No, neither he nor any of the other staffers have heard of a provision camp and presume it is some kind of a place that somehow, you know, *provides.*

Colonel Pritzker says uh-huh, that's almost right. A provision camp is certainly a place that provides a service. But Provision Camp Liberty is isolated for good reason, because it is the largest site where chemical, human, and animal waste is brought to be destroyed in the desert. You lose a leg in Iraq, a finger, a toenail, if it can be swept up, it's coming to Camp Liberty. In fact Provision Camp Liberty stinks so bad that it is known by the TCNs as Camp Crapper. You take several tonnes of human waste, add the insane heat of the Arabian Desert, and you have yourself an intense olfactory experience – but, regardless, whoever is currently in occupation at that site would be mightily proud to meet their commander-in-chief.

Watts imagines the quality of the silence that falls across Colonel Pritzker's comm-link while the information is relayed back to the team.

Two minutes short of their destination the President's entourage return to Camp Navistar on the Kuwait border, where, in the hangar, surrounded by his retiring troops, the President himself announces the New Strategic Plan, and here the terrible mistake is made. In an answer to a question about the apparent failure to rebuild Amrah City the commander-in-chief mentions that there is a new scheme under consideration. Somewhere, he says, *here*, in southern Iraq, in a place he would not identify, the Corps of Engineers are preparing to build a new military outpost, and this outpost will become the largest military staging-post yet built. Once completed, and once its mission is fulfilled, the base will be converted for civilian use and will become the first new city in a peaceful Iraq.

At this announcement HOSCO goes wild. The lines are crazy. Speculation crosses the globe. One hour after the commander-in-chief's unguarded statement the Secretary of State back in Washington confirms the details, but adds, with caution, that the intended base is still little more than 'a good intention'. They're looking at four sites and are sending point-men to evaluate these sites *as we speak*. While this, initially, is to be a military 'advisory' base, an integral part of the New Strategic Plan. Never again will a foreign power enter Iraq territory and occupy its oil fields (a chuckle from the Press Corps to this one).

In a voice of creamy sincerity the Secretary of State insists that the administration is looking to the future. And then that smile. Everybody loves that smile.

You know what this means? Watts asks. You know when this happened? This all happened pre-withdrawal plans and pre-basic implementation. Which means that something has to be done about this now. Like, *yesterday*. Because there's money attached to the idea, and the period in which that money remains available is near its expiration.

This is how government works. They make decisions, they appoint money to those decisions, and they expect others to bid and take on those projects. There's a whole complicated structure for this which has government agencies and private businesses at each other neck and neck. It's in everyone's interest to have this money used up before it gets sucked back. That's how everything works around here. At the last minute whole schemes suddenly materialize.

Watts salutes the air.

Goodbye, Southern-CIPA.

Hello, Camp Crapper.

☆

The convoy gathered at the Transport dock.

Rem hadn't met the men as a group before. Santo, Watts, Pakosta, Samuels, Clark, Chimeno, Kiprowski. Six of the seven picked from Fatboy's list, seconded from their units and placements. Kiprowski added as a late concession. *He rode Jalla, Death Row, on a push bike.* Kiprowski, by rights, should be a legend already.

Clark held court as they waited. 'This is all good news,' he said, 'they're shutting down projects, moving people on. This is the last, last chance.' Clark believed, as did many others, that the section base would soon be closed. 'The commissary,' he asked Kiprowski, 'they've cut down on supplies? Am I right? Same with stores. It's happening. You know it is. The TCNs have their exit papers. The convoys are going directly to the camps. It's over. The only thing remaining in Amrah is Southern-CIPA because that's where the money is.'

Rem walked from vehicle to vehicle, shook hands, gave his name and repeated theirs.

Rem took the first Humvee behind the lead and picked Watts and Santo for company. Pakosta, Clark, and Samuels would follow, with Kiprowski and Chimeno coming after with most of the supplies. Behind them a long train of trucks, gun muzzles spiked out of windows. For the first leg they would accompany the convoy on the southward route to Kuwait then separate before the border and make their own way west. As promised Geezler had arranged security for the final stretch, two Cougars, front and back. Pakosta had experience in recovery along Highway 80, and advised that they should keep the spacing between them uneven. Rem couldn't see how this could be achieved. The map showed nothing west of Highway 80, simply lines indicating the grades of hills and berms, the lengths of dry windswept ditches. No villages, no installations, no pre- or post- war encampments. Nothing until Camp Liberty. A map so blank it might as well be an ocean chart.

'Doesn't mean nothing's there,' Watts advised. 'It just means they don't know.'

Clark's smile slipped off his face.

Watts slapped his shoulder. 'If they take anyone out it's usually the second vehicle. The first pops the mechanism, the second takes the hit, after that they'll take anyone in their sights and the whole convoy lights up.'

Clark began to buckle his jacket. 'Much better,' he spoke to himself. 'Thanks. Feeling so much better.'

'I told you what you say if they capture you.' Santo drew his finger across his throat. 'Remember. No one loves us. No one's paying any ransom. We won't be missed.'

Pakosta standing on the running plate kept up a slow solo jive and paused every now and then to mime being shot in the head, the heart, the crotch.

An hour out of Amrah City and the palms and the villages thinned out and knuckled into the slopes – primitive, Santo called them, pointing as he drove, so that Rem couldn't be sure if he meant the place or the people. In many ways the villages appeared as tight as the old centre of Halsteren. You'd hear your neighbours, every detail, and you'd know them well. A few of the houses sported satellite discs and long aerials. Santo pointed them out. 'If you want to fuck with someone, you go right to that house.'

Rem looked back at the line of trucks, Kiprowski's head struck out of the second-to-last Humvee.

'You see that?'

Santo turned in his seat and took a while to find what Rem was talking about. 'Is that boy a retard?'

'Thinks he's on vacation.'

Rem called on the radio and asked Kiprowski to draw his head back inside the vehicle. Kiprowski gave a wave as he complied.

Santo tutted. 'Certified.'

Beyond the groves and villages the land tired itself out, the bluffs and hills became distant, and the sky bifurcated, blue up top and a dirty skin-like pink along the horizon. Not a desert in the way Rem thought of deserts – as something tide-like, the wind working sand into ripples and banks – but instead a scabby gritty wasteland, hammered, used up, not a place of possibility, but a place with an over-busy history. Knackered. After a while they swapped drivers: Watts day-dreamed and Rem drove and Santo chattered to himself.

Rem focused so hard on the vehicle in front that the rough tarpaulin of the square back appeared to float, a soft fluttering box set at a fixed distance. He needed to thank Geezler and couldn't decide the most appropriate method, then figured that saying nothing would be fine. People have their own reasons for helping you out, and in satisfying his own agenda Geezler probably didn't realize the extent of the favour anyhow: eight men transferred to safety and security. For the first time he began to think seriously about re-establishing his business.

Santo asked Watts why he was here, and Watts explained about his wife and expected child. 'I get back when it's done. No point being there until it needs paying for.'

Santo looked to Rem and began to tell Watts about Matt Cavanaugh. 'The guy who walked across the highway. You heard about this? The walker. The guy in the news?' He cocked his thumb at Rem. 'That's his friend.'

'I saw that. Why would a person do that?'

'I had a business.' Rem cleared his throat. 'House painting. He worked for me, and he helped himself to a few things while we were at some of the houses. He didn't take much. A ring, some watches. The watches were part of a collection. Just enough to cause trouble.'

Watts and Santo shook their heads. 'You knew this man? A friend, you say?' Then after a respectable pause: 'So, how come he ended up walking across a highway?'

'Details,' Santo urged. 'Details.'

Now Rem shook his head. 'I don't know much more. It happened while I was here. Maybe the question is why didn't he do it sooner?'

'You ever done anything stupid? I mean really stupid?' Santo blew his nose into his hand. 'Look, I'm still bleeding.' He shook his hand out of the window and the gesture came as a shock to them, an invitation for trouble, a signal deserving a shot, an ambush.

'As in, coming here?'

'I mean stupid stupid. Animal stupid.'

'Sober or what?'

'Doesn't matter. I mean insane.'

Rem watched the vehicle in front, teased forward, played with the space between them. 'I stole a dog.'

Santo sucked air between his teeth in dismissal. 'OK. Close. Like a prank? A joke, right? When you were a kid?'

'Just before I came to Iraq.'

Both Watts and Santo laughed. 'You did what?'

'It's complicated. I had a dog. A Staffordshire bull terrier. He went missing. I came home one time and he was gone. Doors were open and the dog was gone.' Rem asked Santo to open a can for him. Red Bull was making him sick and he wanted something less sticky. 'I thought I had a good idea who was responsible. So I went to that person's house and I stole their dog.'

'You got yours back?'

'They didn't have it. In fact, I doubt it had anything to do with them.'

'But you have this other dog, right?'

'I did. It was one of those small dogs. I took it back once I realized what I was doing. Sometimes these things seem like a good idea.'

'You should have eaten it,' Santo deadpanned.

'You have issues. You know that?'

'I have issues? I'm not the person who kidnapped a dog. Kidnapping is a felony, man or beast. Seven to nine.'

'So why are you here?' Watts asked Santo.

'Because, Paul, is it Paul? I'm here to put the f in freedom.'

An hour after they'd separated from the convoy the road stopped. Rem woke to find nothing but rock and sand ahead of them. A blank field of sun-split stone that rose and ended in a haze.

'Rem. We're out of highway.'

Rem slowly sat up, looked past the lead Cougar at the desert, the absence of a road, looked back at the small line of vehicles idling behind them. Pakosta jumped out of the last truck. He'd taken off his flak jacket, changed into shorts and boots, a T-shirt, made an effort to look casual. Santo drew out the maps.

'The road goes all the way, runs right along the border.' Watts pointed out a fine and continuous line on the map, then looked to the desert, incredulous. The highway stopped at a line of barrels, metal oil drums. 'Right here. See? There's a road on the map, but nothing even close to a road out there. No tracks. Nothing.'

Rem rubbed his eyes, got out of the vehicle. Stood right where the road stopped and thought it strange how it looked new but just ended for no reason. He called to Pakosta. 'Did you come this way before?'

Pakosta coolly shook his head.

'None of this looks familiar?'

'Nope.' Pakosta straightened up, dropped his cigarette. 'We came a different route out of Amrah.'

Rem shouted back to Watts and asked if he could bring the map.

As Watts came out of the Humvee, Rem checked the horizon, anxious that they were being watched.

'Don't worry.' Pakosta turned a slow complete circle. 'If there was anyone out there, we'd know by now.'

Watts spread the map over the hood and cursed the heat.

'Show him where we are.'

Watts pointed to a line that ran alongside the Saudi border. Rem raised his sunglasses so he could see more clearly, but found the light too bright.

'As far as I can make out,' Watts traced his finger along a short section of the road, 'we should be about here. We turned at the right place, but there's no road.'

Rem nodded, he could see that.

'Thing is,' Pakosta advised, 'without that road you have to go all the way back to Amrah, then take Jalla Road to get back out to Route 567. The way we came before.'

Rem started walking before Pakosta had finished. He called to the men in the security vehicles. If they returned to Amrah could they gather more security?

The first guard stepped down, settled his gun over his shoulder, mirrored sunglasses on so Rem couldn't see his eyes. These men were ex-military, most of them brittle, unsympathetic. Santo called them Sparts, as in *spare parts*. 'These guys are experiments. They come here to be entertained. The whole thing gives them a hard-on. They keep coming back until something gets shot off. Then we're supposed to feel sorry.'

The man stared hard at Rem. Santo leaned toward the guard. 'You know, dressing in black is only going to work at night? You know that right? We – can – see – you.'

The thing Rem had to understand was they had another job. 'If we go back to Amrah we stay there. We only have time to take you back. After that you're on your own. We're needed at CIPA.'

Clark asked about the road they'd crossed shortly after turning off Highway 80. It looked like a service road, nothing much to it, but where did that go?

Rem returned to the vehicle with the map, stood beside Watts and swore. 'Can you find that? Is that marked down?'

'It looks like it heads north. We want to be heading west.'

Watts traced Highway 80 almost to the border and found the route Pakosta had mentioned. '567, is that it?'

Rem called Pakosta back out of his vehicle. 'What did you say the highway was, after Jalla?'

'Route 567.'

'We crossed that when we changed drivers. After 80.'

Pakosta shrugged, like this was common sense, something everyone knew.

'We don't need to go back to Amrah?'

'Not the whole way.'

The four security men approached Rem. 'We can take you to 80, but after that we need to head back to Amrah.'

'You can take Route 567. See us to Liberty, continue on Route 567 to Amrah.' Rem began to fold up the map.

'Route 567 north is unsecure. We'd have to come back to 80.'

'Then you come back to 80 after you've seen us to Liberty.'

'We don't have time.'

Rem took off his glasses and wiped sweat from his eyes. The heat and the brightness bore down, and nothing around them but stone. He asked the men what they suggested he do. He asked Watts if they had anything. Any kind of protection?

'Nothing legal or useful.'

'Anything?'

Watts apologized. There was one more thing. He drew Rem across the road. 'What's the name of the redhead?'

'Samuels.'

'He's not looking too good.'

Samuels sat on his own on the blacktop with his back to the wheels, arms hugging his legs, head rested on his knees.

'What's his problem?'

Samuels' problem had to be Fatboy. The last time Samuels sat in a Humvee Fatboy had shot himself. 'Tell Santo to leave those guards alone and swap places. We'll have Samuels with us.'

'You're going ahead?'

'They said the trouble was north, after Camp Liberty. According to the map there's nothing between here and Camp Liberty. No villages, no houses. Just desert.'

Watts wasn't convinced. 'According to the map there's supposed to be a road.' He pointed at the desert.

'I don't see a choice. Returning to Amrah, driving down Jalla isn't an option, with or without security.'

Rem clapped his hands and told everyone to get back into their vehicles. He walked to the front Cougar, climbed up to the cab, and leaned in through the window.

'We're going back to Highway 80,' he said to the driver. 'We're taking Route 567. It's your choice whether you go back to Amrah or see us on to Camp Liberty. If you choose to return to Amrah, I'll guarantee all of your contracts will be cut before you reach the city. Your choice.'

The security guard looked back, impassive.

They reached Highway 80 with the sun behind them. As they turned the two security vehicles pulled to the side of the road. Rem told Watts to ignore them and keep driving.

'Don't give them the satisfaction.'

As they turned north the sun struck into the cab and gilded Watts' arms and shoulder, the back of his hands.

'There's nothing ahead. No villages. Only the road, then the camp.' Rem checked the mirror to make sure the others followed, and without breaking pace they kept in a tight line and left behind the two security vehicles. The guards sat atop the Cougars with their guns trained across the desert. Highway 80 and the embankment quickly receded to a thin light band, a trace of amber, horizontal planes of colour. Samuels sat with his head down on his arms as if asleep or poorly, sweat beading on his neck.

Pakosta dominated the radio. Entertained them as they rode up Route 567.

'They have these *systems, ways of seeing*. They've created these computer programs, these avatars, that learn. They empathize. They predict. They dream. They know the food you eat, how long it will take to digest, the quality of the shit you're about to take. The heft, the colour, the weight. These *things* don't even exist, they're programs, right, pathways and electrical pulses. But they *know you better than you know yourself*. We're just meat to them. I tell you. We aren't even necessary any more. The future is here. This is where they test it out. It's not *chemical* warfare. It's *digital*.'

Pakosta sang as many songs featuring the word *hero* as he could recall. Asked every single one of them by name if they were all right and demanded an answer.

Watts turned down the volume.

☆

Cathy sat for two hours in the library and stared at the screen, willing the download counter to creep to full. She didn't dare touch the keyboard, and moved the mouse every five minutes to stop the screen from going to sleep. *How does everyone else manage this?* She was learning new words, could distinguish between KB and MB in terms of time, and how long each download would demand. She knew the difference between a gif, a doc, and a jpeg. She knew now to delete her history before closing the browser and logging out.

In his email Rem spoke about assigning cabins to the men, of clearing out bunks. He spoke about a squabble over who would take the cabins closest to the showers – although he couldn't see the advantage, because the toilets and the showers were stupidly at opposite ends of the camp. He used the word loosely, he said. *Camp*. In the end they opted to draw straws, but having no straws or anything that would make do, they fell into a game of paper, scissors, stone. Grown men grouped under a temporary canopy playing a child's game to settle a territorial dispute. He left them to it. Provisions were arriving, but without the proper equipment food would spoil: potable water was shipped in plastic bottles, non-potable water was stored in two large underground tanks set halfway into a hill that relied on gravity to drain into the showers. For the moment they would get by day to day. He didn't mind, he said, he really didn't mind, because they had enough vehicles and enough fuel to drive right back to Amrah City if they had to – not that he ever wanted to go back, but if they had to, they could manage themselves out of trouble. The main problem, he confided, was heat, and adjusting the work day so they'd be up before dawn to receive the trucks for the burn pits. All in good time.

He'd posted the videos to an email account, and she found them accidentally – a stray click on an underlined link.

Once downloaded, the first, smaller message began to play. Rem's voice broke into the library, until Cathy fumbled the headphone jack into the correct socket.

Rem huddled in a dark room, back to a wall, knees up, the camera close to his chest, his face greased with sweat, his eyes deep, closed at first, compressed. And then: his face sulking, baby-like, mouth rising, brow falling, and sobs, awkward and girlish. Rem cried noisily, he choked in awkward bursts that made this difficult, ugly to watch.

Out on Clark, the few lime trees planted along the sidewalk – always the first to suffer the heat. She took a break, called Maggie, asked ordinary questions, surprised at the control in her voice, how cold she could sound as she asked about the orders, about details, about shifts, the possibility of more work, because money, you know, was always welcome, especially now. When Maggie hesitated she said, 'Forget it. Forget I asked. I don't know why I called,' and Maggie took the insult badly and cut the conversation short.

Cathy returned to the computer, grateful that this was only one room, nothing more than a storefront, but disliked how her private life played out on public computers. She found a different image playing, the second message downloaded and running footage of a stony road-side that fell back to an endless palm grove. The jolt of the vehicle punched the image up to the sky, blinding white then blue, whipped by the feathered tops of palm trees, a rustle of green. Date palms, she knew this, not coconut. And would those be almond trees, or walnut, some kind of fruit? Olive trees broke the rhythm, pleasantly squat and pale, and locked between them the brightest sky, a thin block of air. In breaks between the groves the irrigation channels, the ditches, the dusty roads, and further back more fields and groves, an unfamiliar sight for a country she'd imagined only as stone and desert.

This world looked old by design. She put on the headphones, taken by, but not quite believing, the wearing brightness and the bare sunshine. The waters of a great river brought sparingly to the plains, passed plant to plant through channels and tubes and tight little ditches, and the transformation from flat desert to a continuous road-side oasis struck her as ingenious, hard-earned, and beautiful.

She could distinguish voices under the drone of the engine. Rem, and one, maybe two other men, laughing, discussing how the village wasn't on the map. *How wild is that? Shouldn't be there.* Across the radio, she could just about hear a voice singing and sounding like a taunt.

*

The next morning, stopped on Lake Shore Drive, Cathy smoothed the apron over her stomach, and thought again of this oasis: a clear image of water channels, low mud walls, a wild pampas-like grass, but mostly the palm trees, strong leaning trunks, a wild bush of fronds – home to what kinds of bird? What right did Rem have crying, homesick, in some boxy room, when he was free of this monotony?

She wasn't eating regularly, she'd lost too much weight too quickly, enough to stop her periods. These things happened when she became stressed. Outward, she appeared to manage. Inward, everything became a mess: eating, sleeping, shitting, menstruation, every basic function thrown out of whack.

☆

Rem could smell the camp before they came across it. A smell, from a distance, of newly turned earth, slightly foetid, not entirely unpleasant. Closer still the stink fastened to the back of his throat, turned penetrative and meaty.

Forty minutes earlier they'd come through palm groves and an ordered grid of dry irrigation channels surrounding an unmarked village, Khat. Now they sat at the head of an incline, a great plate of desert about them, falling on all sides – except to the west where a small bare hill concealed the camp. The tops of two water tanks half buried in the hill, a wire fence, and a cable-wire gate were all that could be seen from the road.

They drove slowly down the track into Camp Liberty. To their right a Quonset hut with a ribbed barrel roof and a long garage door, rosy in the late sun, with two blackened diggers pulled-up behind. To their left an uneven line of HOSCO cabins. This, Rem understood, was the camp, barely enough to justify the journey. The track continued in a wavering line toward the burn pits. Behind them, the highway struck straight, north–south. Further to the west the land lost distinction, the wind drove up a fleshy haze and the horizon faded to flat tones. He couldn't figure why the camp was based here, nothing established its reason, no commanding feature, water, nothing, except that it lay equidistant between the Kuwaiti border, the Saudi border, and a small town called Khat.

When the vehicles stopped the men stepped out, and one by one looked about, expecting more and failing to find anything. Each one of them took shallow breaths and looked to Rem as if he was the source of the stink. Samuels sloped out last, a spanked dog, all tremors and passing terror, the only one not appalled by the stench.

Rem asked Pakosta if this was it.

'Just about.'

'Dead things. It smells of bad meat, animal fat.' Santo pinched his nose, swatted the flies matting Watts' back.

The plastic cabins were raised on wood pallets. Their fronts and sides, pitted by the sand, were so badly weathered that grit stuck in them and gave them a soft furred look. Santo gouged out the screws, and when the door opened he jumped back. 'Something in here!'

The men gathered in a huddle and peered cautiously inside. The floor, black, appeared to move.

'It's ash.' Santo thought this funny, and wafted the door and the ash stirred, disturbed as the surface of a lake.

The bed, a simple cot, at least had a mattress but the room was otherwise bare. Rem had the common sense to make sure the men brought fresh bedding and bed rolls, something more comfortable at least than their accommodation back at Amrah. He charged Samuels and Clark with checking each of the cabins. Fleas, bugs, roaches. Scorpions. Rats. Spiders. He had no idea what was out here.

Rem asked Pakosta to drive him about the camp. He wanted to see the burn pits as he didn't yet know how to speak to the men about their work: everything was new and unfamiliar.

A home-made sign outside the Quonset pointed to 'The Pits / The Beach'.

Pakosta turned the Humvee aggressively about. 'I have one more property. I think you'll like what we've done here. Honest to god.'

Pakosta drove first to the Beach. If Rem wanted to get a measure of this vast nothing, then the Beach was the place to start.

'I was here in February. We had to haul a truck out of one of the pits. We should have just pushed it in.'

The Beach, a long dune, almost as high as the camp, formed a crescent-shaped gulley around an open tip of abandoned vehicles and equipment – most of it stripped of usable parts. The Beach rode up behind as a steep roll of sand.

'This is where they dump hardware which won't burn.' He strode up the dune expecting Rem to follow. Once on the crest he struck a pose and swept out his arms to the north and north-west. 'Nothing of interest until the border. Belongs to A-rabs, scorpions, camels, and desert rats. Nothing going out, and nothing coming back. If anything did happen to come at us we'd see it several days before it got here. Not so from the other direction.' Pakosta turned to point south with two fingers, pistol-fashion.

'Our closest neighbour is Khat. Sometimes the support and supply convoys from Camp Navistar to LSA Anaconda in Baghdad are obliged to take this road: and on occasion the good citizens of Khat choose to stone the vehicles, to slow them down and rob them, because the convoys come from Shuaiba or Camp Arifjan, and bring eggs, milk, bread, flour, you name it. Foodstuffs. Fuel. If we're smart we'll have nothing to do with them. Fortunately most of them believe that the pits are used to destroy chemicals and toxic material.' Pakosta swept his hand to the east. 'Which brings us to Camp Crapper, the largest and last burn pit in southern I-raq, which, to my knowledge, has never been permanently manned.' Pakosta spat into the sand then levelled his arms. 'So, what the fuck are we doing here?'

Rem gave Pakosta an honest answer. 'Because this is the last job in town. Everywhere else doesn't look so good right now. Why are you here?'

'This is my career.' Pakosta gave a laugh. 'I'm serious. This country is my future. I'm never going back.'

Before returning to the cabins they stopped at the burn pits. Five long and shallow trenches, each as broad as a truck. Inside the pits a mess of black glue and scorched semi-recognizable detritus: a freezer unit, gypsum boards, a bicycle frame, half-burned boxes and bags melded together, yet to properly burn, but mostly an uneven field of papery black and grey ash.

As soon as he shut the cabin door Rem didn't know what to do with himself. Tired? Certainly. But ready to sleep? He wrote a list of what he wanted to say to Geezler, and outlined their abandonment by the security unit, the highway that stopped in the middle of the desert, the stink of the pits, and how the camp was more remote than he'd imagined. Even so, despite these aggravations, he didn't doubt that Camp Liberty would be better and safer than Amrah once everything began to settle into place. Rem couldn't see there being much to report on, day to day. Whatever Geezler wanted from him had already been satisfied. The pits were now manned.

Neither his cellphone nor the satellite phone could pick up a signal. Rem wasn't sure how to use the satphone: a handset with what looked like a folding hotplate. Tomorrow they'd resolve this. Watts would know. Communications would need to be established with Amrah, no one would be happy if contact home wasn't possible.

Each of the men secure in a cabin. No wind. No traffic. Rem turned off the flashlight and lay on the bed in utter darkness. Wide awake.

Part way through the night the lack of sound finally bore into him. A stillness compacted by his heartbeat, the changing pressure in his ears, the random babble in his head, his stomach, his breath, mostly his breath: so that the night slowed down to these small things.

He'd covered himself with mosquito repellent. Thought it better to show caution and hope that the mixed fumes of repellent and sweat would deter anything Clark and Samuels might have missed.

Rem fretted over Cathy. He wanted a little home comfort, a presence, some body warmth. He couldn't think of Cathy without imagining her falling down. He pictured endless scenarios of Cathy suddenly falling, sometimes heavy: on the El platform, crossing a road, climbing stairs; and sometimes slow, as if asleep: driving, in the street, in the shower, at the stove, the room catching light as she lay on the floor. And on, and on. Cathy tumbling, striking her head, not being found. All of this trouble for a ring and a couple of watches.

A sound grew from outside, the fast mechanical cut and chop of a helicopter, the twin rotors of a Chinook. A helicopter, twin rotors. By the time he'd found his boots and made it outside the drop was completed. Four crates lowered behind the Quonset, dust settling, the helicopter already leaning backward into the sky. Hard spotlights and a lit interior cabin.

He looked down the row and saw Santo smoking outside his hut. The two men waved liked neighbours in any neighbourhood.

☆

In the news the bombing of four Amrah City markets in the same day, sixty-seven dead in a strip-mall that looked much like the local K-Mart with its parking lot and a broad, stippled concrete hood sheltering the sidewalk. Both the *Times* and the *Post* ran photographs of men stumbling over rubble, startled, dusty, hands to their heads. After waiting at the checkout Cathy changed her mind and left the newspapers on the counter. She didn't need this. Although she'd known his return was indefinitely delayed, it was today that the information sank through and began to hurt. It meant an anniversary alone. It meant reorganizing the payments on their loans. It meant that she would not move apartment until the next summer, and they needed somewhere smaller, cheaper. She'd made and cancelled two appointments at the Howard Street clinic, thinking *this can wait*, better to go when Rem returned. No more fainting, and no dizziness, instead a lack of appetite, a general exhaustion she carried as a weight, which could be something, but could simply be sadness. This *vacation* had opened up a world of trouble. She kept newspaper clippings every time she found a report mentioning HOSCO, simply for the habit. In the *Tribune* she found a report on military wives and infidelity, and wanted to call the paper to complain, to ask what they thought they were doing? Were they really so short of ideas? Cathy took herself to the loading dock, phone in hand, ready to make the call. Not that she could bring herself to make it, because she wasn't a military wife, just someone in the same position, and she didn't want to have to justify herself, she just wanted to complain to someone who had to listen. The news of the bombing alarmed her; while she trusted Rem's word that he was safe, the notion that he could be harmed stuck as a superstition. She could imagine him dead but not wounded, or if wounded not maimed, a scar perhaps, but that alone. Photographs of men lying in streets shocked and scorched made no sense to her: families would look at these images and recognize their sons and husbands.

The arrival of a package with a military frank was a reminder that Rem really was absent. He'd left her to an artificial world, and she lived expecting news from elsewhere. She drove home still dressed in the store uniform that made her itch, a ring on her finger, the *Happy Shopper* stitched on the breast pocket, and felt owned. Cathy settled her hand on the package. She had her mail delivered to a post-box because packages could not be trusted with her neighbour, Mr Liu.

Three hours at the library. Stops. Starts. Disconnections. The messages recorded on Rem's mobile and transferred to their email account.

Behind Rem a digital fuzz of flat desert and rising heat broken into shifting tonal zones of spoiled muddy ochre. The image assembled out of crude blocks, bold as thumbprints.

Rem squinted into the sun, leaned forward to speak, self-conscious and awkward. The camera propped on a car bonnet. He spoke in a fake Mexican accent, a private joke. (They played a game where he, invariably, was subordinate to her, garden-boy, pool-boy, waiter, bus-boy, and these seductions were always brief and hasty. It could happen on drives, at restaurants, at home minutes before guests arrived. Nobody they knew would guess this of them.)

'So this is home,' he said. Rough as it was it beat the crap out of Amrah. He'd watched the razing of entire city blocks, and for what? The idea that you could rebuild a city was messy, wrong-headed, and they hadn't done one thing right.

Rem took off his shirt, ran his hand over his chest. He coughed before he spoke, his expression serious. 'It makes sense,' he said, 'I know you don't like it, but if I came back there wouldn't be any work. It's coming into summer. You know we'd be right back where we started. Anyway.' He scratched his nose (a habit of his when he wanted to move a conversation off a sticky subject).

'I picked these people,' he said. 'I get to be a manager again. I run my own team.'

Pointing to the desert, Rem said that this wasn't anything much. It was safe, a little quiet, but definitely secure. The only trouble here would be trouble they brought on themselves through boredom. The camp was a good distance from habitation. Nothing but sand and rock and maybe a few scorpions: nothing until the border.

Cathy had her own news, wasn't sure if she had already told him. Cissie had taken Matt back to Kansas. *I'm sorry if I've already said.* Cathy spoke into the phone and couldn't help but stage her voice, pick and pronounce her words with more than her usual care. The truth is the doctors hadn't expected him to make it this far, and now he had, they didn't know what to do with him. They start with one thing and it affects what they do next.

She didn't like the cadence of her voice, all Southern sing-song that made light of any trouble: every *burden* being a *blessing* in disguise. Christ, wasn't that the word they used? *Blessing*? This was her family's doing. How even the worst news came sugar-glazed, every word freighted with *blessings*. How had she escaped this life? And how was it, even after all these years, that her voice betrayed this last tail of home?

She started up the recording and spoke into the phone. Mike and Jenny have moved. *See? Even this sounds happy?* Drove by yesterday. They're gone. Packing cases on the porch which makes it look like they were in a hurry. There were four signs of foreclosures along Ravenswood. That's four in one block.

She'd seen a dog in the park just like Nut, except he was on a lead and barking. Nut never barked. Far across the park the dog strained against its lead, gave the man a struggle, and while it wasn't Nut, couldn't have been, she felt guilty for not making sure.

Cathy ended with the realization that everyone had gone. It's me, she said, and Maggie. Ten years in this town and I know one person. How can this happen so quickly? We had a full life, didn't we? Now I know one person.

She paused the recording and then deleted the message, and resolved to start again in the morning.

☆

The satphone worked only in the late afternoons, communications dropped and stuttered alternately compressing and stretching distance and expectation. Watts sat with Rem beside the water tanks and tried to help Rem send messages back to ACSB, when the news came back that it was closing.

'You knew this?' Watts asked.

'First I've heard.'

'Clark said something when we were leaving.'

'He knew?'

'Rumour.'

They looked down the highway.

'Haven't seen one vehicle.'

The highway trailed back, an empty spine. Not one thing on it.

Geezler wanted to know about the map. He'd consulted the maps at HOSCO and none of them had a highway running alongside the Saudi border. Rem asked Watts where the maps had come from.

'Stores.' Watts shrugged. 'The usual.'

Rem asked Kiprowski: if the maps came from Stores, then where did Stores get them?

Kiprowski took the map and looked it over, held the paper close to his face to read, and found printed in the corner a small tagline, S-CIPA. This one came from Southern-CIPA, he said.

Rem managed to send his reply before the lines dropped. Pleased to have a result, he'd forgotten to ask the main question he'd had since they'd arrived: now they were here, *exactly what were they supposed to do?*

On the second morning they were woken by the arrival of six yellow garbage trucks. Groots. The same back-loading garbage trucks he'd seen on the streets of Chicago. The convoy arrived early, pre-dawn, and the men duly rose, curious, to greet them. At first sight they thought this funny: dump trucks with the municipal labels and signs stripped from the sides, here, in the middle of Iraq. And yellow? The driver of the first truck, a Ukrainian, Stas, was surprised to find the camp occupied, and when he jumped out of his cab he asked if Rem needed a permit or a manifest now, like at Bravo and SCB Alpha. Rem admitted that he didn't know, and Stas assured him that there wasn't too much to it.

'Here we come with no permits.'

Stas carried about a small towel, which he used to wipe his hands and forehead. He spoke briefly with the other drivers, called Chimeno to him, and asked him to drive the tanker from the Quonset and follow them down to the pits. A line of blocked shapes, dim in the pre-dawn, headlights busy with insects, slowly followed the track downhill, their vibration humming through the night air.

Pit 4, closest to the Beach, was the deepest. Stas explained in broken English how he'd helped excavate the pit.

'You dug this out?' Rem couldn't quite follow. 'You made this?'

Rem's question made him laugh. 'You dig! Yes? You. Every week, maybe.'

The idea horrified Rem. 'Every week we dig a new pit?'

'No, you dig *the same* pit.'

This was the reason for the two diggers parked behind the Quonset.

'How do you know when?'

'To dig? You'll know.' The pits, Stas indicated, became full, and with

355

a chopping motion he demonstrated how the pits were extended by cutting and in-filling, and by this process they grew at one end and shrank at the other. Continually dug out of the sand they crept, caterpillar-style, into the desert. Now it made sense why they were placed in a star-like configuration, radiating away from one another.

'How often?' Rem wanted to make this clear.

'Depends.' Stas pinched his nose. 'Sand will stop the smell. But not so much.' He wiped the back of his neck then waved the towel in the air. 'The fire will stop the flies. You have clothes?'

Rem had found a crate of protective suits in the Quonset. Firemen's bunker gear, rubberized suits with reflective belts and black zippers. He sent Chimeno back to the compound and told him to hurry.

Stas tied the towel over his mouth, bandit-style, and supervised the dumping. The trucks began to unload one at a time at the near end of the pit. The first truck shivered as the pistons struggled to tip the container high enough and the contents slipped out in a dense and mudlike mass.

Pakosta started laughing. 'That's disgusting.' The men watched as the black waste flopped into the pit. 'Man, that's graphic.'

The second truck spewed out a muddle of white bags and they watched them roll and slop, getting now a sense of depth and scale.

'My parents,' Pakosta shouted above the noise, 'won a vacation on a game show. A week in Kenya. For five days they saw nothing. Some giraffes. A couple of hyenas. Someone brought them a dead snake. On their last night they stopped at this water hole and saw, like, fifty hippos – and all these hippos did was back up to the water and shit in it for something like half an hour. They made a video.'

Chimeno returned with one suit folded over his arm. Reflective strips caught the light from the trucks. 'There's five complete, and another one without the mask-thing, and a whole bunch of different filters.'

Stas told Chimeno to dress in the suit, then showed him how to unhook a hose from the side of the tanker, then clamp the mouth to a faucet on the back. Satisfied, Stas walked a good ten metres from the pit and scored a line in the grit with his heels. 'Here,' he shouted to Rem. 'Everyone come here.'

Once the hose was fastened, Stas warned everyone to keep their distance. 'No smoke! OK?'

He stood Chimeno at the edge of the pit, kicked the kinks out of the hose, and made Chimeno hold it up, indicating how he should stand, and how the hose should be gripped with both hands, and secured under one arm. When he turned the spigot on, Chimeno staggered back, but managed to stabilize himself and hold the nozzle up to send out a broad spray of fuel. The remaining trucks drove back to the camp. A sharp, head-splitting fume rose from the pit.

'Jet fuel.' Pakosta clapped his hand over his mouth and nose.

The men naturally backed away.

After two minutes Stas closed off the spigot and called Chimeno back for assistance. Once the men had tucked the hose under the tanker he drove a good distance away, then returned running to the group.

'Now this,' he held up his hand. 'Watch.'

It took Rem a moment to recognize that Stas was holding a hand grenade.

Stas held the grenade upside down, twisted the base, then lobbed it softly overarm into the pit. A gesture so casual, Rem expected nothing to result from it. As Stas stepped carefully back, Santo, Watts, Clark, Pakosta on one side, and Chimeno, Samuels, Kiprowski and Rem on the other, all followed suit.

'And now we see.'

Less than a second later with a dull thud and a plant-like plume, spidery tufts and trails of mud sprang from the pit – in itself a disappointment – then, in one sudden conflagration, the air above the pit broke into a vast orange fireball. The heat shoved them back, then rose, startlingly dynamic.

The men hooted, clapped, slapped each other's backs. Santo swore, punched the air. Pakosta yipped and hollered. Even Samuels smiled. Kiprowski and Rem stood side by side, hands on hips, heads upturned, awe-struck. The fire, now a single branching column, sucked air from the desert and transformed into a thick pillar of grey-flecked smoke high above them. Stas stood with the towel covering his mouth and nose.

Pakosta spat then shook his head. 'That, right there, is exactly what we're here for.'

The second convoy arrived an hour after the first. Dawn broke as a sour orange band, across an uninterrupted plain. Rem distributed the remaining environmental suits, then returned to the Quonset, unfolded a deckchair, and sat behind the crates, feet up, cap pulled down.

Rem woke to Pakosta's shouts. Chimeno had collapsed. He needed to come quickly.

After loading Pit 2, Santo had discovered Chimeno on his knees right at the pit edge with his back to the mounting fire, disoriented. Santo and Samuels had hauled Chimeno to one of the trucks. Rem found him still in the cab, his suit unzipped and mask pulled to the side. Sweat stuck his T-shirt to his chest, rucked up and sodden, and his hair slicked flat to his head. Chimeno, head nodding baby-like and unable to keep his eyes open, had still not properly revived and slowly swatted away their hands. The driver, a wiry Indian, sat aside to watch, smoking. Rem asked if he could cut it out, and the man looked to his cigarette, a little put out.

'The suits are too hot. Someone's going to fall into one of those pits.' Santo unbuckled the mask and unscrewed the nozzle. 'Look at this.' He held up the filter, a thin grey fibre disc. 'I don't think this is right?'

Chimeno breathed slow and deep and appeared more connected. He shuffled himself upright and wiped his nose.

'It's too hot. Look at him. He can't move in the suit. They're not fit for purpose.' Santo refitted the nozzle to the face mask and took several attempts to align the threads. 'Maybe just the masks, then?'

Pakosta had spoken with one of the other drivers. 'He said this has happened before. It's the heat.'

'Where was this?'

Pakosta shrugged. 'Bravo? Alpha? I didn't ask. He was talking about another burn pit.'

Rem opened the door to let air inside, asked the driver to take Chimeno back to the cabins. He called Samuels over to ride back with Chimeno then asked Santo if they could have a word.

They both agreed the suits were a bad idea.

'That other driver just had a towel over his face. Maybe we don't need these things.'

They walked back to the cabins, the slope nothing more a low-grade ridge, the sand soft at the roadside, but trenched in the centre into deep curved ruts which obliged the trucks to progress slowly and steer carefully. Santo wanted to know about food, water, general supplies. Rem assured him there would be a delivery every other morning.

*

In the evening the cloud collapsed. It was such a strange phenomenon, a column of smoke that rose from the ground and obscured the pit, as if the ground belched black breath, Rem realized he'd had his eye on it throughout the day, and noticed as the day drew on how the quality of the smoke and the colour changed (black first, then thin and white, then rolling bruised purples, then blue, then orange). As it fattened it began to resist the wind and lean toward the camp. The smoke darkened and slowly descended, came down as a shower of black flakes, small papery wisps thick enough to smudge.

Astounded by this, Clark stood outside his cabin, arms outspread, while everyone else scampered for shelter and watched from doorways. Their hurry drew the flakes in a whorl behind them, statically attracted, so their backs and shoulders, their heads, were quickly dressed. This snow absorbed sound, made the men quiet, and fell as a slight stickiness so delicate it itched.

The ash worked its way through cracks and gaps into their cabins.

'Jet fuel will strip the skin off your hands and rot your brain.' Watts set about cleaning the masks. Took each filter apart and laid out the composite parts.

Rem returned to the pits with his camera. He brought Kiprowski with him and made the boy take photos.

'Got that? Let me see.'

Kiprowski handed back the camera.

Rem scrolled through the images. 'You think you can manage this? Not too taxing?'

'No, sir.'

'What about Samuels? You speak much with him?'

'He keeps to himself.'

'He's settling in? This is just between you and me.'

'He's good.'

'You think that, or you know?'

The boy looked to the pit and reconsidered. 'I think the others could ease off, maybe.'

'In what way?'

Kiprowski brushed flies from his eyes and squinted back. 'I don't know.'

'But he's OK?'

'I guess. They play jokes.'

'What kind of jokes?'

'Someone put sand in his bunk and he was up all night.'

'Who did this?'

Kiprowski turned to the Beach. 'I did.'

Rem looked up from the camera, surprised. 'Why would you do something like that?'

Kiprowski looked out at the pits again, smoke whorled from a spill of black round bags. 'I don't know. It wasn't a major plan or anything.'

'Was it Pakosta?'

'There was a group. I don't know. Just something that came up, I guess.'

'But you did it?'

'There were other ideas that weren't so nice. I thought this was less mean.'

Rem turned off the camera, set his cap back on his head. The men were bored, new to each other, settling in and testing. He understood this.

Kiprowski stood with his hands clasped behind his back, cadet-style.

'Back in Amrah. I heard you rode alone up Jalla Road?'

Kiprowski smiled and shook his head. 'I got a ride at the last minute.'

'But you were going to do it?'

Kiprowski said he didn't know. He guessed so. Maybe. 'Seemed as safe as anything else.'

Rem had no idea who he was speaking with and the temperamental connection didn't help, neither did an audience. Throughout the discussion he was faced with idiot grins from Chimeno and Clark, teamed up as some redneck glee-club in matching blue T-shirts. (Chimeno: 'Lock and Load', with an arrow pointing to his crotch, and Clark: 'Why Does This Keep Happening?' The T-shirts had arrived that morning in a care package from Watts' brother.)

Halfway through the conversation Rem held his hand over the mouthpiece and asked Chimeno and Clark if they could do him a favour. Keen to please, Chimeno leaned forward.

'Get Santo and find out who Paul Howell is. See if he's heard of this Markland.'

The two men left and he returned to the conversation. He asked the man his name: Markland. Tom Markland, secretary for Paul Howell – offered as if he should know.

The problem, Markland insisted, was that they couldn't transport explosives, not in the quantity Rem needed, not by road. Even if he could – just supposing – under the current directive non-combatants weren't authorized to handle munitions of any kind.

This, Rem pointed out, was madness. The burn pits had been running long before his arrival and they had managed to start fires, with explosives, with fuel, without trouble.

Markland's voice sank, as if explaining a very easy point to a very simple person. 'Because the convoys have military escort. They bring their munitions with them. They set the fires by themselves. It's their business to start the fires. Not yours.'

Rem explained about the Ukrainian, Stas, a driver, and how he'd started the fire on the previous night and how there was no military or security escort.

Markland's voice sank further and he offered a three-line defence.

1. 'That's news to me.'

2. 'They're out of my jurisdiction. We have no control over the GST, the CMDN, or over any Ukrainian nationals, only directives on what procedures everyone should follow. If they aren't following these procedures then you have to report this.'

3. 'They find their explosives out and about.'

'There's plenty out there. There are munitions dumps any place you care to look. How do you think the insurgents arm themselves? Most of what they use is ours. Walk in any direction and you'll find what you need.'

'I can't send someone out to recover explosives that aren't secure.'

'I'm not telling you to do that. What I'm saying is you need certification to get what you want.'

'How do I get certification?'

'You don't. It can't be done, unless the Deputy Administrator gives you special dispensation.'

'And how do I get permission from the Deputy Administrator?'

'You talk to me.'

'*I am* talking with you.'

'You come to Amrah and you make your case to me, and then I make your case to the Deputy Administrator.'

This, to Rem, sounded deeply unsatisfactory.

'It can take six weeks,' Markland seemed to crow. 'And I'm due to leave, so the process might not be completed if you don't start it soon.'

In the late afternoon Geezler called Rem directly. 'The map,' he wanted to know. 'You said it came from Southern-CIPA?'

'As far as we know. Usually we pick them up from Stores or the PX, but this came from one of the convoys, and they get their intel and commands routed through Southern-CIPA.' Rem said he wasn't sure who they were, but he'd had dealings with a man called Markland. 'I need permission to handle explosives so we can start the fires. Otherwise the pits fill up and we live with the stink and the flies. It's not wholesome. The man I need to see is Paul Howell.'

Geezler said he was listening.

'From what I know he's the government man for the sector, handles the money and keeps the locals involved. I'll ask around.'

He asked how everything else was going.

'It's basic. No doubt about that. Supplies are due every other day. It's pretty much hand-to-mouth right now. We've no way of keeping anything cold or fresh, so we've moved from A-rations to MREs. I had the feeling that Southern-CIPA didn't know we were here.'

Geezler advised Rem to come up with a list of what he needed. 'Go to Southern-CIPA as soon as you can and get this organized. Everything in Amrah is under reorganization. ACSB will shut down within a month. You'll be busy.'

☆

After work Cathy returned to Touhy Park, picked up some tacos on her way and sat opposite the fire station and faced the road. She never did this, and wasn't comfortable with the shift in her day, but stopping in the apartment would mean cooking, opening a rotgut bottle of wine, losing another night to the same routine, and this routine, she'd decided, was holding her down. Besides, she could go to the library and check the internet when she returned, fix something else if she was still hungry. There wasn't one thing that couldn't wait.

Done eating she rolled the foil and paper into a wad, looked about for the trash – and saw, across the park, a dog, not unlike Nut, the same dog as before, with the same owner.

Cathy closed her eyes. She had to deal with it. Go, check out that this definitely wasn't Nut, otherwise she'd have another spoiled night fussing over yet one more thing she'd failed to attend to. From a distance the man looked rough. Dressed in a white tracksuit with a blue trim, a Bulls baseball cap, he walked with a spongy stride – of course he'd have a dog like Nut. It just figured. She decided to walk by, keep it nice and casual, didn't even have to look at the man, but just wander by and check out the dog.

She cut across the grass, already threadbare, patches spreading out from the path. The dog, as before, lunged and started barking, almost in response to her. Nut never barked. The man yanked the leash and pulled the dog back, other people walked off the path to keep wide of them. As the man tugged the leash the dog chuffed and pulled in resistance.

Despite the barking, the dog became more and more like Nut with each step.

Closer, she realized that the man was not a man at all but a boy, who despite his height could not be older than fifteen. Closer, she realized – no doubt about it – the dog was definitely Nut.

The boy understood what was happening even before she reached him. With the fuss and lunging it became obvious that Cathy was not *any* person walking toward the dog, but *someone* who was known. She stopped a little ahead, looked to the boy, and pointed at the dog.

'I'm sorry but I think that's our dog.'

Nut tugged and strained and coughed, his backside swung powerfully, front legs pedalled. Cathy settled to her knees and opened her arms. 'Nut. Nut.'

Unable to hold the dog back, the boy loosened his grip and the dog bounced forward.

'Where did you find him?' She cradled Nut, closed her eyes to breathe him in, ran her hands over his back. Nut fell upon her, force of habit, licked her face and neck. She looked up at the boy and repeated her question. The leash, a piece of rope, had chafed Nut's neck, and rubbed the fur to a sore red line.

She asked a third time where he'd found the dog, and kept her voice even, friendly.

'He's my dog.' The boy's voice pitched high.

'I think you found him. Where was he?'

The boy attempted to draw Nut back to his side.

'He's very gentle. You don't have to pull so hard. You're hurting his

363

neck.' Again she spoke firmly but with care, did not want a confrontation, but wanted to lay out the facts. 'That's my dog.'

'He's mine.'

'What's his name? Call him to you.'

When the boy failed to answer, Cathy settled again on her knees. 'We both know that this is my dog.'

The boy's pants were dirty, grey not white, hand-me-downs.

'Look.' She stood up, closer than she intended, and was surprised that the boy flinched. He gripped his fists round the rope, looked to the ground, neither at Cathy nor the dog.

'I can give you a reward. I don't have money with me, but if you let me have your address.'

The boy shook his head, a small movement of defeat.

'We've had him from when he was a puppy.'

His mouth tightened. Cathy couldn't hear what he was saying and had to lean in closer than she felt comfortable. Still she couldn't hear him.

'He really belongs to my husband.' Cathy wasn't sure what to do. Why did this have to happen? 'We put up signs. Here. In this park.' She pointed to the few spare trees as if this would make the lie more truthful. 'It would be nice to have him back.'

'So?' The boy's voice came as a whisper.

'So, his neck is sore. Is he trying to run away?'

The boy nodded.

She thought to snatch the leash. Take back what was hers. Get angry.

'I think he's been trying to come home.'

He didn't resist when she took hold of the rope. Nut came immediately to her side and leaned against her leg. The boy wiped his nose with his cuff.

'I want to thank you for finding my dog.' Now Cathy could not look at him. Oh god, was he crying? 'How can I thank you?'

The boy followed them six blocks south to Lunt. Cathy thought to walk around the corner as she didn't want him to know where she lived, then realized that he seemed to know this anyway. *He's not right*, she told herself. *He has some kind of disability.* The way he dresses, the way he walks on tiptoe. As she unlocked the lobby door the boy leaned forward, a gesture not unlike the dog's, one of intent, of someone rousing determination but failing to push himself to action. When she turned to him he walked away, then after a few paces he began to run, his hands to his face.

Cathy crouched down to hug the dog and asked why did every god-damned thing have to be so hard?

☆

Santo travelled with Rem back to Amrah City. Rem didn't like seeing the camp from the air: the pits laid out in a rough star, the Quonset's rounded hood, the row of cabins, the shower block, the toilets all looked provisional. Once the craft had risen high enough to see the Beach, the camp dissolved.

'I told myself I wasn't going back.'

Santo nodded, sullen. 'They have women at Southern-CIPA?'

Rem looked to Santo as if he was mad. Santo pinched his nose and in a sudden flush, a stream of blood ran between his fingers. Rem moved his knees to avoid the mess and asked over the comm-link for a towel or something. The navigator said he didn't have anything.

'Nosebleed?'

Santo, with his fingers blocking his nostrils, blood running through them, looked sourly at the man and answered sarcastically, 'No. It's that time of the month.'

The man handed Santo what he had, a piece of cloth, and Rem said thanks. 'He gets moody,' he said, 'it's always like this.'

Every morning, Santo complained, same thing. A headache. A nosebleed.

On arrival at Southern-CIPA they found that the meeting was to be held with both Tom Markland and Paul Howell. Howell, being Deputy Administrator, would be able to give immediate approval to what they wanted.

The offices for Southern-CIPA were concealed behind security walls: first the heavy concrete blast walls cordoned off the entire block, and then inside, a running wall of sandbags and an untold number of security detail. In contrast to Camp Liberty the compound, formerly a school, was otherworldly: busy and sealed, and occupied by white Americans and Europeans. Most of the personnel in Operations spent their entire tour inside the compound.

Rem and Santo were escorted through a series of offices – small interlocked Portakabins.

Markland, dressed in tan trousers, a long-sleeved shirt, cuffs rolled ready for business, led them into Howell's office and told them to sit at the desk. Paul Howell was running late – a little trouble this morning – but he would be with them shortly. Markland leaned over the desk to shake Rem's hand. 'I'm sorry you had to come in but it makes things easier.' None of this sounded much like an apology, and there was no explanation about the nature of Howell's delay. The room appeared provisional, flimsy, much like a film set, with a heavy desk, a wall of cabinets, a few trophies: silver boats on dark wood mounts. Behind the desk hung photographs of the Deputy Administrator, his white hair singling him out. Paul Howell with tribal chiefs. Howell with a team dressed in Olympic colours; Howell quayside in an anorak, his arm about a sportsman Rem thought he recognized but couldn't place. Behind Rem and Santo, taking up a good amount of space, an old-fashioned safe. Squat, heavy, and incongruous.

Rem asked Markland if the Deputy Administrator really was coming. Surprised, Markland gave a tight nod and drew his chair back from the desk. Howell would join them just as soon as he could.

Santo sank a little lower into his seat, fists bunched into his armpits, his nose red and sore.

Markland set the papers in front of them and read as he spoke. 'So, what can we do? The issue is about gun permits for non-combatants and the handling of controlled items. Fuel. Explosives. Which goes beyond current licensing and permission.' Markland pressed back into his chair. 'You have any Iraqi nationals working for you?'

Rem shook his head.

'Shame. We could allow them to handle the materials, but we can't allow you, and we can't allow you the permits. Iraqis don't require permits and they can handle what they like. This is internal so we have to run to the same safety standards as we would Stateside.'

Rem couldn't place Markland's accent. Mid-Atlantic, crafted and insincere, deliberately unspecific. His hair cut English-style, parted, short back and sides.

'We're out on our own. There's no perimeter fence. If there's any kind of trouble we'll be defenceless.'

'And why are you there?'

'To man the burn pits.'

'They manage themselves. This is purely a HOSCO initiative, we have no funding assigned to this.'

Rem shrugged, unsure if Markland was making a statement or asking a question. 'Ask HOSCO,' he replied, 'they want someone there.'

Markland compressed his fingers tip-to-tip. 'Can I ask who set this up? Whose project is this?'

Rem wasn't sure how he should answer.

'Is this Brendan? Or David? Is this David Mann?'

Rem gave a small nod, his reticence seemed to provide an answer. Now Markland appeared to come to a decision.

'There is, perhaps, one way forward. But it's not straightforward. If you want, the Deputy Administrator can grant authority if the men are working directly for Southern-CIPA *in some capacity.*'

'But they're working for HOSCO?'

'No matter. They can work for Southern-CIPA, on occasion, on contract. I need men to work on a security detail, once or twice a month. If they work on security then they can receive training, and they can carry arms.'

'You don't have enough security?'

'Believe me,' Markland glanced up with a sly quick smile, 'everything we have here is committed. We're under-resourced. We have three security details for the entire Southern-CIPA, and on occasion, when the Deputy Administrator makes his trips, we're caught short. I need more security. You need explosives and men who can carry guns. I can have them flown in for you. Today even. Look.' Markland sat forward. 'I can't pretend we aren't cutting corners. But I can advise Howell to let you have everything you need.'

The problem with shipping explosives, it was explained to him, was the most complex problem of all. If news of the shipment leaked out of the office then every convoy, Christ knows, would be sabotaged. The solution, simply, would be to airlift the munitions as soon as possible, before any rumours could spread.

As they left the compound Santo sucked air between his teeth.

'How do they find people like that?'

'Like who?'

'Markland. You see that safe? Wasn't even locked. You ever seen so much money? The whole thing packed. How much you think was in there? You see the whisky? He had whisky. There were bottles in the safe.'

Rem said he didn't want to know. 'We have what we came for.'

'And they do too.'

'What do you mean?'

'Now they have us managing some security detail. That's all they wanted. Stop.' Santo held Rem's arm. 'Is that a woman?'

Rem took Santo's arm and led him on.

When they arrived back at Camp Liberty they found Watts and Clark waiting for them. A message had come ahead of their arrival. Markland had spoken with Howell and everything was agreed.

'They'll send the first shipment with the next food drop. You need to pick men out for training.' Watts explained the message. 'They want to send a team to Kuwait for a certification course in firearm safety.'

Rem passed the note to Santo. 'You'll know more about this.'

Santo asked Watts what this was about.

'They want a security team.'

Santo held up the paper. 'So who are we going to send? It says you need to select them.'

Watts had already considered this. 'Send the men who already have basic training.'

Clark immediately began to protest. He wouldn't do it. He wouldn't go. 'Don't put me on that list. I want nothing to do with it. Once they start taking notice they'll pick you out for all sorts. You put your head up a little and they pick you out.'

'Clark, that's what people call a career.'

'Whatever they call it. I don't want it.'

Clark gave a gesture like he didn't care.

'Did they say how many?'

Rem looked over the note. They didn't say.

Santo counted out the men. 'Pakosta, Clark, Chimeno, Kiprowski, me.'

'Kiprowski? With a gun? I don't want to see that.'

'He's done basic already. He'll do fine.'

'Kiprowski was in food services.' Watts disagreed. 'There's no way he ever did basic.'

'Then Samuels. But that hound won't hunt.'

Santo grimaced, but Clark protested. If they wanted everyone who had basic training, then they needed to include Samuels. It was only fair. And why not take Kiprowski if he wanted to go?

Rem asked if they could keep it down. 'Tell them we can only spare four. We still have to run the pits. Even with four down this will leave us short. Find out more about what they want.'

Watts steered clear of the ruts, and the Humvee lost traction and slipped sideways, a small slip, almost imperceptible.

Watts called on Rem late in the morning.

'We have a connection. Praise the lord.'

'You have a signal?'

'I know. Who knew. A *connection*. Different thing, same result.'

Rem sat in his doorway with a towel over his head and poured water on occasion to keep himself cool. 'Who was it?'

Santo stretched out in the shade, feet dug into the dust. 'Probably your boyfriend Markland.' Santo rolled to his side, wrapped his arms about himself, spoke in a squeaky voice. 'Oh Rem, tell me about HOSCO. Kissy kiss kiss.'

Watts pulled a face. 'Actually, it was Markland. He said they'd fixed what you wanted and you should expect him to arrive this afternoon. Fourteen hundred hours.'

Rem didn't understand. 'You said *him*?'

'Or *it*. I'm not sure.'

Rem asked if he knew what *him* or *it* was.

Watts shook his head. 'I just wrote down what he said.'

Santo sat upright, 'Markland's pimping for you now? You even remember what you asked for?'

Rem shrugged. 'You were there.'

'Me? I lost all interest the minute you started talking.'

Watts held his cap up for shade. 'Well. It's coming in two hours, whatever it is. He just wanted us to be ready. That's all.'

Rem looked up at the man. 'I'm ready. You ready?'

'Sure,' Santo laughed, 'I'm always ready.' He kicked down his heels, folded his arms, and closed his eyes. 'Ready for anything, me.'

Rem stood at the cabin door and watched as Chimeno wandered from the latrines to the Quonset to the latrines. As far as he could tell Chimeno didn't want to go to the latrine or back to his cabin and was caught tracing the ground between them.

The afternoon gave itself to reflection, the strangeness of being here. Rem took out his phone, turned the camera to video, and panned about the camp. *Goldrush*, he thought. We look like prospectors.

Chimeno's movements made little sense, and when Samuels came out of his cabin Chimeno sank back to the Quonset door. Rem watched as Chimeno watched Samuels walk to the latrines. After one moment inside Samuels came out running, helter-skelter.

'You should see this.' Samuels pointed back at the latrines, eyes agog, face bright with surprise.

Samuels' shout brought Pakosta and Santo to their doors. Rem couldn't immediately see the reason for the fuss. The latrines were a simple row of open-topped huts with a sandbag wall, head height, built as a blast protection. Samuels pointed to the ground where the bags slumped into the dirt, at what Rem first took to be a kind of hairy crab, brittle and spindly: an insect, with a body as long as the palm of his hand. The creature straddled the first sandbag, legs splayed on one side, tucked in on the other.

'Ten legs. That's not right.'

Not keen on leaning any closer Rem took Pakosta's word.

'You know what this is?'

'Camel spider.'

Samuels ducked back. 'That's no spider.'

'You're right. It's not a spider. It's not a camel either.' Pakosta straightened up, matter of fact. 'I wouldn't stand so close.' He stuck out his boot and the creature braced. 'See that? Instinct. They only come out once they've bred. Females. They inject you so you can't feel anything, then chew a hole in your guts and lay their eggs. They run at thirty miles an hour and jump five, six feet at a time. Spring right up. See those legs? Man, you don't want that on your face.'

Pakosta flicked his cigarette and the spider sprang right at them. Pakosta, Samuels, Santo and Rem careened out of the latrines, the spider, already ahead, scuttled under the cabins. Chimeno ran full pelt past the Quonset and the fuel dump until he couldn't be seen.

Pakosta pointed in Chimeno's direction. 'Spider-boy moves to number one.'

Rem wanted to know if these creatures were harmful.

Pakosta laughed. 'Sure. If you give it a chance to bite you. There's other things, much worse. Scorpions for one. They'll sleep in your boots and get you five times before you pull your foot out. You can't get help fast enough.'

The three of them looked along the cabins for the spider, each armed with a section of tent pole taken from the Quonset. Chimeno waited at a distance, hands on hips, and couldn't be coaxed back to help with the search.

'Vibration. That's what they don't like. Most times you see them at night, if you see them at all. Then you wake up and it's chewing your dick off.'

Pakosta made a munching sound and Santo told him to shut up. Some things they didn't need to know.

'Fine by me, just don't sleep.'

Santo raised his pole as a threat. 'I'm not sleeping.'

'It'll still get you. They hide in holes smaller than your fist. Come out at night and rape your ass.' Pakosta stood with the pole over his shoulder, satisfied. 'And they love dark meat.'

Santo levelled his pole at Pakosta's neck and prodding him, warned: 'You say shit like that *one* time.'

Pakosta backed away with a small laugh.

Watts and Clark stood at their doors curious at the fuss. Watts suggested they get Kiprowski out to help find it, and Kiprowski, already behind them, came to the front, sank to his knees, and swept his arm under the steps.

'Woah!' Watts jolted back. 'You don't do that. You don't know what's under there.'

Kiprowski smiled up, still reaching. 'There's no way a camel's getting under there.'

'Spider,' Santo corrected, 'a motherfucking egg-laying turd-breeding bastard camel *spider*.'

'Yeah?' Clark nodded thoughtfully. 'I heard about those.'

'Place is infested.' Santo spat.

'No shit.'

Kiprowski stood and dusted off his shirt.

Pakosta stabbed his pole under the cabin. 'Seriously, no shit. This is serious business. They crawl up your ass and eat their way out to your face.'

'That won't feel good.' Watts began to collect the poles.

'Got that right.'

'Hey, Watts, what it's like to have something eat out your ass?'

Watts paused on his way to the Quonset, gave serious consideration to the question. 'Ask your mother, Pakosta. Go ask your mom.'

For a moment Pakosta's reaction, a slight collapse in his expression, showed him to be nothing more than a boy. Santo stumbled back,
mock-shot. Clark doubled over and laughed into his fist. Kiprowski
looked about, undecided, checking for a cue.

Rem followed after Pakosta as he walked toward the pits, wanting
to know what Pakosta had meant by saying Chimeno had moved to
number one, but Pakosta's smart stride made it clear that he didn't
want to talk.

At 15:40 the sound of the convoy could be heard, a rick-rack rever-
beration clattering off the cabins – seeming to come from the huts
not the desert. Rem looked out to the road, hands shading his eyes, but
still not able to see. The noise increased, adding a bass sound and
becoming insistent, internal, felt. The craft, when he saw them, five
army Chinooks, smooth, black pods, almost too distant to justify their
noise.

The men grouped behind the Quonset to an area where the ground
levelled, big enough they imagined for the five craft to set down. Rem
asked Santo if this was good enough and Santo gave a gesture, he had
no idea. None of them had any idea.

Beneath the helicopters hung vehicles strapped to platforms, a
truck, a Humvee, what looked to be an ambulance, another Humvee,
a boat. The five craft came out of the blank white sky. Holding a loose
'V' they swung wide of the Quonset and rode over the cabins and
kicked up a sharp blister of sand. Watts and Clark backed into the
Quonset, hands holding down their hats.

Chimeno pointed to the Beach and gestured to Rem that they
should take the Humvee.

Rem cupped his hands round Watts' ear and had to shout. 'Call
Southern-CIPA. Find out what this is about. I want to know what's
going on.'

The wind ripped between the cabins as the first craft hovered
above the Quonset, dwarfing the camp. The cover on the Quonset
rippled wildly and threatened to tear. The cabins, otherwise solid,
shivered and strained against their footings – Rem feared the downdraught would destroy them.

*

By the time they arrived at the Beach the first vehicle had been unloaded. One corner of the pallet slipped into the sand and the ambulance shifted as the sand settled. One by one the packets were carefully lowered and released. The boat, improbably beached, tilted precariously, the bow pointing downhill. The cables wound back up as the helicopter yawed away.

Watts said he knew what that was, and Clark slapped him on the back. 'In my culture we call them boats. Buh-oats. Normally we like to use them in the sea or in the ocean, or on some kind of water, on which, my friend, they glide as if by special powers.'

Watts ignored the taunt and couldn't resist running his hand along the boat. 'It's a Sunshine Fifty-five-O. I was raised on the Sunshine Forty. Five years, from when I was nine.'

'I took you to be a trailer-boy. Same as everyone else.'

'Benton Harbor, before we moved to Missouri.'

'Hippies?'

'Something like that.'

Pakosta couldn't do much but laugh, a boat in the desert being too strange to make sense.

The fifth helicopter set down the truck then veered away toward the camp. Rem and Santo followed in the Humvee. Irritated not to know what was going on, Rem drove into the dust barely able to see.

The helicopter settled behind the Quonset and left two long crates and one man. The man stood by the boxes as Rem drove round, and the helicopter hovered then swung away. Whorls of sand drawn by the craft's swift rise twisted about the man, then dissipated. A clear sky began to break through the yellow dust.

The man stepped forward and introduced himself as their translator, Amer Hassan. He repeated his name and his duties until Rem was clear on both.

'*Translator*?' Rem couldn't help but smile. 'But everyone speaks English.'

'He say translator?' Santo leaned out of the vehicle and shouted: 'You sure you're supposed to be here?'

Amer Hassan took the question seriously. He was certain. Camp Liberty. This was his destination.

'Who sent you?'

'My previous position was with Security at Southern-CIPA. I will be working with Paul Howell and his security team.'

'Howell? Here?'

'Yes. With the security team based here. I received instructions this morning.'

Now Rem scratched his head. 'Paul Howell is coming here?'

'No. This is the equipment.' Amer Hassan indicated the two crates. 'For the security team.' He paused, eyes closed. 'This is only what I have heard. When Mr Howell makes his visits he requires a security detail and a translator.'

Rem gave a soft 'oh'. 'OK. You didn't hear anything about those vehicles that were just delivered, because they don't look much like junk?'

Hassan closed his eyes and shook his head. 'No. There was some talk, the men who brought them also did not understand why they were bringing them here.'

'And this was organized by who? Tom Markland?'

'By Howell, I believe. This is what they said.'

Rem offered a ride to the cabins. Santo gave Rem a quick look and slipped into the back seat. Watts, Clark, Chimeno, and Pakosta, they agreed, could move the munitions boxes back to the Quonset – under strict instructions that they should not be opened and stored securely away from the other provisions.

Rem found the man disarming. It wasn't his handsomeness, but his softness: big eyes, long lashes, his slender shoulders and small frame which conspired to one delicate effect.

He led Amer Hassan to Kiprowski's cabin, apologized, and said he hoped it wouldn't be inconvenient, sharing a small cabin with another man.

'That's Kiprowski's cot. Don't worry, we have plenty in the Quonset.' Kiprowski, he assured him, was a good person, quiet and unassuming.

As Rem walked back to his own cabin he shook off this coyness. There were things he was missing, he told himself. Things that weren't good to be so long without. Santo wolf-whistled and asked if Rem was interested in seeing what they'd been sent.

Rem found Kiprowski in the Quonset and explained the situation.

'This will only be temporary, but we don't have enough cabins and sharing is necessary. I can't see any of the others being . . .' He wasn't sure what he wanted to say, *accommodating*? 'You speak Arabic?'

'No, sir.' Kiprowski shook his head and looked like he had something to say.

'I thought you spoke Arabic?'

He worked in food services. Remember?

'No matter. Obviously he speaks English. This whole thing is some kind of mix-up. I can't see him staying with us for long.'

Stopped at the doorway Rem began to make the introductions and suggested that Kiprowski help find a cot and whatever else Amer Hassan might need.

Kiprowski and Hassan greeted each other affectionately with smiles, a handshake that fell into a brisk hug.

'We were at Southern-CIPA at the same time.'

The silence that fell after this explanation made it clear to Rem that he should leave.

That evening Kiprowski brought the translator to the area they'd set aside for eating. Hassan helped Kiprowski start up the portable stoves and watched as they brought water to the boil. He shook hands with the other men, but once Kiprowski had passed out the rations, they sat separate from the group – and about the two men grew a private air.

Pakosta, Clark, and Santo settled to play cards. Samuels and Chimeno returned to their cabins, and sat at their doors, one reading, one writing, while Rem and Watts struggled to find a clear connection to Southern-CIPA.

Markland confirmed the arrangements for the weekend. Chimeno, Clark, Pakosta, Santo, Samuels, and Watts would undertake a firearm safety training course at Camp Arifjan. Howell, who had business in Kuwait, would be there to meet them. With these details settled, Markland began to speak about Route 567, which was now re-designated as a Secondary Supply Route. Neither Rem not Watts understood Markland's instructions.

'If anything happens on 80 then we need to have Route 567 secured for military and supply convoys.'

Rem asked if anyone at Southern-CIPA had actually seen the road. 'In some parts it's just a graded track. You know that?'

Markland didn't care. 'It's not perfect, but it's what we have. We've had trouble on Highway 80 before, and there's no option but to use 567 as an alternative.'

A forty-mile stretch either side of the camp was to be checked and regularly patrolled. All activity along 567 was to be monitored, a zone cleared along either side.

Rem caught Geezler up on the details and found him more interested in Howell's vehicles than the munitions and the arrival of the translator. They had two new generators and more fuel, which meant, for the evenings, they'd have light. A freezer wouldn't go amiss. Watts was stringing up a line of lights for the front of the Quonset now, lights also for the food area, such as it was.

Geezler was stuck on the vehicles. He wanted to know how many were now at the Beach. 'Send me some pictures. I need to see this.'

Rem explained about the new duties, and how they would be expected to monitor part of Route 567. 'We have a translator. Sent by Southern-CIPA.'

This threw Geezler into confusion. 'You're there for the burn pits,' he argued, 'not patrols. You work for us, not CIPA. Why has Howell given you a translator? I don't see why he's even involved?'

Rem said he didn't know, doubted there was a good reason, that everything was largely random. Over the coming weekend most of the men would accompany the Deputy Administrator to Kuwait to take a basic weapons training course.

Geezler asked Rem to repeat this. Could he clarify? The most senior government representative in southern Iraq was taking time out to accompany contractors on a weapons training course? 'Your contracts come from HOSCO. He can't give you work unless he raises a contract which goes for public tender.'

Rem couldn't help but laugh. Geezler seriously didn't understand the territory, the deal with Markland on security was separate. He shouldn't have mentioned it. As for Howell, what did it matter? Nothing here was logical. CIPA had college graduates running entire government divisions. Why worry over five contractors and a Deputy Administrator who probably only want a weekend off?

The next morning Rem took Santo on a drive north along Route 567, and found parts in worse condition than he'd reported. In an hour's drive they encountered no other vehicle. Santo pointed to the roadside, he'd seen something, a dog, or maybe a coyote.

'They have cats out here. In the middle of the desert. I've seen their tracks about the cabins.'

Brooding over his discussion with Geezler, Rem wasn't listening. 'You know, when Southern-CIPA speak about contingencies that means something's going on.'

Santo agreed. They send arms, they send a translator, equipment, vehicles, all without explanation. They shut down the section base in Amrah. Something was afoot.

'I'm talking about the road, this whole security detail.'

'Right. I mean, what do we know about him? We don't know anything. They drop him in the desert with a box of guns.'

'The translator? You know what he's doing here. Howell sent him from Southern-CIPA.'

'That's what he told you. He could be anyone.'

'Kiprowski knows him.'

'You just said you don't trust them.'

'Who are we talking about here? Kiprowski, the translator, or Howell? I was talking about Southern-CIPA, and maybe Howell.' Rem pointed to the vast space about them. 'Everything about this place is backwards. I think there's something we don't know. Those vehicles, this security team. I think there's information we don't have yet. I don't think it's mysterious. I just think we're not in the loop.'

'Think about it. He could be anyone, someone they want isolated, kept away from trouble. Someone we aren't supposed to know about.'

'He speaks Arabic, Farsi, and English. He's a translator.'

'*Think about it.* You didn't know he was coming. And why do we need a translator?'

'Santo, who would he be exactly?'

Santo backed down. 'I don't know. He could be anyone. Who do you think they'd drop in the middle of the desert with two boxes of weapons and enough ammunition?'

'A translator?'

'I'm being serious.'

'So, who is he? Tell me who you think he is? The translator is here because Howell needs him. The security detail is necessary because we're remote and Howell wants a team when he does his travels. And for this he needs a translator.'

'Then why hasn't he asked the translator to come tomorrow?'

'For the training? It's in English? Surely?'

'And those vehicles? What about the vehicles?'

'Maybe that's part of it? I don't know. Santo, this isn't anything different. We just don't have the details.'

'And the guns?'

'They stay in the crates.'

Santo leaned away from Rem, folded his arms, a slight edge of disbelief in his gesture as if he didn't agree, but he was prepared, for the time being, to leave it alone. 'One last thing. Is Kiprowski officially retarded?'

Rem refused to answer.

'I don't want him coming tomorrow. There's something not right about him.'

'He isn't going anyway. You know this? They didn't ask for him. I thought it was Samuels you didn't like.'

'Samuels is run-of-the-mill chicken-shit scared. Kiprowski isn't normal.'

'He's nineteen.'

'They're all nineteen, give or take. That's not the problem.'

'I hope this has nothing to do with the translator.'

Rem pulled the Humvee to the side of the road and they agreed to return.

Rem rose early to see the men off. Lined up in front of the Quonset, Humvee at the ready, he found Santo, Clark, Chimeno, Samuels, and a groggy Pakosta.

Rem asked Santo if he was sure about the group. 'You have Samuels?'

Santo shrugged. 'You want him to stay?'

'I don't care who goes. Take him if that's what he wants.'

'I'm poisoned.' Pakosta held his stomach. 'I can't eat those MREs any more. You seen this?' Pakosta rolled up his sleeves to show a rash, large, palm-sized blotches, map-like and raw.

'Looks like a reaction?'

'No shit it looks like a reaction.'

'See if there's a medic when you're in Kuwait.'

At the mention of a medic, Pakosta rolled down his sleeves and said it was nothing. 'Better today than yesterday. Itches like a bitch.'

Surprised to see Clark, Rem asked if he was sure he wanted to go. 'Never been to Kuwait,' was the only justification he offered for his change of heart.

Neither Kiprowski nor Watts came out of their cabins. 'I don't want any problems to come out of this,' he told Santo. 'Tell them Watts is sick or something. He isn't interested in going.'

Rem watched them clamber into the single Humvee, then slapped the side and sent them off.

He stood on the spot long after the vehicle had pulled out, its lights furred and faded along the curve of the road. The cabins buzzed with the hum from air-conditioners, the air vibrated, then, with a click, the generator turned off. The only people in the camp were Rem, Kiprowski, Amer Hassan, and Watts.

Watts joined Rem at Burn Pit 5 just as the trucks were unloading.

'How many is it today?'

'Twenty-five. Fifteen shit-suckers. Best stay up-wind.'

'Do you know what the problem is between Santo and Kiprowski?'

Watts said he had an idea.

'I wouldn't worry about it. It's a small thing. Kiprowski's a nice kid. He sticks to a routine. Makes his bed. You've seen how orderly he is? He's not from the same planet as the others. He's struggling to fit in.' Watts held his hand to his throat, his voice husky from the smoke. 'I'm too old for this,' he said. 'You do it for so long, and you begin to ask yourself that question.'

'Why?'

'Exactly. You start asking *why*. I tell you. I don't have an answer any more. But this is it. As soon as that child is born I'm done. I married late. I've done everything backwards. I know that. But I'm telling you. Once I'm done here, I'm done. No more contracts. No more of this.'

'You know what you'll do?'

Watts looked out over the pits. 'That's the problem. You do one thing for twenty years and you're no good at anything else. Who's going to hire you? No one wants to take that risk.'

Rem agreed. 'Nothing's easy.'

'And if it is there's something wrong with it, right?'

'Right.'

The smoke cleared, and the fire blistered across the pit.

'You see what went in there today?'

'Looked like powder? Something white.'

Watts nodded, eyes on the fire. 'Building materials. Four loads, whatever it was, shipped from the US, not even opened. And yesterday, food cartons, those plates they use at the commissary. You know how many of those we burn?'

'Must be in the thousands.'

Watts craned his head back, followed the trail of smoke. 'Can't be doing any of us any good. I was checking the news yesterday, looking for information on the closure of ACSB. You know they've closed down Bravo? Those pits aren't operating any more, manned or unmanned. Which means we'll be busier here.'

Back at the cabins, Rem found Kiprowski and Amer Hassan returning from the showers. The men walked side by side, a towel over Amer Hassan's shoulders, and Kiprowski animatedly describing Chicago. His hands formed the ideas, drew rapid shapes in the air. He'd seen the lake freeze only once, he said, great rucks of ice packed against the shoreline, the water steaming. You can't imagine how cold it gets in the winter, he said, you can't even imagine it.

Rem returned to his cabin. Lying back on his cot, he congratulated himself on taking up Geezler's offer.

☆

For the first night Cathy allowed the dog to sleep in the bedroom. He picked the rug on Rem's side of the bed, then part way through the night came round to Cathy's side and settled close. For the first time since Rem's departure Cathy slept well, aware of the dog, his breathing, his musky smell. When she woke she thought again about the boy. She hadn't properly thanked him. She turned to her side and looked at the dog. As always, of a morning, Nut sat right beside the bed and looked up, innocent enough, with a little pink hard-on. His *chilli* as Rem called it. *See, he likes you.*

'You're disgusting. You know that? That's just vile.' She sat upright. 'I can't even look at you.'

It was no surprise to see the boy outside. Dressed in the same clothes, the cap pulled back so he could look up, he stood by the sign for the currency exchange, hands in pockets.

Cathy came down to the door, brought Nut with her. Out on the street she approached the boy and offered him the leash.

'You want to walk with us?'

The boy nodded, hesitated.

'Go on.'

He ran with the dog in a half-jog, then stopped at the corner and waited for her to catch up. When she caught up he crossed the road, then ran ahead another half-block. She wondered what stopped the boy from taking the dog and disappearing. But the dog sat at the kerb, and the boy sank to his knees to hug it.

'I don't know your name.'

The boy set his arms about Nut's neck and kissed it.

'My name is Cathy.'

The boy didn't speak until they returned to the apartment.

'What's his name again?'

'Nut. My husband named him. It's his dog really.' She didn't want to explain that the dog only had one testicle.

'Nut.'

'What did you call him?'

The boy shrugged and walked away, and Cathy realized it didn't matter, whatever name he had chosen was irrelevant. The boy turned the corner on Greenleaf and did not look back.

☆

The men returned from Kuwait in army fatigues. Samuels had tied his jacket about his waist. As soon as the vehicle stopped he stepped out and walked stroppily to his cabin. When Rem asked what the problem was, Santo told him not to ask.

Pakosta, happily gave an explanation. The training wasn't what they had expected. On arrival at the camp they'd waited almost the entire day before they were hustled through an improvised assault course. At the end of this, at something like two in the morning, they were handed automatic rifles with live rounds.

'Only Sammy mustn't have heard the part about live rounds. Because the first thing he did was sling the gun to his hip and blast a round over the camp.'

Rem turned to the cabin to look for Samuels.

Santo corrected him. 'No, he didn't. He shot a couple of rounds into the desert.'

'My version's better.'

'He shot one round . . .'

'. . . took off a camel's head, went postal, emptied the rounds into thirteen NCRs . . .'

'Did no such thing.'

'Left the camp looking like a high school.'

Rem held up his hand and asked Santo for the story.

'We were doing this simulation where you go into a mock-up of an Iraqi village.'

'It wasn't a mock-up. It was an actual village. And we were in Kuwait.'

Santo held his hand over Pakosta's mouth. 'He's right. At some point in history it was an actual *Kuwaiti* village. Anyhow, he didn't have his gun on safety. That's all he did. No big thing.'

'And?'

'And the instructor took it off him, said if he couldn't look after his weapon then he couldn't have one.'

'That's it?'

'That's the story. No one was shot, no camels were hurt.'

Pakosta wrested himself free from Santo and asked what the time was, then held up his wrist with a half-mocking flourish. 'Oh, look, I forgot.'

'That's the other calamity.' Santo pointed at the watch on Pakosta's wrist. 'Pakosta now has a fake Rolex.'

'It's not fake.' Pakosta held up his wrist. 'You know it.'

'The only way you can tell is if you smash it open. They have a number etched under the seal. It's the only way you can tell for sure.'

'It's real. I'm telling you. Gen-u-ine.' Pakosta slipped his wrist behind his back.

In private Santo caught Rem up on the details of the weekend. 'Samuels didn't want to be there, shouldn't have gone, just about shat himself every time a gun went off. Maybe he had some other idea about what he was doing there. Once the instructor took notice of him, he just wouldn't leave him alone. To be honest, it was embarrassing.'

'And Howell? You spend much time with him?'

'Howell?' Santo looked ready to say something but backed away. 'Let's just say he's not your usual bureaucrat.'

The expected convoy didn't arrive the next morning. After dawn Rem drove to the camp entrance, but even with Santo's binoculars he couldn't see any problem, and wasn't sure in any case what he expected to see. No timetable, orders, or instructions had come through about the regularity of the convoys and their deliveries, so he decided to think nothing of it. Santo thought otherwise and encouraged Rem to call Southern-CIPA to see if there was a problem.

'We'd hear soon enough if something wasn't right.'

Santo wasn't convinced. There could be a convoy in trouble, people being held to ransom, the trucks themselves stolen, damaged, or burned. Heads being severed. There was no telling what could go wrong.

'We need to prepare. We should protect ourselves, be ready.'

Rem didn't want to argue, but Santo insisted. 'They sent guns, right? For this very purpose. We need to get ourselves ready. We're exposed, completely vulnerable. This is what they trained us for.'

'No guns. There's nothing to be concerned about.'

'*Yet.*'

'There's no delivery today, that's all.'

Rem said he was going to call his wife, an excuse to be alone. In truth he didn't want Santo's company. Santo was fine, he supposed, although he couldn't understand his fretting over the convoy, just as he didn't understand his automatic distrust of the translator.

He wrote notes on what he wanted to tell Geezler: news on the training, the translator, nothing of particular urgency.

Rem was woken at noon by the sound of gunfire. He sat up, immediately sweating, believing himself to be back at the section base in Amrah. Recognizing his surroundings brought fresh fears: Santo was right, they were vulnerable, and he immediately regretted not distributing the guns. The shots were close.

As soon as he was on his feet he realized that the gunfire was too regular, and in the spaces between he could hear Pakosta laughing. There was no shouting, nothing to indicate trouble, and he guessed that the guns had been unpacked against his direct instruction.

He found Samuels and Chimeno idling at the back of the Quonset.

Santo stood by an open crate giving instruction to Pakosta and Clark who lay side by side on their stomachs. Each man dressed in military drab. Each man armed. Pakosta took aim and fired. The dirt tufted far in the distance. They stopped when they noticed Rem.

'We needed the flares,' Santo explained, 'something to start the pits, they're all packed together.' Then, as Rem did not reply, 'I didn't see any harm.'

Rem drew the gum he was chewing between his teeth and bit down and decided not to react. He wouldn't say a goddamned thing.

'They've had training. I've given the basic safety instructions. We were just about to finish.'

Rem nodded.

Pakosta looked to Santo. 'We only just started?'

Santo began to dismantle his weapon. 'Disarm the weapon and put it away.'

Pakosta stretched out in the dirt, belly down, eye to the sight. Santo set his boot on the small of Pakosta's back. 'I said, put the weapon away.'

This was – Rem couldn't decide – insubordination? While he was in charge, his position was, at best, merely supervisory. They held no rank, had no formal organization. He had little authority. His best decision lay in practical monitoring: managing the weapons and not the men.

Santo began his defence as they packed the guns away. 'What's the problem? They're no use if they don't know how to handle them.'

'Supplies are limited.'

'They need to practise.'

'And what if there's an accident?'

'What if we're attacked?'

'An accident. You're ready for the consequences?'

'That's more of a reason for them to train. They have two hours' experience on a firing range, they have certificates saying they know what they're doing. They need to practise. Not everyone is Fatboy.'

Rem didn't appreciate the reference. He looked Santo up and down. 'You're wearing a military uniform.'

Santo tried a different approach. 'We have no security. No one will protect us. If something happens they aren't going to send anyone. It's not going to happen. We burn shit. And what's the point in having guns if we can't use them? What was the point in going to Kuwait if they can't practise? I can train them so they know what they're doing.' Santo stopped, folded his arms. 'These men aren't stupid. They know what's going on out there.'

☆

Cathy's hostility to her customers didn't go unnoticed: how she leaned over the rheumy Mrs Dempsey with her hands on her hips as if the woman was stupid as well as deaf. She lost her patience counting out change, waiting, then scanning coupons. Couldn't focus. Took breaks which became longer and more frequent. Maggie waved a pack of cigarettes and brought her onto the loading dock.

'You have to be nicer.'

'Nicer?'

'Kinder.'

'Kinder *and* nicer. Let me see?' Cathy narrowed her eyes as she inhaled. 'You know? I'm fresh out.'

Maggie allowed the idea to sink in.

'Oh, come on.' Cathy tried to laugh. 'I mean, seriously. Don't they get to you? Their stupid questions when everything is so obvious.'

'I mean you. I mean you have to be nicer to yourself.'

'To myself? This is crazy talk.' Cathy looked for a place to put out her cigarette, then paused. 'It's just a bad day. That's all it is. I shouldn't be smoking.'

'It's not just today. You know that. You're too hard on yourself. You need to talk to someone.'

'You're saying I need help?'

'No.' Maggie rolled her eyes. 'Yes. But not like that. You need to talk with someone who knows what you're going through. Someone who has a better idea. You're on your own here.'

Cathy leaned back against the wall, arms folded. 'There isn't anything to say. There isn't anyone to talk to.' After a while she appeared to soften and allowed her shoulders to drop. 'You know what I got yesterday? I got an email, one of those round robins – I'm not even sure what you'd call it. I don't know how she found me, but she sent this email to all of the wives who have husbands or partners out in al-*Narnia*, maybe even some of the parents.' She took up the offer of another cigarette. 'I don't know. It just seems so *dumb*. All she talked about was her kids and how much they missed their daddy, and how blessed she was . . .'

'Blessed?'

'I know. Everything is a blessing. All this praying, and Jesus, and – I don't know, just all of this shit about how everything has a purpose, about being happy that today was a good day. She has a child in hospital and she writes to strangers about being blessed. It wasn't enough to delete the message, I had to print it out so I could throw it away.'

Both women paused as the loading-bay doors opened. Outside a van reversed into the dock. Cathy murmured that they should get back.

'Why don't you write to her?'

'I don't want my business to be on their minds. I don't want anyone to pray for me, or Rem. I don't need their Jesus, and I don't want to know about their lives. I didn't ask to hear any of this. I don't want it in my head.'

'And that's what she's doing?'

'That's exactly what she's doing.'

As the truck reversed it cut out the daylight and Cathy and Maggie retreated to the storeroom doors.

'She's just the same as you.' Cathy dropped her cigarette and stepped on it. 'I don't see the difference, actually. I mean, sure. Maybe you're right. Maybe everyone should just leave you alone. Maybe all you need is some new batteries in that Jack Rabbit of yours.'

Cathy logged online and waited for messages to download. The dog sat outside, tied to a bike rail. Once she was done with the library, she decided, she'd take a longer walk, maybe down to Loyola along the lake. The inbox remained empty. With no word from Rem and no other business to distract her she returned to the round robin and clicked 'reply to all'.

> We know that this is as hard on the families and loved ones and pray that this trial will soon pass over.

Cathy began typing unsure of what to say, except, she wasn't going to ask anyone to pray.

> I don't know who you all are and I apologize for writing without permission. My name is Cathy Gunnersen and I'm the wife of Rem

Gunnersen, and this is the first time we've been apart. I was born and raised in Seeley, Texas, and I now live in an apartment on the North Side of Chicago. I don't know what else to say except 'hi'.

She read the email before sending it, unsure what she expected back.

☆

Rem counted the traffic through the morning. Forty-eight: Kia, Renault, Daewoo, Toyota, Hyundai. The first vehicles he'd seen on the road since his arrival. Among them, the occasional Mercedes and BMW, all battered and distressed.

He returned to the cabins to see Pakosta exercising, still wearing the military drab trousers. The sun turning the sweat on his back to silver. The exercises, determined, structured, weren't anything Rem had seen before. Rem found Watts and asked him to contact Markland.

As Watts made the call Rem returned to the road with Santo, and found it empty.

'No one drives in the day. Too exposed.' Santo stood with his arms folded. 'How many?'

'Forty-eight. Domestic traffic.' Rem turned back to face the camp. 'No one knows we're here, but as soon as those fires are lit the smoke will tell everyone.'

He attempted to reach Geezler, a little surprised not to have heard from him after his promise to find out more information about Paul Howell.

Within an hour of contacting Markland, Watts had an answer. He found Rem in his cabin. The intersection between Highway 80 and Route 567 had been hit – an IED. A convoy, intended for Kuwait, had headed right back to Amrah.

Rem ate while he considered the news. The air-con unit in pieces about the small cabin. His hands black with grime. The air grotty with heat.

'Two things.' Watts hesitated at the door, a little sulky Rem thought. 'First, we're supposed to make reports. Every day. CIPA want a log of when the trucks arrive and when they leave.'

'You can manage this?'

'Sure.' Watts remained at the door. 'The second thing – they want you to check Highway 80, see what the problem is. They'll send a team from Amrah to fix it.'

As Rem stood up he told Watts to pass the news to Santo, as Santo, Pakosta, Clark, Chimeno, and possibly Samuels, were now working security.

'Tell him to take the guns if he's confident they can use them safely.' Rem didn't see much choice. If they were to go off-base, they shouldn't go unarmed.

While Santo organized the new detail, Rem took Kiprowski with him to Highway 80 to see the damage for himself.

As he drove off the camp, Kiprowski pointed to the east. At some distance, four Chinooks approached with vehicles slung beneath them, all heading toward the camp.

The vehicle ran well, Rem could feel it in his grip, an easy thrum, a satisfying throaty roll.

'Another delivery?'

Rem said he didn't know, but it looked that way.

'You look at that boat? It's all new.'

Rem asked if Kiprowski had ever been to Europe, if he'd ever travelled before. It didn't matter if he hadn't. Kiprowski didn't respond.

'We've never spoken about Chicago. What neighbourhood are you from?'

'West Ridge.'

'I don't know where that is exactly.'

'Back from the lake. Bryn Mawr to Howard.'

'I'm Rogers Park. Clark and Lunt.'

'Rockwell and Coyle.'

They both nodded.

'You know it?'

Rem shrugged. 'I have – I had – a dog, so I spend most of the time closer to the lake.'

'Some parts of it are fancy.'

'You mind if I ask something personal?'

The boy looked right ahead, and said cautiously he didn't mind.

'It's just most people have their reasons for being here, and I was wondering about yours . . .'

Most of their stories ran to the same narrative. While Pakosta was dodging personal debt, and maybe some unspecified trouble (same as

Clark, Samuels, and in his own way, Watts), Kiprowski was avoiding debt of a different kind: the near-poverty that locked his family to a small railroad apartment, night school and service jobs. The promise of money was more than enough to draw him to Iraq – food services couldn't be a safer proposition. Rem tried to curb his impatience as Kiprowski told his story, about how he was the first in his family to travel to the Middle East. In every story the same tidy tax-free $100,000 figured as the basic lure. This money would be used to provide a decent house, settle parents' or spouse's debt, or children's medical expenses, be seed money for a business they would start with a brother, father, cousin – who knows? Everyone had the same idea, or something close. That money would turn around a life that otherwise had no direction but forward and down.

Kiprowski had the idea more polished than others. He'd picked out a storefront on Howard, right at the Chicago–Evanston border. A café, a small restaurant. Maybe buy into a franchise. Kiprowski's plan sounded dryer than the landscape they were passing through. If Rem breathed deeply enough he could smell the boy's future: a body sweating labour through unbroken years.

Not that Rem wasn't prone to this romance himself. Weren't there properties in Evanston he'd imagined Cathy inside, perhaps even a family, but no matter how much money he earned, this wouldn't be his leafy lane. *And wasn't this the point of Evanston, somehow, to offer up modest but unattainable possibilities?*

They found the damaged intersection shortly after they left Route 567. An oval pit, about nine metres in circumference and one metre at its deepest, broke the highway. Upside down, on either side, lay the stripped blown fragments of a car.

'This isn't good.'

Until Highway 80 could be repaired Route 567 would need to handle the traffic between Kuwait and Baghdad, which brought potential danger to Camp Liberty.

'Doesn't look like much to fix.'

Kiprowski was right: one or two days and the highway could open. Rem wound down his window, leaned on his forearm and smoked. 'It's just a hole.'

His optimism didn't last. On the journey back the radio buzzed with news of two bombings on the outskirts of Amrah City. Jalla Road. Looting stirred up by the bombing had spread from the city centre to the outlying neighbourhoods with less protected FOBs. The sooner the section base closed the better.

As soon as they passed Khat they could see the black plumes from Camp Liberty, two separate strands conjoining as a single cloud to signal the precise location of the burn pits. Rem punched the steering wheel. 'Look at that!' He opened his hands at the horizon. 'Could they make it more obvious?' The convoy from Amrah had made it through. He should have left instruction that there were to be no fires until the highway was secured. He should have considered this.

As they drove in silence the columns grew fatter and more ominous.

In the late afternoon Rem held his first 'three-point' briefing. Southern-CIPA had divided Route 567 into zones. Zone B15 included Camp Liberty and would be monitored by Rem's team. The men were to build two blockhouses out of sandbags and set chains across the road. Signals would alert them of the convoys heading to Amrah City. The plan would become operational immediately.

Markland had specified that all vehicles holding potentially looted goods should be stopped, searched, and held. Rem looked about the group from man to man. 'If you see anything, step out of the way. Let the people at Zone 14 or Zone 16 deal with it. We can't hold people here, and we don't have any kind of authority.'

Clark had a different idea on what was causing the trouble, discussions roiled with conspiracies peeled off the internet. Pakosta agreed. 'Sixty per cent of the oil that's shipped overland is stolen. Fact.'

Amer Hassan had stories from other translators. 'There's no gas,' he said. People queue all day in Baghdad, in Nasiriyah, even in Kurdish Mosul. Families risked breaking the curfew to get in line early, and violence while waiting, snipers who would shoot at the cars for sport. 'It's no easier buying fuel on the black market.'

Chimeno couldn't see the logic. They'd seen the convoys on YouTube, the dirty silver tankers in long heavy lines. How was this possible? 'Just yesterday on CNN, an entire caravan of thirty trucks with Iraqi Ministry of Oil logos was hijacked. It was nothing if not brazen.

Amer Hassan concurred. He'd also heard of this and knew it not to be uncommon.

'You don't stop anything,' Rem repeated. 'Leave it to the military.' If there was going to be any activity, he warned, anything which threatened them, it would likely come at night.

Rem held his hands up for silence. 'Two days. At most. That's all we have to get through. The highway will be repaired, guaranteed, in two days.'

A groan passed through the group at the word 'guarantee'. HOSCO, Southern-CIPA, they all knew, were not dependable.

After the briefing, Rem contacted Geezler and left a message explaining their circumstances. While he didn't ask, he made it clear that he wanted advice. Geezler's misgivings about them working for CIPA now made sense. 'I'm concerned that we've worked ourselves into a situation we can't manage.' He spoke briskly wanting his concern to sound controlled and confident. At the same time he didn't want Watts to hear him.

Rem joined Pakosta, Kiprowski, and Santo for the first shift. The men held back behind the sandbags and allowed the traffic through.

'Looks like everyone's moving house.' Kiprowski couldn't quite believe his eyes. Anything that could be pilfered was being pilfered, and in the first night they saw flatbed trucks loaded with bathroom fixtures, toilets, baths, slabs of ceramic tiles, metal rebar hammered out of concrete, metal doors and window frames. One vehicle crammed with the entire contents of a hotel room: a television, telephone, self-assembled furniture, in another, mirrors and bed frames, doors and shower units. A whole truck of dried semolina, a cloud of flour, white from the distance as the top bags were split. Semis came toward them as a hard vibration, a mirage unwrinkling on the road, approaching and promising strangeness as they passed.

'Guess what we have in this one. Just guess.'

The road brought everything. It brought the dead and the living. It brought people and livestock; oil, kerosene, diesel, and petrol. Hospital equipment, scanners, beds, cots, mattresses, dentists' chairs. Crates marked 'popcorn', 'peppercorn', and 'processed meat'. Milk and honey, and every type of foodstuff. It brought CDs and DVDs. Concrete and tar, stone, brick, clay, paint, and bales of material, canvas, cotton, and silk, stuffed into family cars. Cars, and cars towed by other cars, cars on trailers, car parts, and motors. Machines to break down buildings, military supplies and vehicles. Humvees and Bradleys. One car stuffed entirely with socks and baby clothes stolen from a department store, with the driver lodged into his seat. It was a road of wonders. At dawn, Kiprowski watched a painted stone head with a silent pursed mouth and wide blue eyes agog at the desert, with thin spangled hair flapping in streamers behind it, strapped to the roof of a family car. There were cars with other pieces of cars and sheet metal welded and battened to them for protection, and there were the SUVs black and clean with tinted windows.

Hassan told stories of how women were taken from their houses and brought across the border to Syria or Jordan. Clark had heard similar news on the British World Service. There were hotels in every border country where women were set up as cleaners and prostituted. It was hard to guess how many were involved. Hard also to say what happened to the women who escaped or returned.

The idea was especially repugnant to Kiprowski, who compared everything back to his own family, his three sisters, his mother who'd raised him. He pestered Amer with questions. How could such a thing be conceived? And Amer said that there was always worse, always one more degradation possible. It would be better, he said, that they should die. Amer Hassan instructed them. They should not speak directly to the women, only the men.

Later that night Clark and Pakosta pulled over two black sedans. With the cars stopped off-road Pakosta called Kiprowski and Rem to come immediately. In total there were three men and seven women, all young. Their passes showed the men and women to be unrelated.

Clark shone his torch into the back of the first vehicle and one of the women shielded her eyes and shied away. Clark shook his head, he just didn't feel easy about the situation. They separated the three men, took them out of the cars. One of them spoke English. Pakosta later described his manner as servile: the man was a snake. Kiprowski and Clark spoke with the women through Amer Hassan. Hassan translated in a calm voice so that he seemed to defuse the problem. The conversation, with many pauses, was oiled by smooth and conciliatory OKs.

Clark asked why two of the women were from Baghdad and the others were from Sadr. The women claimed to be related, but did not know each other's names. They all gave the name of their driver as Mohammed.

Hassan asked where he was heading and why. The man replied,

astonished: 'Because I am leaving.' His papers showed that he came from Egypt, and was a businessman in imports and exports, but gave no particular detail. Hassan repeated his questions and they slowly learned that the women's families had paid for them to be to be taken out of the country to safety: instead of kidnapping, these women were being taken to a safe house. They were all married, and were being sent ahead of their husbands for their own safety.

As the men climbed back into the cars, one of them looked for a long time at Amer Hassan.

'He knows me,' Hassan said. 'That man knows who I am. Word will get back that I am working with the Americans.'

Kiprowski asked who would know that he was working here, and how that would matter. Amer said that there were many people who could not leave. His family were still in Baghdad, and if word got back to them there would be trouble.

'What do they think you are doing?'

'They think that I am finishing my studies in Damascus.'

Pakosta held up his gun and tracked the vehicle as it disappeared. He could solve the problem, he said. Hassan only had to give the word.

☆

The next morning Cathy received a reply from Marianne Clark.

> Dear Cathy,
>
> It was very good to hear from you. I live in St. Louis, although I have family in Aurora and have spent some very happy times in Chicago. I don't want to presume anything, but I was very pleased to hear from you as an earlier message had me a little confused. I am new to the internet, and much happier with the telephone if you should ever want to talk. It would be nice to talk and please do not hesitate if you should like to call me. It was a great comfort to hear from you and know that there are others in our situation.
>
> Sincerely,
>
> Marianne Clark

Cathy returned to the library after work and found messages from John Watts, brother of Paul, and Sara Morales, girlfriend of Mark Samuels.

Thnks for yr message. Write when u want, wld be interested in hearing
more. Have pics from Camp Liberty to share & willing to
set up a chatroom if u and others are interested.
JW

and

I haven't heard from Mark since he moved from Amrah City,
and hope that everything is all right with him. I don't know if the
messages are getting through, can you let me know? Have you
heard anything?
Sara Morales

One day more and Cathy was surprised to see a whole number of
messages, each copied to all of the recipients.

I'm angry, this isn't what we were told . . . we were told that his wage
would be $19.45 an hour, but the rate so far is far below at $11.25!!!!!
Has anyone else experienced this?
Paul Pakosta

. . . same here, annual income indicated at a minimum of $87,000
to $95,000, starting wage at $21 an hour – so far, hasn't come close.
Plus travel deductions for the first seven months of $750 to $1,000.
Why are they taking money out? I have copies of the original contract
which says nothing about this?
Sara Watts

. . . and vaccination charges, shipping costs, this is not what he signed
up for!!!!! This is not what was promised!!!!!
Paul Pakosta

. . . Mark's first contract was with U-Tech who recruited him, but
he was asked to sign another at the induction in Virginia, where he
was told he was working for HOSCO, who charged us $7,000 for his
transport to Iraq and for the seven days they kept him waiting in
Dubai, which is paid with interest? Is this legal? I don't think they
started paying till he arrived in Iraq, which means those ten days in
Austin were unpaid. It's confusing. Can anyone get information on
where he's placed? All we've been told is that decisions are made
'on the ground'. He was at ACSB. Where is this? Please advise.
Doug & Marsha Samuels

P.S. our neighbors have a family member who was in an accident in Iraq and he worked for HOSCO and he had to pay all of his medical?

Cathy wrote to John Watts and enquired about the chatroom and received an immediate reply inviting her to an online discussion board and suggesting a login time of 19:00. Once she completed the form she noticed a new icon at the bottom of the screen. When she clicked on it a message-box opened up.

JONNIEWATTS92: ;) it's cathy, right?
CATHYGUNNERS: Hello?
. . .
. . .
JONNIEWATTS92: i sent emails to everyone in the earlier email did that even make sense ???
JONNIEWATTS92: you've not used messenger before?
JONNIEWATTS92: you have to hit the spacebar
. . .
. . .
JONNIEWATTS92: hit enter.
CATHYGUNNERS: OK, thanks. Sorry. Is this live?
JONNIEWATTS92: it's real time, yup, happening now :)
CATHYGUNNERS: Can we speak with them at Camp Liberty?
JONNIEWATTS92: it's 4am in iraq now --- you can send an invite :) click on the red icon at the bottom that looks like a man with a hat -- type in the email address and they get an invite
JONNIEWATTS92: you've not done this before?
CATHYGUNNERS: No
JONNIEWATTS92: seriously!?
[DSAMUELS has entered the chatroom]
CATHYGUNNERS: It's all new
JONNIEWATTS92: it won't take long -- it's not rocket science
DSAMUELS: This is Doug.
CATHYGUNNERS: Hi Doug
JONNIEWATTS92: hey
DSAMUELS: Sorry we're late.
JONNIEWATTS92: s'ok -- we've not really started.
DSAMUELS: My wife is here, Marsha, I'm typing, she's dictating...

Cathy, we were happy to hear from you. Did everyone get the same message?

JONNIEWATTS92: i sent the invite ;)

CATHYGUNNERS: I don't know where to start.

CATHYGUNNERS: I had all these questions.

JONNIEWATTS92: No worries ;)

JONNIEWATTS92: we have time

DSAMUELS: Has anyone heard from Mark? Does anyone know how he is?

JONNIEWATTS92: i heard from my brother -- he didn't say anything was wrong.

JONNIEWATTS92: u said he was at ACSB... I think he's at camp liberty now

DSAMUELS: He's ok?

JONNIEWATTS92: paul didn't say otherwise -- tho he sounded bored.

JONNIEWATTS92: my brother sounded bored -- said they weren't up to much -- out in the desert -- just them and some scorpions --

DSAMUELS: Why are they there?

JONNIEWATTS92: the company picked them for the job

CATHYGUNNERS: I think that was my husband.

DSAMUELS: We don't understand. What is the job?

CATHYGUNNERS: He was asked by the company director to pick a team.

DSAMUELS: By U-Tech?

CATHYGUNNERS: HOSCO.

DSAMUELS: Sorry? It doesn't make sense?

DSAMUELS: ...like everything else. But you're sure he's ok?

JONNIEWATTS92: my brother sent pictures. I have photos.

DSAMUELS: You're sure he's ok. We don't understand why he hasn't been in touch.

[you have three attachments WY8959001.JPEG: WY8959002.JPEG: WY8959003.JPEG]

. . .

. . .

. . .

DSAMUELS: Thank God.

DSAMUELS: Thank you. Thank you. Thank you.

DSAMUELS: This is the first we've seen him since he left. Thank you thankyouthank you. Tell your brother thank you.

JONNIEWATTS92: most welcome

DSAMUELS: How can we get a message to him?

DSAMUELS: Why is he there? When will he come back?

[Invitation from JONNIEWATTS92 to CATHYGUNNERS for a private chat]

JONNIEWATTS92: this makes me feel bad

CATHYGUNNERS: I know. I don't understand why they don't know anything?

JONNIEWATTS92: it's weird --

JONNIEWATTS92: their son is in Iraq and he's not contacted them -- they can call anytime they want -- that's really really sad

CATHYGUNNERS: Do you know what's going on?

JONNIEWATTS92: paul said that there was a real oddball -- won't talk to anyone, is kinda ocd, and another guy who's gay -- probably -- suppressed -- seriously -- they're stuck in the desert with some guy with ocd and a gay

CATHYGUNNERS: You can't write that!!!

JONNIEWATTS92: no offence, but they're in the desert with a guy who does tippy-tap sh*t who wants everything nice and tidy -- that has to be a problem right?

JONNIEWATTS92: I work pt at borders my boss has ocd

CATHYGUNNERS: Seriously? What does he do?

JONNIEWATTS92: she chain smokes

JONNIEWATTS92: honest to god... she's killing herself.

DSAMUELS: When will he come back?

. . .

DSAMUELS: When will he come back?

[DSAMUELS has left the chatroom]

JONNIEWATTS92: did you see that???? -- that has to be hereditary

At work Maggie commented that Cathy seemed less tense. If she needed more batteries, she said, she could just help herself, as and when.

☆

Pakosta liked the movie, would have wiped the outline of a five-pointed star in the dust on the vehicles if it didn't run the risk of making him look like some kind of fanatic – Maoist, Zionist, or Russian. But he really liked the movie.

Rem had to hold his tongue.

'See,' Pakosta explained, 'these two brothers slaughter this guy. Gut him. Cut him to pieces, then drop him all over this city. This old woman finds the tongue in a bag. Anyhow, that's it, job done, these brothers slink back to their farm in France, where they become totally normal. *No one would suspect*. The Italian police have no idea what's happened. No clue. And they start to look at other cases that look something like the same thing. Other missing people. And this is twisted. So in their investigation the police find that this woman has gone missing, right, and because they don't really know what's happened, they don't have a clue, they really don't, they have no clue, they make this announcement that whoever killed the first person has – more than likely – killed this missing woman as well. Follow?'

Pakosta drew in breath, a ball of energy stuck on a desert road, a vast stretch of night surrounding him.

'So, these brothers. These psychos, playing normal in their French farm, see this announcement in the papers that whoever killed this first person probably also killed this second person – which isn't true, right, we know this. But they learn about this, because the whole thing has everyone interested, and they realize, *fuck*, we didn't kill no woman. Uh uh. Not us. So what do they do?'

Pakosta held his arms open, turned about, offered the question to the others.

'Come on. What do they do? What would you do? They're up for two killings not one. So, they only go back to the same city, right when this film is being made because, I forgot to say, because it's all based in fact, and pick up a woman, completely random, and kill her. *Because they've already been accused of a second murder anyway.*'

Watts slowly shook his head. Kiprowski stood with his arms folded over his chest, and Rem, who at least had seen the film, decided not to speak.

Pakosta looked about for support, confirmation. 'It's out now. Just before we came here. Look it up. Go online. What I'm telling you is true. They were making this film about these brothers and while they were making it they came back and they killed someone.'

Everyone agreed that this was publicity.

Rem looked out to the desert anticipating stars, a horizon, a suggestion of life through some hint of light. Instead the moon blotted the sky black, kept the land dense, undiscoverable. Nothing out there to be seen.

☆

JONNIEWATTS92: did you hear about the samuels?

CATHYGUNNERS: Doug?

JONNIEWATTS92: doug & marsha right they were in a fight someone didn't like a sticker on their car ---- totalled

. . .

. . .

CATHYGUNNERS: When was this? How did you hear?

JONNIEWATTS92: he was online a couple of days ago i wondered if you'd heard

CATHYGUNNERS: They stopped writing. I haven't heard any of this.

JONNIEWATTS92: last week drove into the local Dominics with an i-heart-our-troops sticker i don't know maybe jesus-hearts-iraq and some loon rammed them and knocked them one side of the parking lot to the other

CATHYGUNNERS: No?

JONNIEWATTS92: seriously!!!!

CATHYGUNNERS: Because of the bumper sticker?

JONNIEWATTS92: supposedly i wouldn't put it past the old man to have given some verbal

CATHYGUNNERS: Because of a bumper sticker?

JONNIEWATTS92: that's not the worst of it they smacked the car two or three times -- Doug Samuels managed to jump out and the person kept ramming the car with his wife still in it, all he could do was watch

CATHYGUNNERS: I can't believe it. Who did this?

JONNIEWATTS92: god's truth someone who'd come out of wholefoods -- a woman -- just saw the bumper sticker and went postal -- thing is, Marsha Samuels has some kind of dementia -- no clue what was going on

JONNIEWATTS92: apparently she's ok -- shaken up but ok

CATHYGUNNERS: Just awful.

. . .

. . .

JONNIEWATTS92: i don't tell anyone about paul -- no one's business
CATHYGUNNERS: You don't talk about your brother?
JONNIEWATTS92: not worth the grief
CATHYGUNNERS: I'm sorry to hear that. Is this among friends?
JONNIEWATTS92: work friends everyone just about
JONNIEWATTS92: not worth the trouble
    can't handle it
    his wife's pregnant
. . .

. . .

CATHYGUNNERS: Because it makes life easier?
JONNIEWATTS92: even family
JONNIEWATTS92: easier?
JONNIEWATTS92: they don't like the idea of him being there
CATHYGUNNERS: In Iraq?
. . .
JONNIEWATTS92: pretty much
JONNIEWATTS92: not worth the trouble
JONNIEWATTS92: what about you? how does your family handle this
CATHYGUNNERS: There's only my family. Rem's family are in Europe.
    My sister just married. I don't know what she really thinks. It all
    came out of the blue. It doesn't make sense to me. I don't know.
JONNIEWATTS92: so...
JONNIEWATTS92: ...he just went?
CATHYGUNNERS: Pretty much
JONNIEWATTS92: ...and you don't want him there?
CATHYGUNNERS: It's not easy to answer that.
. . .
. . .

CATHYGUNNERS: It's different for me. Rem's parents aren't alive,
    his brothers and sisters are in Europe. His family is big and they
    all do different things. I don't know if it would matter if they had
    a problem with it. I don't think that would be an issue.
JONNIEWATTS92: but you don't want him there?
CATHYGUNNERS: I guess I don't
. . .
. . .
. . .
. . .

CATHYGUNNERS: What about you? What about Paul?

. . .

. . .

CATHYGUNNERS: I don't mean to upset you.
CATHYGUNNERS: This is just how I feel about it.
　　[JONNIEWATTS92 has left the chatroom]

. . .

. . .

　　[CATHYGUNNERS has left the chatroom]

☆

On the second day a message came through from Southern-CIPA that Highway 80 was now open for traffic heading north. Markland sounded blasé. They would see the results in about three hours. If they kept to their post until then, an army vehicle would bring the last convoy through.

As always with CIPA another message arrived within the hour. The final convoy from Kuwait would arrive at Camp Liberty at 02:00 Zulu, and they would need volunteers to accompany the drivers as there was no security.

The traffic stopped two hours after the notification of the convoy. Both Kiprowski and Chimeno waited at the compound entrance.

Rem took the opportunity to speak with Amer Hassan.

Hassan answered the door and stepped aside for Rem to enter. The two beds, both made, both tidy, and so close that once they sat down their legs interlocked. Rem found himself embarrassed, uncertain how he should start the discussion.

'I have made a decision. I have no choice. I have to leave. I was recognized. The men in the car will tell everyone I am working for the Americans.' Hassan paused, looked quickly at Rem. 'At Southern-CIPA I always covered my face. Then, one day, they said that the interpreters cannot cover their faces any more. They killed two interpreters. The same day. My wife and children are in Britain. My son is very sick. My father and my brothers are here. I should not have come. I have placed my family in very serious trouble.'

'We can help.'

'You cannot help.' Hassan briskly shook his head. 'There is nothing you can do.' He looked up. 'Everything makes trouble. You give our names to the Ministry of Finance, who sell this information to anyone. Anyone can find our names. Sooner or later.'

'You could stay here?'

'And what about my family?'

Rem stood up in surrender and said that he understood.

The convoy arrived forty minutes ahead of time: Scanias and MANs, large bull-headed flatbeds, long bodies, camel-packed, mounted incestuously so that one could drag four.

The men gathered round them as they parked, dust colliding upward. The drivers were small, Indian and Sri Lankan, thin and anxious, exhausted from the drive.

Pakosta punched Rem on the arm. 'You heard? We get to ride in these all the way to Amrah and they fly us back?'

Rem asked Santo if this was true. Watts stood beside Santo and nodded. 'Apparently. This is the understanding. They won't go any further unless they have an escort.'

'I was sitting at the stop lights when a semi ran right over a car loaded with Muslims . . .'

Rem checked that Hassan was nowhere near earshot, and caught Pakosta's arm. 'You need to watch your mouth. You understand?'

Pakosta hunched and immediately apologized. 'What? What did I do? It was a joke. Nothing but a joke.'

Bolder, Pakosta tugged back his sleeve. As he walked out he directed a comment at Kiprowski Rem did not quite catch. 'What did he just say?' Kiprowski shrugged. 'I heard him say something. What was it?'

'It was nothing.'

'It wasn't nothing. He said go fuck sand out of his ass. Right? Is that what he said?'

'It wasn't anything.' Kiprowski pushed through the group of drivers. They were hollow-eyed but wired and decided on continuing.

Santo slapped Rem on the back. 'You coming?'

Rem said no, he'd stay. 'You can take Pakosta and Kiprowski, and Clark. Clark can follow and bring everyone back. I'll stay here with Watts and Samuels, and Chimeno.'

Chimeno immediately complained. He wanted to go.

'Let him come along if he wants.'

'Fine with me.' Rem stepped back and bumped into Amer Hassan. Hassan offered his hand. If he returned with the convoys, he said, he could find his family.

Rem asked him to reconsider.

'I don't have a choice.'

'Is there anything I can do?'

'Give me two days before you tell anyone.'

Rem slowly nodded in agreement. 'You should say something to Kiprowski before you go.'

Hassan looked puzzled.

'He's young. He doesn't have too many friends out here. I think he likes you in his way.'

Hassan nodded briskly, decided.

'Do you need to get your things?'

Hassan had packed what he could in a small backpack. Kiprowski climbed into the cab behind him.

☆

Most mornings the boy waited for Cathy to come out with the dog. She wanted his name but the boy wouldn't give it. On the final morning one of the cashiers from the currency exchange came out, unlit cigarette in hand, she squinted into the sun and asked Cathy what she was doing.

'We know you, don't we, Roscoe.' She spoke with mean and nasty intention to the boy, who immediately started walking, hands in pocket, head down. 'Yes, we know all about you.' She pushed her glasses back up her nose, looked to Cathy, and told her to watch herself. 'He's bad with women. Like his father. And watch your things. I wouldn't trust him with anything. That entire family is handy, if you know what I mean. He's always around here. Waiting for an opportunity. Helps himself to what he sees.'

Cathy wanted to defend the boy, but found the dog pulling in the opposite direction. She watched him walk up Lunt, but Nut had other ideas.

She still hadn't told Rem. When he came back she'd surprise him.

☆

Three hours after their departure, Rem received a report that the convoy was involved in an incident on Route 567 in which the unit translator had been killed.

Chimeno and Kiprowski were flown to hospital at Camp Buehring, and brought back the next day by Catfish Air. Chimeno had no difficulties talking about what had happened. Straight off the transport he called his girlfriend in Ohio, told her the story in detail, said that he missed her and made her cry. Immediately after he called his sister in Lansing, and after that his mother in Denver and did the same thing, improving on the story with each telling. By the time he talked to the unit it was smooth and elegant and properly composed. They listened with reverence.

Chimeno's driver was a man from Nepal, only just tall enough, he swore, to reach both the pedals and the steering wheel of his rig. Two hours into the drive the guy was standing up waving his arms, insisting on some point Chimeno couldn't recall. The floor of the cab was drecked with candy wrappers, and he was making plans about how he'd have to drive if the driver had a heart attack. In the event, the man drove courageously into what would have been the line of fire to protect the rig that went down. At that point all they knew was one of the lead trucks had taken a hit. Kiprowski was riding two trucks ahead with Amer Hassan. Once it happened, Chimeno did exactly as he was trained, and when they came to Kiprowski's truck they found him banging and shrieking to get out. Amer Hassan had landed on his head and snapped his neck, and when they pulled him out there was black blood in his mouth, a limp head, but no other sign of damage.

Rem spoke later with Kiprowski. The plainer truth was that Amer hit his head when the truck went over. Not at the beginning of the fall when it was tipping, when he slid to the side, and not while the truck was still going forward, but once it was past the point where it could correct itself, when gravity pulled it down. For Kiprowski it was a question of velocity and force and how it was impossible not to fall, how everything happened in one compressed moment with his back against the glass and feet up to the seat. He was hit in the face, a coffee canister, CDs, pens, a map book, torch spun down, and dirt and sand and whatever else was on the seat or dashboard, everything thrown into the air and falling with them – a vague memory, or was this invented, of Amer slipping past. The moment before Kiprowski had turned to see Amer, curled up on himself in the small daybed at the back of the cab.

Amer had told him he was leaving.

Kiprowski had sulked at the news, so Amer had curled up and slept, or seemed to sleep, and before Kiprowski could explain himself the vehicle had come off the road.

Kiprowski was the first pulled out of the truck, they tugged him free over the body of the driver who was concussed. His first thought, much like Chimeno, was that this was an attack, and they would come to the front of the truck and shoot them through the glass.

Out of the cab, Kiprowski heard small-arms fire, a hollow clap sent out over the desert, and it took him a while to realize that these were the shots from the other drivers, who carried, illegally, their own weapons. There was no ambush, no roadside bomb, no attack. The driver had fallen asleep and they'd lost the road.

The death of Amer Hassan was like every other, he supposed, except he counted this man as a friend. It all came down to a curve in the road – that was it. No junction, not even an intersection, just a simple slight change in direction.

Rem understood that the problem, Kiprowski's attachment, was not that simple.

He called Geezler again and began reading his notes, but felt the words slip from him, the call itself to be useless. 'You know what, there's probably some legitimate reason for not hearing from you, but some contact would be appreciated.'

As soon as he hung up he immediately regretted the message. It wasn't what he'd said, so much as his tone.

Rem wanted to speak with the men in the Quonset the night before Kiprowski and Chimeno returned. He let them gather first, and when he came in he surprised Santo, who had money in his hands, a note-book.

'What's this?'

'Nothing.' Santo tucked the money behind him, slipped it into his back pocket. 'They owe me.'

'They owe you?'

'It's nothing.'

Rem looked to the group, Clark, Watts, even Samuels with hangdog expressions – all except Pakosta, who also had money in his hand.

The realization that they were gambling left him dumbfounded.

Santo said it wasn't quite what it looked like.

Rem struggled to speak. 'How much?'

'It's not like that.'

Rem pointed to Santo then Pakosta. 'How much?'

Now Pakosta lowered his head.

'How much?'

Pakosta drew the money out from his pocket and folded it round his fingers.

'Seventy dollars.'

'And you?' Rem asked Santo. 'How much?'

'It isn't like that.'

'I want to know what he was worth.'

Pakosta gave a snort, something small, either derisive or nervous, Rem didn't care to know.

Rem sat outside his cabin and watched them leave the Quonset one by one, none of them speaking. The temperature dropping. The sky an unbroken black.

☆

On Saturday mornings Cathy made a point of going to Evanston Farmers' Market on her own – she regarded this as part of her independent life, and did not mind so much that she had erased Rem from the routine. She bought exactly what she wanted: basil, tomatoes, olive bread, and when she could make the expense, cut flowers. Hot with her walk from the station and irritated at the shoulder strap for her purse (over her breast, to the right, between, under? None of the options felt comfortable) she pointed out two bunches of gladioli, and as she searched for the correct change she became distracted by the conversation beside her, two women, one making the choice for the other and explaining in a hurry: 'Four months ago I had no idea. Now? Now I have a whole new language.' She replicated the action with three pained gasps. 'He's lost weight. His appetite. None of the specialists will admit this has anything to do with the smoke.'

Cathy took her change and backed away. Had she heard the words *burn pit*? The cut stems bled through the paper, a little repellent. She left the market and made her way back to the station, sure that the conversation was not what she now imagined, then changed her mind and returned to the market to seek out the two women – but could not find them among the stalls and the crowd.

She walked to the library without the decision being properly made and found herself coming up the stairs, sweating at the effort, tired as usual (why always so tired?), and before she could properly rationalize what she wanted she was facing a volunteer and explaining that she was looking for information on burn pits, HOSCO, and everything associated with their dealings in Iraq. She needed to sit down. Damn it, no, she needed to pee.

Phyllis, her name pinned to her jacket, stood with Cathy's packages as she hurried to the restroom. As Cathy returned she adjusted her top. It wasn't that her clothes were small exactly, not all her clothes, and maybe it was just because her breasts this past week were as sensitive as hell.

Phyllis helped with the bags and walked with her to the computers. As soon as Cathy sat down she thought she'd need the restroom again – and Phyllis said yes, with a small laugh, *it was exactly the same for me.*

When she came to say goodbye, Cathy sought out the librarian, and found her collecting books from the carousels. Phyllis asked with interest if Cathy had found what she was looking for.

'I hope you don't mind me asking,' the woman stepped forward, hands precise in their movements, shaping an idea, 'but how far along? Eight weeks?'

Hands full with bags from the market Cathy looked down and couldn't see what the woman was talking about. Did she think she was pregnant?

They sat outside the Unicorn Café, Phyllis with her black coffee, a smart air, with her hair drawn back in a style from another era, one where women smoked, occupied kitchens and dining rooms, took lunch, held dinner parties – her mother's generation, where women worked to appear sophisticated, nurtured, *that look.*

'I shouldn't have said anything. You aren't very far along, are you?' It was only intuition, she explained. 'You won't know, properly, until you see a doctor.'

Neither did she apologize. Cathy had cried. Her first thought that she wasn't much of a woman if she didn't know this about her body. How stupid could you be? It wasn't just the dumbness of the situation, but that she'd missed two months of the experience. Here she was, by her calculation, reaching the end of her first trimester without any of the usual indicators. No specific weight gain, no obvious hormonal changes, no morning sickness. Yes to a change in her complexion. Yes to sore breasts, off and on, of all things the nipples, especially today. Yes to the constant need to pee – although wasn't all this a little early? Yes to the void of her periods, which usually came irregularly with irregular flow. Christ. She'd heard examples of women making it right to the birth without knowing. If she had to admit she thought this was pathetic. *How can you not know?* She could excuse herself, what with the fainting, and having given up some time ago on her gynaecologist, who'd pronounced her womb to be a hostile environment. Something like Mars. Not very likely to sustain life. Not in those words, not from a professional who couched the judgement in gentler terminations: *unfriendly* being the favoured phrase. She must have conceived the night Rem left. This, at least, almost had some kind of logic.

The realization came with other fears. A warning once that it would be unlikely that she could carry a child full-term. This is what she'd been told. Christ sake.

The idea that they hadn't taken precautions was ridiculous. Rem was messy, boisterous, and sex became a kind of combat, so physical she often lost herself. Metaphors wouldn't cut it, because Rem, being so helter-skelter, was not one man but parts of many. She had no complaints. There might be long periods of inactivity, of barely even touching, but when there was, she thought of this as a kind of fission. But the idea that they should have been careful just didn't fit the project.

Phyllis listened without overt sympathy. Doctors always draw the worst picture. 'I lost two,' she said, 'with my first husband. On the second marriage it all seemed to work out.'

Earlier today she was one person, now she was two, which struck her as remarkable and horrifying.

THE MASSIVE

Christ. A baby. How much will that cost?
She wouldn't tell Rem until she was certain.
Secret number two.
Number one: a dog.
Number two: a baby.

INLAND CITY

A single helicopter brought Stephen Lawrence Sutler from Amrah City to Camp Liberty. The eleventh drop since they'd arrived. Rem jumped into the Humvee as soon as the craft came close and drove toward the Beach. Southern-CIPA usually alerted them to deliveries. The unannounced arrival came as an interruption. With his eyes on the craft's black underbelly Rem watched it hover and dip, load-less.

The craft did not settle, but came close enough for the man to disembark, his pack thrown after him. The man crouched in the downdraught then ran directly toward Rem, hand on head, backpack on his left shoulder, a professional pause and dash as if he had military training. Behind him the helicopter slipped back and upward pillowing sand.

The man, Caucasian (unlikely then to be the replacement translator) and dressed like Markland, in a long-sleeved shirt, tan chinos, buckskin boots, the casual uniform of the HOSCO manager – hurried toward Rem, his voice lost to the noise. His paleness, his short back and sides, the picky way he stooped to brush himself down, marked him as British. Army-trained, public school, Rem would put money on it, a latecomer ready to scoop up those final contracts. A profiteer down to the bone. Infinitely readable.

'Stephen Sutler.' He offered his hand, his accent, as predicted, British. 'Can you take me to the unit commander.'

Rem turned the jeep about and explained that there was no unit commander. 'This concern isn't military. It's civilian. There's nothing much here except burn pits.'

Sutler leaned sideways to listen and didn't appear to understand.

'I said *burn pits*. You know what they are?'

The man indicated that he couldn't hear and shook his head.

'They didn't give you ear defenders? Head gear? Headphones?' Rem gestured to his ears and raised his voice. 'Don't worry. It'll come back in a couple of hours. I wouldn't make a habit of it. You heard what I said?' Rem now shouted. 'This is civilian. We manage the burn pits, five of them.' Rem hoiked his thumb in the general direction of the pits. 'Not much else. So, why are you here?'

413

After a moment Sutler nodded and spoke in a clear English accent.
'I need to speak to whoever's in charge.'

'We're speaking. How can I help?'

The man looked at him, blank.

'I'm preparing a survey.'

'A survey? What's this for?'

Again the man couldn't hear.

'I asked *who for? Who are you working for?* Are you working for HOSCO?'

Sutler gave a curt nod.

'So what are you surveying? What are you looking for?'

Sutler answered that it would take about a week. He'd been assured that he could work with some of the men already based here, which is why he'd asked for the unit commander.

'There's eight of us. Including me. What kind of work do you need them for? I need to know the kind of work you're planning. How long will you be at Camp Liberty?'

Again, the man didn't answer.

'You said something about a week? Longer? I said longer? More?'

Rem took a long look to measure the man, to gauge if he was serious or not, because he sounded much too vague. That he was working for HOSCO meant little, the only option for non-nationals was to work private (HOSCO) or government (CIPA). So far Sutler had told him nothing, and from the size of his kitbag he didn't intend to stop long.

Rem presented the options. 'I'll have to put you with someone else, unless someone doubles up. We don't have much in the way of accommodation.'

He saw the camp through the stranger's eyes and realized just how mean the site appeared. It wasn't the lack of provision so much as the scruffiness: the lines of washing and the seven men, hanging around, worse than strays. And here was this guy from England, from somewhere green and wet and moody, stranded now in this unrelenting flat of stone and grit.

'Welcome to dust and ash.'

Kiprowski sat outside his door, sullen, feet and arms crossed, and seeing him Rem changed his mind about where he wanted to house the new arrival.

'What did you say you were here for?'

'HOSCO. A project.'
'What kind of project?'
'A planning project.'
And still *nowhere*.

After the suspicions raised by the arrival of the translator, Rem decided not to bed him with one of the others, especially Pakosta with his paranoid notions about HOSCO, or the increasingly morose Kiprowski. Until Rem had a better measure of what the man wanted, it would be wise to keep him isolated, which meant surrendering his own cabin.

Rem took less than five minutes to gather his clothes and bedding. He asked questions as he packed: how long had Sutler been travelling, where had he come from, and Sutler remained evasive. The answers – eighteen hours, transit through Germany – dry facts, told him next to nothing.

Sutler took the room without thanks, set his bag beside the bed and stood, arms folded, clearly waiting for Rem to leave.

Kiprowski stood up when Rem came to his cabin, a little astonished: too polite to be put out.

'This won't be for long.' Rem dropped his clothes on Hassan's cot and scooted it back to the wall. The other men (notably Santo and Pakosta) found unpleasant amusement in this, grinned as he carried his bags from one cabin to another as if this proved some idea they had. If Rem had signalled Kiprowski out for special attention by pairing him with Amer Hassan, he was making a statement of it now.

He returned to his old cabin and waited at the door while Sutler unpacked.

'We have rations. Army rations. MREs. There's bottled water, it's warm but drinkable. You'll get used to it. Don't expect to get used to the heat. It's best to keep these doors open during the day, otherwise you'll cook. Once the generators are running you can use the air-con, but at night it'll get cold.'

Sweat stuck Sutler's shirt to his back in two small wings. 'I'd like to see the facilities. I'll need somewhere to work.'

'I'm sorry?'

'I have supplies coming from Amrah City tomorrow.'

The man had little idea what to bring to such an environment.

Long socks and long pants – not one piece of common sense – and no keepsakes to speak of his family, personality, or interests.

Facilities. Right. Rem leaned against the doorpost, swung about to point out the Quonset hut, the water tanks, gas storage, the latrines, and over there, the showers. 'What you see is what we have.'

Sutler stood beside him, hands on hips. 'And that hut?'

'The Quonset?'

'What's that used for?'

'Nothing much. Storage. The men use it for shade when they work on the vehicles. We keep the drinking water there.'

'I'll need a table. A chair.'

Rem told him to make use of whatever he found. There wasn't much, maybe a worktable, which he was welcome to. 'Make it yours,' he said, 'for as long as you need.'

☆

Cathy undertook two web searches. First on pregnancy, a general search: *"first trimester" +nutrition +fainting*. She'd speak with Maggie, but what did Maggie know? For a short while Maggie and her girlfriend had openly debated approaching Rem as a donor. Something Cathy had found endlessly funny, although she couldn't see what had amused her so much now. She stared at the computer, at charts, read testimonies, the endless bossy chit-chat on what she needed to do, she found the subject intolerable. And the idea that Rem would make a father. Please.

The second web search came out of pure idleness. Paul Geezler. The author of their separation. That's the word she used now: *separation*. Rem in Iraq, in some godforsaken desert, some dried-out, pre-biblical dust bowl. Nothing if not separate.

A search for "Paul + Geezler" brought up nothing. Not even company reports. She eventually found Geezler on the HOSCO website, and couldn't understand why his page was placed on the European section, not the Middle East, and assumed that this had yet to be updated. Point of fact, there wasn't much information: a bare statement naming him as the Advisor to the Division Chief, Europe. End of.

She had more luck finding Geezlers on a general search. A basketball coach. Two school teachers (mathematics and physics). A teenager whose hobbies included 'Jesus'. These people had Facebook pages, Twitter feeds, but above all, implacably duller lives than her own.

She found the largest collection of Geezlers in Wisconsin, alongside a collection of Geislers. A website on family genealogy, maintained by Annie F. Geezler and her husband BJ (seriously), clarified the link between the Geislers and Geezlers. Annie F. had devoted much energy into gathering the family's history and building a website based on the trivial details she'd found. The Geezlers came from Hamburg. They'd bred in moderation. Conceived of businesses (clothing, printing, transportation). They suffered from bad luck, bad timing, and over-ambition (the Great Depression stopped the clothing business, a warehouse fire terminated the printing, loans crippled the transportation). They fought in wars and died pitifully, and with anonymity (in dockyard bombings, warehouse fires, and on Russian Fronts). Anne F. had married into the Geislers, and Cathy wondered why women always carried the memory of a family. Who else would take on the job? A husband called BJ, she figured, could only be useful for lame innuendo. Christ.

She brought the printout back to the apartment.

Nut followed Cathy from room to room, brows tightened, pained, as if in apology, and she found herself unusually affectionate toward him. She fed him scraps. Cuddled him. Spoke endless nonsense, tolerated his need to be close, and found him to be good company. Except, of course, for the gas.

'Listen to this.' She read details to Nut. 'The American Geezlers changed their name in World War Two.' She looked down at the dog. 'To Greeves.' She held out a piece of toast. 'If I give you this toast I don't want to be smelling it in a second.'

Cathy had a retentive mind for facts, and hadn't Rem said that the man was Southern? South Carolina? And hadn't he mentioned Pittsburgh? She hadn't found any records for a Geezler, a Geisler, or any other variation from South Carolina, Pittsburgh, or, in case she hadn't remembered correctly, Philadelphia. The references she did find were for Milwaukee. After the war the Greeves returned to Geislers and Geezlers, respectively.

Cathy dropped the toast.

The only other reference, a slang dictionary, listed *geisler* as an image of two girls kissing. Something traded, covertly, among adolescent boys.

Done with Geezler, she checked a second set of papers, information found from a metasearch: *"burn pit" +lawsuit +exposure +Iraq, +legislation, +"sleep apnea" +sores +asthma +"respiratory problems".*

Maggie sat with the papers about her, picked at them at random, and said it still didn't make much sense. So? Loads of veterans come back and get sick. It doesn't mean anything. And anyhow, wasn't this all from some rumour she'd heard at the Saturday market? Hardly reliable?

Cathy apologized and Maggie became conciliatory.

'You know what I mean. You have a habit of running away with ideas. It's just what you do.'

'Look, there's more online, more about the materials they're burning and how they're causing all kinds of problems. Headaches, nosebleeds, skin irritations. Healthy people are getting asthma. People who shouldn't be getting sick are getting skin and respiratory problems. Cancer-like cysts. All this is happening as soon as they get back. People losing weight for no reason, people who have no energy. Problems with their immune system. It's wrong.'

'But how do you even know it's true?'

'There's a lawyer in Tucson. Phyllis, at the library, found him. So far he's contacted thirty men. He has a website, he's working with doctors. He said all they need to do is prove what's being burned in those pits.' She handed Maggie a list. 'Contaminants. This is what you get from burning plastic and polystyrene. You get sulphuric acid, you get these chemicals, you get carcinogens.'

'Then why don't they stop it?'

There was a difference between being wilful and dumb, and Maggie was pushing it.

'They need proof. They need someone to take samples and photographs. They need documentation of what's happening out there.'

Cathy itched to smoke. Her fingers lost for activity.

'The thing is HOSCO have made a public statement about stopping the burning in the camps, so they know something is wrong. Everything is now sent to remote locations and burned, and where they used to classify and separate the waste, now they just burn everything, get rid of it as fast as they can, and they can't be touched, because they have contractors to do the dirty work, people like Rem who won't complain.'

She looked at the papers, disorganized now, and wondered why she'd tried to explain anything. It wasn't that Maggie was stupid, she just didn't need to care.

'I found this.' She held up a separate sheaf of papers. 'There's another burn pit in Camp Bravo. The people working there have just walked out. They abandoned the camp.'

'Why did they do that?' At last Maggie was interested.

'Because they were burning illegal waste. HOSCO have said that they closed the camp. Here it says they walked out.' Cathy offered the papers to Maggie.

Cathy sat at the kitchen counter and outlined the questions she wanted to ask Rem. Maggie wanted to know what this interest was really about, and the question troubled her. The answer, that this was about making sure that Rem wasn't messing up his future health, she knew to be only partly true. It's an occupation, she told herself, a way to organize the day. But this wasn't quite to the point either.

Nut sat at her feet, satisfaction vibrated through his entire body; he focused completely on her, attentive to every move.

Stacked across the counter, a permanent feature now, were four box folders, each tidily marked: HOSCO/US; HOSCO/Iraq; Burn Pits & Case Examples; ARTICLES. Phyllis, a sharp reader, had made copies of articles from the *New York Times*, the *Washington Post*, the *New Yorker*; she had transcripts of interviews and CDs of podcasts: *Alive in Baghdad, American Microphone, This American Life, War News Radio,* all of which Cathy now stored.

1. What are you burning? Paper? Plastic? Particle board? Polystyrene? Plywood? Wood? Rubber?
2. What protective clothes do you wear?
3. What type of masks / breathing apparatus do you use?
4. What kind of ash is produced?
5. How large is the particulate matter (PM)?
6. What are the smells? Compare to other smells, e.g., egg, sulphur, rubber, etc.
7. Does the smoke ever fall across the camp?
8. What are the symptoms, long term / short term (inc. shortness of breath, skin problems, asthma, headaches)?
9. What instructions have you received from HOSCO?

Much of this could be discovered through simple questions, nothing too challenging or direct. Below the questions she wrote a second list:

Dioxins
Lead
Cadmium
Formaldehyde
Fungicides
Hydrochloric Acid
Arsenic

If he hesitated she'd get to these, and outline the conditions they caused, to shake out the details.

☆

Kiprowski, Chimeno, Samuels, and Clark worked with Sutler to clear out the Quonset. Rem, a little put out that the men had so readily stepped up to Sutler's request for assistance (his own response was a curt 'knock yourself out'). Midway through the morning Samuels found a logbook which he brought to Rem.

Rem sat at his cabin's door with the logbook open on his lap, and guessed he was supposed to keep some kind of record of the fires: which pits were used, the number of vehicles in each convoy, the contents. He smoked as he read through the book, although smoking lately left a bad taste in his mouth. Tucked into the back page he found a copy of a manifest which listed safety grades with ash measured as Particulate Matter.

Sutler didn't make sense, seemed out of place: *why this man*, and *why here*? No fan of the British, he found Sutler typically smug and superior. The man's efficiency also counted against him: who stays fresh and on-message after eighteen hours in transit? Stephen Lawrence Sutler was much too keen.

As the dust threatened to worsen Clark's cough the men worked carefully, carrying packs of canvas, rolls of tent poles, drums, and boxes, and setting them in front of the Quonset with as little disturbance as they could manage.

Sutler picked through the stores, at what now looked like a HOSCO yard sale, and cut a lanky figure in his tan trousers and white shirt, his hair almost ginger, his skin whiter than crab meat.

Rem watched as Kiprowski and Clark lumbered a large poly-sack out of the garage in a sloppy embrace. Sutler assisted as the men shook the package out of its sleeve, then stepped aside as they opened it out to reveal something like a sail.

Sutler pointed to an area beside the Quonset and said they should set it up here. That way they'd have some shade when they ate.

Between them, over the course of an hour, the men erected the awning. Chimeno supervised, and they stretched the canvas, raised it, secured it, and worked for the first time without argument. One by one the men sloped away, beaten by the heat, leaving Kiprowski and Sutler to drive in the final pegs and tighten the wires.

Rem came to the Quonset in the early afternoon, freshly showered, a towel draped across his head and shoulders to protect from the sun. The fires needed restarting, as sometimes happened; whatever the trucks were bringing this week wouldn't burn, not even with jet fuel. Sutler had cleared an area to work and set out a table laden with maps, unrolled and weighted with pebbles, along with a shoulder bag, a small black notebook, four books, a selection of pencils, a separate roll of papers, none of which he'd noticed that morning when Sutler had arrived. In five hours the man had laid out his patch. Rem examined the maps but found nothing of interest and was surprised by Kiprowski who sat by himself, half-dozing, snug at the back beside the stack of water bottles. Sunlight from a small window sparked through the plastic containers and cast a webbed path.

'Not exactly a whole lot to look at.' Rem leaned over the maps, ducked close. 'Is this us? Right? I can't tell.' Conscious that he'd been caught prying, Rem made conversation for the sake of it. He nosed through the black notebook, no point being shy now. 'Has he spoken to you about any of this?'

Kiprowski shook his head.

Rem flattened the pages, pointed at a diagram. 'Any of this make sense to you?'

Kiprowski reluctantly came forward.

The diagram could be the camp, although the details appeared wrong – a group of seven cabins, not eight, with names pencilled beside them in the wrong order. It disturbed Rem to see that the man was collecting information on them. Rem attempted to read Sutler's slanting script. 'Any idea what this says?'

'It's a list of the buildings in the camp.'

'So, what's the map for? He must have drawn this before he arrived?'

Kiprowski didn't like to guess and couldn't help, but was pretty sure he'd just drawn it.

'He hasn't said anything about what he's doing?'

Nothing on the desk gave away Sutler's job. One book of tables marked 'Quantifying Densities' and a HOSCO account tablet gave little information. Dissatisfied, Rem stepped away from the table. 'You'll let me know when he says something.'

Rem drew the towel back over his head and stood at the open door. Everyone asleep in their cabins. The air vibrated with the drone of air-conditioners; silence, even here, couldn't be held. One man coughing, the miss-stroke of the generators, the wind catching on wires and buffeting the sides of the cabins; a general restlessness of people lying low.

Sutler walked from the showers in a wayward arc, clearly at ease, a towel and washbag tucked under one arm. He offered an unsmiling hello as he approached.

'There isn't anything like a fan, is there?'

'No, and the power will go off in an hour. We have to conserve fuel.'

Sutler looked about, a little startled. His hair damp. 'I'll need to see the camp perimeter. If I can do that today?'

'Later,' Rem promised. 'When it isn't so hot.'

Sutler nodded without thanks. 'You took a look?' He drew Rem back inside the Quonset, pointed to the table and the maps.

'You draw that?'

'No. It's eight years out of date. These maps go back to when Camp Liberty was first set up. See. There used to be a village. Kitrun. When the burn pits were dug what remained of the village was levelled.' He opened his notebook and tapped his finger on one of his sketches. 'The marshes started a little east of here. And the land was irrigated, it wasn't always desert.' Sutler closed the book and began to roll up the maps. 'You all seem to be managing with the news?'

Rem thought the statement underhand. 'News?'

'HOSCO.' Sutler half-turned, the drawings gathered in his hand. 'This.'

'This?' Rem didn't like playing the stooge and he allowed his irritation to show.

'You've come all this way to work at the burn pits and now they're shutting them down.'

'And you heard this where?'

'I read it in the paper coming over. It's probably why they chose this place.'

'Chose it for what?'

'As one of the four potential sites for the Massive.'

Now the man wasn't making sense.

Done, Sutler excused himself and returned to his cabin, leaving Rem with the notion that he had been lectured and dismissed.

Geezler, again, could not be reached.

☆

Back home, Cathy sat herself at the kitchen table and began writing, by hand, a letter she would later type and send by email from the library.

Dear All,

Please excuse my writing to you all like this. Before you read this I should caution you, and I apologize for any alarm or worry that this email might cause, but I have become aware of some problems to do with the burn pits – I'm sure some of you will know about this already – and some of this information will be difficult and worrying for you to read.

The problem I have is that I need to share information which is going to cause you a great deal of alarm. I have thought hard about what to do, but I can't in good conscience not notify you now that I know.

So I'll ask you to read through this – and to take time to consider the content. I've copied in web-links (I think I've done this right) so that you can look up the information for yourselves, and also, among these, are some other resources that should be able to help. I'd be happy to talk with anyone, although I don't know much more than what's included here.

First: there are a number of health risks associated with the burn pits. Some of these are very serious and are currently being documented by Peter Strauss, a lawyer based in Tucson on behalf of a number of returning servicemen and contractors. According to their website, Sue Williams (HOSCO director of personnel and head of human resources) states that the burn pits at Camp Liberty are no longer in use. (If you know otherwise, please let me know as it's important to document this and get the facts right.)

Second: it is possible that the effects of inhaling and being in close proximity to the fires and smoke will cause damage – just because they have stopped doesn't mean that there isn't a problem (also if you have information about how the pits are being cleared and how the materials are now being handled, I'd be grateful for it).

Third: and this is by no means a definitive list, the pits have been used to incinerate plastic, polystyrene, metals, hospital waste, army waste, metals, oil-based products, oil and gasoline and jet fuel, mattresses containing treated plastics and rubber (as a point of interest, it's illegal to burn these here).

Fourth: this is the frightening part. These items, when burned, produce toxic gases and particles. Particles are measured in PM (Particulate Matter). Anything that is smaller than PM2.5 (this would be a regular flake of ash – comparable to a snowflake) can be ingested very easily. The smaller the particle, the more dangerous it is, as it can be breathed in deeper. The chemicals are scary, and include: PCPs (banned), hydrochlorine, benzene, dioxins, cadmium, arsenic. Alongside heavy metals: lead and mercury (from batteries). It's a serious list.

Five: To some degree the health problems help to indicate what has been burnt. Throat, mouth, and nose problems can be caused by exposure to smoke over any period of time. Dry coughing, numbness anywhere (chest, arms, legs), heart problems (palpitations), headaches, migraines, problems with sight, passing out – all indicate a smaller PM and a bigger problem. This is a crude outline, but if you can look back over your correspondence and see if there is any mention (nosebleeds, headaches, passing out) give me the dates, as far as you know, and the length of time that this lasted.

Please. If you know anything different, or have any information, please send it to me at this address: cgunnersen@hotmail.com

I hate to send you news which can only make things harder. Remember that most times a headache is simply a headache. But if you are hearing of other problems, then we have to think carefully about what our men have been exposed to, and we need to consider what kind of action to take.

If you have any questions, please use the above email.

Cathy

☆

In the late afternoon Rem drove Sutler around the compound perimeter, and they found most of the fencing gone or in poor condition, the posts leaning forward so that the fence could be easily straddled. In some places there were no signs, or wire, or posts to delimit the camp. On the map the compound ran roughly three miles by one, a panhandle cut by the Beach into the top left corner gave it the same outline as Utah.

While Rem drove with care, the ground changed from pockets of sand to hard shale and the drive took longer than he wanted. Beyond the Beach the land dropped and Sutler agreed that the view was missing something. A strong wind pulled toward them and the horizon gave out to an itchy pink fuzz. Every half-mile Sutler told Rem to stop and he hopped out to hold up a piece of equipment, a compass, as far as Rem could tell, which he kept in a small worn leather pouch. Rem cautioned him about the sun. If the vehicle broke down they'd face a hot walk. It might be late in the day but the sun could still cause trouble.

Sutler's paleness distressed him, the man wasn't covered up, and skin that delicate would sear in no time at all. He explained how the sun here cooked you, how you wouldn't feel it until it was too late, and in that thin shirt the man didn't stand a chance, but Sutler seemed not to listen.

'Your first time in a desert?'

Sutler weighed a compass in his hand, shook it, and held it up. 'I didn't have much of a warning. Put together what I had at hand. Didn't have much time to think it through.'

Sutler couldn't get a proper reading as the compass would not lock onto GPS. He held the device up, shook it, studied the screen.

They both looked at the screen, Sutler's hand providing shade, and watched it register north, then north-north-west, then twist suddenly south.

'It shouldn't be doing that.'

'It's the same with the phones. They work fine in the evening. Any other time it's hit and miss.'

Sutler strode about the vehicle. 'It's something in the car.' He held up the compass. 'No. Now it's indicating north again.'

Rem asked if Sutler could help him out.

'I'm thinking maybe you should have someone working with you? Kiprowski, for example. Someone to drive you about? If that's what you need?'

Sutler slid the compass back into its cover. 'Kiprowski? You'll have to point him out.'

Rem said he'd give the compass to Watts. See if he could take a look. 'I need to ask something else as well.'

Sutler looked up, eyes tight from the sunlight.

'I need to ask that you don't share the information you have on the camp closing.'

'It's public. It was in the papers. If I found it—'

'Keep it to yourself for now. Until we're told something definite, I'd like this not to be discussed.'

Sutler set his hands on his hips. 'They should close these places.' He looked at the smoke rising over the shoulder of the Beach. 'You don't even know what's in that. If any of them ask what I'm doing, I'll have to say.'

'And what are you doing?'

Sutler's expression became weary. 'I'm here to gather basic information about the site before it's developed.'

'Developed into what?'

'You should get everyone together and I can address this in one go.' Before Rem could ask for more particulars, Sutler added. 'Tomorrow would probably be better.'

Once they were back he left Sutler to it. Watts set up the satphone and Rem failed to speak with Geezler again and told himself not to fret. He ate supper, a pack of plain couscous, and realized when he was eating that he'd used non-potable water. He sat with Chimeno, who pressed for details about Sutler.

'So what's he doing here?'

'I don't know.' Rem shrugged. 'I don't think *he* knows. In fact, I don't think he has a clue.'

They both looked to the Quonset. Sutler sat deep inside, leaned over the table, occasionally animated, but mostly bent close to his maps, studying. As far as Rem could see the maps showed next to nothing, the desert being marked as a blank and featureless expanse.

'He's surveying what? The desert?'

'I guess. As far as I know.'

'They send one man? That's not right.'

Rem agreed.

Chimeno sat back and folded his arms. 'Think about it. When they dig up a street they send an entire crew, they mark up the road, they take measurements, they make all kinds of inconvenience for the utilities alone. A whole desert, you'd reckon they'd send a team. A whole delegation. Some support. No, this is something else.'

No longer hungry, Rem offered his bowl to Chimeno, who said he wasn't hungry. His stomach, he complained, just wasn't good these days.

Rem checked on Sutler before returning to his cabin. He took a quart of water with him and suggested that Sutler should make sure he was drinking enough. The man hadn't eaten, hadn't come out of the Quonset.

At first Sutler didn't pay any attention. His concentration didn't appear genuine, the way in which he referred to the map, returned to his notebook, drew small designs quickly on one page then another, then leafed back to earlier pages struck Rem as self-conscious, performed. Sutler set down his pencil then seemed to become properly aware of Rem.

'Which would the men prefer? Beer or whisky?'

'Beer. I guess.'

Rem didn't state the obvious, that alcohol was not permitted. The camps and municipal units were dry, and Southern-CIPA demanded compliance. Sutler's confidence that he could run against regulations bothered him. He spoke about importing booze – an almost impossible task – as if this would incur no effort at all.

What would Rem say, he asked, if he could guarantee one crate for each man in the unit, *if* Rem could get him a secure long-distance line out of Iraq? Sutler gave a quick smile. 'There's equipment arriving tomorrow.'

Rem said he would speak with Watts, they should be able to find a secure line to Southern-CIPA.

'You know anything about the Mormons?'

Rem said no, and Sutler drew his attention to the plan in front of him.

'They built three cities. The last one at Salt Lake. Each city designed on a grid, the houses set on rectangular plots. Where there's a cross-road the houses sit together. See? With this kind of design you can keep building as far as you like. It won't appear crowded.'

'And that's what they want? HOSCO? You're designing buildings?'

'Then there's this.' Sutler drew out a second plan. 'In Morocco the houses are communal and surround a private inner courtyard, there isn't much in terms of public space. It's a different idea. Each building provides shade so the streets are constantly in shadow. Traditionally, they're not much more than one or two storeys high.' Sutler set the two designs side by side. 'Which do you think is easier to police?'

'The Mormon.'

Sutler nodded.

'It's simple. It's clean. For security it makes sense, but that means you can't have as much determination over the environment. This is just a desert with houses, some shops, an airport. The *closer* the houses, the more compact, the more potential trouble, but also the more control over the environment.'

Rem understood the problem, but couldn't see the point of the lecture. 'So, they're building a new camp? An airport?'

'Something like that.' Sutler picked up a cardboard tube from beside his chair, turned it upside down to draw out a bottle of scotch.

'Where?'

Again, Sutler wouldn't give details. 'All they need is confirmation that the site is suitable.' Sutler offered the bottle to Rem. 'At the moment it's all about making sure everything gets onto the map. Mines. Armament. Disused sites.' Sutler waited for Rem to take a sip.

'I used to live in England.' Rem handed back the bottle. 'This is going back some years. Your accent. It's northern. I'm right? Right? I lived in London with a plasterer from Northumbria and another man from Yorkshire.'

'Neither.'

'So further north?'

Sutler shook his head. 'Would be Scotland.'

'But northern, no?'

'No.'

The men sat in silence and the temperature began to drop.

'So what did you read about HOSCO closing the camp?'

Sutler looked directly at Rem.

'You really don't know about this?' Sutler's smile looked a little too comfortable.

'We don't hear much.'

'It's not just you. They're all closing down. HOSCO is facing criticism. Soldiers are getting sick and they're blaming the fires.'

Rem said they'd keep doing what they were doing until they weren't paid or the trucks stopped coming. 'But like I said,' Rem stood up, 'keep it to yourself.'

As Rem left, Sutler reminded him to speak with Watts.

He found Watts lying on his bunk and realized that he had not come out that morning to assist with the fires. He let the matter slide and asked if Watts could contact Markland. 'Find out what you can about this man, Sutler. Stephen *something* Sutler? See what he's here for, and be subtle. He wants to make a call. International. When he comes to you make sure it looks like an effort.'

Eyes closed, Watts said he'd see what he could do.

'Good. There's beer in it.'

Watts sat up, amused. 'I asked already. I spoke with Markland and I asked who this person was. He said he didn't know and hadn't heard about him. Whatever he's here for has nothing to do with Southern-CIPA. It's all private-sector-contract related. HOSCO like us. Whatever he's doing they've yet to hear about themselves. There's a big fat disconnect between them and HOSCO. Neither really knows what's going on.'

Rem agreed that this was probably what was happening.

'It's a game. Southern-CIPA didn't know we were coming so they sent the translator. HOSCO didn't know about the translator, so they sent the Brit. This is how they work. I'd say this is business as usual. You asked him what he's doing?'

'I asked.'

Watts paused, now curious. 'He said nothing about why he's here?' He couldn't make the question casual.

'Not to my ears. If you hear something, I'd like to know. We're a thousand miles from anywhere. We burn every kind of shit known to man, but it's still shit. So why would HOSCO send someone else?'

Rem returned to the Quonset to let Sutler know about his call. Returning to his cabin he asked himself what he was doing here. Never mind Sutler. Was there really nothing else he could have found for himself? Geezler hadn't answered his messages for days and wasn't available for calls.

Watts secured a signal, it wasn't strong he explained, as it was rabbit-hopped across the desert, every fifty miles they had an uplink that would boost and propel it, but routed through the Engineers' line, it was shunted station to station all the way to Amrah, sometimes it went down. It was the best he could do. (This, Rem knew, was nonsense, but sounded feasible enough.) The satellite system frequently failed. Atmospherics. Interference. It shouldn't happen, but it did, and Watts had no idea why.

Sutler asked if the line was secure and Watts shook his head. 'No, it's pumped way too high. Anyone with a bucket or too many fillings can pick it up.' He could do better later, if Sutler wanted to wait. But right now, if the call was important, this was what they had.

☆

C,
Now you've done it –
JW

Mrs Gunnersen,
    You have no right to send these messages and stir up trouble in the way you are carrying on. We have no wish to hear from someone who has so much hate.
    D. Samuels on behalf of Doug & Marsha Samuels

Dear Cathy,
    I have read and given great consideration to the letter that you sent recently, and I have followed and read the articles that you provided in your message – but has something happened that I am unaware of? Is there something that has started this enquiry? I don't understand.
    I don't understand why they would send people to these places if they are so dangerous? It makes no sense to me that they would

behave like this, and I am confused by what you say about the camp being closed. I can't see how this helps the company at all? I can not accept that they would contravene health and safety regulations which must be in place?

There is so much that is confusing. I do not like conversing in this way and would appreciate speaking directly with you. Could I ask you to call me? This is upsetting and disturbing.

Marianne Clark

Cathy made several attempts to speak with Marianne Clark but received no answer. Finally, she called early in the morning and caught her.

'But they are there because your husband selected them? Am I right? Why would he do this if he knew that the work was dangerous? I don't understand?'

'He didn't know. I don't think anyone knew what was involved. This isn't only happening at Camp Liberty, this is how they destroy all waste. Very few places have incinerators.'

'So why don't they build more?'

'I think they haven't properly considered the problem. Maybe they have, but it's too large to do anything else.'

'But why? I don't understand?'

How should she explain this? 'The troops and the contractors have to bring everything in. The country has nothing. It doesn't produce anything. All of the bases have a McDonald's, a KFC, some of the camps have shops and malls. Everything is taken out there, the goods, the people who work in the shops, and then they also have to be looked after, fed, housed.'

'It doesn't make sense? Why would they need a shopping mall?'

Why indeed? It wasn't only food, they imported ammunition, clothes, vehicles, medical supplies. This is how it worked.

'They eat and drink with polystyrene cups and plates,' she explained. 'Three times a day.' Three plates, three cups, three sets of knives and forks. Every person out there adding to the problem.

☆

The light from Kiprowski's alarm lit the room. A small battery radio with shortwave and FM, which picked up nothing but static. Kiprowski

431

slept on his side and faced Rem, and in his sleep he shunted the sheet and blanket down to his feet. In the morning, before the temperature rose, he curled up tight with his arms locked about his knees, and while he didn't snore he breathed through his mouth with a slight rasp. He appeared restless, on guard, inward, wrapped up.

Rem lay for as long as he could manage, then rose and collected his clothes and boots to dress outside. When he looked at Kiprowski he was surprised to see him awake.

'What's the time?'

'Still early. There's no need for you to get up until the convoy gets here.'

Kiprowski gave a small nod. 'I'll get up.'

'There's no need. There's another hour.'

The boy swept his hand down to his calves to find the sheet.

Two convoys arrived pre-dawn, a total of thirty-two trucks loaded with trash accompanied by a military escort. The first driver jumped out of his cab in a white suit with a hood. The man, already short, appeared shorter because the leggings rutted from his ankles to his knees, showing orange rubber boots, white gloves with red palms.

'I'm thinking circus.' Watts coughed, struck his chest to clear his throat. 'Maybe Christmas.'

Rem watched the drivers disembark, one after another, in white hazmat suits, full-body, zipped up, protective boots and padded gloves. The military also wore breathing gear, visors, and gloves. A few had wrapped scarves about their heads.

'This is not my favourite part of the movie. This where we learn bad things.'

Rem was told to keep his men away. The fires would be started and they would not be required.

'That's Level C. What they're wearing.'

Rem took his cue from Watts, who didn't appear worried.

'Known contaminants which aren't airborne. You have any idea what they've brought?'

Pakosta joined Rem and Watts outside the Quonset.

'The bags inside the trucks are white. That's medical. Those bags are medical waste. That's thirty-two trucks of medical waste.'

'They shut the hospital at Amrah?'

'I don't want to know.'

'Look at the dirt.' Watts pointed at the wheels as the trucks rolled slowly in line toward the pits. 'Looks like they've come a ways.'

The men remained at the camp and gathered under the new awning, a little concerned by the change in procedure.

Sutler followed after Watts and pestered for a comm-link. 'I'll take what I can get. I need to get a message through this morning.'

Watts said he would stay on it. If something came through he'd find him immediately. Watts made a face to Rem signalling that he wanted to talk.

'He wants to speak with some guy in Washington, DC, not state.' 'Any idea who?'

'Some guy called Jesus. I'm not kidding.'

From the direction of the burn pits came a soft percussive bump, followed seconds later by a similar noise, louder, harder.

The men came out from under the canopy and looked up, puzzled. Some shielded their eyes – all focused on the rising block of smoke.

Fires burned in one, two and four. And from Pit 4 the smoke began to change from black to brown to yellow.

Santo sought out Rem. He thought he'd recognized one of the drivers from Anaconda. White bags meant plastic and polystyrene, right? 'Nothing but plates? Right?'

'They were in hazmat suits. White bags are bio or medical waste. Black or blue bags are plastics.'

'You think it was military?'

The base of the column roiled a thick pure yellow. 'Any idea what makes smoke turn that colour?' Rem asked.

'No idea.'

Rem shielded his eyes. 'You think that's chemical?'

Santo nodded. 'There's no telling what they're getting rid of now.'

Rem returned to the awning. 'I don't want anyone going near those pits today. Keep an eye on it. If you see that smoke descending, if the wind changes, if you smell anything different, I want everyone out of the way. In future no one goes near the fire without protection. Masks. Suits. No excuses.' Captivated by the smoke, the men nodded. 'Watts.' Rem walked with Watts back to his cabin. 'I want you to contact Amrah, get Markland, and find out what was in those loads today. Get back to me as soon as you can.'

Sutler, Rem noticed, walked to the Quonset.

*

433

The smoke flattened above the camp, thick enough to block the sun and rob the colour from their lips. Chimeno, as a joke, dressed in one of the protection suits and staggered zombie-fashion between the cabins.

Sutler sat with Rem as they waited for their calls. Watts came first for Sutler. Sure enough, the same guy, *Jesus*, he was talking with the other day.

Sutler, a little irritated at the name, made his excuses and hurried to take the call.

Rem looked to the cabin and noticed that Sutler had closed the door. 'Any luck getting hold of Markland?'

'He's not available. I asked someone at his office to get back as soon as they can. Apparently Markland's the wrong man for the job. This comes under someone called Rose. He's the environmental specialist. Guess where he's gone? Damascus. And the way things are going he won't be getting out any time soon.'

An idea struck Rem and he asked Watts to repeat the name of the man calling for Sutler. 'Just humour me, what was the name again?'

'Jesus or something. Cheese. Cheeser.'

'Geezler?' Rem gave deliberate emphasis to the hard gee, as in grease.

'Greesler. Right. That's what I said.'

Now Rem was interested. What was Sutler doing talking with Geezler? And why was Geezler available to Sutler but not to him?

'Did he ask you to call him?'

Watts said yes, then thought for a moment. 'He didn't give me the name, I overheard it. I thought he said *Jesus*. I recognized the voice.'

Clark walked by, towel in hand. 'What's all this talk about cheese?'

Watts turned sharply. What was Clark talking about?

'Jesus? Cheeses? What are *you* talking about?'

'You think I talk funny? You don't like how I talk? I'm not fancy enough?'

Clark held up his hands. 'Jesus Christ, Watts, what did I say?'

Watts walked off to his cabin, leaving Rem with Clark and Pakosta. 'What was that about?'

Pakosta blew out his cheeks. 'Time of the month.'

'Pakosta, just once, leave it alone.' Clark unwound the towel from about his neck. 'It's his daughter's birthday.'

Sutler came out of Watts' cabin rubbing his hands together.

'You know Paul Geezler?' Rem asked.

'No. Just as a name. He was passing on some information, third party, contracts.' Sutler smiled, satisfied, an explanation so thin it carried no conviction. 'The delivery comes this afternoon. Did you have any luck finding out what was in the load this morning?'

Reluctantly Rem admitted that he was wasting his time. But seriously, Geezler? From Europe?

'Why?' Now Sutler sounded suspicious.

'I've been trying to speak with him for a while.'

'Well, I can't help you. Try calling him back.' Sutler looked up to the cloud. 'You need to speak with someone about that. There's no telling what they're getting rid of. What was wrong with Watts?'

Watts came to his cabin door, red-faced, a sheet of paper in his hand. He called to Rem, asked if he could have a private word. 'That was from Markland. CIPA have pulled the plug on the burn pits. We're to stop immediately. If HOSCO send any more trucks we're to turn them back. According to CIPA we can't burn a goddamned thing.'

Rem asked Watts to get hold of HOSCO.

'I tried.'

'But he just spoke with Sutler.'

Watts shrugged. If they don't answer, what could he do?

Rem stood at the door, and worried that Sutler and Pakosta had overheard them. 'We keep this to ourselves until we hear something definite.'

Watts agreed. 'I guess they can do that. Shut us down whenever they like.'

'No one's shutting anything down. At least, not until we hear from HOSCO.'

Sutler appeared uncomfortable, he spoke with Pakosta, his hands dug into his pockets. 'Those fires. There's no telling what they'll be trying to get rid of. Do you know what's wrong with Watts?'

'It's his kid's birthday or something. So he's having his period over it.' Pakosta shook his head, disgusted. 'It's not like she'll remember, just take a photo of any party, tell her how great it was. She won't know any different.'

Santo said Watts' child wasn't born yet, so it probably wasn't that.

Rem watched Sutler return to the Quonset, and wondered how he'd known about the closure, so early, long before anyone else, and why he would have Geezler's attention.

Pakosta asked Rem if he thought Sutler could use an extra hand. He stood at the door to Rem and Kiprowski's cabin.

He'd spoken with the man that morning. Seemed like things with Kiprowski weren't working out.

'Things with Kiprowski are working fine. They're working together right now. Has Sutler said anything about what he's doing here?'

'Nope. Nada.' Pakosta looked about the room, slowly taking in Kiprowski's cot, then Rem's. 'So what's wrong with him?'

'Wrong?'

'I got the idea from Watts that you aren't happy. You think he's CIA?'

'He's HOSCO. I don't think the CIA are interested in a place that burns shit.'

Pakosta gave a tight nod. As far as he could gauge Sutler was just another POG, a company man.

'So, we aren't getting paid any more?'

Rem had to admire Pakosta's directness. 'And you heard this how?'

'So it's true?'

'If we're working then we're being paid.'

'But are we working?'

'I haven't heard anything from HOSCO. If anything changes I'll let you know about it.'

'Well, I've heard they're closing down the pits. All of them. Not just here. They just haven't reached us to tell us, that's all.'

Rem asked how this could be true. They received supplies every other day. Trucks arrived with waste every morning. Pakosta wouldn't say where the rumours had started.

☆

Cathy,

2 points to make here. 1. It isn't your business why my brother is out there, just as it isn't my business that you don't want your husband out there. 2. I'm guessing you haven't been following the chatroom, but you've stirred everyone up and the discussion isn't healthy. There's all sorts of rumours about the contracts. HOSCO won't think twice about getting rid of you. Their contracts are in iron.

You stay there until they say you're done. There's someone posting on the forum now – *boston_adams* – who has a son at Camp Bravo. He says they refuse to work and now HOSCO are suing, breach of contract. He says people are coming home sick. He says HOSCO holds them responsible for what they were burning and it's becoming a mess of lawyers and litigation. And (this is probably point 3), I don't know anything, but it seems like this man is a good place to start.

JW

P.S. You don't know what other people go through. I forget that. It's my fault Paul left because he has to do everything when he's home. I don't know. Now everyone is angry with him.

P.P.S. I couldn't talk with you when you said you didn't want your husband out there. This is all I hear. They pretty much take it out on me now Paul's not around. I think of leaving every day. I go to work and I think of leaving. I get home and just don't want to be around. These people are strangers to me.

Paul is the kind of brother who'd do anything for you. That's who he is. He brought me up and pretty much I can tell him anything. People don't see that side of him.

There's no one who supports him except me, and I've been thinking that if I thought what you thought then he'd have no one, and he's always stood by me, no matter what. I can't talk with you if this is what you think, because I can't think like that. If he doesn't have me, he has no one.

I'm sorry you feel like you do, and I hope your husband comes home to you soon.

Dear JW,

I am so sorry. I didn't think before I answered your question, and I am so, so sorry. It isn't that I don't support Rem, and it isn't that I think what he is doing is wrong. I don't know either what the answer is. I just think it isn't our problem, and now, somehow, it is. I don't understand why it should be like this? I know all the reasons why he felt he had to go there, but don't understand why he chose to go there.

But that's how things are with us. How things are with you and your brother isn't something I have any right to make an opinion about. It isn't my business, and if it sounded like I was judging you, then I'm truly sorry. As you can see I'm just as confused by this as everyone else.

I have been on the chatroom, but can't find *boston_adams*.

If you could forward my email and information to him (or tell me who he is), I would appreciate it.

Your brother sounds like a kind and decent man.

You can call me anytime you like. Day. Night. Any time.

Sincerely,

Cathy

☆

The call-back came at 15.30. Sutler's delivery would arrive within the hour. Watts took the message to Rem then drove with Santo and Samuels to watch the three helicopters come in, changing formation as they descended. They settled behind the Quonset, one after the other, and deposited thirteen crates and boxes, and with them, a day earlier than usual, the mail drop. Sutler supervised the loading of the crates inside the Quonset, and asked Kiprowski to help organize the unpacking so that everything would be stored correctly.

Sutler stood with Rem beside the empty crates. Whatever Sutler had asked for Markland had provided: a portable freezer, frozen meat, vacuum-packed steaks, two barbecues, packs of tortillas, a box of tortilla chips, packs of dips, packs of cheese, packs of cookies, Cheerios, long-life milk, new respirators, complete masks. Included in the drop were three sealed cases marked: *S. L. Sutler. HOSCO-ACSB*. The final crate contained the beer Sutler had promised. German beer in packs marked AFCS Ramstein.

'How did you get all this? You spoke with Geezler?'

'You keep asking. I've nothing to do with this man.'

Watts sidled up to Rem and asked what he was going to do about the announcement. 'You going to tell them?'

Rem said he didn't rightly know. How come they were making deliveries when they wanted the pits closed? He couldn't see the logic. 'I need to speak with Geezler.'

'I tried again, just now. Nothing. Do like he did and use email.' Watts nodded to Sutler.

'I'm getting nothing from him.'

'We're on someone's radar.' Watts pointed to the Quonset, to the stacks of provisions. Clark and Chimeno squatted in the dust and assembled one of the barbecues. 'Who is this man you both want to speak with?'

'Making ice,' Samuels loaded up the freezer with bottled water, 'ice. Ice. Cold water.'

'Just someone at HOSCO.' Rem watched Samuels, the man diverted, possibly even happy, bottles of water tucked under his arm. 'Let's take it easy and see what happens. See if I don't hear from HOSCO by tomorrow. No point ruining a good night. We'll talk tomorrow when there's no delivery.'

The men gathered under Sutler's awning with an open crate of beer, the cans packed in a bucket with ice, and they waited, grouped in silence to read mail and open packages. Occasionally news was repeated, read out loud, simple facts or loose comment, but the men mostly read to themselves or listened to messages on headphones. Clark sat with the satphone, his back to the Quonset, contented as he downloaded his emails. 'See,' he said, holding up his fist. 'It's working for me. Oh, hang on. No it's not.'

Kiprowski received packages from his mother, and he softly repeated details to Samuels: she'd caught a report on NPR about a contractor who'd handed out footballs to the kids in Nasiriyah, and this had spurred her to speak with the local Wal-mart, who were keen on the idea but hadn't got back to her. She sent him care packages with candy, Hershey's Kisses, bars of chocolate, messages from his sisters, cards with found poems, details she thought would interest him, substitutes for the conversations they were not having. 'She hates Skype,' he said, 'email, anything that involves a computer.'

Pakosta butted into the discussion, and zoned in on the poems, and while Kiprowski was willing to share what he'd been sent, he resented the cards being read out loud. Pakosta snatched a card from Kiprowski's hand, and Rem (surprised to see this) watched with interest as Kiprowski stood up to the man and took the card back without a word.

Clark moved the satphone closer to the Quonset. Watts told him to be careful.

'You fuck with that and we're all in trouble.'

Clark looked over his shoulder, sheepish. 'It kind of gets through then breaks off.'

'That's what it does. Try later.'

Samuels moved away from the group, in his hands a bundle of unopened letters.

'You aren't reading those?' Thwarted by Kiprowski, Pakosta sorely needed entertainment.

Samuels tucked the letters into his pockets and mumbled that he'd get to them later.

'Christ, Samuels, what you waiting for? The Dead Sea to freeze or something?'

'Dead Sea?'

Pakosta gestured toward Kuwait.

'You think we're near the Dead Sea?'

'Sure we are.'

'You don't know where we are.'

'Yes I do.'

'Which province are we in?'

'Al-Muthanna. Al-Amrah?' Pakosta answered smartly.

'Which one?'

'Muthanna.'

'Al-Muthanna's a desert. Al-Amrah's a district. I'm asking about the province.'

'I knew that.'

'How many provinces are there?'

The men, interested in Pakosta's cluelessness, began to guess wildly. Santo said nine, Watts said four. Pakosta said he could give a crap.

'Name the governor of our province.'

Chimeno stabbed his finger in the air. 'That's a trick question. I know for a fact there isn't a governor.'

Samuels slowly shook his head. 'Yes there is. There's a governor who decides on the mayors and the chiefs of police. And there's the local council, which the governor convenes, which is overseen by the Administrator. The governor would be an Iraqi, the Administrator is someone from Southern-CIPA.'

'Paul Howell.' In this they sounded unanimous.

Samuels again shook his head. 'Howell is the Deputy Administrator. He's the finance, the guy with the money. The Administrator is responsible for governance. It's the Administrator we're missing, not the Governor.'

Chimeno couldn't keep up. 'What? How many people run this place?'

Sutler, who was shucking peanuts, interrupted. 'Actually, they haven't replaced the Administrator,' he paused to recall the name, 'because the English and the Americans can't agree on his successor. And as it happens, HOSCO is also missing its regional chief, a person they've yet to appoint.'

'So there's no one running the place?'

'Howell. Paul Howell.'

'That's what I said!' Chimeno became exasperated. 'I said that.'

'But he's like some deputy, right?'

'Deputy Administrator. That's the title, which isn't quite what you mean.'

'But he's the one who got us all this stuff?'

Sutler blew the husks off his hands. 'No. The provisions are HOSCO but CIPA helped expedite the transport.'

The men raised their beers, clanked cans. Samuels, disgusted at the conversation, said he didn't see why everyone was so smug. 'And you guys get to vote come November.'

Santo held his hand to his heart and said he felt a great stirring of hope.

Pakosta laughed. 'That's not hope. That's gas. Won't make a bit of difference.'

'You think?' Samuels picked out a fresh beer and popped it open. 'Once we're out of here they'll start looking for people to blame.'

Kiprowski and Clark worked together to assemble the second barbecue. Sutler announced that he had ground steak, flown in from Germany. The whole lot was defrosted so they had to eat it tonight. The group cheered, opened fresh beers, and toasted Sutler with cries of *The man! The man!*

When Sutler saw Watts, he handed the tongs to Kiprowski, rooted through the food crate, and called Watts to him and asked casually how he was. Watts replied, 'Fine,' sullen enough not to invite a discussion. Sutler, box in hand, approached the table.

Clark returned his attention to the satphone. 'I'm on! No, I'm not.'

'It's not much.' Sutler offered the box to Watts. 'You could take some photos and send them to your daughter.'

Beer in hand, Watts looked at the box, a pack of Entenmann's cinnamon rolls. He looked up at Rem, puzzled.

'We don't have candles.'

Pakosta suggested they use cigarettes.

'Maybe something else? Everyone could sing. I don't know how you do these things out here.'

Watts cleared his throat and spoke quietly, 'I don't have a daughter.'

'Sorry?' Sutler froze. 'I heard it was your daughter's birthday?'

'*Wife*.' Properly considering Sutler's gesture Watts softened. 'And that's nice. We could do that. I think she'd like that.'

Pakosta immediately complained he'd rather get ass-raped than sing happy birthday over a couple of cupcakes to some woman he hadn't met. 'Once that shit gets on YouTube it goes viral.'

Watts hung his head, huffed out a laugh, and Pakosta slapped him on the back and called him *pops*.

'What are you talking about?' Watts looked at Rem as he spoke to Pakosta. 'I never know.'

Rem heard his name being called and Clark, now sat beside the barbecue, held up his phone. 'Why is your wife writing to my mother?'

Rem held his hand up to his ear and said he hadn't heard.

'Your wife is called Cathy? Cathy Gunnersen.' He held up the phone. 'Why is she sending emails to my mother saying HOSCO have shut down the pits?'

The men all turned from Clark to Rem. Santo took the phone from Clark.

Watts hung his head.

'HOSCO haven't announced anything.'

'Is it true?' Clark stood up.

'I've not heard anything from HOSCO. I'm waiting to hear from them.'

'But they've said something?'

Pakosta shook his head, spat on the ground, said in a low voice, 'I knew it. I asked you, and you said there was nothing going on.'

Santo didn't appear to understand what he was reading. 'What's this about contaminants? There's a whole list. Dioxins. Lead. Cadmium.'

Rem said he'd seen it.

'You've seen it?' Santo sounded alarmed. 'Why don't we know about this?'

'It's what she does. Pay no attention. She's caught up in a debate that's happening back home.'

'About the burn pits?' Santo pointed toward the pits.

And now Sutler weighed in. 'CIPA have ordered the pits to close. HOSCO haven't complied. If they comply then they're admitting to illegal burning.'

'Bullshit, they're just trying to get rid of as much as they can.' Pakosta also pointed to the pits. 'That's what this is about.' He turned to Rem. 'You knew this?'

'I saw the email yesterday. I'm waiting to hear from HOSCO.'

'They've closed Bravo?'

Sutler stepped in front of the barbecue, his hands raised. 'It's why I'm here.'

All heads turned to him.

Sutler asked if anyone liked whisky. He invited them into the Quonset.

'I don't know if you've heard the rumours – about a city. If so, they're true. There are four sites under consideration, but I can tell you this one is looking like the favourite.' Sutler couldn't suppress a smile. 'It will be Camp Liberty. It's not official. But it's almost certain.'

The men looked to each other and the maps on the table.

'A city. A new city is going to be built here.'

'Here?' Samuels looked from the map to the view outside the Quonset.

'Right here.' Sutler was serious. 'Supplies start arriving tomorrow from Southern-CIPA.'

'I knew it,' Watts preened. 'What did I tell you? There was a rumour.'

Sutler smiled beneficently. 'They haven't made it official – yet.' He folded his arms, an authority now. In nine months they'd flatten the Beach, and the plain would be divided into lots designed to hold a new city with its own water supply, schools, an intel centre, an airport, accommodation (buildings not huts), there would be a PX, a shopping complex, a cinema. In nine months the largest military base would begin construction in the southern Iraqi desert. The Massive, as the project was known, would have its own advanced medical unit, air-field, water, and waste-processing. You name it.

'The size of the fuel dump is where the Massive gets its name. It isn't the size of the military base but its capacity to store oil. We're bringing a city here, right where you're standing. The first job will be to build a proper road, something more substantial than the existing route.' He'd calculated the support a place like this would need. Equipment would be flown to Amrah City and dropped on site. The base would be snapped together out of pre-manufactured units shipped from Singapore, Kuwait, Bahrain. The Massive would be assembled in situ, but until the word came from Washington, they had to wait.

'So what about the burn pits? It's true then, they're closing them?'

Sutler shrugged, and looked to Rem. 'We're all waiting on news.' He knew only what he'd told them.

☆

The entrance to the apartment was also the entrance to Mr. Liu's Tai-Chi School. The classes began in the early evening, and in the winter the hallway became a harbour for men sheltering from the cold. In the summer it became a latrine. Cathy had a habit of holding her breath as she unlocked the lobby door.

With the key in the lock, she was surprised by someone coming up from behind and signalling for her attention. With some relief she recognized the boy from the park – dressed in the same white, blue-rimmed tracksuit. The same Bulls cap.

'Someone was here.'

'I'm sorry?'

'They left a note.' The boy offered Cathy a folded sheet of paper. A receipt for ninety-five boxes of mouthwash. At first she thought the boy had handed her a piece of scrap paper. If it wasn't for her name and address printed on the receipt. Mouthwash?

She invited the boy to the taqueria, sat with him, had him describe the men in detail, but could not guess who they were. They'd come in a car, he couldn't remember the make, looked casual, like any other man on the street, dressed in jeans and a T-shirt, sunglasses, and pushed the paper in between the doors because they were locked.

'Roscoe, right? Roscoe. I need to ask a favour.'

The boy took off his hat, she couldn't decide how old he was. His head shorn, a stern look about him, but still baby-like.

Cathy explained that she needed to go to Cleveland. She might drive and stop somewhere overnight. Just one night. 'The thing is,' she hesitated to ask, 'Nut.'

'Sure, I'll come.'

'I wasn't asking . . .' Cathy paused and laughed and started to explain how this wasn't what she was asking, because – what about his parents, what about, I mean, wasn't there school somewhere in the mix here, apart from the fact that, however likeable the idea, because it seemed so inappropriate, apart from the fact that they didn't know each other. *I could be anyone.* But still. Easier to agree. If there was somebody else in the car the dog would be manageable.

Roscoe waited for Cathy to explain herself. He didn't live at home, he said. He was eighteen and he lived with an aunt, and pretty much did what he wanted.

He explained himself so plainly that Cathy lost her argument, retreated to a standard *let's see*. And the boy sat back, knowing exactly what this meant.

They sat in silence after this, the boy with folded arms, his cap on the table. Cathy looked across the road to the apartment. She could have seen this boy a thousand times and not paid attention to him once.

She said goodbye to Roscoe at the taqueria, and decided to check her email at the library. She found fourteen emails from *boston_adams* with twenty-seven attachments. As she opened the documents she found information from a Senate Sub-Committee on burn pits, affidavits from doctors, but more interestingly documents from HOSCO including manifests of waste shipments to Camp Bravo, SB Alpha, and Camp Liberty. Included with the emails was one brief message: *Cathy, I believe you will find this interesting.*

Rem couldn't sleep. The idea stuck on replay. A city? Nothing about it made sense. HOSCO were scrambling to finish the few jobs they could manage, and it was no secret that much of what was promised would not be achieved. It was common knowledge – even Cathy knew this from the news and papers back home. So a city? Here? From scratch? In a desert?

Just supposing it was true, where would you start? You'd have to build a sewer system, electric, water, roads, everything from nothing. A city built on sand? Wouldn't that be the first problem? And what was that story about building a house on sand? An idea so deep in the culture, so ingrained, that going against it invited collapse and godly punishment.

He stretched the idea in his head, exercised it, and found it lumpen, illogical. If it was a joke – and surely it was – he couldn't see the point.

Kiprowski slept with his back to the room, silent enough and still. Rem had opened the blinds a crack to keep an eye on Sutler at the Quonset, and noted that the man finished his work about one thirty, a little later. The lights dimmed and Rem listened as Sutler hauled down the Quonset door. After that all sound was lost to the generator, before it too shuddered and stopped.

Still no word from Geezler. So if they had closed the burn pits, he had to ask himself, how would he know? And Cathy. He needed to speak with Cathy.

Alerted by the noise (a rough crank of gears and brakes, of a truck reversing at the camp gates rather than coming directly through) Rem came out of the Quonset, first walking then running to the gates. What were they doing? Just what was going on?

Strapped to the flatbed of a long trailer sat the burned-out front of a truck, a Scania – immediately recognizable as the vehicle in which Amer Hassan had died. Glassless and gutted, fire had stripped the interior, seared the seats down to their springs, left a sharp stink of burnt rubber, but the door, scorched and dulled by the heat, still held the HOSCO logo.

Rem stopped the truck as it backed through the gate and clambered up the footplate to ask Clark who was driving to tell him that this was not the vehicle he thought it was.

Pakosta and Santo looked one to the other.

'Just tell me that you aren't this fucking stupid. Tell me there is a sensible notion behind this.' Rem jumped down and signalled Pakosta and Santo to get out. 'Santo, tell me. Why would you bring this vehicle back to the camp?'

Santo began to explain that a call had come earlier saying that a convoy had passed through the previous night and the vehicle was on fire. Southern-CIPA had asked for it to be removed. Clearly, the vehicle couldn't be left where it was, it was a danger to the other convoys, and could be set with IEDs, it was a hazard, a potential danger, and wasn't this part of their job?

Pakosta pointed wearily to the cab on the flatbed. 'Look. We're doing exactly what we're told. Stephen said we should move it.'

'Stephen?'

'Sutler. He spoke with CIPA this morning.'

Rem sprang close to Pakosta, face to face. 'So, how, if it's such a fucking danger, did you have the stupidity to approach the vehicle in the first place?'

Clark, half out of the cab, began to explain that the vehicle was upright when they arrived – it had been dragged upright, and they'd simply hauled it onto the flatbed. There wasn't any choice. They couldn't leave it there.

Santo folded his arms and muttered that he wasn't paid for this.

'Take this vehicle away. You back out, you dump this a million miles away, and you take some charges and destroy it.'

Rem drew back and pointed south to indicate where they should take the truck, then walked away without looking back.

Rem couldn't bring himself to sit with the men at supper. Instead he started up the barbecue and picked out two of the burgers and watched them shrink as they cooked. On the other side of the awning he could hear Samuels and Clark, then Chimeno talking about the morning, and it was clear that they did not know he was there. Sutler came to the tent looking for ice or cold beer but found the coolbox empty. The men were sullen and when Watts asked what that was about earlier, Sutler refused to be drawn. As he left he said he had no idea.

Chimeno couldn't figure it out. Everything was tits up. Did anyone know if they were working any more, and if so, who for? What was going on?

Clark sounded defensive. He still didn't get it. What else were they supposed to do, and what was going on last night? His wife, what the hell was she doing? What was with that email – and there were others, they'd all seen them.

Rem could hear them re-load the coolbox. Chimeno struck a conciliatory tone. 'You should have nuked it right where you found it.'

Clark opened his beer and swore.

'About the truck.' Chimeno attempted to reason through the morning. 'It's obvious. He feels responsible. Gunnersen sent the man out there. Think about it. There wasn't any need for a translator, but Gunnersen sent him out. You should have talked with him first. Maybe if he'd known what you were doing there would've been a different reaction. Who knows? We've all been there. It's not so unreasonable.'

Clark said he didn't care. It wasn't just about the truck. 'What are we burning here? Does anyone know? Are they closing the camp? What exactly are we doing here? I mean, how do we know were not breaking some law burning this shit? Are we in trouble when we get back? You saw that list. How can any of this be legal?'

Rem waited for the men to disperse, then came around the awning to pick two cans out of the coolbox. He walked to the Beach to find Kiprowski.

He sat in the sand beside the boy and said he was sorry: about Hassan, about the men in the camp, about the camp itself. He offered Kiprowski one of the beers, and as Kiprowski accepted he asked if he'd seen the truck that morning.

Kiprowski nodded. 'I heard,' he said, 'I didn't see it.'

Rem waited before asking how he was doing.

'I'm fine.' Kiprowski cleared his throat. The beer unopened in his hands, his hands between his knees. 'I'm good.'

Rem had to hold his breath before he spoke. 'This is doing good?'

Kiprowski hung his head and his voice came low as a whisper. 'I don't want to talk about it.'

They sat in silence for a while, the sky barren, pinched of colour.

Kiprowski dropped back into the sand, his arms at his side, unanimated. 'Something like this was always going to happen. You can't have so much against you and expect to come out of it without something – I don't know – happening.'

Kiprowski opened the beer and let the foam pour over his hand, where it hit the sand the grains gathered together as if contracting. 'You said something to Pakosta about making a mistake you can't afford.' Kiprowski took a sip. 'What did you mean?'

Rem had said this off the cuff after Pakosta had thrown a second flare into the pit, causing the gasoline, now airborne, to ignite and sweep over them; harmless enough, but unexpected.

'He – I don't know – has a particular talent.'

Rem looked over the abandoned vehicles at the foot of the dune, and felt a faint whip of disappointment. He'd watched them arrive, slung like dumb cattle and dragged by helicopter over the desert from

Amrah City. There were older items, parts of a cart, a wagon without wheels. Un-funny. Mule-less. Foolish.

'You remember that map. The route we came in on. The highway that stopped in the desert.'

Rem half-laughed. 'Seems a while ago now, doesn't it.'

Kiprowski drew his legs up. 'I've been looking at Sutler's maps. There's never been a road there. The new maps he brought with him don't show that road either. It's only on the map from Southern-CIPA.'

'Well, some of it does. We were driving on it.'

'That turn on Route 567. Where we came off. That's not on the map either.' Kiprowski cleared his throat. 'You look at any map and you'll see there isn't a turn anywhere on that road. It comes up straight from Kuwait and heads straight to Khat, then straight to Kamkun, *then* it starts turning, *after* Kamkun. You know how many accidents they've had on that road in the last nine months?'

Rem had no idea.

'Twenty-two. I checked. Most are people following a map like ours, or people who haven't driven that route in a while. Everyone expects it to be straight.'

Rem stood and brushed off the sand, tired at the useless compression of grief, the struggle to find plots and reasons to explain events that just happen because they can happen. 'Look, I'll leave you alone.' He straightened up and pointed at Kiprowski's beer can. 'There's more back at camp. It won't last long.'

'I'm stopping here.'

Rem warned that it was getting cold. The sky sucked the heat from the desert, and the temperature dropped quickly. Kiprowski said he'd be fine, for the last couple of nights he'd searched through the hulks of the scrapyard, a blue light in his hand, scanning under the vehicles for scorpions. The creatures absorbed the light and threw it back a spectral green, luminescent. 'Did his nosebleed stop?'

'You mean Clark?'

'No, Spider.'

'Spider?'

'Chimeno.'

'I didn't hear about it.'

'It looked like someone punched him.'

Rem made it halfway back to the cabins when he realized that Kiprowski wanted to say something about Chimeno but hadn't quite managed. As he passed by the tent he avoided looking at the men, and they quietened in any case when they saw him approach.

☆

Cathy arrived late at work to find the store closed, the aisles empty except for the four clerks standing hands on hips or arms folded, nonplussed, an accusatory pitch in the way they leaned back to watch her. She greeted the guard as he unlocked the door and thought he also had some problem, something she couldn't guess.

'She's at the back taking stock.'

Cathy hitched her bag higher on her shoulder as she walked through the store.

'Maggie wants a word.' The first of four girls pointed to the loading dock. Chewed black fingernails. *And she handles food.*

What was it with these people, anyway? Voices sharp as pickle-juice, first jobs, more or less, hair dyed whore-black, punched-face make-up, all younger by a good fifteen years, and the attitude. What was it with the attitude?

'She's in the back.'

Cathy walked through Produce, through the soft rubber slats to the loading dock to find Maggie with a man in a short-sleeved shirt and glasses, *George* stitched in orange on the pocket. The man counted while two boys emptied a van, their arms loaded with white and pink boxes. On every surface the same pretty boxes: stacked on pallets, blocking the freight elevator, the firedoor, falling back from the dock to the open back of the truck. Maggie's gesture, hands held in flat-out refusal, pushing, indicating she wanted everything gone, out of here, now, and when she saw Cathy she hurried forward, relieved.

'Tell him to take them back. We can't store these. It's a mistake. Tell him he has to take them back.'

The man set his feet wide apart, folded his arms, leaned back, stubborn, a stance that might have appeared manly, except the girls in the store stood in the exact same way. He did not instruct his men to stop.

'What's going on, *George*?' Cathy conspicuously read the name on his shirt. He didn't look much like a George. With a tattoo edging under his shirt-sleeve she guessed he'd have a nickname.

'Insanity. Mouthwash!' Maggie waved, exasperated, at the boxes.

Mouthwash. Cathy asked to see the order-sheet. She still had

Roscoe's receipt in her pocket. 'We don't have any orders for mouth-wash, George, and we don't sell this brand.'

'I told him.' Maggie held out a docket, shook it. 'Look at the name on the delivery. It's yours.'

Cathy opened the paper, looked to the top and found her name, *Cathy M. Gunnersen*, underneath the name of the store.

'I didn't place this order. We can't accept these.'

The man folded his arms, a finite *no*.

'I'm serious. You have to take these back. We won't pay for them.'

'No one's being asked to pay. They're yours. I'm paid to deliver. That's all I know.'

Maggie looked down to her feet. 'This is the wrong day for this.'

Cathy looked over the invoice, searched for a name, a number to call. 'You've come all the way from Connecticut? Who's PrimeCut? I've never heard of them. Says here that the order has come from PrimeCut Supply.'

The man nodded. Now they all had their arms folded.

'Let me make a call.'

Cathy strode back through the store determined not to show her confusion. She ignored the sales clerks who turned, magnetized, to watch her. She paused at the checkout and turned slowly about to face the shop.

'Why are you all standing around? Get those doors open.' She turned her back as she placed the call, not wanting the see the girls disobey her, but feeling better in any case to have said something decisive.

After an hour speaking with different people at PrimeCut Supply in Connecticut, Cathy finally convinced them to cancel the order and take back the goods.

The woman, a clerk called Martina with a summer voice, explained that the order to deliver ninety-five boxes of mouthwash had come to them via a third party. It wasn't an error.

'I don't understand why you have my name?'

The woman couldn't explain. There was one shipment of ninety-five boxes to Cathy M. Gunnersen placed through this one third-party order.

'*Third party*? I don't understand what that means.'

451

'It means the order is coming from a customer who wants the goods to be shipped to another party, someplace else.'

'And what address do you have?'

The clerk read out the address for Happy Shopper, then the address for Clark Street.

Cathy looked out of the window at a small line of shoppers, all static, lost, because the store was closed but the lights were on, and they could see the staff standing about, useless, and it was already one hour and twenty minutes into trading time and the girls had not done what she'd asked. Zombies, she told herself. Undead. Slow. Soul-less. Zombies. In a film they would invent ways to dispatch them one by one.

And why mouthwash?

☆

Sutler brought beer to Rem's cabin and asked if he could have a word. Rem pointed to Kiprowski's cot.

'I have a little scotch left,' he said, 'if you'd prefer.'

Rem paused from writing. 'You manage to get your hands pretty much on anything.'

'What was that earlier today?'

'A man died. An accident. Before you arrived.' Rem paused and closed his eyes for a moment. 'His name was Amer Hassan, and he had two sons. His wife is now a widow, and she's barely in her twenties. She's in another country and doesn't speak the language, and there won't be insurance or compensation from HOSCO. He comes from Yemen, and has family, who came with him to Iraq who will be in danger once the word gets out that he was working for us.'

'You're not responsible.' Sutler offered the beer. Rem did not accept.

'This isn't about me. This is about a deep and meaningless fuck-up.' Rem looked hard at Sutler. Was he asking because he was interested, or because it was information? 'Look. I don't mean to be rude, but I'm tired of trying to figure you out.'

Sutler set the beer on the floor.

'This whole thing? It doesn't look like you know anything about cities. Why are you talking with people from HOSCO? What business do you have with Paul Geezler?'

Sutler nodded as if there wasn't anything to explain. His arrival came down to a simple fact: he had the skills the company needed. Skills and availability. Right place, right time.

'So how long are you here?'

Sutler didn't know. 'If they pick Camp Liberty – and I'm confident they will – I could be here for the duration. I don't know. If the company has some other notion of what they want me for I could be somewhere else tomorrow. That's how it works. Until then, I collect the information, work on the timetable and costs, and submit the bids. That, in a nutshell, is what I do.'

'Why are you talking with Paul Geezler?'

'I'm talking with HOSCO. He was involved in a minor capacity. You keep mentioning this man. What's your business with him?'

Rem looked up to the ceiling. 'Geezler organized some work he had an interest in, and I guess he's done with it now. I don't know. We haven't spoken.' Rem decided to accept the beer. 'Next time you have a little chat ask him why I've not heard from him.'

Rem opened the beer and drank so that he didn't have to talk, and gave Sutler the opportunity to leave.

The next morning Rem rose early enough to work on the burn pits. He followed after the trucks and worked side by side with Santo to guide them into place at Burn Pit 3. He asked the drivers if they'd received any instructions about the possible closure and each of them knew nothing. The work orders were coming in, as usual.

Santo worked without talking, seeming to be drowsy or exhausted. Dust washed about them, kicked up as the trucks backed to the pit-edge. The sound, he thought, belonged in a city: the choke of a reversing vehicle, the accompanying steely beep.

Once the trucks were in position, Santo slapped the sides, spoke with the drivers, made sure that they unloaded with care, and it was Santo who set the flare and returned as close as he could to the edge once the fire was burning, a wall of smoke so black and angry it looked like it might suck him in.

He asked Rem if he was all right, and Rem, already walking back, waved a hand over his shoulder. He was all right.

Santo wanted to know what was happening. 'You believe all this about a city?'

Rem took a weary look at the camp: the tables outside the cabins, the awning straining against the wind, the same dirt that rubbed alongside the Quonset stung his neck and ears. 'I've no opinion.'

'That's an opinion.'

Rem stopped walking. 'OK, you want to know. I think he's putting us out of work. I think he's here to shut us down.'

Santo looked up to the cabins, the sky beginning to brighten, the quality of the air becoming thicker. 'There's a lot of frustration. Did you speak with your wife?'

Rem started walking again.

'I'm just asking because she can't write to everyone like that. You have to speak with her. You have to put everything in order.' Rem walked a pace or two behind. 'Fuck, Rem. Sutler isn't the problem here. He isn't the problem. Once he has those plans made and those bids in place he'll be gone. You need to make your own plans and think about what's best for the people you brought here.'

Rem agreed, Santo had a point. He needed to start making plans so they would know where they were heading.

When he returned to the camp, Rem set about making coffee.

He should contact CIPA. Find out exactly what was going on and confirm these details with HOSCO. Too tired to bother he sat under the awning, put up his feet and refused to move.

With the coffee made a second convoy arrived.

As Pakosta walked past Rem he hissed, 'I thought we were shut down? Looks like there's more.' And he was right, Pakosta counted the trucks as they came through. 'Twenty-five shit suckers.'

Rem roused Chimeno, Kiprowski, and Samuels.

'Take them down to Pit 4. We might have to dig 4 out later.'

For a moment Rem thought the men were going to refuse him. Chimeno and Samuels looked to Pakosta, and Pakosta said they wouldn't work without those masks. Rem waved them toward the Quonset, and told them to go ahead.

Sutler spent a good amount of time at his table writing in a small note-book. Preparation, he said, ensured success, and there were details which had to be sought out and recorded. He hadn't worked like this since he was a student.

The map, stuck together from separate sheets, took up most of the table, and Sutler hovered carefully over the paper, forefinger tracing the fine lines demarking the existing camp, the shaded areas and zones for development.

'I'll be speaking with HOSCO tomorrow,' Sutler said without looking up. 'If there's anything you want me to pass on.'

'The only thing I need to know is when they intend to shut us down.'

Sutler appeared to hold back from saying something and Rem asked him to speak his mind.

'Isn't that a moot point at this stage? Don't you know that already?' Sutler leaned against the table. 'The idea is – they will work for me.'

Rem stood in the dust with his hands on his hips.

'Once you close the pits they will work for me on the Massive.'

'I need to hear this from HOSCO.'

'You are. I'm telling you. I've sent requests for money and supplies. I'm waiting on HOSCO and Howell for the final word on budgets.'

'Perhaps today.'

'Perhaps.'

'You'll let me know?'

'You'll be the first.'

☆

The choice: contrive an excuse for missing work – being ill, fainting, anything – and make up her shifts later. *I'm pregnant*, she could say. *I need to see a specialist.* That's right, start using an unborn child for leverage. Alternatively she could speak honestly with Maggie about her plan to drive to Cleveland.

Maggie would see through her, whatever reason she gave: you're over-reacting, you should wait, you shouldn't interfere. Wait and see what happens? A sensible perspective was exactly what she didn't need.

She called Phyllis at the library and found a sympathetic ear. 'Ask yourself why they agreed to see you. If everything is normal, if they have nothing to hide, why would they agree to speak with one of their employees' wives? They're a business. About as big as it gets. It's not like they need to be nice. Besides, you want to look them in the eye when you show them what you have.' Cathy checked through the documents forwarded by *boston_adams*.

'Have you heard any more from him?'

'I get about three emails a day now.'

'More documents?'

'Mostly HOSCO manifests about shipments, a report yesterday from the EPA.'

'Why don't you take him with you? Might be useful to have him along.'

'I asked, but he's not –' she wasn't sure of the word, *personable*? 'He's not big on the chit-chat. He just forwards the documents.'

'Sounds like you have a whistle-blower.'

'His son was at Bravo. I think he just wants justice.'

Despite herself Cathy called Maggie and started to explain with an apology, 'I know how this sounds.'

The office overlooked a parking lot, an unbending canal, a modelled lawn with gravel paths, all new, and beyond it the greased slip of a highway. The office didn't impress her: stained carpet tiles and mis-matched furniture that looked borrowed, an empty feel as if this were somehow a sham, a movie set, although the tiredness of the atmos-phere, the piles of paper proved otherwise. She sat opposite Sue Williams, *overseas personnel* on her door, not the title she'd used in her correspondence. Three windows offered a solid block of sky and Cathy thought only about how hard she'd have to push to get that woman, that chair, that self-assembly desk through a plate-glass window.

Sue had her answers practised: 'While HOSCO coordinate the proj-ects the responsibility for the health and safety of sub-contracted workers belongs to their employers.'

And: 'There are no functioning burn pits in Iraq now. All waste is handled through monitored sites and controlled incinerators.'

And: 'Authority over the monitoring of illegal dumping and burn-ing has been passed on to the Iraqi authorities.'

Cathy sat with her arms folded, happy to inform Sue Williams that whatever nonsense she came up with made no difference to what she knew to be a fact. Her husband and seven other men were out in the desert in southern Iraq burning waste which arrived in trucks marked HOSCO, and their uniforms and protective gear were also marked HOSCO. Which wouldn't look good in any court or newspaper.

'Don't make the mistake,' she said, leaning forward, 'of think-ing this is about you and me.' Cathy laid out the manifests sent by *boston_adams*, one by one. SB Alpha. Camp Bravo. 'You might want to look at the dates. The most recent is from two weeks ago.'

Sue Williams ran her tongue over her teeth, then asked as an aside where Cathy had obtained the documents.

Cathy slid the papers forward. 'I think a more interesting question would be: how come there are manifests in the first place, when, according to my husband, there are trucks arriving at Camp Liberty without any kind of documentation. You'll see the waste they were taking to Camp Bravo is now being taken to Camp Liberty. Medical. Plastics. Paint. Batteries containing lead, cadmium, zinc.'

'I can't comment on these documents, and I can't comment on Camp Bravo.' Sue Williams, to her credit, held Cathy's gaze. 'I can show you the papers that record that there are no functioning burn pits in southern Iraq. The facilities that *were* in use are now closed.'

Cathy shook her head. 'They are in use.'

'I can assure you that all waste processing in southern Iraq is currently managed by Iraqi firms and businesses. Our facilities are being converted for other use or are in the process of being shut down. If burnings are happening, it's without our authority or consent.'

'What about the health concerns?'

'We're awaiting rulings on this,' Sue continued through Cathy's objection, 'we have excellent medical facilities in Austin; when these individuals return they will be offered a full screening. We will honour our responsibilities.'

Cathy stopped at a bar. Sat outside with a Diet Pepsi too flat to drink. She'd learned nothing, and failed to profit from the journey. She looked out at the farmland and knew this wasn't quite the case.

Nut sat in the driver's seat. Smudges greased the passenger window, and when she came close his expression, a little dumb, a little guilty, reminded her of Rem.

She waited for Roscoe to return from the restroom. In some regards a bad idea to bring him, but he sat in the back with the dog, and kept to himself.

He was eighteen, she couldn't believe it, just as he'd said. And he worked, on occasion, with the Park District. His aunt was sick and couldn't be bothered with him, and Cathy had driven by the house intending to have a word with her. Aunt Bea had stood on the porch and looked at the scrubby front yard like she detested it. A woman with emphysema who smoked. Cathy drove on. One look at the house and Aunt Bea and she knew enough about the boy's life not to ask any questions.

Roscoe. Another detail she would not share with Rem.

☆

Watts woke Rem with a communication from Southern-CIPA.

'This is from Tom Markland. Some instructions about the security team.' He held the paper out. 'He wants to hear that the pits are shut down. He wants confirmation. He thinks we're working for Sutler now.'

Rem dressed quickly and took the paper outside to read it. *Pakosta, Clark, Chimeno, Santo*, it read, four of the men recently qualified with C3-5 firearm training, were to be picked up at 14:00 and brought to Amrah City where they would accompany the Deputy Administrator to a conference in Amman to work as his security detail.

News had filtered through and Pakosta, Clark, Chimeno, and Santo ambled conspicuously between the Quonset and the cabins.

Chimeno punched the air as Santo read the list out loud.

'Pakosta said there were two cars stopped on Route 567. We have company. A couple of cars with Kuwaiti plates.'

Santo suggested that they both take a look, and Rem signalled that this wasn't a problem, his hands smoothly cutting through the air.

'Tell them Watts is sick or something. He clearly isn't interested in going.'

Rem stood on the spot long after the vehicles had pulled out, their lights furred and faded along the curve of the road.

Once the security team were dispatched, Watts drove to the camp entrance and found two cars pulled off the road, shabby and dust-caked – a small group sat in them looking hot and quarrelsome like any family that needed a break during a long drive.

'They had a tarp laid out,' he reported back. 'Four men, three women, a girl of four or five. Kuwaiti plates.'

Wanting to know how much of a threat these visitors might be, Rem decided to check them out.

'Call Amrah,' Watts suggested, 'have one of those Chinooks blow them back to the Gulf.'

Rem asked Sutler if he'd brought protective gear.

'I've a jacket with panels, a helmet, it's pretty standard.'

'I'd like to borrow it.'

'I was hoping I could come with you.'

They dressed in their cabins then met outside Watts'. Rem helped Kiprowski tie the straps that held together the chest and back flaps. Kiprowski shook a little, an edge of nervousness or too much coffee, and Rem regretted not properly considering this jaunt: he didn't want Kiprowski along. Kiprowski, and Rem, dressed in an odd assemblage of worn kit, looked end-of-credit, the characters left standing, and Rem badly wanted to tell Kiprowski that his family had a specific word for ill-advised ventures such as this: '*jammer*'. Sutler wore new kit with shiny black shoulder pads, a smart jacket with quilted pleats, more suited for fencing than blast and bullet protection.

'I'm missing the crotch.' Kiprowski held out the front of his jacket and looked enviously at Sutler. 'There were flaps for the neck but I cut them off.'

Rem looked Kiprowski up and down and swore under his breath. 'We look like kids on Halloween.'

'We can't all go.' Rem designed an excuse for Kiprowski. 'One of us needs to stay in case there's contact from Amrah. Where's Watts?'

Rem found Watts in his cabin, splayed on the floor, collapsed and wheezing, his jacket beside him opened out. Watts didn't respond when Rem turned him over, and saw, on his shirt, a fine spread of aerated blood. He shouted for Sutler and began to haul Watts to the side of the room to lean him against the wall.

Watts opened his eyes and looked at Rem as if he were a stranger, and would not answer his questions.

Sutler came hesitantly into the cabin, and knew better than Rem how to manage. He lay Watts on his side. Raised one arm out and hoisted the other under him to keep him on his side.

'You've checked his pulse? How's his breathing?'

Sutler held Watts' head, looked into his eyes and asked him questions. 'Can you hear us? Can you raise your arm? Try lifting your arm. Clench. Make a fist.'

Watts looked at Sutler, entirely unable to respond.

'You need to call for help.'

Rem didn't have a clue how to work the equipment. This was Watts' territory.

'Get Kiprowski,' then shouting, 'Go!'

They carried Watts to the Quonset and sat him upright, and slowly, in increments, he revived. The men hung close, silent and anxious. Sutler guessed he'd had a stroke, although, in truth, Watts was missing most of the typical symptoms – but nothing else would explain his disconnection. Watts moved slowly, turned his head, turtle-like, and indicated that he was thirsty. As soon as he had water he began to appear more alert.

Kiprowski sat beside Watts and said that they were shipping him out. 'You get to fly,' he said, 'any minute,' and then, in a less certain voice, 'you'll be all right.'

Kiprowski returned to Watts' cabin to call CIPA and check on progress.

Watts, considerably improved, acknowledged only Rem.

When Sutler came forward with water, Watts looked sourly aside. 'Watch him.' He pointed to Santo's cabin. 'He's no friend to you.'

Watts began to struggle again for breath. He looked about the Quonset in panic, and held Rem fast, his grip locked about Rem's arms. He couldn't feel, he said, mouth now struck in a gawp.

Rem asked Sutler what was happening, and Sutler said they needed oxygen.

'Lay him down, he can't breathe. Give him some space.'

The sound of the helicopter came as a mercy.

☆

When Cathy returned from work she picked up Roscoe and they walked to the taqueria. After eating he took Nut to the lake while she worked an hour at the library. She asked little about him, and kept her curiosity to one question: why he was living with his aunt. His answer was honest, and not quite the story she expected.

'I was in some trouble, about two years ago. I have a younger brother and my mother wanted me out of the house.'

Cathy returned from the library and talked through her findings.

'Two good things. First, an email from Jonnie Watts.' She read out a portion of the message, repeated the name. 'Stephen L. Sutler. I didn't find anything, some people from Cleveland. Nothing in the UK. Less even than Paul Geezler. Speaking of,' she laid the paper on the table, 'the man is coming to Detroit.'

Roscoe looked to the paper, turned it about, still couldn't see what she was talking about. 'He's giving a paper at a business conference. Here.' She pointed out the abstract. 'Where it says *Proteck*, it's a talk about supply chains.'

Roscoe asked what this meant.

'It means a visit to Detroit.'

Roscoe asked if that was the second point, and Cathy remembered. 'No. There's a second message, from *boston_adams*.'

Dear Cathy,

I'm not surprised by the news of your meeting with Sue Williams. At every turn HOSCO have sought to absolve themselves of all responsibility. I can confirm that the documents are genuine and from the company. I can't tell you how I got hold of them. I'm sure you understand. I can't take this further, but you can make these documents public – I have no objections. I would advise that you act quickly – I'd say you're right to worry about your husband and those other boys at Camp Liberty. With that in mind I attach two copies of contracts the company have recently issued – note the changes in items 5 through 9.

Sincerely, Bob Adams

☆

Rem asked the men to gather outside the Quonset. Watts, he explained, had collapsed and was currently at Camp Buehring, where they'd stabilized him, with the intention of sending him, as soon as possible, to hospital in Germany.

'This is because of the pits?' Pakosta stepped forward.

'They think it was a stroke.'

'Of course they do.'

'They don't know yet. I don't think there's anything here to cause a stroke.'

'He looked healthy when he arrived. We were all healthy.'

'They just don't know at this point. They've done some tests, they'll do more. It could be a number of things. Stress, or heat, or exhaustion.' Rem struggled for an explanation. 'We just don't know yet.'

'So that's it? You're happy with that?' And then as a dismissive aside, 'Your friends don't do so well, do they?'

Rem asked Pakosta to say that louder.

'I said your friends don't do so well.'

Sutler watching from the Quonset said he was sorry about Watts. 'It's unfortunate. This next step is crucial. And it's important that we work together. I need a team to pull toward the same goals now.' Sutler began to lay out his plan. 'From tomorrow you'll be working on the Massive. The pits are closing. It's over. I've organized a team to come from Southern-CIPA.'

Pakosta interrupted. 'Who is this team?'

Sutler looked to Rem.

'Do you know who they are?'

'They're an environmental safety – I don't know – I haven't properly . . .' Sutler hesitated. 'The idea is they'll advise us on the best way to deal with whatever's left over.'

'Is this the same team that went to Camp Bravo?'

'I don't know anything about—'

Pakosta asked Rem. 'Is this the same team that went to Camp Bravo after it was closed? Has he called in the EPA?'

Rem shook his head.

'Because they didn't advise on anything. They took samples to see what they'd burned. They were collecting evidence.'

Sutler took his hands out of his pocket and folded his arms. 'I don't see what you're getting at.'

'I'm saying, if you want your project to go ahead you don't want to invite the EPA in beforehand. They will shut this place down, just like they shut down Camp Bravo. We should bury the pits ourselves. Dig them out, bury them, get rid of them.'

Sutler agreed. 'We can do that.'

Chimeno and Pakosta lingered in front of the showers after the meeting had broken up. Before Rem could settle with Pakosta, Chimeno asked, 'Why are you letting him do this? He's taken over.' With the light on in the Quonset they kept their voices low so they would not be overheard.

'That's why HOSCO sent him. It's his project and we can't keep the pits open.' Rem shook his head.

'You're kidding, right?' Pakosta, hands on hips, leaned to the side and spat. 'You seriously expect us to do this? He doesn't know what he's doing. He's talking about inviting the environmental agency to inspect the pits for fuck's sake. He doesn't have a clue.'

Rem held up his hands. 'This is something else.'

'Fuck you *it's something else*. It's not something else. We didn't come here to get nailed for burning waste.'

Rem leaned forward, his shadow falling across Pakosta's face. 'Keep pushing Pakosta. Say one more thing.'

Chimeno tugged Pakosta by the arm and drew him away.

Back in the cabin Kiprowski said that he was comfortable with the arrangement staying as it was.

'It would be weird to move into Watts' cabin.'

'I think you're right.'

'It has all the communications.'

Rem nodded, uncertain where the discussion was heading. Kiprowski folded then unfolded his arms.

'Sutler could move his office there. He uses comms all the time.' The boy had a point.

'There's no point moving the equipment,' Rem agreed, and Kiprowski immediately appeared to soften, as if this had been a source of some anxiety.

'Tell Sutler he can have that cabin. Move him out of the Quonset. We need the stores.'

Kiprowski nodded, clearly satisfied. He'd get right on to it.

Rem waited for Kiprowski to leave and found himself a little relieved also. It hadn't occurred to him that he'd need to reassign Watts' cabin, and being used to Kiprowski's presence, he thought it would be odd to be alone now.

☆

Cathy wrote directly to Paul Geezler and explained that she would be in Detroit the next weekend and wanted to meet him. He might remember that he hired her husband to work in Iraq, and had assigned him duties at one of the burn pits. She didn't want to waste his time, but a short meeting would be enough. Say fifteen minutes before or after his presentation.

The librarian waited by the desk, impatient to close. Cathy logged off and apologized. She played the housewife in such circumstances, gave a little story about her husband being in Iraq, and could see from the turn of the librarian's shoulders that she'd ruined the woman's night, made her feel bad.

'We open tomorrow at nine,' she said, a sweet apology in her voice. 'Tomorrow, then.'

☆

The work began in earnest the next morning. Sutler and Kiprowski drove out and began to calculate the distances, set up flags as markers first in a broad circle, then, inside this circle, a spiral of posts, and for the first time Rem began to understand Sutler's dogged involvement in the project. Sutler began to describe the form of the city, the districts, the relation of one sector to another out in the field, plotted with small posts and paper flags. He stood in the centre of the plain and pointed out. There: *a centre for transport*, there: *commerce*, there: *housing*, there: *education*, there: *entertainment*. Sutler returned to the jeep to sketch, as Rem and Kiprowski followed his instructions. He drew patterns, spirals, and complex internalized webs, spoke about how the city should be low-lying, with broad avenues and tiered squares. If the desert was formerly green, he would begin with a new system for irrigation. Whole zones would be planted with vetiver, grasses which bound the desert stone and sand, drove down deep roots, made stable environments. Concrete, yes, but also, of much more importance: water and grass.

Rem looked over the drawings while Sutler slept in the back of the jeep with his feet propped up. He turned the sketches round and over and couldn't follow what Sutler was aiming for, because he was drawing shapes now, patterns, blocks of colour which bore no relation that he could see to buildings or figurable structures. Etched small in one corner Rem recognized the form of a ziggurat, and as they talked he slipped his foot out of his shoe and drew out a small shard of shell.

'How about that?' Sutler held up the rounded white fragment to Kiprowski for inspection.

*

Rem asked to be dropped at the pits on their way back.

He found Pakosta supervising Clark and Santo with the diggers. The others stood about watching and advising. The atmosphere a little easier than the previous night.

'You're making progress.'

Chimeno said he didn't understand the point. 'I don't see how getting rid of the pits will change anything. They measure trace amounts.'

'Who?'

'The specialists. They take samples. We can bury the pits, but whatever they're looking for it's in the sand.'

Pakosta finished talking with Santo, jumped from the digger, and pulled off his mask. 'You're not thinking right. If everything is churned up, there's no way they can say we were responsible, because they won't be able to tell what happened when. If we leave the pits as they are then they can tell what fires were lit and when shit was burned. They can read them like a book. With no pits, they just have random samples, and no timeline. We could have been burning paper.'

Pakosta had devised a workable plan. Burn Pit 5 would stay in use for the interim – in this pit they'd burned mostly electrical equipment, vehicle parts, computers, chairs and tables, on one occasion a whole store of cabinets, and something like forty sprung cot beds and thin mattresses, all marked from a hospital. A mass of metal frames and a strange puzzle of blackened wires were all that remained, but they needed compressing, or a hotter fire. Pakosta suggested just blowing them up, an idea not too ridiculous. The smaller the pieces, the hotter the fire, the easier the task.

The other pits would be filled in, but first, the sides need to be bought down, which meant, impractically, excavating a ramp into each pit and using the diggers to collapse the sides. Anything unburned would be dug out and transferred to the final pit. The men working in the diggers would wear full protective clothing. Everyone else would stay east, upwind, and away.

Pits 2 and 3 didn't pose much of a problem. Sand and shale could be heaped up beside them and pushed in. These they would flatten later.

They ate at the Beach. Flares stuck upright into the sand about them, a can brought from the camp to hold the coals for a fire, the last of the beer brought in a coolbox.

Sutler set up the area, then sat with the men on the prow of the dune and passed his camera about so they could look at the photos he'd taken earlier. Below them the fire deepened the shadows on the boat, the ambulance, the two jeeps, the Humvee, all fettered to wood pallets. Further down, the jumbled wreckage of civilian cars, burned and flattened, alongside stripped pieces of military hardware. And while their conversation seemed comfortable, they avoided speaking about Watts, and sometimes looked over the scrap, silenced by the evidence at their feet.

Clark, compelled to spout the same fact each time he came to the Beach, insisted: 'It took six hours to get here from Kuwait. Then six days to take the rest of the country. They fucking threw Iraq at us.'

Pakosta complained that he'd missed out. 'I was too young.'

'I wouldn't worry about it.' Santo joked. 'The military won't take people like you. You have to pass basic psychometric tests.'

'Why are you always riding my back?' Pakosta cracked open a can and blew off the foam. 'We're sitting here like turds attracting flies. We should be doing something useful.'

'You are,' Sutler interrupted. 'You'll have plenty to go home and talk about.'

'I said something *useful*.'

Sutler didn't react, and Santo asked where Pakosta got a word like *turd* from. Samuels started to laugh.

'You're not the only one with an education, Samuels.' Santo took the roll-up out of his mouth and picked at his lower lip. 'Isn't that right, Pakosta?'

'I can read.' Pakosta pointed at Kiprowski, who sat apart from the group beside one of the flares with his head down to a book. 'Like Kiprowski-boy there. Is he reading? Is he seriously fucking reading? What are you reading, Kiprowski? *The Princess Diaries*?'

Kiprowski continued to read and ignored the taunts.

'Hey, Kiprowski,' Pakosta needled, 'how do you know your dad is gay? *Cause his dick tastes like shit.* Hey, Kiprowski. Kiprowski. Come here, I want to tell you something. Kiprowski. Come here, man. Kiprowski, don't ignore me. I love you, Kiprowski. Hey Kiprowski, come on, what's with the book? I said don't ignore me.'

Kiprowski closed the book about one finger, stood up, and walked off.

Pakosta sat upright, kicked sand after Kiprowski. Sutler handed

Rem a beer and Rem brought it to Pakosta, stood close in front of him and held it out.

'We didn't finish our conversation last night.' Rem held on to the beer as Pakosta took it.

'I'm not Arab enough for him.' Pakosta huffed, snatched the beer, and wiped his mouth. 'Why are you always looking after that boy? And by the way, how's everything at home?'

Rem walked with Sutler to the fire, and suggested they start cooking.

Sutler battered the side of the barbecue and said he had an announcement. Rem split open packs of meat and handed them to Santo and Chimeno. Santo squeezed the meat to check it wasn't frozen and muttered something Rem couldn't catch. Chimeno gave a nasty laugh.

'Things are starting to move. Like I've said, we're the top choice for the Massive, and in preparation they've released funding to start the development of this site.' Sutler held up his hands. 'Tomorrow I go to Southern-CIPA to collect the first funds.'

The group looked to each other, unimpressed.

'That's a big fat nothing, then.' Pakosta held up his steak and seeing Kiprowski come slowly back up the dune said: 'You've come back for me. I'm fucking irresistible.'

Again, as earlier, the team divided into clear groups. Only Santo and Kiprowski would directly acknowledge Rem or Sutler.

Sutler rose early, and as Rem sat outside the cabin and slipped his feet into his boots, Sutler came at him busy with ideas.

'You don't check for scorpions?'

Rem looked down at his boots and admitted that he only ever remembered after he'd put them on.

Sutler wanted to hustle Southern-CIPA. 'It isn't just about the money, they need to get behind the project. Show some support.' That's why he wanted Rem along. 'Support. We're losing more than time just sitting here doing nothing.' Sutler laid out his plan: today they would go to Amrah City, collect the first amount of money released for the project. Paul Howell would set up the accounts. Everything was in order. As soon as the decision became official HOSCO would send in workers, more than likely, who would need a work camp, which meant a need for more amenities. This would take time to put together. 'This is what we should be working on. So today we can make a proper start.'

Every conversation with Sutler now revolved around the Massive. Even Kiprowski had commented. Any subject could be bent to the project.

'What time is Steven getting up?'

'Steven?'

'Kiprowski.'

Both men looked at the cabin.

'About five minutes after the transport arrives.'

Sutler folded and unfolded his arms, checked his watch.

Cathy,

Paul was taken to the ER after collapsing at home. They've taken scans and he has scars on his lungs and reduced lung capacity and what looks like asthma. That's all they can tell us, they don't know what's happening, they tell us they don't have any idea what's causing this. Before this happened P was contacted by a lawyer who was asking a load of questions about the kind of work he was up to and said that the company don't give a shit about the risks and get away with whatever they want. He's lost 30lbs, he can't breathe right, and we don't know what to do.

Jonnie

Jonnie,

I'm sorry to hear this. I've been doing my own research and am worried about what they have been exposed to out there. There seems to be no accountability, and there's a great deal of confusion. I have documents from *boston_adams* which give an idea of the materials they have been burning, which might be of some use. I've good reason to believe that these are genuine, and that they come from HOSCO. Please see the attachments to this message.

Please know how sorry I am to hear about your brother. I'm praying that he is making a good recovery. I have some information on the chemicals and the effects of the chemicals – which doesn't make good reading, which I want to send to everyone. But I wanted to know how Paul is doing, and how you are managing with what is happening.

I'll post what I know on the forum.

Until I hear from you – Cathy

Dear All,

I'm sorry to be sending this information in this way, but this is the quickest and most effective way to make sure you get to hear everything you need to hear.

Some of you might know that Paul Watts collapsed at his home and has been in hospital since. He has been diagnosed with sudden onset asthma. He has also suffered contusions on his lungs. It's possible, just about, that this has nothing to do with his work in Iraq (given the weight of evidence, the numbers of people returning with similar conditions and problems, and the nature of the work – it probably seems self-evident that this is the outcome of the work he, and our partners/loved ones are engaged with). I must stress also that while this is serious, it might be the case that not everyone will be affected in the same way. There are no studies yet to show how this will affect everyone, which makes this all the more frightening. You will find five documents attached. These are from HOSCO, and they clearly show that they're aware of what's being burned and the associated health-risks.

Again, if you have any questions, please use the above email. Cath

☆

It wasn't until Rem was in the helicopter that he considered he didn't know what 1.4 million dollars looked like, and while he doubted that it would come in fives and tens, it would be difficult to barter for equipment with anything larger than a hundred dollar bill. He couldn't imagine how big or heavy the package would be, or if it would be one package or a number of packages. When Sutler spoke with CIPA they asked him when he would be collecting the shipment, and the word *shipment* sounded large and heavy and difficult to secure. And why bring the money back here? Wouldn't most of the services, equipment, arrangements be made through Southern-CIPA in any case? Wasn't it their duty to ensure they hired Iraqi labour, brought in the right local services (which were all, again, based in Amrah)? Not including himself or Sutler, the six men they had on base weren't enough, and despite Sutler's assurances, their contracts didn't cover them for this work. Would Sutler pay them separately? In cash? All Rem knew was that they would be met as soon as they landed and taken to the Southern-CIPA's Regional Office for Procurement. It was his assumption that they would bring them back to the airfield. Nevertheless he asked Pakosta to come with them for added security.

Rem assured Sutler that neither Pakosta nor Kiprowski understood the real intention of the visit. But given the porousness of information at Camp Liberty it didn't surprise him to hear Pakosta brag that he had worked one summer delivering diamonds and cash from the mart on Wabash to jewellers and banks in the Loop. This was in Chicago, about three years ago, when he was seventeen. The pay wasn't great considering the risk – it only occurred to him later that the work was actually dangerous. The diamonds were carried in a backpack, nothing more. There were no guards, no one to watch his back, just him and a backpack coming in and out from the cutters' and setters' studios to the shops and dealers on State Street. He blended in with the students and tourists, no one had any idea. He would be crossing the road with dirt-poor people, and if you've ever visited Chicago you see some dirt-poor people, who had no idea that right next to them, right within reach, was more money than they would ever make, all in one bag.

Pakosta leaned forward and asked Kiprowski if he missed Chicago. Kiprowski nodded, and Pakosta sat back.

'Shut your face. It's a shit-hole. The whole town is a shitty place.'

'I like Chicago.' Sutler shook his head at Pakosta, and straightened the headphones.

Kiprowski turned away and smiled to himself.

Pakosta shrugged. 'Why don't you two just get a room?'

When the blades fired up, the vehicle shook so violently that it seemed to Rem that something was wrong, but no one else appeared alarmed. Kiprowski, shoulders shaking, kept his face turned to the window. Sand curtained up and pillowed out, and they rose with the blades' vibrations riveting through them. The motion made Pakosta laugh, and the pilot asked him to switch his comm-link off. Pakosta whooped and cheered, he loved this, he said, his hips, his shoulders, his head shivering, everything about it. Shot out of a gun. He slapped Kiprowski's thigh and asked if he liked this. He wasn't nervous, was he?

*

Following Sutler's example, Rem and Kiprowski ducked as they disembarked, and ran in a squat. Pakosta swaggered across the airfield with his pack on his back. Sutler held out his badge as he approached the hangar and said to the first of two guards that he was supposed to meet Tom Markland.

The guard held out his hand and stopped them. The pass wasn't enough. Immediately exasperated, Sutler said it would have to do. 'Tom Markland,' he said, 'is waiting.'

The guard conferred on his radio. No, there wasn't any Markland at CIPA any more.

Sutler struggled to explain. 'Markland. The secretary to the Deputy Administrator. Tom Markland?' When this produced no result he asked to meet with the bursar.

Behind them a group of vehicles waited to mount a ramp into the open dock of a C-130 Hercules – the entire tail split open for loading.

The guard struck his hand up to his earpiece. As far as he knew Tom Markland was no longer at Southern-CIPA. 'Howell likes to rotate his boys. He's gone already. You can speak with the bursar but it won't do you any good.' The officer pointed to the aircraft.

If they walked over, he'd radio the bursar for them.

'What's his name?' Sutler fell back as they walked toward the Hercules.

'The bursar?' Kiprowski looked shocked. 'I thought you had it?'

'I can't remember.'

'I think it's Hispanic. Like Ramirez? Hernandez?'

'Leave it to me.' Pakosta walked confidently ahead. 'These are my people. I know the language.'

Sutler pinched the bridge of his nose. This wasn't helping. Rem kept pace, fascinated to see Sutler flustered. A forgotten name could be a bad omen.

While Rem had seen these aircraft before, it was only now, on approaching, that he appreciated its size. Pakosta craned to see inside and laughed. Two forklifts worked in alternation, one in, one out, each picking up one pallet at a time. The pallets were loaded with square white blocks wrapped in clear plastic, each about the size of a washing machine, which the forklifts brought down to the runway and set on either side of the ramp under the aircraft's vast stubby grey tail. Inside, two other forklifts drew the pallets closer to the loading bay.

'That's money.' Sutler pointed at the pallets.

Rem didn't believe him. Pakosta swore. Kiprowski wanted to take a closer look.

'I'm serious.'

'How much do you think that is?'

Sutler shook his head. He had no idea.

A man of tight proportion, the bursar, came out from the aircraft's belly, a clipboard in hand, clippered hair, pressed shirt, a figure from another generation.

'You're Stephen Sutler? You're looking for me?' He picked Sutler out of the group and offered his hand. 'How can I help you?'

Sutler explained that they had come to collect money and that arrangements were made by HOSCO directly with Tom Markland.

'It doesn't quite work that way. This is earmarked for the ministries. Some goes to the projects, but that's not my say.' The bursar held the clipboard up to his chest. 'But I can tell you yours isn't on my list. You'll need to speak with the CAs at the regional office. They hold some currency in the offices, so he might have it there for you. Now I'm afraid I'm going to have to ask you to leave.'

Rem couldn't take his eyes off the pallets, bright white blocks, with the sun hard upon them. One block alone must surely represent more money than he would earn in his entire life, and there were how many? Twenty-three, twenty-five, nine, thirty-four pallets, so far, sitting about them.

Sutler explained the shipments: the money was divvied up prior to shipping and sent directly to the regional offices, in this case from Newark to Amrah City, as they could not trust ground transport once they were on site. The first batch had been set with dye packs which had burst when the pallets were off-loaded and set in the sun, necessitating the destruction of $1.5 million. It wasn't just a myth, they'd brought in a special team to dispose of the money, incinerated it right on the airfield. The men Sutler needed to suck up to were much like the bursar, wormy officials, thinner than starved cattle, whose selfworth, it seemed to Rem, was increased by their proximity to so much money. These were the managers. The men who guarded the money and manned the transports were from Special Services provided by HOSCO – heavy-set men, wrestlers dressed in police-department drag, with black flak jackets and automatic weapons, sunglasses so dark you couldn't see their eyes, so they struck a kind of irony and seemed to be playing themselves, feature-version, not quite real.

Security had increased since Rem's first visit, and they found the compound barricaded behind a concrete blast wall and double wall of sandbags topped with razor wire. Out on the street a guard post and a row of concrete bollards with chains reached between them cut access to the road. The worry of a car bomb (or suicide bomber bounding over the barricades making it right to the front of the building) made security a clumsy affair of blocks and stoppages. Inside, sandbags obscured three-quarters of the windows so the offices took on a dry air of reflected, indirect light.

They were met inside the entrance by an officer dressed exactly like the bursar, who introduced himself as Howell's clerk. Squires, Markland's replacement, would see them in Howell's office. Rem had seen some young people working in Iraq (among them Fatboy, Samuels, Chimeno, Kiprowski, and Pakosta, who ranged from their late teens to their early twenties), but this boy looked like he didn't yet shave, and Rem found this disturbing. He wasn't an *officer* but an *intern*. The clerk assured Rem that there would be protection once they'd taken possession of the money; someone would see them back to the airport. There was also money for that. 'People watch the office,' he gestured to the street, 'they know what happens here. Somehow the word gets out.'

Sutler struggled with the information that Markland had left. 'I spoke with him yesterday. He said nothing. Everything was set up with Markland.'

'Squires has been briefed.'

While they walked to Howell's office the boy made a casual comment that the building needed retrofitting. They were going to ask HOSCO to make a survey to see what needed to be done to make it more secure. 'These aren't solid, these are prefabs, not much more than a trailer. We're a whole lot more vulnerable than we look. You could kick your way into here.' The boy spoke in a flat voice. 'You'd be surprised what you have to think about.'

The clerk knocked on Howell's door.

Squires called out that the door was open: on Howell's desk sat a small packet, a box which might, in other circumstances, contain a cake.

'Just you two.' He pointed his pen at Sutler and Kiprowski and told them to close the door.

The clerk made his excuses and Rem waited with Pakosta who still seemed steamed about the earlier exchange with Kiprowski. He dressed his agitation with further indignation: Sutler.

'You're sure you're not making a mistake?' he asked. 'He's soft. He has stuff going on you know nothing about.'

'There's no other *stuff*, Pakosta. He's employed by HOSCO the same as you and me.'

'Why don't you ask your wife? She knows more about what's going on here. You have no clue.'

Kiprowski came out of the offices and signalled to Rem. 'You'd better come in.'

Rem found Sutler standing in front of Howell's desk, looking small. Kiprowski stopped at the door.

Squires spoke without looking at Rem, his fingers spread to play chords at the edge of his desk. 'Can you tell me how HOSCO know about the shipments to Camp Liberty?'

'What shipments?'

Squires pushed his chair away from the desk. 'The shipments of military property to Camp Liberty.'

'You mean the boat?'

'What has this to do with HOSCO? This is none of their business. These matters lay outside their interests. I'd like to know how they know.'

Rem shrugged. 'I don't see the difference?'

Sutler bowed his head. 'He's telling us we can't have the money. He wants to know how HOSCO managed to hear about the transports being made to Camp Liberty.'

'I told them. Why wouldn't I?'

Squires shook his head. 'Those vehicles and the property on which they are kept are managed by the United States military under our authority. Why didn't you come to us? This is Southern-CIPA's business, it has nothing to do with HOSCO. You will leave them where they are.'

Rem said, 'I wanted to know what we were supposed to do about the vehicles on the Beach.'

Sutler held up his hands in submission. 'I'm here for money. That's all I'm here for. This doesn't involve my project.'

'Well, you've wasted your time.' Squires slapped his hands on the armrests, satisfied with himself. 'I can't just hand out money. You've raised these orders without any permissions from the divisional director. They need to come through the proper channels.'

'There isn't a director for this region in post. You know that.' Sutler leaned over the table.

Squires continued unabated. 'Once you have those orders properly countersigned we can see about distributing whatever amounts you need. I can't give you the money until you've followed the proper procedures. It takes twenty-one days.'

'This is childish.'

'No. This is about 1.4 million dollars. That's what you're asking for. We can't release any monies without the proper guarantees about how it's going to be spent.'

'I've been through all of this with Markland. Let me contact HOSCO.'

'No. It can't be arranged over the phone. You need the proper authorization *on paper.*'

When Sutler protested, Squires folded his arms. 'I've explained what you need to do, I don't understand why you're still here.'

Sutler walked out of the office, bypassing Kiprowski and Rem.

On the return flight Sutler sat apart from the crew. HOSCO would deal with this, he said, and they would still be paid for what they'd done today, and maybe there would be something extra in it for them as this wasn't any part of their normal duties. Pakosta and Kiprowski exchanged glances.

Sutler spoke more privately with Rem. 'We have to come back.'

'I'm about done with these people.' Rem enjoyed the certainty of this thought.

'Did you notice the photographs?'

Rem said he hadn't.

'In Howell's office. Did you notice the photograph behind Squires?'

Rem said no.

'I've not met Howell. I take it he has white hair?' Sutler appeared to refigure the idea as he expressed it. 'In the photograph there's a man with white hair on a boat. This is Howell. Do you know what his hobbies are?' Sutler waited for a guess, which Rem didn't provide. 'Sailing.

He likes boats. Do you know what he did when he took Pakosta and the others to Kuwait?'

'No.'

'He went sailing.'

'I don't see the problem. So the boat belongs to Howell?'

'After I left Howell's office I went to speak with the CA. The Civil Authority coordinate everything that happens at Southern-CIPA. These people are the muscles to an overworked brain. There were no records of any deliveries coming to Camp Liberty. You've seen those Chinooks, every other day something new comes over, but there's no record. They're all missing. The equipment was moved without proper authorization. I don't know why, but it looks like Howell is using military resources to move his own property without proper authority, Squires and Markland must know this, that's why they aren't pleased that HOSCO knows. Have you seen the boxes? Have you checked what's in them?'

'Explosives for the burn pits.'

'But have you looked?'

Rem said no. The boxes were all marked the same. He assumed they all held flares and grenades for the burn pits.

As soon as they arrived back at Camp Liberty, Rem and Sutler checked the crates stored in the Quonset.

'Have you spoken with anyone else about this?'

Sutler said no. It wasn't something he'd properly thought through. Not that it made absolute sense to him at this moment. 'I don't know Howell. And I don't know why anyone would be doing this. But it seems bizarre.'

The crates could not be moved by two men, so Sutler found Kiprowski, and when they still couldn't move them Kiprowski was sent to find Samuels. These two, Rem believed, could be trusted.

Inside the first crate, packed in moulded sections, they found industrial equipment. None of them could make sense out of the parts or tell if they were weaponry or machinery. The oiled metal left a residue on their hands, retained their hand and fingerprints, and Rem said they should just leave it as it is.

In the third and fourth crates they found explosives, the same baton grenades they used for the fires. In the smaller pits they simply used flares, set trails of gasoline, lines of fuel to light the fires. The quantity of explosives surprised Rem, it wouldn't be possible to use everything they were supplied with – but this also didn't seem out of the ordinary. They had more water than they needed, they also had a surplus of toilet rolls.

Rem and Sutler sat by the Quonset door, which reminded Rem of a gas station: the open door, the scrappy road, a building busy with crates and boxes, the smell of oil.

☆

Cathy checked her emails after work.

C,

No change. He hit his head when he fell so they don't know for sure what's causing the problem. They give him something to make him sleep, and yesterday he said he had more feeling back in his arms. Thnx for the info – the doctors said they needed to know exactly what he was exposed to, so this helps, I guess, but the list is so long they're going to wait for the results of the earlier tests first. Otherwise, we don't know what to do for him.

JW

Jonnie,

I've spoken with the lawyer I mentioned earlier who has represented people like your brother. He's collecting information, and I've given him everything I have. I've also given him your name, if that's ok, and he'll be in touch once he gets it all together. I think I told you that I met with the company and I have a recording of that meeting where she says that all of the burn pits have been closed and they're sending an assessment team to take samples and see what they've been burning. I've no faith in this actually happening, but she said it to my face and I have it on my cellphone. If this moves fast enough there might be some money for the medical expenses, if not now then later.

When I hear more I'll be back in touch. In the meantime, I hope Paul continues with his recovery.

Cathy

☆

Santo gone. Pakosta gone. Kiprowski gone. Sutler gone. Chimeno, Clark, gone and gone, a weekend in Bahrain with Howell, and Watts back home: everyone away except Samuels (which, to Rem's thinking, was pretty much like shepherding a lame, wet dog).

Rem couldn't sleep in a room on his own, nor in his cot, so he moved to Kiprowski's with the notion that this would compensate: a different perspective on the same room, a relief from his own stale mattress and pillow – not that he could distinguish Kiprowski's smell from his own. He attempted to sleep in his shorts and T-shirt, then naked, then fully clothed, then just for a laugh, tried on clothes he found in a bag under the cot, and realized once he was dressed that these were Amer Hassan's trousers and T-shirt, unwashed. A dead man's clothes lovingly folded in a doubled plastic bag.

Samuels' company was worse than no company at all. The boy, a lanky blankness, came to him panicked with a message from HOSCO saying that inspectors would come to confirm compliance with the closure of the burn pits.

Rem asked Samuels to join him on a drive through the camp, and found the boy unsettled by the news because he didn't want to return home. Rem didn't press for details.

'Your contract with HOSCO still runs for the next couple of months, but you'll be working with Sutler, and he'll organize what happens, and there'll be more work if that's what you want.'

This confused Samuels even more. 'You're leaving?'

Rem didn't want to answer. The air stank of burning oil, a sense of trouble coming toward them, faint at first, a little doubtful, but definite as they came to the pits. Fires sparked up independently once in a while. From Pit 3 rose slow wisps, the soft green-black of a mallard's neck. Not trusting the smell or the colour Rem took Samuels up to the Beach and they both looked out at the horizon. Samuels held his hand up to his face, sheltered his eyes, his watch caught the sun.

'What's that on your wrist?'

Samuels looked at the watch.

'Nothing.'

Rem took hold of Samuels' arm and looked closely at the watch.

'How did you get a Breitling?'

'I bought it from Santo.'

'Santo sold you a Breitling?'

'I won it playing poker.'

'Do you know how much a watch like this is worth?'

Samuels looked at his watch with a little more curiosity. 'Sure,' he said. 'It's a Breitling. Santo picked it up on his way back from Kuwait.'

'And how did Santo manage to buy a Breitling?'

'Maybe Howell gave it to him? I don't know.' Samuels began to sound uncertain.

'Howell?'

'It was part of the pay. He said we were working for him, not HOSCO, and this was on top of the work we were doing.'

'Was this just for Santo?'

'We all had a choice, cash or pick out something. Everyone picked a watch.'

'A Breitling? How many did he buy?'

'I don't know.' Now Samuels sounded defensive.

'What did he give you?'

'A watch and cash.'

'He gave you cash? How much, exactly?'

Samuels muttered his reply.

'I didn't catch that.'

'I picked a different watch and he made up the difference because it was cheaper.' Samuels nodded. 'A hundred, a hundred and fifty.' Then in a smaller voice, 'Four hundred and seventy, something like that.'

'He bought you a watch and he gave you over four hundred dollars, and you accepted these gifts?'

'He said it was pay. He said it didn't matter.' Samuels shrugged, a little insulted by Rem's questions. 'It wasn't just me.'

'And none of you thought this was strange? From the Deputy Administrator?'

'There's no harm done. It's his money.'

This, Rem recognized, sounded more like Santo than Samuels. Samuels held out his hand, flat, palm up, a gesture meaning, *look about you, come on, take a look, exactly what is normal here?* And Rem considered this gesture to be borrowed, although he could not place the quote.

☆

Rem's relief at the return of the men to Camp Liberty lasted as long as it took them to disembark. Pakosta came first, striding as usual, unbowed by the downdraught, the force of noise from the engines – and something wrong with his face Rem didn't catch – then Santo, then Sutler, who hurried out with papers tucked under his arm. Everyone but Sutler said they would walk to the camp or just continued walking without any word to Rem, and they set off in a broken line, no one talking.

Sutler sat beside Rem, red-faced.

'What's going on?'

'You need to speak with them. They started fighting. Santo and Pakosta and Clark, a proper fight. I've never seen anything like it. Halfway through the flight Clark just got up and punched Pakosta in the face, took his mobile and smashed it.'

After returning to the camp the men stayed in the cabins so that the camp still seemed empty. Rem left them to it, allowed them to keep to themselves through the day. In the early evening he joined them and began chatting with Chimeno. The boy, unaccountably sullen, spoke about his father. He'd worked with him one summer, and one time, he remembered, 'They had to close off Michigan Avenue to fly in an air-conditioning unit, a coolant system for an entire building. Bigger than a house.'

'All well and good, Chimeno, but I want to know what happened in Bahrain.'

Chimeno ignored the question. 'The unit was carried to the roof by helicopter, and they dropped it through a hole in the roof.' He couldn't describe how perfect this was, that something so massive could be matched so exactly. Rem listened to him and thought nothing of the story, except, in telling it, Chimeno sounded sad, regretful.

'Bahrain?'

'It's real isn't it? The Massive. It's happening.'

'What happened in Bahrain? What was the fight about?'

Chimeno shook his head. He didn't know anything about any fight.

'Sutler saw it. Everyone saw it. None of you are talking. What happened? Did Howell give you anything? Did he give you all gifts? Is that was this was about?'

Chimeno picked up a pair of gloves, shook off the sand, and said he should get back to work.

Rem found Sutler and said he was getting nothing from the men.

'They're working.' Sutler pointed across the lit plain at the men digging shallow pits in the shale.

'Everyone's blowing smoke.'

'I don't know anything more than what I've told you. Clark was playing with his phone one minute, the next he was on his feet thumping Pakosta.'

'So Clark started this.'

'It might have started earlier. None of them looked happy yesterday morning.' Sutler indicated that he was busy. 'I'm going to Amrah tomorrow morning. I need permits and money. I need to get ready.'

Once the work was completed Rem found Pakosta at the Beach with a small hurricane lamp beside him. He was sullen, untalkative, and Rem stood over him with a bottle of whisky, a gift from Sutler.

'You're quiet.'

'I'm often quiet.'

Pakosta shrugged, so Rem sat beside him and offered him the bottle. 'So why are you here?'

'I have a deep and sensitive side. I'm misunderstood. Sometimes I like to come out here and write poetry. I don't fucking know.' Pakosta took the bottle. 'What did you say this was?'

'Malt. Single malt.'

'I prefer bourbon.' He swallowed and winced. His tooth, he said, needed seeing to the next time he was in Amrah.

'You're going with Sutler tomorrow?'

'Sutler. He's keeping us here scratching our balls for nothing. We're wasting time. Tell me, why did you pick me?'

Rem let the sand slide over his shoes. 'I had a list.'

'Oh, I heard about this list.' Pakosta couldn't help but smile. 'The Kennedy Club.'

'Is that what they called it?'

'What was his name again? The boy who shot himself.'

'Billy. Fatboy.'

'Fatboy kept the book. Santo ran the club.'

'It doesn't make any difference.'

'You want to know how Santo made his money? He managed the rotas.'

Rem said it didn't matter any more what the list was or what it meant or who managed it.

'You're really interesting, you know that? I just told you that your friend deliberately manipulated the work rotas. He sent people out on the streets of Amrah increasing the chances that they might get killed. He worked the odds. And you just suck it all in.' Pakosta shook the bottle and rolled the bourbon about the sides. 'You had no right bringing us here. Whatever the reason, you had no right.' He took another mouthful of scotch. 'You know this is all fake? It's all a scam.' Pakosta held Rem's eye until he turned away. 'There isn't going to be a *Massive*. Ask Howell. Stephen Sutler doesn't know what he's doing. The whole thing is a scam. And the burn pits, ask Howell about the burn pits, and ask him about the enquiry that's coming, and how they're coming to see exactly what was being burned here. Ask him about how HOSCO manages any complaints, how they've screwed everyone who worked at Camp Bravo and how we'll be hung out to dry because what gets burned here is our responsibility. Ask Howell about that. See,' Pakosta jabbed a finger at Rem, 'you always have to read the fine print.'

Rem said that HOSCO was responsible for the shipments.

'What I don't understand is how you ever got involved.' Pakosta's expression turned pinched and nasty. 'Santo says you have a friend. Someone in HOSCO. Why don't you ask him some of these questions, because you won't want any of us talking with him.'

'What happened in Bahrain?'

'Nothing.'

'Why did Clark attack you?'

'Because he has issues.' Pakosta stood up and complained as he slipped down the hill that nothing could be done around here without it becoming some kind of complicated ass-fucking. At the bottom of the dune Pakosta shouted up.

'Tomorrow, you're going to thank me. I've sorted everything out. If we'd left it to you we'd be in the same shit as those sorry-assed fucks at Camp Bravo. I'm changing the landscape, Rem. Tomorrow.'

Rem woke Clark up. Knocked on the door and walked in.

'I need to know what this is all about. Someone needs to talk to me.'

Clark sat up, addled. Rem switched on the light. Across the room in tidy piles were drawings, sketches of the burn pits.

'I don't know what you mean.'

'You punched Pakosta in the mouth. You assaulted him. Everyone saw it.'

Clark looked down at his feet, considering.

'So what did you fight about?'

'I don't know.'

'Why did you go for Pakosta?'

'I don't know.'

'So why did you volunteer to go with Pakosta to Amrah tomorrow.'

'To keep an eye on him.'

'And why would you need to do that?'

'Because it's something I want to do.'

'What's happening tomorrow?'

Clark shook his head. 'Just leave it, Rem. What you don't know can't hurt you.'

On the way to his room Rem saw Chimeno out by the Quonset. When he walked toward him Chimeno signalled that they should go inside.

Chimeno immediately began to talk about the trip.

It wasn't like any of them had wanted to go, but once they were on their way they were up for it. Howell had booked himself one big suite, the others had rooms on the floor underneath, except Sutler and Kiprowski, who were on the other side of the hotel, and he didn't see much of either of them. Sutler and Kiprowski didn't have to wear uniforms either.

The hotel was made out like a palace. Howell's room had a foyer with an actual fountain in the middle. All over there were pictures of this one guy in Arab dress. Completely over the top. The second floor wasn't even finished, and the pool was this massive thing, lit up at night. The whole place was over the top, although it wasn't like there was a Motel 8 round the corner, or any other choice, just this palace smack in the middle of the desert. The security also was over the top.

He'd never seen a place so large in his life.

Chimeno said he had trouble sleeping. The room was too big, and he could hear this couple, you know, above. The room, nice as it was, caught everything. The front was glass, pretty much, a window and a balcony, so he heard every little detail. First off it was just the physical sounds, the man's effort, and later instructions, it was hard to tell how many people were in the room. At two o'clock the noise quietened down but started up again at around three, and when it turned bad, shouting, he got dressed and went down to the pool.

'I found Clark by the pool. He looked a mess, his shirt all over the place, like he'd been drinking. He'd been up in Howell's room with the others.'

Chimeno stopped talking. Rem asked him to continue, it didn't matter what he had to say.

'The thing is, the noise I could hear, it was Santo and everyone, and they were having a party with a girl laid on by Howell.'

'Where was Howell?'

'That's the thing. The noise came from Howell's room, right above mine.'

'Was he at this party?'

'I don't know. I'd guess so. In the morning I went up and changed and got ready. The others, when they came out, didn't say anything. But they looked bad, all of them.' Chimeno became anxious. 'I wasn't anything to do with this. I only heard stuff, I wasn't in the room.'

'So what was the fight about between Clark and Pakosta?'

'Someone sent him an SMS, and it had a link. Someone had taken a video.'

'And what was it?'

'Pakosta and a woman.'

The flight left early. Running out across the sand Pakosta held on to his helmet, wincing into the blast.

Rem, who hadn't slept much, asked Pakosta how his tooth was, and buckling up his harness Pakosta said *what tooth*.

'I want to speak with you when you get back.'

Kiprowski slipped out from behind him and climbed into the helicopter, a backpack in his fist. He sat on the far side and did not speak as he sorted out the straps. Sutler also appeared stern, unhappy, not quite his usual self.

Rem ran back to the Quonset and watched the helicopter rise then veer sideways above the Beach.

☆

Geezler's response came just as she was preparing to leave.

> Dear Cathy Gunnersen,
>
> We would like to thank you for your communication with the Advisor to the Division Chief, Europe, Paul Geezler. We have consulted with Mr. Geezler who is unfortunately not available to meet you in Detroit this weekend, and who has no knowledge of meeting or working with your husband.
>
> If we can further assist you in this matter, please contact our employment services and HE division based in Cleveland, particularly Sue Williams, Overseas Personnel Director.
>
> Sincerely,
>
> M. Waites for Paul Geezler, Advisor to the Division Chief, Europe, for HOSCO International.

Cathy sat on her own at the taqueria. It wasn't usual, she thought, for a woman to eat on her own, and she came here often enough. The only other women were girls who stopped briefly to flirt with the cook or the boys waiting tables, or family friends, who in any case always took their food with them. She wondered if she made them uncomfortable.

Geezler's email was what she'd expected, more or less. As far as Rem had explained the man was working independently anyhow, and she should have contacted him some other way. She noted that the notice listing his participation in the conference had been taken off-line.

A woman watched her from the doorway, and it took Cathy a while to recognize her as Roscoe's aunt. The woman scowled at her through the glass, but wasn't bold enough to come inside. Cathy finished her meal, took a while to wipe her fingers on a napkin, and thought, whatever this was, she could really do without it.

The woman came at her with surprising speed, so fast that Cathy backed off, arms up for protection.

'You stay away from him. You're disgusting. How old are you? What do you want with him? He's a boy. You come anywhere near him and I'll call the police. You hear me.'

Cathy froze in place. The woman bowed, wheezed, the energy required suddenly spent. Then, without warning, she took out a container and threw the contents over her.

*

485

Nut jumped as Cathy came into the apartment. Cathy kicked the door closed and clawed to get out of her clothes. It was urine, she was sure of it, the woman had thrown urine over her, and most of it had hit her blouse, although some, she was certain, was in her hair. Cathy stripped in the entrance then ran to the bathroom and stood in the shower. Appalled by what had just happened.

She threw the clothes away. Couldn't be entirely certain of the substance thrown at her, but understood the intent. She held up her hands and was surprised not to see them shaking.

When things happen, she told herself, as long as you're not harmed, you have a choice over how you handle it. This meant nothing. It closed an episode, perhaps, but as an event it was unattached to anything else that was happening. Not everything connects.

☆

The first explosion came an hour after Sutler's departure. A hollow pop from the burn pits. Rem walked down the track and when the second explosion came he saw smoke rise from the Beach, not the burn pits.

He arrived as the third and fourth bursts broke above the dune in a hail of debris and sand that hissed as it fell – and saw Samuels standing on the Beach with grenades. Little remained of the boat, an outline, flats and scraps of fibreglass spread across the dune.

Rem asked what he was doing. 'Did Sutler tell you to do this?'

Samuels looked at his watch and asked if it mattered. Anyway, he was done now.

The news of the assault on the regional government at their offices in Southern-CIPA was quickly followed by the news of Kiprowski's and Sutler's deaths.

A small convoy of military police arrived late in the afternoon and immediately cordoned off Pakosta's and Clark's cabins, and took Rem into the Quonset to answer questions. Southern-CIPA had come under mortar attack. The offices of the Deputy Administrator had taken a direct hit. The Deputy Administrator was in the adjoining office at the time and had suffered burns. The two men inside his office, Kiprowski and Sutler, were killed, and they would be identified by their DNA, there were specialists flying in from Germany who would assist.

Rem couldn't see why Pakosta's and Clark's belongings were being taken, and the guards would not explain, except to say that both of them were unharmed, they were at the front of the building when it came under fire, and had suffered nothing more than a few scratches in their scramble to get clear. In Sutler's cabin they found a mason jar with a number of red and black scorpions inside. The man who found them hurled the jar over the Quonset before Rem could stop him.

THE PLAINS

Rem kept a newspaper transcript of an interview with Paul Geezler.

In its way, he thought, it was a work of art.

On hindsight: *We could see how things were going, I doubt anyone knew the scale exactly, but it was possible, early on, to see the circumstances, if you like, the pre-existing conditions, but none of us knew what would happen. The system was more vulnerable than any of us realized.*

I can see why this has drawn the attention it has. We're six weeks on from the assault, and we're still finding out what happened. We're coming up to an election and if there's a new administration they're going to want answers. I want answers, and we're working hard to find them. Everyone wants to know why this happened and how it happened, and hopefully this is something the hearings can resolve next May.

On Sutler: *We're committed to finding this man, to bringing him to justice. Like everyone else the first I heard about him was the day Southern-CIPA was attacked. We have good people out there looking for him, and I'm confident he'll be found. It's only a matter of time.*

On the burn pits: *We know a lot more now than we did two, three weeks ago. New information is coming to light about these rogue operations. The pits at Camp Bravo were abandoned, and we've since learned about the illegal burnings there, and given that the same thing was happening at Camp Liberty it's clear that projects like these were not appropriately monitored. More globally, it's clear that the speed at which everything was ending wasn't manageable. Anyone could see that the burn pits were a problem at a number of levels. You can't close down an operation of that size in such a short time.*

On his culpability: *By the time we get to the hearings it will be almost a year after the fact. The enquiry is digging in all sorts of directions and we'll have to see what comes up. Given the work I've done since, the responsibilities I've undertaken, and all of the changes HOSCO has undergone, it's not a surprise that my name has come up. It's after the fact. I have to accept that the work I'm doing will make me a target in some way. I did, it's true, accompany the European Division Chief to Amrah. We were there one night. I think we made fourteen visits to other sites across Europe also in the same month. You have to look closely at the other testimonies, and how they say I was involved. I'm supposed to have spoken with Sutler on the phone. On the phone. There's no record of those calls. More importantly, there's no record in Southern-CIPA of any involvement from any of the staff from Europe. Southern-CIPA handled the money. Paul Howell was the man responsible for the funding, he's the man to concentrate on. This, I hope, is where the enquiry will focus.*

On the day of Geezler's appointment as Deputy Director to the Middle East, Santo called Rem. 'He stepped on our backs, he rode us the entire time.'

The Chicago train arrived early morning at Kansas City. Bound for Los Angeles, it paused in the station for several hours, and while this was Rem's stop he decided to wait for the moment, sleep, get off the train before it departed. But when the heating clicked off the carriages quickly cooled and the dim light and bustle on the station kept him awake. It made little sense to him that the train would be so slow, that something so American could be so backward, so of another period. The trains in Europe were sleeker and faster.

He walked stiffly at first, and made his way through to the terminal, then set his cases beside a bench and decided to sleep sitting upright until a reasonable hour. Samuels lived in a town called Topeka several hours away. As he wasn't expected, Rem imagined that any time between midday and late afternoon would be the best time to arrive, the best time to conduct the kind of conversation they needed to have.

He drove over the plains, the rising downs, a soft snow slipping into rain already settled in the bristled fields. The roads rode the backs of the hills, small and regular enough to suggest an endlessness. Little changed, and when he came to Topeka he thought it familiar: the Holiday Inns and motels bordering the highway, the closer lots of white clapboard houses, the train line skirting the centre, an unremarkable main street of coffee houses and closed-down stores. You'd fight hard to leave such a place, and it would live on in you in some way, a measure for every other town you'd visit.

At first he couldn't imagine Samuels living here, and drove through the centre to see how far the town stretched. When he arrived at a golf course he turned about, and thought that the place was hollow, dropped down rather than evolved. This definition was Cathy's. Having come from a small town herself, she had the belief that these smaller places followed one of two possibilities. Either they morphed out of the landscape and had a peculiar logic (grain stores at the railyard), or they were deposited, designed elsewhere and dumped. Much like Camp Liberty, Topeka could be erased by one strong wind. The evening before the trip Rem had sought out Camp Liberty on the internet, located the very spot identified by Watts by GPS and found nothing: in six weeks they'd wiped it clean, packed it up like it had never happened.

On his second approach he made a more direct route, and found the Samuels' house without trouble. Sat on a corner lot, fenceless, slightly raised from the street on a small hill; the lawn rode up to the house, which, being raised and ringed with posts, gave the impression that it stood on tiptoes. A familiar variation on familiar features: a sunroom, an enclosed patio, a raised veranda, a separate garage.

A woman, Samuels' mother, came to the door, head down, unsurprised at the call, old and disorderly. She listened while Rem asked for Samuels, then looked up, dithering, and Rem could see that she was almost completely blind, her irises clouded, her face used and lined and white. She turned away, squinting, lips slightly parted as if thinking, and walked slowly back into the house, leaving the door ajar, her house-shoes scuffing the floor. Dressed in a nightgown and cardigan, her hair flattened from sleep, she looked not long out of bed, although by now it was almost mid-morning. Samuels came through from the kitchen, leaned toward her and asked impatiently what she thought she was doing, then led her further back into the house. *Come on*, he spoke, half cajoling, half encouraging, *come on*.

In the six weeks since he'd last seen Samuels the boy had hollowed out, not a boy so much, but someone like his mother, who looked weary – and how thin he appeared, his stomach scooped out, his T-shirt hanging between his shoulder-blades. Samuels guided his mother to the kitchen, and turned only at the threshold as if remembering that she had only just answered the door – and saw Rem, half in, half out. Unsurprised. He signalled with one hand that he would be a minute.

Rem stepped into the hall to show his determination, and found the house not to be quite so grand inside, a little bare, undusted, unkempt.

Samuels returned with the same sloping stride, feet barely rising from the floor. He couldn't leave her alone, he said. 'It's just us. My father's at work. You can come in.'

He didn't ask why Rem had come, or even how he was, and made no comment about how he looked, but brought him into the family room with resignation.

'We don't use this room much.' He indicated a choice of seats. 'She likes the kitchen. Or she stays in bed. Most days.' Samuels remained standing, shoulders braced, hands dug into his pockets, he looked at the floor and wouldn't look directly at Rem through much of their conversation.

'I heard from Watts.' Rem offered a gentle start.

'I heard he had a lung removed.'

'They took out part.'

Samuels dug his hands deeper and still would not look up. 'They can do that?'

'He's better. He's out of hospital and back with his wife.' Rem sat forward and cleared his throat. 'I'll get to the point.'

'I don't know what I can tell you. I don't know anything more than I've already told the enquiry. I told them everything I know.'

'They're saying Sutler wasn't his real name. They're saying Sutler was working for Howell.'

'I don't know anything.'

'I'm going to see Kiprowski's family. His mother wants to know what happened. The family have a right.'

'I still don't know anything.'

Rem stared hard at Samuels' downturned face. 'They picked him up in pieces. You know that?'

'You should have called. I could have saved you coming. I don't know anything. I'd like to help you, but I don't know anything.'

'He was running from the office, that's what they said. They said he was running away. He had his back to the office and he was heading toward an exit.'

'I work for my brother. I'll have to go soon.'

'He was running away. He was trying to leave the building.' Rem waited. 'Which means he had an idea about what was going to happen. I think there's some other story to this.'

'I'll have to go. I don't have my car.'

'I can take you.'

'I can walk. I have to go.' He looked back toward the kitchen. 'Once she's up we have a neighbour look in.' Samuels turned away.

'Kiprowski talked with you. He would have told you what he was thinking. He would have explained himself to someone before he did this.'

'I told you, I know nothing. The same as I told the enquiry. The same as I'll tell them at the hearing. He didn't speak to me. He never talked to me. I don't know anything.'

'I can wait. I can sit in the car and I can wait.'

Samuels, now in the hall, wiped his face with his hands, his cuffs rode down his arms. 'I'm sorry you wasted your time.'

'You don't wear your watch any more?'

'They took it. They took everything.'

Samuels watched as Rem drove away.

Rem drove about the block and passed the house a second time to see Samuels still at the window. His face behind glass, static, the house bright about him, grander on the outside.

☆

Santo wasn't surprised at Samuels' reaction.

'That's how he was,' he shrugged, 'so it's not strange to hear that's how he is now.'

Santo kicked aside a small footstool, made room on the couch for Rem.

'I don't mind talking.' He cocked open a beer, handed it to Rem, then opened a second for himself. 'I don't see the sense in telling this at the hearing, but I don't mind telling you. I don't mind at all.'

In opposition to Samuels, Santo agreed to talk but would not allow himself to be recorded.

'There's no use for that. No point at all. This is for your ears only.' He sipped his beer and waited for Rem to switch off his phone. 'Kiprowski always stood up for Sutler, but Pakosta had it in for him from day one. You knew how it was. The boy was too sensitive, less use than Samuels. He had no business being there. You should speak with Pakosta. Once Sutler arrived everything went south. The pits were closed, Watts left, the translator died.'

495

'It didn't happen like that.'

Santo paused, thinking. 'You're right. It didn't. We took those trips, you know this, and there was everything you'd want, and we knew that Howell had his own thing going on. It was obvious the first time in Kuwait. He was spending money and it was clear that he didn't want for security, he just wanted us there. I don't know why, but he wanted us there alongside him. He had us shoot, that first time. He had a car – we were coming back from basic training, we had our guns with us, and he just pulled up the car, drove it off-road a ways and had us shoot it. He wanted to see us shoot. He wanted to see how the car stood up to it. No one wanted to do it at first, but once it started. So we wasted the car, for no reason. I think Pakosta knew something was up even before then – the others? I don't know. I don't think they wanted to know. Clark might have had some idea. We talked a little about it, about how strange it was that we'd be in these hotels, and how Howell was always pushing to take this, or use that, or do something. The man knew how to push. Pakosta didn't like it at all. And then there were those gifts which we didn't say no to exactly.'

Rem watched the cat stretch out on the newspaper and wanted it out of the room.

'You know he's from a religious family.'

'Pakosta?'

'Both his parents run some kind of ministry, some kind of nut-jobs. He talked about it once. Said he wasn't into any of it, but that they didn't like him being in Iraq. They were against the whole idea, but he owed money to his father, couldn't get himself ahead, and this was the quickest solution. It didn't hurt once those gifts started coming in. At first it was a watch, then some cash. On the second trip there was a whole lot more money going around, and Pakosta used this to pay off the debt to his father, which meant he could keep his house. Which isn't how things turned out. It was after that second trip that things started happening. Howell had been speaking with all of us, sending emails like he was our new best friend, and he knew what our situations were, and he started helping out, saying he could make a loan, help with payments on this and that. The third trip was a mistake. I don't know why Howell wanted Sutler and Kiprowski there. Like they were some kind of tourists or something. Kiprowski just wasn't made the same way as everyone else and he wasn't having any of Howell's gifts and couldn't see why we would either. You know Kiprowski stood up for Sutler? Kiprowski was convinced he wasn't involved. Said he was convinced that Sutler had nothing to do with it. But when Sutler explained how the money worked, and how much money was involved in the contracts he was writing, it started to make sense that Howell was just messing things up. Sutler said something about an inspection, that all of the finances for the civil projects were automatically investigated by HOSCO. I didn't understand, but it sounded like there was no way that Howell would get away with what he was doing. This all came out one evening, Sutler was just talking about business, I don't think he realized, and when he left, we all got to talking about the things Howell had done for each of us, small things, some not so small, and we realized he'd done that with everyone. The truth is we all talked about what to do. We all agreed that something had to be done but didn't have the nerve. The final straw was the news from Camp Bravo, and how lawyers were going after everyone involved in the burn pits. We didn't know what we were burning. No one knew. It wasn't any one person's idea. But we all agreed that this wouldn't go away unless we did something, and it wasn't like you could just tell Howell to stop. Pakosta put it all together. The idea was to get rid of the records. Howell's records, and the records for the burn pits. We knew that they wouldn't be able to trace anything if those records were destroyed, and that was the basic idea. Kiprowski volunteered because he didn't think Sutler was responsible, and because he didn't trust anyone else to do it properly. Sutler said that everything was recorded and kept in the Deputy Administrator's office. Pakosta had the idea that if it were all destroyed then there wouldn't be any proof.'

Santo leaned back and downed the last of the beer. 'It's not what you want to hear, I know that. But everyone agreed. As soon as we heard there was an inspection we knew we had to do something. You understand? We were all of us working toward something, it's not like we had a choice. The only thing we could do was destroy whatever records were in Howell's office. Make some chaos. Divert attention. Kiprowski just got it wrong, that's all. He knew what he was doing, but he just got it wrong. It was unfortunate, but he knew what he was getting himself into. He volunteered. Everybody had too much to lose. I know how that sounds. But that's exactly how it was.'

☆

Rem called Cathy from the motel room and sat on the bed counting folds in the curtain while he waited for her to answer, one wall a yellow curtain dressed with sour streetlight. How much time had he spent in such rooms: a room with two beds, a door beside a window, a bare light, centre-ceiling. The room, depressing enough, had no effect against the idea that he was alone, and how he'd never imagined this, could never have conceived that he would be separated from her in such a way.

After a shower he found a message from his wife in which she talked about HOSCO, only HOSCO, the information was accurate, certain of its facts. All of the men at Camp Liberty had received payment of some kind. A watch. Cash. A car. Rents paid. Loans paid. Advances made to mortgages. Medical payments erased. Debts settled. None of these payments were ever over five thousand, so they were easy enough to hide, and in each instance the payment or donation came directly from Howell himself or was traceable to him through his manipulation of the account system used by Southern-CIPA. 'I don't see anything in it but greed.'

Cathy, but not Cathy.

'There *is* a kind of logic. If you think of him like a child in a candy store, the unpopular kid buying friendship, that kind of thing, but it's clumsy, and he wasn't very good at it. There's evidence he was spending money then making it back by pilfering from other accounts. I'm guessing that storing the vehicles was a crude way of stocking up, putting together a marketable resource. One thing I don't get is how the companies he was working for, HOSCO, Credita, SIMLAC, Venture, given the contracts these companies were managing, especially HOSCO, how none of them were on to him sooner? They all have separate account trails. I'll have more of this together by Friday.'

When the message ended, he realized she'd called the wrong number, and when the phone began to ring again he leaned over the bed, watched *Cathy – Cell* light up the screen, the small phone vibrating the sheet.

She'd called the wrong number. She was sorry, but not sorry in a way, because she needed to speak with him. *Actually*, she didn't need to speak with him, but she had something to tell him. She had some things to say. First, she hadn't changed her mind. It wasn't *didn't want* so much as *wouldn't have*. She wanted to explain the distinction because, yes, she still loved him, she thought she still loved him, in fact she knew this to be the case, but she couldn't bear to go through this. After working so hard at the separation, she couldn't see herself working equally hard or possibly harder at getting back what they had. And there was no guarantee that they would even get back there, not really. All that work and no guarantee. She didn't have it in her, and doubted that she would find it. She wanted to explain, but couldn't find anything that wasn't clichéd, and wondered if that was how it worked? You get so tired that even the words, the phrases you need, are exhausted? She was worn out, and maybe if she was any other age and not thirty-seven she'd feel something else about the matter and find the energy to continue, or the fear not to be alone, but no, at thirty-seven she found she had nothing to invest and no real fear in starting over.

She wanted to say more, she said, but knew that this would be cruel.

She didn't want to see him, not at Thanksgiving, not at Christmas, that the effort required just to be in the same space with him right now was beyond her. She'd switched off. It was sad, but that's exactly how she felt about it, and she didn't imagine that this would change, although, who knows, she could be wrong.

As one final favour she gave him her final analysis on Camp Liberty: her idea on what had happened.

'You let people take advantage of you. It isn't that you're stupid, it's just that you don't see it. They were all running circles round you right from the beginning. The simple fact is you just continued to make the same mistake for the same reasons. You took a job without properly knowing what it involved, you stumbled into it and couldn't see your way out, so rather than drop what you'd gotten yourself into, you just continued.' And this, she thought, was the reasoning of an animal, something caught in brambles that pushes deeper into a briar without calculating and reasoning the best way out. 'It isn't your fault that you were used. Someone saw you coming, they recognized the kind of person you are, the opportunity was waiting for someone just like you to come along, and once you did, well . . . Did you ever seriously think any of this through? Did you ever sit down and ask yourself what you were doing? Did you ever think through the possibilities of what might happen? The consequence of this is real. One man is dead, another missing. Two men are sick, perhaps all of you, because you can't work yourself out of trouble.

'I know this isn't fair. I know this is holding you responsible for other people's actions. But you were part of it, and you'll have to come to terms with that. One way or another. You are, at root, entirely responsible.'

Rem lay in bed, sleepless. Sounds from the highway pressed upon him, busy, irregular traffic with no real lull or rhythm – the room disturbed with other people's noise, sliding doors, walls that unaccountably cracked, the air-conditioner's poorly tuned complaints. Just noise, and too much of it.

She didn't want him.

This idea made no sense. There wasn't anyone else. Baggage. This is what it all came down to. Trouble. *You're all inside out. You start where other men stop. Everyone else bears their trouble inside, but you, you dress yourself in it, it comes flying at you, attaches itself. You're too expensive to be around, it just takes too much.*

He parked opposite the store and asked himself if he couldn't do this in some other way?

Phone, email, letter?

This didn't need to happen face to face.

The car clicked with the heat. Midday and no other traffic, which couldn't happen on any other main street.

He couldn't see into the store with the sun hard overhead, a sign saying 'Kiprowski' in small gold script.

Kiprowski's mother – he knew the woman from first sight – with a crate of mangoes, leaned forward as she elbowed sideways out of the door.

With the mangoes set on a stand the woman still leaned forward, straightened when she saw him, noted his hesitation and told him he'd have to hurry if he'd come about the job as she was expecting some-one.

In the window: a hammer, replacement blades for a bandsaw, a single dead wasp.

Back in the car one block on, he could remember the wasp and how it curved into itself, but couldn't form the woman's face, except the hair, that brown bob. Young hair, old face.

He hadn't told her that her son was not liked. That he wasn't popular. He hadn't explained how distraught her son had become on the death of the translator, a man from the Yemen who was married, had children, and who'd died in an accident, a death only slightly more pointless and senseless than the death of her son.

What had he said? He'd said what anyone would say who did not know her son, blank niceties about his popularity and character and how sorry he was, mostly, just about how sorry he was.

He started the car and checked the mirror and found her standing on the corner, not coming toward him, and not retreating, but fixed with the sun hard on her shoulders. He could drive, he thought, leave, as none of this was his business, but he wanted to know how long she would wait, and if this waiting would produce any kind of result. Finally, the smallest of gestures – an unclasping of her hands – drew him out of the car.

She waited for him to approach. 'I have work and I have a room if you're still looking.'

Rem, now fixed in place, squinted back at his car, everything in this town hard and unrelenting, concrete, brick, and glass, laid flat or vertical.

☆

She returned to find Nut on the sidewalk, sat beside the door, and came into the apartment to find it also unlocked.

Nothing appeared to be disturbed. She checked the bedside cabinet for her jewellery – small pieces from her family, all of little value. Money she'd left out on the counter was not taken, and as she walked about the apartment she thought of Roscoe. *Would he do this? Doubtful. He'd have taken the dog.*

Papers were missing from her desk. Her files also, but not all of them, and the chair was set at an angle, as if someone had, at their leisure, sat down and read through every single scrap of paper.

As far as she could tell, every piece of information about Paul Geezler had been removed.

Mud on the porch threatened to make its way into the house courtesy of three sets of feet, despite her mother's agreement that she would keep the heating on if they all but entirely disrobed in the entrance. Jackets, pants, boots, anything spattered with mud should stay in the *vestibule*. Cathy's mother had used this word once, years before, as a joke and it had stuck. A word that sounded like boiled candy. There had to be a less formal word. Cathy settled against the shoe rack, stacked with coats and boots and hats, and the soft wall of coats to read Rem's letters.

He called her 'honey' in his letters, a word he never used in person, and she liked that he found this tenderness when he addressed her, although she felt none of this herself. If he can still love me, she reasoned, then he can love someone else. She liked how he fought to keep his writing legible, how he insisted on writing as well as sending emails, and that these letters arrived without anticipation. Rem was awkward, easily embarrassed, not so unlike her father, or perhaps any man, and did not like to appear to be a fool. She held the letter to her stomach, now tight, and still she hadn't told him. And there was more news to tell him.

In the afternoon she would speak with a student radio station, a friend's daughter's project, a favour she did not mind making. The call had come through, a request that took some time to organize because she was becoming a figure, she was told, a name, someone hard to get hold of. Unpractised, Cathy worried that she would say the wrong thing, or that she would somehow become part of an aural wall, that anyone who listened to her would hear the same words of any other soldier or contractor's wife, and she did not like that category. She would instruct the student not to mention her pregnancy, the material would be available on the web, anyone could hear it, her pregnancy was private business.

The reporter, a girl of about seventeen, left her boyfriend in the car, who would not be persuaded to come inside. Cathy looked through the kitchen window and watched him, a boy wearing sunglasses on an overcast day, strong short black hair, head nodding, and the slow thud of some music. It was easy to imagine his body under those loose clothes. The girl, she kept forgetting her name, had an unbelievably bad complexion. She needed sun, make-up, a make-over. She needed not to be eating whatever she was eating as her lower jaw was lined with a rash. The girl appeared so sticky-looking that Cathy wiped the surfaces in her mother's kitchen as she talked to keep from staring. She wasn't pretty, and she imagined that the girl would allow her boyfriend to do pretty much whatever he wanted with her, because that's what it would take to keep him interested, *a girl who would do anything*.

Cathy talked about Howell, Southern-CIPA, about HOSCO, but most of all about Geezler. Contracting work to civilians in a military zone was really the single and entire origin of this problem. She used the idea of Howell as a child, selfish, greedy, lonely, buying friendship and influence, but wasn't so convinced this time. Geezler was harder to quantify. He'd moved up in the world, as the head of HOSCO in the Middle East he was disassembling the company, and she still didn't quite understand the logic of his manipulations. She couldn't prove anything she was saying about Geezler because she didn't have evidence. 'You have to look at who's still standing. There's only one. Paul Geezler.' She gave the girl the documents forwarded by *boston_adams*, and when the girl asked where these had come from, Cathy answered, HOSCO, although she couldn't prove it.

The girl wanted simple answers, but Cathy resisted. 'If we reduce this to one source,' she said, 'to one man, then we've failed to see what's really happening. No one wants to talk about it because it's too painful. Think about it, we had the public enquiry open one month after the death of the boy at Amrah, and soon we will have the hearings. Think about how long this has all taken.'

The girl's complexion seemed to worsen. This wasn't the interview she wanted. Cathy looked at the small digital recorder set on the counter between them, the mugs of coffee, her attempts to be nice.

'There's a man called Paul Watts.' Cathy leaned forward, decidedly maternal. 'Go and speak with him. He is missing a lung because of the work he undertook at the burn pits. Go and speak with him, speak with the other men who worked at Camp Liberty and ask them about what happened. Ask if they were told anything about the dangers of their work. Then speak with HOSCO, speak with Paul Geezler, and speak to the people who know him.'

Cathy sent the article as an attachment to Rem. In the subject line she typed a row: ?????? The attachment was an article about the country singer Grey Wills and the dispute on a house outside of Santa Fe, New Mexico, with his neighbour, Paul Geezler, who had bought the land and developed a property without apparent permission, then cut down the bordering trees in order to build a second building closer to the ridge and river. The property, a five-bedroom country house in the

English style, was built without the appropriate approvals and on inspection violated several county and state codes – and was, to Grey Wills' satisfaction, ordered to be demolished.

The article, dated five years back, was intended as a last gift to Rem. A kind of statement about the men he'd done business with, how they had always been this greedy, this disregarding of other people, and how they would not change.

☆

Santo drank and insisted on driving. He knew the route, he said, so Rem wouldn't have to pay attention to the maps. He knew how to get there. South, then west.

Rem watched the last of the city pass behind them. One remaining building from the Robert Taylor Homes, the last out of a scattered wall of high-rise blocks. It didn't occur to him until later that they were heading east not south – toward Michigan – a mistake which took a further two hours to correct.

The men hardly spoke, and Rem could not be certain what this drive was about, except that they would end up in Austin, see what work they could hustle from one of HOSCO's subsidiaries, although any debate about this idea soon dissolved into argument: both of them unhappy to return to the company, but neither seeing a choice.

'Would you go back?'

'Iraq? No.'

'Me neither.'

They could make it to St Louis before dark, find a motel on the other side of Memphis. It wouldn't be beyond him to drive all night, he said. 'We make Highway 10 at Baton Rouge.' Once in Louisiana they would soon be in Texas. Sealy first, then up to Austin, after which, who knows.

At Sealy they would locate Cathy. Find her at her parents or her sisters. 'She's sending you this information. She's still thinking about you. See?'

Rem rolled in and out of sleep. Santo opened energy drinks, answered his own questions and did not seem to mind if Rem was or was not listening. The smell, nutmeg and honey, of cold spice, brought back memories of Fatboy, and Fatboy's small room – the cab of Santo's car feeling almost as tight and airless.

'Your parents alive?' He'd never asked Santo about his family, but understood it to be large, that the Hernandez family were spread generously across North Chicago, Milwaukee, and Minneapolis, St Paul.

'At one point we lived close. My grandparents, aunts, uncles. There was a fire, but up until then we were all together. After the fire my father had to start over. His business was destroyed, so he had to find work elsewhere. After the fire we started moving around, things were spread about. It happened quickly, but I don't remember much. To me there was this fire and then people left, and there were new people about us who we called aunty and uncle. Things were hard for a time.'

Santo smoked, opened the window to flick out his ash. Commented on the landscape.

'This place needs hills. Seriously. It needs landscaping. It needs the Hernandez family to sort it out. You know, there's some pyramids out here. Maybe Indian, I don't think they even know, but they found these chambers where they'd buried people alive. I don't know how they know this, but there were these stone chambers underground that you could get into but not out. Like a sacrifice or something. A slow sacrifice.'

Rem half-listened, looked out at the fields of corn stubble.

Across the road from the parking lot Santo found a private members' casino. He won $50 in his first game and then lost every time after. Nevertheless his mood lifted, Rem could see it in his gestures, how he became broader when he was playing, his arms widening to express his failing luck. He accepted the free drinks, sent beer over to Rem who sat apart, alone, the appeal of the place not extending beyond the ring of tables and slot machines. Sat next to a sticky wall in a vast half-darkness, Rem drank and waited, tapped his foot along with an entertainer who sang to a backing track, and wondered how the police didn't shut the place down, and realized, it was all police – the gamblers, the drinkers, the investors.

When Santo came back, smiling, he shook Rem by his shoulder. 'I know exactly what you need,' he said. 'After tomorrow, you're going to feel better.'

As they walked out Santo leaned on Rem for support.

The countryside out of Santa Fe appeared contradictory, the air thin, mountain-like, but the land flat and stony, a desert, sure, but not the desert of Al-Muthanna. Here there was scrub, spiny and dusty-green, even some grass in place, piñon trees, larger boulders, a substantial flat plate of sky, a numb blue, a breathless blue, and the definiteness of the rocks, their honey colour, their solidity.

Despite Rem's questions Santo still wouldn't explain himself. This wasn't Route 10, it wasn't Louisiana, this desert wasn't the swamp. Not even close. They were so far from Louisiana, he said, he couldn't even imagine it. The further they drove the dryer and more weathered the land became, and as they turned off the highway and came slowly through a gate Santo hitched forward in his seat and drove with more attention. 'Not long now,' he said, and appeared to look for clues. 'This is Peterstown.'

'This is where Geezler lives?' The name struck Rem in an instant.

'Not quite. This is where he *had* a house.' Santo couldn't hold in his smile. 'You think we might call in?'

'He won't be here. Neither will the house. This whole situation is five years old. The house will be gone. Besides, it's a bad idea.'

'It's here all right. I looked it up. The man just can't live in it. And anyway, we've arrived.'

He pulled the car round a long curve, the land opening out to a gravel paddock, and a low-lying building, roofless, but with long tan adobe walls.

'The man likes horses. Can you imagine? And what was he? A *deputy*? An *assistant*? This was going to be a stud farm. He fucking breeds horses.'

Not a picture to keep in your head, Rem agreed.

'I had to see this. I love this story. He built this house, and then they made him take it down – only one floor though. So that's it. That's what he has. One floor of nothing.'

'Why are we here?'

'It's no accident. We're not calling because we happen to be close. You think we're the only people he fucked with?'

He let Santo get out of the car, watched him walk to the boot, take out a crowbar, then saunter toward the building and clamber over one of the low-lying walls. He waited, determined not to follow, but also curious.

The land split in front of the house, a vast narrow canyon, so that the house topped one side. The rooms were laid out, concrete, cleaned, and roofless. The walls had been cut, so the entire house held the appearance of being sawn horizontally in half. The range of the rooms, laid out like a villa, something you'd see on a holiday programme, where the presenter would speak about the possible activities that might once have happened in such a place, evoke a lifestyle by look- ing at stunted walls, views and prospects.

In what Rem took to be the lounge, the largest defined space, a staircase, a clean oblong dropped through the concrete.

'Get this,' Santo called up. 'There's more down here.'

Rem came carefully down the steps and found Santo in a concrete chamber, working on the door. With nothing else to take out his frus- tration on, he swung the crowbar and knocked off the handle. Still inside, he let the door close.

Rem stood on the bottom step. Santo, unable to get out, banged, first with his fist, then with the crowbar. The sounds seeming soft, distant. Rem had to push hard to open the door.

'That's not funny.' Santo stepped out, alarmed. 'There's no win- dows. You know how dark it is in here?'

'Shouldn't have messed with the lock.'

Rem returned up the stairs, there was nothing to be gained by looking at this place.

He sat in the car and waited for Santo.

'There's one thing I don't understand.'

Santo dug in his pockets for his cigarettes.

'Kiprowski. He didn't have to go to Amrah. I don't see why he did what he did.'

Santo set the cigarette on his lap. 'He wanted to go. He had his own reasons.' He found the lighter and tested the flame. 'You remember that map? The road that didn't exist.'

'It came from CIPA.'

'CIPA funded projects just to get rid of money. That road where the translator died – it used to be straight. They had a roadwork project that was supposed to improve connections between remote villages. Only they didn't do anything. They dug up roads and re-laid them. They put a curve in a road that used to run straight.'

'How did he know this?'

Santo lit the cigarette. 'He asked Howell. Said the road was straight on all the maps. Howell came right out with it, told us about a number of projects just like that. None of them any use. Just a way to spend money.'

'We're here because of a curve in a road?'

'I think you know there's a little more to it than that.'

Santo blew out smoke. Both men looked ahead at Geezler's house. Another incomplete project.

He woke with a headache, and felt more tired on waking than he had when he'd lain down. The room was otherwise empty, and Santo gone. The car also gone.

Santo had left an envelope on a small Singapore Airlines bag. The envelope contained a DVD and a note: *Watch the DVD, I'll call.*

Santo sent two SMS messages mid-morning. Rem had risen properly, showered, and sat on the bed. He watched the sunlight slip across the floor and considered how he was going to get back home. It wasn't just about deciding the next moment, the next couple of hours, but a larger, more difficult question. Why return? What to do?

After the second message, Rem slipped onto his knees and figured through the small complications of playing a DVD on the motel monitor. He sat on the floor and watched with the sound turned low.

On the first segment, a small image sank into the screen, large pixels vibrated unevenly, unstable, material shot on a handheld phone. The image dipped and opened to a figure in a doorway, silhouetted by giddy light, a voice, male, off-camera, close and wet: <How about that>, a white hand pointing into the room.

A woman on her back on a bed, a sheet pulled up over her crotch, her breasts shining, her hand dug between her thighs. A man with a cigarette and credit card was told to <Fuck her, just get on top and fuck her>, and the woman kicked the sheet back to her ankles.

Rem couldn't guess her age, young, surely, without doubt, long black hair, dark eyebrows, so that she might be Middle Eastern, he could not be more specific, the camera divided her body into flat plains, light and dark.

Santo, now close, smoking, rubbing his gums, <Try this>.

Another man, Pakosta, standing over the girl, <I'll leave you here>.

Instructions: <No, fuck her, get on top>.

Pakosta in another shot, closer now, seen from the back, labouring, flopped forward, slow then active, naked on top of the girl. A leg in the way, interrupting. Then on her side with two men, Clark and Santo, the woman propped between them, their skin shining, making one animal out of the three.

<You up her ass? Fuck her, fuck her, she doesn't care>.

Pakosta walking into the room, undressing and thrusting his hips as an example. <I'll have some of that>.

A soft downlight now, a different shot a different camera, infinitely more detailed. Pakosta, bleary-eyed, face messed with powder, opening perfumes and smelling them, pouring out the contents. The woman spread-eagled on the bed. Then Clark thrusting over her head.

Pakosta laughing: <You're gonna choke her>.

Santo again, aggressive with the woman, working on top, turning her over, hands gripping her breasts, pinching hard, and no reaction from the girl. In this shot it is clear that she is young, clear also that she is not aware of her surroundings.

<Thank you, thank you>.

<That was inspired>.

Santo rang about an hour after Rem had watched the footage. 'Who was she?'

'This isn't about the girl.'

'She was, what? Fifteen? Fourteen, fifteen?'

'She was working at the hotel. What does it matter? Howell paid for her. You have no idea, and when we came back it was like nothing happened. You didn't want to know. I don't think you even asked.'

'This has nothing to do with me. This is you, Pakosta, Clark, and Howell, and whoever that girl was. It has nothing to do with me.'

'See. The thing is. That wasn't the problem. The problem is that Howell had us. He took that footage for pleasure, and he wanted more, and he would have kept it going for as long as he wanted. He owned us once he had that material. He made that happen. The day after we returned he sent us emails with these attached.'

Santo wanted to know what Rem had done with the DVD.

'We were toys,' Santo said, his voice unnaturally flat. 'You get that? Howell. Sutler. Geezler. We were the entertainment.'

☆

509

THE KILLS

When the news came that Howell had died of his injuries, Santo called Rem. 'That's everyone except Geezler.'

'You're forgetting Sutler?'

'You think he survived? They just haven't found him yet.'

APRIL

Rem played games with the landlord's dog, a small wire-haired terrier, to distract himself while he waited for Santo. When Rem blinked, the animal blinked, or it blinked then he blinked – impossible to tell. The woman held the dog to her bosom and cleaned the animal's eyes then her own using the same tissue, only slightly less hygienic than when she kissed it on the mouth.

He searched for jobs in the paper, found a couple, none too promising, and wondered what time Santo would show. Blinked at the dog, and the dog blinked back. Chimeno's death, still recent, gave a perspective to the upcoming hearings.

The car, a Lincoln, sat low on the back axle. Santo leaned against the driver's door and appeared to be making a call – and sure enough, Rem's cellphone began to ring. When Santo looked up Rem guessed he could be seen, framed by the window.

'What's up with the car?' Rem asked.

Santo held up a hand in a static wave. 'Heavy load.'

As Rem came out of the apartments to the adjoining lot, Santo walked about the car and unlocked the boot. The lot, filled with oil patches, stumpy grasses, pea gravel, and building blocks, in-filling for a building long removed, was overshadowed by the brick side of Rem's building, blind except for one vertical strip of windows.

Santo opened the boot. 'Don't worry. I've covered his face,' and showed Rem what he took to be a plaid bedcover. Even when he recognized an area of skin, a white upper arm, it still didn't register that he was looking at a person. The smell – sharp, sweet – of an animal in fear, some beast that sweated.

Stooped to look into the boot, Rem figured out slowly, rationally, what he was looking at: here, hands bound at the wrist with silver duct-tape; there, a single fleshy bend, a knee; and there, a towel wrapped over a head with a wet and frayed breathing slit, as if a man, and this had to be a man, had chewed at the cloth.

Santo shut the boot with two hands, fingers sprung, with an expression of achievement, a man happy with a sale, or maybe even a

513

little prideful, a man with something to prove. The boot, punctured on the left side with a set of six indented holes, had to be punched down to close. Rem assumed from the hot stink, the arcs of sweat, the natural turn of the man's head that he was alive, although there were no proper signs, no sound, no evidence of breathing.

The two men stood over the boot, an unsteady edge to Santo, aside from the evidence of a bound man locked in the trunk of his clapped-out car.

'You know who this is?'

Rem could not move, felt absorbent, like he was taking in water, becoming heavy.

'It's Paul Geezler.'

Now Rem couldn't think – couldn't manage much more than a blink.

Santo gave a presentational gesture, a *what do you think* flourish, and appeared, if Rem had got this right, disappointed at his reaction.

'That's Paul Geezler?'

Santo nodded, pinched his nose. 'You need another look?'

'In your trunk?'

'That's what I said.'

'Alive?' Rem couldn't see, on any level, why or how such a task would be decided and managed. 'I don't know what to say to you, Santo. This is insane. You have to get him to a hospital. This is wrong.'

'I gave him –' Santo clicked his fingers – 'can't remember the name. But, yeah, he had to climb in first.'

Rem looked across the lot to the corner diner, but could see no one inside, only the reflection of the street, the sky, the long avenue.

'You have to let him go. Call the police. Let them find the car. If he dies …' He shook his head. 'Santo, what is this for?'

'It's about you, Rem.' Santo began to walk toward the diner. 'Let's have a coffee,' he said. 'We'll talk. And then I'm gone.'

Three police officers sat at one booth. The sun full on the floor also caught their boots, the sides of their legs. Guns clipped to their holsters, weighted so they pulled away from the men's sides. The officers had about them an irritated look, and Rem could not imagine the explanation he would have to give to impress on them the fact that a man was tied up in the boot of a car in the opposite lot.

Had he touched the car? Left any kind of trace? His connection would not be difficult to establish. Had these men seen him?

Santo picked a table by the window, deep in the glare. He asked Rem not to do anything. 'Just stay as you are. Calm. I'll get the waitress. I'll get us some coffee. Something to eat. You can just sit there and do nothing. Let me get the coffee. We'll talk. Just coffee, that's all we need right now.'

This discussion, at least, sounded normal. Not knowing what else Santo might be capable of, Rem agreed with a nod: the police across the room, Geezler jammed into the boot, everything held in the window.

Santo spoke with the waitress, who nodded while he placed the order. They needed cups, and water. If she could bring water. He pointed to the cooler at the back.

While the waitress fetched the coffee Santo took a tissue from his pocket and opened it out to show two off-white pills. He covered the paper with two hands when the waitress brought the coffee, and smiled at her as she poured.

When she left he asked Rem to hear him out. 'You're drawing attention to yourself. They're watching you now. Put your arms on the table, sit back, and look like you're relaxing.'

Santo pushed the napkin toward Rem. 'First. You have a choice. You need to decide to take these pills. If you don't take these pills, if you make any kind of move, I will stop you.' Santo looked into Rem's eyes. 'I don't want to do that. So you have this choice.'

Rem looked from Santo to the pills.

Santo cocked his head. 'Rem, listen to me. This is all done. This is all decided.'

'Why are you involving me?'

'Because this has everything to do with you. We are in this situation because of you. I didn't want it to be like this. The others wanted you to come along.'

'Which others?'

'Clark and Pakosta. We've worked this out. And this is the deal I have made with them. You have to know about this, and you have to live with this. The pills, that's my idea, to make it all a little easier. We can do this two ways. You can just go ahead knowing what is going to happen and leave us to do what we are going to do, or you can tell the police and try to stop this.' Santo looked sorrowfully at Rem. 'But I don't want you to do that.'

'Why the pills?'

'This is my idea. I gave these to Geezler. It will make things easier for you. I didn't want you involved, but Pakosta thinks you know too much, and he holds you responsible. He wants you to know what we're doing. I agreed to come and sort it out.' Santo pushed the napkin up to Rem's sleeve. 'It's enough that you know.'

Rem looked to the car to make certain that this was true: the apartment block, the open lot, the car strangely weighted.

'Take them. You know Geezler. You know what he's done, and don't tell me he hasn't got this coming. He's laughing at us, he's laughing at Kiprowski. Every day above ground this man is laughing at us. Take the pills.'

'The hearing starts in a week.'

'And what good will that do? You've heard what he says about everything. He's the last man accountable for what happened.'

'Are you going to kill him?'

Rem drew the napkin between his hands. He licked his forefinger, pressed down on one of the tablets and put it in his mouth. 'What will it do?'

'Take both.'

Rem took the second pill, swallowed it with the coffee. 'They will catch you.'

'And who are *they*, Rem? No one has any idea. People should thank us for what we're doing.' Santo sat back. 'He's untouchable, they can't find a thing against him.'

'It isn't Geezler.'

'Nice try. Keep telling yourself that and maybe it will help.' Santo lifted Rem's hand and let it drop, and Rem felt a sensation run through his arm, a fuzz of heat. His stomach also tightened.

'Don't worry. Just relax.' Santo pinched his mouth. 'Don't try to stand up. They give this shit to horses. You'll be OK.'

'You know I have to tell someone.'

'To what point, Rem? It's already too late. This is almost done now. It's almost over.'

Rem began to panic and when he attempted to rise his legs gave no support. Santo took out his wallet and threw down five dollars. 'I'm going to take you back.' He slipped out of the booth. 'I'll need your keys.'

Rem attempted to resist, his fingers now feeling too fat to control.

'I'll take you home. You'll begin to feel sick. You shouldn't look so scared. I promise nothing will happen to you. We'd better get going.'

He hitched his arm about Rem and hoisted him out of his chair. 'You're going to have to help me a little if you can.'

The officers watched as Santo shuffled Rem upright then walked him sloppily to the door, and Santo joked to Rem, although he couldn't focus on more than the bright light, the welter of sounds, the hectic displacement of planes. Two of the officers rose, one to get the inner door, the other to get the outer, both with a little laugh as Santo explained himself, tapping Rem on the chest, and pointing out that he needed to get him home, that this wasn't anything to worry about, he didn't need any assistance, he just needed to get him home and back on his meds. The second policeman stepped sharply back, and Santo looked down, apologized. He does that. It's just what happens.

Santo managed Rem across the road, into the lobby, a fireman's lift up the stairs, Rem's physical senses condensed now down to his guts, to his skin, prickling, and then the realization that he had wet himself.

Santo wrested the keys out of his pocket, leaned Rem between his hips and the wall, Rem's arm struck out crazy into the air, pointing.

'I'll sit with you till you sleep, and then I'll be going.'

Santo sat him in the chair. Propped him up with cushions and clothes so that he was lodged upright. Rem had messed himself, Santo noted, he was sorry, it sometimes happened. I should have brought you back first.

Rem focused on Santo's mouth and could no longer clearly follow what he was saying. The words came dog-like, chewed, shapes made out of his mouth, a cracked lower lip, uneven teeth, looking small in such a big mouth.

Santo talked about a room, a drive, a story about people stopping at motels, about meeting a girl, some beautiful woman, and how things might work out, you just don't know, about how he would not come back, and would make no attempt to see him again. Sutler had been discovered in Syria, he said, out in some desert, half-dead. Smoking now, Santo held back to exhale. Can you even believe that? He's dying in some hospital in Damascus.

Santo held Rem's head in his hands. 'I'm taking Geezler back to his house. I'm going to leave him in the basement, and I'm going to shut the door. In nine hours he's going to revive. Alone. In a room he can't get out of. You have to live with this. You have to deal with this on your own. We can't let him continue, we can't allow him to make more profit from what he has done. We're all adults, and there are consequences to every action that we take. What happened to Kiprowski wasn't right, and Pakosta will have to live with that, but Geezler, he doesn't have to deal with anything, not unless we do this.

'In fourteen hours you'll come out of this. You should throw away these clothes, burn this chair, get rid of anything which attaches you to any of us. You will not go to the police. Pakosta is still sore at you. I've talked him round and this is the deal. You live with this, like we have to live with this.'

Rem slipped out of himself, backward and away.

☆

Picture yourself above a highway, right below you a mess of trucks, cars, motorbikes converging on a slick turn on a rising road. Imagine, right before the scene gets complicated, that you can drop down, right out of the sky, pick someone up, and take them out of harm's way. Imagine that. The car spinning behind you as you rise. The truck jack-knifing. The bike scudding the rock. Imagine not one person, but every one of them. That you could spirit them away. Every single one.

Oftentimes, at night, bordering sleep, the same sensation of hovering above a bright and broadening field would overtake Rem – and sometimes this sensation would annihilate him, at others he would hover with expectation that someone else was readying to join him.

THE KILL

Mr Rabbit: He gives them a choice. It's the same in the film.

Mr Wolf: What kind of choice?

Mr Rabbit: They don't know. He flips a coin, and they have to choose. Heads or tails.

Mr Wolf: What if they don't want to?

Mr Rabbit: Not an option. Heads or tails. They have to choose.

Mr Wolf: And this is what you want to do?

Mr Rabbit: They get to decide what happens. Only they don't know. They have no idea.

Mr Wolf: It's a place to start.

YEAR 1: VIA CAPASSO 29

SUNDAY: DAY A

Early on the last Sunday of July, Amelia Peña, supervisor at via Capasso 29, rented a tiny basement room to Salvatore, who, with his sons, ran a modest grocery and eatery set into the corner of the palazzo.

They met at the small service door on via Tribunali, and Peña escorted the man across an inner courtyard to the basement stairs. The courtyard was cluttered and unswept, and as they walked Salvatore answered Peña's questions but did not chatter. He spoke quickly and in a soft voice, mellow enough so that much of what he said was lost to her. *No*, he said, *in all these years he hadn't seen these rooms before.* The windows overlooking the courtyard were closed and shuttered. *This wasn't for him. This wasn't for his business.*

The basement, Peña explained, was what remained of an earlier building: small square rooms carved into the tufa with barrel vaults that might have been used as storage for food, oil, wine, nobody really knew, as nobody knew how old they were. Every building abutting the Duomo had similar rooms dug at different levels, each sunk deeper than an ordinary basement. Their layout didn't conform to the layout of the buildings above and there were signs that they were once linked. Peña took the steps one by one, her hand fast on the side rail, and hoped that this effort wouldn't be wasted. The temperature dropped as soon as they stepped out of the sun. The walls, rough as pumice, shed a white grit, a kind of static.

The previous tenant had left the room in a poor state: flattened boxes scattered across the slab floor, a stained mattress tied into a roll and tipped against the wall, a stove stripped of fittings turned into the room out of square. A window slit let in a little dull natural light through a shaft carved up to street level. *And was that via Tribunali or via Capasso seven or eight metres above them?* Salvatore couldn't quite tell.

Salvatore stood under the window, cocked his head and appeared to listen. In all these years, he admitted, he'd assumed the door led to another apartment, or street-level rooms. Although he knew the city had subterranean vaults and passages, he'd never given it much serious thought. *In the war,* he said, and nodded. *Yes, in the war,* Peña supposed, *they would have been used for shelter.* Salvatore measured the room with strides. No one comes down here? he asked. It's secure? Peña showed him the key-ring and chain. If he was worried about security, there were only two keys, he would have one and she would have the other. The last time these were used – she had to think back – would be seven or eight years ago. Whatever he wanted to store down here would be safe. Nobody knows about the place to steal from it, she said. Pay the rent in full and on time, and everything will remain secure.

Salvatore took two or three photographs with his mobile phone, although, in truth, there was nothing to show, and he didn't seem to know what he was looking for. When he was done he snapped the phone shut and said he needed to return to the courtyard to get a signal.

Peña locked the door and laboured back up the steps. Not even halfway she paused for breath and asked if he was or wasn't interested and the man became flustered. It wasn't for him, he said. Hadn't he explained? He was working as an agent, a go-between for his associates. They were brothers, businessmen, French, they didn't speak Italian, and they were busy, so he'd agreed to check the room for them. Just as soon as he could send the images they would get right back to him.

He pressed ahead, and hurried through the door, and by the time she joined him Salvatore said he'd spoken with the brothers, they'd looked at the photos and they were happy. They'd take the room for one month, but they'd pay for two to cover any inconvenience or deposit. He could pay her now, in advance.

With money in her fist Peña repeated the terms of the lease. This was for one month, renewable before the end of the month. The first key would open the small door at the main entrance and the door to the basement from the courtyard. The larger brass key was for the room itself. Salvatore and his associates could come and go as they pleased, but they should not disturb the residents. As an afterthought she asked for the brothers' contact details, just in case, and he wrote a number on the back of a business card. The room would need painting, if she could arrange this, and the men would require a driver.

It was only later, once she was back in her apartment that she looked at the card and read: *Room 312, Hotel Grand, CMdS.*

MONDAY: DAY B

For six weeks Mizuki Katsura's clothes, hands, and hair reeked of a sweet vanilla. During the summer the bakery three floors below the language school on via Capasso produced small star-shaped biscuits, dipped in syrup and covered with paper then plastic and left to drip and dry on trays on racks in the courtyard. Throughout the day the sugar attracted a good number of wasps and the perfume rose as a fume and seeped, thick and unwelcome, into the schoolrooms and offices above.

The train arrived late at the Circumvesuviana station and Mizuki, phone in hand, stood at the door halfway reminded of the scent of burnt sugar. The morning sun cooked sweetness from the furnishings, the rubber seals, and the sticky floor. Idly stubbing her mobile against her cheek she squinted at the docks and recalled details of a detective story in which a man paused to smell jasmine before he was shot, but couldn't remember the title or the writer. She could chase this notion on her phone and hunt down the reference, but did not like the idea that she was leaving trackable data every time she switched it on. Even so, she quickly checked for messages, emails, SMS.

The train stopped with a gentle shove. On the platform, immediately in front of her door, stood a young and thin man with shorn hair and a drawn face: tall and puppet-like and handsome, as European men can be angular and handsome. A creaturely intelligence about him that held a kind of stillness. Sunlight, softened by the humid station air, cast a broad square over the man as he waited. Handsome, yes, and maybe even cunning.

Mizuki rode the escalator and the idea of this man stuck with her as she dug out two euro for a bottle of water. Once on the concourse she found, to her surprise, the same man already ahead of her, waiting. A little more alert now. The man stood with his arms folded, chin down, attentive to the steady line of commuters rising from the lower platforms.

The realization that there were two men, not one, came slowly, an idea she only properly understood after she'd paid for the bottle of water and turned to find both men waiting side by side under the station's awning. Dressed alike (one in a powder-blue shirt, the other in seamless white), and surely brothers; the man in the powder-blue shirt looked directly at her: a simple turn of his head as if he knew precisely where to look and what he would find.

Out of the station the traffic was stopped bonnet to boot. Horns sounded above the market and rounded hard off the buildings on either side. Mizuki walked by the market stalls and between the round walls of Porta Nolana, alongside tables of shoes and purses and undershirts, and a stack of birdcages. Agitated by the traffic the finch and quail squalled against the bars. Looking, even briefly, at their skinny necks made her skin itch. On Corso Umberto she found the focus of the delay: a long, low-slung tow-truck with a crushed taxi loaded on the truck-bed. Other cars looked only like cars, but the battered taxi had the bruised, gummy face of a boxer, its side compacted, slumped, the roof cut off and strapped back upside-down. At the head of the intersection by the newspaper stands and cash machines and racks of clothing the police fussed over an orange city bus stopped sideways and within metres of a smaller coach. The coach like the taxi had a mashed hood and a shattered windscreen. An ambulance turned in the corso, and Mizuki pressed her fingers to her ears and wished that she had walked some other way. When there were sirens it meant that someone was hurt, but worse, no sirens, according to Lara, meant that someone had died.

She deliberately turned her thoughts back to the brothers and sketched the differences between them, but couldn't measure the look the man had given her: clear and direct, an assessment. The man was taking weights and measures. Mizuki brought her phone from her pocket and regretted not taking a photograph. No messages. No email. In this way she avoided thinking about the accident.

Access to the school (on the third floor at the back of the building) was gained through a courtyard, and before that a set of massive carriage doors of solid black beams with a small inset port door, through which you had to be buzzed. Such buildings, a feature of the city, were referred to as *palazzi*. Palaces. The word lent a formal air and a sense of protection to the apartments and businesses inside, so that ducking through the smaller door was very much like escaping the ordinary world: except this ordinary world had narrow streets, black cobbles as big as shoe boxes, the constant buzz of Vespas. The hidden world housed wasps. Mizuki always paused at the door, tucked away her hair, drew her sleeves over her hands, and worried over the wasps and how she would cross the courtyard without being stung.

☆

At seven o'clock on the first Monday in August, Marek Krawiec picked up the coach from its lock-up on via Carbonara. Marek drove a small eighteen-seat transit bus and shuttled American servicemen between the military base at Bagnoli and the airport at Capodichino. He took civilian aircrew between their hotels and the airport as and when required. English Tony arranged the work, provided the vehicle, and paid him cash in hand. The job ran scattered: two being the fewest, and eighteen the most runs he'd managed in a single day. Marek didn't like flying and didn't much care for the people he transported about the city. While he tolerated the servicemen, he disliked the aircrew. The men were effeminate, the women aloof, and once they settled onto the bus they ignored him and talked among themselves, unless there were complaints to be made about the traffic, the congestion at the airport, or the delays before the tollbooths.

While the work was light the morning was hot and Marek began to sweat. He'd gained two kilos since the beginning of the year and felt himself to be slowing down, although he could see no reason for it, no change in habit or diet. As he sat in the driver's seat he avoided his reflection.

Tony waved him off with a floppy gesture, half-ironic and half not bothered.

At seven twenty, Marek returned to via Capasso to pick up his partner, Paola. *Partner*: her word. Marek waited outside the palazzo as Paola hurried about the bus, made no comment as she loaded the bags of shirts and struggled to close the door, then drove the short journey down via Duomo to take her to a machine-shop close by Porta Nolana that manufactured sports clothes. Paola worked at home, seldom less than a seven-hour stretch stitching sportswear logos onto pockets and collars for three cents an item. The house sang with the crank of the sewing machine and a kind of intense concentration she had with two hands down to the material, lips tight, willing the thread not to break, the material to hold. Most mornings Marek collected the shirts and vests and ran the loads back and forth, but on this day Paola wanted to negotiate the workload and the pay, and, he suspected, use this time to talk with him again about money, about why they never had enough. While Paola knew they were in debt, she didn't know the full extent: the loan from his brother Lemi, the payments for his mother's healthcare, a bank loan he could barely service, and back-standing rates and taxes on his mother's apartment. Running between his mother in Poland, his brother in Germany, his *partner* in Italy, was costing Marek more than he was making. His mother's unkempt slide into dementia hit his temperament and his pocket with equal force. To add to this Paola had decided that they would take a holiday this year. Somewhere nice. Not Poland. Not Germany. Maybe the Croatian coast? Like they were the kind of people who sat on beaches.

Paola remained testy from the previous night's argument and it became clear that she didn't want to talk. Where their disagreements had once refreshed them, they now brought drought. Delivered to her work in silence, she opened the door, tugged out the shirts, and muttered that she did not want him to wait.

Marek drove up Corso Garibaldi with a burn of irritation. At the corner of piazza Garibaldi he noticed a small red patent-leather purse in the passenger footwell, the kind of purse sold by African traders at the Stazione Centrale and along via Toledo. While he hadn't seen it before he guessed it was Paola's. Inside the purse he found a single twenty-euro note, a lipstick, and a small roll of receipts. She would be inconvenienced without the money and sorry to lose the purse. Without the money she'd have to walk home with the shirts.

With the purse in hand Marek missed the lights and failed to pull into the intersection. Horns sounded behind him, a taxi cut directly across his path – so close he automatically braced – the shock of this barely registered when the cab was struck by a city bus, punched sideways and shunted into Marek's coach.

Marek dropped to his side as the airbags pillowed over him, as the windscreen blew out, and found himself straddling the gearbox on his hands and knees. The impact itself seemed to come later, after its effect, as a mighty shove, something divine, out of scale.

The accident left a buzz in Marek's ears and dampened all other noise. He'd hit his head, not hard, but a knock nevertheless. Scattered birds came soundlessly down, and a kind of wonderment spread through him: if he hadn't been preoccupied with the red purse he would be dead, he would have driven directly into the path of the taxi, of this he was certain; being caught on the rebound was nothing, nothing at all. Glass in his hair, a shirt ripped in the seam, but no real damage, except to the coach.

Passengers stepped off the city bus and walked in a disconnected stumble to the kerb. To Marek's right a woman with bags tipped at her feet, groceries spilling into the road, pointed at the traffic lights and shouted, *red red*, in disbelief.

The instant it was over a bevy of car horns sounded along Corso Garibaldi and Corso Umberto. The first pneumatic punch brought people onto the balconies overlooking the intersection. Others hurried from the market stalls to catch sight of a crushed car and coach, a city bus stopped at an acute angle to the sidewalk. From under the cab rose a thin, violet quiff of smoke.

Marek studied the car in front of him, astonished that this – how many tonnes of steel? – had spun out of nowhere, as if the car had landed smack-bang out of the sky, as if the people stumbling from the bus were drunk. As if the men – the passenger slumped across the seat, his head resting on the driver's haunch, the driver lolling over a battered door, shirt rucked to his shoulders, arms flung out so he appeared to be reaching or pointing – were some soft part of the car.

A man in a doctor's coat, skinny and bald, hurried to the taxi. He leaned deep into the cab and as he drew out he sorrowfully shook his head, nothing could be done – an intimate gesture, Marek thought, which implied kinship: as if they knew each other.

Traffic locked the length of Corso Garibaldi and Corso Umberto, and in a slow outward spread the smaller side streets began to seize up. Marek could smell oil and rubber and the sun's heat rebounding on the smooth black cobbles. He looked hard at the taxi and the dead men and resisted the urge to lie across the seat and see how long it would take for someone to come to him. He didn't know what to do with himself. His job, he knew, was over. Without the coach Tony would not be able to hire him. The vehicle, too damaged to repair, would not be replaced. Without a vehicle there would be no work. Paola would need to be told.

Security guards from the Banco di Napoli escorted passengers from the bus; as the bus driver passed by he looked hard at Marek, his expression still and blank, one of shock, and Marek felt pity for him. The man in the doctor's coat helped passengers to the kerb and looked at Marek as if he knew him, and Marek realized the man was his neighbour, Lanzetti, Dr Arturo Lanzetti, the pharmacist who lived on the fifth floor with his wife and his son. He knew his son, knew of him, heard him almost every day.

The first police arrived on motorbikes and rode the pavement alongside the piazza. The corso sang with their alarm. Firemen trapped in the traffic abandoned their trucks and clambered between the cars to the intersection, and everyone stopped to look at the taxi, the two dead men, then Marek and the coach, and shook their heads at his undeserved good luck.

Lanzetti came to the coach and opened the passenger door. He brushed the glass from the seat with slow sweeps then sat down, uninvited.

'This will take a while.' He offered Marek a bottle of water and told him to drink. 'Will you let me?' He signalled Marek's head by tapping his own. 'You have a cut.'

'It's nothing.' Marek leaned toward his neighbour. Lanzetti looked and nodded, it was nothing to worry over. The pharmacist could give no information; a passenger on the bus needed to be taken to the hospital and although they had managed to get an ambulance to the intersection, it would be another matter getting it out. The medics were already in control.

The police slowly re-established order: the gathering crowd kept to the pavement, and drivers ordered back to their cars.

Marek leaned away from the sun and waited for the police to come to him. He showed the purse to Lanzetti and explained how it had delayed him, how otherwise, without the purse, matters would be very different. Lanzetti nodded as he listened, a slow gesture, one of comfort, as if he understood how the smallest coincidences of place and time could be of such startling importance. The difference between what did happen and what had nearly happened – which didn't particularly require discussion, but needed to be acknowledged.

The road was hosed down before the roof was cut from the car and both men watched, silent and respectful. A ring of firemen held up blankets to block the crowd's view and to prevent the curious from taking photographs. As the bodies were lifted from the squat wreckage Marek finally gave his details to the police and Lanzetti slipped quietly out of the cab.

The sight of the young men being laid carefully on stretchers and then covered with blankets struck Marek deeply; he looked hard, expecting some break in their stillness.

And what was their argument about? Money, sure, because every argument is about money. But this one started with a discussion about children, about how they could not afford, as a couple, to have a child, when really, the simple fact was that Paola did not want his child, and he wanted her to admit this truth. We have enough to look after, she said, with me and you. We have enough. Their arguments concertinaed, one to another, and while Marek remembered the insult he lost the particular words and phrases; Paola, however, recalled intricate points and details so that nothing was properly resolved. They each had their triggers: the uselessness of their work, their mismatched schedules, how lonely it was to go to bed alone or wake alone, how weekends when they finally spent them together were listless, empty, and how they both felt unattractive. Beneath this ran their own dissatisfactions (for Marek: his recent weight gain, his thinning hair, how easily these days he started to sweat. For Paola: the veins thickening on the backs of her calves, how tired she was and lately forgetful). Some of their disagreements grew out of their daily routine. Paola resented cooking, and Marek resented the half-efforts she would make, and how much food was spoiled through lack of care. How could someone prepare so carefully for sex (the gel, the foam, the condom slick with spermicide), and not have the wherewithal to make a simple meal? How could an Italian woman not cook? How could this be possible? And then there was the issue they usually avoided, the heart of every disagreement: Paola did not want his children. Who would want the children of a man who had no work?

When Marek returned he found Paola in the kitchen, deliberately positioned at a bare table with nothing about her, no cigarettes, no drink, so that her waiting would be obvious.

Tony had called. She'd heard everything from him, about the accident, about the coach, about his job. She stood up and walked to Marek and held him tightly.

'He'll find something. I know it.'

Feeling ugly and argumentative Marek closed his eyes. There wasn't any *something* out there for Tony to find. In his mind a sign in the building supervisor's slanted script, pinned under the mailboxes, 'Painter Wanted'.

Letting him go, the recriminations started. Why hadn't he spoken with her? Not one call. Why? 'I called. I sent messages. Why didn't you respond?' Wasn't she his partner? Didn't this mean anything to him? Didn't he have any idea what she was going through? My God, did he do this to her deliberately? He could have been killed.

She would be glad, he said. Happy if something had happened to him.

Paola's hand fluttered in front of her mouth, and then, inexplicably, she began to laugh. She waved a hand in defeat or exhaustion and surrendered, tonight she wouldn't argue. Instead, Paola walked queenly to the bedroom.

Once alone Marek looked for something to justify his meanness, and found Paola's keys and mobile phone beside the sink. He took the phone to the bathroom and checked through the log. The only number dialled that day was his. The incoming calls came from mutual friends. He recognized every number stored in the phone's memory.

In the wastebasket lay the packets of condoms and the spermicide he'd brought to her the night before in his demand that they be thrown away, and here they were, thrown away. Marek searched through the basket to see what else she had discarded, and found among the foil packets a slender box of contraceptive pills and didn't understand exactly what this meant, although he could see, right there, that this was exactly what he'd wanted.

That night he lay awake and fretted over his work. *Painter Wanted.* It wasn't a simple matter, even if the coach was replaced, he still didn't have the proper papers. The insurers, the police, would want details about the driver. When he finally managed to sleep he was woken by the sound of drilling, a sudden racket from the street.

He struggled to read the time on his watch. From the balcony he could see two workmen. Another man stood bare-bellied on an opposite balcony and shouted: *What are you doing?* The workmen ignored him, and the man shouted louder. A magistrate lived in the same building. If Marek leaned forward he could see the apartment on the top floor.

During the day via Capasso appeared respectable, students from the language school took coffee at the Bar Fazzini, but at night women worked the corner. They sat on mopeds, indifferent to business. Marek wasn't certain they were all women.

Behind him Paola drew the sheet over her shoulder.

The noise didn't matter. The sound of the men drilling gave him a reason to be awake, a reason not to be in bed, and another example of how this city drove him crazy. As he watched the workmen he again considered the accident and wondered if the police had yet identified the men and informed their families. He wanted to thank Lanzetti, he wanted to find the pharmacist and thank him, because the man's calm had made an impression on him. As he stood on the balcony a message came on his mobile from his brother Lemi, *call me*, which would give news of his mother wandering unsupervised from the care home a second time. A search by the police, and a requirement from the home to find her somewhere new, somewhere that could manage.

☆

At midday, as Peña returned to her apartment, she decided she would ask Marek Krawiec if he knew of a driver for the men who had rented the basement room. She took the stairs one at a time, her head swam with the effort. On top of the Duomo, perched on the dome, a hawk bobbed against the wind, sometimes sleek and sometimes ruffled. Peña watched from the second landing and felt her pulse calm and her head clear. When the bird launched the wind held it in place. Wings out, the hawk tested the updraught before it tipped backward and away. She watched it eat on occasion, some small bird held down and plucked, elastic innards and meat. A strange thing, if you gave it thought, a little repugnant, a bird eating a bird.

Ten years before, when Peña first arrived in Naples, Dr Panutti's apartment was halved by a flimsy dividing wall to make two apartments, one for Dr Panutti, Snr., the other for Dr Panutti, Jnr. The wall once had a door, so the younger Panutti could steer the older Panutti through his final illness. Peña, employed as a companion and respite nurse, made herself indispensable and invisible, and earned the right to stay in the apartment as specified in Panutti Snr.'s will, much against his family's desire. In taking out that door and sealing the wall, they turned the room into a sound-box, so that Peña heard the intimate comings and goings of the family who now rented the apartment: the pharmacist Dr Arturo Lanzetti, the voice coach Dr Anna Soccorsi, and their son, Sami. She knew when they ate, bathed, fought, and reconciled. More than this, the room duplicated the movement of sound: if Sami ran in some hectic game, his escape mapped a similar higgledy path across Peña's room.

They called the boy Sami although she knew his proper name to be Francesco. With his dark hair and olive skin the boy could be taken for a full-blooded Neapolitan. He mostly resembled his mother, a woman Peña believed to be ill-suited to city life: unable to shift and adapt she pressed too hard in one direction. Peña could read this stubbornness in the woman's thin-lipped mouth, in the sessions with her clients: the repetitive 'peh-peh-peh', 'zseh-zseh-zseh', 'tah-tah-tah' exercises, the insistent singsong rhymes she gave to stutterers, language students, and lisping adolescent boys. Their boy, Sami, often alone and unsupervised, played with his toys at his bedroom window, and Peña sometimes found these toys scattered in the courtyard. Small plastic figurines of crusaders, Roman and American soldiers, robots, caped action characters, and other figures she couldn't place. She would find them and she would pocket them, and she would take them to her room.

Most mornings before Arturo Lanzetti went to the pharmacy he sat with his son and read through the headlines from the previous day's paper. The child's voice, sweet and high, carried easily through the wall, and Peña, who spent her mornings cleaning the stairwell and courtyard, made sure she finished in time to enjoy the company of their voices. She began to associate the boy's voice with the morning light that flooded her room.

At night he dropped tokens into the courtyard, sometimes lowered on string: small figurines, notes, coins, folded scraps of paper, wads of bread, pieces of his mother's make-up. In the morning she would retrieve them.

Today, as on other days, Peña climbed into the armchair, restacked the cushions and scooted herself back so that her legs stuck out. Of the four places where she could listen to the family, three offered views into their apartment (the kitchen, the hallway, and the boy's bedroom), which ran around the courtyard and mirrored her own apartment. When the shutters were open their lives were offered up one to the other in merciless detail.

Sami read out the world's news with sticky precision. His ear was good and he repeated the phrases he couldn't grasp, softly correcting himself.

'Brasilia. A fire . . .' he read.

'Brasilia,' Lanzetti repeated, 'a fire . . . in the centre of the city.'

'Brasilia . . .' Peña softly whispered.

The older Panutti had taught her Italian in exactly the same way. Reading, repeating, reading, until her Portuguese bent to Italian. Later he helped in other ways, providing medication, then braces to help straighten her legs. The more you use them, he said, the easier this will become.

As she listened Peña took her medication. She laid the pills along the smooth walnut side-table and took a sip of water, a tablet, another sip. *The boy dropped toys into the courtyard and she retrieved them: the small soldiers, crayons, pens, a racing car, a diver with the yellow aqualung.* She listened to him read. The boy's pronouncements outlined a chaotic world. The tumble of an aircraft into open water; a fire erasing an entire city block; a mudslide sweeping houses, cars, caravans into a widening canyon, events which described nothing godly or divine, but simple laws of opportunity, matters Peña understood to her core. There was nothing, she considered, not one thing, which could truly surprise her. After reading the headlines Sami turned to the local section to read stories of disagreements, strikes and train stoppages, contracts for uncollected trash. After this he read the sports, although this was news they already knew.

A sip of water. A tablet. A sip of water.

Propped forward with pillows, Peña sat upright and motionless, her eyes fixed on a length of sunlight vibrating into the room. Her medication amplified her waywardness, a potential to slip away. Tiny things tumbled down the side of the building. A steady rain of falling toys: a cowboy, a diver, a mule, a racing car, a lipstick, a robot that was also a car, a troll or what she took to be a troll, a key-ring, a mobile phone, a face cut out of a magazine flickering down, a hawk – wings open, a number of pigeon eggs, one by one, a series of keys, an open can of paint, a boy who could swim through air.

*

THE KILL

At night Sami hitched himself onto the window ledge and pushed open the shutters. Too short to see into the courtyard, the boy shuffled on his forearms like some kind of creature, Peña thought. Dust stirred and sparked in the void between them. Peña stepped back from her window. It troubled her not to remember things. Names mostly. Places. But sometimes plain words.

It took some moments for her eyes to adjust; she watched as Sami edged himself forward, one hand set in a fist. With his chin on the stone lintel he stared into the courtyard. Small sounds skidded beneath them: televisions in separate rooms, honks and voices, the settling rattle of air-conditioners and the steady clap of water on stone, the less attributable snaps and tremors that came from deeper sources – the entire building contracting in the cooler night air.

There was something in the boy's hand, and he took time to stand this object right at the edge. Another toy soldier, Peña guessed by the size, another trophy.

About an hour after Sami had set the toy on the ledge Peña heard the clack of the lock on the small portal door, then a muffled conversation as two men came from via Capasso into the courtyard. Sami came to the window then quickly ducked away – and although she could not see him she guessed that he was standing in the dark away from view.

The voices were soft, too quiet to properly understand, and when a soft chuckle rode up the side of the building the boy cautiously returned to the window ledge. They were speaking to him in whispers, words she couldn't quite catch. *Come on*, they seemed to say. *Come on.*

The men continued talking while they smoked, the rising whiff of tobacco, their voices becoming a little less discreet. One of the men became boisterous and shouted through the courtyard, 'Hey,' for attention, and then softened into laughter. Peña slipped back into her room. The boy slid himself forward to watch.

In the kitchen, unaware, Anna Soccorsi stood over a kettle with her arms folded, wearing nothing more than a man's T-shirt.

Peña slept in her armchair. She woke once and heard the voices again, men whispering to the boy words she could not hear.

Arturo Lanzetti did not always live with his family. He stopped two months in Naples, sometimes less, but two months was his median stay, then he would be gone, leaving Anna with the child, or Anna alone. The period before his departure would be plagued with silences and bitter argument so that Peña could tell even before he was gone that he was going. While Lanzetti was away the phone rang late at night, and Peña became used to Anna's thin and unpersuasive voice sounding always like a complaint. Anna sometimes wore a ring and sometimes did not, and as was common she kept her own last name so there was no clear indication of their status. For Peña the mystery of their relationship was solved at different times to a different result.

TUESDAY: DAY C

As the train drew slowly toward the station in one long curve, Mizuki, by habit, stepped up to the door and watched the reflection, phone in hand. The towers of the business district, superimposed on the glass, slipped over the long grey container park that faced the bay. On this day she remembered a story about a woman who'd lost a bracelet, and again she couldn't remember the title: she found the lapse funny, because wasn't this also the subject of the story? In learning a new language she was forfeiting memories, or maybe she was simply tired? For two nights now her sleep had been broken. Nothing particularly troubled her, and neither was she hankering for something – the usual causes of unrest. She simply couldn't sleep. Both nights she'd lain awake with the notion of a river suspended above her, a current flowing through the room that would occasionally descend and engulf her (and she would sleep), then rise (and she would wake). The water looked nothing like water: black and slick and infinite as volcanic glass. The sensation was not unpleasant, but it left her unable to concentrate. A memory of the dream stuck as an insistent ache in her arms and a pressure in her chest as if she had wrestled a strong current.

Mizuki did not purposefully look for the brothers, but was pleased to recognize one of them as she stepped off the train. *Which brother is this*, she asked herself, *the older or the younger?* Once again the man appeared to be waiting, a little less present than the previous day, perhaps even bored. This time he leaned back, puppet-like, with one shoulder bent to the grey pillar and his hands dug into his pocket, so that his body turned – loose-looking, something set aside. When she passed by she hoped to catch his eye and paused to make sure that this would happen: when he finally looked at her he registered nothing. This, then, was the younger brother.

On the upper concourse she spied the older brother at the station threshold, beside him the newspaper vendor, magazines pegged in a line, others stacked in bundles, and drinks, water, cola, wrapped in packs. She stood beside the man as she bought a bottle of water, felt her pulse quicken. If she leaned to her right her shoulder would touch his upper arm. She paid, turned about, passed directly in front of the man – and noticed how he turned his head to watch her with the same intensity as the day before. Today the men were not wearing similar clothes and she could easily distinguish one from the other. French, she decided. Definitely French. She had an eye for this. The clothes (a summer suit jacket with new jeans, expensive shoes when sandals would do), but best of all a studied casual air, a kind of self-possession she had to admit she found attractive even while she found it arrogant. Generalities, sure, but she was usually right. And was he wearing perfume, some fresh aftershave or shaving balm? Or was it just the sight of him, so clean, a man in a pressed shirt, a man in a suit jacket, European, that made her expect this?

Today the corso was clear and Mizuki reached the school before the start of the lesson, and realized, again, that she had failed to take a photograph. At the large wooden doors to the courtyard she tucked her hands into her sleeves, pulled back her hair, and turned up her collar to protect her neck, readying herself to run from the wasps.

☆

Marek rose early. He walked about the house in his shorts, prepared breakfast for Paola and laid a place ready at the table, and considered what he needed and what he didn't. For example: he didn't need Paola on his case, organizing him, making plans. She would bother him with schemes and details. Finding him work would become her project. He didn't need this bother and he didn't need his brother calling or sending messages. He needed his mother to stop her midnight walks. He needed less advice and more money.

His first idea was to visit Nenella. A *fattuchiera*, a woman from Pagani reputed to have second sight. Pagani was Paola's village, and Paola had known Nenella as a girl. Nenella, she swore, could call out the bad fate of the most cursed. Often Paola would say that such a situation, or such a hope, such a notion could be divined by Nenella. The woman was able to advise, solicit, or intervene in any situation. Marek had no such faith, and ridiculed Paola whenever she expressed this belief, but today he thought he would see her.

A slow trickle came out of the pipes, not enough to shave and not enough to wash. He remembered the workmen and how the drilling continued intermittently for three hours, driving sleep out of the neighbourhood. He leaned over the balcony and looked for the pit the men had dug, but there was no sign of water, only a dry hole surrounded by bollards, nothing he could see, and no signs that explained the drilling. It was typical. They came in the middle of the night to disrupt his sleep and after all that noise they had achieved nothing. Further up the street he could see the magistrate's car and his driver leaning casually against the side. As he looked down he thought he saw the man look up. Glancing back at Paola it occurred to him that the magistrate's driver spent a great deal of time outside the apartment.

With what little water he could draw from the tap he made a coffee. As he waited for the coffee to boil he checked the wastebasket in the bathroom. Marek brought a small cup to Paola, and waking her set his hand on her stomach, and thought perhaps that he felt her flinch. Light bloomed between the shutters and Paola blinked, slowly wakening. Marek ran his hand softly over the curve of her hips as an overture, but remembering the discarded contraceptives decided against it: a child conceived today, out of duty, out of surrender, would be an unlucky child.

'Speak with Tony.' Paola hugged her pillow. 'See what he has. He promised he'd find something.'

Already. Not yet up and she's making plans. He told her about the water, happy to annoy her.

Marek hid in the café beside the *tabaccaio*. He watched Peña sweep the pavement, Lanzetti leave for work. The youth, Cecco, hung around the *tabaccaio* during the day and the Bar Fazzini at night, and seemed, oddly, to be friendly with Stefania, who otherwise sat at the counter and stitched all day without much of a word for anyone. For the boy she ordered coffee, Coke, *limonata* allowed him to sit with her and run errands on occasion.

At eight o'clock Paola sent Marek a message asking what he was doing. When he answered, *Speaking with Tony*, she responded immediately, *IMPOSSIBLE!!!! I just spoke w. him*. Moments later a third message: *He has a car for you*. Then a fourth. *Can you pick up more shirts? I need them this afternoon?*

I'll ask Tony.

As long as it happens.

He watched the palazzo. The supervisor, Peña, sat on an upturned crate in the long shadow beside the entrance. She looked like a doll, not only because she was small, but because of her high forehead, thin hair, tiny mouth and hands, and the way she sat with her legs stuck out. When she moved the action appeared mechanized. Unlike everyone else on the street she seldom spoke and he felt something in common with her because of this.

As Marek came out of the café Peña shuffled forward to slip off the crate. She waved to him, straightened her clothes, and signalled that she wanted a quick word.

Peña spoke formally but not coldly. 'You are a driver? Yes? I'm looking for a driver.'

'For how long?'

Peña didn't know. She'd ask Salvatore. Two men had rented a room from her. Two brothers. She believed they were French. They weren't from the city, and had an idea that they wanted to hire someone to drive them. She offered Marek a card with a handwritten number and asked him to copy it down. She also needed a room painted if he knew anyone who could manage this.

Marek said he'd see what he could do.

He found English Tony at the garage with Little Tony and Antonio. The three men discussed two cars raised on the loading bay; another car, a cream and grey old-style Citroën, sat on the sidewalk. English Tony broke away to speak with Marek.

'Use this one.' He signalled the Citroën. 'There's a pick-up in Bagnoli. Bring it straight back.' Tony looked him over with sympathy, and said he wouldn't know the extent of the damage to the coach until he'd taken a proper look. At an uninformed guess, worse scenario, the frame could be shunted back. If this was the case it would take a while to fix. Marek wondered what story Paola had told him, why he sounded calm about the matter, and why he would loan him the Citroën – a man who lost his temper at any provocation, and had once thrown a hammer at his son, Little Tony. Tony also did some dealing, nothing more serious than dope and maybe some light recreational blow for his American friends, and Marek clumsily implied that he could help, you know, deliver, you know, but English Tony didn't take up the invitation.

'Can I use the car this afternoon?'

Tony gave an expression Marek couldn't read.

'Paola needs some packages for her work. Some shirts.'

'Sure. Take it. But when you're done you bring it back.' English Tony gave a half-hearted wave, then added as an after-thought. 'But no accidents. OK? No damage. There's just one thing. Fuel. Don't go by the gauge. Sometimes she just dies.'

Marek drove to the *lungomare* at Mergelina and called Peña's number, and at first, because what was being said didn't exactly make sense, he thought that he was speaking to an answering machine – then realized that the phone had been answered by accident.

'If it's not in,' the voice said, 'we don't do it.'

After a rustle the call cut out.

Marek called a second time, and the answer came as a curt *pronto*. He spoke carefully, in Italian, and explained that he was a driver, and that he understood that they were looking for a driver. So . . . The call cut out a second time. Marek waited a moment before calling back. This time he spoke quickly and apologized for not having a name and said that he was a driver. The supervisor at the palazzo on via Capasso had given him the number. He understood that they needed a driver.

He felt that he had the man's attention.

'You need a driver?'

In the background he could hear another voice, in French, a man demanding to be given the phone.

'Hello. You are a driver? You know the city? Can you come at four this afternoon? We can discuss rates when you come. Room 312. Hotel Grand.'

The man gave an address in Castellammare di Stabia. Did he get that? 'It's on the hill,' he said. 'On the mountain. Looking at Napoli. The big white hotel. You will find us, yes? Room 312.'

Marek said yes, and once the call was cancelled he realized that he had not taken a name, just a room number.

They called an hour later and cancelled the meeting.

By the afternoon Marek found himself in the basement stripped to his waist with two tubs of white emulsion and a roller that didn't apply paint so much as drag grit off the walls. He couldn't quite believe how quickly the walls absorbed the water, and then flaked. Four hundred euro made the job worthwhile. Good money from the same men who'd wanted a driver then changed their minds.

Marek worked through the afternoon and grew resentful while he painted, what choices had he made to come to this: making do by driving cars and painting rooms? Falling deeper into debt while his mother slowly lost her mind. He set himself to the task, bought new brushes and a third tub of emulsion from the hardware store at the back of the palazzo. He stripped down to his shorts and felt the air wrap round him blanket-warm, and as he worked sweat stung his eyes. Once he was done the room seemed little improved. Brighter, yes, but otherwise no different. Four hundred euro would barely service his debt. Four thousand euro would pay the debt and leave enough, perhaps, for his mother or for Paola, but no money for himself.

He took a call while he waited in the courtyard for the final layer to dry. The men who'd rented the room wanted to know if the room was ventilated. Marek picked up a toy dropped by the door. A scuba diver, a black figure with moveable arms and legs, the mask missing and two small round holes in his back where an aqualung would fit. He described the room, said there was a window, high on one of the side walls, but the basement was a good six or seven metres below street level so there was little chance that air could circulate. He wasn't sure quite what they needed, because the air was dry and stale and the walls flaked as soon as you touched them.

The man became hesitant. That wasn't good news. 'It's going to be used for storage,' he explained. 'It's important that everything remains clean, you understand?' He seemed to think something through. 'You need to line the walls and the ceiling with plastic. Do it properly, nice and neat.'

Marek listened as the man outlined the job. Behind a row of railings stacked against the wall he found another toy, a small figurine of a green plastic soldier. He wasn't sure how to ask for more money, and broached the subject cautiously. The man appeared to sense his unease. 'We can pay, of course.' Marek could buy the materials, see to the work and they would reimburse him. If this could be done by Thursday they would double the money.

Marek returned to the hardware store and bought a roll of plastic. He explained what he needed to the clerk, a man with grey rheumy eyes.

The man swept his hair from his face and shuffled to the back of the store between racks of shelving.

'It's not the best way to do it. It's dry now, but when it rains the damp will come through the stone. You need to build walls.' The clerk returned with a long box on his shoulder, his expression – as if setting Marek's face to memory – remained stern. 'You need to know what you're doing. These days people don't know what they're doing.'

Back in the basement Marek cut lines of plastic to the length of the room. He carefully trimmed the sheets and set them side by side ready to tape together. He left enough plastic to make a lip to double over as a seam. By late afternoon he'd managed to cut the all pieces for the ceiling and walls.

Determined to complete the project in one day he worked late and found satisfaction in this labour, a level of pride, a return to the normal world of work and reward. The walls and ceiling were smartly lined, the floor scraped clean and painted, and the room reeked of a fresh chemical smell.

He called the brothers a second time. 'It's ready,' he said. 'It should stay up for as long as you need.' He crossed the courtyard for a better signal and blinked up at the square of pure blue sky five floors above him. Two windows open – Lanzetti's, and opposite, the supervisor, Peña – all others shuttered or blocked with the purring back-ends of air-conditioning units.

The men said they were pleased, one on the phone the other prompting in the background.

A helicopter crossed overhead, POLIZIA, too small for the noise it was making, smaller even than the swallows diving for ants. Marek waited for it to return but the clapper-like sound soon faded.

In the evening he sat with Paola, he drank two glasses of water without speaking, then started on the wine, and mentioned, because he couldn't help himself, that he was being paid eight hundred euro to clean up a room.

'It's hot down there,' he said, to excuse his appearance. He realized his mistake, regretted bringing up the money because now she would make plans. 'It's good to work with your hands.'

Paola explained that the water wasn't running but she'd set aside some buckets so he could wash. They could think about that holiday, then? Croatia, maybe? There was a place on the coast. 'The hotel is

close to the port and the beach and there are places to eat. It's convenient for the ferry. Easy.' How many nights did he think they should stay?

'Let's see about my mother.'

'One week,' she said. 'Six nights. No more.' She looked at him
closely. 'Good, we can decide this tonight otherwise the money will
just go. If you found work today, there will be more tomorrow.'

☆

Lila scooped up the bear and hid it under her jacket as she came out
of the room. On the dresser sat a number of other toys from a suitcase of examples, some unfamiliar – hand-stitched felt with glass
eyes – and others more recognizable, rubber-formed figures with hard
faces and outstretched arms: Topolino, Goofy, Pinocchio. Picking up
the toy to put it right and taking it was one continuous action.

Out on the landing Lila checked that the door remained closed
then wrapped the jacket about the bear. She shimmied her skirt the
right way round and fastened the zip. The tang of stale talcum still with
her, and right before her, looking down, a city bright with bare sunlight
and the rising scents of braised meats: infinitely busy, infinitely small.
Lila didn't like heights, or holes, or any kind of drop which presented a
proposition: to jump, throw, or hurtle into, difficult to resist.

The man had deliberately sat the toys upright in the suitcase, row
upon row, stadium-style, to face the bed: three stacked lines that
would have taken patience to arrange. He was happy to finish himself
off, he said, just as long as she watched, so Lila watched, ass tipped up
and head twisted on the pillow. Out of his shirt the salesman looked
underfed and pale, a dry man with a pinched, soapy face, and the same
soft eyes and calf-like lashes as Cecco – a coincidence she didn't like.
Once he was done he asked her to pass him the hand-towel and complained that she hadn't paid attention, but slipped off somewhere,
present but not attentive. He spoke Italian in a northern accent and
every comment came as a complaint. On the floor beside the bed lay
an open map, a pencil stub, and a single new shoe. When she thought-
lessly used the towel to wipe her thighs the man lost his temper.

Light on her feet Lila scooped up her clothes, took the abuse, nothing more than shouting, and snatched the panda as she opened the
door. If there was ever trouble Lila knew how to smartly break a nose
and run. Four times now she'd sped out of a building, clattering onto

some corso or piazza, her heart in her mouth and clothes in her arms. She wore plimsolls, large and loose, as per Arianna's advice to keep her shoes on – because *men can't run after sex. They just can't do it, as their energy, momentarily, lies elsewhere.* The shoes' loose slap drew memories of a wheel-less camper in a dry pine wood, in which she'd tolerated the same kind of attention she tolerated now. Memories of running across sand as a skinny girl, a spider – all legs and arms, all knees and elbows – weren't especially real, but this is how she saw herself, as something in flight.

Cecco was gone. Disappeared as soon as he'd received the money. The deal, arranged by Rafí, was simple: *Cecco goes along to make sure the men pay first, after which he does as he pleases, just as long as the money reaches Rafí by the end of play.* Lila became used to Cecco watching from a doorway, stairwell, or window (stealthy enough to keep out of plain sight and always a little sulky when she returned). Cecco, Arianna said, was a picture. She couldn't work out if he was dumb or not, and supposing he was an idiot, just how deep it ran through him: if you offered the boy too many choices he simply sat down, confused, head shaking, and he only washed when Rafí reminded him. Who could guess what Cecco wanted, coming back each night with pizza, *aranchini*, some days a bottle of wine, and other days pills? And who could guess what his business with Rafí actually involved, he just hung around without purpose, almost as if he loved him?

Lila headed down the wrong flight of stairs to a sudden view of the Albergo dei Poveri, a building so monumentally solid that she paused when she knew she had no time to pause. How in four months had she not noticed this? Finding herself at a secured gate she threw the bear and jacket first, then climbed over, eyes fixed on the long red roof of a building that could be a prison, or a barrack, or maybe a workhouse. Three flights down the air reeked of petrol. Everything about the day scorched and hard except the view of distant hills; Capodimonte, Vomero, and there, Vesuvius, the tip of it seen through fumes, blunt, jellied green.

She squeezed the bear as she picked it up and found a pocket stitched into the back, a pouch large enough to fit four fingers up to the second knuckle. She could feel the seam inside, the stitches beginning to loosen.

*

Lila avoided the traders grouped in the lobby at the Hotel Stromboli. Nigerians, Kenyans, sweaty men twice her height with blankets folded into sacks filled with belts, handbags, sandals, goods they sold on the streets. Quietly up the last of the stairs she paused to take off her shoes and slowly unzip her skirt. She stepped barefoot into the room, into the heat, breath held, toes testing for the edge of the mattress that took up most of the floor. In the late afternoons she preferred to lie beside Arianna, who was softer, less agitated, easier company than Rafí.

The salesman had worn two condoms, insisted on the detail, then was brief and rough, and she could feel him stuck to her guts and hated the idea that the man stayed with her and how it was getting harder to leave everything in place. Rafí told a good story about how she was stolen from her family, how she was naive, maybe even a bit simple, and while no one seriously believed this there wasn't a man who didn't find pleasure in the notion.

Arianna slept with her back to the window, a blade of sunlight across her shoulder. Lila shuffled out of her clothes then sat carefully on the edge of the mattress and waited for her eyes to become used to the dark. She set the panda against the wall then curled beside her friend and settled down as if slipping into water. She held her breath, slowly exhaled, attempted to empty her mind. As soon as she relaxed Rafí's dog began to bark, he sounded close, as if from a neighbouring room. Two floors below, tethered by a chain to an upright pole, Rafí kept a skinny white bull mastiff on an open rooftop. The creature slept outdoors without proper shelter or shade, it loped from one flat of cardboard to another to stay cool, ate whatever was thrown at it, and barked in pitiful, chuffing coughs. Scabbed and hairless, the animal stank.

Arianna slowly woke and reached blindly behind her, tap-tapping Lila's hip. 'You're back already. Oh? Cecco didn't wait?'

Lila's chin nuzzled Arianna's shoulder. Her arm crossed under her breasts, and she thought for a moment that she could smell Rafí's aftershave, a smell not locked to the skin but hovering above, separate.

'He wants us to go to the Fazzini.' Arianna yawned into the pillow and gave a sour chuckle. 'Tonight. I don't know though?'

There were whole days when Lila wouldn't speak. Not one word.

They began to prepare for the evening at nine o'clock. Arianna gathered clothes and make-up onto their shared mattress, along with what remained of Rafí's favours – crushed pills, halved tabs in foil and brittle plastic packs, treats from his associates at the hospital: for this, at least, he was useful. Arianna made no bones about it, these gifts were the only reasons she would tolerate him. For Lila the matter was entirely transparent. She knew three people in Naples: Arianna, Rafí, and Cecco. Between the four of them they knew only the district pinched between the Stazione Centrale, the Hotel Stromboli, and via Carbonara. While they could name the hotels alongside the marina they had little idea what lay inland.

Lila sat still as Arianna brushed her hair. She squeezed the panda between her thighs, teased its fur, and plucked stuffing from its pocket. Arianna worked herself into a sulk and asked why they should go tonight, what was so important about the Fazzini? Why did they always have to do what Rafí told them?

Lila looked up because the question made no sense.

'He has this man he wants us to meet,' Arianna scoffed. 'We can find men by ourselves. We can look after ourselves. We should never have come here.' By *here* Arianna meant Naples.

Lila sorted through the make-up. Rafí had his uses, even Arianna had to admit, and it wasn't like they had any choice. Rafí, in his scattershot way, provided clothes and food, arranged this room at the Stromboli and made sure they were secure and they had something to sleep on. Rafí found business for them, ensured the men paid, he picked out new names and refigured their histories so the whole mess of Spain was forgotten. It was Rafí's idea that Lila and Arianna should work together as sisters, and he bought them small gold pendants, an A for Arianna, an L for Lila.

In private they thought him ridiculous. To his face they were sulkily obedient. Arianna had forgotten how difficult life was before Rafí, how the traders harassed them for sex and money, and she was forgetting the trouble they'd had from other women, from the police, how easy it was now they didn't have to hustle for business: you couldn't work the city on your own.

Still, while he made business easier, he couldn't make it any more pleasant. Preoccupied by the salesman Lila imagined him checking out of the hotel, the toys secure in their suitcase, a phone nudged between his shoulder and ear; the man talking and walking to his car and speaking with his wife, his girlfriend, his mother, or perhaps a daughter who might be close to Lila's age. She couldn't understand why this especially bothered her.

Arianna brushed Lila's hair in measured sweeps. All in all Rafí demanded too much of their attention. She dropped the brush and drew Lila's hair back through her hands. 'I'm serious,' she said. 'We don't need him. And what about the dog? I hate that dog. Every day, bark, bark, bark, bark, bark.'

Lila found the lipstick she wanted. She held up the mirror, stretched her mouth to a smile, then drew a finger across her lips.

Arianna, now standing, said that Lila looked like the panda. Adorable.

As Lila drew the lipstick across her lower lip she had the idea that the salesman was polluting the toys, showing them something of the world before he handed them over to families and children who would take them into their homes, their beds.

They found Rafí at the bar, shirt unbuttoned to a grey T-shirt, sleeves rolled up, Cecco beside him with his elbows on the counter looking more boyish than usual. Rafí signalled out the man he wanted Lila and Arianna to meet.

'You know him?' Rafí asked. 'He's here all the time. His name is Salvatore, goes by *Graffa*. He lives in the palazzo opposite.'

Reed-thin, static, heron-grey and bald, the man wore workmen's trousers and a workman's shirt. Lila found his bird-like sharpness a little sickening and thought the man didn't belong in the bar. If such a man wanted company he'd pick up women along the marina. Such a man, being fifty-five, maybe sixty, would be married or separated, and almost certainly would prefer young girls.

By the time Lila and Arianna reached the counter, Rafí was already at the man's side. He rested his hand on the man's arm and whispered to him. Cecco, watching, appeared bereft.

Lila watched Cecco as Cecco watched Rafí.

Rafí bought the man a drink. Salvatore, he said, persuasive, overusing the name, Sal. *Graffa* then followed him outside when he wanted to smoke and stood so close that when the man exhaled he blew smoke over Rafí's shoulder. Arianna leaned close to Lila and said they should be going, her voice now hoarse. Although the bar was busy there would be no business, and she didn't like the way things were going with Rafí. The man, this Salvatore, wasn't interested – anyone could see. Lila shouldn't encourage Rafí. Tomorrow she'd have a word and find out exactly what was going on with their money. They shouldn't depend on him.

'Have you heard him talk?' She nodded toward the street. 'These stories?'

When they tried to leave Rafí stepped up to the entrance, sly and pleased with himself.

'It's good,' he said, his head turned so the man couldn't see him. 'He's interested.'

'In what? What have you told him?' Arianna steered Lila toward the street, and there, on a low stone wall, with the dark furred shafts of palm trees behind him, Salvatore sat waiting, expectant. Music from other bars slipped through the night air. Lila could smell jasmine, and looking up she saw a rusted sign of a star and realized that what she could taste in the air wasn't jasmine but scorched sugar and vanilla from a bakery. From the windows came the hum of fans and extractors.

Rafí whispered into Arianna's ear then stepped back. 'It's agreed. Right? You agree?'

Arianna looked to Lila then nodded. 'We do this, then we go.'

For a reasonable fee Rafí took the women to a car parked in the alley behind the bar.

Rafí shone a flashlight along the cobbles and spun the light over the sunken bags and newspaper packets bunkered into the doorways. Lila held her breath against the sweet boozy stink. Arianna became argumentative. A flashlight? A car? What was this exactly?

Salvatore turned his back to the group and spoke on his phone. When he was done he clicked his fingers to draw Rafí's attention. He nodded at Lila. 'Seriously. How old?'

'I told you. Fifteen.'

The man sucked on his teeth and shook his head, certain. 'She's not fifteen.'

Rafí gave a small confirming nod and called to Lila. 'Tell him. Fifteen?'

Lila nodded. Fifteen it was.

They kept their voices low, aware that above and about them were open windows to kitchens and bedrooms, the warren-like pockets of apartments dug side by side into sheer unornamented walls.

Salvatore repeated the information into the phone, one hand to his ear. 'Is she clean?'

Rafí held out his hands, palms up, as if insulted.

'Where's she from?'

'Originally?' Rafí blew out his cheeks, and slowly, indifferently, spun a story about how Lila was Sicilian, how her dark complexion came from Arab blood, but being too live a firecracker her family had packed her off to Mostra to the sweaty attentions of a retarded uncle and cretinous second-cousins. He'd found her in the Veneto, he said, picked her up on an autostrada, or some such flat un-sunny hinterland. Lila was a naive unfortunate who surrendered her ass night after night to every male member of her family, who might be imbecilic but knew enough about business to save that other temple for a paying stranger. So, in a sense, she was untouched, and yes, definitely clean. Unschooled but not uneducated. Dumped at the side of the road by her uncle after a final refusal she was making her way back home. This story played better than the earlier version where Rafí claimed that the women were sisters, who slept cat-like, entwined on a single bed in a small stone hut in some dumb coastal village. Driven by misfortune to the mainland to sell themselves, Lila and Arianna delivered nightly shows on hollow mattresses in dry, dirty basements right across the peninsula. In their primitive understanding there wasn't even a word for what they were, Arianna being a weird boy/girl hybrid so you couldn't actually call what they did lesbian. Any story played better than the truth, which, in Lila's case was nothing but bland. Lila came from Modena, and before that Skopje, the entire family uprooted when she was less than two years old, although she had no memory of this. End of story. Her father was a mechanic, as were her brothers. Her mother, gone too long for her to remember, had worked as a domestic. Now, Arianna, half-Spanish, was a more interesting bundle and told stories about her brothers who threatened her with knives, locked her in a room for an entire week the first time they saw her dressed as *Arianna*. The second she fled they told the neighbours she was dead. Rafí discovered her at a gas station ten kilometres outside of Pavia, where, he explained, she'd learned to suck the small change from a vending machine.

Salvatore listened without interest and repeated the information into the phone, and this time Lila could hear him repeating himself, as if the person he was speaking to could not follow the discussion. While the man listened he looked hard at Lila. 'Is what he says true?'

Lila shrugged.

Rafí pinched his tongue between his teeth and nodded.

Salvatore cleared his throat. 'What about the other one?'

Lila for her part was starting to tire; she couldn't see why they were waiting, or why they were doing business outside and on the phone. She hoped these men weren't Italian. Italian men talked everything to death, explained themselves and their sorry situations in endless preparation, each one of them secure in the notion that buggering a prostitute wasn't hard-line adultery. As soon as they were done Lila didn't exist, and this disregard seeded a real and terrible shame.

Rafí stepped away and shone the flashlight on Arianna, who stood with her arms folded, clearly unimpressed.

'And she has a—' The man whistled through his teeth and waggled his little finger. 'This one, she has a cock? Yes? A pistol?' He translated into the phone and then, speaking to Rafí, said that he needed to see for himself before they could decide.

Rafí turned the flashlight through the window to the back seat of the car. 'Just to look,' he cut his arm in a flat cross-swipe, 'anything different and you pay more.'

Arianna shot Lila a glance as she ducked into the car. She signalled Rafí to come close and whispered to him, the streetlight stroking his jet-black hair and greasing Arianna's forehead.

Inside the car Arianna sprawled across the back seat in an attempt to find a comfortable position. She raised her knees, struck up her feet and shimmied her hips lower and lower until her shoulders jammed against the door. Salvatore let her settle then took the flashlight and hunched through the front passenger door, folding himself inside as a man undertaking an unpleasant task.

Lila backed off and waited ten, fifteen paces away, poised on her toes. It wasn't fruit she could smell, ripe and spoiled, but a heap of flowers brought out of the chapel beside the music conservatory. The air fizzed with their perfume. On the brighter cross-street a woman sat side-saddle on the back of a scooter and whooped at friends out of sight on another bike. Hearing the scooter Rafí shrugged, indicating to Salvatore, ducked inside the car, that this was nothing. The scooter's buzz zipped across the shuttered shop fronts and the woman's shouts echoed up, teasingly unstable, mapping her route down via Tribunali, up via Atri, and back about the hospital. Lila listened knowing they would return, because that's what they did, these kids, they ran feckless circles round the Centro Storico until the police, or someone, stopped them.

Throughout the inspection Arianna lay across the seat, legs high and wide. It was hard for Lila to look without getting a little anxious. She wondered what it would be like if this car, the bags and newspapers, the armfuls of faded flowers, the mordant sticky stink itself, dislodged and tumbled down the hill with Arianna riding a tide of muck into the delicately detailed courtyard of the music conservatory.

Salvatore clambered out and straightened himself, tut-tutting, unimpressed. He wiped his hands on his shirt with the same distaste he'd demonstrated earlier. It wasn't Arianna that disgusted him, so much, but the task itself. The man spoke into the phone and then turned to Rafí. 'OK. They're interested,' he held the phone to his shoulder, 'but they want to see. I'll pay for one photo.'

'How much?'

The man ducked his head to listen. 'Twenty,' he said.

'Fifty.'

'Twenty-five. No more.'

Salvatore took less time on his second visit, and while he didn't touch Arianna, he shone the flashlight directly into her face.

Out of the car he straightened his shirt, and spent some time composing a message. Once he was done he shut the phone. Rafí stood with his hands in his pockets and bided time while they waited for a response. Lila wanted to go.

The phone gave one sustained trill. As he answered Salvatore coughed to clear his throat. He nodded as he listened. 'How much do they earn?'

Rafí shrugged and stepped back, his hands in the air.

'No. Don't walk away. These girls. How much do they earn?' Salvatore gestured at Arianna. 'Do you know how much she earns?'

Rafí gave no reaction.

'How much? Tell me what she makes in one night. Fifty? One hundred? Two hundred?' The man made a small seesaw gesture. 'How much?'

Rafí pursed his lips and refused to answer.

Salvatore redirected his question to Lila. 'You tell me. How much? You understand? How much do you earn?'

Lila kept still and refused to look up.

'They want to make an offer for both of them, for one night,' he said. 'What do you say? One hundred? Maybe two? Two hundred? Two hundred, let's say?'

Lila looked to Rafí then Arianna. If they made two hundred a night their debt to Rafí would have been paid a long time ago.

Salvatore held up his hand, and listening to the phone he appeared confused. 'How much do they weigh?' He kept the phone to his ear. 'Fifty kilos? Do you think she weighs fifty kilos? And the other? Sixty-nine?' Salvatore cleared his throat. 'I will pay you two euro per kilo.' He squinted as he made the calculation. 'So that's – what – that's the final offer. There's a party tonight. A party with important people, business-men, judges, people from Rome. Name a price and I'll pay you now, and the women are ours.'

Rafí looked to Arianna, who now leaned out of the car. She shook her head at that final phrase, it suggested intention, sleight of hand, a game with uncertain parameters.

'I have to be honest,' Rafí explained. 'Usually, the way this works, I bring men to them, or I take them to the men. Hotels, private parties, saunas . . .'

Salvatore nodded.

'. . . if people know they are working, then other people are going to start expecting things. Money. Favours.' Rafí softly rolled his head from side to side. 'You understand? And everything becomes difficult. If everything is quiet then everything is good.'

Rafí looked back to Lila, then Arianna. Arianna curtly shook her head.

'OK. You can all come with me.' Salvatore made a final gesture of agreement, and took out a wallet fat with cash. Fingers flicking through the notes he peeled off five, six, seven, and held them out. 'Here. OK? For you.'

Rafí accepted the money, but his eyes remained fixed on the man's wallet, on the new, unspoiled notes.

'It's for you, OK?' he said, 'and something for the photograph.'

Rafí counted the money as he folded the notes into a small roll.

Salvatore walked ahead and crossed the street diagonally. Rafí followed behind, arm in arm with Lila and Arianna. The street cut directly through the old quarter, a broad barricade of shop-fronts. The build-ings rose six or seven storeys in one face, a long line undercut by an arcade, with regular balconies along the upper floors, shuttered windows, and huge tarred carriage doors. Salvatore hesitated at the entrance to the palazzo and appeared to have trouble opening the small portal door. In the shop beside the entrance, spelled out across the glass were the words SALVATORE-GRAFFA/ARANCHINI/PIZZA, the end of the sign obscured by a banner.

Rafí stepped back to Lila and Arianna. 'They have a room,' he said, 'here, in the basement.'

Lila leaned backward to take in the full height of the building.

'They?'

'These brothers.'

'How do you know this?' Arianna blew smoke directly into Rafí's face. 'He said there was a party.'

'They want to look. The brothers. First they take a look, then they take you to the party.'

'You'll stay with us?'

Rafí handed the flashlight to Lila and told them to wait.

With the door now open Salvatore signalled that they should be quiet.

Lila followed Arianna into a square courtyard to find Salvatore struggling with a second door – this difficulty set Arianna into a giggle, and the man stopped, held out his hand and indicated that she needed to be silent. The door, metal, smaller even than the first, refused to pull open.

Lila stood in the centre of the courtyard and shone the torch up the wall. A square of low cloud yellowed by the street lamps stoppered the opening. All but one of the shutters were closed, and Lila thought she could see a figure leaning out. When she shone the flashlight directly at the window the socket appeared empty. Lila switched off the torch but kept her eye on the spot, and there, too indistinct to be certain, appeared a face – what she took to be a child. Lila tapped Arianna's shoulder, looked back up, but couldn't quite tell in the darkness if there was someone at the open window or if this was her imagination.

Salvatore finally turned the key, unlocked the door, and beckoned them forward. Lila looked up a last time, and there, bumping down the wall, came a small object tied to a piece of string. Arianna fussed with her skirt, Salvatore and Rafí ducked through the doorway. Lila, captivated by the thread and the lowering object – a toy, a small plastic figure – walked to the wall and waited for the toy to reach her, watched it twirl as it came down. Salvatore, irritated at her dawdling, hissed at her to hurry.

She raised her hands, let the toy settle into them, looked up as she drew the thread away from the wall. In the open window four flights up, she could clearly see a boy leaning over the edge, holding the other end of the thread and a torch. The boy flashed the light, twice, and Lila signalled back with two blinks. She directed her beam at the window and was surprised to see how young the boy was, his face all moonish, round, a little startled. Torchlight from the window strafed the paving, settled on her face. Lila smiled up and raised her hands so he could see the toy.

Salvatore shoved her out of the light so hard that she fell backward, and without thinking she punched, open hand, heel first, and blunted the man in the face, struck his nose – then scuttled to the doorway, and further, to the street, so fast that she didn't stop until Rafí and Arianna grabbed hold of her. What was she playing at? What was she doing? Arianna pulled her upright, drew her quickly into the streetlight toward the noise of the Fazzini while Rafí reasoned with Salvatore, salvaged what he could, saying: 'Calm. Calm. Let's all keep calm.'

Lila didn't understand the problem. Arianna stroked her face and said she shouldn't worry, 'but these men, they don't want to be seen. It's not so good to draw attention to yourself. You shouldn't have hit him.'

Arianna hectored Lila on the walk back.

'He was laughing at us,' she complained. 'What was he saying? How much we weigh?' She waited for Lila to catch up. 'The price of what, of meat? Who were these brothers? Who talks like this?'

Lila wanted to find something to eat. Michele's would be open, they could pick up pizza, Pepsi, *frittura*, but Arianna walked ahead without a word. She walked wide of the doorways and the shuttered booths, suspicious of every man they passed.

Back at the Hotel Stromboli, Lila settled against Arianna. Arianna complained about the dog, her long body stretched out, head turned to the window, straw-coloured hair loose about her face. Bark, bark, bark, she complained, every time they come back. No end of trouble. She spoke slowly, lazily, as if the words were too weighty to heft out, her arm hung over the side of the mattress. On the floor between them, mismatched shoes, a scrap of foil, three lighters – all spent – an envelope with two remaining pills, egg blue on one side and white on the other. Lila pressed her head back into Arianna's thigh.

'Did it hurt?' Lila asked. She could feel her voice vibrate through her collarbone. There had to be some science behind this, the way that people intuit sound, how some people sense danger, or how animals, dogs for example, or birds, know that trouble is coming, or feel threat in their bones, a coming earthquake, a lightning strike, a wall of water. The dog's barks also passed through her.

'Did it what?'

'Hurt. When you were in hospital?'

Another pulse ran through Lila's shoulders. She could smell Rafí's aftershave, a metal tang to it, old and sour.

Arianna crawled out from under her and sat upright. 'We need to think. We need to plan what we're going to do when he comes back. If he had to give back all that money . . .' She rested her hand on Lila's head and apologized. 'I should have been watching you.'

☆

In the late afternoon Peña swept the courtyard and kept an eye open for Sami's toys but found nothing. When Dr Lanzetti returned to the palazzo he passed by Peña and continued to the stairs without a word. A man who walks with his head down, his hands in his pockets, a man who used to show politeness, who passes now without the time of day, is a man in trouble.

That night Peña waited until Arturo Lanzetti and Anna Soccorsi were in bed. Neither of them had spoken much through the evening; Anna's mood infected the air. Again the palazzo settled into its own subterranean sounds, the tiny clicks of cooling tiles, the snap of contracting wood, of pipes tightening.

Sami appeared at the window some time after midnight, awake and ready. With his shoes over his hands he slowly pushed open his shutters. The boy must be standing on a chair, or a box, something to raise him level to the window so that he didn't need to scramble up.

This confidence made Peña anxious. The boy was becoming bolder and she worried that with any misstep he would fall, but he stood, framed by the window, the room a black hollow behind him. After half an hour she could not help herself and drifted into sleep.

The first disturbance of the night came as a scuffle, a woman's shouts and a confusion of voices, how many men how many women she couldn't tell, although one of the voices, she was certain, was Salvatore's. By the time she made it to the window the fuss was over, the entrance door shut, the courtyard silent. The boy's window and blinds now closed.

The second disturbance came several hours later when Peña was woken once again by a soft call, men's voices rising though the hollow. She looked out and saw the boy standing on the window ledge, one hand timidly touching the shutter, his toes tipped to the lintel. Four floors up and the boy stood at the lip of his window, knees slightly bent, while from the courtyard voices seemed to coax him forward with a baritone coo. Unsure of what she should do Peña picked up her water glass. Terrified that she might startle him and cause him to fall. She thought to drop the glass, but instead simply struck it lightly, a spoon against a glass – a slight sound, clear and distinct. The boy looked up. He stepped back, and Peña moved forward so that he could see her. The boy slipped further back from the edge, clambered down, then closed the shutters. With the shutters closed, the voices stopped, and she thought that she had imagined this. A startling image, a boy in a window, so high above the courtyard.

The third disturbance came at four in the morning. A shout from the boy's room, cries, the clatter of shutters thrown open: light cast directly across the courtyard to brighten her room.

A scene of unity, the three together in the boy's room, Lanzetti holding the child, the mother bent beside him, insisting that she look at his hand, prising it open, and the boy twisted away, stuck to his father crying slow ow-ow-ow's.

Anna came to the window, looked down into the courtyard and then shouted across to Peña. 'Who did this? You saw. You must have seen.'

Peña shook her head.

'It's impossible. You must have seen who did this. You see everything.' Anna leaned further over the ledge, fierce and unwavering.

Peña again shook her head.

Anna left the boy's bedroom. Lanzetti followed after – the boy fast to his side – asking where she was going.

'I'm going to talk to her,' Peña heard her say. 'I'll make her tell me who did this,' she said, 'that shrunken little bitch.'

Peña stood at her door and opened it knowing that the woman would shout at her, that there would be no containment, no reserve. Anna Soccorsi came across the landing with a toy held in her hand, a small metal car, the front end blackened.

'They heated this. Do you see? He burned his hand. It was deliberate. Do you understand? This is assault, and you saw who did it.' Now warmed up, she looked over Peña's shoulder and caught sight of Sami's toys laid out across Peña's kitchen table. Her voice immediately slipped gear, became incredulous, alarmed. 'What is this?' She turned to Peña. 'Those are my son's toys. Look,' she shouted to Lanzetti and pointed, 'look, she has his toys. It was you? It was you! I'm calling the police.' One hand covering her mouth, Anna turned and ran back to her apartment.

Back in her apartment Anna vented her rage at her husband. In one long monologue she lay out her dissatisfactions, her outrage, her unhappiness, and this, this assault, was the natural result of how they lived. A burn on his hand today, and what tomorrow? Lanzetti could not soothe her and found no consolation for her outrage.

Lanzetti came to apologize. Peña stepped aside and allowed him into her apartment. His eyes settled first on the table. She had cleared the boy's toys away, hidden them in a drawer. Uncomfortable, the doctor nodded at the windows – the closed shutters.

'All these people,' he said, 'so close. The way we live now.' Lanzetti meshed his hands together.

She asked if he would like a seat, but the man remained standing, the size of him, filling the room. 'How is your son?'

'It's not so serious. He has a blister.' Lanzetti forced his hands into his pocket. 'He was fishing,' he said, 'playing a game with people he couldn't see. He sent down a toy on a piece of string and they heated it up.' He began to apologize. 'She spends all of her time with him. She won't let him go to school. It's difficult for her. And Sami,' he said, 'believes all of these things, these ideas. He mixes them up.' Lanzetti smiled and shook his head. He spoke slowly and chose his words with care.

'He says that he can hold his breath for fifteen minutes. Fifteen minutes. This is what he says. He believes that he has special powers,

Check Out Receipt

Parsippany-Troy Hills Library
973-887-5150
www.parsippanylibrary.org

Thursday, February 4, 2016 10:48:39 AM

Item: 0102905631390
Title: The wolf at the door
Material: Book
Due: 03/03/2016

Item: 0102903127425
Title: The price of power : a novel
Material: Book
Due: 03/03/2016

Item: 0102902902851
Title: Time to hunt : a novel
Material: Book
Due: 03/03/2016

Item: 0102906430594
Title: The kills : Sutler, The massive, The kill, and, The hit
Material: Book
Due: 03/03/2016

Total items: 4

Please note the hours at the Mt. Tabor
Library have changed. The new hours are:
Monday-Thursd   11AM-7PM
Friday & Saturday: 9AM-1PM
Closed Sundays

that he can control things. He believes that if he concentrates hard enough he can shatter glass, or start fires, or flood a room. He believes that he can make the building shake.'

Lanzetti cleared his throat. 'He does not like to sleep, because he thinks that when he sleeps he cannot control these powers. He believes that when he is idle he makes bad things happen, that when he is asleep he is responsible for earthquakes and landslides. For accidents. I read the paper with him every day to teach him that these things are coincidental. That they have nothing to do with him, that the world works without him and he is not responsible. But unlike other children he isn't able to let this go. He thinks that there are people hunting for him. I'm not sure what we will do.'

WEDNESDAY: DAY D

Mizuki told the story in class about the brothers at the station. An ordinary moment, easily told, about how, on three successive days, she had noticed one man on the platform, the other up on the concourse, and how on that first day she was confused to see a man she assumed to be behind her, suddenly, so quickly, ahead. Today she'd found the men waiting side by side at the top of the escalator: both men had watched her walk by, hands in pocket, one without much interest, the other with a certain intensity. This time she had her phone ready, but didn't dare take a photograph, and didn't pause to buy water. In crude and cumbersome Italian she explained her confusion and delight in seeing one man doubled. Today, the couple (could you even call brothers a couple?) followed her to the station exit – although she couldn't be certain that this was deliberate. She used the words *attractive*, *handsome*, when what she wanted to say was brutish. *Bruto* in Italian meant ugly, and the word caused confusion.

The tutor nodded as Mizuki spoke: not in agreement, but collecting mistakes. The group discussed what the men could be waiting for – some crime no doubt, Mizuki should watch her bag. Those stations are dangerous.

The tutor shrugged. 'It's part of our culture to observe. It rarely means what you think.'

The women disagreed, and began speaking in English. It wasn't the looks, so much, but the comments, or the tutting, what was that about? Men tutting at women? And wasn't it worse in southern Italy than anywhere else?

Mizuki found nothing problematic in the men's interest. Nothing troublesome. It wasn't quite interest in any case. She knew the word in English, she knew it in Japanese: one of the men was *assessing* her. Collecting information. He'd looked at her, three times, with a kind of assessment that had little to do with catching her eye. When men look at you they usually expect a response. But this man didn't appear to want anything.

Although her story had nothing to do with coincidence, the class became busy with stories of happenstance: a woman who missed a flight that crashed into the ocean off Brazil, only to be killed one year later in a car accident in Austria; a man who survived one bombing in London to die four years later in another. Mizuki could not follow the logic. Europeans, she thought, Americans, are like birds in the way they collect information: greedy and undisciplined. How foreign this all seemed in comparison to the look she'd received three times at the Circumvesuviana, a look of solid concentration, a look signifying intelligence, a focused assessment.

With some effort the tutor drew the conversation back to the previous night, to conversations the students might have attempted in Italian. But the discussion slipped into rumour and could not be retrieved.

'I don't like it here. It isn't safe.'

The group nodded in agreement.

'It's no worse than anywhere else.' Mizuki shrugged and added that the city was beautiful, knowing this would please the tutor.

'It's not the city. It's the people.'

The other students keenly agreed. Something about the city just didn't feel safe. Mizuki flushed with embarrassment.

One of the military wives spoke up. 'They warn us not to go into the centre on our own. We aren't allowed into the Spanish Quarter. Don't even think about it.'

While Mizuki had spent time in Berkeley there were still some American accents she couldn't follow.

The tutor clapped her hands, 'Italian! We speak in Italian!' This was not what she wanted to discuss.

A French student shifted her chair forward. 'I couldn't live here. It's all the same. The restaurants serve Italian food and nothing else. There's a Japanese restaurant in Vomero, and guess what? They sell pizza.' She held up her hands, exasperated. 'Seriously. This is old Europe. It's important what village you come from, or street, or neighbourhood. It matters. People actually care about that kind of thing.'

Mizuki couldn't accept the point. How different was this, say, from New York, Paris, Tokyo, where people took you more seriously depending on your street, district, zone.

The American student held up her hand. And what about the Spanish student in Elementario Due who was chased through the Centro Storico *by a man with a machete?*

The tutor dipped forward in defeat. She knew this student, she said, and Erica, point of fact, wouldn't run even if her head were on fire.

'I heard this from an Italian,' the American continued regardless. 'There's an earthquake in the middle of the day, OK, and a house shared by two families – one family from Milan, the other from Venice – and it's totally destroyed. Which family die?'

The women fell silent.

'A family from Naples who broke in while the others were at work.'

Mizuki could not look up and didn't want to face the tutor. The class fell silent: when the tutor finally spoke she suggested they take an early break.

Mizuki waited in the stairwell for Lara to finish her class: she checked the messages on her phone then switched it off. She thought to leave, to return to the station although she guessed the brothers would be gone by now. A young man flapped a dishcloth out of a window; the sound dislocated and came softly across the courtyard to her, undiminished. People knew their neighbours because the courtyards amplified every detail: the TVs, radios, the clatter of plates and cutlery, the arguments and supple conversations, the flushing toilets, the water running through pipes, and with surprising frequency, people singing or coughing. To live here was to sense your neighbours at all hours, to taste the food they ate, to bear their good tempers and bad. It made no sense that she would like this city, being so opposite to home, so permeable and messy.

When Lara finally arrived the friends kissed in greeting. Lara said she looked tired and asked if she still wasn't sleeping.

Mizuki shrugged, who knew why these things happened?

'You should rest this weekend.'

They sat on the cool marble steps of the open stairwell, quietly sharing confidences, while other students (the military wives, the vacationing teachers) on their way to the café mixed with priests and clerks from the seminary offices. Mizuki, closest to the courtyard, kept an eye on the wasps, small specks chaotically charging the air two floors below. No one else appeared bothered.

She repeated the joke, knowing it would annoy Lara.

'They talk about this place like it's a zoo,' Lara slapped her hand to the step. 'Come on. I need a cigarette.'

Mizuki followed Lara through the courtyard and kept close to her side; her hands tucked away, her collar drawn up. Wasps zagged over the biscuits in untold numbers, their tiny shadows flitting across the wax paper, antennae dipping for syrup. A horror show. Mizuki covered her mouth, held back her hair, half-ran to the door with her eyes closed, suppressing a squeal – bad enough to be stung, far worse to swallow one.

Once outside Lara lit up, indignant now, unaware of her friend's small panic. Mizuki held her hand to her heart.

'And where does she get these ideas? She lives in Bagnoli.' Lara huffed out smoke. 'These houses are behind gates, no one can visit. Americans keep themselves locked away. They aren't houses, they're safes.'

The buildings overshadowed the street and drew out a cavernous darkness. A clean blue sky pinched above tight black alleyways of old stucco facades, of dim intestinal yellows and pinks. Above them hung a sign for the bakery, a simple tin star in a circle. How familiar this was now, this depth: straight lines buckled to time and gravity. Streets designed for walking, for carts, made perfect runs for scooters and dogs and channelled their noise.

'If they don't offer me something soon I'll have to go back.' Due to finish her course, Lara taught sessions at the language school as part of her placement. 'It's good to have work, but it's always temporary, and it's not enough. Everywhere is the same.'

They watched students return from the cafe one by one, each buzzing first, then ducking through the small portal door. Mizuki looked over two dusty violas displayed in the window of an antiques store. She held her hand to the glass to see into the shop.

'They never sell anything. I've never seen it open,' Lara paused. 'You're wearing a wedding ring?'

Equally surprised, Mizuki looked at her own hand then held it up for Lara to see.

'I've never seen you wear a ring.'

'It was my mother's.' Mizuki automatically began to screw the ring about her finger. 'I wear it at home. Sometimes. I forgot to take it off.'

The first bell rang and they returned to the courtyard. Lara hesitated at the door, half-in, half-out, unconvinced by Mizuki's answer.

Mizuki let Lara walk ahead, worried now that Lara would ask bolder, more direct questions. She hurried by the bakery, did not look at the trays of biscuits, but noticed, up on the third landing, the American, Helen, arms up, flailing, and couldn't make sense of her gestures, how her hands slapped uselessly at the air. Up the stairs Mizuki kept behind Lara to avoid her questions, and the reason for the waving came to her. A wasp.

Mizuki fell immediately on the first sting, sudden and heavy, and upturned her bag even as the wasp, caught in her hair, stung her throat a second and third time. She frantically ruffled her hair, felt the insect between her fingers as something rough, like a seed head, caught then swiped free, she saw the pen, a red tube, tumble out of her bag with her lipstick, face cream, sun cream, tissues, hand mirror, mascara; her course books scudded down the steps, her phone. She snatched up the pen, snapped off the top, stuck it to her shoulder and injected herself.

By the time Lara reached her, Mizuki was done. The wasp, flicked out of her hair, spun circles on the marble.

And now the part she hated, a light woozy bafflement, how she might even seem a little drunk. How inevitable this was because of the biscuits, the syrup, the wasp's natural aggression, and how day after day for six weeks the odds were getting thin. Inevitable now that Lara would ask questions about the ring and Mizuki would have to explain herself.

Lara brought her to the office then returned to the stairwell to collect her bag and books. Mizuki sat by the computers expecting to feel sick, an awful anticipation. She took the water offered to her, insisted that she was all right, and explained to Lara once she returned that she took antihistamine each night as a precaution. Who could say if this helped, if this time there would or would not be a reaction?

'When I was a girl,' she explained, 'I was stung.' Once, on her foot – and her legs, her arms, her face swelled like she was some kind of windbag, or some instrument. And while her throat had not sealed, a mighty itch had troubled her afterward as if her neck was fur-lined, and the threat that one day she might choke stuck with her. Ant bites, spider bites, a scratch once from coral, and she swelled up, ballooned.

As if to prove her contrariness the insulin depressed her. She could feel the immediate effect. Not sick now but tired. A nurse from Elementario Due came out to check her pulse, her throat, and declared if something was going to happen, it would have happened. Mizuki wasn't sure that this was true. She hid in the toilet and hoped that Lara would leave her, but Lara stuck outside and waited in the corridor.

An undiscouraged Lara accompanied her to the station. Because of her tiredness, Mizuki felt a general disconnection from what she was doing; more than this, she felt empty, and this emptiness seemed evident in every spoken word and gesture, to the flow of passengers rising on escalators or paused on the stairs, the deepening sunlight, the presence of the scaffolding, of paint pots and rollers laid across the platform. She insisted that she would be all right; two hours now and there were no serious fears, no reaction. She just wanted to be home. Home? In the hot and still air it seemed possible that she could haul herself above the hubbub and swim free. In her dreams flying and swimming were the same action, but even when dreaming she never really lost what was troubling her, she never really became free.

Mizuki took off her sunglasses and shook her head. She pointed at the stubby towers of Porta Nolana, close by there was a café, she said, she had something she wanted to say.

Lara paid for the coffees, brought them to the window where they stood and faced the Circumvesuviana station. The sun sparked off windscreens and chrome of passing traffic. She couldn't help but scan through the waiting groups outside the station for the brothers.

Lara dusted sugar off her hands.

Unsure about how she should start, Mizuki took out her passport and passed it across the counter, the text inside was printed in Japanese and English. 'My name is not Mizuki Katsura,' she began. 'I didn't intend to lie to you. I haven't told you everything. I'm married. It's true that this ring belonged to my mother.' Mizuki rubbed her finger as Lara paged through the passport, conscious that her friend would not look at her. Mizuki looked to the station forecourt. 'When I first met my husband he told me he had two ambitions. He wanted to marry before he was fifty, and he wanted to see every building designed by Kenzo Tange. He likes this architect. Back home, in Tokyo, he has an office in a building designed by Tange. He sometimes arranges his business so that he can go to a new city and see Tange's buildings, and he has seen almost all of them, but he hasn't come to Naples. He hasn't seen the

Centro Direzionale. After we married he became busy with his work. He's away most of the time, and I was looking after his mother, who is very sick and very difficult. When I decided to leave, I couldn't decide where I should go, or what I should do. And one day he was talking about Tange and Naples. I don't know why, but I made up my mind to come here.'

Lara closed the passport and left it face down on the counter.

'Why did you leave him? Why change your name?'

'I don't know. I could say that he is nineteen years older than me. That he knows his mind. He never makes mistakes. He is always certain. I could say that I always make mistakes. I make too many mistakes.' Mizuki bowed her head. 'But I don't know that these are the right reasons.'

'He doesn't know where you are?'

Mizuki shook her head. 'Nobody knows. Not even my family. If they knew they would tell him.'

'What about your friends?'

'I had friends before I was married, but he didn't like them. He told me they were bad people, or they were stupid, or strange, and that they were not a good influence. Then, slowly, they stopped calling or inviting me out. It's complicated. When I'm with him I don't know my own mind.'

'But if he can't find you here. If he doesn't know where you are, he can't bother you.'

'My husband is very wealthy. I thought that if I told somebody they would find out how wealthy he is and they would tell him where he could find me. I don't think they would want to – not at first. But I'm certain that this would happen.'

Lara propped her elbows against the counter. Both women looked hard at the coaches and taxis under the station awning. 'This is my second attempt to finish my studies? I never finished – the first time – because I met someone. It was a terrible mistake. I gave up everything. When it was over, when I came back, I had to start from the beginning again. I had nothing. Nowhere to live, no money, no work. I had to start everything from the beginning.'

Mizuki fell quiet for a moment. It was sad, she said, when one person gives too much and the other takes for no proper reason.

'It's never that simple. But why don't you tell him where you are?'

Mizuki paused then closed her eyes. The story was not true, not quite. She hadn't left her husband exactly, but run away for an adventure, something happenstance, the kind of encounter suggested by the brothers at the station: one thing couldn't end without another starting.

Lara saw her onto the train and then left.

Immediately out of the station the line ran between empty warehouses and loading bays stacked with rusted shipping containers, the shore visible between the gaps. Mizuki sat beside the window, her shirt stuck to the small of her back, and she regretted explaining herself to Lara. Why had she done this? After spending six weeks as Mizuki Katsura, she had spoiled this illusion in five, less, three minutes of careless chatter. She couldn't understand why she would do this, and couldn't see what she could do to correct it. In an attempt to dismiss the day's events she began to take notice of the passengers, and sensed among the men an air of opportunity. They looked at the women dressed in thin skirts and tight summer tops with long glances and lowered heads. A dog-like expression, she thought, common, hopeful, indolent, and nestling threat.

Mizuki looked at the sea through breaks between the apartment buildings. Her mobile rang as the train came into San Georgio, and she was bothered to see that the call came from Lara. More questions. More explanations.

One man dressed in a business shirt, his tie loose about his neck, stood too close. Mizuki shut off the phone and closed her eyes. How disappointing these men were, and how unlike the brothers. If she saw them now what would she do? Would she speak with them, follow after them? The idea of two brothers took on a new shape and possibility. It wasn't the older brother who interested her, no, it was both of them, together, and how would it be to spend time with two men? One intense, the other removed.

The train slowed as it approached Torre del Greco; men drew out cigarettes, lighters ready in their hands. The businessman paused on the platform as he lit his cigarette. He caught Mizuki's eye as the door shut between them, then gestured, hands raised, unresolved.

Anxious that her sleep would again be interrupted, Mizuki prepared carefully for bed. She ate early and moderately, and then focused on completing her assignments. Once she was done she sat at the dressing table and declined verbs, then answered simple questions with direct answers and watched Italian bubble out of her mouth. Mizuki practised the tricky rolling consonants, the unchanging vowels, and wondered at how her expression, fierce with concentration, appeared to show anger, when she was seldom, if ever, harsh or bad-tempered.

In the hour before bed Mizuki set her books aside and took a long shower. She bathed the stings with antiseptic. She double-checked her tongue and throat. She turned the sheets, opened the shutters to refresh the room, laid out her clothes for the next day, so that even the smallest decision would not trouble her, and she knew, even as she did this, that she should call Lara and attempt to undo what she had said.

The call came after Mizuki had gone to bed. The line fizzed and a voice, immediately familiar, crackled out, saying nothing except an inquisitive, 'Hello, hello?' in Japanese.

'Hiroki.' She said her husband's name without inflection then cancelled the call. She checked the screen to make sure that the connection was cut.

The phone rang again, two bursts, and stopped.

Mizuki sat up, turned on the lights, assured herself that she was far away, that it was only her husband's voice which could carry to the room. How had he found her? Less than five hours after she'd spoken with Lara. How could this happen so quickly? Mizuki set the phone on the pillow and lay beside it so that her ear was close. She watched it ring and stop. Ring and stop. A counter clocked the number of incoming calls.

Lara answered on the first ring and asked Mizuki if she was all right. 'I was worried,' she said. 'You didn't answer.'

Mizuki wasn't sure where to start. 'What if everything I told you wasn't true?' she asked.

Lara said she didn't understand.

'What if everything I've told you came from another person? All of the details. What if I'd taken everything from somewhere else?'

Silent for a moment, Lara said she didn't understand. 'Why would anyone do that?'

A silence grew between them. Mizuki wanted to know details, she wanted to understand how Lara had found him so quickly, how she could have come to such a decision with so little thought. Not five hours even. Not even one night. But all she could ask was why.

'Are you in trouble?' she asked. 'Because if you needed money, I could have given you money. You could have asked me.'

Lara said she didn't understand.

Mizuki turned onto her side and changed her mind about talking. 'It's not important.'

Mizuki cancelled the call, rolled onto her back and looked up. The ceiling fan stirred hot air to no result. The phone rang and she looked at the small screen and decided that she wouldn't speak to Lara again.

Despite her best efforts Mizuki lay awake, aware of the passing minutes, the tread of traffic, the supple chuff of voices outside the all-night *farmacia*, and later, much later, the sharp and mournful caw of gulls – sounds so ordinary that ordinarily they would cause her no trouble. She wouldn't return to the language school. Naples had not provided what she wanted after all, or rather, if she was honest, she didn't have the courage to follow opportunity when it occurred. The brothers provided a perfect example: supposing these men were interested in her, she doubted she could follow through. She began to consider other cities. Milan, perhaps. Rome. Palermo. Genoa.

When she finally did sleep, in the moment she succumbed, Mizuki felt a weight descend upon her, a rolling tide that brought anxious but unspecific dreams.

☆

The sun crossed obliquely over the building and spilled through the window, drawing with it the noise of traffic, buses idling outside the station, car horns, the hiss and snort of hydraulic brakes, shouts from the market stalls. Lila woke to the dog's barks, which sounded less alarmed than usual, a colour to them, frisky, expectant. Today she felt soft, gummy, not one hard bone in her body, not one joint. She liked how Arianna inclined toward her, leaned on her, almost nestling, how their skin brushed lightly when she breathed in.

Rafí returned in the early evening and said nothing at first about the previous night but kept himself busy fetching water for the dog.

'So I'll make the arrangements, then?' His foot nudged Lila's thigh. 'What do you think? I'll get everything organized.'

Arianna turned over. 'Organize what?'

'With the brothers.'

Arianna cleared her throat and began to cough.

'Tonight. I'll set something up. They'll come and pick you up.'

Arianna rose herself onto her elbows and frowned at Lila, her face red. 'What's he talking about?'

Lila shrugged.

'I'm talking about the two men from last night,' he said, 'they'll pick you up in front of the station.'

Arianna shook her head. She blinked into the sunlight. 'You told them where we live?'

'I told them to meet you at the station.'

Rafí stood over Lila, raised his foot and pressed it onto her stomach. 'You're going to be nice tonight,' he warned.

They waited under the station hood, anxious about the police, the carabinieri, the station security, the taxi drivers. This surely wasn't a smart idea. In front of the entire square, fenced off and dug up, cranes reaching over, the belly of the piazza dug out to a vast black pit. A white car drew up to the kerb and the headlights flickered. Two men sat inside and watched the women approach. As they came alongside the passenger opened his door and stepped out. Lila looked across the piazza to the Hotel Stromboli and picked out the windows on the upper floor, imagining herself already in bed, and thought, How is it that this building always appears to be wet? Arianna began to heckle: who did these people think they were? I mean seriously, to pick them up at the station like common whores?

The passenger leaned on the car roof, smug, hands clasped, smiling. They only wanted to be nice, he said. Nice. Nothing more than that. Behind him, from a ring-fenced lot, steam rose from the building work, a new line for the metro, a pipe impossibly crusted with ice.

Arianna gave a huff. 'Nice. What is this nice?' She settled her hands on her hips and leaned forward, neck stuck out. With slender shoulders and waist, large hands, the passenger looked out of proportion, a long body of mismatched parts. Not a boxer, Lila decided, but a swimmer.

Now the driver stepped out of the car and Lila could see that the men, unaccountably tall and trim with similarly shorn hair, were undoubtedly brothers. The same features – noses, brow line, small inset eyes like field mice – the same swagger. Men who considered themselves handsome. The driver pointed to Lila and indicated that she should get in.

The driver approached, slid his arm about her waist and brought Lila to the car and opened the door, something gracious about the gesture, his hand in the small of her back. When Lila sat down she thought to open the opposite door and slide out but did nothing. On the pavement Arianna stood with her arms out wide, palms up, face set with disapproval. Ignoring her, the younger brother and the driver returned to the car, leaving Arianna alone on the pavement, behind her the long swoop of the station front, black windows of empty restaurants, chairs on tables, the certain presence of security guards. When the car started Arianna reached for the door handle.

With Arianna in the car the younger brother locked the passenger doors. Lila sat with her arms crossed and looked up at the Stromboli, a thought came to her, *wasn't this what they had talked about*, but she kept the thought to herself.

The passenger set his hand on Arianna's knee and shoved clumsily under Arianna's skirt. 'Now you are the one with the cock? Yes? Show me,' he grinned.

Arianna stopped the man's advances in a small gesture, a hesitation rather than a refusal. In response the man twisted completely about – and with a swift and sudden jab punched Arianna in the face. The sound of it, a snap, then Arianna's howl accompanied their acceleration about the piazza.

When they arrived at the farmhouse Arianna bolted from the car, hurtling into darkness, leaving one sandal in the footwell, another tipped on its side in the gravel, pointing to an orchard, a long wall, dimly lit by the car's red tail-light. Lila sat with the door open, the night air a soft drift across her shoulders, the realization slowly occurring to her that they would not escape this trouble. The passenger shot swift as a rat after Arianna and leapt on her with poisonous certainty. The driver pulled Lila out of the car, hefting her forward by her hair and dropping her at the threshold so that her elbows struck the flagstone. While Arianna fought and struggled, Lila shut down and made no attempt to protect herself. She focused hard on the details before her, the uneven floor, the tiles, broken but still in place; the peaty stink of rotten furnishings. She knew these smells. She knew this air, how the wind picks salt from the sea so that it can be tasted many miles inland.

THURSDAY: DAY E

Lila and Arianna were abandoned twelve miles outside the city on a slip road off the Domiziana. Hired pickers and farmhands working in the lower fields watched the women struggle out of the car naked and shoeless – and for one bad moment the vehicle jolted backward threatening to reverse and run them down but drew instead hastily off the side road. They had seen women squabbling in awkward brawls, hairpulling, kicking, ugly slap fights at the roadside, or more usually cars pulling slowly into the tree-line and dropping some girl off, often as abrupt, but never with such threat. Later, confirming the story among themselves, the workmen easily described the women but disagreed on the model of the car, mistaking its dusty coat for grey or tan or silver. The men had barely started work, and the last thin breath of mist clung stubbornly to the irrigation ditches, and there, right before them, two naked women scurried chaotically, chicken-like, across the fields.

First out of the car, Arianna zigzagged across the mud then clambered back up the embankment and stumbled alongside the road, falling more than walking, cars veered wide, her focus set on the distant lilac mountains, her hands covering her crotch. When the labourers caught up they beat their sticks and tools on the road and whooped to drive her down to an irrigation ditch. Trapped in the shallow black water Arianna began to bellow in a language they couldn't understand, and they could see for the first time cuts and bruises, soiled red skin and fatty white grazes, evidence that she had been brutalized – and they could also see, despite her skinny figure, her long hair and hard breasts, that she was a man.

Deaf to the labourers' hoots and jeers Lila tottered through the mud and slippy rotten sops of cut greens, her underarms, buttocks, stomach, legs, caked with dirt. She fled diagonally across the field, and ran with quick picky steps, but when she heard Arianna's shouts she simply stopped, sat in the mud, hung her head and covered her ears, waiting for whatever would catch up with her. Startled, the men also stopped. Keeping their distance they waited for the police.

In the ambulance the women faced each other, eyes wide at the strangeness of being brought from an open ploughed field into a box where they could hear themselves breathe. Wrapped in a rough red blanket Arianna shivered violently and would not look up, her ankles and forearms crossed with deep bramble scratches, her neck scored purple, swollen to show the clear imprint of a belt. Lila refused to be touched and sat forward, head down, hands tucked under her thighs. This was her fault. Clearly all her fault. As she slowly warmed, the punctures on her back began to suppurate. She fought against sleep, fearing the sensation that she was evaporating, becoming lighter than air; but sleep, or something like it, brought on by a mess of drugs came in soft buckling waves, impossible to resist. The accompanying officer, dressed in a smart and faultless uniform, looked out of the back of the vehicle and watched the road and fields recede. In full daylight the mountains took on the soft contours of a strong man's arm.

They were separated at the hospital and taken to small bright booths set side by side. Alone, Lila slipped off the high examination table and hid under it with the thin tunic drawn over her head. She squeezed hard against the wall. The pressure and the cool tiles soothed the sores on her back and the penetrating ache in her shoulders. Crouched under the bed she could smell cigar smoke in her sweat, and the sweet, cold stink made her retch. She did not want to sleep and she did not want to be awake, neither did she want to be alone. She called for Arianna. Her voice sounded separate, not of her making, so that the sound itself became something to fasten on to.

Almost two hours after they had arrived at the hospital a second woman officer returned with a photographer, a doctor, and two uniformed police. The woman spoke to Lila in a whispered singsong, supposing that Lila was as degraded as she appeared.

'Can you come out? Can you stand? Can you sit?'

Lila allowed the woman to coax her out. She sat where she was told and did not flinch as the doctor opened the back of her tunic and unpicked the temporary dressing.

The man spoke in a flat and practised tone, almost a private whisper as he described his actions. 'I'm going to lift and extend your arm. Let me know if this is too painful.'

Lila allowed the man to hold out her arm and softly turn her head, and made no complaint when he compressed the skin either side of the wounds. The dry sound of dressings being unsnapped from their packets identical to the sound of that first punch – a sharp crack.

'These are cigar burns.' The doctor began to count the blisters across her neck, shoulders, back, behind her knees, and on the soft underside of her arms. 'And these,' he said, 'are bites. Here, and here. Here. These marks are older.'

She said nothing.

The brothers, trading places, warned that if either of them spoke they would return to finish what they'd started. Lila didn't doubt their threats, she wasn't lucky, a simple fact, and she knew when to take advice.

The photographer took pictures of her back and shoulders. He took photographs of the nape of her neck, showing where her hair had been tugged out. Coming round to face her he photographed the bruises and lacerations to her thighs, wrists, and breasts, then took a single photograph of her face. The men who touched her now wore gloves. Lila waited for them to be done.

After searching for traces of fluids, the doctor began to inspect for matter, dirt captured on the rough skin on her feet and in the grazes on her knees, traces of ash and tobacco swabbed from the wounds. He measured the bruise about her neck, then one by one the bites, burns, the lacerations were swabbed, cleaned and finally dressed. The sounds of utensils set in their trays, of metal against metal, and metal against glass, sang unnaturally sharp in the small booth, sharp sounds tightened by the hard walls, unabsorbed and brittle, unexpectedly invasive.

With the examination complete Lila was left alone with the promise that someone would return with clothes. She waited, stared at the door until her eyes watered and wished herself, uselessly, elsewhere. The woman returned, apologizing, with two T-shirts held to her chest. A charitable order provided the clothes and this was all they had at the moment. The clothes were new, both with designs, smiling cartoon characters Lila did not recognize. She sounded apologetic. It was OK; no one else had worn them.

When the police returned she'd changed her mind, come around to the idea that it didn't much matter if she did or did not speak, and that the effort not to speak would require resources that she knew she didn't have. The choice was a simple economy.

They met the men at the station, she said. If they wanted to know exact details they could speak with Rafí at the Hotel Stromboli. They'd raided the hotel a number of times and they would know him.

The brothers were tall, slender, active, with sporting bodies, trimmer and fitter than the men she was used to. Their hair was cropped military-style. They had clipped their body hair, and one of them, the younger brother, had waxed his arms. Except for a thumbprint mole under the older brother's right nipple there were no tattoos, no distinguishing marks. She couldn't guess their ages, but they appeared younger than the officers now questioning her. They almost certainly weren't Italian, and weren't familiar with the city nor the autostrada: when they were driving they took a number of wrong turns. She couldn't swear to it but there were times when they spoke to each other in pidgin French, or slang, or in a private invented language.

After the first punch, when the passenger, the younger man, hit Arianna, the brothers had joked with each other. The older man was persuasive, and he kept talking about a party in Livorno, and that other women were being brought there. Rafí had promised this earlier, maybe the day before, and Lila in particular liked the promise that they would be introduced to influential men; judges, lawyers, businessmen, but knew that this was unlikely. In their long slow afternoons Lila and Arianna had concocted a loose plan where they would move to America, to Los Angeles, or stay in Europe and work together in Milan, Paris, or maybe even return to Barcelona. They wanted to be kept by one man, why not, or better still, to be able to afford an apartment of their own where they would establish themselves with a select and limited number of clients, men that they would choose, and their working lives would run to a timetable of regulated and well-paid fucks. This hope had underscored every discussion, and the brothers' hint that they understood this was one of the night's enduring cruelties.

The second officer asked for other details, he could tell from her accent that she wasn't Italian. Lila nodded, yes, she'd come to Naples and worked for a while in a shop on via Duomo. Her family needed money. She often used this story, and Rafí laughed at it, because, let's face it, she'd never worked upright in her entire life, and, best of all, even if in some crazy alternate universe she did find herself a job men would always smell her out, because first and foremost she was a whore: where would she be without those American servicemen she was so fond of, and those good clean Scandinavian boys from NATO who were always so generous with their drugs? Lila also cringed at the idea, but it made a better story than the way she passed her days. For Lila time divided between doing something and doing nothing, and she dreaded time spent on her own. Alone at the Stromboli she felt like baggage, like substance without worth.

The officers began to ask questions she couldn't answer, and Lila began to tire. Perhaps she needed a moment to herself. Lila shrugged, she'd told them as much as she knew. Nothing further would occur to her.

When the door reopened Arianna leaned into the room. Her neck now purple, her face swollen and pulpy, her eyes panda-wide and bruised. Stopped at the door she leaned slightly in and whispered, 'Lila. Lila? We can't stay.' Arianna looked back into the corridor then stepped into the room. Behind her, and this made no sense, stood Rafí. 'We can't stay. We have to go.' Arianna held out her hand. 'You understand? We can't stay here.'

Lila called to Arianna, and a second, more formidable wave of nausea overcame her and she thought that she might faint.

'I had to call him,' Arianna whispered. 'This is only for tonight. We take our money and we leave like we planned. Tomorrow. We go tomorrow.'

Rafí hovered at the door, anxious and uneasy, eyes on the corridor.

Arianna was right, they should leave, but Lila couldn't rouse herself, all energy and self-determination gone. Arianna held out her hand, now impatient. 'Now. We have to go now.'

Rafí supported Lila on his arm, one T-shirt held to her chest, the other across her shoulders. As soon as she stood a chill passed through her and she thought that she might collapse. Rafí lumbered her through the hospital corridors without a word, taking an emergency exit so that they came out onto a parking lot edged with trees that seemed to her to be another country perhaps. Not Italy but America. A flat periwinkle sky. A low-lying mall too wide to be part of the city she knew. Barefoot, Arianna walked ahead and scanned the lot for the car. A technician in blue overalls sat smoking in the shade, the ground soft with pine needles. He looked at the three and blew smoke into the branches, indifferent to their hurry and disorder.

☆

Marek waited until the afternoon to call the brothers. He sent them photographs he'd taken of the Citroën, and asked if they still needed a driver. *I know the city*, he wrote, *if there's anything you need during your stay. Don't hesitate.* He tried to imagine what they might want, two men in Naples, and couldn't picture taking a holiday with his own brother, who in any case would never know his own mind without his wife. A hot summer, almost too hot to move, and hadn't Peña said the brothers didn't know the city, and they barely spoke the language. He knew from military service the kind of trouble men could make for themselves, it wasn't that they specifically sought it out, but given the opportunity, trouble would happen. If they wanted opportunity, as in *company*, he could help with that.

He waited in the cafe and stood at the window, an eye on his apartment and the magistrate's driver, who lounged against his car, half-hopeful of a call from Tony. A call came mid-morning from the brothers. Did Marek know of a doctor? One of the brothers had been punched in a fight and he needed a doctor. Could Marek bring someone to the hotel? It wasn't anything that needed any fuss. They would appreciate his discretion.

At first Lanzetti wasn't interested.

'I'm a pharmacist. Take them to the hospital. Take them to a clinic.'

'They don't want trouble,' Marek reasoned. 'They know how things work here, how simple things become complicated. They just want a doctor.'

'They don't want the police. This happens all the time.'

Marek shrugged. It was possible, a fight in a bar could lead to all kinds of problems, and no one would want to make a report, no one would want the police involved. He needed the work, but didn't want to spell it out. 'If I do this. If they trust me—'

Lanzetti turned his hands over, palms up as if to ask, *And this should involve me? This should be my problem?* 'You drive them to a hospital. You take them to a clinic. You bring them to a *farmacia*.' Out of politeness he asked where they were, and offered to find out the nearest clinic or pharmacy.

'Hotel Grand, in the hills.'

'Castellammare?'

'On the mountain.'

Marek stepped back from the counter. Before leaving he thanked the doctor for his advice. Before he reached the door Lanzetti had changed his mind.

Marek followed two white vans along the escarpment's terraced walls, vines and fig trees and creepers close on one side, a blue hole on the other. As he came up the hill, Lanzetti pointed out the view, and told him how the Americans at the end of the war had first seen Naples from the very same place. The view struck Marek as a piece of information: a set of facts. So this is where the Americans stood, Lanzetti explained. First they came over the top, then round the side through the valley, and others, even later, came by sea. In four days a mongrel group of partisans with a wise eye on the Americans' progress had rid the city of the Germans. It wasn't just a view about recent history, the capped top of the volcano, the thick plates of lava, and the dangerous proximity of the city spoke as a present reminder to an ancient event every boy knew by heart. Marek patted his pockets for cigarettes as the car crept upward and asked Lanzetti if he smoked.

Lanzetti said they could stop, if he wanted. They needn't hurry? He asked this as a question, and Marek drew over and said no, there was no particular hurry. He stopped at the crown of the hill where the road levelled out to a viewing station.

'I have decided to spend more time.' Lanzetti paused and lit a cigarette and Marek rolled down the window and blew smoke out over the view. 'More time *being present*. Does that make sense? To make sure I enjoy what is around me. My son. Good food. A beautiful view. I know how ridiculous it sounds.'

Marek looked past Lanzetti to the view, mindful of the edge, which fell at a discomfortingly sharp pitch. He saw the view as a phenomenon, a plate of land bounded by mountains and sea with an imperfect cone smack in the centre. If you drew up the centre of a tablecloth you would have yourself a model of the bay, the same flowing curves, the same dimensional scope.

'Last year I lost my father. Now I am the adult. He brought me here a number of times. It is always a good view. Don't you think? There are walks from here to Vico Equense, or over the top to Ravello.'

In front of them a man sat on his motorbike, head turned to the view.

'My wife has taken my son to her brother's.' Lanzetti looked out at the view as he spoke. 'There have been some disturbances at the palazzo. She's unhappy. She's always unhappy. She makes the boy unhappy.'

Marek remembered finding the purse on the coach. The accident wasn't his first death, and certainly not his first accident. The summer before, driving on the Tagenziale, a motorcyclist, a man in black and red leathers, had inexplicably sprung from his bike and spun over the parapet, head over heels, gone. The bike toppled as soon as the man was loose, parts shattering and spinning across the lanes, and Paola shouting in pure disbelief. Did you see that? A cross-wind, the smallest of bumps, a curving bridge, elements long in place that predetermined the young man's startling tumble and thump onto a roof, a balcony, a road. There were other deaths that summer, his father, Paola's grandmother, relatives dressed and laid out in grey rooms in sombre calm, a little dignity returned to them, but these two incidents where men appeared to be snatched, grabbed and thrown, were the measure to him of how life, and the taking of it, was a matter of simple whimsy.

Marek parked between the same two white vans, now being unloaded of decorations and tableware. They followed a man bearing flowers into the hotel lobby. The bouquet, a generous spread of cream-coloured lilies and green ferns, swayed a little obscenely as the man scampered up the steps. Marek, out of place in combat shorts, waited at the entrance and phoned the brothers. All about the lobby and the entrance staff prepped tables, windows, carpets, cleaned and arranged with practised focus. A wedding, without doubt.

A man came out of the hotel, brisk and direct, hand extended and asked Marek if he was the driver from Naples and was this the doctor. Marek shook the man's hand and the man indicated that he should come with him.

They drove in silence down the mountain. Once they joined the autostrada Lanzetti began to ask questions.

'Did he say how this happened?'

'His nose? A fight.'

'A fight?'

'In a bar. I think he said.'

'Did he say where?'

Marek said no. 'It was broken?'

'Yes, but not so bad. There is a bruise, a small swelling.' Lanzetti unfolded his arms. 'And how do you know these men?'

'I don't. They've asked me to drive them.'

'You work for them?'

'I will. They need a driver while they're here.'

'And you know what they do?'

'I only met them today.'

'So you know nothing about the fight? Because there were scratches. It would unusual for a man to scratch.'

'He said it was a man.'

'Perhaps he didn't want to admit.'

Perhaps, they agreed, perhaps. Marek dropped Lanzetti at the palazzo then returned the car to English Tony. He walked back along via Tribunali, a small and indirect detour, but he wanted to think. It wasn't his business what the brothers were doing, now they had guaranteed a steady two weeks of work.

☆

When Lila woke she found herself at the Stromboli lying on her side on the mattress, the T-shirt twisted about her midriff, a clear enough memory of the journey back but nothing after they arrived. An argument swelled about her. Arianna's voice rose hard above Rafí's, insistent on one question. 'My money. Where is the money? My money. I want my money. Where is my money?'

Rafí shouted back, face to face. 'You think you can work now? You think anyone wants you?'

Why had they gone to the hospital without coming first to him? It was the wrong day for this. The men he owed money to would not be happy to know that he wasn't in control of his women. 'Do you have any idea what this means? How this makes me look?' The difference between having something or nothing now depended on them.

Arianna settled on the bed, one argument streamed from her.

Wasn't he supposed to watch out for them? Wasn't that the one small thing he was supposed to do?

Hands dug deep into his pockets, Rafí slipped back to the doorway.

Lila couldn't work after the beating. Arianna insisted. 'She can't. It isn't possible.'

Slumped back on the mattress Lila let the argument fly and felt the small room collapse about her.

She woke a second time to see Arianna lunge from the mattress and spit at Rafí. Rafí cowered and blocked her blows with his forearms. Arianna flailed, untiring. The dressing flapped loose from her wrist.

Throughout, awake or gone, Lila could feel the unending arrhythmic cough of Rafí's dog. She'd let that dog free sometime. She and that dog would go separate ways. She'd rather see it dead than live out on the rooftop.

When she woke a third time the argument had shifted pace, and Arianna sat on the floor hugging her knees and Rafí leaned over her, swearing that he would find these men. He was emphatic. If Arianna knew where these men, these brothers, were now, where he could find them, he would kill them, he swore. He would find them and he would castrate them.

And later still Arianna sat with her head in her hands, sobbing, saying this is crazy, crazy. Alongside this, Rafí talking. It was the wrong day, entirely the wrong day, he had somewhere else to be, he was in default of a debt, the total, by default, now doubled. Lila and Arianna needed to understand this, because he couldn't run around after them, waiting on them, doing the things that needed to be done for them *all of the time*. In any case the Stromboli was closing down, in two months they would be out of a place to live.

In her sleep Lila pawed at her arms, wanting to wake but unable to rouse: she recalled details of the assault with a terrifying clarity – the sour breath of the younger brother as he beat her and how boyishly happy her fear made him, how bold he became, how certain. How he drew on the cigar before he stamped it onto her skin. When she held up her arm to protect her face he grabbed her wrist and bit deep.

*

THE KILLS

She woke with Arianna crouched over her, whispering, sobbing, eyes an unreadable black: 'I can't stay here. I'll find somewhere. I will come back.' Arianna stroked Lila's hair, a roll of cash in her hand. 'I'm sorry,' she said. 'I'm so sorry.' A kiss and a promise to return.

☆

Peña returned the boy's trophies: the small soldiers, a racing car, the diver with the yellow aqualung. She set them in a single line close to the door then returned to her apartment to call Salvatore to find out who these men were and exactly what had happened. But Salvatore was not at work and refused to answer her call, although she left message after message. 'I'm not happy,' she said. 'I was very specific that there should be no trouble with the residents. Tell them that I want to speak with them.' But she knew, even as she spoke, that these words were nothing more than a gesture.

The toys remained in place for the entire day. Afterward, the only sounds to come from the apartment came from Arturo Lanzetti, and slowly Peña came to realize that Anna Soccorsi and her son Sami were gone.

FRIDAY: DAY F

Paola wasn't sure she could find the time. Today? Tonight? This week-end, she excused herself, she had plans, work to complete. He could see for himself. All of that, that right there. All of those clothes needed stitching, they weren't going to do themselves. And when she was done it would start again on Monday. Marek couldn't believe his ears. He laid out the brochure, pointed to the hotel. Was she crazy, or being delib-erately stupid? This was a five-star hotel with a spa, a swimming pool, a gym, a chef of international renown, with three fully-staffed restau-rants one of which sat on a promontory with a view of the entire gulf, and all of it was for free. The brothers were away for the weekend, and they could use their room. Why was she was turning her nose up at the opportunity, except to be spiteful?

He expected a denial, but no, Paola admitted, if that's how he chose to see it, that's probably how it was. But think about it, she said, who-ever gives anything away for free? Things that looked too good to be true, as a rule, are pretty much always too good to be true. 'We aren't the kind of people who get given things for nothing.'

Out of his building Marek saw the magistrate's driver again waiting beside the car. The car was parked in almost the same place and the man adopted the same position – leaning against the car door with his arms folded. The difference this time was that the man faced Marek's building, and not the magistrate's. The driver's expression appeared stern and focused, expectant. Aware that he was being watched Marek stepped into the café and decided to take a coffee.

To his surprise the man unfolded his arms, stood upright, and came across the street.

Standing next to Marek the driver took off his sunglasses and asked for a coffee.

Both men stood at the counter and slowly stirred sugar into their coffee.

'It's hot.'

'Indeed.'

'The coffee is good.'

'Very good.'

Both men nodded and then drank their coffees.

The driver smiled. 'The thing about coffee,' he said, 'is that you can never make it the same yourself. It's impossible. It always tastes better away from home.'

Wishing Marek a good morning, the magistrate's driver put his sunglasses back on and walked back across the street to take his position leaning against the car. This time he faced the magistrate's building.

It always tastes better away from home.

Marek was certain that the man was mocking him.

He returned to the apartment and found Paola in the shower, and became intensely aggravated, as if she was preparing herself for a man and not for work. He couldn't believe she wasn't yet working. Marek waited in the bedroom. He stood back from the window and watched the driver to see if there was any signal, any interest even. He searched quickly through her belongings, the pockets in her jacket and trousers, then in her bureau, looking for receipts, notes, messages, anything that would indicate a separate life. But still, he could find nothing, except a life that was ordered, regular, and constrained by work.

Paola came out of the bathroom with her robe open, her breasts and her stomach equally round and white, and appeared surprised to see Marek. She ruffled the towel under her hair. 'Look, I'm not going to change my mind.'

'Who is that man?'

Paola covered herself and peeped quickly out the window to see the driver, her expression indicated that the man, clearly, had some appeal.

'I've no idea.'

Marek was not convinced.

'Everyone knows who he is. He's there all day, every day. He's the magistrate's driver.' The whole street could recognize the man and Paola could not? It simply couldn't be true that she hadn't seen him before.

'And why are we talking about him?'

'If he arranged a weekend in a five-star hotel would you go with him?'

Paola had no idea what he was talking about; she let the towel fall from her shoulder. 'This isn't about you, Marek. It's about work. You know? Work? I don't have time – I really don't have the time for this.'

'But you'd go with him?' Flustered, Marek gestured out of the window, and pointing at the driver he said that he would go down there now, and he would tell the man that he could have her.

Paola, still confused, called him ridiculous and returned to the bathroom. 'I'm going to dry my hair.'

Suddenly angry she returned to the room.

'I don't know what you want, Marek. Tell me? Tell me what you want, because it isn't clear to me. You want a child then you don't want a child. You don't want a holiday then you want to go away for the weekend. You complain about the city, all of the time, and yet you stay here, you talk about going to a hotel which has the best view of the city when you hate the city. I don't know what you want. And now this? I mean seriously, what do you think is going on? How can you not trust me? How dare you say these things when you are disloyal yourself? Tell me, which is worse, doing something, or constantly considering it? You are such a child, Marek. You're this little boy who believes all these things about women. I'm tired of having to work so hard.'

Stopping herself Paola returned to the bathroom, an apparent calm settled about her as she leaned toward the mirror, her mouth set firm as she drew the brush in long forceful strokes through her hair. Marek watched her hand search across the counter top and fail to find her lipstick. 'Fine. You want to go to this hotel. Let's go. It's free. Great. Let's go and see how free it is.'

Once again Marek had the feeling that he had won nothing.

At ten o'clock Marek reported back to Lanzetti that he had returned to the hotel the previous night. The brothers had called him with a proposition. Lanzetti excused himself from work and invited Marek for a coffee at the *alimentari*. They stood side by side at the counter. Marek checked the street and was happy not to see the magistrate's driver nor his car. Lanzetti asked after Salvatore and left the change in the dish. Marek leaned into the counter with a book and a map in his hand: *Napoli, Ischia, Capri. Touring Club Italiano*. On a sheet of notepaper Paul had written out street names and features.

'Paul?' Lanzetti pointed out the name.

He knew their names now, Marc and Paul. 'Paul is the younger brother.'

'And you know where they're from?'

'South? You know I'm not sure. Gap? Gad? Gappe?'

Lanzetti said he didn't know. He hadn't spent time in France, but he could ask his wife when she called this evening. 'Everything French,' he said, 'she loves it all. She loves the wines. She loves the food. She likes that man. That singer.' He couldn't remember names, admitted to it. 'Faces. I see faces and remember the medicines, the strengths. But names.' He shivered quickly to change the subject.

'How long have you lived here?'

Marek counted the years. Three, he thought. Perhaps a little longer.

Lanzetti picked up the book and fanned through the pages. Did Marek speak Spanish?

Marek shook his head. He hadn't meant to pick it up, but it was with the map, and maybe, thinking about it now, he could look up some of the names, at least he could pick out the names of places and see if he knew them.

'And you don't speak French?'

'English. It's easier, their Italian isn't good. It's basic but it isn't good.'

'They don't speak Polish, then?'

Now Marek smiled, he was just getting the measure of the man's sense of humour.

Lanzetti read out loud from the book. Did any of this sound familiar? He didn't know it. 'A mystery? *The Kill*. It must be?'

Marek thought as much. 'It's Paul's, he says it's about Naples.' The book wasn't old, and the story was set in the mid-forties, just after the war, but they were curious about seeing places mentioned in it.

Lanzetti asked if he could borrow the book, just for the night, just to take a look. 'I always have a book. I like to read to my wife,' he said, 'at night. When she's here. My son reads to me, and I read to my wife. If it's any good I will order it for her.'

'They were looking for places from the book.' Marek opened the map. 'I'll take them after the weekend. They wanted to find a farm, a vineyard. In the city.' Marek spread his hand to flatten the paper, from what he could see on the map there was no such thing.

Lanzetti asked him to repeat the question. There was one possibility, up above the neighbourhood marked as Cariati. He didn't know what the neighbourhood was called, or if it had a particular name, but just under the Castel San Elmo and the Certosa, there was an area, a hill, he explained, steep, and terraced into small and spare fields. As far as he knew it was run by an association, and there was an orchard, a place to grow asparagus also, some olive trees, from what he remembered: maybe there was also a small vineyard. He'd been there twice with Anna, once for a wedding, then a second time for a feast to celebrate the end of the harvest. There were some sheds, lean-tos, one with a wood-fire oven, and food was brought to be cooked there. Tables were set out in a double row under the shade of the olive trees. 'It's steep, and it's not anything you'd notice, but the area is entirely countryside. You can see over the city, the whole bay, from Capri to Nisida. It's very beautiful, but from the city it doesn't look like much except wasteland.'

Lanzetti folded the map in half.

You could reach the place by a church. 'Here,' Lanzetti pointed to the map. San Sepulcro, first an old path with proper steps to start, then a small rural path. 'The association keep goats up there, a donkey.' From what he could remember. 'Wild cactus, olive trees, and yes, I suppose a vineyard, grass, not at all what you'd expect in the middle of the city, and it's very steep. But why would they want to see this?'

Marek said he didn't know. They were just interested, he said. But it didn't seem so important.

So this is what they want? Not a driver at all, but someone who knows the city. Someone to confirm a few ideas taken from a book? 'How well do you know the city?'

Marek shrugged and said he had a pretty good idea.

'But you drive? For how long?'

'Two years.'

'In Naples?'

'In Naples. Yes. To the airport. To the city.' Marek wove his hand back and forward. Lanzetti laughed a little.

'What do they want with the room?'

Marek looked up, blank. He hadn't asked. At first, because they were businessmen, there was the idea that they needed the room for storage, but now, meeting them, they clearly weren't here on business.

'They are away for the weekend, and they've offered their room.'

'At the Grand?'

'At the Grand. Tonight and tomorrow night. They've already paid, but they have to be somewhere else, and they want the room when they get back.'

Lanzetti saluted him. 'You must have made an impression.' Marek smiled and said it seemed so. 'You are a lucky man.'

He drove to Salerno and parked beside the docks under the overpass. It was a good place to smoke dope. Marek set the tobacco pouch on his lap and began to make himself a small joint. At midday the prostitutes came out to meet the long-haul drivers waiting for the ferries and deliveries, the men who slept in their cabs before the drive back north. The police drove regularly along the road beside the docks and parked between the bulky red containers off-loaded from the ships, so that it wasn't always possible to see them. Marek watched the docks and the road, and made sure that all of the doors were locked. One prostitute wandered through the shade, made her way dolefully between the trucks and flat-bed lorries parked up alongside the pillars supporting the motorway. Leaning into the windows, or climbing up to the cabins and calling to the drivers, the woman solicited business. Marek smoked and watched, with his hands cupped over his crotch.

And this was the deal: if he wanted the hotel for the weekend, if he wanted a little luxury, he had to find two women. One (and this was easy), an Asian woman, Japanese, who worked for or attended, or lived above a language school close to the palazzo. This was pure curiosity, someone they'd seen a number of times at the station and going into the school, and they wanted clarity, they wanted to know her name. The second woman (a little trickier) worked as a prostitute. A she-male, Paul had said, a very particular she-male. Looks just like a woman. Exactly, every part, with only the one small exception he supposed (ha-de-ha). Paul spoke with fascination and mock-horror, and wouldn't let the subject go once it was raised. The task was simple. Marek didn't have to find her, as in *bring her back*. They just wanted to know her location, where she was, because, as far as they understood, she wasn't in Naples any more. They just wanted to know either way. Marek didn't like Paul's humour. He didn't like the word *she-male* either, and if he thought about it, he didn't like much of anything that came out of Paul's mouth. He knew Paul's type: the wiseacre loud-mouth who became quieter and more unstable the more he drank.

Marek asked for his money upfront, and wanted assurance that the arrangement with the hotel was legitimate.

Marek thought he knew who they were talking about, from watching the women outside the palazzo, he thought he knew. He concerned himself with this, the familiarity, not the issue of whether or not he should be helping them, because, in truth, he didn't understand what this was, and yes, the offer of a luxury hotel for one entire weekend was worth a few hours of idle enquiry. They wanted to know where she was, this she-male, this star. Simple and straight.

The woman walked with her hand out to steady herself. Her hair, an acid yellow, long and crimped, tugged back from her face. She wore a silver jacket and a frayed denim skirt, short and too small to allow her to step easily onto the kerb. From the way that she walked, busy but unsteady, she veered toward the cars in thick-heeled sandals that slipped from her feet, it was clear that she wasn't sober. When she approached Marek he wound up his window and looked blankly ahead, ignoring her. He needed to take a photograph and he didn't have his phone ready. The woman waited at the window, and then knocked. Marek continued to ignore her. He watched her walk on and lean into another car, once he had his phone out of his pocket he flashed his lights. The woman drew out of the car, turned and paused, and Marek flashed the lights a second time.

When the woman returned Marek ignored her and re-lit the joint. The phone sat on his lap. He didn't know why he was doing this, but he wanted to ignore her. The woman tried the doors, front and back, but found them locked. She knocked on the window again, but quickly tiring of him she slammed her hand against the glass and walked off. Marek waited until she was back at the car, and again flashed his lights. Leaning half-in half-out she shouted at him, and gestured that he should go fuck himself, but this time Marek held his wife's small red leather purse up to the windscreen. The women squinted back. Marek continued to flash the car lights and the woman returned, a little unstable on thick heels, shouting, what, what, what did he want? Marek opened the window just wide enough to squeeze the purse through, and he held it there, undecided whether he would let it go or not. When the woman came to the window she curled her fingers over the glass, and asked what it was, what was in the purse. Her voice and hands unfeminine, her make-up crudely defined her lips and eyebrows. Close to the glass he was certain now that he recognized her but doubted that this was the one the brothers wanted. Her face, thickly powdered, eyes and lips drawn with delicate care, but her eyes were dark, a little red, and very distant. She took the purse, looked quickly inside, and tried again to open the door. Finding the door locked, she pulled down her top and pressed her breasts to the window. He took the photo and managed to catch her face before her breasts spread against the glass. A small necklace, the letter 'A' on a chain, trapped against the glass. Laughing, she backed away, then hitched up her skirt and waggled her ass.

Marek squinted into the sun as he drove away. Between the shipping containers he spied a man on a moped. He doubted that the prostitute would keep the purse. The money would go to the man on the scooter.

As he drove back he regretted that the lipstick, which had passed over Paola's mouth, would now belong to a prostitute.

Marek came through the hotel to a terrace and a lawn prepared for another wedding banquet. The Grand Hotel sat on a wide plate high above the gulf; the walls and stuttered tiers of gardens could be seen from the city as a series of white slim-stepped blocks on the mountain-side. As he followed after the waiter (a waiter, a clerk, who exactly were these people?) he made a note of the pool, the Jacuzzi, a sign for the spa, the viewing terrace called *Napoli a Piedi*. The man led Marek by tables laid out across a lawn to a lower terrace and a view of the city starting at Castellammare and ending only where the broad sweep of coast rubbed out at the horizon. Marek, as invited, sat at a table with his back to the cliff feeling the suck of all that space behind him, made worse by a swimming pool built right into the edge. He sat with his arms folded, thinking how odd it was to have so much water abutting so steep a drop when the whole point of water was to find the lowest point in any landscape.

'Would you like something to drink while you wait?'

Marek lit a cigarette and blew smoke out over the terrace. A day spent zipping back and forward, but not unproductive. The smoke hung over the drop. The idea of it, suspended, slowly dissipating, made him uneasy. Two nights, two days. Paola would be in her element. When the man returned he told Marek that the brothers had already checked out, but that the room was ready.

He wanted to check the room before he brought Paola, see if the brothers had left anything, luggage, belongings, so that he might get a better understanding of them.

The room faced the bay, and he was surprised to see a large bed and a single cot, but no luggage, and no keepsakes.

Late-afternoon Marek waited outside the language school. He recognized the sign for the bakery – he'd come to the small square many times and sat under the palms, drank at one of the two bars because it was literally just around the corner from the palazzo, a last stop on a night out before going home. The faint whiff of dope hung in the shadows under the long and weedy palms. The older parts of the city divided into micro-neighbourhoods (he'd heard Americans talk this way about their cities), so you could speak of Forcella, Sanita, Fontanella, as if they were distant towns, when in reality they might be side by side. Those really in the know could shave these districts even closer, so that you might refer to half-streets, blocks, as if they were distinctive, unique cultures with particular habits and codes. This idea only served the city's bad reputation, despite the mythology that the poorest neighbourhoods held the best eateries, the finest tailor, the original pizzeria, the freshest mozzarella / *sfogliatelle* / pasta / *limoncello*, the cheapest shoes, it spoke louder about the mysteries of clan-like associations, habits of use, of gangs, of safe and unsafe, when in reality after three years all Marek could see was a jam of dog-poor neighbourhoods scrabbling for breath. In Poland that kind of romance would be seen for what it was, a useless snobbery about poverty. As an outsider the best way to see Naples was from a boat or a hill, where it looked coherent as one single effect; come down to street level and everything started to fracture.

Marek couldn't quite work out what he was expected to do. If he asked in the school he would have to give reasons for looking for the woman, reasons he didn't understand himself. He had no name, which made this stranger, and he didn't understand the aim of this – except for his reward. In the end it wasn't hard at all. He stood at the doors, buzzed the doorbell and said he was looking for . . . and then he mumbled. When the reply came that they didn't know who he meant he gave the brothers' description of the woman.

'She's Japanese. Short. Black hair. About thirty-five but she looks younger.'

'Oh! Mizuki?' The voice sounded mechanical, metallic.

'That's right. Is she there? I'm supposed to meet her.'

'She isn't very well.'

Marek got the information he needed, the girl had been stung by a wasp two days ago and had to go home. She was all right, they insisted, but she was staying in Portici. She'd be back next week. They expected.

Marek said thank you. He'd done his work. Now it was time for his weekend.

SATURDAY: DAY G

Rafí had a new watch. A Seiko. He told Lila that he didn't want her to leave. He wanted to find the men, he wanted to find them and hurt them. This was a promise. Arianna had gone. It would be easier without her, and Lila would be safe as long as she remained at the Stromboli. She couldn't help but follow the reflections from the watch, the way sunlight splintered off the face, bright and sore.

'She took everything,' he said. 'We have nothing. She took your clothes, money. The rents. My savings. Everything. It's all gone.'

Lila pressed for details, had Arianna said anything about where she was going? Why had she left? Had he seen her? Had she called? Lila could see herself wearing upon him. Pushing.

He liked her more when she talked less, he said. What was so hard to understand?

'She took everything. Your friend. This is how she treats you.'

And this was true, Lila remembered Arianna crouched over her, promising that she would return, money in her hand rolled in the same way that Rafí rolled his money.

And later: Lila wasn't the only victim. Arianna had also spoiled his chances. This was typical, just his luck, to get stuck like this. The money he'd saved, yes some of it was Lila's money, but most of it was money set aside from the rents, the money he'd borrowed, money which could have set them up anywhere they wanted. Madrid, why not, or Barcelona again? Barcelona hadn't been so bad. He could probably go back there now. He could have opened a nightclub, a nice little place with a select membership. He could have, it would've been possible. A private club providing for every taste, every possible experience, but no, in robbing them Arianna had ruined these chances. He was done with Naples and with this way of living.

Rafí took off his shirt and straightened his back. He asked Lila how old she thought he was. His family were mixed blood, Spanish and Arab, and this was where the fine dark looks came from, the olive skin, the heavy balls. The women were freaks, he said, weak, feeble, little more than creatures, but the men were vital and strong. It was a pity for Lila that he didn't go for whores, because he knew how much she liked him.

Arianna would not come back. Couldn't Lila see this? Rafí held Lila's face close. Why would she come back, he asked. Think it through. What would she come back for? Every cent was gone.

Rafí left her in the afternoon. Lila lay awake, aware for the first time of other noises hiding behind the dog's incessant barks. Behind this animal hid a whole city, and deeper even, behind the traffic, the crude honk and buzz, the gasp of brakes, the market shouts, beyond these sounds were others, more ancient. Bells first, through which you could map the entire plain, the distinct differences between one church and another, the tinkering off-colour sounds, out of tune and out of time. And something else, something more than the city's daily shouts and murmurs, sounds she could not calibrate. When she couldn't sleep Lila saw herself poised above the muddle, neither rising nor falling, but holding place above the rucked red roofs, the churches, the palaces, the archives, the ancient halls and houses. No longer running, no longer falling, but suspended above the city.

Lila woke to smell burning. A small column of black smoke curled and collapsed on the balcony. She recognized, without interest, a pair of her shoes, the T-shirt from the hospital, and Rafí dropping these items one by one onto a grill. He was burning her clothes. From the flat roof two floors below came the crazy coughing barks from Rafí's dog.

Rafí, done, stood in the doorway, with blackened hands and a pair of tongs, telling her that she should stay where she was.

'I've thought it through,' he said. Lila didn't have to work at Fazzini or on the corso. She didn't need to go to hotels any more. Until they had to leave he would bring men to her. She didn't need clothes. She didn't need shoes. 'I'll provide what you need.'

And one more thing: with Lila momentarily out of action he'd devised another plan, involving Cecco. Everything now depended on Cecco helping out and pleasing a few of his friends. They had to take opportunities when and as they came. These friends, they wanted a boy.

Rafí dug his phone out of his pocket, and worked a bad smile as he scrolled through finding photographs. Cecco on a bed, soft, loose and compliant on Rafí's dope. Cecco arranged across a bed with his shirt hitched up, eyes closed to half-moons, arms propped behind his head. Cecco with his legs spread wide, so deeply relaxed that he appeared as something hunted, a trophy. He showed Lila the photographs and said they weren't half-bad, given that the camera on his phone was a piece of shit. Rafí's concentration did not last long, and while Lila could not guess the details of this new plan, she didn't doubt that he would replace her.

She came down in the late evening and waited outside Rafí's door. Hungry, she wanted food. Rafí stintingly provided what they needed, going out after midday to bring back ready-cooked meals from an *alimentari* opposite the Fazzini, usually something simple, pasta and beans, or pasta and tomato, which they shared sitting in front of the small balcony overlooking the roof. While he ate, Rafí would coo to his dog and taunt it with scraps. Lila had never needed to remind him before, but there was no coffee, no bread, no sugar, nothing sweet at hand, and she had woken hungry and dizzy.

She sat on the stairs and waited and listened, but could hear nothing inside. When she knocked there came no reply. The door was unlocked, and opening it she found Cecco asleep in Rafí's room. She'd never slept in Rafí's bed.

SUNDAY: DAY H

Amelia Peña returned on the Sunday morning, and found the basement door ajar and a white plastic shopping bag tucked inside. The bag was heavy and the sides scuffed with what she took to be brown paint. Inside she found a hammer, a pair of pliers, and a saw-tooth blade on top of a bundle of damp rags. The rags were wet and sticky, and looked like clothes. When she looked at her fingertips, she recognized that this was not paint or thinners, but blood. Beside the clothes curled to the plastic lay a piece of meat, pink and mottled and dry, and beside the meat a single tooth with long white double roots. The tooth, perfectly formed and specked with red pith, convinced her that this was real and not some kind of fakery. It took her a moment to realize that the meat, with its velvet upper surface and slick underside with a single ridge, was, as far as she could tell, a human tongue.

☆

Marek's problems started when he checked out of the room. While the brothers had paid, they'd also left a package at the desk for him: a box containing a pair of latex gloves (large), a disposable white suit (large), covers for shoes (size 42 to 50), what looked like a shower cap (medium), a pair of industrial goggles (one size, adjustable), and a two-litre bottle of bleach. Paola stood by the windows to the patio, her back to the desk, her bag between her legs. Marek asked when the package had been left and the clerk replied, on Friday, when the gentlemen checked out.

'And there was no note?'

'Just the box.'

'Why didn't you just give it to me when I arrived?'

The clerk pointed to a note which stated, quite clearly, that the package should be presented to Marek Krawiec when he checked out on Sunday.

600

Marek asked when they would be back, and the clerk looked blankly back at him.

'I'm sorry?'

'What time do they get back? Do you know what time they return?'

The clerk logged on to the computer, found the reservation and said no. The room was booked for another couple for the entire week. They had no reservation for Mr Wolf and Mr Rabbit. He smiled as he read the names. Funny that. Funny names.

Marek said no. Those aren't the names. 'Check for Marc and Paul.'

'Last names?' The receptionist looked from Marek to the screen.

'It will be the same last name. First names: Marc and Paul.'

'No,' the clerk adjusted the monitor. 'These are your names. Marek and Paola.' He made a creditable stab at pronouncing Marek's last name. 'Car-wee-ack.' No one could pronounce his name.

'No, no. I said Marc and Paul. Not Marek. Not Paola.' Marek spelled out the brothers' first names and the clerk still couldn't find them. First or last.

They'd paid in cash on Friday morning (everything in cash from Mr Wolf and Mr Rabbit), and there was no further booking, no apparent intention to return.

Marek didn't want to talk this through with Paola. Mr Wolf and Mr Rabbit? There were people with nouns for last names across the globe. Everything in English sounded funny: Mr Vest and Mr Trowzer (lawyers in Gdansk), Mr Grass (his French teacher years before in Lvov), Mr and Mrs Shyte (Pennsylvania, backpackers he'd met in a London hostel, unremarkable except for their last name); it didn't even have to be translated into English: Frau Frau (a nurse in Dusseldorf). In New Zealand a town pronounced Papa-fukah. Not quite right, but there it was. Wolf and Rabbit were probably spelled some other way (Wulffe? Wapett?). Although, weren't they brothers, Marc and Paul? They hadn't said they were brothers, because, being obvious, it hadn't needed saying. Marek had just assumed that this was fact. Wolfe and Rabbit was some joke between them, another example of their humour which he just didn't get. If Wolf and Rabbit was a joke then what about Marc and Paul, apostles both?

His telephone began to ring on the train back. Ring and cut off. When he checked his messages he found five calls, all from the supervisor Amelia Peña. Peña's messages were incoherent. The situation wasn't helped by a poor connection. Something terrible had happened and if she could not reach him she would have to call the police. When Marek called back the line was busy. As the train came into Torre Annunziata he made another attempt, and when Peña answered she spoke in a rapid staccato, repeating herself and the exact words from her last message. She was sorry, she said, sorry she couldn't reach him. She had called many times. She was sorry, the basement door, she said, a bag. Something about a bag? Salvatore wasn't around, she said, he wasn't even in Naples right now, and she didn't know who else to call.

Marek didn't understand her urgency or why it was necessary to call the police. Whatever her problem he had plans for the day. As far as he knew everything at the palazzo should be in good order. Paola spent the journey looking out of the window, head turned so that he couldn't see her face, not even in reflection. This gesture, if that's what it was, summed up the weekend, where she had participated but was barely present.

Mr Wolf and Mr Rabbit.

He would be back, he said, he would not be long.

At this Peña's voice became fearful and brittle.

She had found a plastic bag in the entrance. A shopping bag. There was blood smeared inside the bag, and worse, much worse, something so bad she didn't dare say. She hadn't dared go down to the basement. Couldn't.

They walked from the station to the palazzo and found the door locked. She's made this up, Marek told himself, Peña has concocted some plan or she's stupid, or maybe crazy.

He rang Peña's bell and her face appeared briefly at the bottom of the grille in a small square peephole cut into the door, her eyes wide and red, glassy and fearful. She had locked herself inside and in her anxiety she could not draw back the bolt. Paola drew an impatient breath, and said more to herself than Marek that Peña was a drunk dwarf. She wasn't even the proper supervisor; no one paid her. It's not official. 'And now she's locking us out of our home.'

When the door finally opened Peña stepped away in a doped slowness and slipped back to the whitewashed wall.

Paola pushed through, and used her overnight bag as a block between her and the supervisor. She gave Marek a look as if Peña was drunk, as if this really was all too much.

'I'm going up.'

She was sorry, Peña said, hardly acknowledging Paola as she walked away. She reached vaguely to Marek, feebly caught his arm, her voice fragile and diminishing, and whispered, sorry. So sorry.

Impatient with these apologies Marek asked what was she sorry about. What was this exactly? What did she want?

Peña pointed to courtyard, to the basement door, to a white plastic shopping bag. Even at this distance, Marek could see the blue lettering that served as a logo for *Salvatore Alimentari*. The bag looked fat, the sides folded over as if tucked, as if waiting to be collected, the sides scuffed with muck.

Marek walked directly to the bag and gruffly pulled it toward him and was surprised at the weight. Inside, he found a hammer and a sawtooth blade, a pair of pliers, some shorts, and a T-shirt sopped with something like oil, sticky and dirty. He opened the T-shirt with his fingertips, still not thinking, a little repelled at the feel of the material, but just not thinking, and out skittered two teeth, two human teeth, with long white double roots. At the base of the bag a piece of meat, impossible – a tongue. He dropped the clothes. '*What is this?*' Wiped his hands down his shirt, looked to Peña and said he didn't understand. What was this? Blood? Real blood. Teeth. A tongue?

Peña held out the keys and said that he should go to the basement, she would not go, and Marek said she was crazy, why had she waited, this was a matter for the police?

Except.

It wasn't a matter for the police.

Not at all.

When he returned to the courtyard Marek came quickly out through the service entrance onto via Tribunali. Certain that he was going to be sick, he leaned forward and regulated his breathing. The room's heavy stink followed him out, and the effort not to retch brought tears to his eyes. Marek curled up in the doorway and hugged himself hard.

It was impossible that this could happen. Impossible to accept what he had seen, a room fouled with thick gouts of blood, a pool of it misshapen with skids and slides, the colour bright-edged and black-centred, wet and crusting.

He had bought the plastic.

He had prepared the room, painted it, left it white, layered with plastic, not draped, but taped and nailed and dressed, and what he returned to was far beyond his understanding, a room so thick with blood that someone had dragged and swum through it, soaked themselves and left their imprint.

Plenty of people would have seen him coming and going over the past week.

He called the brothers, could hardly hold the phone with shaking, but let it ring and found no answer. He called again, and again, and thought he heard a sound from the bag – and there, in fact, was the phone, set to vibrate, beside the tongue.

Outside, distant, he could hear sirens and car horns. The traffic on via Duomo stopped and began to stall along via Capasso.

Sensing Peña behind him he spat on the pavement.

Had she called the police?

She could not remember.

'You must remember. Have you called the police? Have you spoken with anyone else?'

Peña shook her head, no she had not called anyone else.

'Nobody has seen this?' He pointed to the bag. 'And the room? Has anyone seen the room?' A T-shirt with a star.

Again Peña shook her head.

Marek shook his head. 'You haven't been down there?'

Peña gave another quick shake. No, no she hadn't looked. What was down there?

'Nothing.' Marek shook his head. 'Nothing.'

They shook their heads together, willing this to be true.

'There's nothing down there.' He held up the keys. 'Let me keep these for now.'

Peña nodded, eager to be rid of any responsibility.

'Has anyone come in or out? Anyone from the palazzo? Has anyone seen or looked into the bag?'

Once more she shook her head, and Marek again felt hopeful.

'Did you see anyone go down into the basement this weekend? What about the brothers? Has anyone seen Marc or Paul?'

She didn't understand him. She hadn't met the men.

'The men who rented the room? You haven't met them?'

'Salvatore,' she said, but according to his sons he had returned to

Bari, for his health. They knew nothing about a basement room, and nothing about two businessmen.

Lanzetti. Marek decided he should speak with Lanzetti.

What was he going to do about the bag? Peña pointed back to the courtyard. Marek followed after. He picked up the T-shirt, returned it to the bag and again took note of the pattern, badly stained: a white star in a white circle.

One of the brothers had killed the other, he was certain of it. He pinched the keys hard into his fist. A white star. A white circle. The same star and circle as the bakery. The bakery and the language school. A far worse idea occurred to him. They had murdered the Japanese girl. This was why they had asked him to find someone. This was why they had paid him so well. The clothes in the bag were not clothes likely to be worn by either of the brothers, but neither were they women's clothes.

Marek had painted the room. Bought the materials. Dressed the room in plastic. He'd helped them search for a woman. He began to understand his part in this, the realization yawned open, the bleach, the gloves, the package at the hotel. An expectation that he would clean up. And the tongue? An emphatic demand that he should shut his mouth.

He told Peña that it was a joke. The tongue, the blood, were fake. The clothes were real enough, of course, but everything else was some kind of elaborate joke. Peña appeared to accept the answer, although the idea produced no change in how she appeared.

Paola, seated at the sewing machine, leaned through and gave a hi, as if the weekend had not been awkward, as if nothing had happened, which was in many ways the problem. Nothing had happened: no arguments, but no agreements either. She'd tolerated the weekend, suffered through it as if this were something he'd especially wanted to do, and just this one time they'd do it, right, but it wouldn't become a habit, OK, it wouldn't be anything she'd care to repeat. Paola leaned from her chair, hands holding a T-shirt steady under the needle, to peep into the room with an apologetic hi, as if she realized now just how childish she could be sometimes. 'What's that on your shirt?'

Marek answered *paint*. He'd wiped his hands down his shirtfront. Two smears that looked nothing like paint.

Paola slipped back into work, and left him alone while he sat at the toilet, tried to control his breathing, tried to hold down his retching or keep it to the moments when she was sewing, when the machine peckered through the material and the sound stammered through the walls. His eyes were watering from the effort to regulate his breathing, he didn't know if he was crying.

She asked if he was OK, what was keeping him?

'I think, I don't know, maybe I've picked up something. The steam room.'

'The chicken,' she said, 'undercooked. Oh god, we both had it. I'm feeling a little that way too.'

He'd never thought of her as superficial, but now it struck him. If he was feeling sick, she had to be sick too, or sicker. The idea of Paola came to him, entirely apparent. As ridiculous as a small dog. It wasn't stitching clothes she hated, not in itself, it was the dread that this was the limit of her expertise, that she wasn't any better than any other peasant who stitched and sewed. Italian through and through, she felt she deserved better. She hated him, treated him with contempt. This was clear. Because he was Polish, because he earned his living when and where he could. They weren't a couple. They were two people making do.

He thought that he should like her more. That he should want to hold her, be close, feel someone living, just to feel loved. But he just felt sick. He thought he should be able to tell her exactly what he'd seen and she would know – without pause – to offer comfort. But she would blame him, she would tell him: *nothing is free.* Didn't you see what you were doing? Didn't you ask yourself: *what is this for*? Did you have no understanding, no perspective? She would tell him nothing that he did not know.

He stayed in the bathroom, lodged his foot against the door just in case she had the bright idea to check on him. He always knew what to do, in every situation, he always knew the answer. He'd speak to his brother. Lemi would know. And then he realized his brother couldn't begin to calculate the complications or the dimension of it. Every way he looked at this he was in trouble. He would be held responsible. Culpable. To the end of his life.

The room would have to be cleared. Either him, the police, or someone else would have to tear down the plastic, pack it in bags, take it elsewhere. It would not stay like this. It could not.

*

Marek kept the basement keys in his pocket, where he could feel them digging into his leg. He closed the shutters, lay on the bed, tried to sleep so that he didn't have to explain himself, but didn't want to close his eyes because the room stayed with him. He told himself it wasn't real. It couldn't be, he'd taken it wrong. They'd butchered an animal, that's all, some dog picked off the street. That's all this was. Not a joke but a prank, although how could this in any shape be seen as something funny. A tongue in a bag. Teeth. A room drenched in blood.

At five o'clock he heard a knock at the door, and felt his heart stop then quicken. This would be the police and they would take him now. They would want to know why he was asking at the school about the Japanese woman. Why had he bought those materials? Whoever were these people, Mr Wolf and Mr Rabbit?

He heard Lanzetti's voice and rose immediately. Paola at the door – uncommonly nice, even welcoming. She held the door open and invited the pharmacist in, explained that Marek wasn't feeling well, a stomach bug from a short trip, but here he is.

'Ah, the hotel.' Lanzetti smiled and looked to Marek then Paola. 'How was it?'

Paola nodded, too eager, surely she knew she didn't need to play it this way. 'He's picked up something. Stomach.'

'Have you been sick?'

Marek shrugged. It wasn't much of anything. A little rest and he'd be fine.

'Water,' Lanzetti smiled. 'Make sure he drinks lots of water. He's sweating. People dehydrate quickly. You have no idea how quickly, it's so hot. If he isn't well in the morning come by and I'll give you something for it. Some salts. Something also for the stomach if it doesn't go.' Lanzetti held the brothers' book in his hand. 'I came to return this.' He offered the book to Marek.

Paola stood at the door, looked hard at the book, and Marek felt that he needed to explain himself but couldn't think of anything.

'It's . . .' Lanzetti paused, turned the book in his hands, his expression showing some distaste. 'It isn't nice.'

'Nice?' Paola gave a short scoff.

'It's hard to say,' Lanzetti looked like he would rather explain this to Marek alone. He held the book out. 'It isn't what I would usually read.'

Marek didn't want to touch the book. He turned and Lanzetti

stepped into the apartment. Paola asked if he would like a drink, and Lanzetti appeared relieved. He asked for water, if that would be all right. It was hot this afternoon.

Once Paola was in the kitchen Lanzetti asked Marek if he knew what the book was about.

'The subject is – it's a little strange.' Lanzetti looked quickly to the kitchen. 'It's about a building, a palazzo such as this, a place where a lot of people live, and how the main character takes revenge on them because they didn't stop an event from happening, an event which involves his sister. He has a room, a basement room . . . and he turns this room into a slaughterhouse.'

And now Marek was paying attention.

'He prepares this room . . .'

Paola returned with the water, ice clinking in the glass. 'I have to work.'

Lanzetti accepted the glass with a smile. He gave a small and formal bow and apologized for stopping her. He stood and Marek stood as if in a confrontation, then they both walked to the kitchen.

'I'm not sure I understand. But there are elements from the book that are familiar.'

'Elements?'

'A word was scratched on the door, on the main door. This word was painted on the doors of collaborators at the end of the war. It's mentioned in the book. I think your friends, although this doesn't make sense, believe that this is the same palazzo as the place described in the book.'

'And the room?'

'The room. The room is where a killing takes place. Only it's staged. It isn't real. He wants the people in the building to be punished. So he pours blood onto the walls and floor and makes it look like a slaughterhouse. He makes it look like the people in the building have been killing American soldiers and selling them as meat.'

'It isn't real?'

'No. It's staged. It isn't real. The man uses blood he's stolen from a field hospital. He uses body parts. A tongue. A hand. A foot. All taken from the hospital. He leaves these where they will be found to incriminate a doctor, a lawyer, a magistrate, because he blames them for something that has happened to his sister.'

Marek accepted the book.

'It's not even a good book.'

Paola slept beside him, uncommonly affectionate, first spooning, then, because of the heat, lying separate but keeping a hand at the small of his back. Marek lay awake, now confused. So they had a book, a story, a script to follow, and what had they done? He knew blood, he knew the smell, but had no way to know if this was real. If this was animal blood, how could such a quantity be stored? A human has seven litres of blood. This they had taught him in the army. Seven litres, which, with an arterial cut will vent a fountain two or three metres, and take three to four minutes to bleed out. There were ropes hanging from the ceiling with tethers made from duct tape, and spatter on the ceiling and the wall. An elaborate hoax if it was a hoax. He wanted to ask Lanzetti about the mechanics of the hoax, the similarities with the book. He wanted to know the ending.

It was clear that Marek needed to return to the room and remove anything that would identify or connect him, and then he would leave the city. Take his money and go.

MONDAY – TUESDAY: DAYS I & J

Marek spent the day in bed, turned to the wall, the same thoughts racketing endlessly without result and couldn't sleep. In the late afternoon he rose, and decided he had no choice. Before he returned to the basement he contacted English Tony and asked for a car. It didn't have to be the Citroën, but he needed a car as soon as possible. Tony said that he could take the Citroën and Marek asked for something different. Anything would do, it was just to move Paola's bags, and he didn't want to spill anything in the Citroën. Already he was explaining too much.

'Take the Citroën,' English Tony insisted. If something happened he could clean it. Just take a little care and fill it up. It's only shirts, right? This is what she does, she stitches shirts?

Marek drove back through piazza Garibaldi, passed by every kind of police imaginable, municipal, state, carabinieri, finance, firemen and paramedics, you name it. Every one of them idling at the piazza.

Back in the basement he waited at the door, dressed slowly in the white suit, the slip-on booties, the hairnet, the goggles, the latex gloves, stared at the door, a heavy door like something from a ship, painted and repainted so the surface had a roundness, a way of appearing smooth when in reality it was deeply scratched and picked. He couldn't enter the room, couldn't make himself touch the door handle, and found himself stuck.

One week ago – was it? – the argument with Paola, a joke of hers about him being gullible. It wasn't that he was stupid, that wasn't what she was trying to say. Maybe it was the military training, or something, but he always did what she told him, always. She just had to speak in a certain way and he'd jump to it. He couldn't remember the comment but she'd said it was almost the same thing – doing what you're told and being stupid. Almost the same.

How could he not have thought of this?

A room covered in plastic.

610

How could it not occur to him?

He made the decision, physically leaned into the door until he had no choice but to step forward and touch it. Once inside he walked about the perimeter, his nose and mouth buried in the crook of his arm as he tugged the plastic sheets free from the walls. He shielded his face as the plastic slipped down, and trod carefully, because whatever this was, it wasn't only blood. Although he had carefully covered the walls and double taped the seams, the sheeting had separated on the floor and a large pool of blood had settled underneath, and there were bare footprints, already dry, tracked across the concrete. Marek attempted to fold the sheets without coming into contact with the blood. With only one side torn down, he looked about the room and understood that what he was doing was unwise.

Behind the door, set beside what remained of the roll of plastic, he uncovered a shoulder-bag. Under the bag, placed tidily next to the wall, he found a pair of brown trainers and socks, left side by side as if someone had undressed there. None of this seemed fake to him, the hairs caught in the tape strapping, the pattern and pooling of the blood, the hanging tether – but he told himself that none of this was real.

He packed the plastic into six black disposal bags, slopped bleach onto the floor and left it as it was.

Back on the street he found Cecco leaning nonchalantly against a parked car, happy with himself. Marek checked the street and when he saw that it was clear, he came out with two of the bags. Cecco watched, then offered to help him load them into the car. Marek signalled a gracious no.

'If you need a hand,' Cecco offered, 'I could drive.'

Marek opened the car door and began to load the bags onto the back seat, and wedged them behind the seats with his foot. Straightening as he backed out of the car, he smiled back at the boy and wished that he would leave. It was the car he was after. This is what held his interest.

Marek parked the car on via Consolo. He washed his arms and neck in a fountain in a piazzetta with boys playing football around him who knew better than to pay attention. He rinsed out his shirt then he checked himself in a shop window and was surprised by his expression, stern, sober, and pale. Inside the shop the owner sat in a chair fanning herself and avoiding eye contact.

Out on Corso Garibaldi the police attended to the traffic. A cat-call of sirens, close and threatening, ran down Corso Emanuele. Marek walked the long way round to via Capasso avoiding the groups of police, mindful not to appear suspicious; he had never seen so many police before, but realized that he must have, he'd just never had a reason to fear them.

He waited in his apartment, certain the police would come, told Paola that he was still feeling unwell. He waited curled on the bed, arms wrapped tight about his chest, and stared hard at the wall, convinced that the police were playing a game. His fingerprints would be all over the room, all over the car, and he didn't doubt that they would soon come after him. The police would trace the car, contact Tony, then they would come for him.

After midnight he began to feel hopeful. It was possible, just possible, that they hadn't discovered the car. Parked alongside other cars one road away from the palazzo it would not be so obvious. What was there to notice? Even if they did find the car, how would they know to come to him? Fingerprints would take a while to process, by which time he would be out of the city. No. A new problem struck him. The car and its contents combined were less of a worry than Peña. The woman was so stupid that if the police came to speak to her information would pour out of her, unstoppable, and she would tell them everything about the bag, about Marek preparing the room, and once they associated Marek with the room, they would quickly piece together what they needed. And Salvatore? What was the deal with Salvatore?

At two o'clock Marek decided to return to the car. He came carefully down the stairs and checked the courtyard to see if there were police in the building, and was surprised to see the entrance as it usually was at night, the hefty wood doors closed, windows and shutters open on the upper floors, only one or two lights showing in the front of the building.

The car was still on the bridge, undisturbed. He walked by it, not looking at the car, but looking up the street for any sign that something was not right. Satisfied, he turned about, and hurried back with the keys in his hand.

The late afternoon heat had drawn out a fatty stench from the clothes. Marek wound the window down. The car started on the third attempt with a rough choke. Marek drove with his head toward what draught there was, a buffet of hot air with the soft feel of cloth.

He took the smaller roads following the coast south toward Ercolano and sensed, for the first time, the possibility of success. The headlights broke across concrete walls and glasshouses, on one side were simple townhouses and workshops, on another a broken line of warehouses which appeared largely abandoned. Turning a narrow corner he was forced to an abrupt stop, in the middle of the road an abandoned dumpster, so solid, he thought of it at first as some kind of creature, something ancient. Marek laughed, tension broken, he turned left and headed inland and soon he was back among housing. He drove now with the lights off, aware that the car would draw attention to itself. He turned again and headed for an unlit area and found himself on a pumice track with stark concrete high-rises on either side. The road came to a halt at a dry sloping scrubby field.

Marek stopped the car, turned on the headlights: from what he could see he was far enough away from the housing estate and into a wasteland. He could burn the clothes and bags here. This, he thought, was too easy, as if he had some natural talent. The idea disturbed him.

Under the plastic bags he found a litre can of engine oil. He threw the clothes into the field and when he returned to the car he thought he heard a cough, a definite cough. Marek stopped and listened and squinted up the track. It was nothing, he was certain, but nevertheless he needed to hurry. As he reached for the shoulder-bag he thought he heard the sound again. Not a cough this time but someone walking, the crisp break of dry grass underfoot. Marek paused and again stared hard into the night, and again discovered nothing. He swung the shoulder-bag out into the field, then, following the light cast by the headlamps he walked after them opening the can of oil. It wasn't a cough this time but a huff – Marek stood over the clothes, he doused them with oil and was surprised that the clothes would not ignite. He attempted to light them with a handful of dried grasses, but again it wouldn't catch. He plucked more grass, wound the strands into a knot and tried again. This time the grass caught, but the flames died as quickly as they had started. Behind him the first handful he'd thrown aside quickly caught fire – and just as swiftly died. If he couldn't burn the clothes he would bury them. Unable to see where he had thrown the bag he searched the field and stepped carefully through the grass

– and there, again, a rustle. This time he was certain he heard someone approaching.

When he turned back to the car Marek was surprised to see a dog. Bleached white in the headlights, the animal appeared big and strong, with fluorescent eyes, a heavy black mouth; it stepped lightly through the grass. Head dipped it picked up the scent of blood and took a position between Marek and the clothes. As Marek moved forward the dog hunched in threat. He kicked sand, threw stones, a clod of earth, and the animal dodged and weaved back, swift and lithe, it came threateningly close. 'Just go,' Marek hissed, gestured. 'Go. Go.' But the creature set its shoulders back and gave a slow rolling growl. Behind the dog and the clothes the grass again began to burn with a soft crackle.

It was just becoming light, a pink hue opening at the horizon, the hills, barely described, becoming distinguishable in the last of the black night, a smog caught about the bay.

Marek returned to the car aware that it was becoming bright enough for him to be seen. People would shortly be rising, heading to work. The car would be easy to remember, the clothes would not, just clothes on a wasteland, dried and dirty. He saw the estate now, highrises built on a flattened section of land, turned to the bay, closer than he'd imagined. Further away, at the edge of the wasteland were the abandoned factories he'd driven by. He would dump the plastic in one of the buildings. The dog, now settled in front of the clothes, watched him back away.

He drove slowly back down the track. In the early morning light, the warehouses appeared less ominous. At the junction he remembered to slow down for the dumpster. He turned the car into a small alley and parked. Along the verge lay a pile of rotting flowers. He hauled the dumpster inside the factory. One wheel caught on the threshold and he hoisted it up, then shunted the dumpster across the room, the noise starting up a dog in the distance. The floor was gritted with broken glass, cushions taken from a couch set beside the remains of a small fire, among the ashes were several syringes. It was light enough to see now, and he quickly took the plastic out of the car, bag by bag, to the dumpster. Breath held, head turned, he worked quickly. By the last run it had become bright enough to see that the small alley ended in a steeper slope of smooth black basalt which tipped directly into the sea. He walked to the edge, and decided to dump the bags into the sea.

THE KILL

Hefting the bags back out of the dumpster was an unpleasant business, and one of the bags flattened at the bottom of the dumpster was difficult to reach. Once most of them were down to the shoreline he began to look for stones to weigh them down. He found pieces of concrete in the building, but not enough, so he tethered the bags together and weighed down the first.

He undressed by the shore, washed out his clothes then laid them on the stones which held a body heat from the previous day. He worked naked, made sure the bags were securely knotted one to the other, then carried the heavier bag with him and he picked his way slowly into the water. The sea was cold, welcomingly so, and gave him the odd sensation of being both awake and revived, while also being exhausted, so much so that he seemed to be observing his own movements, how he waded slowly through the water, how tedious it was to draw the bags one by one in a slack chain behind him.

He dropped the bag at his feet when the water was head-high, nudged them still further with his foot, and was pleased to see – at last, something was working – that all but one bag was submerged. Gouts of air belched from the bags as they sank, and holding the last bag he squeezed out the air, compressed it, turned his head away so that nothing would spill over him, then ducking under the water he felt for a stone, and lifted it over the last bag to secure it.

A shoal of small silver fish began to gather about him. The bags now submerged sent out a powdery rust. Marek also, his chest and arms specked and fouled, gave off a dusty cloud, and the fish, tiny, glass-like, sparks of light, flashed about him, feeding, and seemed miraculous.

Marek sat on the rocks and smoked. He had done well to separate himself from the basement room and the brothers, but while he might have broken the obvious links, there were, he guessed, many other connections. A body, if there was a body, which would have its own story, then Peña, and Paola, Lanzetti, and maybe even Salvatore, who could each connect him to the brothers. Without evidence, without the room, there would be nothing concrete. He didn't know how he would manage if the police questioned him. Brushing away mosquitoes he looked back along the coastline at the grey outline of the city and thought that he had never seen a place so beautiful or heard a sound so lovely as the slap of the waves against the shore.

Marek dressed and returned to the car, relieved for the moment.

The car, however, would not start. He had run out of fuel. Marek returned to the shore, swearing, cursing his bad luck. Hadn't Tony said as much, warned him she just runs out and dies. How could he possibly have let this happen? If he bought fuel in Ercolano he would be remembered, he would be connected with the place. If he left the car, he risked it being damaged or stolen. His only option would be to return to Naples, buy fuel in the city and come back for the car. This, he guessed, would take no longer than two hours.

Half an hour after he caught the train, the first of the bags, tugged loose by the current, floated free from the stone and came to the surface. The incoming tide drove it back to the shore and it pulled behind it the others so that they could be seen from the shore as black rounded humps bobbing at the surface.

The solution came easier than he expected. As soon as he arrived back at the palazzo he found the boy Cecco idling in front of the *tabaccaio*. Marek signalled to him and called him to the palazzo and asked if he could drive. Of course he could drive. Did he want money? Of course, he could always use money. If he wanted he could come with him to Ercolano. Marek laughed while he explained the situation: I need someone to buy some fuel, that's all. 'I can trust you?'

Cecco nodded. He could be trusted. He would be careful.

Marek took the train back to Ercolano with Cecco, had the boy buy a canister, then walk to a garage to buy fuel. At the last moment he decided that Cecco could also collect the car. He didn't want to be seen, and thought no one would pay attention to the boy. He gave clear and direct instructions. Find the car beside the warehouses and bring it back. Did he understand? If he brought the car back to the station he could pick up Marek. 'I've someone to meet,' he lied, 'come back to the station. I'll meet you here.' That's all he was asking. How difficult could that be?

Cecco nodded. He knew nothing, and that was good. The less he knew the less he could blab to the police.

Marek traced his change of luck back to the accident. He did not know how to describe it. It wasn't that he was unlucky; it was something infinitely more complex.

He paid Cecco generously, told him to be quiet about the errand, then left him at the station. He drove away from the city toward Salerno and with the mountains to his left and in front, determined to perform one last task. Pagani was joined to Torre del Greco and the larger sprawl of Naples, one town blending without break into another. Smaller barn-like houses butted beside villas and developments. Paola always pointed out Nenella's, a family house shared by three generations, isolated by busy roads that cut by on all sides.

When he arrived Marek parked and waited. He smoked and considered the absurdity of driving so far to meet a woman he had often ridiculed. He wasn't sure either what he wanted to ask.

The door opened directly onto the street, he watched a woman come out and manhandle a wheelchair onto the road. The chair was cumbersome, and strapped into it was a young boy, one arm on his lap the other held up to his chest, crooked, his head slightly twisted. The traffic could not see her, and came fast round the turn, coming dangerously close to the wheelchair. The woman lumbered the chair out onto the road, and once it was on even ground it seemed to move by itself. The woman, the child's mother or aunt, walked beside the boy to protect him from the traffic. She walked with a little difficulty, a slight twist in her hips, an awkward gait, a plastic shopping bag hitched into her elbow that flew over her hands as the traffic passed close by them.

Marek considered returning to Naples.

The house sounded busy. Children upstairs, shouts coming from the kitchen, full of people who could not be seen. As no one answered the door Marek came timidly into the hall and then into the kitchen. Two women worked together, busy, preparing food, and they didn't immediately notice him. When they did they sent him back down the hall and said he should go into the room on his left. Behind the building, through the open kitchen door, was a small courtyard, and he could see parts of cars and scooters parked up beside stacks of salvaged wood.

Nenella was younger than he expected, not much older, by appearance, than Marek himself. She wore jeans and a shirt with an embroidered design across the shoulder. Her hair was short and dyed a deep chestnut; she had none of the airs that he associated with faith healers and readers. There were newspapers spread out across the floor to either cover or collect, and at the back of the room, dark because of the drawn shutters, a fat old dog with rheumy eyes stretched out. Nenella appeared momentarily unsettled, surprised by Marek.

Disappointed that the woman appeared so ordinary, and a little ashamed to be explaining his doubts and troubles to a stranger, Marek began to stammer. Starting with the accident he described the difficulties and indifference that had settled upon him. Now anxious about what he was saying Marek began to sweat, and admitted that he did not know what he was doing.

After five minutes Nenella stopped him. There was nothing she could do. There was nothing to fix. She sent him away saying that she would not read for him. He would not conceive, she said, because he should have died that day. Every day after the accident came from a new life. He was a baby, she said, new-born, and there was no business between them.

He called Paola as he drove back and said that his mother was not well. He gave no details and used the tired language of those who don't have time to explain. *She'd taken a turn for the worse.* She was seeing a specialist, he didn't know when exactly, but it looked like they were running out of options. As far as he knew there were no further treatments possible. Lemi was coming from Frankfurt, they would stay at his cousin's then drive to his mother's house in Lvov. He didn't know how long this would take. He hoped to be back in a week.

He returned to the palazzo one last time, collected his passport, left what money he could on the table. Just as he was about to leave he heard a key in the lock, and Paola came into the apartment on her own. He waited in the bedroom and said nothing as she crossed through to the bathroom. He wouldn't normally be in the apartment at this time. So it was strange to him that she locked the bathroom door after herself, a piece of information he would not have guessed. He crept out of the bedroom and came slowly up the hall not wanting to make any noise, and not wanting to alarm or alert her. He thought of her without him, how his absence without an explanation would be cruel, and would hold her unnaturally to one place, where ordinarily, if they simply parted, she would be able to continue. She would understand the shape of such a departure. She would stay in the apartment, he could be certain of this. It wasn't easy finding a place as good as this to live, certainly not at the rate she paid. He would stay with her, while apart, for long enough to ensure that he could hear about the palazzo. If anything happened, if the police started to make enquiries he would need to know. For the interim he would stay at his brother's. He would wait, bide time until he could feel confident.

Then he would disappear. This much he had decided. Without Paola, without his mother, he would be untethered, and while this felt like a necessity, he realized that he had expected more with Paola, that while they weren't perfect, they fitted, and that – he'd never thought of it so clearly before – he had expected to grow old with her.

The last details: the edge of parquet meeting the marble floor at the main entrance. The marble yellow and cracked at the wall, but bleached where it had been cleaned over many years. The weight of the door, and how, slow to draw shut, it became easier mid-swing. How the key needed to be turned twice to get the latch to properly cross the gap. These details would stay with him longer than the physical memory of Paola, how she lay beside him on their final night, her hand curved to the small of his back, how she muttered in her sleep when she slept on her side, small whispers, the subject: he could never guess.

WEDNESDAY: DAY K

Early on Wednesday evening Niccolò Scafuti, a security guard for the Persano-Mecuri chemical dye plant in Ercolano, reported the discovery of bloodstained clothes and a small black cloth shoulder-bag a few metres from the road on scrubland behind his apartment.

Built in the early nineteen-seventies, the Rione Ini estate dominated the south-eastern boundary of Ercolano. Poorly constructed of pre-cast concrete sections, the buildings overshadowed the surrounding wasteland. Only four of the planned twelve high-rise apartments were completed, although the foundations, drains and sewers were laid for the entire complex. The land about the estate remained tracked and broken, levelled in the spring and summer by a sloped field of grasses busy with red, papery poppies.

Niccolò sat out on the balcony and waited for his sister to return. At five o'clock the incinerator on via Tre Marzo burnt paper waste and sent up a plume of white, feathery ash. In the late afternoon a cool breeze blew in from the sea, and the heat rose off the concrete and caused the falling ash to momentarily pause, hover, then rise.

At six o'clock Niccolò took a plastic sack and slingshot and headed directly for the wasteland. As he walked through the scrub he followed a path running parallel to the road, his eye open for small pea-sized stones. The day had been frustrating, much of it spent manually raising and lowering a barrier as the new security passes would not work. The drivers coming into the compound waited for his service but did not acknowledge him. When they did talk they'd look at him, take a moment, then deliberately slow down.

Beside the track, partly hidden by the tall grasses, lay a brown shoulder-bag. Further to his left, in a one-metre-wide clearing, he discovered a small rubbery hump of clothes, as brown as the bag, which appeared to be dug out of the ground from a small scratched hole. He cautiously inspected the clothes, busy with ants, set hard and coated in sandy dirt. It was only when he opened out the T-shirt, saw the cuts, a series of small slashes, and noticed how the heavy stains stiffened the cloth that he realized they were stained with blood.

Niccolò looked back along the path to see what else he had walked by. Close to the road the grass was scorched in a wide path, and he guessed that an attempt had been made to burn the clothes and the bag. Alarmed at what else he might find, he checked carefully to see if there were other areas burned or flattened in the field – then he returned to the bag when he was sure that he was alone.

He waited a long time before deciding to open the clasp.

There needed to be a certain kind of hush before it would happen. A kind of white noise filling the background and him focusing down, concentrating on the one thing – and then without any kind of prelude or announcement he would disappear inside himself. Just vanish.

There were triggers. Flickering or flashing lights, almost any tight pattern; reading – the simple action of casually passing his eye along a line of printed words was often enough to snag him. A length of sunlight slatted through a blind, or light cutting into a room catching dust and vibrating, and he would lose focus and become fixed in a kind of endlessness, a loop. In such moments the world flew away from him, a kind of flutter, and gone. Words within a moment of being spoken became lost. His sister would coo to him, singsong, 'Hey, hey, Niccolò? Where are you?' sometimes kindly, sometimes impatient, as if there was a destination, a place he retreated to, but these events were nothing but absence, the moment of leaving knitted to the moment of returning, and while they were brief, he had no notion of their length. These weren't jumps forward, sudden segues, but steps out, lapses. He'd worked in security for two years, or nine, depending on how good his memory was that morning.

Bent over the brown hump of clothes with a breeze running through the grass, Niccolò couldn't be sure how much time had slipped by, if those were the same dusty clouds burning off in a late-afternoon sun, the same flies rising, so dizzy and fired they batted into each other and into his face. His thighs ached and he settled onto his knees. He couldn't figure out how long he'd waited, just as he couldn't be sure, exactly, what he was doing. His hand settled on the clothes and information began to return: the sack, the slingshot, the heat, the ants, the flies, the clothes, the field, the reason for walking through the field, the time of day, the scents of scorched earth and something less pleasant. He couldn't stand cats, never could, he remembered now.

The material, crusted with dirt, unfolded to a T-shirt, a pair of shorts, and a fat wad of rags. The T-shirt slit with two parallel cuts at the navel – one long, one short – and slashed on either side at the lower stomach and just below the armpits. Ants ran up his hands and he shook them off. Done with the clothes, Niccolò carefully opened the shoulder-bag. He pinched the clips to release the buckles then cautiously opened the flap. A natural thing to do. You find something so you check inside just to see who it might belong to, naturally.

Niccolò returned to the estate with the contents of the bag tucked inside his sack and then he decided to contact the police.

Within an hour of Niccolò's discovery the police had cordoned off a small area of the field, and the clothes – a pair of corduroy shorts, boxer shorts, a T-shirt with a five-point star design – were photographed on site and carefully packaged. A preliminary search was made of the area but nothing of interest was immediately discovered.

Against all logic the evening wind brought heat. Reporters began to assemble at the perimeter of the wasteland. People hurried from the estate toward him to be stopped by the police. A slight haze wrapped about the figures. Still dressed in his uniform, Niccolò stood beside the police vehicles and folded his arms high over his chest so that the company insignia could not be seen; but the police had gathered the information they needed and asked him, not unkindly, to return home with the assurance that they knew what they were doing now, and thank you. You've done a good job. You've done all you can. We know where you are if we need you. Certain they would want to speak with him further, Niccolò took a new position outside the taped perimeter. With the sun low over the bay, light began to strafe between the buildings and their shadows reached almost to his feet – for one moment every detail held his attention. The gathering crowd, the police unpacking their equipment, the waiting huddle of reporters, the sun and the shadows and a light wind raising dust between the buildings, grey in the street and white in the sky.

Niccolò returned to his apartment and waited for the police to seek him out. Even without him the event drew interest. More people idled in the street than usual, and they stood in small groups, the men with their shirts open or rolled over their stomachs, an expectation that a body might be discovered. He practised his explanation about how he'd come across the clothes so that he would not sound confused. On the table he laid out two books on forensic science, course textbooks bought second-hand at Porta Alba. He waited, but the police did not come.

Frustrated, Niccolò returned to the balcony and waited for his sister, mindful of the street outside and the television inside playing an American detective show, dubbed well enough for the mouths to almost match the sounds. Away on the wasteland, under bright arc lights, the police walked in a line across the scrub. A second team combed the edge of the floodlit field, and he felt a slight anxiety and exhilaration as the line progressed through the field – but none of them, not one, looked like they would come to speak to him any time soon. Inside the apartment the sack with the contents from the shoulder-bag lay on the floor. If he wanted, he could simply walk out there and tell them what else he'd found, then they might speak to him, only he wasn't even sure what he'd taken and he knew that this might not be a sensible idea.

When he decided the police weren't coming, he put everything back in the sack, and tucked the sack where Livia wouldn't move it. He looked through drawers, and found in the kitchen where Livia had stacked photographs of his wife and daughter, removed them from their frames, although he could not see why. Tomorrow he'd take the sack to the paint factory, sort through what he'd found and dump what he didn't want to keep.

Niccolò stood on the balcony with his hands on his hips. He could feel the attention of his neighbours, and knew that he was being watched with small quantities of something that resembled respect. Police vehicles remained parked alongside the wasteland, and the press and crews assembled a temporary camp at the head of the field. The bright lights, the gathering crowd gave the evening the appearance of a festival. Two police teams worked their way toward the shoreline, one passing through the abandoned paintworks, the other passing through the rows of greenhouses, uncertainty in their staggered movement. Niccolò watched the white vehicles crawl along the road while the men walked ahead.

When Livia came home, he insisted that she watch the news with him. Niccolò described his discovery and his discussion with the police, and just as he began to work himself up a little (*they told me to come back. I waited, I was here. I did exactly what they asked*) a report from the Rione Ini estate came live on the television. It was a jolt at first to recognize the estate and they both pointed at the screen with surprise. The item was presented once in the main news and again on the summary fifteen minutes after, and later still on the local bulletin. Each time the segment appeared it came as a small shock, and he watched the wasteland on both the television and in reflection in the glass in the balcony door, satisfied that he, Niccolò Scafuti, security guard for Persano-Mecuri Ercolano, was the root cause of this. As soon as the clip was over, Niccolò scanned through the stations to see what coverage they were giving the event. He described the discovery to his sister again to fix the moment he came across the clothes.

Livia sat with him, occasionally dozing, legs stretched across the floor, her back to the wall, because these days this was the only way to remain comfortable. It was sad about the clothes, she said. It was the saddest thing.

THURSDAY: DAY L

Eight days after the assault three men came to the Hotel Stromboli for Rafí. Warned by a telephone call, Rafí scrabbled for his clothes and told Lila to get downstairs and tell them he wasn't about. The men, already inside the Stromboli, banged on doors and drew out residents to the landings. If she could delay them he could get out onto the roof where they wouldn't find him. They were peddlers, kids, he said, petty dope dealers he owed money to, and while they didn't pose much of a threat, he didn't doubt that they could do some damage if they decided on it.

As Lila searched for something to wear Rafí shoved her to the door and told her to hurry.

She met the men on the stairs, already halfway up, halfway running. Behind them the traders who sold belts and purses shuffled at their doors. Lila flattened herself against the wall and allowed the men to pass without comment or resistance, and they looked, as Rafí had said, young, like people playing a role, nothing much to worry about.

The two rooms on the top floor led one to another in a simple inverted 'L' and offered no place to hide. Lila followed after, immediately behind, and watched them turn over the mattress, search through the bedclothes, and when they found Rafí crouched behind the kitchen door – eyes squeezed shut, hands clamped to his face, groaning child-like, volume rising, as if this game was being played to the wrong rules – they demanded money. She watched them wrestle Rafí out, and backed away bumping into the door, the doorway, the wall trying to keep out of their way. Rafí at first pliant, disbelieving, snapped to life and began to struggle. He twisted, thrashed, kicked, lunged at the door, grabbed the lintel. The three men stumbled over the mattress, dropped him, scooped him back up, each of them shouting instructions. Rafí writhed in fury, octopus-like, took over the room with a pure and vicious energy sucked right out of nowhere.

As the brawl shoved past her out onto the landing, Rafí, face up, back arched, flipped over and grabbed a fist-full of Lila's hair. With Lila as an anchor the group collapsed to the floor. Too stunned to think, Lila punched out and hit Rafí in the crotch – at that moment the fight was lost and Rafí rolled into a ball, gawping, all of his fight gone.

Bowed forward, dizzy and wincing, Lila pressed her hands to her scalp, not quite sensible of the fact that she was the cause of this lull: three grown men, each twice her size and strength, had failed to subdue Rafí, and with one nudge (it really wasn't that much more), she had levelled him. One of the men helped her to her feet as the others took time to laugh and swear and rearrange their clothes, tuck in shirts and smooth their hair. For a moment they looked back at the room, taking account for the first time, and she felt in the way they looked from her to the hurly-burly of bed sheets and upturned chairs, that there was no difference to them between the battered room and the people who occupied it. As if she had no idea of the shabbiness of it all.

But she was all right? Right?

When the three men finally dragged Rafí down the stairs his expression, his final look before he was hoisted out of view was of surprise and betrayal, as if she should be running after him, shouting at least, putting up some kind of resistance. Instead, Lila listened to the men clomp and struggle down the stairs then returned to the room, stood tiptoe on the mattress to lean out the window and watch the sidewalk – but no one came out of the door. Hearing shouts downstairs, she hurried to the kitchenette to see Rafí sprinting full pace across the flat roof. Two men half out of Rafí's window withdrew as the dog went crazy, spinning at the end of its chain, lunging for them. When she looked for Rafí he was gone.

Lila sat on the mattress and waited for the men to return. She heard them come up the stairs and stop on each landing to demand payment from the traders, who each, at first, feigned disbelief, unable to understand Italian, some spoke in French, some in English, and she slowly understood that the men had come for the rents, rents that Rafí had collected. Collected and kept.

They searched the entire building. Room by room. Insistent that there was money somewhere, that the boy had stowed away the rents. How frugally he lived. By the time the men came to Lila they were irritated and tired.

'And you,' one asked, 'know nothing?'

Lila would not move, and the man drew up the blind to take a good look at her, to get light into the room for the search.

'Did he do that to you?'

Lila drew her hair forward and shook her head. While the men searched the room she sat on the floor, and when they left the man who had spoken to her said that they would be back. 'Why,' he asked, 'are you still here?'

Alone, Lila waited at the window, the day already a shape she did not recognize. She waited expecting Rafí to return or Cecco to appear, knowing it was unsafe to stay. Clearly, this would all be her fault. She counted the pins that fastened the hotel's name to the wall, she noted how they were corroded through, and how people coming out of the station squinted up at the building as they came into the sunlight, and how, tethered to the flat roof two floors below, Rafí's dog lunged at the length of its chain as if to choke itself.

It was impossible now to look at the room without seeing it for what it was, chaotic and dirty. She could smell Rafí on her hands, a stink of sour bedding and stale clothes and his sweet and peppery aftershave.

Rafí's keys lay on the landing with his shirt. Further down, almost to the wall, she found his lighter and cigarettes and a silver mobile phone. Her scalp stung, and she carefully straightened her hair and drew out loose strands. It was shit that he was caught, shit that he was so stupid or unlucky or both, shit that she knew no one better to be with and no better way to live, shit that there was no food and only three cigarettes, shit that there was no money, shit that she would have to wait for him, and it was shit that she could not find his drugs. The pills, which should have been in a hole behind the light switch, were not there. The dog's bark cut through to unsettle her; hard and loud, its whole body concentrated on the task.

She returned to the upper windows overlooking the piazza and watched the station. She stood with the sun in her face and made noises to the dog to gain its attention.

The dog sat down and looked up, suddenly placid.

Determined to do something about the dog, Lila made her way down to Rafí's room.

An old wood-framed bed dominated the small room. The sheets rucked back. The pillows bunched together. Rafí's clothes and shoes were scattered in loose heaps across the floor. His shirts hung on hangers on nails above the bed. Kicked from under the bed were cartons of cigarettes, contraband with Greek markings that he sold in clubs. The small sink was ringed with stains, above it a set of scents and colognes on a glass shelf. There were newspapers on the floor, kept as wrapping.

As Lila took stock, the dog tugged on his chain, followed as she moved through the room, paused when she paused, peered through the window as if intelligent. As she sat on the bed and summoned the courage to deal with the dog, it lunged forward, the chain snapped tight and slumped behind him, striking the roof with the sound of dropped coins.

Now the idea seemed foolish: it would be impossible to loosen the animal's collar without being mauled.

Under the window she found a patterned blanket, little more than a rag. She'd watched Rafí thrash the dog, whip it with the blanket until it cowered, thin-ribbed and panting, as far as its chain would allow. Lila braced herself, stood up, and opened the window.

The instant she opened the window the dog cowered back, shivering, haunches flinching. She held out the blanket and the dog slunk off, tail tucked tight away, ears back.

There was little out on the roof, a cardboard box of a kennel, an upturned water bowl, the dog's chain and the pole it was attached to. Padlocked to itself the chain wrapped about the pole and the pole lodged into the stub of a vent that butted out of the roof. Unless she could lift the entire pole out of its socket she would not be able to release the dog. The idea wasn't going to work. As the dog circled wide of her the pole jolted in its housing, and when the dog stopped tugging the chain slackened and the pole straightened up. Once the chain was slack Lila found that the pole could be twisted with ease. A small plastic wedge poked through the lip of the stub and kept the pole upright. With this removed the pole slid out of its housing, and as she hoisted it up the chain rode down and slipped free. Unaware, the dog lunged forward for the blanket and hurtled over the lintel into Rafí's bedroom, the chain snaking after.

Money poked out of the empty socket.

A single twenty-euro note.

Lila laid the pole down and picked up the note in disbelief. Pulling out one note, another came with it, and with that note came another, and another. She sat down to look at the money, checking either side to make sure that it was real. She was not lucky. Never this lucky.

She reached into the hole and unthreaded more notes until she held in her hands more money than she could count. Deeper still the hole was stopped with a scrunched plastic bag. Lila knelt down and tugged out the bag then reached further into the pipe, finding another bag containing yet more money, tight rolls of ten-, twenty-, and fifty-euro notes. The pole itself was also stoppered with plastic, and still deeper were tucked more rolls of money. Gathering the notes together Lila stuffed her sleeves full, then left the plastic and the pole out on the roof.

Back in Rafí's room the dog leapt onto the bed and turned first on the shirts, tugging them off their hangers and worrying them. Spoilt for options the dog began to nip and tear at the sheets, then the mattress, and wrenched out hanks of stuffing until it could squeeze its head into the holes. Done, the dog sat on the bed and looked back at the roof, the mattress now ragged, with hollowed-out pockets. Thick drifts of polyester, a fine white fibre, settled about the room.

Lila held the blanket up, ready to throw it over the dog's head. She crept cautiously back through the window. The door was closed and the dog watched her edge slowly about the side of the room, her back to the wall, and he growled with rising threat. When she opened the door, just wide enough to squeeze through, the dog sprang to its feet and began to bark.

Safely in the stairwell she leaned her head against the door, and thanked the dog. It was impossible to know how much she had taken, as it was impossible to guess where the money had come from – in such a quantity – or why it was stored on the roof. The only certainty was that the money was either Rafí's or belonged to one of his associates, and Rafí, the little shit, had done nothing, less than nothing, to earn it. What Lila had not earned she deserved.

Lila made her way directly to the Stazione Centrale. Dressed in Rafí's shirt and trousers and a pair of plastic sandals – the toy panda clenched in her arms – she walked out the door taking a simple A to B route, off the pavement, between the bollards. She headed across the road, under the station awning into the darker concourse to the ticket booth to the first free window. She walked in a daze with a crisp fifty-euro note pinched ready in her fist. She'd tucked money into clothes, arms and pants, before remembering the toy. The toy panda, mis-shapen, stuffed with money (loose, scrunched, wadded, rolled and folded) appeared more forlorn than before. Heat bloomed from the blacktop. And in making that walk Lila understood that she was breaking something which could not be fixed. She would never be able to return, she would not see Rafí again, if she did, she was certain he would kill her.

Once at the booth she stood blinking, sunspots in her eyes, thinking 'oh' to herself, 'oh' at her alarm to be standing exactly where she intended, 'oh', to have completed the simple walk without interruption. To her left the police lounged in a glass-walled office. To her right the carabinieri loitered in pairs, some on motorized carts scooping through the terminal in predatory arcs. Youths, boys she recognized, hung about the automatic ticket machines and lazily scanned the station, the groups, the people waiting, the small queue forming behind her. Lila kept the toy clutched to her chest.

She looked square at the man behind the glass, his hair slicked back in one smooth hood, dwarfed by his computer and the broad desk on which he leaned. Feeling queasy with the heat, Lila kept her composure.

The teller leaned toward the glass.

'Rome,' she said. 'No, Milan. No. Yes. Milan,' then, to be certain, 'Milan.'

He twisted his head to hear her. He tried Italian. English. French. Then returned to Italian.

'*Dove?*'

'*Milano.*'

'*Che giorno?*'

'*Si.*'

'*Oggi? Stamatina?*'

Lila pushed the money through the tray before he asked, before the details were decided. It was an effort to stand still, to not shout at the people behind her that they needed to back off. She picked the first of every option.

'*InterCity—*'

'*Si.*'

'*Diretto?*'

'*Si.*'

The man looked at the money. '*Eurostar?*'

'*Si.*'

'*Andata e ritorno?*'

'*Si.*'
'*Andata?*'
'*Si.*'
'*A che ora? Adesso?*'
'*Adesso?*' with some exasperation.
'*Prima o secunda? Prima?*'
'*Si. Prima.*'
She held her breath as she watched him type.
'Fifty-four euro.'
Lila leaned into the glass.
'You need four more euro.' The man held up the fifty-euro note and four fingers. Lila's stomach tightened, she couldn't see the problem until the man pointed at the price. Jittery at the realization that she would have to open the small pocket in the panda's stomach in the middle of the station, Lila wasn't sure what she should do.

The clerk twitched the fifty-euro note between his finger and thumb, and before her eyes the note divided into two.

The teller, equally surprised, saw that he now held two fifty-euro notes. 'Together!'

'Oh?'
'*Cento euro?*'
'*Si . . .*'
'*Cento.*' The clerk slipped the money away and drew out her change. After counting her notes and change he slid the ticket and the reservation stub into the tray then wiped his fingers on his cuffs.

Lila walked by the police and caught her reflection in the long smoky stretch of glass. She began to lose confidence, and doubted that she had properly thought through what she should do. A skinny ghost of the person who had arrived at the same station five months earlier, she doubted that she could manage without Rafí and Arianna.

With the ticket in her hand, Lila found the exit and stood facing the security cameras mounted over the automatic doors, defenceless in the station's broad angular forecourt.

The concourse and forecourt were now full and people moved slowly through the muggy air. Among them a young girl, slack and dead-eyed, hand feebly held out for money. Lila recognized her. The women who were out of favour, untrustworthy, or most likely sick were sent to the station to beg and steal. Lila watched the girl and felt again an extreme urgency that she should leave. Police waited by the barriers checking tickets. Above her, with infinite slowness, the clock ticked up to the hour.

Forty minutes after the train should have departed it was still at the station, delayed without announcement or explanation. The air-conditioning struggled against open windows and open doors. Lila sat beside the window with Rafí's silver phone tucked under her leg and the panda safely stowed on the rack within view. Three other women sat in the same compartment, one with her feet curled onto the seat, a large suitcase wedged between them so that Lila was obliged to sit upright. She wore sunglasses with a small diamante cut into the frame.

'I'm going to miss my flight,' she complained to the other two women in the compartment. She made the calculation, totting hours on her fingers. If it took two hours to get to Rome, one hour to get to the airport, plus, because you never know, another forty-five minutes waiting for the bus outside Termini station, then she was already running late, and you were supposed to be there two hours ahead of time. She would be in trouble if she missed the flight.

The other two women, students, sat with heavy textbooks open on their laps. One of the students' arms was bound in a sling and her friend tended to her, opened a drink, and asked if she was hungry. They stretched out side by side, shoes slipped off, bare feet on the seats, blocking the exit.

Lila sat on her hands to stop them shaking. It occurred to her to switch to another train, but none were leaving the station.

The longer they waited the more likely it would be that Rafí would return to the Stromboli, in which case he would find the dog loose, his room destroyed, and he would know to check for his money. Lila looked up at the toy, she couldn't remember if she had set the pole back in its slot.

Indifferent to the delay the two students tried to sleep, and the woman opposite Lila stared out of the window, arms folded, clearly angry. Passengers loitered on the platform, resigned. Some talked on their mobiles and others leaned out of the windows, smoking and watching the station, buying iced water from the vendors, everyone loose in the heat. Lila kept her eye on the panda and began to believe that she would never leave the city.

When the first announcement came the passengers on the platform applauded. The next train to leave was bound for Messina.

The trains were running again and surely the train for Milan would be next?

Rafí's phone gave a sharp trill and vibrated against her thigh. Lila jolted.

The woman opposite pushed back her sunglasses and pretended not to watch.

Lila listened for an announcement, a sign that they would soon be gone. If the train started now she swore she would never return, this was a final warning to underscore how urgently she needed to leave. Once they were out of the city she would talk with the women and ask what they knew about Milan.

The phone rang a second time.

There was no need to answer, no need to know who was calling. She was on a train and would soon be gone.

Looking at the small screen Lila saw the two calls from Cecco's mobile. She pressed her forehead against the cool window. The train on the opposite platform began to move, starting with a slow and smooth tug. Messina, she could have been heading to Sicily.

An announcement came with the small singsong of the station's call. The next train to depart was the Eurostar to Rome. Caserta would be next. No mention of Milan. The station stops were read out and she listened to the list and decided that she would take the very next train that was leaving.

She recognized him immediately. Rafí. Running headlong up the platform beside the grey Caserta train. Unmistakable in his loose white shirt, his scruffy black hair, that sloppy mouth, open, fish-like. Lila tried to draw the curtain but found it fixed in place. Throughout the night with the two brothers, through all of the brutality, it had never occurred to her that she would die, but she understood as a cold and clear fact that if Rafí found her and the money she would die. Rafí would have sent Cecco along one platform to check one set of trains while he checked another. The two of them would be here. Rafí hurried along the carriages pushing through people, passing parallel to Lila but searching, for the moment, the wrong train.

The woman flying from Rome sat upright, alert, and passed a glance to the students.

The announcement came, the next train to leave would be the Eurostar to Milan from platform eleven.

Lila sat down and looked up at the toy. The women also looked up. Passengers on the platform gathered at the doors.

If she held her nerve she would soon be gone. She was unlucky, she knew this, but how unlucky?

Rafí returned down the platform looking, as he ran, toward her train. He was much too far down the platform to see her. The announcement came a second time. They would soon depart. He would not make it.

And there he was, suddenly, as swift as a devil, hands up to the glass, looking hard, staring into the compartment, his face red and tight. Lila fled the compartment. She stumbled over cases, she made her way down the narrow corridor busy and blocked with people finding their seats. At the door she stopped and thought to ask for help, but Rafí already stood before her. For four hours Lila had been lucky.

Rafí walked Lila off the platform with his arm locked about her shoulder. She looked down as she walked and watched herself return, the toy tucked under her arm. The train began to slide out of the station.

'Where is Cecco?' Rafí's grip tightened, fingers digging. 'Was he with you? Where – is – he?'

Two carabinieri loitered at the entrance and Rafí steered Lila through clustered groups of travellers and past the news kiosk to the food hall. Walking through the food hall they came out of the terminus to the corner of piazza Garibaldi, to banks of white taxis, loitering passengers, men smoking, and he pushed her along the side of the station. Seeing two more policemen, a van marked 'carabinieri', he tugged her back and they returned to the food hall. Lila cringed as she walked, the toy tight under her arm. The station tannoy echoed through the concourse. More departures, a second train to Roma Termini.

He made her sit then slid beside her to keep her at the table. What was she doing? Why was she leaving? Did she think she wasn't being watched, that there weren't people who would tell him what his women were doing? Did she think after Arianna's little trick that she could slip away, just disappear, and do whatever she fancied? And where was Cecco? What did she know about Cecco? What had Cecco told her? Did she know where Cecco had gone?

Lila could not speak, and Rafí looked at her expecting information, his face red and his eyes small. What had Cecco told her? 'Was he on the train? Did you meet him here? Was Cecco with you? Was this his idea?'

She knew nothing and shook her head. Cecco was not with her, she said, and she didn't know anything. The men had frightened her this morning and she didn't want to stay on her own. That was all she knew. Lila forced the panda into her lap, fists on its belly.

Rafí shook his head and scoffed. 'You're lying. Who found the money? Did you see anyone on the roof? Did Cecco take the money?'

'What money?' Lila looked up and met his eyes, surprised that her voice could be so small and so convincing. 'You said Arianna took everything.'

Rafí rolled his fist across his forehead. A station guard hovered close to their table and they both became silent until he moved on.

Lila repeated blankly that Arianna had taken the money, hadn't she? She wiped her nose, then her hand on her trousers. As soon as the men had come this morning she'd left. She was frightened. They told her to go. She didn't understand what was happening. They told her to get out. Arianna had the money. Hadn't he said so?

'Where is it?'

Maybe the men who came this morning took the money. They let the dog free.

Rafí shook his head. 'No. No.' This didn't make sense. 'They're still looking for me,' he spelled out the situation. 'Why would they still be looking for me if they'd found the money? That's what they came for.' And as for the dog, no stranger had let that dog free, no stranger could come anywhere close, he'd deliberately under-fed it, kept it mean, for this explicit purpose. Whoever let the dog free had to know the dog. Which meant one thing: Cecco had let the dog free. 'Did Cecco come back to the Stromboli?'

Lila shook her head.

'Don't,' he said. 'Don't shake your head, don't cry, and don't draw attention to yourself.'

Lila nodded and wiped her eyes.

Rafí leaned closer, wrapped his arm about her shoulder, the table cut into his gut, he wiped her tears from the tabletop. 'I know what happened. I know that Cecco came back to the Stromboli. I know he found the money. He's the only one.'

Lila's hand closed over the scar on her wrist.

'Now tell me where he is.'

She took Rafí's phone from her pocket and slid it along the table. *Cecco – 3 Missed Calls*, registered dimly on the screen. She leaned forward and spoke clearly. 'He hates you. Every time he talks about you he says how stupid you are. He can't stand you.'

Rafí froze. So it was true. 'Where is he? Where is my money?'

Lila sat back, drew the toy to her chest and hugged hard. Her expression set as if she didn't know, as if she didn't care.

Unwilling to return to the Stromboli, Rafí arranged to meet Cecco at the Montesanto station. Lila watched from the station steps as Rafí became increasingly anxious. The waiting crowd grew thicker and mixed with the more active crowd scouring the market, so that commuters stood static beside the busier shoppers.

She thought it impossible that so much could go wrong at such speed. She looked down upon the market hating the stink and bustle, and uncomfortable to be out in the open she held the panda tight to her stomach and let her fingers press into the rolls of cash, outlining their shape even as she looked at Rafí, and she wondered why she had ever thought of him as smart.

Rafí came back and called Cecco a second time. How long could this take? Why wasn't he here already? As he listened to the reply he slowly straightened and looked up, patience draining out of him.

'What do you mean you're in Pozzuoli?'

Rafí listened, appeared to agree, then said he couldn't stop at the Stromboli, the men who were after him would be back, and he wasn't going back. He needed money and a place to stay. Lila noticed that he did not mention her. Rafí repeated: he had a handful of coins and that was it. He needed money.

'No,' Rafí disagreed. 'It isn't the same.' He hawked phlegm to his mouth then spat on the pavement and looked to see if anyone would disagree with him. When he said he only had a couple of euros, that's exactly what he meant. He needed money and he needed a place to stay. Lila watched Rafí cock his head, and for the first time look square at her. He held the phone up, his expression a mess of irritation and pure disbelief. Cecco had hung up. When he redialled the call would not go through. Rafí held the phone out and swore at it.

Cecco, Rafí said, the fat bastard, was dead to him, dead to the world.

He grabbed Lila's arm and pulled her up the steps toward the station. The platform, busy with people returning home, made it easy to bypass the gates and the guards. Slipping onto the train they stood close to the doors in the thick of the crowd and Rafí looked among them for bags that were open, and people who were distracted. When the train doors closed with a final decompression, Lila realized that she would not escape and began to hope for some other intervention. A wreck. A flood. A fire. A derailment. Some terrible affliction.

Within an hour of arriving at Pozzuoli they found Cecco at one of the bars facing the small port. Keeping their distance they watched from the shelter of the small tourist shops; if Cecco intended to go to Proceda it would be difficult to follow, but even he had enough animal cunning not to trap himself on an island. Rafí had managed to steal a pack of cigarettes on the train, slipped from a woman's open shoulder-bag, but for the moment was still without money. Lila smoked and found herself strangely unbothered, a little dizzy. How delicately Cecco held himself when he was alone. Two fingers pricked out as he held his beer.

'Get rid of the bear.'

'No.'

'Get rid of it.' Rafí raised his hand. 'You look stupid. People are noticing you.'

Lila tucked the toy to her stomach, leaned over it and drew on her cigarette. She couldn't help but shiver.

'You look stupid.'

'Stupid.' Lila repeated, her voice flat and factual, her arms clamped about the bear, shivering. 'Stupid me.'

Cecco stayed at the bar all evening and kept to himself, contented, perhaps even self-satisfied. Later, after talking on his mobile, he left the bar and began to walk away from the small marina. The road curled up the hillside and ran under the railway through a short steep tunnel carved into the tufa. Rafí stopped at the mouth of the tunnel and Lila followed after. They watched as Cecco entered an apartment block set on its own. Four storeys high, the building squatted into the hillside beside a small orchard raised from the road, paint peeling in soft folds on the undersides of the balconies. The street was open and Rafí decided to return when it was dark. Until then they would wait at the station and keep an eye on the road.

☆

Niccolò woke early. Livia could not sleep; uncomfortable and nauseous, she asked him to feel her brow. Brother and sister slept in T-shirts and shorts for decency, side by side, back to back, although this was becoming uncomfortable for her. Livia swore in her sleep, cursed and muttered so that she was always present in his thoughts. Sometimes the child stirred inside her and she would exclaim, often nothing more than a sharp intake of breath, but enough of a disturbance. The notion that something swam inside her turning, shifting, possibly even dreaming, made him uneasy.

'Am I hot? I feel hot.' She worried that something might be wrong but wouldn't say so directly, and it was left to Niccolò to divine this information out of her. Having slept poorly / very little / not at all (her status changed with each mention of her night), Livia demanded attention. Niccolò sat with her, clumsy with sleep, and when he reached for her stomach, because this is what he thought she wanted, she flinched and told him not to touch her.

'Why do men do that?' she asked. Angry now, Livia told him to get up and prepare for work.

By the time Niccolò had dressed Livia was sitting at the table drinking hot water, calmer and less concerned, colour back in her face. 'I'm OK.' She gave a tight smile that said she was still not quite herself. It had been a hot night and the heat had made her uncomfortable. 'I'm fine,' she said. 'Go. You'll only make me more anxious.'

He said goodbye from the door and as she waved she told him to head directly to work.

Niccolò returned to the wasteland to find the cordon taken down from the field. After only one night the police and reporters were already gone. The wasteland was still sectioned with stakes and tape, but the vans and cars and massive steel stanchions that held the arc lamps were gone. With nothing left except a few posts and lengths of tape snagged in the flattened grass it was hard to believe that the wasteland had attracted any attention at all.

He drove his scooter by the abandoned factories on his way to work. You could walk to them quicker, straight down the hill toward the bay. After the crossroads the road led directly down to the shoreline, the factories, the railway, the water. He drove slower by the market gardens and the rows of covered greenhouses, the plastic sheeting fogged and tracked with condensation. To his right the factories now: most of the buildings were without roofs, many had their entrances and windows bricked up and sealed. Heat rose from the stony fields of sparse and scorched grass which, some summers, held a lone mule.

The scooter made a feeble warble as he passed the first buildings, a thin wail thrown off the concrete wall to the road and fields. He slowed as he came to the last building, an old paint factory, and stopped at the small alley that led down to the railway bridge and the shore. Discarded on the steep slope lay bags of trash, ripped open with papers and plastic. Bound, rotten and dried bouquets of flowers spilled out. Flies broke loose from the weeds as Niccolò hitched the scooter onto its stand. He shouldn't be riding. He shouldn't be lifting. The agreement was that he would walk to work. When you've come this far, remember, it doesn't have to be everything at once. Niccolò checked to make sure he was not being watched or followed. A loose group of boys played football on the pumice road above the wasteland, and a white dust hung in the air.

The police had searched the paint factory the previous night and strings of black and yellow tape stretched across the doorway and lower windows.

As he approached the entrance Niccolò walked as if he intended to follow the alley down to the sea, but ducked quickly under the police tape and slipped inside, where he waited, head up, attentive, to ensure that the building was empty. Children often played in the building (possibly the same children who sometimes pelted him with stones when he rode to work). With its shattered walls daubed in graffiti the factory made an attractive haunt. Slogans and obscenities scrawled across the concrete named people he did not know.

Safe inside, Niccolò no longer felt the urgency he'd felt in the apartment. In the first room, cut into the floor, was a square metal tank with a round mouth, in which he dumped objects he no longer wanted. The animals he'd caught on the scrubland, cats mostly, stunned or dead, things he'd found, items he didn't need. Niccolò walked about the hole, scuffed a half-brick to the rim and tapped it over. The drop could only be a couple of metres, three at the most and the water would not be deep. Now disturbed, the water stank. He thought of the things he'd dropped into the water – the cats, the cans, the playing cards – as things which passed through a mirror to an inverted world: from his hands to someone else's.

He sat close to the hole, then carefully laid out the contents of the bag along the edge. After considering them for a moment, he divided the objects into two groups.

In the first line he laid out the blue notebook, a charger for a mobile phone, a black and white postcard of the port at Palermo, a wallet containing only receipts.

The second line, closer to the edge, included a receipt for the Hotel Meridian in Palermo, a mini-audio player with a crack in the plastic face, a small bottle of medication for insect bites, an open pack of chewing gum, a soap packet, a razor with a used blade, a novel with the cover torn off, a pocket-sized Italian–English dictionary.

In one last pass he looked through the items again and selected only the small blue notebook, which he returned to the sack. Its pages were greasy with oil, the ink smudged, and the paper translucent. Written in a small slanted hand that he couldn't read or in any case understand.

With one gesture he swept everything else into the tank.

The two other members of the B-4 security guard at the Persano-Mecuri chemical dye plant, Federico Taducci and 'Stiki' Bashana, met late on Saturday afternoons and occasionally in the evenings before work to play cards, sometimes at Bar Settebello in Ercolano, and sometimes at Federico's small apartment on the outskirts of town, less occasionally at a place closer to Stiki in Torre del Greco. Two years ago the shifts were managed with only one guard, but after the theft and assault, two men now monitored the facility during the night and one maintained security at the gate during the morning and through the afternoon.

Federico, a widower, always failed to invite Niccolò – not that Niccolò especially wanted to play Scopa or Sette e Mezzo – but he did want to be invited, and besides, Niccolò was the closer neighbour. Stiki lived in a single room in one of the larger blocks overlooking the train station at Torre del Greco. Younger than Niccolò by only two years, Stiki seemed much younger. He studied engineering, and worked nights to subsidize his studies. Always obliging, he smiled frequently but seldom laughed, and Niccolò mistook Stiki's poor and formal Italian as a sign that he was uninterested. At night Stiki slept while Fede played cards solo or taught himself English. Fede bought one American newspaper a week and made a show of completing a word puzzle. Niccolò often looked at the paper, but could make no sense out of it.

On this morning Federico stopped to speak with Niccolò. Fede greeted Niccolò warmly and asked for news about the investigation, they had both seen the news before the start of their shift and followed the reports on the radio. This is why he was late, no? The police had business with him? Stiki, ready to leave, loitered for a while, his backpack slung across his shoulder.

Niccolò bowed his head modestly and confessed that both the police and journalists were gone.

'Gone? Already?' It was mysterious, he said, very strange, they had listened to the news through the night. 'Are you sure?' Fede narrowed his eyes. 'You're not hiding anything, right? If there was something you'd tell me?'

Niccolò opened the windows and started a small fan. The booth carried a stale smell of sleep that Niccolò found unpleasant, but he could smell something else, as if the stink from the paint factory had clung to him, stuck to his hands or clothes.

'Don't you think it's strange?' Fede gave a reasoning shrug. 'They leave after one night? One night. Think about it. It's suspicious.'

Stiki agreed. It was suspicious.

Niccolò recognized that the two men were not entirely serious and said he didn't see how.

'It makes you think, though? No? Something is going on,' Fede considered. 'I'm telling you, there'll be more news tomorrow and they'll come back. This isn't over yet. You'll see.'

The men laughed as they walked away, an earlier conversation continuing between them. Niccolò completed the discussion: 'So you're helping with the investigation?' He looked at his reflection in the glass, ran his hand through his hair, ran his finger along a crease that started at the crown and circled round to his left temple in a perfect groove. If he tapped his head he could hear the difference, seriously, a completely different sound because it wasn't bone underneath the skin.

'Yes, I'm helping with the investigation.' He answered himself in a shy mumble. 'There are very many details to consider. It will take some time.'

Niccolò spoke to himself now, where before he used to sing. During the night he used to stand in the stairwell in the empty offices of B-19, call his wife and sing to her while his voice, hollow and lovely, drew strength from the darkened halls.

*

Once Fede and Stiki were gone Niccolò settled down to read the note-book. The wind carried sage and the slight scorched scent of fire. He lit a cigarette although they were not permitted to smoke in the booth and the memory of sweeping the evidence into the cistern came back to him. This gesture, a simple and decisive swipe, dismissive, was not in his language. A gesture borrowed from his sister. The thought, once solid, unsettled him. He took the notebook out of his bag, swept it off his desk, picked it up, and swept it off again. No, this was not his ges-ture. He sniffed at his fingers, and it became immediately obvious that the cover of the notebook, saturated with fat, was the source of the smell.

Livia returned home as the evening news concluded. She sat heavily on the side of the bed and twisted off her shoes, her mouth set in a tight line as she smoothed her hand over her shoulders.

'They stand at the entrance,' she said, 'those boys, right by the door so you have to push past them. How old are they? I don't like it. Always a group of them. My neck,' she complained, 'and my back, all day. There's something bad in the kitchen. I could smell it as I came in.' Livia made a face. 'What is that smell? Something smells bad. What is it?'

Niccolò leaned into the doorway with his arms folded and said that he was careful now to smoke outside and lean over the balcony so that the smoke did not enter the apartment. Afterward he washed his hands and brushed his teeth as she didn't like the stink of cigarettes on him. The bother of it meant that he was smoking more at work and less at home.

'I'm not talking about cigarettes.' She screwed up her face. 'Can't you smell it? It's like something has died.'

For an hour Niccolò indulged his sister, he moved the furniture around, checked behind and under the fridge while she sprayed with disinfectant, but the source of the smell could not be discovered.

'Men are so dirty,' she said. Which was not true as Niccolò kept his rooms clean and in order. Livia's clothes, her cups and plates, her shoes and papers littered the small apartment.

She asked him to sit down and said they needed to talk about the upcoming assessment. 'They will want to know how you've managed,' she said, 'they'll ask you questions, they'll try to trip you up, and you know not to tell them that I have been here. They won't want to know that I was here. You know not to say anything about that. You also shouldn't say that you've been using the scooter. Not right away. They'll want to know that everything is fine, that you are coping well. Tell them about work. Tell them that you cook and clean for yourself. Just tell them what they want to hear.'

Niccolò said he understood, this didn't need talking through – he didn't say, although he hoped that this was true, that once the first assessment had occurred that she would also leave. She hadn't come to look after him so much as to punish her husband.

FRIDAY: DAY M

As Niccolò steered his scooter around the barrier Fede came out of the booth, a little swagger to his walk, the *Cronache* folded in his hand. Stiki slumped in the booth, asleep, with his head to his chest. On a single-ring stove beside him was a pot of noodles.

'I imagine you haven't seen this?' Fede thrust the newspaper forward.

Niccolò set the scooter on its stand then brushed his hand over his hair. He took the paper out of Fede's hands.

'He was American. The man who was stabbed. A student or a tourist. Have they told you this?'

Niccolò shook his head as he read.

'And . . . there's a witness. Someone at the Circumvesuviana station on Friday morning – that's five days before you found the clothes.' Fede squeezed Niccolò's shoulder. 'What did I tell you? Didn't I say there would be news today? It says that a woman has come forward who recognized the star on the T-shirt. She saw someone at the station wearing the clothes you found. On Friday. In Naples. The T-shirt comes from America, it's unlikely there are more like it in the country. It's exactly as I told you.'

Niccolò looked hard at Fede and saw that he was serious. He didn't remember Fede telling him any of this but didn't want to openly disagree. Fede's face being creased and rubbery, was the hardest of faces to read.

'The police are certain it's the same person. They're looking at videotape from the security cameras to see which station he came from. It also says the person is almost certainly dead.' Fede pointed to the article. 'Here. Wounds to the lower stomach, chest, upper . . .' he ran a finger across his neck, '. . . within four minutes.'

The two men sat side by side on the concrete step beside the security booth.

Niccolò opened the newspaper across his lap and focused on

where the hillside dropped to a smooth blue plate of sky. Aquamarine. The tips of the city's towers visible at the edge in a tawny haze.

'I know,' Fede interrupted his thoughts. 'It's a bad world.' He slapped the paper with the back of his hand. 'But you know what. Everything moves forward.' The man stood up and looked down at Niccolò. 'Some family is going to thank you for finding the clothes. If it wasn't for you this might not have been discovered. When they sort this out some family is going to be grateful. I wouldn't be surprised if there wasn't some kind of recognition, some kind of a reward.'

Niccolò slowly re-read the article. Please, no more rewards, no more meals / speeches / flowers and plaques, no more interviews, no more presentations. He studied the two articles with care and re-read sections that were unclear to him until they began to make sense. The police wanted to hear from anyone who'd travelled on the six thirty Trento express or the six thirty-five Circumvesuviana into Naples on the previous Friday, or anyone who was in or around the station from seven fifteen in the morning until eight thirty. An image of the five-pointed star was reprinted, bold, white on black, accompanied with a map of the Circumvesuviana line marking all stops to Naples. An editorial called for witnesses to come forward, and an appeal was made to hoteliers asking them to report unfilled or cancelled bookings and ensure that all visitors were properly recorded as required. He began to count.

'I know,' Fede sucked in his breath, 'four minutes is a long time.'

Niccolò took the night report and logbook to the main office and waited a little while in the entrance, knowing that Fede would not be able to linger. When he returned he sat with the small blue notebook on his lap and kept it concealed under the counter. Happy to be alone he studied the tidy, sloping handwriting, his eye ran over words he couldn't understand. A fan blew warm air into the booth. On the first page, written in capitals he found an address and what he thought to be a name and serial number. N. CLARK, -0626.

The police had said that they would get back to him if they needed help, and given this new witness he was certain that they would need more information once they understood a little more about the situation. He wouldn't wait for the call, he would make his own investigation. It was almost two days now since his discovery, and during those two days Niccolò had been walking in a different world, breathing different air, separate and expectant. In the long hours sat monitoring cars and staff in and out of the dye plant, he nursed the idea that he was being tested and observed, as if the event itself, the murder of this student, was some kind of creature.

Closing the book Niccolò decided that he would conduct his own investigation, then he would contact the police and hand the note-book over to them along with his findings. He would say that someone left the little book outside his door, or that he had found it in a part of the field that they had not searched, or perhaps that he had found it a place that they had searched just to make a point of their uselessness.

Disappointed with the day Niccolò re-read the articles in Fede's newspaper and could not shake the idea that whatever had happened was predetermined, that all of these people and coincidences com-bined to make the event not only inevitable, but possible. As if the event itself had some kind of intelligence, an ability to decide what would happen and who would be involved.

The evening was slow and Livia contrary, whatever mood he was in was bothersome to her, and she had no interest in speaking about the investigation, nor in hearing his ideas.

'Stop,' she told him. 'Don't make this into something it isn't. Just stop. Take a walk.'

Avoiding confrontation Niccolò did exactly as Livia asked and took a walk and returned to the wasteland and the line of empty factories with his slingshot in his pocket to smoke and think a little about Livia and the baby, but more about how he would start his inves-tigation. When he reached the factory the stink was now so foul that he couldn't enter. And then it occurred to him. If the clothes were dumped on the wasteland, and the person wearing the clothes had been seen on the Circumvesuviana train, then they must have walked from the station to the wasteland.

He couldn't decide which station the student would have taken. If he was a student or a tourist he would have alighted at the Scavi stop. This seemed the most logical. It was always possible, of course, that it was not the victim who took the train in the first place. In which case whoever had committed the crime would have taken the train from the city and brought the clothes with them, and they could have used either stop, Ercolano, or Ercolano Scavi.

As he walked the route, he began to think his logic was wrong. If the student was heading into the city, then why were the clothes found here, outside the city? And supposing the person who committed the crime did travel to Ercolano to dump the clothes, then there was no guarantee that they, like the victim, had taken the train. This walk was a waste of time. He needed to go to the station in Naples to see who came on the trains, and who left. To think about this properly, he needed to be at the station himself.

Later, when he settled into bed beside his sister and lay on his back, he doubted that he would sleep. It didn't help either that Livia slumbered soundly beside him, out almost before she laid down, mouth open, breath softly chortling; even in sleep she sounded dissatisfied. He longed for the baby to be born, and he longed for her to go.

As he lay in bed he retraced his walks from the wasteland to the station, the night leaning on him as a palpable pressure, thick with possibilities: an American on a train, a woman at the station, clothes on the wasteland, and the hint that this all connected to him. It was likely that the person who killed the American student was also on that train with him that morning.

☆

Mizuki rose early, dressed, sat on the balcony, then fell immediately into a deep, recuperative sleep. At seven thirty she was woken by a call from Lara. She watched the phone vibrate and allowed the call to go to message.

Mizuki took her morning shower then returned to the balcony. She held out her phone to read the screen and saw two missed calls.

'Mizuki. The police came to the bakery yesterday. They wanted to know if the bakery have ever printed their logo onto any clothing.' Lara paused, little more than a short intake of breath. 'I'm talking about the bakery under the school.' She paused again. 'The sign, the star sign. Mizuki. Are you there? They were asking about a T-shirt. Call me.'

Star signs? Mizuki didn't understand. She looked out at a wall of closed shutters and thought about the school and the palazzo, then remembered the small tin star that hung above the portico.

Lara called again, and again Mizuki allowed the call to go directly to message. 'Mizuki. Have you seen the news? Call me. Have you heard? It's on the news, right now, on the radio, on the TV.' Lara carefully explained: a T-shirt with the same design as the bakery logo had been discovered cut and bloodied on wasteland outside the city. But stranger still, someone, a commuter, had come forward convinced that they had seen a tourist, a young boy, wearing this T-shirt at the Circumvesuviana station last Friday morning. Mizuki felt her chest tighten, and was surprised that this was anger, not fear. She had come to Naples to experience something, and here was that something – and she'd missed it. *She wasn't there.*

Lara left a message asking to meet.

'I'm worried,' she said, 'you haven't called me back. I thought it was you. Did you contact the police? I'll be at the station before class. I'll meet you outside the station at eight.'

Mizuki came directly into the city. Once at the station she looked for the brothers, but they were not on the platform, not on the concourse, nor waiting, as before, under the long overhang from the station to the street, nor in the bright sunshine waiting by the taxis. Their absence came as a heavy disappointment, just to see them would offer some kind of solace – but what would she have said that wouldn't have ended in some kind of disappointment?

Lara waited outside the station. Not ready to talk, Mizuki took the exit through to the main station and walked from Stazione Centrale all the way around, through piazza Garibaldi, back to the Circumvesuviana so that Lara would not see her, but she could see Lara. Her phone sang in her hand.

Mizuki returned to the cafe she where she had spoken with Lara and listened to the message as she watched the station through the window. She had seen the clothes on the news and felt sad that a relative would have to identify them. Until they found the young man these clothes would be the only record of what had happened. The clothes were made in America, this is what they were saying now. But the coincidence about the star was very strange.

'I thought it was you,' Lara said, and as Mizuki listened to the message, she saw Lara come into view. 'The person who came forward. The woman who spoke with the police. I thought this is why I haven't seen you.'

Lara's final call came later that night while Mizuki was considering if she should or should not pack. Mizuki accepted the call but did not speak.

'I know how this is,' Lara spoke. 'I know how this feels. My father, when he died – I had to collect his jacket from the police.' At four thirty one summer afternoon her father had taken off his suit jacket, laid it carefully across the passenger seat, and before he could settle into the car had suffered a heart attack. 'I brought everything back. Things they had taken from the car, and my mother, the first thing she did was check through the jacket, to empty his pockets as if she didn't trust him.'

When Lara began to ask what was wrong, why had they not spoken, *She didn't understand what she'd done*, Mizuki hung up.

She would not pack. She did not need these clothes. She did not want them. Everything that was bought to fuel this character, this failed escape, would be left.

☆

Rafí had spent the night watching the flats while Lila attempted to sleep in the shelter of a small hut, her head resting on the toy bear, her arms locked securely about it. Several times she woke up, immediately alert, and thought she could just walk away, sneak down the hill: to where though, and to what? Woken by the sun and troubled by mosquito bites along her arms and neck, she watched Rafí, who in turn watched the apartment block, eyes fixed on third floor, which he believed to be where Cecco was staying. When he stood up, she stood up. When he walked she followed. Stray dogs, curious at this early activity, followed lamely after. Weak from lack of sleep, Lila ached and was thirsty, and despite the sun she was cold. How strange to have so much money in her arms. She could buy food, she could buy cigarettes, she could buy cola and Sicilian pastries. She could hire a taxi to take her anywhere she could imagine, but she couldn't find a certain opportunity to escape from Rafí. All this money.

They lingered at the port for an hour, dissatisfied with each other, unspeaking and uncertain. The bear clutched tight in defiance. Rafí sat with his back to her and turned on occasion to give a look of utter disgust. Both were surprised to see Cecco walk immediately by them, close, but so preoccupied he saw nothing but the pavement ahead. Cecco wandered along the promenade, paused to see what the fishermen had caught, then ambled by the ticket office.

Rafí tightened the distance between them. He was learning

nothing, he told Lila, this watching and waiting was a waste of time. If he wanted his money he would need to get closer, and when Cecco clambered delicately down to the rocks, Rafí came closer. He signalled Lila to stay back.

Cecco sought out a broad flat rock and settled down, he rolled his shirt high over his stomach and gave himself up to the morning sun. Rafí climbed down and Lila hurried after: if she ran now Rafí would catch her, she wouldn't even make it off the promenade. Cecco lay with his belly exposed, his hands flat to the rock, defenceless.

'So this is what you do with yourself.'

Rafí stood with the sun over his shoulder so that Cecco had to squint at him, hand shielding his eyes. Cecco managed a small hello and looked feebly about him. His gestures, his expression were the sure signs of a guilty man.

'You're sweating.'

It would be easy to pick up one of the smooth black rocks and belt Rafí while he was preoccupied, and who would stop her? Maybe not to kill him, but leave him useless for the rest of his life, with just enough brains to understand what had happened to him and why.

Rafí squatted beside Cecco, patted his friend on his shoulder and asked where he was staying.

'So? Pozzuoli?'

Cecco gave a nod and then shrugged. He noticed Lila and appeared momentarily relieved.

'Tell me about it.'

'With everything. I thought. You know. Why not? Just.'

'Just keep your head down.'

Cecco sat up on his elbows and nodded earnestly. 'I was going to call you today.'

'That's funny, because I've been trying to call you.'

They looked at each other, stalemate.

'Where are you staying?'

Cecco pointed up the coast to Lucrino, but looked back at the town. There was a woman, he said, a friend, but it was a small place.

Rafí settled on the rock beside him. 'I don't mind,' he said. Big or small it would suit him fine. He'd had a rough night.

Cecco's woman was not what Lila expected. Cecco passed her photo about. In the picture Stefania sat beside a man in workman's overalls, perhaps on the same rocks they'd come from. In another she held a ball, just caught or ready to throw, a posed picture. Ridiculous. Shapely, old, homely and content, with deep black eyes drawn in kohl and dark hair bleached to a brittle gold, the woman had married twice and more or less lost both husbands, Cecco explained. She worked at the *tabaccaio* on via Capasso, and every time he went in he'd spoken with her and got to know her a little.

'Enough that she looks after you?'

Cecco couldn't look at Rafí, as if ashamed. He took back the photograph and set it on the small side table. Rafí joked that widows were accommodating, especially the fat ones. He bent down to squint at the photograph and said she looked familiar. The apartment comprised three small rooms, a bedroom, kitchen and a sitting-room cramped with a plump couch and a large television beside a small veranda. There was no evidence of children, and few photographs or certificates.

Rafí sent Lila out to the small hallway. She backed out and watched him scope the room, possibly figuring where Cecco might have concealed the money. The room was busy, unkempt, with small girly keepsakes, china dolls, and soft toys with embroidered clothes that she sold at the shop. On the couch in small boxes were more soft toys with names and hearts sewn onto small jackets, and china ballerinas with real lace skirts. In the kitchen along a small folding table lay lengths of pastel-coloured ribbons cut to the same length with a package of porcelain figurines ready to be assembled and decorated, and she understood that this was how Stefania spent her evenings. Cutting and stitching.

Lila smoked at the veranda doors and took long considered draws. Cecco also smoked, fingers crushing the cigarette. When he caught Lila's eye he gave a private shrug, a *what is he doing*, and Lila, in response, shrugged back. How odd this was, how interesting, everything Cecco did just made him look like a thief.

'You have a paper? A newspaper?' Rafí asked Cecco.

Cecco looked down in deference. He wiped his hands on his shirt.

'I need a paper. Go,' he said, 'get me one. And get some food.'

Cecco nodded, yes, he'd go. There was one thing though, something important he'd forgotten to explain.

Rafí said that he could tell him when he came back.

Cecco shook his head. No, it was important. Her first husband was a security guard at the port.

'And?'

'And he's dead.'

Rafí, lost for words, looked like he might hit Cecco. Exactly why was this a problem?

'Because her second husband was in the carabinieri, and he isn't dead.' She spoke of him as if he was dead, but he wasn't. The man was violent and she'd finished with him years ago, but, and this was the problem, he was obsessed with her and sometimes watched the house and deliberately caused trouble.

'Just get a paper and get me some food.'

Cecco backed out of the room to the door. Lila could hear him running down the stairs.

With Cecco out of the apartment Rafí hurtled through the rooms. He swept the ornaments off the table, took a paring knife from the kitchen and searched swiftly through the boxes, first opening them then turning them upside down, emptying the contents onto the hard tiled floor until it was covered with small bites of packing foam and shards of shattered china, tiny painted heads and arms and legs, whiter than sugar. The money was not in the boxes. It was not in the drawers, the side cabinet, the dresser. It wasn't in the cupboard. Under the couch, under the cushions, under the bed. Neither was it stuffed into the pillows or mattress. Rafí reached over the bedroom cupboard and again found nothing. When he stepped back, hands on hips, he looked to Lila, then beyond her, and Lila followed his glance to see Stefania at the doorway, dark eyes, silent, aghast at the chaos and destruction. In five short minutes Rafí had emptied every container and destroyed everything he touched in his search for the money. Scattered among the broken porcelain were pieces of dried pasta, lentils, and pulses. Stefania cringed as he came quickly after her. With the paring knife pointed at her neck he told her to sit down and keep herself absolutely silent.

Stefania swept aside the brittle shards of figurines and slowly sat on the floor, her back to the veranda door.

'Tell me where he has hidden my money.'

Stefania shook her head and Lila shook her head to warn her.

'Where – is – my – money?'

Rafí held back her head to expose her throat and drew his arm full out, ready to swipe.

'Where?'

Stefania pointed to the television. Behind it was a package containing thirty euro, a measly find compared to the size of his loss.

Lila could see Cecco returning through the tunnel, a newspaper in his hand, an anxious hurry to his step, and in total contradiction, a broad smile – when she pointed, Rafí turned, and for no reason she could understand, his face tightened with fury and he bolted out of the room.

Rafí rushed upon Cecco in the stairwell and stabbed him in the gut. As Cecco tumbled back Rafí criss-crossed the knife over his face, then fell upon him.

'Where – is – my – money?'

Rafí stuck Cecco until the blade became slippy. Lila hurried partway down the stairs, the bear in her arms, and stopped when she saw the fray, the mortal horror on Cecco's face, how Rafí pinned him down so he could not protect himself, and how Rafí could not hold the knife without also cutting his own hand.

Cecco babbled, and Rafí let him talk. He knew nothing about the money, nothing. He'd come to the Pozzuoli because Rafí wanted him to do things with those two men. Rafí, his one true friend, had asked him to do things he did not want to do and he had come to Stefania confused and troubled and Stefania had taken him in without question. She was his friend like Rafí was his friend. He'd done nothing, nothing. He swore. What had he done? Rafí was like his brother. Whatever he had done he was sorry.

Rafí fastened his hands about Cecco's throat.

Lila flinched away as Stefania passed her, swift and ghost-like. She saw the woman, saw the hammer, but did not properly figure what was about to happen until the act was done. Stefania stood over Rafí and without pause or haste swiped him on the temple with one hefty clout.

Rafí fell sideways, turned, rose on his hands and knees so that he straddled Cecco, then stopped and hung his head. The four of them stuck in place: Rafí on his hands and knees, Cecco under him, Stefania poised with the hammer ready to strike again, and Lila, witness to it all, on the stairs.

Rafí squatted like a dog. Cecco, bloody chest, stomach, and nose split open, cheek gashed, slid from under him, mouth open. Lila could not calculate how long they waited, attention fixed on Rafí, who slowly leaked – blood dripping from his nose – but otherwise remained completely still. Finally, Stefania turned to Lila and offered the hammer and Lila came slowly forward, the toy clutched to her chest. She took the hammer, stood over Rafí, but could not strike. Instead she sunk to her haunches and looked closely at Rafí's face. Wall-eyed, he stared both at the floor and through it, and remained fixed in place.

Cecco raised his shirt in disbelief. The wounds, four small and bloody mouths, puckered his stomach. He looked to Stefania and asked why, and she said she didn't know. Cecco shook his head in a small shiver and asked again, 'Why?' Why had she hit Rafí? He didn't understand.

Stefania brought towels and a bucket of water. She locked the door, pushed the bolt to secure it, then threw the towels across the floor, gave Cecco her apron and helped him tenderly to his feet. With Cecco on the stairs she took a plastic bag out of her pocket and drew it over Rafí's head, when Cecco began to sob she stopped and explained that he was bleeding everywhere.

They laid Rafí across the back seat of Stefania's car then covered him with wet towels. On Stefania's instruction Cecco and Lila were to take Rafí and leave him, she didn't care where, but not the police, and not a hospital.

Cecco, wrapped in bandages, sat at the wheel, sweating, mouth drawn, his breath compressed, his face swollen, already black and plum-like, pulpy at the cuts. He drove carelessly, indecisive, as if driving some route from memory. Lila peeled the towels back from Rafí's face – also swollen now but bloodless, eyes black and blown, eyelids fat and slug-like, his hair matted flat. Not dead, certainly, but not fully alive. She held her hand, then the bear over his face and wondered what he could see, if anything registered. There was a warehouse, Cecco said, an old paint factory. They'd take him to Ercolano, call the police, tell them where they could find him, and then, as Stefania had instructed, he would return to Pozzuoli where she would again check his wounds. Lila wondered if she had any part in these plans.

They followed the bay, houses and developments on either side, until the bay-side, gorgeous with sunlight, swung close to the road, leaving room for abandoned factories, train tracks, a few open fields of scrub, then row after row of long plastic sheds running down the slope, greenhouses, the plastic sweated and tight. Cecco, bleeding from the cuts to his nose and face and the deeper wounds in his side and back, said he was beginning to feel sick and weak. He pointed out the road to the station and said, not unkindly, that they were here, and she should go. It was better if she looked after herself now. He was sorry that he didn't have any money. His voice came faint and exhausted, and he shook his head. She should hurry. She should go.

Rafi's eyes were dry and fixed. His breathing now shallow and brief pulls, too brief to be of use. Cecco wept with his head down, his hands on the wheel. When Lila closed the door he drove away. In the end it was that simple. She opened the car door, slipped out, then watched it drive toward the bay.

Lila waited on a bare platform with the sun full on her shoulders. From the stairwell she could hear voices, a couple arguing in Spanish, and their words rose sweetly recognizable, a sound intermittently lost to passing traffic on the nearby autostrada. She read the sign, ERCOLANO SCAVI, and spoke the words out loud, repeated them until they fell into a rhythm. She looked left to right, then approached the rail and looked down the road at a campervan, rust running along the roof. She would speak with these people, or she could wait. Or she would sneak into their vehicle. Or she would walk to the service station she could see beside the motorway and clean herself up. Or she could find himself a car parked outside the services. Or she would wait in the shelter on the platform and tell someone how she had been mugged. Or, she would call the police and describe to them how Cecco could be found in an abandoned factory hugging the body of his friend who was not dead but almost dead. Or?

As she stood in the sunlight, dizzy and sticky, the toy in her arms, possibilities opened one by one by one.

SATURDAY: DAY N

Mizuki sat looking at herself. Her hair freshly cut and treated, heavy, black, so that it curled just under her ears. She'd never worn it short before. With the right glasses she would look boyish. No disguising her features, but an extreme enough change to mark a distinction between the woman who had come with such disorganization to Naples. It irritated her to have her nails manicured, and she did little to disguise her impatience with the woman – who asked, in any case, too many questions.

Her mouth, small but full, took on a slight shell-shaped plumpness, and the plum colour took attention away from what she considered now were heavy jowls and the distinct flatness of her eyes.

When the dress arrived she left it on the bed and waited for the woman to leave.

Mizuki took the box out of the bag, slipped off the lid and parted the tissue. Her hand ran over the material, a warm grey flecked with gold, wool threaded with silk so that the dress found its own weight and smoothed itself to her hands – and she could see, just in the whiteness of her hands against the colour and heft of the cloth, how well this would suit her.

Once dressed, she opened up the jeweller's box, set square on the table. She leaned forward to buckle the chain about her neck. Her eyes small and black. She was again a woman not out of place, a handsome woman, lucky enough to afford her tastes.

Lara's Saturday class would be over in ten minutes. Mizuki watched the clock. She could invite her to the hotel and they could speak one last time before she left for the airport. There would be time.

As the car pulled out, the grand facade of the opera, the Castel Nuovo, the fountains and piazzas reflected across the window. But she sat looking forward, scanning for men on the street, her mind elsewhere, her hand resting delicately at her throat. Keiko, she said to herself. Keiko. Possibilities. Always. Possibilities and happenstance.

MONDAY: DAY 0

He woke certain that what he wanted would be found in Naples.

Niccolò rose quickly, closed the door between the bedroom and the kitchen and called Fede to explain that the police wanted to speak with him. He needed to go into the city. It would take all day.

Niccolò was careful to sound perfunctory.

Fede agreed to cover the first two hours of his shift, after that he would tie the barrier back and they could manage without a guard. If it couldn't be helped, it couldn't be helped, but couldn't the police give them more advanced warning? Uninterested in debate Niccolò said that he had to go.

Niccolò dropped his keys. As he stooped to pick them up he caught his reflection in the frosted glass of the bedroom door. Behind the glass, in the dark, Livia slept. Fearful of spiders, wasps, mosquitoes and blood-borne diseases she preferred the shutters closed. 'I'm a magnet for disaster,' she claimed, 'any kind of trouble,' although this was simply not true. The air from the room was still and warm and baby-sweet. He reached for the keys and caught his face half-lit, and believed for a moment that the reflection was someone else's. He waited expecting the reflection to move independent of him, to pick up the keys before he picked up the keys.

He prepared breakfast knowing that Livia needed to be away early. He took his time showering and dressing. He dressed as usual in his uniform, but once Livia had left he changed into casual clothes and laid his uniform out across the bed ready for the end of the day.

Checking his watch he made sure he had plenty of time. Niccolò stood in front of the mirror and took measure of himself. Uncomfortable, he undressed, folded away the clothes, took a second shower, selected new clothes and re-dressed.

He rubbed oil into his hands and tousled his hair, then combed it, then gave himself a parting, a clean straight cut, so that his hair no longer fell forward to disguise the edge of the plate. He studied himself in the mirror and began to feel satisfied. While he found it difficult to associate with this face, he understood that it was his and how it felt, increasingly, less like a mask. The student's notebook wrapped in plastic safe in his pocket. As he came across articles about the case he clipped them from Fede's newspaper and folded them between the empty pages in chronological order.

At the station Niccolò bought a ticket from the tobacconists'. After franking the ticket he walked up to the platform and stood where he could watch the other passengers.

The train was not crowded. He stood with his back to the door so that he could see about the carriage without having to move. People read newspapers or sat looking out of the window, there were few discussions. At Torre del Greco passengers began to move toward Niccolò's end of the train. At the far set of doors he could see two men in carabinieri uniforms. While most people avoided looking at him, the officers caught his eye, and Niccolò nodded back, and couldn't help but smile at the idea that they were probably on the train for the same reason.

Niccolò studied the passengers and considered that none of them looked strong enough to abduct and stab a young man. He knew that it was a mistake to assume that the person who committed the assault would stand out in some way or even look interesting. He knew that once some discovery was made, the assailant would, in many ways, be a disappointment. But still, the possibility remained that the man responsible for the stabbing would be on the train.

The station in Naples was busy with police and carabinieri. Up on the concourse, the police watched people coming out of the station and up onto the street. Uniformed men stood in threes and fours, armed and prepared, and immediately outside the station, under the shade of the concrete awning, carabinieri waited beside black vans marked with official insignia, and Niccolò guessed that there was to be a parade or demonstration.

Niccolò came slowly through the market stalls at piazza Nolana, his hands in his pockets, hoping to see why there were so many police, for some kind of reason to materialize. But no demonstration emerged. Disappointed to have discovered nothing Niccolò walked through piazza Garibaldi and further, along via Carbonara, hoping that something would occur to him now that he was in the city. As he hadn't read the paper that morning, he bought *Il Mezzogiorno*, and decided to take a coffee and see if there had been any developments overnight.

The front page carried an image of the star: a simple black square with the white outline of a star set in a circle. Inside, on page seven, he found an article about the graphic and how it was used in the city by a publisher, a printer, a chain of bakeries, and as a logo for a biscuit produced by the bakery. He read slowly, took breaks so that he would not become addled, so that he would not lose himself. This is what he needed to focus on. The star. This was the reason for his journey. Niccolò remembered the biscuits. Surely everyone knew of them. The tins were stacked in every shop and market for weeks before and after Ferragosto. It wasn't a tradition, as such, but this is when he always remembered seeing them. He also had an idea where the bakery was located – although the newspaper had indicated that a number of bakeries produced the star-brand biscuits.

Uncertain of the neighbourhoods Niccolò walked first through I Miracoli and found the roads forced him up the hill; the streets became steeper and narrower and took him away from where he sensed he should be heading. At first, catching his reflection in shop windows, he did not recognize himself. But this was no confusion, instead he saw himself as someone who lived in the city, someone who belonged on the streets, a man with authority. The almond sellers, the gypsies asking for money, the shoe salesmen, the women at the markets, they all knew him, or knew his type: an independent man going about his independent business.

The further he walked the quieter the streets became, until he was surrounded by buildings five or six storeys high, their fronts rose directly from the black-cobbled road and their backs stumped into the hillsides. One row of houses topped another, butting higher at each level, so that the road appeared to rise through a canyon of dank grey rock. Turning back, he returned through the market on via Vergini, then seeing a street sign, via Arena di Sanità, he followed the street through to a long curved piazza and regretted that he had no address and no map. Even so, he couldn't find the bakery.

Stopped on the piazza with only a general notion of his location, he decided to return to the station. Once on via Carbonara his thoughts now ran on other subjects. When he stopped at via Capasso to wait for a break in the traffic, he looked down the small street directly at a red tin sign of a star in a circle mounted under a porch.

The dimensions, colour and design of the star were identical to the star on the missing student's T-shirt, the sign duplicated in Fede's newspaper and this morning's *Mezzogiorno*. The discovery astounded him. He walked to the entrance and found the small portal-door open. Niccolò peered into the courtyard to smell fresh bread and see what looked like apartments rising above the central courtyard. On the brass plaque beside the doorbells he read the names of the businesses: a language school, a furniture 'fabricator', a lawyer, a seminary. It took a while for the information to sink in and seemed oddly coincidental, so odd that it might not be a coincidence at all, but some deliberate design.

Niccolò stopped at the entrance perturbed, unsure of his discovery. The longer he looked at the tin sign, the more significant it seemed.

He waited two hours, standing first immediately outside the door, so that every time it was opened he could see into the courtyard and understand a little better what was inside. He thought it best to wait, to stay open to the coincidence and see what might develop. Contented with the discovery he was happy to allow whatever might happen to unfold without prompting. At eleven o'clock he heard voices echoing as they came to the door, and a whole group of people came out of the courtyard. They came out in threes and fours, Americans, French, German, busy with chatter. The students from the language school held the door open for each other, they ducked as they came out, and Niccolò waited with his back to the wall, close enough to see each individual, and some, noticing him, nodded politely. The students, mostly women and girls, spoke English, although he heard German, and a little tentative Italian. Two boys, Japanese, ducked out through the doorway, and Niccolò waited, not sure if this also meant something. When the door closed behind them the students walked on and the street became silent.

After twenty minutes with few people coming in and out Niccolò began to consider moving on, and just as he debated the idea the door opened, and out stepped a young girl dressed in a short skirt with black skin-tight leggings.

The woman crossed directly in front of him. Short, with black hair cropped in a boyish cut, she hurried, half-running, through the shade of the street out into the sunlight, and headed to the broader piazza where she joined a small group of students and followed after them into an *alimentari*. Niccolò, with nothing else to do, came cautiously to the shop. Looking through the long windows he couldn't distinguish her from the other students. Finally she emerged from the shop alone with a blue bag tucked under her arm. As she walked the strap slipped from her shoulder and she occasionally corrected it.

The student crossed directly in front of him. Niccolò automatically shied away, when he looked up again she was heading through the market and the tight streets of the Centro Storico, stepping aside for the cars and motorbikes and making her way to the open parade of via Cavour. Turning once the street opened out she hurried toward the metro, and came directly down the subway steps, walking so purposefully that he was sure she was taking him somewhere he needed to see.

Niccolò followed the student down to the platform, and stood close enough that he could have touched her shoulder without having to stretch. Niccolò seldom came into the city, he disliked the forced proximity of strangers, the crush and chaos; through the rush of the morning he had found no time to consider where he was, but now, deep under the city, he felt at ease. He fidgeted with the student's notebook in his pocket. His fingers slipped over the plastic sheath.

Nothing particular singled out the student, she was a plain girl, thin, possibly haughty, a little masculine. There were other women on the platform and girls dressed in shorts or short skirts shouting as they came to the platform, heading to the northern beaches. One talked to a friend and lazily looked him up and down.

He stood beside the student on the train, turned three-quarters away from her, and refused a man asking for cigarettes. The girl appeared not to notice as the man spoke to her. Coming through to Campi Flegrei the train broke to the surface. Looking directly out of the window he watched the hotels and apartments on the broad cliff surrounding the back lots. He waited for her reflection when the train hit shade to show in the window.

Alighting at Campi Flegrei, he let her walk ahead, and followed via a bridge over the platform down to the street, it was clear that she was familiar with this route. The avenue was broader than the tight city streets. Ahead, running behind apartment blocks was the steep sweeping rim of a crater, the crest edged with finer houses and palm trees.

He followed her through a car park to the doors of an apartment and stopped at the steps as she paused at the doors and checked through her shoulder-bag for her keys. As she leant over the counter she looked back, and for the moment, before she turned and walked into the building he was certain that she had seen him. She seemed, he thought, to be looking for someone.

A group of four men playing cards inside the entrance looked back at him, and he thought that he should leave.

He returned directly to the train station.

Finding Niccolò just out of the shower Livia asked why his work clothes were laid out on the bed.

'You need to help put things away. They're going to be here at any minute. Why are you taking a shower now? You do this deliberately.'

In an attempt to broker reconciliation, Livia's husband's parents had invited themselves for the evening. They were passing through, they said, nothing more. Livia begged Niccolò to stay. 'Do this one thing,' she begged. 'For me. I ask very little of you. They are checking on me. They don't like that I came here, and they are suspicious.'

Niccolò knew how critical her father-in-law was and was well acquainted with her mother-in-law's particular fussiness. The evening would be soured by the couple's disappointment in Livia.

'I've bought cold meats, cheese, and bread. Do you think that's enough? They said they wouldn't eat.' Livia stood in the bathroom and watched Niccolò dry himself. 'Don't,' she asked, 'please, please, don't mention the clothes. Say nothing of the clothes. I'm begging you. They are going to be here soon. You need to hurry up.'

Niccolò stood naked in front of the mirror. He parted his hair in the same way he had parted his hair that morning. He refused to be hurried.

'So? Why are your clothes on the bed?' She didn't understand. 'And why is your hair different? You didn't go to work?'

Niccolò shrugged and said the police had called and asked him to come into the city.

Livia immediately appeared alarmed.

'You went to Naples?'

'I took the train.'

'I don't understand why they would want to speak with you? What else do they need to hear?'

Niccolò said he didn't know.

'What did they say?'

'I didn't see them.'

'You didn't see them? They called you in and then they didn't speak with you?' She shook her head, immediately angry. 'Do you have a name? Who was this?'

'It wasn't anyone. It doesn't matter.'

Livia paused, then made herself smile. She stepped closer to Niccolò and apologized. Her tone became lighter, easier. 'You're right? This is your business. If they call you in and then they don't speak with you it has nothing to do with me. I promise I won't interfere.'

Niccolò nodded. There were things that she didn't want to hear. Details about the clothes. Details about the murder. New ideas.

Livia waggled her hands. 'I don't need to know. I don't want to hear how many times that boy was stabbed, or what else they've discovered. I don't want such details in my head.'

Niccolò watched from the balcony as Livia kissed her in-laws good-bye. She waited as they got into their car and kept her hand raised in a minimal wave, crisp, precise, until they had driven out of sight – then immediately dusted her hands. She glanced up before returning to the building. Hearing the door close behind her, Niccolò flicked his cigarette into the street and returned to wash his hands and brush his teeth. On the table the remains of their small supper: olives, cold meats, bread, cut tomatoes and artichokes.

As Livia cleared the table she said he should not let them talk to him like that. 'You could defend yourself a little more, you know.' She stopped and grimaced, hand at her stomach. 'I shouldn't have eaten so late. Why do we always eat so late?' She gathered the plates together. 'Did you notice how they agreed with me? You watch, he'll call tomorrow. I'm telling you.' She paused and asked: 'Don't you mind how they speak to you? You barely said a word. It wouldn't hurt if you stood up to them. Just once. That's all you have to do. Stand up to them, and they will respect you.'

She spoke to the police later in the evening, broke her promise and called them to complain. She held her hand over her stomach, sometimes looking at Niccolò, and sometimes at the wall as she cleared up the confusion.

'Someone called. I don't think he would make that up. Someone invited him into the city,' and then, with genuine anger. 'That isn't how it works.'

He knows what she will say. This is his story, although, to be honest, he's sick of hearing it. Two years, she'll say, he nearly died. They held him down, she'll say, a foot on his neck, she'll say, they beat him with a metal pole. She'll try not to tap her head as she talks. She might give the detail about how he came across them, a band of men in one of the warehouses stripping out the units. She will explain how, even after the police had caught them, they couldn't really explain why they'd done it. *We'd already got what we came for.* When it was done they took the pole with them and drove away, and nobody knows this except Niccolò, how he managed to get himself to the security barrier. From the warehouse to the barrier. It wouldn't take two minutes to walk, but it took him all night and he made it on his belly, with his fingers in the dust and his toes pointing and pushing to drive himself forward across a concrete lot, across a rough stretch of scrub, across the open parking lot, all the way to the security barrier. The report says that the men dragged him, propped him up against the barrier and left him, but no, Niccolò had focused on the barrier and made it the whole way by himself. He knew what lonely was, he knew what effort was and what it cost him, that crawling on his belly to that barrier was something almost beyond him, an ocean to swim, or like turning bone to metal through pure force of will. He knew that when you have to focus on your breathing you are in trouble. He understood that everything comes at you one moment at a time, and when it came down to it he either made it to the barrier or he didn't. He either survived or he did not.

Livia had one or two stories about her brother depending on her mood. Story one was always the attack, how she had heard this on the national news, about how she had stood up and screamed and screamed with grief. Story two, more often than not, was the story about how his wife had left him, taken their daughter and moved back north to Rivara, because he did not know who they were. He knew who they were in common ways, he could remember their histories, the birthdays, the courtship with his wife, but these events no longer had content, and while he knew enough to sometimes feel guilt, even that was not sustained. He knew that he had loved his wife. He just didn't currently understand what that meant. She told this story when she was angry, or when she wanted to become angry. She didn't speak about the day he married, his daughter's birth. She didn't explain that she had taught him to swim, and how beautiful he was, my god, how incredibly handsome, floating free of her arms, just loose, present, so very alive, and that every day she had to steel her heart because she was looking at someone who both was and wasn't her brother, and how her only wish was to have him back. She didn't speak about how easy he was, about how, before all of this Niccolò Scafuti didn't have one miserable bone in his body. She hid the photos in his apartment for herself because she no longer believed in that perfect world.

TUESDAY: DAY P

Niccolò arrived early for work and sat in the booth frustrated. On the horizon hung one long grey cloud, smog rising from the city.

Fede sent Stiki up to the main building with the report and the logbook, he wanted to speak with Niccolò. Out on the counter were his study books, an English-language primer and an English-language newspaper. Niccolò was in no mood to talk, but seeing the newspaper, he asked Federico if he could read English.

'Yes. Of course. My reading is better than my speaking. With reading,' he explained, 'I can take my time. As long as the subject isn't too technical. That's why a newspaper is good.' Fede set his books away, and slipped the small and worn dictionary into a drawer beneath the desk. 'I can manage. So did they say anything? Yesterday. The police?'

Niccolò took the student's notebook from his pocket and set it on the desk. The notebook was almost full now, fat with newspaper clippings.

'What's this?'

Niccolò pushed the notebook across the desk.

Fede picked up the small book and looked through the pages, slowly turning and reading. 'Do you understand any of this?'

Niccolò shook his head and asked if Fede could make any sense out of it.

'No, it's difficult.' Fede frowned at the pages. 'Tricky.' The writing was small and slanted, difficult to read. He glanced quickly through the other pages; his head made a small bird-like peck when he came to the clippings. 'What are these? What is this book? Where is it from?' Fede closed the book and looked at the cover. He didn't understand. 'Surely this is evidence? Why haven't you handed it to the police?'

Niccolò said that the police didn't know about it, yet.

'But I saw them myself, they had a whole team of men, they wouldn't have missed it?' Federico placed the book down on the desk. 'You found this in the field? Why didn't you give it to them yesterday?'

Federico opened the cover. 'If this is the American's notebook it might be important. It belongs to his family. You can't keep it. You understand? They might be able to tell who he is. His family will want to know. You should call them immediately. I mean now. You should tell them now. Any news about this person is important.'

When Stiki returned he stood outside the booth and asked what was wrong. Fede shook his head and said it was nothing. Nothing he needed to explain.

Sparrows squabbled in the dirt.

Once they were gone Niccolò attempted to settle into work. Taking out Fede's books he spread them across the desk, then adjusted the seat, raising it so he could sit comfortably and face the view.

Little happened for the first hour. The plant was located on the outskirts of the town and the road led directly to the factory. Lovers searching for discreet roads and parks would make their slow way up the hill, but few stopped long. From the cubicle he could see the edge of Naples, a vast yellow spill slipping into a solid blue sky. Aircraft coming in and out of the airport slid slowly beside the hill, gaining height over the bay.

Disturbed by his discussion with Fede, Niccolò could not settle. He spread out the newspaper and kept the notebook underneath. Throughout the morning he considered what he should do, and the problem bore into him. He should take the notebook to the police, he decided. He could say that he'd found it on the wasteland after the search, that there was an area close to the houses where everyone parked their cars. It would be better to be rid of it.

Fede returned in the early afternoon and asked directly, coldly, if Niccolò had gone to the police. Irked by the question, Niccolò shrugged him off. He'd come all the way back to ask him that? Fede stepped into the office and asked immediately, 'What's that smell?' He saw ash on the ring burner, saw how the wall was scorched, and turned in disbelief to Niccolò. Niccolò, as usual, was due to take the report forms and ledger to the central security office, and he used this as an excuse to leave Fede. When he returned from the main building he was pleased that Fede had gone. He sorted through the newspapers stacked under the desk, and looked quickly through them to see if there were any reports he might have overlooked before he threw them away. The day was bright; a soft wind came off the bay directly onto the mountain, and with it came a sweet smell, and again the faint brittle stink of fire.

Livia had wanted to talk that morning. Her in-laws wanted to visit again on Sunday afternoon, there was progress she said, real progress this time, and if her father-in-law was as rude to Niccolò as he had been on the previous night, she wanted him to say something. Niccolò could not remember what the man had said. The man wore glasses with thick black rims and thicker lenses so that his eyes appeared glassy and wet, he was short, and his teeth were yellow from smoking. Niccolò could not see why Livia was so intimidated by him.

At four o'clock Niccolò was called to his supervisor's office.

The supervisor's office was in the central administration building, a set of concrete oblongs abutted one to another; the windows zipped in a long black line across the entire complex. The dye-production plants were glass boxes with slanted glass roofs, surrounded by concrete offices. It was only his second time in the office, the first when he picked up his employment papers and the Chief of Security who had seen him came out to shake his hand, and from that one gesture Niccolò had always thought well of the man.

Niccolò had seen the chief a number of times, talking at meetings and holding discussions. The man habitually spoke in an unbroken monotone so that he could not be interrupted.

Now, on his second visit, Niccolò walked quickly wondering what this could be; the reviews were completed for the year, and in his report he had done neither well nor badly, which his manager assured him was a good sign given the length of his employment.

As soon as he entered the office Niccolò could see that his guesses were entirely wrong. Three senior officials stood about a desk: his manager, the section manager, and a police officer. The police officer asked directly for the notebook, and Niccolò, in honesty, said that there was no book. After speaking with Federico he had set the book on top of the stove and burned it.

The three men appeared surprised. The officer invited Niccolò to sit down.

'You've destroyed evidence? Do you understand what you are saying, what you are admitting to?'

Niccolò shook his head. He locked eyes with the police officer. Pinpoints of light vibrated on the tabletop, the floor, the tawny walls and doorway shifted in relation to each other. The pure complexity of the moment he found himself in. Unlike other absences this one shuddered down on him, and Niccolò fell heavily, his cheek on the floor, his shoulder hammering his chin as he quickly seeped away. Light first, voices after; the officer calling for attention.

FRIDAY: DAY Q

In the late morning Niccolò returned to the abandoned paint factory with the police, and it was a shock to leave the confines of the cell and return to Ercolano.

That morning two magistrates had come to question him. They wanted to hear again about the factory in Ercolano.

Was there anything Niccolò wanted to add to the list of evidence he had thrown into the tank?

Niccolò shook his head. It was hard to be exact, he had thought through the night, trying to remember, but nothing else had occurred to him. Cats, he said. Mostly cats.

Was there anything particular about the factory, anything he could describe?

Niccolò apologized. No. Nothing occurred to him.

The chief magistrate said that it was of no issue if he could not remember, and Niccolò said that he was thinking, but it was difficult to describe an empty room. He had only ever gone into the first room. He didn't much like the building, and didn't feel safe going in there, as there was only one entrance and no windows.

The men waited in silence.

Could he describe the factory?

Niccolò nodded, and looked to the chief magistrate as he answered. There was only one that you could get inside, because the commune had recently sealed the others. And this factory was on the opposite side of the road to the wasteland and the market gardens. A path ran down from the wasteland across the estate and eventually brought you to the road and the factory. The other factories, as he had said, were fenced off.

Could he remember what was inside the room?

Again, he shook his head. There was nothing in the room. Nothing at all, and he hadn't looked into any of the other rooms. As he'd said it was entirely empty except for a tank, in the first room. A tank set into the floor. Is that what they wanted to know?

There was nothing else to remember about the place? The tank. What shape was it? Was it square or round?

The hole into it was round, but the tank itself might be square. The water was about three metres down from the hole. It probably wasn't that deep. It was filthy, the water was black and it stank.

The magistrate asked if Niccolò could draw a map, and could he show where the building was in relation to where he lived. Niccolò said that he could, it would not be as hard as trying to describe the place. Even though he'd seen it a good number of times, he couldn't remember anything distinctive. There was graffiti. Writing on the walls.

As the magistrates left, Niccolò rose in his seat, and raising his voice a little, began to repeat what he had said. It was easy to know which building it was because all of the other buildings had been sealed by the commune. Some of them had been bricked up, but for one reason or another they hadn't sealed this one. He didn't know why. The others were all secured, and there was no way into them.

Leaving the room the chief magistrate quietly thanked him, and Niccolò thought that there was sadness in his voice.

The officers' heads jolted in unison as the squad car came steadily down the grey pumice track, silhouettes in their flat caps. Dust rose behind them in a long and low plume, obscuring the steep rise to the mountain and the two cars behind them.

The three police cars drew up beside the building. Two policemen waited on the opposite side of the road, between them stood an old man whose trousers were tucked into his socks. Further up against the wall leaned a bicycle. Niccolò recognized the old man as Italo, one of the market gardeners. He didn't know his last name, but knew that the old man was difficult and disliked. It was the only reason that he knew the man. Italo grew dahlias in an allotment opposite the factory, and earlier that morning he had cycled by the building and heard boys inside throwing stones. There was something about their haste, the way they ran away from the factory and their pause on the hill that made him curious about what they were doing. Inside the warehouse he found cushions from a couch, and a split bag of lime, the room was empty. The boys had taken the dumpster from his land two weeks ago, he complained, a theft he had reported to the police. They had slashed

the plastic in his hothouses and cut the irrigation pipes, but it was neither the theft nor the vandalism that justified his call to the police, it
was the stench from the factory.

In one day the smell had become much worse, the boys had disturbed something, and as the police stepped out of their car they
paused, recognizing the smell, and unwilling to go closer to the building they decided to wait. The investigating magistrate joined the police
and the old man, and discussed what they were to do.

Niccolò sat alone in the car. He could see into the factory through
the doorway, and he watched the two policemen approach the tank,
hands covering their mouths. Standing at the entrance another officer
threw a small stone. The stone hit the metal plate with a round boom,
and a black storm of flies rose in a malignant buzz.

The three policemen backed out of the room and agreed that,
clearly, something wasn't right, and this was perhaps a matter they
weren't adequately prepared to handle. The magistrate shouted across
the road to the men that nothing was to be disturbed. They were to
wait.

Italo complained to the investigator that he knew exactly who the
boys were, their parents worked for the cooperative, and he'd spoken
with the police a number of times about their thievery and the damage
they caused. He knew their names, and he knew where they lived. He'd
given them the names before.

The first officer called across to the magistrate and said that they
should take a look in the tank and see what it was. Supposing the
experts and specialists arrived and all they found inside was a dead
dog, or rotten fruit, or any of a number of things that had nothing to
do with their investigation? How stupid would they look?

The second officer disagreed, it was unlikely that anything vegetable could smell that bad. Had he smelled anything that bad before?

They all knew what it was.

Both men hesitated and agreed they had never seen so many flies
in one place. It was a bad sign.

Italo asked if they were going to do anything now that everyone
agreed on how bad the smell was. The magistrate stood with his hands
on his hips. Turning slightly he agreed that they should pry back the
plate and disturb as little as they could. He looked at Niccolò as he
spoke, but Niccolò sat still, his hands cuffed together on his lap.

Is there anything we need to know? he asked.

Niccolò shook his head. The heat was making him sleepy.

The first officer returned to the room with a stick. He pushed the cushions away, then tapped the metal plate covering the tank. On the floor were marks indicating that the plate had been recently dragged into place. He grimaced at the stench and shoved the plate back with his foot. Flies swarmed up as the lid slowly shifted back. The officer leaned over the pit, hand to his mouth as he squinted into the hole. He turned his face away but kept his place. He needed a torch, he said, it was too dark to see or guess what might be inside.

The second policeman shrugged and gingerly approached and he seemed to stare for a long time, squatting over the hole, squinting. Cupping his hand over his mouth he walked briskly out of the building. Out in the sun, a good distance away, he breathed fresher air. Then standing upright he said that there was something in the tank. The white back of splayed legs. It looked like a body.

Turning to the squad car, the magistrate asked Niccolò if he had any idea who it was.

Niccolò held up both his hands to scratch his neck, in the heat it was impossible not to yawn. What, he asked, what was he asking?

The police set up a barrier along the road to redirect traffic through the town. The only vehicles that arrived were the ones attached to the investigation, squad cars, a forensics van, and almost as an afterthought, an ambulance.

The magistrate sat beside Niccolò and said that he should just tell him now what he knew. Hey? Why not? Identification would be attempted on site to see if the body in the tank matched the basic description of the missing student. So why didn't he simply tell them what he knew?

Livia was allowed to speak to Niccolò on the evening of his second day in custody.

'They came to the school and brought me home.' She sat at the table with her head down. She tapped her head, indicating the bandages about Niccolò's head. 'They told me you didn't want me to know.' She spoke calmly, her voice fading into the room.

Niccolò sat upright, he remembered to set his shoulders back and raise his head. There was work in Rome.

Livia caught her breath. She listened to him silently and appeared

startled by the news. Niccolò continued to talk. There would be opportunities in Rome. When they released him he would go immediately
and look for work. Why should he stay and struggle here? His mind was
made up.

'You can't go to Rome because you don't have the money.' Livia
shook her head. 'Niccolò. They have dismissed you from work.' Livia
steadied one hand on her belly, the other at her mouth as if to delicately tease out the words or finish them so that he would clearly
understand her – and looking at her he tried to measure if this was
anger or pity. 'Do you understand what is happening? Do you understand what they are saying about you?'

Niccolò again reminded himself to sit upright. He said nothing. It
was obvious that he was helping the police. She should understand
this. Tomorrow they were to take him back to the warehouses in
Ercolano again, and this would all be cleared away.

'Niccolò?' Livia shook her head, her hand now clapped to her
mouth. 'How have you become so lost when I have always been by
your side? How did you manage these things?'

Niccolò folded his arms and closed his eyes.

Eyes swollen from crying, Livia slowly regained her composure.

YEAR 2: MR RABBIT & MR WOLF

MONDAY

The magistrate agreed to meet with Finn on the understanding that his name would not be mentioned and there would be no direct reproduction of any of the material he would present. Finn agreed without hesitation and arranged an earlier flight so he could make his way directly from the airport to via Crispi in Chiaia in good time to meet the magistrate at *Prima!* – a café he'd picked for such a purpose on his previous trip, the kind of venue that deserves a tracking shot, a slow reveal of the space and the few mindfully solitary characters in it; white tiles, a god-damned chandelier, smocked waiters, a canvas-covered patio (in a word: Europe). *Prima!* sat beside an intriguingly unnamed jewellery boutique just up from Ferragamo, Emilio Zegna, Armani, and further over – piazza del Martiri. Pleased about how his day would focus down from Paris to Naples, to Chiaia. He liked the economy of it – the first day of his second visit to Naples. He'd be working as soon as he set foot in the city. The very moment.

He wanted to use his time efficiently because he only had the summer. He needed to be *effective*. In less than eighty days he would be a student again, one of a number, pushing a student loan, a coffee habit and unsociable hours; but during the summer he was a writer with a project. A writer with a project and a publishing contract. A sophomore (soon to be final-year) student with an agent and a contract, about to hold a discussion about a notorious and unsolved murder with a respected anti-Mafia magistrate. Hard to believe how the year was working out. In travelling Finn had focused his luggage down to two items: a small backpack; a soft hold-all. Both could be slung over his shoulder, and he fostered this image of himself, as someone mobile, focused, unburdened but connected. The contents of his luggage reflected this ambition: in both bags he'd carefully wrapped a wealth of goods, a laptop (new), a portable hard-drive, two USB memory sticks, a DV camera (borrowed at the last minute from his sister), a phone, and less convenient, the assorted cables and plugs because they've yet to figure out the proper portability of these items. Along with this were his notebooks. These books were precious, seven already filled with his tiny writing, a compact concentration of notes from interviews, his own impressions, research from the sites, scraps of papers, tickets, receipts, things discovered while out and about, and he'd been smart enough to choose small books and marked each one with his mobile and home number, email addresses, and a note on the first page suggesting a reward might be paid if they were found and returned.

Finn wanted to test-drive a way of life – this is how he'd phrased it to his sister – see for himself if he was cut out for writing. While he loved college – what wasn't there to like? – he was working it hard and didn't see the point in waiting around, holding on for blind luck and good fortune while amounting debt. The whole point about ambition is making sure it happens (name one other sophomore to secure a publishing contract). Carolyn agreed, besides, he was older than the other students, and that five years made a difference. They talked this over, endlessly refining, because beyond choosing a smart college and a sensible course with professors whose references would really matter, nobody really considers the bigger picture, not really, and just because his family were loaded didn't mean he could ignore these things. No one really figures this through. Most people just let things happen to them, like they're lucky. Not that Finn wasn't lucky. Moderately good-looking, modestly intelligent, white, and with parents who didn't mind bankrolling the project while he waited for the advance, just so they could brag that their not-yet-graduated son had a publishing deal and was writing in Naples, Italy for the entire summer (and your kid has an internship, er, where exactly?). From Finn's perspective everybody gains something this summer: the parents, the college, the publisher, and certainly (not least of all), Finn himself.

Finn ordered coffee, spoke Italian well enough to feel part of the general rush, although Spanish was the language he swam in. The value of the magistrate would come in the form of names, not anecdotes (which Finn already knew), and through inflection – the weight he placed on certain events, and the sequence in which he ordered them. Aside from this, a senior magistrate who wasn't willing to go on public record but still had something to say (unofficially) would make an excellent introduction to his book, not to mention the boost it gave the project: people were still interested. Finn couldn't imagine a better situation. He didn't expect to uncover anything new, not after a year, but he did expect to find new people and new perspectives – much the better if they wanted to remain anonymous.

As a figure, the magistrate didn't disappoint – reassuringly familiar (as if cast into the role) – tall and thin, slightly wild grey hair, a hint of stubble, a man both preoccupied and focused. Distinctive, Finn thought, an air of instinct about the man, an intelligence and concentration he'd like to describe. As expected the information was less than revelatory: the magistrate ran through what he knew to be happening.

1. Since his release from custody, Niccolò Scafuti had returned to his apartment at the Rione Ini estate on the outskirts of Ercolano, where he now lived a solitary life. If the magistrate had any personal regrets, it was the involvement of Scafuti in the investigation and he wished that the man had not taken the walk that night and discovered the American's clothes and brown bag. But he didn't think, a) given the circumstances, b) Scafuti's unwise decisions, and c) what they knew at the time, that anything could have played out any differently. Scafuti had destroyed evidence, it was unfortunate, a criminal offence which had caused great damage. Who knows what might have happened if they'd read the notebook?

2. Marek Krawiec. Now here was an entirely different situation, and the magistrate remained clear and absolute about the fact that Krawiec could not be interviewed, and neither would he be coaxed into any kind of acknowledgement of where Krawiec was being held (most likely Rome). The case was under judicial review. On this the magistrate remained firm. Marek Krawiec could not be interviewed. He could say, though, that investigators were hopeful about finding the missing bodies. Krawiec was still emphatic about his innocence.

3. The palazzo, of course, was indeed the palazzo at via Capasso 29 close to the Duomo and the tourist district – everybody knew this and it had featured in many news reports over the year. This didn't stop a rumour that this palazzo was not the actual site of the murders – that there was some kind of cover-up because somebody important lived in the building where the killing had actually occurred. This was plainly untrue.

4. Evidence. There were many other rumours which were not true: the evidence taken from the basement room on via Capasso and discovered on the shoreline at Ercolano was not destroyed or lost, and was not mishandled or contaminated as many reports had speculated.

Much of the blood evidence was destroyed by the sea, but even so, there was plenty of other evidence to confirm Krawiec's presence in the room (which, interestingly enough, he never denied).

5. The missing student, otherwise known as 'The American', 'The Student', or less frequently as 'The First Victim', seen once and only once at the Circumvesuviana station dressed in the hunter-green T-shirt with the five-point star design, had not yet been identified, and no other remains had been discovered. The DNA from the shirt, shorts, undershorts, matched the blood evidence on the plastic taken from the room and recovered from the shoreline, and these were assumed, until new evidence or Krawiec told them otherwise, to belong to the American. The American was picked up probably before he had a chance to check into a hotel. The only blood evidence belonged to the American.

6. The man known as 'The Second Man' (the body discovered in the abandoned paint factory in Ercolano) had never been mistaken for the missing student – 'The American', or 'The Student'. This death, the autopsy demonstrated, could be attributed to a combination of factors: a blow to the head, the resulting haemorrhage, and drowning after he was dumped in the storage tank. Because of evidence found in the tank with the Second Man – the novel, a wallet, a digital player – assumed to be items taken from the student – this 'victim' had always been looked upon as a co-conspirator, although they were unable to establish his identity.

7. The body of Mizuki Katsura, AKA the missing 'Second Victim', had also not been traced nor recovered. And here the magistrate wanted to talk about what he called the situational context. 'Imagine,' he calmly laid out the facts, 'in a region of four and a half million people, how many more transient people come and go who are not accounted for?' Some legitimate, but a good number without account. There is immense opportunity here for exploitation. Both victims were linked by one known circumstance; they were both known to have passed through the Circumvesuviana station in the early morning. A friend at the language school confirmed that Katsura saw two men, had noticed them at the station, and commented on it in her class. The magistrate believed she had seen both Krawiec and the Second Man hunting, as it were. Katsura's belongings were found in the room she had rented in Portici. The name and address she'd given the language school were not genuine – who knows why?

8. The star. Now here's a coincidence – which might one day be explained by Krawiec when he finally talks. Fact 1: Mizuki Katsura went to school in a building on which there was a sign showing the outline of a five-point star held within a circle. Fact 2: The American, and this is still all they really know about him, wore a T-shirt with the same design. Again, there were theories about this, many wild and ambitious, semi-occult ideas. To the magistrate this spoke of something both deliberate and accidental. A coincidence, which, examined in the right light, would open up a methodology, systems of thinking, habits which could be key in definitively identifying Krawiec and the Second Man as the killers.

9. The existence of the Brothers. From the start the killings were considered as crimes which had to be committed by more than one person. The logistics of erasing not one, but two people would require resources not open to a single individual. Krawiec's story about brothers from France was exactly that, a story, a fancy, implausible at best – a ploy to get the system tied in knots while they chased down phantoms. The people who could supposedly confirm the existence of these brothers, other residents at the palazzo, had never in fact met or seen them. The building supervisor, Amelia Peña, was a fantasist.

Which brings us to, 10. the most contentious issue of all: the relationship between the murders and the book *The Kill*, published anonymously as a fanciful memoir by Editiones Mandatore, Madrid, in 1973, then by Universidad di Seville in 1997, where it was presented without the introduction as a work of fiction: one in a series of novels published as 'crimes in the city'.

The magistrate regretted the coincidence very much, and wished that the link had never been drawn – another attempt by Krawiec to muddy the water, this one, wildly successful. True, a copy of the book (the '97 edition) was discovered in Krawiec's apartment. The magistrate had to be honest. 'The book, this *Kill*, is not about Naples. It doesn't mention the city, the region, the country. Not once. The city in the book bears no comparison to the city in reality. It is a work of imagination and a truly regrettable coincidence.'

'So you've read it?'

'It has been a while now, and I no longer recall the details.'

'But the details are very similar.'

'They appear similar.'

'A room prepared with plastic. The body cut up and left in the palazzo. The blood.'

The magistrate shook his head.

'In the novel, there are other items. What happens with the feet, if I remember correctly. The bones. The organs. An ear. Teeth. Some hair. A tongue. Evidence is deliberately scattered in places to incriminate people who live in the palazzo. There are elements that seem similar, but a number of important pieces aren't there.'

When asked if he believed whether Marek Krawiec and the Second Man had collaborated precisely to realize the murder described in *The Kill*, the magistrate shrugged.

'To what purpose would they do this? They abducted tourists. These were crimes of profit or opportunity. Pure and simple. To recreate a fictional event is something much more imaginative, even intellectual. Something well beyond their scope. And they would have to have read the book. Marek Krawiec does not read or speak Spanish. He has the book, but he can't read it. Perhaps he knew something of the story, and perhaps this is part of his fiction, along with the brothers, another invention.' The magistrate asked Finn to consider. 'The practicalities are more convincing. You abduct someone from a train station. What are you going to do? You rob them, take from them whatever you want, or do with them whatever you want to do, and because you have already exposed yourself to certain unnecessary risks it becomes necessary for you to kill them. This is a city of four and a half million people who live on top of each other and who know each other's business. So what are you to do? Such murders involve dismemberment because you cannot walk out of a palazzo with a whole body, not without being seen, but if you divide something into small enough parts, and if you are a little clever in how you dispose of these parts, it is possible that you will never be discovered.'

'But there are connections between them?'

'Unfortunately, there are general connections, yes. But it has been a year since I read it. Without the book this is not such an interesting case. Without the novel nothing distinguishes itself above other such events. It's possible that this aspect of the case, which has been greatly speculated over, has meant a certain kind of concentration, an inclination toward the more sensational elements, which has, in turn, distracted us from asking the proper questions.'

The magistrate folded his hands together and smiled, closing the discussion about the book.

'Why did the evidence point only to one killing?'

He looked directly at Finn. 'Because we found only one crime scene. They wouldn't have risked committing a second crime in the same place. The evidence from via Capasso indicated only that the American had been killed there. Although this was considerably degraded. It might be possible that two people were killed there, although only one dismemberment took place.'

'And you believe Marek Krawiec to be the main instigator?'

'I do. Krawiec's skill, if this is the right word, is in his "everyday-ness". The issue – let me give you my experience – is that wickedness is not as interesting as you might hope. Krawiec appears normal, a neighbour, someone who can be trusted, because, for most of the time, this is exactly who he is. In most circumstances he is entirely ordinary. There is nothing exotic about him, and nothing immediately apparent in his personality that would show him capable of such vio-lence. If you want to understand him you should speak with the people in the palazzo who were familiar with him. They also were convinced by him, and managed to draw them into his version of the world. This is typical of someone who is dissociative. They will insist on a reinter-pretation of events, and they will draw people into their schemes and ideas. I don't think Krawiec was the sole perpetrator, but I consider him to be the sole author.'

The magistrate had one last thing to say: 'People come here believ-ing all kinds of things about the city – I'm sure you have your own ideas – that it is violent, corrupt. It is hard to refute the facts. The city has its problems. There are many issues. But it does seem, and this is perhaps truer when speaking about Naples than any other city, that stories are written and ideas are decided long before anyone has actually arrived. Do you understand? It is a problem to be spoken about only in one way, to have one kind of discussion, or one common language. To believe in occult signs and coincidences is to lose sight of the facts, and to indulge fanciful ideas. We have enough problems without this becoming more mysterious than it already is, especially because it involves two missing visitors. We still don't have many answers at this point about what happened. At the moment there is very little truth, what we take to be truth is based on rumours and lies.'

As Finn walked the magistrate to his car, the man's driver straightened up and opened the door. Finn's last questions involved Mizuki Katsura.

'Nothing was found in Tokyo. I even hired someone and they found nothing.' Mizuki Katsura did not exist. Had the magistrate ever considered this?

The magistrate paused before ducking into the car. 'We don't have her name. But that doesn't mean she didn't exist. Clearly someone under this name attended classes at the language school, and someone under this name has disappeared. In Europe we should be especially careful of such an idea. Many people who fall victim to crime are undocumented, or have chosen or have no choice but to exist in ways which remain officially off the record.'

'So you believe that there were two victims.'

'There are three, remember. The man at the paint factory is a victim as well as a culprit.'

Finn nodded in agreement.

The magistrate lowered himself slowly into the car, then fixed Finn with a gaze, cold eyes, grey, white-rimmed and a little clouded. 'I will give you the ending of your book,' he said, with just an edge of a wry small smile. 'Consider how smoothly this was achieved. I do not believe that this is the work of a novice. It is possible that Marek Krawiec and the man found at the paint factory had a criminal career which involved the disappearance of considerably more than two people. Krawiec also might have had experience prior to his arrival here. What better place to disguise himself? What you must write about, if there is any need for clarity, is the history of Niccolò Scafuti, and the damage done to the city.'

Finn watched the car draw away then looked with satisfaction at the boutiques along via Crispi. A profitable meeting, which provided both a beginning and the end. As soon as he was on the metro Finn checked his mini-recorder. Nothing you could broadcast, not in terms of quality, but still useable.

Hotel Grimaldi – between Corso Umberto and via Nuova Marina – was close to the palazzo on via Capasso, and cheap (Finn wasn't being irresponsible with his money, and didn't want to make the mistake of being too remote from his subject, just comfortable enough for a good, critical distance). The room held a wardrobe, a dresser, a bed, a sink; the shutters for the window could not be folded back as they hit the side of the bed. Finn left a voicemail for his sister, and then typed. *They have beds here like school beds.* And thought as the message slowly fed its way through, a dial turning on the screen, that this was the beginning of her day, the end of his. She wouldn't yet be in New York, the message would arrive before her. Out in the bay a ferry rounded the jetty, the sea soaked blue.

While he unpacked he began to consider the month ahead. He would find his meals close by, eat during the day with Rino. He would write for four hours in the morning, arrange his interviews and site visits in the afternoon, write late into the night. There would be no evenings out, no time wasted. With twenty thousand words already written – the first three chapters had secured the contract – he had a foundation for the project; although he already guessed this would need to be refigured. Unlike his fellow students, Finn had discipline. He could organize himself, and he could focus. By the end of the month he would transform the notes and the research into a complete and serviceable draft: something in the region of seventy to eighty thousand words. Which meant three thousand words a day. Not a problem. He could achieve this. Having secured a book, Finn had his mind on a larger target, film, and while his mother could advise on publishing and help with contacts, with filmmaking he was completely on his own.

Finn, still busy unpacking when Rino arrived, asked the clerk to let him up. He'd advertised for a researcher at two universities, and picked Rino Carrafiglio, a Ph.D. student at the Orientale. He'd formed an idea of the man from their correspondence, and thought of him as someone in his early twenties with whom he would have easy and intense conversations. He'd pictured himself in bars, cafés, trattorias, which only Rino with his detailed understanding of the city would know, either planning or unpacking their interviews, tapping into the core of the crime and the city itself, stripping back, in long and late discussions, the artifice and the deceptions to discover what was really happening. In reality Rino looked like a taxi driver, end-of-shift bags under his eyes, unshaven, and miserable, with thinning hair, short stature, and a wrinkled shirt; he looked like a dirty old basset-hound. A few hairs stuck over the back of his collar. He could be twenty-something, thirty, late forties even, Finn couldn't tell. Finn did little to hide his disappointment, and regretted sending money in advance to secure assistance (money he could have used on a ticket to Amsterdam, London, or his return to Boston). He had a certain expectation of Italians – which the magistrate had not disappointed. The magistrate looked the part: a long grey face, thin and graceful, a man who appeared cultured, whose knowledge seemed to be reflected in his owlish and groomed manner. Where the magistrate held authority, Rino, on the other hand, just looked worn and sad. It didn't seem right after all of the work he'd committed to the project – two weeks in Naples, two weeks in Rome, two (crushingly disappointing) weeks in Struga, Poland, chasing up a mother who was dead, and a brother who could repeat one phrase in English ('He didn't do it'), visits obsessively described in little black notebooks. He'd already over-sold Rino's abilities to his agent and editor, and determined now that he would take no photographs which included the man.

Finn took a while to hide his valuables while Rino waited. The cash on top of the wardrobe. The traveller's cheques in their envelope under blankets inside the dresser. His passport under the mattress. The laptop inside its soft case slid under the wardrobe. The portable hard-drive in the bottom drawer of the dresser, among dirty laundry. The spare USB sticks which contained copies of all of the drafts of the book and correspondence were easily concealed, one in his wash-bag alongside the shaving cream and toothpaste, the other in the interior side pocket of his soft hold-all. He'd also bought a bottle of rye and he placed that beside the bed.

Rino stood by the door with his hands in his pockets and licked his lips.

On that first evening, for a small additional fee, Rino brought Finn to the Bar Fazzini. As they passed the palazzo on via Capasso, Rino pointed out the carriage doors but didn't say until they were inside the bar that this was the place, you know, that's where it all happened.

Immediately into the bar Rino picked two men and told Finn to keep an eye on them. 'Here,' he'd said, 'are the people you need to speak with.' Finn couldn't guess why he'd singled them out. The men, evidently brothers, had dressed for the meeting; both wore suit trousers and long-sleeve shirts, both combed their hair straight back, and both were clean-shaven with light skin and small wet black eyes. The younger brother, slight, reed-thin, pinched his forefinger and thumb at his crotch as he spoke. The older brother, larger and more solid, was the man to do business with and Rino paid him all of his attention. With broad shoulders and massive hands, the man looked like a chef and was a chef. He looked out of proportion, as if he had built himself, choosing a thick body out of mismatched parts.

'Salvatore and Massimiliano.' Rino grandly swept out his hand. These, he said, were the brothers Marek Krawiec had based his alibi on. From these two men he had invented the French brothers. Massimiliano worked at the *alimentari*, the small kitchen and food shop under the palazzo on via Capasso. His brother Salvatore worked as an accountant but was often at the store.

Finn asked when the brothers had first met Krawiec and the men shook their heads. It hadn't worked like that. Salvatore had only recently moved up from Bari. He'd never met Marek Krawiec.

Rino, thoughtfully, began to explain. 'But there were photos in the *alimentari* of them together when they were younger. Lots of photographs.'

'So he knew you?' Finn spoke directly to the older brother, Massimiliano.

The man shook his head. At that time he also was not living in Naples. 'But in the store there are photographs of us that the man would have seen. It is unbelievable that he would do this.'

Rino nodded. It was true, there were pictures. Their father, who ran the store until last summer, had pictures of his family everywhere.

'It's like that film.' Massimiliano leaned forward, confident about his information. 'Where the man makes up stories from what is around him. He sees something and he includes it in his lies.' He nodded, sincere, eyes closed. 'This way, everything sounds true because everything comes from somewhere. Everything sounds reasonable.'

'So your father ran the store?'

Alimentari. The brothers nodded. They served and sold food and wine. Salvatore wanted to get back into property again, just as soon as he had his licence.

'And would it be possible to speak with him about Marek Krawiec?'

Their father, much to their regret, was no longer with them. The family hadn't managed the shop for very long, four years. 'Do you know what it takes to run a business like this?' The whole fuss with the palazzo last year hadn't helped.

'So what's your father's name?'

Salvatore answered, '*Salvatore.*'

Massimiliano answered, '*Graffa,*' at the same time. 'After the sweet – you know, the pastry with the sugar. Because he's fat.'

'Because he sells them.'

'So he's alive?'

'He's back in Bari.'

'Can I speak with him?'

The men shook their heads. He wouldn't talk. He had nothing to say. They wouldn't want to burden him.

The interview was going nowhere. The brothers knew nothing about the affair. Not one thing you couldn't find in the newspaper or discover on the internet. Even so, this could still be useful. News isn't news, after all, without colour and detail. Information requires the inflection of experience. Finn understood exactly what he had going. What he didn't understand is why no other journalist had jumped onto this. So he asked details about the city, about the Italian south, about what they knew of the crimes. Throughout the discussion Rino kept nodding, and gave his own little affirmations, *yeah, right, OK, like I told you. Exactly.*

The small bar remained busy through the evening. At some point the ceiling fans were turned to the highest setting and the doors that made up the full front were lodged open, all without effect. The sticky night air, honey-sweet, became acrid with sweat. Finn stood at the counter beside the brothers, and while they spoke he took notes in a small black notebook, keeping it as discreet as he could manage, the book held low, at his hip. He wrote about the meeting, small clues and reminders, alongside what he was recording, so that when he had time he could fill out the episode with more detail.

'Is this all you wanted to know?' The older brother, Massimiliano, tipped his finger on the notebook. He spoke in English and set his arm about Finn's shoulder.

'I don't know. What else do you know?' Not his best question, but still.

'What's this?' The man's finger ran down the spine.

'It's nothing.' Finn closed the book and tucked it into his back pocket.

'You write nothing?'

Finn felt himself begin to flush.

The man nodded. 'Where are you from?'

'Boston.'

The man curved his mouth, impressed. His voice sounded softer than his brother's, the accent a little more marked. The man leaned into him, angular and uncomfortable. 'You should be careful who you speak to. Not everyone is happy to remember this story. It might be a big city, but this is personal, and you might want to show some care.'

Finn gave a gesture, a half-shrug indicating, naturally, he would show discretion.

'Do you smoke?' The older brother tapped Finn's arm. 'Do you want to come outside to smoke something?'

The four men walked to the alley behind the Fazzini. Muffled beats came from the bar, the blue lights of televisions hesitantly illuminated rooms in the wall above them.

The older brother took a cigarette out from a packet. He licked along the length and tore off a strip. 'You'll like this.' He smiled as he concentrated on the task. 'This is a nice. A little different. You smoke this sometimes? It's OK?' Gripped in his hand was a smaller packet, a lighter and papers. He looked to Finn for his response.

Finn said yes.

When the joint was made Massimiliano rolled it between his forefinger and thumb and eyed it, pleased. 'This is good,' he said again. A scooter's buzz sounded in the night. The four of them waited but the scooter did not appear. The younger brother lit a cigarette and leaned back against a car.

'Twenty euro,' the man said, his expression held, expectant.

'Sorry?'

'For the joint. Twenty euro. It's good. You'll like it. Twenty euro and we'll all have a nice smoke.'

Finn took out his wallet and tried not to show how much money he had. The older brother took the note, pocketed it, then lit up the reefer. Then handed it to his brother.

The younger brother blew smoke up in a long measured calculation. 'Have you seen the palazzo,' he said, blinking. Then shook his head and sniggered as if he had no clue what the answer might be, and Finn thought in these casual gestures was seated a small element of threat. In the humid air the smoke rose and flattened out above him.

'Do you want to see inside the room? The basement room.' Salvatore used the word *basso*, although technically this was not one of the *bassi*, but a simple underground storage room. 'We can show you the room.'

Salvatore leaned into Finn. 'It's true,' he said. 'We have a key. If you want to see inside the room we can show you. We can take you tonight if you like. Only if you want, of course.'

Salvatore snorted, a little incredulous. 'Of course he wants to.'

Massimiliano spoke deliberately, answering to his brother through Finn. 'He's in a mood. He wanted to go to a party tonight, but instead.' He took the cigarette out of Salvatore's hand. 'So, we can show you the room but it's expensive.'

A light blinked above them, on and off. The four looked up. Rino, who had yet to receive the reefer looked a little disconsolate.

Massimiliano offered the joint to Finn. 'So how much to see the room?'

When Finn raised his hand Massimiliano drew the joint away, then slowly set it to Finn's lips. 'Take a little, breathe lightly and hold it, then let it go down slowly.'

Finn nodded, and did exactly as he was told.

At the first proper toke Finn immediately felt dizzy. He held the smoke in his mouth and felt it soak softly into him. This, he thought, wasn't grass. Not even close.

Massimiliano set his chin on Finn's shoulder and looked up at his face. He smiled when Finn smiled. 'I said it was good.' He took the joint out of Finn's mouth. 'Don't blow out yet. Just let it . . .' He smoothed his hand through the air, and Finn felt the smoke run free through him.

'So how much are you looking for?' he asked.

The men looked eye to eye.

'Three hundred euro and we can take you there tonight. You can have a look now.'

Massimiliano took a drag himself, a deep, slow intake. He leaned his head back, wrapped his arm about Finn's shoulders. Looking up at the sky he held his breath, then slowly, in what seemed to be an infinitely beautiful moment, exhaled with a satisfied hum, a soft guttural roll. He offered the cigarette back to Finn.

'I like the name. Finn. It's a good name.'

The two men held on to each other. Massimiliano, inexpressibly big and soft, seemed permeable, his arm still about Finn's shoulder. 'You have three hundred euro. It's nothing. You can afford this.'

'How do you have the keys?'

'For the shop. Everyone has keys.'

*

Massimiliano opened the small portal door to the courtyard, and as he held it open he warned that there wasn't a great deal to see (now the money had changed hands), but a trained eye could pick out the right details to get a close picture of what had happened. The two brothers led Finn across the courtyard to an unlocked metal door. Rino followed behind, his hands in his pockets. Finn ducked through the doorway and found to his surprise a steep set of steps carved into the rock to form something like a tunnel, the top of which was rounded, the steps themselves small, steep, and worn with use. A blue electric cable threaded down the steps, and Finn, feeling increasingly more of an interloper, consciously ducked to make himself smaller – still feeling a soft buzzing blur from the reefer (surely something more than just a regular reefer).

The four men came carefully down to the basement. The air, cooler underground, set up the hairs on their arms, a stale reek of mildew made them hold their breaths. At the bottom, Massimiliano pushed forward and indicated a door set into the right side.

The door, small, metal, chipped and battered, had the lock punched out and the handle removed so that it could not lock. Salvatore pointed this out. 'They took the door handle as evidence,' he said, smiling. 'Look, they cut it out.'

The blue cable ran along the corridor into the room, and he could see through the doorway a set of photographers' lights to the left and the right. Finn had the feeling that the brothers had brought a good number of people into the basement, and the likelihood of it costing three hundred euro to every person was slim. He took in breaths, held them, slowly released, and thought that he would not be able to stay for long because of the overbearing reek of mould.

The room itself was entirely stripped, smaller and cleaner than he had imagined. A strip-light in the corridor shed an oblong of sour yellow into the room. Of all the reports Finn had read, none had given much of a sense of the space and just how tiny it was.

Massimiliano leaned into one of the corners. 'There are more caves under this,' he kicked his heel to scuff the stone. Then stamped. 'Can you hear that?' A small boom, perhaps nothing. He stamped again. Moments later another faint boom, deep below, possibly imagined. 'You wouldn't think that people used to live here. When they built these old palazzos the city introduced a stone tax. You couldn't bring stone to the city, so most of the palazzos were built from stone dug out from under them. You have buildings five or six floors high which lean against each other and that's all that holds them up.'

Salvatore held out his hands and shook them, made a rumbling noise and Finn realized he was talking about an earthquake.

Rino, uncomfortable, sweating, bowed his head. He was sorry he said, but he would have to leave. The basement had a bad smell, the room was too confining. Finn felt uneasy as the man scuttled out. The remaining men did not speak as the scuff of Rino's footsteps tracked back to the courtyard hollow and fast.

Finn realized that he was alone with two men, brothers, in a basement where two men (brothers according to Marek Krawiec) had cut their first victim, another American, to pieces. Salvatore said that he would turn on the electricity for the lights and disappeared after Rino, leaving Finn and Massimiliano to face each other in the basement. Neither speaking. As if a plan were now in action. The light from the corridor fell on the man's shoulders but not his face, which seemed to Finn to hold a desperate expression. Finn began to compose an excuse in his head. Massimiliano watched him without a word.

With a loud click the basement lights completely failed, both Finn and Massimiliano were swallowed by thick, clothy darkness. This is it. Finn felt himself weaken, become dizzy. He had walked directly into this, and any questions he'd had about how the brothers had enticed the boy to the palazzo were gone. It was that easy. A little curiosity. A little smoke. If he ran there would be Rino and Salvatore to contend with, there would be no escape. His sister, he thought, would be hearing bad news.

A timid apology echoed down from the courtyard, and with a third click both the photographic lights and the corridor lights suddenly brightened. The glare, so instant and so bright, brought Finn and Massimiliano's arms up to cover their eyes. Finn began to laugh with relief. He was sweating and he could smell himself even above the mould, sour and bitter, and he could taste bile. For the boy, he thought, there had been no such relief.

They lowered their arms slowly, blinked and grinned and grew accustomed to the light. Massimiliano cleared his throat, and, as if obligated, explained that the holes, these holes, were where the plastic sheeting found at Ercolano had been pinned to the stone. Starting at this line here, and ending there, close to the doors. The police had brought two sheets back and rehung them, and found that whoever had prepped the room had taken considerable care to make sure that the sheets were held taut and flat. It would have been a difficult job and it would have taken two people. The tape used to hold the plastic together was cut, sliced, and set at regular intervals to prevent the plastic from sagging. 'A professional job.' Massimiliano nodded almost in admiration. The sheets on the roof were stuck with a double row of tape. It would have taken some time to complete. The mattress was taken out of the room before the final attack. It was possible that when they removed the mattress they also disturbed the plastic on the floor, which is how there came to be such a large quantity of blood underneath it. There was, Massimiliano cleared his throat, another possibility. From what they could tell, the American was suspended at the centre of the room with his arms above him, however, it is possible that he was standing. Out in the field they discovered the lengths of tape used to bind him. He was hog-tied, ankles bound to his wrists, and hoisted, belly down. Before this happened he was kept hanging by his arms, possibly for two days. Depending how high and how firmly he was raised he could have disturbed the plastic on the floor, kicking or thrashing. The event itself had probably occurred over three days, two at the very least, as there were three different drying patterns in the blood. They knew one thing for certain: the boy had been bled before the final event, and then slit open.

How the plastic was removed was another story, and it was certainly done in haste. There was evidence that someone had begun to wipe, perhaps mop, but this was only in one small area close to the door and this was started very soon after the killing, thirty-six to forty-two hours. The woman denied cleaning the room, and in truth it was unlikely that she was able or strong enough to tug down the plastic. 'She's a dwarf,' he said, cutting his hands at hip height. 'It's just not a possibility.'

Finn tried not to think of where he was, and that a young man had been strung up and gutted right where he was standing. According to Massimiliano the boy would have died within four minutes, and four minutes, after waiting three days, was a long time. It's also possible that he would have remained conscious for much of that time. Whatever the scenario, there would have been time for him to realize exactly what was happening.

It must have occurred to Massimiliano, just as it had occurred to Finn, that he could do to him whatever he liked.

A line of sweat ran down Finn's side; he held his breath, and despite Massimiliano standing close beside him he felt utterly alone. It was more than this. He felt useless, and sad. And while he could see the logic to how he had come to this place it just didn't make sense once he was there. What he had taken as a public phenomenon, public property, was nothing of the kind. The boy was taken from a train station, brought to a room, any room in any basement, and gutted.

Finn had never properly felt alone. He'd moved from infatuation to infatuation, falling from one kind of love into another, and he'd distracted himself with the idea of it, so that he could not remember a time when he wasn't preoccupied with thoughts of someone else, so that a presence sat with him at all times – except now. At this moment, for the first time he could remember, Finn was not in love, and neither was he surrounded by family, and he felt alone and wretched.

Remembering his mobile phone, Finn took it out and began to take photographs, and used the activity to avoid making conversation, and as a way of concluding the visit.

TUESDAY

Finn woke in the early morning with the sun full on his face, his mouth open and dry, unsure for a moment where he was.

He waited for Rino on Corso Umberto. His chest ached. He felt seasick, out of balance, his throat unnaturally sore. He hung his head and breathed slowly, his conscience was beginning to prick. The visit to the basement had brought home exactly what he was involved in. Confronted with the room itself, he'd felt his interest to be sordid, a little shameful. He was earning money writing about the killing of a fellow American, and it seemed random to him who would be receiving the money to write the book and who would the subject of the book – as if their positions were interchangeable. However he justified his interest and motivation, he came back to this fact, *he was earning money from a death*, and it didn't feel good. Last night had cost him close to five hundred euro.

Rino was late. A bad sign. While Finn couldn't complain about the previous night, he couldn't say either that the basement visit had happened as a result of Rino's research. This had come out of the discussion – which was otherwise useless. Finn waited where they had agreed: Corso Umberto, beside the *farmacia* and opposite the Banco di Napoli. Or was it inside the *farmacia*?

Finn checked inside and found Rino waiting at the counter with a pack of disposable diapers in his hand and a queue of assorted women in front and behind. Rino poked his finger into the plastic wrap as he waited and left divots in the packet. The store, with its glass shelves and white boxes, seemed unnervingly antiseptic, at odds with the muddle outside. Behind the counter stood a woman, a girl, and an older man, each dressed in white clinician coats. When Rino reached the front of the queue he allowed the woman behind him to be served. When the girl became free, he again allowed another customer ahead of him, but when the man became free he stepped immediately up.

While the man said nothing about this, Finn thought the pharmacist had noticed that Rino wanted to be served by him.

Finn picked through the toothbrushes while he waited, and didn't become especially aware of any problem until he looked back at the counter and saw the pharmacist pointing at the door and heard him give Rino instructions to leave. Finn came closer to the counter, not quite sure if this was private business or something he needed to be involved in. Rino appeared to be holding his ground.

'You have a son,' he said, 'what if something like this were to happen to him? What would you do if someone was not telling the truth? What would you say to this man?'

The pharmacist, clearly addled, his face white with outrage, as if unused to being challenged. The man shook his head and asked Rino to leave. 'Go.'

'No.'

'Go.'

'No.' Rino stood firm, a little petulant but unmovable. 'I'm not going.' He pointed at the pack of diapers. 'I would like to buy these.'

The pharmacist picked up the diapers, looked over his glasses at the price, sharply rang it into the till and asked Rino for the money.

Rino laid the coins one at a time into a small dish. 'Imagine. You hold on to something for so long. Keep it inside. Is this healthy? Is this advisable? Imagine when something else comes to light, the trouble that this would cause.' Rino buzzed his fingers at his temples to indicate confusion. 'Imagine also the kind of father who would set such an example to his son? I have a son, and I wouldn't want to set such an example.'

The pharmacist pushed the coins back across the counter, took the diapers and placed them behind him. There would be no sale.

'You think you know what is good for my son, or for my family?' The pharmacist leaned forward his voice now low and threatening. 'If you return I will call the police.'

Rino stepped back, gave a small gesture, and lifted his arms lightly from his side as if this were of no account. The police, he seemed to indicate, would possibly also have these questions. Rino caught Finn's eye as he turned about, then remembered, suddenly, to pick up the money.

The two of them walked out onto the street. Rino, in no apparent hurry despite the pharmacist's threat, patted his pockets for a cigarette. The pharmacist looked after them as Finn closed the door and made a dismissive gesture to the women as if this were nothing. But the gesture, Finn thought, being too emphatic, and grumpy, seemed disingenuous – and the women, who might be expected to be curious, simply continued with their work as if this had happened before.

'This man,' he said, 'his name is Dr Arturo Lanzetti. The very same Dr Lanzetti that Marek Krawiec claims came with him to the hotel in Castellammare and gave treatment to one of the brothers. Dr Lanzetti says that this did not happen. Marek Krawiec also says that Dr Lanzetti told him about the content of the book, *The Kill*. Dr Lanzetti says that this did not happen, although he has read the book, he says that he read it after Marek Krawiec was taken into custody. He says he knew nothing about the room, and knew Krawiec only in passing as they lived in the same building.'

Finn looked up at the sign, a small outline of a neon cross. The store windows almost empty except for posters for eyewash in which a young woman looked to a blue sky, white letters furred with beams of light as if offering a religious experience.

'You think he's lying? Do you believe the story about the brothers?'

'I've no idea. We need to find another *farmacia*. Life will not be worth living if I forget this.'

Rino drove to Ercolano. He pointed out the volcano as they came out of the city and spoke about the earthquake, 'Nineteen eighty-seven. The city was hit. Many of the buildings were weakened and later condemned, but they weren't taken down. At the same time all of these factories were closed down, and there was a plan to build here – hotels, places to live, shops. But this never happened. Instead they made them so they could not be used. After they found the body the commune had the doors and windows closed so no one could get in.'

'This is it?'

'This is where they found the Second Man.'

He drove over a small crossroads and parked beside the building. When Finn locked the door, he said, 'Don't worry, there isn't anything to see here.'

Finn walked down the small alley, a slip-road to the shoreline. A wall of striated concrete on one side, the factory close on the other, so that path – barely broad enough for a car, became deep. A black railway bridge, and the grey shoreline beyond.

THE KILLS

A haze out to sea hid the horizon, hid the sun, so the sky and sea faded one to the other in a glassy bright plain. If they make a film, Finn thought, they should use these locations. The places where it happened. Finn had ambitions he'd yet to formulate properly. He walked along the shoreline, back and forth, stood on the stern grey blocks, smooth, massive and locked together: arms folded he looked back at the factory to imagine the event playing out – not as it might have happened, but as it might be filmed. A crew gathered in the road huddled ready because this would be taken in one long shot, the camera beside the door, a set of tracks for the camera down the alley to the shoreline: and there, the actors playing Krawiec and his accomplice arriving in the Citroën, parking. Krawiec giving instructions: an urgency to his gestures and movement. The Second Man unloads the large bags – unwieldy, tied at the top – and brings them to the shore, while Krawiec smokes with the car door open. Krawiec is the one to manage the body, cut up by this time and sectioned into manageable pieces which are also packed in plastic, blood slipping into the creases. The Second Man manages the sacks, which are full and lighter, and they rustle. Krawiec's packages are heavier, much smaller, and tape binds round them. The camera will follow Krawiec, because this detail is important. They will want to give themselves options, and the entire scene will need to be shot right from the start (the car arriving) twice, because there are two questions the film will need to answer: 1. Why did they kill, and 2. What happened to the body – and this scene will resolve that issue. They wouldn't need to specify the victim, well, not the first, because that would undermine the basic mystery. Everybody knows by now that nobody knows who this was, and there's no point in spoiling this with invention. Instead it would be more interesting to look further into Mr Rabbit and Mr Wolf, now these deserved inventing, fleshing out. These men should be made physical. OK, there was the whole absurdity of it, obviously, it's a crazy idea, but an appealing idea also, who doesn't like the idea of two men, tourists, who kill, and take their instructions from a pulp novel. The very randomness of it. They come and go, and no one is ever caught – it's morbidly satisfying, knowing you'll never know.

In the film, in this first version – Version Number One – Krawiec unloads all of the packages: these heavy little sawn-up pieces of Victim Number One. He lines them alongside the water, and here the filmmakers will need a calm day so there are no waves, just this dopey lapping, the water coming up and folding over, not even touching the bags, although the stones are wet and there are clouds of tiny black flies. And Krawiec, seen from behind, will crouch and open up the packets, slit them one by one, and dump out the contents – piece by piece until he is done, roll them into the water so that the water clouds with blood, until he closes the knife against his thigh. Trouble is, with this version, if they found the bags, you've got to believe they would have found the body.

In Version Number Two, Krawiec will arrive with a small dinghy of some kind. An inflatable. It could even be in its box, bought for the purpose. And this will need to be done carefully so it doesn't become stupid. Krawiec brings this craft down to the shoreline first, and maybe this isn't all one shot, because you're going to want to see him inflate this, and see those details, the nozzle holding the valve; Krawiec working up a sweat because this shouldn't be too easy. If this is shown to be an effort it's going to look more plausible. Once the boat is inflated, he's going to press on it with his foot. He's going to test it and make sure he's satisfied, maybe give it a few extra pumps. Only then is he going to unload the backseat of the small packages, and the Second Man is going to be standing at some distance tying his sacks together and making a job of it. Krawiec will load up the dinghy. Piece by piece. A hypnotic back and forth. Done, he'll tug the boat into the water, then, with his pocket knife he's going to give the dinghy a little nick, just a small – the smallest – puncture, then push it the final distance. He'll come back to the shore holding a rope that's tethered to the dinghy and it's going to take several attempts, and there's going to be some tension here, because if that boat deflates too much it's just not going to make it, because those gentle waves are pushing the boat back alongside the shore, not taking it out. Finally, Krawiec will have to wade, then shove hard, and out it goes, a little slow, a little dreamy. The small craft, obviously weighted down, is picked up by a current and taken out the whole length of the rope.

And maybe here you'll see the boat up close, the shoreline distant with Krawiec standing, rope in hand, the line leading from the boat all the way to the shore, and further to Krawiec's right the Second Man is on his knees still working on those larger bags, still busy with his knotting, and water begins to fill the craft, slowly pooling about the black bound packages, trickling in at first, then faster, so that half the dinghy folds under the waterline, half of it submerged, and the packages tip out, and then the whole thing, flaccid, just sinks, then sits softly under the water making bubbles with this blue line of rope going all the way to the shore. That sea reflecting like it's thick, like sugar syrup.

Back with Krawiec he tugs the dinghy to the shore, hand-over-hand, it doesn't look like much, a more or less empty black bladder that he hauls to the shore, water runs off the rope. Krawiec winds the rope about his arm, the way that fishermen coil lengths of rope. He folds up the dinghy. When he stands up they're almost done. There's no need to show what happens with the bags. Everyone knows this part of the story. He will kill the Second Man with one blow, a rock or a hammer. One strike. And it will mean nothing to him, this little piece of business. Or, alternatively he'll just shove him into the tank like it's an afterthought, and the man will hit his head as he tumbles. Either way, Krawiec will put little thought into it, but great energy. As the magistrate said, Krawiec is ordinary, he's not so special, but when he kills the violence comes with extraordinary force.

Finn took photographs from the shore, 360°, a whole revolution. He wanted to see inside the factory, to see the tank, but couldn't find an entrance. The windows and doors bricked up with some care, small ventilation blocks set up in a row, the holes too small to see through to anything. At first he couldn't find Rino, and didn't understand that the pebbles landing at his feet were dropped from the roof. When he looked up he saw Rino on the flat roof.

'Ready?'

He didn't want to be hurried, and even while he was paying Rino for his time, he didn't like to cause delay and had to think through if he wanted to get to the rooftop or not before they called in at the Rione Ini estate (although he had the feeling that Rino wasn't keen), and wondered if he would he regret not climbing up.

In preparation for Finn's visit, Rino had kept his eye on Niccolò Scafuti for a week but hadn't learned much: Niccolò Scafuti no longer worked, remained in the same apartment as before, but was seldom seen outdoors. Much of what he needed was brought to him, and the days when he was feted and celebrated by the Christian Democrats, the charities, the good people of Ercolano, had long since passed. Finn had a collection of photographs of dinners and presentations held in honour of the hero Niccolò Scafuti. All of this before the discovery of the clothes on the wasteland, before he was taken in and charged with murder – which had to be, as the magistrate acknowledged, the worst mistake made by the investigation. Finn wanted to speak with him, to straighten up the story.

They walked from the paint factory, followed the road beside a line of glasshouses up to the estate. Finn asked why Rino wasn't interested in this, he seemed reserved. Was he reading this right? And Rino said he doubted that Niccolò would want to speak, a good number of reporters had tried, they'd pestered him, and whether or not this was the reason he didn't appear to ever leave his apartment he didn't know. You'd have to figure what kind of trauma that would bring for someone normal, you know? Let alone some guy who has had a fistful of brain removed and half of his skull constructed out of steel.

'I wouldn't stay.' Rino plucked a piece of grass, trimmed it down to the stalk. 'I'd take myself somewhere new and start over. Once you've lost your family and your neighbours you have nothing.' What had happened to Scafuti was criminal, but it was done and there was no way to undo that fact. Rino pointed at the school where Rino's sister had volunteered one summer to help kids who hadn't passed their exams, who otherwise wouldn't move up a grade. 'Most of those kids have family who've spent some time in jail, or were otherwise in trouble, one way or another.' What made this ironic was that Niccolò Scafuti, once a hero, was now seen as some pervert who'd cut up a body, planted the evidence and 'discovered' it, to keep himself in the picture. And nothing backed up these ideas, even the stupid things he came up with, all by himself, about the notebook, about a star. His co-workers had made good money telling his story to the papers. 'Once it's in people's heads, there's nothing you can do. I feel sorry for him myself.'

Rino had a way of making Finn feel responsible. Finn couldn't figure out how he managed it and whether it was deliberate, something in his delivery, the way he spoke without expecting a response, or if it was something Finn felt anyhow but didn't yet understand. It didn't matter because, after less than one full day together, he was tired of the man's company.

Finn rang the number. Took a photo of the lobby door while he waited. Rang again. Buzzed another number to be let in. Photographed the side of the building, had Rino point out exactly which apartment Scafuti lived in (from the right: four along, one down), rang the buzzer, took another photo and then stood back in the street with his arms folded. The buildings, mirror copies of each other, had clothes and plants out on other balconies. Not shambolic and not quite messy, but disorganized, like the people who lived here didn't have much time to consider what was around them, or bother about their clothes being in their neighbours' view. A few people hung about, women at balconies, a small group of boys at the head of the wasteland who stopped to look for a moment and then continued with their game.

'We should go.' Rino encouraged Finn to leave. The two of them walked to the wasteland, as Finn wanted to see exactly where the clothes were discovered, because this at least needed to be fixed in his mind when he was writing. They lingered for a while. The scrubland was dry and tawny with long grasses bent over, paths worn through, some scattered empty water bottles, but not much of interest. He took some pictures, and took pictures of the apartments from the wasteland, but didn't think he'd use them. It didn't look like much, even with the side of the volcano in view behind the shoulder of the school buildings, broody and slightly improbable – a purple slope where there should be sky. He couldn't think of anywhere less prepossessing, only the presence of the mountain gave it any kind of dark mood.

Finn wanted to understand Scafuti. In many ways the man was key. Here you have someone who is celebrated in his community, who has this whole other life going on. Rino didn't follow. What other life? Niccolò Scafuti barely had his life together, two years ago he was just out of rehab for a head injury. Two years before that he was just an ordinary man running security up on the mountain. This man didn't have another life.

'So what about the cats?'

'What about them?'

'The cats he killed. He killed all those cats. Dumped them in the tank.'

'So he didn't like cats.'

'With a slingshot.'

'They were strays. Nobody missed them.'

'But you don't kill cats. That's not normal.'

Rino shrugged. 'Cats are cats.'

Finn didn't want to leave the question alone. 'But it isn't normal.'

'Who knows? They piss everywhere. They shit and breed. They need to be controlled.'

THE KILL

A figure stood out on Scafuti's balcony, leaning on the railing, but when they approached the figure slipped back inside, and no amount of ringing would draw him out.

On the return drive Finn asked questions about Rino's family, but Rino remained reserved and delivered answers as plain facts (My son is nine months old. Portici. All my life. She works for the commune and teaches adult literacy), as if he disapproved of what they were doing. Two weeks before while emailing these facts had come out easier, more conversational (My son keeps us awake, when he sleeps he sleeps for two hours, three sometimes, he has his mother's lungs. How he can cry!), but one week spent waiting outside Scafuti's apartment had soured him, and the visit revived this dislike.

Finn would rewrite the start of his book. It needed a statement, something to set it up, about how, years after, the crime still held purchase in the community: the magistrate who won't be named, a suspect who won't answer his door. He'd start the story properly with the cats. A man killing cats. He wouldn't start at the basement. This image would set Scafuti up as a creep, the villain, but he'd slowly recover the man's dignity, work against type, until, by the end, you would feel the injustice deeply. They'd have to make a film of it.

Finn called his sister, ran through some of the issues. The two-killer theory had its problems. First, how did Krawiec and the Second Man know each other? He just didn't see it. If it was all Krawiec's idea, how he would find another person and then get them involved. Krawiec's theory that there were two other people, the famous brother hypothesis, had its attractions and smoothed out all of the problems, but it just wasn't plausible and there wasn't any evidence to it. If there were two brothers, and if they were following the narrative from *The Kill*, then key elements were missing. This is a story about a man, a fascist, who won't accept his country's defeat and humiliation, who punishes the people living in his building, his palazzo, for collaborating with the Americans by making it look like they are murderers and cannibals, like their acceptance of the occupation is only skin deep; after starving for years, the army is seen as meat. The book is about revenge. It's about creating havoc.

Finn read out the opening of the book, translated it to English for his sister and couldn't be certain if she was or wasn't listening. 'I am not a cruel man. I'm not stupid or vicious. I'm not wicked. I am not an animal. You must not believe what you have read. There are many facts about me you do not know and would not easily guess: I am a sentimental man; I like to help when I can help. I prefer not to interfere in other people's business, and keep where possible to myself and trouble no one. I am a private man.'

Couldn't she see it? This was all about someone being provoked. Had Krawiec been provoked in some way? Was Krawiec following the narrative? 'I am a sentimental man.'

Other structural elements did not stand up, the room, the blood evidence, the organs, the teeth and tongue. The book was about the building. It's all about the palazzo.

And then the magistrate had said something interesting, something he probably should have picked up a long time ago. There were two versions of *The Kill*. There was the version which read as a crime novel, and then there was the earlier version, which had an introduction, which was marketed as a confession, a testimony. The publisher of the second edition had cut the introduction because they felt it didn't work with the main story.

Did she see the difference, he asked? Could she see how different this was?

He could tell she wasn't listening. Finn spoke to his sister about a killing, figured out details, gave her information because he couldn't otherwise talk to her. When she needed money, he asked for it from their father, because she didn't want them to know it was for her.

Finn curled up in bed, couldn't quite fit the frame, the bed slightly too short, so he either slept on his side with his feet curled (uncomfortable after a while), or he stuck his feet between the bars which meant that he couldn't turn over and had to wake in order to pull his feet out and then slide them back once he'd found a new position. It didn't work, this sleeping in shifts.

He finally lay diagonally across the bed, flat on his stomach, arms folded under his forehead, and legs out in the air, and woke twenty minutes later splayed out, superman. At one o'clock the air-conditioner began to squeak so he found his earplugs, which seemed, all things considered, a sensible solution. At midnight he was woken by a small tremble, a vibration – his phone, which he'd tucked under the pillow, as always.

Finn struggled to read the number and found the ID withheld. He answered with a more timid hello than he would have liked, and was surprised to find himself speaking with a woman.

'Where's Rino?' the woman demanded – as if midnight was an acceptable time to call a stranger and ask for someone's whereabouts.

Finn had to think before he understood what he was being asked for: Rino? 'Who is this?'

'This is his wife. Where is he? He's supposed to be home.' She sounded more irritated than worried, her voice an outright demand, as if he had some special knowledge, or was the cause, of Rino's delay.

He told the woman that he'd sent Rino home early, like, really early. He lowered the phone to cancel the call and then couldn't help from asking one last question.

'How did you get this number?'

After a hesitation the woman answered crisply. 'Rino gave it to me.'

Finn thought he could hear laughter in the background – something close to a donkey bray.

'He gave you this number?'

More braying laughter.

'But he has his own phone?'

'He isn't answering, *culo*. That's why I called you.'

Finn bridled at being called an asshole and at the hee-haw laughter behind this. 'Just don't call this number, all right. Never call this number again.'

As he hung up he could hear more hefty chuckles above the donkey-laugh which seemed to choke on itself, a laugh that was also a haughty gulp.

He should have turned the phone off. Right off. Instead he checked his messages and email, and felt that the glow from the small screen, blue and just bright enough to pick out the white sheet, the edge of the pillow, as if sensing and measuring the rising humidity, which now, thanks to the air-conditioner, closed in, a kind of seepage, the air quickly thickening. Finn lay on his stomach, felt sweat bristle in the small of his back and he thought again about the student and wondered if Krawiec had stayed in the room the whole time, watched him strung up, ankles to wrists, and taunted him, or left him alone at times. This information mattered, he wanted to know if the student was toyed with, tortured. He felt the dimensions of the room, could sense exactly where and how he was located, the distance of the walls and floor, the pitch and angle of his body. He could sense it all. The boy had suffered, and it mattered that no one properly knew how much, and that no one knew his name.

The second call came forty minutes after the first. The number, again, withheld.

'If that whoreson isn't home in five minutes you can tell him not to come home at all. You tell him—' and this time the woman's voice tumbled into laughter and she couldn't quite complete her sentence. Once again a donkey-like laugh buckled through from the background like this whole thing was a dare. He hadn't heard Rino laugh. She hung up, then called back immediately.

'I think he's been kidnapped.' Again, that laugh, a little more distant but a little more explosive.

'I'm tracing the call,' Finn lied. 'It just takes a second but I can do it. There. I've got it. I'm passing this on to the police.'

'*Culo*, you'll do no such thing.' The voice sounded angry now, she hung up herself.

The phone rang again. Stopped. Then rang again. Nearly two o'clock.

He resisted answering, allowed the call to go to message, managed not to check the message, until – with the phone under the pillow, his arms supporting his head he realized he wouldn't be able to sleep.

The message started with a string of expletives: *culo, pezzo di merda, frocio, succhiatore, pompinaio, leccacazzi, affanculo.* 'You come here and you think you know who we are.'

The phone rang regularly after this at intervals which cut shorter over the hour. Every fifteen minutes, every ten, every five. Finn switched off the ring, turned off the vibrate, but the small screen still lit up each time a call came through and each time a message was stored, and he fought against the urge to check the messages. Finally, when he decided to switch it off he was surprised to see that the calls had come from Rino's phone.

He checked the messages and heard Rino, at first apologetic: 'I'm in a situation,' he said. His voice a little bashful, hushed, and a noise about him, which Finn identified after replaying the message, as a number of men quietly pushing over some discussion. 'I need money. Badly. I can pay you back.'

The second and third calls reiterated the demand with a little more emphasis. 'Pick up. Answer. Come on. I know you're there.' Finn couldn't tell if this was frustration at receiving no answer or desperation because he really was in trouble.

The phone rang in his hand. Finn didn't intend to answer but his thumb hit the keyboard.

'Hey, hey. Are you there?' Rino sounded indignant. 'I need a little help. It isn't much, I can pay you back.'

Finn didn't respond, and waited for some explanation.

'I need seven hundred euro. I swear I can pay you back as soon as the banks open.'

The phone crackled and another voice cut in gruffly and demanding, 'Just get the money. Do exactly as he tells you.'

Then Rino – 'I need the money tonight. I know you can do this.'

The call cut off and Finn switched on the bedside light and sat upright and blinked, really unsure what was going on.

Minutes later the phone beeped. An SMS, again from an unmarked number, with the simple instruction that Finn should walk to the piazza Nicola Amore, right where Corso Umberto crosses via Duomo, and wait. *Portico, Café Flavia, 20 minutes. €800.*

He arranged his clothes ready to dress, picked the socks out of his trainers, half-hurrying, then paused because he was working up a sweat and something about this whole thing just didn't convince him. He sat on the bed, looked about the room for his clothes, and wondered what he was doing. A demand for money for no reason, coming in the middle of the night: why would he answer this? Rino didn't sound drunk and didn't sound particularly under pressure, and Finn had paid him, transferred a good deal more than this already, in advance. He had no obligation to go out.

€1,000. A new demand.

And how safe would this be? Walking the streets with a thousand euro.

Ten minutes later another message. *You'd better be on your way.* A definite threat.

Minutes after: *Room 32, Hotel Grimaldi. Your light is on.* His hotel, his room.

Then finally: *Bring €2,000. Mr Rabbit & Mr Wolf.*

Finn re-dressed, tucked his shirt into his pants. Two thousand euro? Rino wasn't worth two thousand euro. One, maybe, at a stretch.

But two thousand? Not a chance. A meeting with Mr Rabbit and Mr Wolf would be worth much more than two thousand.

He had the money, as it happened. This was all of his money for the month. It troubled him more that these people knew his hotel room, and, more likely than not, this would make him a target. If he didn't go to the café they would come to the hotel. If he did go to cafe this could all be resolved.

He wrapped the notes in a sock and brought it with him to the piazza. Mr Rabbit and Mr Wolf? The mention of these men, he had to admit, was alarming and deeply unexpected, and sent the whole night off kilter. Finn waited in the portico outside the Café Flavia, the metal blinds down, no lights in any windows along the curved arcade. The road ran in a circle about the piazza and a centre island barricaded by temporary plywood barriers and a sign saying 'Metro'. Above the hoardings some indication of roadworks, or digging: the sketched tops of cranes and heavy equipment. No traffic and no people. Finn stood under one of the arches, in view, in case anyone was watching, the money in the sock in his fist, in his pocket.

He heard the scooter come down the corso – a feeble wavering zip. When it came about the piazza the scooter continued, made an entire circuit, and when it returned to view a second time the man slowed down and crawled hesitantly toward him. A skinny man in shorts, very tight red shorts, with a striped T-shirt, a white helmet, sunglasses, a ratty beard, set his feet either side of the scooter to hold it up. Red shorts and white shoes. No socks. Sunglasses at two thirty-five in the morning. The man whistled through his teeth at Finn and signalled him forward.

'You. Money.'

'No.'

'Money.'

'No.'

'Money. Now.'

'No.'

The man appeared to speak little English, and Finn, although he spoke Italian very well, had no inclination to help him. The man set his hands on his thighs, as if Finn was being entirely unreasonable.

'Money!' he insisted.

'Rino,' Finn replied. 'Mr Rabbit. Mr Wolf.'

The man lifted one foot to the scooter's running board then started up the motor. Finn watched him slowly ride away and disappear around the corner. Something laughable about a tall man on such a small vehicle making such a stupid noise.

He couldn't hear the motor run up the corso, so he followed the arcade round and saw for himself, the man on the scooter stopped at the side of the street speaking into a mobile. Finn crept close enough to hear pieces of the discussion.

'I asked him. I said. I told him to give me the money. That's what I said. I think he wants . . . I didn't ask. OK, say that again,' a pause, 'again. OK. No. OK. One more time.' The man cancelled the call, and stood up to wedge the phone into his pocket.

Finn approached him and asked in Italian what he thought he was doing.

'Your friend. They will slit his throat. You have the money?'

'I want to see him.'

'You can't see him.'

'You can't have the money.'

'Give me the money and tomorrow you will see your friend.'

'He isn't my friend.'

Finn started to walk away. The man started up his bike. He followed Finn with some difficulty, the front wheel weaving awkwardly, the pace being too slow to keep the scooter steady.

'Why don't you give me the money? They will slit his throat. It will be your fault. You will be to blame.' Now the man was sulking.

Finn gestured that he could care less. Before him, he saw a sign for the Questura. 'Call your friends and tell them I want to see Rino, or they won't get the money.' He pointed at the sign. 'Do it before I get to the police station.'

The man stopped his bike, and called OK, OK, to get Finn to stop. He stood up to take his phone out of his pocket, spat on the pavement, sat down heavily and cursed under his breath as he made the call. '*Ciao, ciao*. Yeah. No. He wants to see him. I have . . . I did . . . I said that . . .' He gestured at Finn. 'He wants to see him now. OK.' He handed the phone to Finn. 'They want to talk.'

Finn dug his hands into his pockets.

'Take the phone.'

'No.'

'Take it. They want to speak with you.'

'I want to see Rino first.'

'Take it, *culo*. Take the fucking phone.'

'If I take the phone I'll smash it.'

The man recoiled, and began speaking very quickly into his phone. In a hurry he started up the scooter, and with phone pinched in his hand he swung back into the street and sped off. Finn watched him disappear, then continued walking. The thin whine died away, but didn't disappear completely. He was almost at the doors to the Questura when he realized that the sound was getting louder.

The man rode on the sidewalk and came right at him, head down, and fast. Finn, now past the police station, had reached a long wall and could find nowhere to step into. He began to run, too slow and too late.

Struck by a punch in his side he hit the wall and rolled to the pavement. Unsure exactly what the mechanics of the accident were he fumbled to his feet. The man had driven up and shoved him, hard enough to knock him down, and Finn winced, automatic, just folded over, expecting something else. Instead the man turned his bike around and returned. He used the scooter to block Finn against the wall, all of this within paces of the Questura.

'Give me the money.'

'I don't have it.'

The rider pointed to Finn's pocket.

'The money is in your pocket.'

Finn reluctantly took the sock out of his pocket and handed it to the man.

'You come to the Fazzini. The Bar Fazzini. Your friend will be there. One hour.'

Finn sat down in the street. The scooter zipped up the sidewalk, raced toward piazza del Municipio with a throttled croak sawing up the sides of the boulevard. Denying that he had the money and then handing it over was, well, as stupid as it gets. The corso opened up at the piazza, broadened into a neon-tinted night. Lights on the heights at Castel St Elmo. They'd found a boat in the piazza, hadn't he heard this somewhere, or maybe lots of boats, some entire Greek fleet imprinted in the mud under the piazza, right smack in the centre of town. You couldn't lift a paving slab without history leering back at you insisting your insignificance. Winded, Finn tried to catch his breath.

*

Finn decided to return to the hotel, but wanted first to check himself. He could have been stabbed. You heard about this happening all the time: people in shock who don't know that they've lost an arm, a kidney, half of their spine ripped out, who walked up the street like la-di-dah, to collapse from blood-loss, shock, inattention. Finn found a side alley behind the Questura and stripped down to his boxers and checked himself, and saw in the dull yellow light only a slight graze on his elbow, a round imprint on his right hip that would surely blossom to a bruise. The man had shoved him, knocked him down – the whole thing was immature, barely man-to-man. There wasn't any blood, and once he'd reassured himself that he hadn't been stabbed, he checked his body for broken bones. Pressure? Wasn't that it? You check for pressure points? See what aches or hurts, or is just outright unbearable.

Everything checked out, nothing really wrong here (but how close was that?), no blood loss, punctured organs, broken bones. But seriously – how stupid was that? Why had he even answered the phone? His watch had hit the wall and it grieved him to see the face cracked, but nothing else was damaged.

He walked quickly, limping at first, one side seeming a little larger, the bump to his hip limiting his stride, and elbow aching as a hint of how serious this could have been. He became angry as he walked and couldn't console himself with the idea that this was all experience, all useful, all material for the book. The kind of story he could tell in an interview. *Oh the kidnapping. Yeah. Well, Naples – beautiful by the way – nice place, but troubled, very complicated . . . let me tell you . . .*

Finn took via Umberto back to via Duomo, to via Capasso. He walked fast to walk out the ache.

The Fazzini, as before, bright and busy, with a younger noisier crowd. The bar ran along the back wall, a broad wood counter stacked with glasses, and blocked with people, quite a crowd. But no Rino. No thugs. No kidnappers. No hit-and-run scooter-rider.

He half-ran, half-hopped back to the hotel.

Lights on in the lobby, the door unlocked (at three in the morning) and no night security: bad signs. Unwilling to wait for the elevator he hobbled up the stairs, four floors, to find the door to his room open, *as he expected*, the lights on, the room in disarray looking something like a film set with the bed pulled away from the wall, the cupboard open, his clothes thrown out of the drawers and scattered, paper torn from the blank notebooks littered the bed and the floor. Everything gone.

Someone must have given them a list. Just written out exactly where he'd hidden his laptop. His portable hard-drive. His sister's camera. His phone. The two USB sticks. His remaining traveller's cheques. And not one, but every single notebook from the trip. Even his copy of *The Kill*.

This was no simple theft, but a complete strategic wipeout – erasing every piece of research he'd collected on the murders. In taking the computers and the notebooks they'd stolen every draft and every scrap of information he'd collected, along with the correspondence. Some of this stuff he couldn't begin to consider replacing. Finn buckled over at the doorway. An instant stab of grief at all the detail and experience now lost to him: all of his careful and particular notes that could not now be recreated. He'd sat with Lemi Krawiec for six long hours while the man repeated endlessly that his brother was innocent, and how he didn't know the facts because he didn't need the facts. *He was innocent.* All the while Finn had taken notes, he'd written about the kind of airlessness trapped in that room, the space between these protestations, the protestations themselves and how by their insistence they held a kind of dogma, that the more times they were repeated the more it could be believed, and the more likely it was that this would be true: until nothing else could be considered except that single fact: *Marek Krawiec is innocent*. And this was gone. The precise description of the decor along a mantelpiece, Krawiec's mother's house, the petiteness of it, sullen and ordinary, of Lvov at night, how capsule-like the city seemed, of the people seated facing the windows at the respite home in Lvov, the women on buses, the silent trains and trams. Everything lost: the airport and how coming into it the aircraft pitched through a layer of fog – fog so you knew you were in the heart of Eastern Europe, right on the edge of another period entirely – how this worked as an image of what he would and would not find – *coming through fog*. OK, not great, but apt. The petrochemical works, the roadways, the fields and fields shaved of produce, and the intensity of it all, that one man could come from this flat monochrome to a city so bumpy and opposite and butcher two people. Just how, exactly, is such a notion seeded in someone, so that it becomes essential to act on? He'd formed some sense of Krawiec – not so much from his brother, but from experiencing the same spaces – of how casually cruel the man would become, of how the landscape predicted this, made it so. He was close to understanding how such a crime comes out of a limited number of options, so that it seems both possible and inevitable, something to do; he understood a connection between flat landscapes and wet fields and industrial parks and chemical plants and how an impulse drives an idea to become an inevitable action. He'd come that close to understanding.

On the door handle, a last touch from the thief or thieves: the housekeeping sign saying '*Thank You For Your Stay: Gratuities.*'

He checked the dumpsters outside the hotel, went through the trash, dawn now and his side beginning to ache, and found nothing. The hope, at least, that the notebooks would be scattered somewhere because they were of no earthly use to anyone else. As he bent over the dumpster, moved cardboard around, he remembered a description in one of the newspapers about the discovery of the clothes in Ercolano – and didn't like the idea that there could be more in the dumpster than trash or stolen goods.

WEDNESDAY

He packed his rucksack in the morning. Without his papers and note-books and equipment he didn't have enough to fill the soft hold-all. He hadn't slept, and through the night plans were made and disassem-bled, ideas on how he would return home because he had less than nothing, and how he'd have to undo the publishing deal because he didn't have the material any more, or even the heart to start over. He hadn't slept, and he had to go back to the Questura, chase up his report, because the police who'd come had told him there wasn't any-thing to do until the morning because this crime didn't register to them as being something worthy of any kind of attention. He couldn't even call Rino because all of his numbers were on his phone, his email was on his laptop, and nowhere would yet be open.

After the police, Finn checked in his bag at the Stazione Central. His head rang with humiliation; they'd laughed at him, asked him to describe with particular precision exactly where he'd hidden his valu-ables. *So you hid the money on top of the what? Exactly where?* He couldn't expect any sympathy back home, because this whole thing, he had to admit, was kind of shameful. He'd set himself up: bragged about his summer, his contract, rubbed it hard into other people's faces, and in one night he'd managed to wreck it all. The police had contacted Rino, who said he had no idea about any kidnapping, assault, or rob-bery. Last night was the same as any other, he ate at about eight o'clock, watched TV, argued with his wife, and was incredulous, as was his wife, about this entire idea, and Finn understood that words were said between the police and Rino that undermined him, although he did not know exactly what.

Finn stood in the concourse and looked up at the grey boards flick-ering city names and routes above him. Passengers waited on the platforms, some smoking, most sitting, pressed down by the heat, mopping their foreheads and necks as if expressing regret. It was

716

stupid, foolish to trust Rino, to have paid money to the man. A mistake he swore he wouldn't make again. It was hard to estimate the amount he'd lost, all in all. Now he had twenty euro, just enough to find a place to email his parents and explain the whole stupid episode in some kind of shorthand they would understand. How much would he need to return home, end the summer in Massachusetts? How much would that humiliation cost? He wouldn't ask his parents, he'd ask his sister. Carolyn would lend him money, and he'd pay her back, as long as she swore to keep this to herself.

What to do? Tired and too sickened to eat, he walked through the platform, and found a bookstore. Feltrinelli. And there, facing the door, a small display of *The Kill*, a new Italian translation with the introduction restored, as per the '73 Editiones Mandatore original. The cover: a blood-spattered picture of an Italian palazzo. Finn stood in front of the display completely forlorn. Here it was, a last piece of mockery to rub home his failure. Two days in Naples and he was through. He picked up a copy and walked out of the store without making any effort to disguise the book.

He sat for an hour on the concourse, faced the bookstore entrance, and read the introduction in one sitting.

Finn called his sister collect, could hear her laughing as she accepted the charges – *This is going to be good, bro.* He told her quickly about the theft, about the night with Rino and some skinny thug on a scooter, and how, everything done, Rino denied the whole thing.

Carolyn laughed. Couldn't help herself. Thought this was funny, better than expected. But he was obviously OK, OK? because they were talking. So he's been stung right? This is what it was. A sting. This Rino had orchestrated the whole thing. Obviously.

Finn couldn't see the logic.

'Where did you find him?'

'Online. The university.'

'And you know that he goes to the university? You've seen him there, met his friends, spoken with his professors?'

'I've spent one day with him. His email address is through the university.' And then he remembered, it wasn't. Rino had given an excuse, *The university email is sometimes inaccessible. The server is slow and often fails. Use this address.*

'So he could be a student, but he could also not be a student. Doesn't really matter.'

'They kidnapped him. Someone kidnapped him and threatened to slit his throat.'

'Someone *said* that they'd kidnapped him. Big difference. Do you know anything about him?'

Finn struggled for ideas, of course he knew things about Rino, they had spoken for two months, the man had completed research for him, sent photographs, sat outside the estate at Rione Ini for an entire week and watched Scafuti's apartment. He knew all of the sites and all of the places relevant to the murders.

'Sounds like he just got sick of you.'

'Thanks.'

'Seriously. You can be tiresome. Anyway, it's not like anything bad has happened. You just got played.'

Finn didn't like the term and wouldn't answer.

'So why have you called? Are you really broke? Have you called me to sulk? It's just money. It's just stuff, right? Money and some computers, which were probably holding you back. You've bruised your ass, that's it. I wish my lessons came so easy. There isn't anything permanent. There isn't anything to really worry about. You're OK, and you have yourself a story.'

'I'm OK? I've lost all of my work. All of my equipment.'

'You're fine. It's just some constraint someone's given you. They've taken all of your toys. You just have to work with that. I love you, Finn, but you're a pain in the ass, and someone has played you. Which, you know, you kind of earned. Now you have to work with that. I'll get you money, but you can't come back. You just can't.'

Finn spent the day walking. He tucked *The Kill* into his back pocket and took the *funiculare* to Vomero, roamed through the grounds of the Villa Floridiana, then followed the roads along the steep scalloped flanks zigzagging down via Falcone, Francesco, Tasso, to Corso Emanuele – the bay, sharp silvers and sparkling blues, to his left then his right – all the time feeling the pressure of the book squeezed into his pocket. As the late morning sank into a placid afternoon he slowed his pace and realized that he'd stamped about the city without looking at what was around him. Coming down to the *lungomare* he found a place to sit on the seawall and watched joggers and couples pass by. The idea of coming to Naples wasn't just to write the book, but to gain experience of the city, to prise under its surface and become, chameleon-like, part of the situation, someone tapped into the heat and the bustle, open, as only an outsider can be. How stupid was he? He'd come to Naples one time to test the water, and was startled on a walk to Capodimonte by his first view of the city where he couldn't believe the sight of one unbroken mass of housing, so busy and detailed, so hectic and impenetrably thick, carpeting the hills and the swoop of the plain all the way to the volcano and further to the distant mountains, and he became certain that here among this fractured chaos something would speak to him. Now he had to admit that he'd penetrated nothing.

He pulled the book from his pocket. It wasn't only the city he'd misread, he'd also been misled by the book. Without the introduction *The Kill* was little more than a story about a man who manufactures a crime scene with body parts stolen from a hospital so his neighbours are accused of murder and cannibalism, a strange story, bloody and blunt. But with the introduction it became a story of someone lost in a defeated city, whose actions were prompted by the occupation, a hatred of the occupiers, and a deeper hatred of people he saw as collaborators: his actions, in this context, were justifiably provoked. An entirely different story.

Finn returned to the station feeling less and less happy as he came up the corso. He had to walk by the Questura just to see in daylight the place where he was knocked down, and he began to wonder now how much it would cost him to stay in Europe for the rest of the summer. Six thousand euro? Would that see him clear for the month? He came up via Capasso, and as soon as he caught sight of the palazzo he decided to stay. Maybe losing everything wasn't actually so bad? Carolyn had a point. He could strip everything down to pen and paper. He took a coffee in the café opposite the palazzo. Looked to the shops, the wedding boutique, the *alimentari* with Salvatore and his brother Massimiliano, the doorway with that weird imp of a woman, and thought the story here wasn't the killing, he had this wrong, right from the start he'd had it wrong, the story wasn't even the city, much like *The Kill* the story here was about the palazzo, about what was happening immediately around the crime.

*

By the evening he'd received the money wired by his sister and rented a room opposite the palazzo on via Capasso – procedures, both, which he expected to be much more laboured. Finn paid for one week and assured the landlord that payment for the month would come in two days, and found him not only amenable but sympathetic. By the time Finn returned to his room sweating and laden with supplies (six-packs of sparkling water, beer, long-life milk, biscuits, and chocolate), his head was busy with new plans.

His room faced the palazzo, and if he stood at his window he could see a broad wine-red wall with regular, deep-set, shuttered windows, on the lower floors the small Juliet balconies, the rooms inside black and unknowable. He divided the view into quadrants to guess occupant by occupant who might have lived there for more than a year (most, he assumed). At street level he could see the entrance, the vast black doors, the tops of heads, the fanned black cobbles of the street. Tucked beside the door a wrapped spray of flowers, dirty and bruised, and behind them other flowers, what might be a candle stub, and beside them a small upturned crate with a cushion.

The landlord came to ask if he was settled, and Finn looked about the room and realized that he was settled, and that, with little more than a writing desk, a handful of pens, some paper, he had everything he needed. He wouldn't dwell on last night, because most things are replaceable, right? Everything depended on him, on what he wanted to achieve.

The landlord lingered and Finn realized he wasn't in any hurry to start his work. Tonight, tomorrow. He could write any time, but the opportunity for a discussion would not always be available. So he offered the man a beer and invited him to sit at the window overlooking via Capasso, and gave himself the one constraint – he wouldn't talk, he'd leave it to the landlord.

Window by window the landlord described the occupants of the building, their occupations first, then their foibles: pharmacist, speech therapist, accountant, the two brothers who ran the *alimentari*, a lawyer, at the door the supervisor, in the street the magistrate's driver who seemed to be there at all hours. Outside the Fazzini there would be prostitutes, and while you can't see the bar, you can see the women, loitering among the scooters, talking, loud, calling one to the other.

'The two Frenchmen, the brothers – not Salvatore, not Massimiliano.' The man pointed at the palazzo with his beer, he'd seen them himself. Only one time, but he'd seen them, they weren't fiction. Few people believed that Krawiec was guilty, except the police. 'There isn't much,' the man admitted, 'that happens here that doesn't get noticed.'

Finn asked him to be clear. 'You saw them?'

'I saw the brothers. Plenty of people saw them. They came at night, they never stayed long. Many people saw them, except the driver.' The man nodded down to the street. 'He's there most days, but he says he never saw them. It might be a question of keeping his job.'

Finn took a long look and realized it would be hard for anything to happen here, night or day, without someone seeing or hearing. A figure in the palazzo, faced into the room unaware that he could be seen, practised voice exercises: 'peh-peh-peh-peh'.

As soon as he was alone he set the table in front of the window. He tore pages from the notepad and labelled the days: A, B, C, D . . . wrote a list of the occupants as he could remember them: the doctor, the supervisor, then added the participants: Marek Krawiec and his wife/g-friend, the Second Man, the American Student, Mizuki Katsura, Niccolò Scafuti. Then a list of places: Ercolano, field and paint-factory. Via Capasso. The Language School. The Circumvesuviana station.

MONDAY

Finn called Carolyn and told her he was staying, not just for the summer, but for as long as it took, which might mean deferring his final year. *It's different this time*, he explained. He was considering Krawiec's story, and taking it seriously; no one had bothered to do this. For Finn this meant going right back to the root, which wasn't, as you'd expect, the Spanish novel. He asked his sister if she knew how he'd first heard about the killing. Not the novel, but the *actual killing*? It happened through a chance meeting, in a hostel in Portland, Oregon, on a mid-term break, and in one long evening, after they'd exhausted the usual conversations about the weirdness of campgrounds, fears of bears and deer-ticks, the hassle of travelling by Greyhound, he was told a story by someone who'd spent the previous summer in Italy. Naples, Italy. This man – there's no point even trying to remember his name – said he'd sat opposite two women on a train, and one of them had started talking about how she was the only witness in a murder case. There wasn't much to it. She'd stepped off the train to see a boy at the station with two bags – a shoulder-bag and a duffel bag. Key to this was the fact that he was wearing a green T-shirt with the design of a star set in a circle on his back. There wasn't anything else to it. She saw this boy at the station. Nothing more.

Then one day, on the train again, with everyone reading the newspaper with a picture of the dark T-shirt with the star design, she'd caught a headline saying that the person who was wearing the clothes had, more likely than not, been killed.

It took her a while to figure out what to do, but eventually, she decided to have a word with the police.

Next time she was in town she went to the Questura, and she spoke with the people at the front desk and was immediately taken to the top man. She told him what she knew, and he asked her to describe the clothes, and then he took her to a room where he showed her the actual clothes. At first she thought they couldn't possibly be the same.

They didn't even look like clothes. The T-shirt was cut, stained, so wasn't even the same colour. The shorts were rust-coloured, this weird brown, and she realized that this was blood. Except for the blood, the stains, the cuts, the clothes were exactly the same. She was positive. The only thing was, she couldn't exactly remember what the boy looked like because it wasn't like she'd really noticed him, she'd just walked past him. And this is where the police did something really smart. This investigator had the man who did the photo-fit pictures walk her through one of the offices and ask her to look at the men in the office. As they walked he asked her if the youth she'd seen looked anything like this man, or that man. And the woman, who's really uncertain, started to give answers like: he wasn't so tall, his hair was shorter, his nose was this way or that way, and this gave the photo-fit guy a really good idea of what they were looking for. Clever, no?

At the end, once she was done, they made up a picture of this guy composed from different faces, and with a little work they managed to figure out exactly what he looked like – not just his face, but they managed to get a good idea about his height and weight, just from walking through the offices and her answering questions. I mean, that's really something. That's clever.

Finn told his sister what he was writing, in great detail: three thousand words on Saturday, seven thousand words on Sunday, and today, a day of revision – and then a description of the content. He read passages to her, but nothing too involved. His desk overlooked the palazzo entrance, the doors were right in his eye-line, he could look sideways from his paper and see it, and had quickly learned about the habits of those who lived inside and those who visited. It wasn't unusual for people to come to the entrance and just stand there. People came all the time to loiter in front of the doors, and it was hard to tell exactly what they were doing. Some took photos. But a good number just gawped in a way that could be boredom or grief and left flowers, candles, notes and tokens, and while the supervisor cleaned everything away almost immediately, she was too superstitious to remove the candles and tokens, and they become dustier and greyer by the day. It's the kind of thing that causes more pain over time, he said. Sometimes the Italian sense of melodrama took over: on Saturday three black sedans pulled up just short of the entrance, highly polished and dressed with fine strings of white flowers, and in the middle car sat the bride, who would be married, he guessed, within the hour. The doors either side of the bride were open and a woman attended to her, arranged and fussed over her dress. Beside the car, smoking, the bride's father in a new suit, visibly more anxious than his daughter. The girl's mouth was drawn into a pout and what details Finn couldn't see he imagined: the pearlescent lipstick, the nails impossibly long and polished the same colour as her lips, her black hair carried back in long ringlets and covered with a mass of toile, delicately edged with petals that needed to be plucked away from her face. The girl's face was undeniably round, he could see this, hamster-like sulking jowls, and when she talked she tended to set her mouth in a broody scowl, her neck and arms also were plump, child-like – but when she smiled she became exceptionally pretty, in a girlish way that made Finn suddenly sentimental. It was lucky, he thought, to see a bride among all this bustle, poised before her wedding, it improved his mood to see her in her last independent moment, cosseted and fussed. But it wasn't an accidental pause. The bride's father threw away his cigarette, took the bouquet from behind the bride and laid it at the foot of the entrance. No prayers, no pause, which surprised Finn. The bouquet was placed with care, leant in the corner so that it would not get kicked and would not be in the way, another man handed him a football shirt, Napoli blue, with Maradona's number, No. 10, which the man folded, number showing, and laid beside the flowers. Once the man had set the flowers and shirt in place he returned to the car and settled without a word beside his daughter, and within a moment the three cars continued slowly down the hill toward the bay.

The brother of the bride, Finn thought. It had to be someone close who'd disappeared – and for this boy, as for many others, there was one day when he needed to be accounted for, included in some way in the family's continuing life.

Carolyn repeated, *That's sad. So sad.* He called her every time he saw someone paused in front of the doors. One man, old, knelt for an hour on the cobbles. *Sis, sis. Listen to this.*

Finn took his lunch at the *alimentari*, he sat with Salvatore and caught up on the news. In the evening he began to translate the start of *The Kill*, as it set a context for his book. What I'm writing isn't about the crime so much, he explained, but the people in the palazzo. What he didn't know he invented, and began to find a kind of veracity to this invention.

*

THE KILL

Finn didn't tell his sister about the emails he'd received. The first came the day after an interview in the *Corriere* in which Finn requested new information on the killings. Information he promised to treat with discretion. I'm not the police, he'd said. I write. The email came from a commercial account: *If you want to know what happened*, it read, *we'll be happy to show you.*

More messages from other fake accounts. In each email the same message.

If you want to know.

This also, although he could not put his finger on it, appeared to be another echo. Another book, another film, a way of saying – if this was serious – that an idea once seeded has to yield fruit.

We will be happy to show you.

Future tense. Perfect.

The Kill

Sections previously not published in English

(page 1) 'First. I am not a cruel man. I am not stupid or vicious. You must not believe what you have read. There are many facts which you do not know and would not easily guess: I am a sentimental man, I help when I can help. I keep to myself and trouble no one. I am a private man, and perhaps this is a failing. In sum, I am no different than any other, excepting the reports in newspapers and those written by hired experts in which I am described as a maniac who does not have the temperament to stop or to quell an idea which could otherwise be expressed in violence: whatever boundary prevents you from undertaking an experience is no boundary to me. The accusation stands: that I have murdered my brother.

I do not intend to argue or rehearse my defence. Understand, I have no desire to lie – it is in my interest to lay everything out clearly and honestly, and this is my intention. Even so, the task is not easy as I have been confined for a considerable time and questioned on so many occasions that the most basic facts now seem either to be confused or to indicate some grossly wicked intention – so that I no longer know the truth myself, although I wish, sincerely, to tell the truth. Doctors assigned by the court regularly put questions to me, and these questions – which I am required to answer yes or no – imply readings and meanings beyond the range of a simple answer.'

(page 4) '. . . When asked if I have committed violence, I must answer 'yes', as there are many forms of violence which are casually enacted, day to day. Is it violence to deny food to a person? *Yes.* Is it violence to withhold employment? *Yes.* Violence to portion charity to one person and not another? *Yes.* Is it violence to display your wealth, or at the very least does the display of wealth justify violence? *Yes.* Is it violence to hold a conflicting opinion or position on any given subject? *Yes.* Is it

726

wrong to set yourself above others to take advantage of them? *Yes*. Is it not also wrong to set yourself lower, in such a position that others must take advantage of you? *Yes. Yes*. Ask yourself: if you are weak, why have you not yet been taken?'

(page 5) 'In examining my past experts have found and reported in depth and detail the root causes of my disturbance. If you believe what you have read there will be no convincing you otherwise, and you might ask instead what else has this man achieved? *What other crimes are we unaware of?*

Let me explain myself.'

(page 5 cont.) 'Much of this is nothing, half-remembered (rooms roughly laid out, tables and fireplaces; an afternoon sky edged by pine trees and rooftops. Certain smells which draw images of the city: a skinny dog running the length of a street; a doorstep opening to a courtyard with water dripping on flagstones from wet clothes). There is nothing specific or entire until I am six years old, and even this, I suspect, is borrowed from a newsreel, a history I have mistaken for my own. Although I have a full sense of the occasion I can't claim it is authentic.'

'(. . .) what could be a carnival? Certainly, a celebration. A parade? A boulevard busy with people nudged shoulder-to-shoulder, immobile for a moment, expectant but sombre. A city canyon, the windows and doorways along a route marked with shoddy home-made bunting full on every floor: women, only women, leaning out, waiting, heads turned to the city gate. There are people along the rooftops also – still, poised, silent. These people are silent because they are defeated, and they have come out of cellars and holes and shelters which were intended only to be temporary but have become their homes. And from these hovels they have watched their neighbours and their families die, and many strangers also. Above anything else they are exhausted. Neither do they look like women: they have shaved their hair to rid themselves of lice, they have haggard faces and colourless skin, they wear unbecoming clothes and have long ago shed any kind of vanity in how they present themselves. They are nocturnal, bloodless and famished. This manly crowd is silent, there is no gossip or chit-chat, none of them are bearing a child (although this will shortly change), all softness has been scraped from them, scoured by days spent underground, and nights spent foraging. But still, they know to present themselves when the occasion requires. And then a sudden eruption, a cascade of paper, white and yellow, papers ripped from ration books, passes, identification papers, contracts with the living and the dead, and memberships of now, or soon to be, illegal organizations, all torn to tiny pieces and flung so that the air flickers. Among this paper snow fall petals and flowers – stemmed flowers in what might be my first memory of real flowers – and while I couldn't have seen them before, I knew exactly what they were, and didn't wonder where these would have come from, because this is the end of a war, and where would these flowers have grown? How could we have flowers but not food? With this, just as sudden, another burst, a mighty shout, unified, a roar of loving cheers, arms raised, hands waving and hands clasped, frantic and happy. Children, girls, are heaved to shoulders, held high. I remember being held aloft and seeing only heads, arms, upturned and expectant faces, many in tears, and there, at long last, making slow progress, the first in an interminable line of green-grey military vehicles, the jeeps the tanks the trucks, being struck with flowers and paper. I remember the men on these vehicles, and how they arrived unsmiling, jolting, unimpressed, sober men, statuesque and unmoved, bruised by war, who kicked the flowers from their vehicles, swept the paper away, looked on us, half-starved, with disgust. I remember the physique of these men, how they seemed bigger, broader – a different species – biggest among them, their fat and round commanders. The faces of these generals set with distaste. We welcomed you, we offered you open arms – the soldiers who'd fought in the marshes, the beaches, and lately to our disaster the mountain crests – the men who starved us (our memory is not so short), the army who stopped our water and poisoned the air, the men who nightly bombed our homes and churches, sucked oxygen from the houses with fire, shot us in our streets and squares, killed women and children like bored farm-boys hunting rats: for you we crawled from basements, crypts, and shelters, and stood on the ruins of our city to present to you the last of our politicians, the collaborators, their wives and their children. Under the brightest blue sky we gave you our city, and we gave it to you out of love.[*]

[*] This was not the experience related by the Americans – see Part 2, pp. 64–67, where there is a discussion about resistance fighters in the main square, and the discovery of a building loaded with explosives which did not blow.

The very next week we lined the streets and performed the exact same welcome for the British.

This was not the end of war. Although we believed that it was.'

(page 9) 'I am allowed to read, and have been given histories and accounts both of the war and of the city prior to the war. And while these versions of what happened are not incorrect, they largely miss the point. Remember: your arrival was our defeat. For twenty-two years we happily supported the government and way of life knowing that hard choices needed to be made – unpopular decisions for the benefit of all. The government didn't arrive by accident, and while they disappeared overnight, taken to courts and tribunals, some summarily shot, remember – this was our choice because it worked. Full employment. Acceptable housing. Food. And future hopes – not only for ourselves. And our inclination to that government, our allegiance to those ideas, did not disappear as quickly as their bodies.

(. . .)

The city thrived, ten years before my birth. Everything new: stations, trains, trainlines, trams, roads, the first motorways, an opera house, public gardens, cinemas, a grand post office, municipal buildings and swimming pools. We asked for homes and they built us homes. We lived on the edge of the city, in new houses. At that time ground hadn't yet been broken and the city hadn't overtaken the neighbouring villages, spread out to take over the farmland.

You can't imagine the countryside and how it was. The wine and olives from this region were famous, as was the oil with its curative properties – all of which sounds like Spain, and while there is a strong Spanish community here, it is not Spain. It is, or was, handsome; we enjoy a fair climate and moderate weather. The countryside is, or was, pretty in every season: the vines held the winter mists, spring was brief, the sunflowers followed a full summer sun, and autumn, the longest, truest season, when the twilight is unnaturally long, was the time best spent here – the basic structures remain: there are rivers (now channelled), a close curve of mountains, a bed-like cultivated plain leaning into a broad-curved gulf where the city tumbles to the sea, and while it is not Spain, you might believe that you were in Spain. Now that the city has become so vast these seasonal subtleties pass unremarked: it either rains or suffers an oppressive heat. The winters are wet. The summers are hot. The periods of transition are almost unnoticeable. Outside the city, away from the concrete the climate is more temperate. All this is before the Americans. Before their tanks and progress, their factories, their processing plants, all, now, abandoned.'

(page 12) 'Shortly after the relief of the city, I witnessed, close-hand, a death in the vineyards, a young workman, cut in the thigh with a pruning knife, bled into the dirt, arterial, beyond help. He knew this, self-wounded, and I felt the weakening pulse at his thigh; held my hand close above his mouth until his breath expired. I looked into his eyes for a long time and fancied that I witnessed something, although I am certain now that this was only a naive desire; in any case I found it hard to leave – more out of science than sentiment – and having witnessed the process of his expiration, having watched a great quantity of blood leave him and saturate the ground, I became curious about the other processes now riding his body and in learning what other kinds of collapse were happening inside him: I wanted to know what was occurring deep under his skin. I inspected the cut but left the body otherwise undisturbed, (. . .) there is little point withholding the fact that this man was my brother.

(. . .)

The three-room apartment in which we lived does not deserve attention, situated on the first floor in a building seven storeys high, it housed at any given time no fewer than four, and no more than six of us. We shared mismatched chairs, a table, and little else. Four children, we shared one room and two beds. The boys bundled chaotically into one bed, a habit so ingrained that I still dislike sleeping alone. One apartment among many, our home was no different and no more decrepit than our immediate neighbours on either side. One mystery occurs to me now, which has not occurred to me before. At the start of the war, upon its declaration, the city lost about one third of its inhabitants, who took with them what they could manage and headed for the mountains or the sea and abandoned their homes. We did not take over these empty properties, then or later. Even at the start of the bombardment, when war came to our doorstep, we remained, as did the others, in the places allotted to us. Even in their absence we afforded respect to people who had abandoned us.

It is possible that the building dictated this. There would have been little use us occupying the other apartments. The professors, lawyers, doctors, clerks, the city officials and shop owners had their own entrances, their own stairwells. The tradesmen and labourers, along with those who could not find work, entered through the stairwells opening onto the inner courtyards. So that the building, as with many of the buildings in the city – and I think, in other cities, although I have not travelled much – folded about a core courtyard and kept separate the wealthy and the poor. In other countries these palazzi are known by their more proper names as *tenements* or *slums*, although, I believe, in other countries, they do not house the same variety of people. Opposite these apartments, as I have said, on the other side of the road, and therefore in the country, lay a vineyard, and more immediately a line of stone sheds, a place first for animals or produce, for olives and walnuts, for the safe storage of harvest, some of which were later adapted into workshops in which the goods brought from the fields were prepared. During the worst of the bombardment we temporarily fled the palazzi – taller, and easier targets for the mortars and bombs – and hid in the farm sheds. Although I spent much of my childhood in these buildings, either hiding or playing, I remember very little about the place, except how the musk of animals permanently coloured the air. The city, at this time, took on its own smell, of cooked and rotten meat, of the flesh of the dead.

What of the farm, which is now long gone? The owner, whose father had built the property, was killed early in the war, at the docks during an air-raid. On his death his family managed to buy their way out, and left all of the business (the managing of the land and farms, the harvesting and selling of its produce) to unscrupulous managers. But so productive were these holdings, and so rich the land, that even in the thick of war there was produce available – until, naturally, the final year, when the outmost fields abutting the river and mountains became the front line and the harvest was left to rot.

I have less useful information about my parents than I have about the place in which we lived. Both were sentimental, suffered at every slight grief or injustice, and easily took on others' troubles as their own. Before the war my father worked as a handyman whenever and wherever he could and was periodically busy and absent, or without work and constantly at home. When he was busy he lacked the wherewithal to collect what was owed to him – as this seemed to pain him, and people quickly learned of this weakness and took advantage, delaying and sometimes denying payment whenever possible.

Unskilled, he dug graves, trenches, irrigation ditches, and never received his proper wage. He laboured at the harvest, repaired walls, drains and roofs, and was always, in every instance, short-changed. I remember him in dirty, worn clothes, hands stained by labour, the skin on his face, hands and arms commonly rough and dark from the sun, the rest of him remained whiter than a plucked chicken.

My mother worked for charities and good causes, and before the war she avoided the city proper and worked in the local towns. Coming from the south we were used to working on the land, and while we lived in the city, we looked outward and worked the trades and activities that we understood in the neighbouring fields. Similarly, my mother worked at foundling nurseries and in the hospitals, she cleaned, learned to administer basic care. A skinny woman, she walked bent, peasant-like, head down. Prideful enough to henna her hair, she wore it high and drawn back tight. The pair of them, my parents, made little sense, one constantly robbed, the other constantly burdened as if grieving – and in the evenings they would bring each other to tears, and so, as I have said, they were largely useless.

Was I loved? I suppose so. They bragged over our achievements, small as they were, celebrated their children to others, held us up, but in such a limp way they always seemed on the edge of an apology. My younger brother sang in church, at fetes and fairs, travelled for a while with my mother and then with a band of penitents, and my parents talked about him as you might talk about a man who slurs or stutters, or a man who drinks, with a little shame, as if this were also a small failing, as if he could not help himself, knew no better than to sing in the way he did – and underlying this, always, a warning to my brother that this would not last, or that his ability to sing more beautifully than other boys was also a cause of pride which was to be monitored and kept in check.

The truth is that my sister and brothers gave my parents so few opportunities to celebrate that they were unused to it, and as a consequence did not know what to make out of the small pickings we offered them. A joke in the palazzo that my parents were related, brother and sister, which is patently untrue, helped to explain their simple pleasures, their inability to soundly reason, their love for the church, how they were able to dutifully abide the pressures of the times when others wilted under it. If I'm giving the impression they were attentive: they were not. Our education was a scattered affair. We were taught, sporadically, at the local school by a fraternity of monks, who delighted in my older brother and my younger brother (too stupid on one hand, too naive on the other), but whose interest I managed to escape. We shared the same tutors, the same amount of schooling, each of us managed the rudiments of reading and writing, and the most basic arithmetic, but we were needed in the fields in the spring to plant, train and prune, in the late summer for harvesting, in the autumn for storing – whatever influence the holy fathers had over our young bodies and minds, remained, at best, minimal. Our education came in the fields through practical labour: first we understood the length of the day, our own energies, we quickly trained in agriculture, assisted in making cheese, wine, and then we understood the currency of our bodies, that our labour, four children, was not enough to sustain the family, the fact our combined labours were worth less than the work of one man meant that we were obliged to pilfer food.'

(page 15) 'My younger brother's birth came alongside the first suggestion of war. I should impress on you that once the country was overtaken by war, life became a wholly different matter. First there was the skin, the day-to-day fact of it, and second there was the underlayer, the continuation of regular life: births, deaths (unassociated with the war); people continued to marry, breed, labour, sicken – and in this regard we existed almost as we had before.

My mother, a thin woman, took on a translucent quality when she was pregnant. Her skin became unnaturally pale, as if something fed on her and threatened her life. As her belly grew she became increasingly fragile – and looked, very much, like a fish, a sprat, with some bubo attached, so that she appeared infected. Our neighbours, all farmhands and labourers, bred hard – so little else to do – and as these women grew they took on an unsuppressed vitality and health, of which my mother appeared to be the exact opposite.

My brother's birth came in February. I watched her in the courtyard, cranking the mangle and managing sheets through the rollers, then all of a sudden doubled-up, hand to her belly, and brought to her knees. Secured in her room she bled heavily, and we waited for news, we sat in the kitchen as the midwife boiled towels, brought out spoiled sheets and bedclothes. Her yelps lasted through the night and were accompanied by deep guttural blows that sounded like wind on a roof, a rising storm that came in answer to my mother's cries, a kind of call and response of two animals. As she howled, the sky bellowed – and so my brother was brought into the world. These booms, this noise was neither thunder nor wind, but the artillery of the 112th sounding from the mountains. Already in view of the town, too far to effect damage, they made their guns sing to us little songs of threat, a boom, a drum-beat, an unrealized threat.

One detail. We needed a doctor. Three lived in the palazzo, so my brother and I were sent first to one, and then to the other, and finally, begging (as it looked as if both the child and mother would perish) to the last. While these good men were home, one assured us that he was called out elsewhere, another that he was sick himself, and the third that he would attend (he did not), and that we should return to my mother.

(. . .) On this first assault the Americans were repelled. Perhaps if they had not announced themselves they would have surprised the city, and if the city had fallen then, the region, and maybe the country would have slid quicker into their hands – but no, they told us where they were and were repelled. (. . .) Four years later they would not repeat their mistake. The 112th returned with fresh battalions and with the British in tow (somewhere, dallying behind, paddling up the beaches, moving in like hyenas after the kill). The Americans dropped their troops in the mountains from great aircraft and a great height, scattered them like dandelion drifts along the farther crests, speckled the ledges with paratroopers, and so they silently took the heights ringing the city, and from this vantage they prepared to kill, maim, starve, and punish. The lights of the city can be seen across the plain at night as a condensed and distant sparkle. Intensely signifying the kind of life, the plenteousness of the city, which they must have looked upon with hate: planning, night after night, how they would reduce it.

But this, this is four years ahead still, four years away from the night of my brother's birth.'

(page 19) 'I cannot talk about the American army without mentioning my sister – who I should have more properly introduced. E—, named after my mother's German grandmother, had her own mischief and needed watching. She could be still, as sound and static as a tree, and then gone. If you did not keep your eye on her you would miss her. But I cannot think of her right now. Not at this moment.'

(page 20) 'Against expectation, A— (they gave him a Spanish name) was not a fat baby. The first time I saw him he appeared greasy and paler even than my mother, run through with fine capillaries, as if made of goose-fat and red thread, infinitely vulnerable. So frail and vague he was not expected to live. Announced by the Americans boom, boom, boom, A— brought into the house a new and focused anxiety as we expected him to expire at any moment. As a consequence we lived those moments and felt them dearly, and sustained him second to second, minute to minute. For this period I remember being happy, and my devotion toward A— grew.

This birth brought little joy to my father, who would not approach my brother, feared any further attachment, and resented that the birth had cost so much physical trouble for my mother. As my mother recovered, A— remained delicate, and we all worked toward his welfare, either in the home or at what work we could find.

It is possible that A—'s frailty caused my father to ignore him. He robbed milk from my mother, leeched her limited vitality, he cried through the night, a thin noise, pathetic and unbroken, lamb-like. The midwife kept returning and brought with her chestnut oil, nutmeg oil, light scents to coax the baby to sleep. Even so, I do not remember my brother sleeping, he seemed to fight it, on the understanding, the midwife fancied, that he would be taken the moment he surrendered. While awake, he still lived.

I am not the man they claim. This is the evidence. I lived for my brother. I kept vigil over his cot – so small he was coddled in half a suitcase. We watched over him, and paid him every attention. I learned to feed him a weak broth on which he was weaned, anything to encourage and draw life into him. We raised my brother in the same way in which we had raised cast-off lambs.

(page 24) Here now is a version of an incident that has been used to demonstrate how black a people we are. (. . .)

The first assault by the Americans brought unintended consequences. In landing on the ridges, overtaking the small villages in the mountains on that first salvo, the Americans inadvertently woke a long-standing resentment. This resentment has no logic, or that logic is now lost and there is no pure reason why the cities in the plains mistrust the villages on the mountains (accept that they are thieves; known cheats, unreliable in business. They are cunning as gypsies, oily, calculating, and equally unclean. The women are loose and unprincipled). Accept that this grudge exists: to welcome a man from one of these villages into your home would corrupt your name, spoil your reputation. There is between the city and these villages no trust and no common ground.

Imagine the reaction, shortly after the birth of my brother, when it was discovered that these villages lay within kilometres of the American army. Think also of the outrage when it became known that not one man sought to warn the city (they claim not to have known, and were as surprised, as alarmed as the people in the city when the Americans began to sound their guns). Imagine what nonsense they expressed as justification. The simple fact that an entire battalion of Americans could spread through a landscape they did not know seemed too incredible to accept. These villages, these villagers must surely have helped.

In order to protect ourselves it became necessary to clear these villages. To move the inhabitants elsewhere so they could no longer provide opportunity and support to our enemies. As documented in film, in photographs, the houses of two of the villages were systematically destroyed. While there are a number of other villages, V— and C— were chosen, being positioned at either end of the crescent ridge. A seven-day warning was given to the inhabitants of V— and C—, and so they were driven out of their farms and houses: once vacated the villages were razed to the ground.

The occupants of V— and C— had nowhere to go, and no means of travel. Their animals were slaughtered, and given the poverty of the villages, it is unlikely that more than a few of them could have afforded to leave, or have bribed the officials to provide them with passes and identification. Instead, they came down from the mountains and set up encampments on the outskirts of the city.

By this time many had fled the city, as I have earlier described. And this train of refugees – as this is surely what they were – was moved from place to place and not allowed to settle. The hope being that they would move somewhere distant.

One group, of perhaps forty, certainly no more, men, women and children, settled on the roadside beside the farm in full view of our palazzo.

These people were wretched. They wandered ghostlike without complaint, sat by the roads and track without energy. Idle and indolent, they did nothing to support or help themselves. Discussions in the courtyard of our palazzo grew hot. *These people might seem passive, but they need food, they need water, and they will soon come to us for provisions and who knows what else.*

In less than a week these fears began to be realized. Small shacks were built, from our waste – spare boards and wood and cardboard were fabricated into shelters. The encampment pushed a little into the field, a semi-circle overtook one of the vineyards (it has to be said that no damage was afforded to the vines), and they stretched their squalor alongside the road as an affront.

My mother, familiar with such degradation from her work in the hospitals and hospices, was no better than our neighbours. In practice her charity did not extend far, while her sympathy might have reached other cities and other situations, it did not travel so much as one step in their direction. Her fears, numerous, of disease, theft, murder, were slowly realized with more misery than she would have imagined. First an outbreak of measles, then an unnamed fever the source of which appeared to be the fetid pond that grew in the bald centre, which took with it the babies and the elderly. And then, one night, a fire broke out, which razed five of the eleven shacks. Imagine us gathered at our window to watch the fire. Imagine our attention on the rising brightness, how people fled, approach and ducked, shied from the heat, of how they sought help but found none. This emergency certainly drew out the good people from our tenement who grouped at the road, and seemed for a moment to be ready to set aside their resentments at these gypsies. But no, they did not assist. Instead, as the emergency vehicles made their attempt to approach, our neighbours valiantly held them back, delayed them, detained them from reaching the encampment. What of the police? What of the fire brigade? What of our army? It is true that they arrived in great numbers, a battalion of trucks and water wagons, but while the fire spread they appeared to discuss the situation with our neighbours so that it seemed to be the army, the fire brigade, the police who were manning the very barricade which blocked them from the fire.

(page 28) Both of my parents attended the fire, they knelt with the neighbours on occasion to pray – for guidance, or a clean wind to lift the fire.

(page 29) The Americans, and later the British landed their armies in the south. Swallowed the islands, overran the east and spread like cholera with dangerous and undeniable speed. I do not remember the war, and while its history is physically marked upon the buildings – if you look above the boutique and shop windows you will see bullet holes in the stone and blast damage to the cornices and carved decoration. In some districts, close to the docks, there are still vacant spaces, sockets left by the bombing raids – the vacant lots soon grew a scant kind of grass, so that the city took on, in my early memory at least, a damp aspect, damaged and melancholic.

(page 32) The Americans took the Royal Palace and made the surrounding government offices their headquarters, leaving nothing for the British when they arrived a week later. The British settled at the outskirts, right under the city walls, and chose as their hub the vineyard, to use the old farmhouse and outbuildings as their command base. They managed to settle the land without destroying the vines, seemed to occupy us with an apologetic air. Later, on negotiation with the Americans, after the end of hostilities was formalized, they moved into the city proper and shared the government offices. In their absence, gypsies, who had been encouraged to settle, occupied the vineyard, growing in number from a few makeshift huts and huddled caravans into a larger encampment. They refused to settle in the houses and chose instead the outlying fields. They cared little for the vineyard, and the fields, which had survived the war, were soon spoiled. Our rooms looked down on an undisciplined, unkempt, unsanitary arc of tents and trailers. The vines were cut for fuel. The carefully tended embankments levelled. The irrigation ditches in-filled, so that the terraced field became nothing more than a mud flat.

I remember distinct moments from this period. The fire. The women. The women, brought from the south, were either camp followers, or women traded on the route through the country, from the beaches. Wherever they landed the men, who found almost no resistance, distracted themselves with women, and rather than discard them, collected them, adding to each regiment a sizeable retinue of girls. They were housed in the basement rooms at the palazzo, and I spent my time watching from the courtyard window as the women gathered and washed, or simply spent their days, a kind of endless waiting as if idleness stuck to them, glued them into deeper inaction. The soldiers had gathered women without any particular eye, taking, by criteria, women who were young first, comely second. The trek along the beaches, then inland across the malarial swamps, through the lowlands and foothills, and later, the mountains, had meant that few were lost through combat, but along the way the skinnier girls had become lost, or abandoned, or did not have the fortitude to last.

I have no real idea about how the women came to be in our palazzo. I know only that they were, and how they appeared thinner than seemed reasonable, and how they followed the soldiers without complaint. They washed; they worked on their backs. The British soldiers appeared not to enjoy this. The American, the Polish, the French all took to these opportunities, and there was no small amount of abuse, shouting, little displayed physically. But the women were spoken to as imbeciles. They were paid in food. Badly. Stale bread. Dried meats. Processed foods that were shipped in, offloaded and left to cook in their cans on pallets on beaches further south. One can of corned beef would service as pay, so that these women were worth less than canned meat. These women were worth less than rotten scraps. As supplies improved, so did their pay. One night a week the Americans would arrive and back a truck into the courtyard, and on this truck they would hold a barbecue, cook meats; they were uncommonly generous.

(page 34) Because of the dead the city was overrun with rats. Many had been trapped in basements when the bombing started, others were caught in catacombs, in the churches, in what passed as shelters, so the city took on a sweet smell which sank into a rank stench, recognizable as decay. The Americans brought us cats. This was one of their first gifts. Cats to kill the rats. The rats who had grown fat and large on the dead were easy to catch, and we were soon overrun with cats, who without live rats to hunt, turned to the same food source. They became aggressive and seemed to hold designs upon the living.

(page 35) The Americans reported the truck missing. They came another time in separate vehicles, but the truck was taken, assumed sold, as most other provisions and equipment were stolen away and resold, sometimes back to them. In this instance the truck was found, and inside, littering the truck-bed, were the bodies of cats, necks

snapped, slaughtered in the hundreds. As for the rats we would find our own solution.

(page 36) The loss of D— had a profound effect. While we did not play together, knew each other in passing, I thought of her as someone close, similar. Her proximity and encouragement (while she was free), and a discouragement (when she was incarcerated). Once she was gone – or unavailable – I turned to my brother A— for company. At that time I needed a compatriot. I needed to know I was not alone.

(page 40) Here I must speak about my sister. Here everything comes together and I should speak of the third woman who has held influence over me. So far E— has been absent, and there are many reasons for this, not least of all the considerable pain I feel at remembering her.

The episode of the cats caused a change in how the Americans treated their women. They viewed them afterward more coldly, as a resource, the men arrived now with briskness, as if keeping to an appointment, and no longer delayed to joke and play games, to tease. They also began to play small but cruel games. Through the Americans the black market thrived. In opening the city they brought back trade in two tiers, honest and expensive, dishonest and more various, and double the price. One young recruit, a handsome willowy man, a private from Kentucky, from whom I would not have expected such cruelty, brought with him packets of stockings which he gave to the women, there was one girl he was fond of, young, very small, from the mountains in the south, who had fine and dark features, and was known among the women as Mouse. The youth held back one packet, which he handed over with a kind of pride. Unlike the other sets of stockings, these were coloured, a faint but handsome pink. The women, at first delighted by the gifts, perhaps believing that some normalcy was now returning, that they had been forgiven for the episode of the cats, soon appeared puzzled, and as I watched a wave of doubt flickered through them. While the stockings were in packets, they were not new, some were rolled, and others carelessly folded, a sagginess to them that showed that they had been worn. These stockings, it later became known, were taken from the bodies of the dead or stolen from the homes of the absent. A whole new economy grew about the houses and apartments which had been abandoned, and also the houses of the dead. These places were looted – and I will not lay the blame solely at the feet of the Americans, I will not say that this was entirely about finding treasure, about taking trophies, but they caused this need, and the houses which had remained secure until now were plundered.

The women received gifts from the houses of the dead. Lamps. Carpets. Clothes. L— dressed now in a fine patterned silk nightdress, and wore over this a sheer white nightgown with cascading frills, a silly pretty thing which suited her. I watched as she received this gift, from a commander, who gave it to her in a box, wrapped in tissue paper, so that it appeared as a gift a lover might present his mistress, a fine token brought from Paris, to signify a small, perhaps intimate, occasion. It was of course no such thing. Shortly after other such boxes appeared and we learned that one of the boutiques on via F—, which had remained shuttered and unbothered through the barricade, was now forced open and looted. But this made a better gift, something she was happy to accept as it came from no one's home, from no other body.

She stretched the fine material over her arm, allowed it to smooth over her, the weight fitting itself to her body. In wrapping her arms about the commander she looked up and caught me watching. With one finger she gave a small tick-tick wave, indicating that I should not watch. I should keep out of this business. I should not be involved, because, clearly, all this would invite would be trouble. But even with this small admonishment, I had to admit to a fascination.

L— kept a good eye on the women. She did not interfere in squabbles, but quelled them quickly if they appeared to stay unresolved, or if the irritation escalated into a fight. More like the sultan than the chief of the harem, she signalled her displeasure and her pleasure with gestures: sent girls away, picked men when they arrived. An authority on her that even the soldiers obeyed.

She also gave advice: 'Would it be better to be dead?' 'If he enjoys you now, he won't hurt you later.'

On occasion a darkness fell over the group. The girls would become unhappy, or some incident, an argument with one of the men would infect the air. L— was not immune, and I learned when and when not to observe them.

One night L— came to our door. My father answered and shut it immediately.

My mother and sister wanted to see the visitor, and came after him to the door. I watched also, and saw, with a confused pleasure that it was L—. I could hear her laugh before the door was opened, and sure enough she stood in the landing with arms carrying something wrapped in a shawl. She offered this to my mother – and what might have been a baby proved instead to be supplies provided by the Americans.

Up close L— was pretty, the face of a china doll, round, with sweet small lips, blue eyes. Her cheeks a little chubby made her face while it was settled appear even jolly, although I had seen on a number of occasions that this was not always the case, and that she could set herself from silk to steel in a simple moment.

My mother wanted to refuse. I could sense this, so L— had to drop her hands to let the weight settle in my mother's arms. My brother came forward and took the bundle from my mother, and nodded his gratitude. His face as flushed as mine.

She offered us milk. Packaged eggs. There were cigarettes, she admitted, but they used these to trade for produce. There was no telling what the soldiers would bring, and rather than allow this to waste she thought we might make good use of the food. There were perfumes (she smelled so sweet herself), stockings, scarves, clothes, but it did not seem a good idea to offer those, unless they could be traded. But trade here, she seemed to indicate the building, is not safe.

On seeing my sister L— looked quickly at my mother and whispered, I am sure I heard it. 'You should not keep her here. You understand me? Take her to relatives. She is not safe.'

After this warning my parents did not allow my sister to pass through the courtyard unaccompanied. They attempted to keep her to the apartment, but found this impossible, and needed in any case the money she would bring in. She had to work. They hatched between them another plan, a fatal idea, that they could buy a pass for her so that she could leave the city, work elsewhere, somewhere safer. These passes were almost impossible to acquire and were gained through the permission of an adjutant, one of the military administrative overclass. I accompanied my mother to the offices, and we made our way through the vast lobby of what was once the central office for pensions and war relief, less than insects in the shadows of these lofty windows, which made me certain that this endeavour would not succeed. In front of us, a man who had once been a neighbour, who spoke without bitterness about how he had needed to choose between his daughters, whore one to save the other. He was there, on this occasion, to barter for his wife, and had brought with him what remained of her jewellery: her wedding ring, her engagement ring, a pair of diamond stud earrings, which he feared would not be enough.'

The queue ran through the corridors, my mother told me to keep in place, then checked for herself and despaired when she saw that this line of people ran a ring about the entire floor then through the stairwell to rise, and who knows, run another circuit about that floor, maybe others also. The people appeared comatose, and this frightened her; resigned to whatever they might need to surrender, they brought with them small packages, clothes, food, boxes of jewellery, all to ensure that their daughters and wives would escape the city. It was not clear how many days we would have to wait, and if that wait would in the end be successful. Another plan needed to be devised.

This failure sent my mother into a depression. E— could not remain in the building, it was not safe, neither could she leave. To confirm her vulnerability E— had been stopped that morning by the soldier from Kentucky. Clear that his tastes ran to the more delicate, the more defenceless of the girls, he singled out my sister as she brought water through the courtyard. The man watched as she passed, turned his whole body as she moved alongside him and toward the stair. He looked up as she made her way up the stairs, then gave a long and low whistle. The kind of whistle a hunter might give his dog, a signal that there was quarry to be had here. He had found something to hunt.

A short time after this, perhaps one or two days, the Americans performed a search of the entire building. Whether this was for security, as they claimed, a kind of census taking to ensure who and how many people populated these palazzi. They came to the door in their uniforms. Four men. Clipboards and rifles.

'This is how they find their women,' my mother fretted. Clearly they wanted more than women. They catalogued the rooms and contents, checked our food resources. It was certainly how they found their goods. And we listened afterward as they broke in to the empty apartments. Once those doors were breached, the contents would be pilfered. During the night we could hear the vacant apartments being looted, the soft bumping of furnishing, the splintering of wood: we dared not see who this was.

This situation sustained itself for a while. Once the apartments were looted it seemed that there could be little else that could be taken. And perhaps this might have been the case, perhaps this might have been the story if the women in the courtyard had not caused another upset.

(page 43) The young private, the youth from Kentucky, was found stabbed. The wounded man wandered, trance-like, out of the lower rooms, into the courtyard. He walked through the stairwells, vacant, seeming to have some quiet purpose, stepping as a cat through wet grass, lifting up his feet, but not sensate enough to express exactly what it was that he was doing, what it was that he wanted. His hands, slashed, showed defensive wounds, where, perhaps, he had tried to grab the knife. His handprints along the wall, small slides and smudges tracking his progress from floor to floor. We saw the blood, ignored it, then later, more worried about what fresh trouble this would bring, my brother and my father followed the trail up to the top floor.

They found him sweating and panting. In the darkness his tunic appeared black, the blood having seeped through his jacket.

Unwilling to touch him, they raised the alarm. One dead solder would be no end of trouble and they did not want to be involved, but considered quickly – which would be worse? To allow him to die and suffer whatever consequences the Americans would bring down on us, or perhaps, through intervening, be seen as people who had helped, at the same time appear as collaborators to our own.

My father could not make the choice. My brother, independently, sounded the alarm. Went down to the basement and roused the women, got the soldiers away from their women's arms and beds and brought them up the stairs to their companion, who now lay in a swoon.

They brought him down in a blanket, a makeshift stretcher, and laid him in the courtyard, still alive, but feeble from blood loss. The women came out, one by one, and held back to the courtyard walls, hands to mouths, frightened, recognizing that this would be no good thing. Ten of us could die, twenty, a hundred, and it would mean nothing. But one wounded American signalled a whole world of trouble.

The soldiers themselves appeared stunned. They stripped off the boy's tunic, demanded water and rags and found him stabbed once in the side, and once in the chest. The boy lay pale, his wounds agape. His chest raising and falling with laboured breaths.

The military police arrived alongside an ambulance, and the boy was dressed and taken away with some hurry, and greater fears that he would die. The courtyard trapped silence, no one dared speak, and it seemed that all, even the men who had spent the night here, were under suspicion.

(page 45) Let me describe now what was happening inside our apartment. How this event brought down a deeper distress. My mother at the table, too gone to wail, head in hands, believing that this would be the last that we would see of my brother. My father, useless, did not know what to do with himself and hung, waif-like at the door. My sister kept back, and I urged her to pack. We would hide her in one of the other apartments. They would not find her. We would say that she had already gone, that she was working elsewhere, that she was now in a city in the north, and that we had not heard from her. We could say that she had died. We would take her belongings, all evidence of her and deny that she existed, say that their records were incorrect, that there never was a girl here, that we had no sister, there was no daughter. The Americans would be bound to come and question us now. Our involvement would be examined. This attention would need to be managed if we did not want it to cause us trouble. Looking about the room, about the apartment, as bare as it was, it would not take much to convince them that there was no girl.

We hid her in another apartment, the room a chaos of broken furniture – it was not hard. She dug herself under the broken frame of a bed and slipped from view.

The Americans came in the night. They brought dogs. And now my mother's grief grew into song. She shrieked as they came into the courtyard as they broke the doors and rounded up the women, hauled them into trucks. I strained to watch but did not see L— but watched as the women were roughly gathered, bound, thrown onto the back of the vehicle like meat. They took them away and left a team of men to clear the room, who threw out the beds, tossed the clothes into the courtyard, and then set fire to it; sparks rose and sucked the air, a column of smoke billowed upward. They threw linens, bedding, mattresses, clothes and shoes onto the fire, not caring that this might spread, that the dry night air would carry sparks into other homes.

I saw the face of my neighbours at the windows, brightened by firelight, who each caught my eye, and each turned away, slipped back into the darkness, wanting not to be seen. The dogs howled at the fire, strained at their leashes, and here – finally – we come to the worst.

One of these hounds released by its minder hurtled up the stairs, and found its way floor by floor to the vacant apartment in which we had secured my sister, it sought out the chaotic heap under which she lay and began to bark and howl and scrambled at the furniture.

They found her, the soldiers. Brought her out. Took her away.

(page 47) My mother returned to the new ministry and came back exhausted, used up. They would not speak with her. Threatened her with arrest when she started to make a fuss. She begged, fell to her knees, offered herself in her daughter's place. Attempted to explain that they had taken her by mistake, that she was not one of the women they had herded in the palazzo. She was a girl. Her daughter. Surely they had daughters themselves? Surely they had mothers also, who they would not bear to see degrade themselves? Could they not see that this was a simple mistake. She would make no complaint. She would be grateful. She would spy for them, inform on the neighbours, collect information. She would do anything if they would release her child. She is fourteen. Return her to me.

The man she spoke to appeared not to understand. Refused to listen, and when he had to, sat without expression, a wall. Stones would have wept, she said, but this man saw nothing in front of him, nothing recognizable, nothing from which he could draw the simplest strand of sympathy.

Outside the building she was met by a woman, an American who hurried after her. This girl, she said, had heard her, understood her, and realizing that the adjutant would do nothing, explained with care that there was a magistrate. One of our own people, and that my mother should assemble witnesses, set out a record of what had happened and have this signed by neighbours. The magistrate would not ignore us, with evidence he could over-step the adjutant and speak directly with the military commanders. There was hope in this, a little hope.

On her return my mother explained what we needed to do. Using D.P.'s paper I addressed the facts of the night before. Wrote first our address and date as I had seen on official documents, set out the names of the people in the house, wrote my sister's name in capitals. After this we knocked on our neighbours' doors. If they had refused my mother, they could not refuse the testimony of others. There were men who had witnessed this. Neighbours drawn to their windows and balconies – she had seen them, I had seen them – keeping safe behind shutters, but watching; she had felt them, seen them, knew they were there.

Some, at first, admitted as much. Gave their condolences. Shook their heads in horror. That it would come to this. After everything. Daughters taken, stolen from their houses. Floor by floor we knocked on each of the doors, implored each neighbour the same. Come with us. Come to the magistrate, help present our case, prove that our daughter existed, and that she was taken from us. Sign here. A piece of paper, give some testimony, if not your name then a mark, a simple mark. None of them. Not one. Would sign.

Misfortune is a river, and once it has found its course it will widen its banks, flood wasteland, vineyards and farmland without discrimination, swamp and lay the plains to waste. The same day my sister was taken, the British stood by as the museums were looted. Done with our homes, our palaces and museums were now the target.

We determined to see the magistrate without the petition. If he were one of our countrymen he would surely help us. The streets, which by mid-afternoon would normally be quiet, were hectic with activity. Troops, American and British, lined the boulevards, the shops along the main thoroughfares were shuttered, the ministry itself closed. Police blockaded the main arcade, at the port the ships' guns faced inland. It became clear, as we ran from corner to corner, inching our way to the magistrate's court, that there were fears of an insurrection. By the time we passed the National Museum the looting was done. The doors lay open, and a white thread of smoke blew from the back of the building. There were shards, glass from the windows, stones used to pelt the doors, and papers scattered across the pavement and into the road. Tanks faced the building and the men now guarding (surely too late) wore visors and masks so their faces could not be seen.

The magistrate was not at the court, as we should have expected. Instead, at the height of the looting, the Americans had driven him to the museum, and there was no clear idea what had then happened to him, except that he had failed to quell the trouble.

We waited at his office. His secretary sat behind a desk and told us that it would do no good. 'There will be no other business now. They (meaning the Americans, perhaps the British) were working hand in hand with the looters. These weren't bandits. This was organized, carefully planned. Much of what they wanted, the prize of our culture was gone already by the time they arrived. The people they caught were passers-by. They will be shot. Under martial law. They will be shot.'

He knew nothing of our sister. Nothing about the women at the palazzo. Nothing about the entertainments, and did not seem surprised by the news. 'A car we could find,' he said, 'we know the names of every thief. A person.' He shrugged. 'They disappear. If someone is gone. I am sorry to report. They are gone.'

His office, decorated white and blue, held busts. Heads of state, former kings, and in the corridor also I noticed the bronze likenesses of our philosophers, a great deal of statuary in fact along the corridors and stairwells, none of it particularly fitting the surroundings. Watching me the magistrate's clerk said that we should go. There was nothing he could do, and nothing either that the magistrate could manage. Without verification of our claim we had no grounds to make a petition.

(*page 50*) My sister returned two days later at sunset as we returned, again, from the magistrate's office. (. . .)

I called on Dr P—, begged him to come see her, to help. Knocked hard at his door. Saw that his blinds were slightly opened. Called to him. Insisted that I knew he was in. That I would break the door. His voice, feeble but clear, refused to assist, and told me, directly, and with some shame to go away.

I ran to other doors, to other neighbours and asked for water, for towels, for a trough so we could bathe her. Door after door remained unanswered. About the palazzo hung a thick silence. The silence of people hiding, of people holding their breaths, of people closing their eyes and hardening themselves, making themselves as dull as walls and floors and stone. Not one person came to our aid.

(*page 51*) The morning after the return of my sister, my brother took himself to the vineyard and used a curved pruning knife to slit the artery in his leg. He lay with his back to the vine and bled himself of life. He left no note or explanation, which did not need to be voiced perhaps. I found him, and held him at the end. I sat with him long after, and thought hard over the facts and realized that everything I had done to this point was driven by coincidence. The opportunities opened to me had come through chance alone. The misfortunes were otherwise, and were driven by situations which I believed I could not control. But now, it seemed to me that I could be less undirected. Less blown. More determined. If I did not I would end up used like my brother and sister. Here, as if to give example to the trouble which I debated, I was found with the knife, covered in blood, and arrested.

And so I was imprisoned for the murder of my brother.

YEAR 3

WEDNESDAY

Yee Jan waited in the cubicle until he could be certain that the students were gone. Some stuck around for extra sessions, one-on-ones that lasted an hour at most. Others dawdled to chat and wrap up the day, and took too long to say goodbye. Tonight they were filming at the marina and Yee Jan didn't have time to dawdle. *They* meaning a film crew, technicians, handlers, movers, a mix of lean and professional Americans and Italians (men) from Los Angeles and Rome: people (men) so serious and focused and so used to crowds they saw nothing but the job ahead of them. Yee Jan wanted to watch them for their industry alone. The crew wore military green T-shirts and vests with *The Kill* printed in white script on the front and the outline of a white star in a white circle on the back. He wanted one of the vests, although he was happy to settle for a photograph. Yee Jan leaned into the mirror and considered how this could be achieved. He pinched his eyelashes to tease out stray hairs. He'd come in early that morning specifically to watch the maintenance crew off-load lights from flat-bed trucks and prepare the cabins (technically trailers) and set them end on end on the broad sidewalk that ran alongside the port, and just as soon as he was ready he'd go back and find them.

Inside his satchel he'd packed another set of clothes and a small zippered make-up bag. He laid the clothes across the sink then picked carefully through the make-up and chose the lighter lipstick, flesh-pink, and a foundation which would erase the small open pores on either side of his nose and the oilier skin around his chin. He leaned toward the mirror, smoothed his hand across his jaw and satisfied himself that there was no sign of stubble. Certain now that no stray students roamed the corridors. he puckered his mouth, tested a line of lipstick, and thought it too much. The staff would stay until the evening and students would return for a film screening, a cooking class, a visit to the crypt or the roof of the Duomo, he couldn't remember the programme, but it usually started two hours after the final class.

THE KILLS

It was a mistake to open the week with the story about the wolf: Lara had made a point of showing her disappointment. No stories about Naples, right from the start. Meaning: no bad stories. No bull-shitting the Italians. In fact if you're going to say something that involves Italy or the Italians you better make it flattering: and best remember that as an American you know less than nothing about food, language, clothes, culture, politics, religion, especially religion, especially with Lara. No shit. Yee Jan practised his shtick in his head: remember, this is a country that voted a prostitute into government and a fat clown as Prime Minister, persistently, for like, eighteen years. Italians know every kind of shit about every kind of shit there is to know. They've heard it all. Italians are the Meistershitters. No kidding.

Personally, Yee Jan didn't understand what was quite so bad about the wolf story. It certainly went down easier than the introductions two weeks earlier when he'd announced himself as Princessa Chiaia. He'd given the word a kick, a little hot sauce, a little yip: Key-yai-ya. Bad idea. But like most ideas it came to him in a moment – and you just never know if it's going to work until it's out of your mouth. The group after all were all women, worse, wives, worse, military wives, and they had no sense of style, not one drop, and probably shopped at Target and T.J. Maxx, no Filene's Basement, not because they were poor but because they didn't know any better and had No Idea about the pleasures of Chiaia and the boutiques at piazza del Martiri (was it any wonder that their husbands were so fruity?) – besides, they didn't know him yet, hence, not one laugh. Instead they regarded him with the same kind of horror they might regard a falling phial of smallpox. But this time the tutor, Frau Lara, had taken umbrage, and she seriously couldn't see that a story about a wolf loose in the city was simply a story about a wolf loose in the city, nothing more. He meant it as a fable, if anything. Nothing more to it than that. Wolves are cute, come on. Who doesn't like wolves? Yee Jan pouted at the mirror, narrowed his eyes. Didn't a story about a wild creature slinking through the alleys and piazzas make the city that much more interesting, that little bit sexier, and best of all, didn't it seem ever so slightly possible? Besides, he'd yet to meet an Italian who didn't love to bang on about Napoli's special sense of mystery, a particular ancient unnameable beauty, a special something, a blah-blah-blah-blah-blah-di-blah, all in one breath and then slag it off as *terzo mondo* in the next? Bad logic, freakopaths. You can't have it both ways: you're either something of interest or you're not.

Yee Jan inspected himself in profile. The light in the toilet wasn't great but it gave him enough to work with. He squeezed the foundation into his palm first, presented his chin to the mirror and sneered at the sweet stink of the place, a sickly vanilla, somehow worse in the bathroom, which made little sense – the bakery in the front of the building, the toilet at the side, nowhere near the courtyard. What's that film where the woman rubs her arms with lemons to rid herself of the stink of her job? And what's her name? The man was Burt Lancaster. No forgetting Burt, who might have had an English name but surely, had to be, somewhere deep down, a pure genetic Italian.

In Yee Jan's story the wolf made a habit of coming into the city: she hid in the underground caverns that ran under the old town, or sometimes those catacombs dug into the rock at Fontanella. She didn't live here, no, instead she wandered in now and again, found her way from the mountains by tracking the scent of the city through waterways and irrigation ditches, all the way through those drab flat fields. She came in winter, in February with the denser snow, when the waterways were frozen, and when the meaty stink of the city clung to the earth and spread out for miles, scratch that, kilometres. She came here to give birth. This wolf, magnificent, canny, even wise, and had enough smarts to know when and how to hide herself and her pups in a city of nearly three million people – four point six if you include the entire metropolitan area – and she knew how to disappear, how to find food, taking cats, small dogs, maybe once or twice some impolite fat child (and so many of them good and porky). The people who spotted her (an old woman outside the Duomo, a trader on via Tribunali, the street walkers at piazza Garibaldi, a team of street cleaners on via Toledo / Roma, whatever you will) were luckier than they knew, because the wolf took a particular interest in the people who spied her – call it providence. If the wolf passed by you, if she saw you, if, for some small reason she paid you a little attention, allowed you to see her, you couldn't come to harm, for a day, for a week, it just depended.

Yee Jan's Italian wasn't great, that's for sure, but he could manage well enough to tell a plain story simply. A city. A wolf. The lucky few who stumbled across her. And he could tell these ideas as unadorned facts which provided a handsome certainty. Everybody knows it's not the embellishment that makes the story: it's the cold hard presence of possibility. This is why people play the lottery – because winning is always possible. Improbable. Really-fucking-remotely unlikely. But *possible*.

Yee Jan pouted at the mirror. A finger at the corner of his mouth. He held up the mascara brush but decided against it. The thing about make-up is making sure there's just enough, too much is a problem, but finding that distinctive point where you both are and aren't familiar is all about precision. More often than not it's the mascara and lipstick combination that tips the balance. These military wives could do with some lessons. Seriously. Why would you leave the house looking like a monkey had a party on your face?

By the time he found the film crew they had progressed from the portside to where the road curled about the bay, right beside Castel dell'Ovo. A line of silver-white screens bounced light from the sea to form a bright path across the road. As far as Yee Jan could make out, the shot involved a woman scurrying along the promenade and a man following after. Time after time the woman walked in a quick romp, skirt tight between her legs, hand up to her shoulder to keep her bag in place. The man came after in a long stride, close enough, smoking, sunglasses and a pinched face. People only walked like this in movies. When they stopped both the man and the woman wiped their faces with towels in a gesture that reminded Yee Jan more of tennis than filmmaking. Tedious wasn't the word. The woman walked, the man followed. Walked. Followed. Their movements matched by a camera running alongside, then everything stopped, tracked back to the start, and after long and digressive preparations (make-up, discussions, cables hauled back, the camera itself in one instance appeared to be dismantled, while screens were adjusted to accommodate for the changing pitch of sunlight, and plenty of pointing, everybody pointing) they began again. Tired of watching Yee Jan sat and finished a slice of pizza which he picked into pieces, this at least couldn't be faulted, mozzarella so fresh it sat in a light sap, only just set. He took a photo of himself with the slice held up to his mouth and didn't mind that people were watching. After eating he wanted to smoke, Bacall-style. It's the head that moves, never the hand.

THURSDAY

Before the class could properly settle the secretary knocked on the door and asked the tutor if Yee Jan and Keiko could please come outside. As soon as they came out the secretary asked if they could sit in the hallway for a moment.

'What do you think this is about?' Keiko whispered to Yee Jan in English.

'Fashion police.' Yee Jan whispered back. 'You're wearing two kinds of stripes.'

Keiko gave a complicit shrug and said she didn't think she'd done anything wrong. Not anything she could remember.

'You think we're in trouble? It feels like high school. Maybe it has something to do with money?'

Yee Jan thought it strange that they would be called out of class and then asked to wait. He was, after all, paying for the lesson he was missing. He listened to the tutor's voice through the door and the measured laughter of their fellow students, all a bit predictable. People didn't like Lara as much as they liked the other tutors, but he had to admit she got the job done. Yee Jan splayed his hands and inspected his nails. Today he wore mascara but no foundation.

When the office door opened, a student from Elementario Uno came out, book in hand, and returned to her class.

'It looks like they're speaking to the Asian students.'

Yee Jan strained forward. Printed on the back of the student's T-shirt a picture of a smiling cat, the face not entirely unlike her own, broad, almost round. He had to admit she was pretty. Inside the office sat two police officers. 'Why are the police here? Are we supposed to have our passports?'

Keiko took out her passport from a small wallet hung about her neck.

'You're such a victim,' Yee Jan said. His statement of the week, which he applied with sincerity, insincerity, irony, love, or anger to any situation. *Such a victim.* 'I told you about those stripes, didn't I?'

As they both leaned forward the office door was carefully drawn shut.

After a few moments the secretary came out of the office and in a low voice she asked if Keiko would come with her – then seeing Yee Jan's bag, she stopped cold. The secretary curled her hair behind her ear then pointed at Yee Jan's bag. '*Questa è la vostra borsa?*'

'Sorry? Am I going?'

'Your bag,' Keiko interrupted. 'She's asking about your bag.'

'This is *my* bag.' Yee Jan held up the bag so the secretary could see, then pronounced emphatically. 'Mine.' It was one thing learning Italian, quite another using that knowledge out of class.

The secretary looked seriously at the bag. Maybe the job didn't pay that much. Maybe secretaries across the city had to snatch and grab whenever they could.

'It's from Macy's.' Yee Jan pointed in the direction he thought was west. 'I know. Ironic. It looks like Ferragamo. You'll have to go to New York yourself.'

Used to Yee Jan's oblique ways the secretary straightened up then returned to the office.

Keiko looked at Yee Jan's bag. 'I don't think this has anything to do with visas or money. I think it's something to do with the bag?'

'*My* bag, victim. *My* bag. *I* paid for it.'

The news that a man had followed him was nothing extraordinary. This is Italy, Yee Jan told himself. As far as he could tell everyone seemed to be watching everyone else, and apart from an obvious, often hostile, curiosity, Italian men liked to make their likes and attractions clear. It wasn't much of a surprise that someone would take it further. Only this wasn't a simple harassing call, a bothersome stare, a whistle or a gesture. This wasn't a joking profession of love, a cock-grabbing insult, or a scout for a sexual service. This was a grown man waiting outside the school for him on three, certainly, possibly even five consecutive evenings.

When they showed him the footage the secretary Sandra burst into tears and had to leave the room. The police, uncomfortable with the procedure, continued, their faces red, flustered. Yee Jan wondered to whom they felt the most sympathetic, him, or the man who'd mistaken him for a woman – as this was the scenario from their perspective.

THE KILL

Everyone knew the story about the language school and the disappearance of the Japanese student (which explained Sandra's tears), but none of the students were aware that this had any effect day to day on the school or had anything much to do with the slightly heightened security around the palazzo, because, let's face it, this is Naples, so a camera above the intercom wasn't odd. A camera above the courtyard doors wasn't odd. A camera mounted in the window of the antiques store wasn't odd. The police knew next to nothing and seemed genuinely bored. They couldn't even be sure how many times the man had followed him. Three times captured on tape, but maybe four. Four or five, then.

In gritty black and white, from three separate vantage points, the image showed a man standing, and sometimes leaning, by the wall opposite the entrance. In the first tape the man stood with his arms at his side, he wore an unmarked baseball hat and a lightweight jacket despite the heat and humidity. Yee Jan thought he looked a little (and while he didn't like the word, he couldn't avoid it) *retarded*. No one stands that still for that long without having some kind of an issue going on. It didn't help that the crudeness of the image flattened everything into tonal plains. The longer Yee Jan looked, the harder he concentrated, the more the grey plains appeared to vibrate. In two of the segments other students came out and the man showed no interest, but as soon as Yee Jan emerged with his bag tucked under his arm (that handsome ersatz-Ferragamo with a white and brown body and long double-stitched brown straps, a serious piece of equipment), the man turned his head, then, once Yee Jan walked away, he followed after, looking ever-so-slightly undead. It was the walk. Definitely the walk. Evidently, Yee Jan or his bag had some kind of zombie-magnetism going on.

In the set of images from the second day the man waited in almost the exact same spot. This time he leaned back, shoulders against the wall, and bowed forward as soon as Yee Jan came out of the doors and followed after, not quite so zombie-like (in fact pretty ordinary, though somewhat languid) one hand running along the brim of his cap, a ring on his finger. The ring passed too quickly for him to see which finger (he suspected it was a signet ring, it would be too much to hope that a married man with some secret vice was following him, smitten). On the third day the man waited, hands in pockets, a little more anxious perhaps and wary of the street. When Yee Jan came out, among a burst

759

of other students, he waited, held back, his right hand wiped his face and he walked out of view, more zombie than not, again following Yee Jan.

The director of the language school cleared her throat throughout the viewing. She spoke softly with the two policemen, then directly addressed Yee Jan in English.

'This isn't the first time. I think the film, it's possible, is making things worse.'

Yee Jan sucked the skin on his knuckles – which film? Did she mean the movie they were shooting on the seafront? The policemen didn't appear to care and he wondered at how Italians seemed to love their uniforms, however stupid they appeared wearing them because they always looked a size too small and were over-dressed in ornament. Just dumb.

'Do you know who he is?'

'No. Most of the people who come, come only once. And sometimes, once they're here, they wait for a while. It's not clear why, exactly.' But this time there was a complaint from one of the students about a man waiting outside, and when the secretary checked the tapes, she noticed it was the same man coming time after time. 'We don't know for how long.'

Yee Jan sat forward, and repeated his question. 'Why is he here?'

The director shifted back in her seat. 'There isn't much we can do. It's a public street. There is the sign outside. Every time something comes out in the newspapers or a book – and now this film – we have people who come to the school, they go to the palazzo on via Capasso, then they come here to look at the sign outside. I have asked them to take down the sign. But I don't think it would make a difference.'

It sounded to Yee Jan like this would be the preferred option. Take down the sign, rename the school. Easy.

'Why is he following me?'

'Was. He was following you. This footage is from last week. He hasn't come back this week.'

'So why was he following me?'

At this the director looked deeply pained. 'Because,' she answered carefully, 'one of the people who disappeared was one of our students. A Japanese student.'

Yee Jan nodded, he knew the story. 'I'm American. The features are Korean.'

'I don't understand it either. But it's always the same. People are curious. It's an unfortunate mistake. I think this is what happens when an idea spreads. I think someone has seen you and just become fascinated with the idea.'

While the error was just about plausible – in a general sense – it was a simple fact that Yee Jan looked nothing like a Japanese housewife, not even close. In any case, Yee Jan had shown utmost sensitivity for the first couple of weeks at the school over the issue of his mannerisms and his clothes, and toned everything down. He'd kept to a simple wardrobe of dark T-shirts and black jeans. Although he sometimes changed after lessons, not one person from the school had seen him. Only slowly, over several weeks (and the difference becoming more noticeable this week), had he allowed himself to relax, to return to being human, feminine; his body becoming less constricted, his gestures broader, larger, and he'd started wearing a few more bangles, a little more make-up. He'd began to laugh again, that double laugh, the supple ripple that underscored and lit up conversations, and that coarse horny bellow that singled him out of any crowd. Yee Jan's laughter was a gift given generously. He began to address himself in the third person when he was forgetful, or if he made a mistake. He began calling the boys *girlfriend*, *girl*, *ragazza*, or sometimes *she*, in a manner which suggested affection, and enjoyed making a mess of the genders in class to amuse himself, his tutors, the other students.

It was possible with his black hair, the occasional clasp, the eyeshadow, the hint of eye-liner (nothing even close to the amount of make-up he wore at home), the plucked eyebrows, his mannerisms (that lazy, sexy walk, those smooth gestures where his hands followed one beat behind every motion), his height, his skinniness, that he could be mistaken for a girl – a girl – but not, no way, a middle-aged Japanese housewife.

There were too many questions. Did this man follow him because he looked the type – Asian and petite? Did the man have some kind of problem with his sight, or was he crazy? Was he certain about his choice, or did he consider, vacillate, become certain then uncertain? How long did he follow? Did he come all the way to Vomero, door to door, or did he give up at the *funiculare*? Did he intend to harm him? Or was it something else? Yee Jan had seen in movies how a slight gesture made without deliberate intention could fashion a whole world of consequences, happenstances, and while he didn't believe that this would occur in life, he wanted to know if the man believed that he had given him a signal, a please follow me? In any case: how curious was he, this man who wore jackets in the middle of the summer?

The police had a slightly different idea. Some of the people who came to the palazzo were from families with missing people. Since the disappearance of the first victim, and possibly because he wasn't identified, the case had brought the attention of almost everyone who had lost someone. There were forty-five similar cases in the region, of people who had just gone missing without any indication or any obvious plan or prior warning. The case was a touchstone, and sometimes people came to the palazzo or the school in the faint hope that there would be some kind of discovery or realization. Yee Jan found this unbearable.

The director said she didn't know what to do, because there wasn't really much that could be done. They had debated whether they should let Yee Jan know, and thought it sensible to see if he recognized the man. 'But really . . . other than that . . .' She raised her hands in submission.

The police asked him to watch the images again, just to make sure, and this time, Yee Jan noticed some differences. The clothes were the same, the baseball cap, the jacket, the hand to his cap, the same hand to his face. Yee Jan asked for the images to be replayed. Now he was used to the idea, something didn't quite fit. There was a something else, a piece they hadn't shown him on the first viewing where the man had made some kind of gesture to the camera above the door. It looked like sign language, he couldn't tell, being brief and perfunctory it passed almost without remark.

'It's a wasp.' The director dismissed the gesture before Yee Jan could say anything.

'That isn't the same man.' He cocked his head to think. 'Look.' He pointed at the monitor. 'They aren't the same. Their shoulders, this one is smaller, he's a little shorter and he isn't so broad.'

The policemen couldn't see it.

'His hand. He has a ring on the second day and not on the third.'

They all leaned toward the monitor. Yee Jan was right. On the second day the man was clearly wearing a wedding ring, on the third day he was not.

'It isn't the same man. I'm telling you.'

The police struggled to see the difference, but once the idea was suggested they couldn't claim to be certain that it was the same figure on all three occasions.

'It's all right.' Yee Jan gathered up his bag. 'It's happened before. I'm used to it, kind of. Seriously, I know what to do if there's any trouble.' Yee Jan pushed back the chair. The police shuffled to their feet but looked only at the director.

'I – we – want you to know that you are safe.'

Yee Jan didn't understand.

'Nothing is going to happen to you.'

'I don't know what you mean? You said this was nothing.'

The director corrected herself. 'The police have been keeping an eye on the school, and they –' she indicated the police, 'want you to know that you are safe.'

'Do you mean I'm being followed?'

The director shifted her weight. 'You were,' she said, 'but they don't think there's any need any more. It has been a week.'

Yee Jan's friends waited at the *alimentari*. When he came out of the school he looked first to the wall knowing that this was where the men had waited, then crossed the alley to the broader piazza in a skittish hurry – and it was easy to allow the sunlight, the promise of waiting friends, their expectation of news, and such strange news also, to diffuse the threat he felt. He knew that if he could talk this through a good few times he would be able to wrap the event in a protective shell, reform it as a harmless anecdote. Stranger still was the idea that he had been monitored by the police but had no idea about it. Yee Jan looked about the palazzo, but could not see anyone in uniform, or anyone who looked like the police.

The news came out in a flood. A single explanation delivered standing at the head of the table. He held his hands up against the flurry of questions, ordered a beer, then sat down.

'You don't understand,' he said. 'I'm losing my touch. He wasn't interested in me. He didn't want me. He wanted an ancient Japanese hausfrau.' Yee Jan shuddered and whispered to Keiko. 'It's so insulting. Epic eyesight fail.'

No, he didn't know what this man / these men, wanted, except to look, that it was probably some pathetic kind of curiosity that brought the lame and the inadequate to the language-school doors. They wanted to know about the Japanese student, the housewife, that's why they were there. It wasn't really much of a mystery, just people who had nothing better to do, and no other accident to gawp at. And it was all so last week.

'Aren't you frightened?'

'No. I mean, maybe if I'd known about it, then yes, but I had no idea. And there's nothing to be frightened of.'

The woman who asked the question was French, and she sat low in her seat with her arms folded, making herself as small as she possibly could. 'I don't like it,' she said. 'This place isn't safe.'

Yee Jan saved the best piece of information till last. 'I had an escort. All last week. And I didn't even know it. I had police, secret police, following me just in case. Who knows, maybe they're still here?'

On the *funiculare* back to Vomero, Yee Jan scanned the commuters, and wondered how many of these people, just out of curiosity, had walked by the language school at some point, just to place it, to know exactly where the school was located; to confirm for themselves that this was the very same sign they had seen a hundred thousand other times. He looked for a man with a baseball hat, a lightweight summer coat, but found no likely candidate. He looked among the passengers for someone who might be a policeman, and again found none, everyone looking so tired, so fed up and everyday he couldn't imagine any one of them rushing to his aid if things got sticky. What worried him most wasn't the current threat that some stalker might be after him – but that he hadn't noticed. The whole event had come and gone and he'd known nothing about it.

FRIDAY

Yee Jan decided to overhaul his look. He rose early and made sure he was first into the bathroom, where he washed his hair, then spent an hour sitting at the end of his bed waiting for it to dry with his make-up laid out. It was time, he decided, to do the whole business. He wedged a small hand mirror between the slats of the window shutter, and as he prepared himself he occasionally paused and looked out at the city, at the backs of apartments and closed metal shutters, over rooftops busy with aerials and satellite dishes. He took out the clothes he'd thought too risky to wear, and thought that unworn, as loose items without specific shape, the blousy almost translucent shirt, the chequered neckerchief, the mini-skirt (tartan, naturally), the chain-link belt from which hung raccoon-like tails, the black herringbone stockings, the patent-leather black Mary Janes, were nothing, literally nothing, elements of something perhaps, but of little substance in themselves. He stood naked in front of the window, hands on hips, then posed in front of the mirror and thought he was tiny, without clothes he barely seemed physical: I dare. I don't dare. I dare.

He wanted to see the video again, slowed down if possible, the man or men outside the language school, leaning against a wall, sullen plains of grey like this was early TV, Ernie Kovacs maybe, some kind of gag. He wanted to click through frame by frame, give the men the same attention they'd given him: only this time they wouldn't know it. He wanted to see that gesture, to see if this movement was conscious (a deliberate sign, a series of calculated motions) or something automatic (a wasp in his face, a complicated nervous tic). The director's answer had come too readily: it wasn't enough any more to know if one or two men had followed him, no, he wanted to know if one of the men had left a message.

There was no reaction on the *funiculare*, but crossing piazza del Municipio two boys shouted at Yee Jan and ran ahead, finding them-

765

selves funny, and these shouts were reassurance that he'd established himself: if someone followed him now, police or maniac, there would be a reason for it, an explanation. With his white face, finely drawn eyes and eyebrows, with his hair pulled back over his scalp, a broad soft collar (he'd chosen a butch office number over the blouse – hints of Chanel), he walked with the manner of a courtier, with delicate but confident steps, not quite primping, but mannered, definitely mannered: each footfall an assured but subtle, *me, me, me, me*. The wide reach of the piazza, this volume of space about him open and hollow, the air close enough so that he could feel himself swim forward, and he felt honest and good and happy.

The students of Elementario Due returned with clippings from the week's newspapers and chatter about the film, the visiting actors, and news of where they were staying. Everyone expressed amazement at Yee Jan's transformation, how perfect, how delicate he appeared, and how he seemed to flutter in front of them as someone they knew and someone they did not know. He soon bored of the attention, and became exhausted by the constant struggle to pick the simplest phrases, he ached to get outside and find the film crew (although, even this could offer only a momentary interest). As a boy in Washington State he'd felt the same kind of boredom, days on end. A dry dissatisfaction. Something akin to taking a journey, the sedation of watching the world slide by a window and holding no influence over the persistent slide of it all, of being both inside and outside, a passenger who is never really present.

The newspapers revived the story of the clothes, the assault, the missing Japanese student, Mizuki Katsura, the missing American student, and it all began to assemble itself. At first, Lara refused to answer questions. Everyone had an idea about what had happened, and while the tutor would say nothing the students became busy with speculation.

With some effort she attempted to steer the conversation to easier subjects: toward whatever they might have attempted in Italian on the previous night – but the news of a killing made for a better discussion than food or culture or travel and these students, now roused, became inexplicably fluent and direct in their new language. This was no ordinary Friday. Lara wouldn't just tell them directly to stop, to shut up, to do exactly what they were asked.

'She was singled out at the train station. They were waiting for her.'

Then Lara, provoked: 'There are people who have family – missing family. They come here to make a film, to tell the story about this, but they bring everything with them and have no interest in the city, and no interest in the people who have lost members of their family and who have no idea where they are.'

Tonight there was to be a demonstration. A silent protest, an hour-long vigil organized over mobile phones, devices seeking people from the region, calling them to a specific point at a specific time. They would find the location of the film crew and they would silently materialize and surround them in their hundreds. This, anyway, was the plan.

The second session did not improve. Having answered questions all week about why they'd come to Campania and what they liked best about Naples, students fixed on the subject. What they liked best about Naples today involved killing.

Yee Jan was surprised how uneasy the discussion made him: when he left the building for the coffee break he waited deliberately for a group and struck up a conversation so that someone would escort him across the courtyard and outside.

'Did you see him?'

'You know I can't say I saw him. I mean, the police said he was right at the main door.'

The question was repeated, time and again through the break. Have you seen him? What do you think he wants? What are his intentions? What do you think he is going to do? It was only when they returned to class and came round the corner to see the thin dark alley, the glass of the antique shop window, wet-looking, eye-like, that Yee Jan understood – these people are no better than the people who came to the school and stood outside. Everybody wanted that thrill of proximity. There wasn't one speck of difference.

Keiko met Yee Jan on the stairs and Yee Jan spelled it out. 'I have a theory,' he said, 'about why people are so curious. There's only one question, really. What's it like to watch somebody die?'

He refreshed his face at the end of the day, and when he came out of the toilet he found Lara at the entrance, waiting, somewhat deliberate, he thought. He planned to find the film crew at the Duomo and did not want to be delayed.

Lara sat in a folding chair beside the door, an invigilator, hands clamped between her knees.

'I thought you'd be here. If you have a moment.'

Lara had not spoken to him in English before and Yee Jan found this slightly alarming. 'You want to speak?'

'It's about what happened last week.'

Yee Jan waited but Lara couldn't formulate the question. Finally, she gave up and stood up and said it didn't matter.

'I know about the police,' he said. 'They told me I had my own secret security guard, or something like that. I had no idea. Did you know?'

Lara gave a small nod. 'They told us last week.'

'So everyone knew except me?'

'The other instructors were told.'

'Did you see them? The police?'

Lara shook her head.

'I should have been told.' Yee Jan smiled. 'Someone should have told me.' He let the statement stand. 'Have you seen it?'

'I'm sorry?'

'Did you see the footage?'

Lara nodded. 'They showed it to all of the instructors last week.'

'It was two men, wasn't it?'

'I don't know. It isn't clear.' Lara dismissed the question as she did in class when the answer wasn't what she wanted.

'Did you know her? The Japanese student. The woman who disappeared? Were you teaching then?'

Lara made a small gesture which Yee Jan took as a no.

'Has to be weird. The whole thing. Is there anyone here who knew her?'

'I was here. I was finishing my teaching placement.'

'So she was in an advanced class. But you'd know about it.'

'Everybody here knows about it.'

Yee Jan nodded and thought to leave. 'It's just, when something like that happens people treat you differently. If they know you were involved.' He could sense Lara measuring him.

Yee Jan made one single nod. 'And people don't know how to talk to you. Like you're sticky. A little toxic.'

'Look.' Lara dipped her head, eyes closing. 'This has happens a lot. People come all the time. Even though nothing actually happened here.'

'They said.'

Lara zipped up her bag. 'You said this happened to you before?'

So this is what she wanted to know? 'Not quite like this.'

'Sorry?'

'It wasn't the same.'

Lara looked up and waited.

'OK, the first time there was a guy in a car. He just drove up and told me to get in.'

'And you got in?'

'I recognized him. I knew who he was. I wasn't sure there was much of a choice. Anyway, *I always do what I'm told*. After I got in the car I changed my mind and he wouldn't let me out. I managed to get out, but for a moment I didn't know what was going to happen.' Yee Jan explained the situation directly and without fuss, his voice gently flattening as if what had happened was a little tedious or had happened to someone else, to a person perhaps that he didn't like.

'Did he threaten you?'

'He didn't need to.'

'But he didn't?'

'I don't know. I thought when I got out of the car – that was it. He'd – I don't know.' Yee Jan shrugged. 'I was just scared.'

'And nothing happened?'

But that wasn't really nothing. Yee Jan gave a polite smile. 'No. I saw him again. He tried the same thing. Told me to get into the car. This time he made threats, said he would tell my family things, make trouble for me at college, at work, and then he started making threats, just general threats. Stuff he'd do to the people I knew.'

'He knew you?'

'No. I found out later he didn't. I'd seen him around. I'd noticed him. But I thought he knew me, or knew of me, and he might know where I lived – and I thought he might do something.' Yee Jan looked up. 'It was two men, wasn't it? Last week. Outside. Not one.'

Again Yee Jan had the sense that he was asking the wrong question.

'You sound certain?'

'Do you think they thought I was her, this Mizuki?'

'I don't see how. She's been gone for two years.'

'Then why were they waiting for me?'

'I don't know.'

'It's because of the way I look.' A statement of fact.

'I don't think it's that specific. Or clear. The police think you fit a general profile. Being Asian. Something more general.'

Yee Jan didn't answer. 'So this has happened to other Asian students?'

Lara shook her head. 'We've had some trouble with younger women, girls – but I think that's not so unusual. That's an entirely different thing.'

'So, I don't understand. Why are the police interested if this happens all of the time? They have someone don't they. Isn't he in prison?'

'Everybody thinks he's the wrong man.'

Yee Jan nodded. 'Even the police?'

'I don't know.'

'Did they say anything else?' Yee Jan was surprised when Lara paused. 'They did? They said something else?'

'Not about you. There's a type of person who gets obsessed with this kind of thing, and there have been lots of people coming by because of what had happened. It's a problem the school have to do something about. They understand it's a problem, but they haven't done anything about it.'

'I know. They said. But did they say something else?'

'Not about you.'

A siren careened from the corso behind the school. Yee Jan cleared his throat. 'I'd like to see the tapes again. One of the men made a gesture.'

'It's an ambulance, that's all.' Lara stood up.

'So what else did they say if it wasn't about me?'

'It wasn't about you.'

'So it was about the men, then?'

'It was nothing.'

'They think it was two men, don't they?'

'Nobody knows. It's not so clear. And maybe not so important.'

'But they have been speaking with people here, so you know what they think. I mean people must have some idea?' Yee Jan stopped and became more direct. 'I think you know something.'

'I don't. There are so many rumours. Where are you staying?'

'In Vomero. It's OK. An apartment. You know. Why?'

'Are there other people with you?'

'Why are you asking where I'm staying? Is there something else going on?'

THE KILL

Lara folded the straps of her bag around her arms. 'There is a rumour,' she looked directly at Yee Jan, 'about the tapes. It isn't anything the police have said directly. But after they spoke with you they were interested in the tapes again and they spent some time looking at them.'

'So they do think it's two people.'

Lara shook her head. 'There's something else, and I probably shouldn't be telling you this, because it is a rumour, and it's only a rumour. But the gesture the man made, they think that he's saying something.'

Yee Jan waited. Lara slowly ran her tongue over her lips.

'I did know her. Mizuki. I thought I knew her. She came here to get away from her husband. She told me this. Before. Mizuki wasn't her real name. She paid for everything in cash, she gave many explanations, to me and to her class, about who she was, and she didn't seem to be someone who would not be telling the truth. Anyway. She stopped coming.' Lara's voice became quiet, the words less than vapour. 'She was here at the school and then she wasn't. We don't know what happened to her.' Lara cleared her throat and spoke louder, her voice caught in the room. 'I've watched the tapes. I watched them with the police. They think he's saying something to the camera. The man who followed you is saying something to the camera in the video. There are some gestures, but they think that he is saying something to the camera about a woman. They think this is a reference to Mizuki. They think he is saying that they did not touch her. They didn't touch the woman. They think the person who was waiting outside was involved, and they think he is saying that there was only one person who was killed and that they did not touch the woman, but it isn't clear.'

Yee Jan stepped back to the counter. 'Why were they following me?'

Lara reached forward to calm him. 'It's over. The police were watching you. Just in case.'

The film crew took up most of via Duomo in a one-block radius of via Capasso with their vans, stalls, and equipment. Lights raised on stanchions and scaffolding burned sharp into the street, silver caught in the shop windows and along the cornices and ledges. Yee Jan tried to push ahead to see what was happening and found his way blocked by a line of security guards and behind them a row of boards. He caught glimpses of the crew, but had arrived too late to find a good position –

and what he could see didn't interest him. They were filming the murder in the place where the murder occurred: a little bankrupt, he thought, a little unprincipled.

Yee Jan came out of the small street, walked by the palazzo onto via Duomo and found papers taped and pinned to the door – photographs and photocopies – on each sheet a face or a figure in a scratched monotone, and beneath each a date. A familiar kind of memorial. At the bare piazza in front of the Duomo he found a disconsolate group of six or seven protesters each holding a placard with one of the same images from the doors of the palazzo. The protesters, a shabby group, had dressed in black and wore black armbands, and looked, being such a small number, foolish. One of the group approached Yee Jan and offered him a handful of flyers believing him to be one of them. The man's expression was stern, possibly disappointed, so Yee Jan accepted without saying anything.

DOVE SONO I 41? / Chi sarà il prossimo?

Yee Jan took a piece of paper, on one side a list of names: Pascal Entuarde. Johannes Blume. Emilio Santos. Mizuki Katsura. In two years there were forty-one unaccounted people, forty-one missing.

The film crew divided into two groups. A group busy with the production, and a looser group at the margin, who waited, arms folded, some smoking, a little edgy at what was beginning to develop: as if a group of ten people was something to worry about. Yee Jan also felt that energy, as people began to gather in twos and threes at the Duomo steps. Eight people to start. Thirty people within ten minutes, and in twenty that number had tripled: the day, the fading light, began to hold an expectation.

Yee Jan picked up the flyers scattered across the piazza and added them to his own. And as the Duomo's bells began to ring a charge ran through the air. From the side streets, via Tribunali, along via Duomo more people arrived, many dressed in black, many with posters and all with unlit candles, the groups gathered without sound, all facing via Capasso and the film crew, so the noise of the gathering became a hustle of bodies and feet. Yee Jan stood in the centre and handed out the sheets. For Pascal. For Johannes. For Emilio. For Michele. For Mizuki. The vigil formed about as the small open square in front of the Duomo stopped with people – when the bells struck midnight the candles were lit and all conversation stopped without any instruction to do so. And there, brightening the darkness, a sea of light.

TUESDAY

The men wear baseball hats, one grey the other blue with a black visor. Both men wear lightweight summer jackets, windbreakers, similar to the film crew. Both men wear sunglasses in what seems at first to be an affectation, because approaching midnight on the piazza the only light comes from candles and the floodlights brightening the front of the church and the blank ends of the buildings either side – so in analysis there's little to distinguish them apart, regardless of how many cameras, how many phones catch them as they push through a crowd too dense to make room. The image loses focus with the candles, the fuzz and blow of light, as an undulating plain speckled soft and obscure, a sudden brightness dazing the image as the two men lug the boy through. The blackness – night sky, gaps between figures, hair – appears liquid.

Monica watches the image on her own, sits at the side of her bed, the remote in her hand to change to another channel. The image switches, a kind of flicker, as if something has been edited, and loses colour completely, shows the men as they push through, bodies angling sideways, shoulder first. In every example it's almost the same, or a version of the same sets of information: two men, on either side of what you'd take to be a petite girl, Asian, who appears to be drunk or stunned or stoned. The two men look like boxers in the way they duck forward, although the association makes no sense to Monica, perhaps because of how lean they seem, and their clothes, the caps, the coats, an attitude to them of stern and focused business. And the girl – who she knows to be a boy because this has already been reported and discussed, and because the screen carries his name – Yee Jan Lee – although this could be the name of a girl as far as she can tell, because this is the face of a girl, deadpan white, and eyes so small, would it be wrong to call him pretty? And something wrong with him, seriously wrong because he isn't walking properly, he's being held up by these two men who bully him through, propped on either side, and

773

move as one brusque unit, no gentility about the shove and shunt and push, and there, in the register of the boy's mouth a turn, a down-turn, that might be pain. He's being swept through. Monica thinks of him as a girl because this is how the boy is presented, a painted face, luminous white, delicate eyes drawn in, a painted face with a slender feminine mouth, so much about this boy is soft. The boy's face sweeps by the camera, nothing more than a blur, his eyes are certainly looking into the camera, and there, a hand gripped on his upper arm. If he or she passed by you so close you could free him, hold him, keep him from harm. The videos insist that this is a present action, something happening continuously: the ongoing abduction of a boy in a crowded piazza. A counter beside the name marks the days he has been missing. 4.

She watches again.

A different view taken from the Duomo steps so that the field of people is specked with a pulsing light, the candles too many to account for, star points, a map of light, and she can see the disturbance, how the light appears to grow dense, block together as the three bodies push through, a small hole behind them which soon, waterlike, refills itself. The buildings opposite glow with ominous long, hollow windows.

Again. Another view. Closer.

The crowd barely move, the threesome press directly toward the camera, shoulders first. No one steps aside to allow them through so they have to shove and lumber past the person taking the shot. The camera jolts, is held up to show a brighter set of lights, the film set beside the Duomo and the scaffold holding floodlights which turn night into day. Something about the crowd reminds her of an execution, a public trial. She's old enough to remember Tiananmen Square.

Monica watches because she has promised to do this, and tries to concentrate on the men, the boxers, the brothers, as they bump deliberately, shoulders set to knock people out the way, some small cries of protest. But every time she can't help but focus on the boy, it is impossible not to watch him, and she can't imagine how this could happen – an abduction during a silent protest, one body selected and removed.

She has to understand how this could happen. How someone could be picked out when surely all attention would be on him, everyone would notice him. She cannot help but watch the boy. The boy appears drunk, ill, out of it. The men have purpose, threat in their speed, which dares to be challenged – and this, the greatest shock of all, almost unaccountable, is their pure nerve to show themselves, join the very crowd protesting their actions two years earlier. Everybody is here because of these two brothers.

The news today is worse, if this is even possible. There is footage from the police, not from the demonstration but images taken a week before of a man waiting in a small street. This image is almost black and white, and at one point, showed slowly, the man appears to leave a message, make a series of gestures, his hand up, a signal she cannot read. The same baseball cap, the same jacket. A one point a group of people come out from under the camera, and there, among them, the boy from the piazza. Yee Jan Lee.

Monica sits and watches, unsure of the limits of her body. She can't feel her fingers, or sense anything other than her breath and chest, aware that it hurts to watch, but now, exhausted, she feels like she is starting to disappear. There is nothing about the brothers that she recognizes. Although they must have been there, two years ago, on the platform, in the station. They had to have been close, she must have walked right by them, there is no possible way she could not have passed them. She has taken the very same walk many times in the intervening years and looked at every detail and wondered, in a space so small, how could she not have seen them?

On his first visit the man made it from the door to the rack of magazines. On the second he managed a further two metres to the desk before changing his mind. On his third visit, which comes minutes after the second (they have all occurred in the space of one morning), Elisa, who always keeps an eye out for the weird ones, announces as the man steps in from the street that this is a travel agency for the purpose of booking flights and holidays. OK?

'You come here when you want to go somewhere.' She slides a brochure across her desk. 'If you want anything that isn't travel-related then you're in the wrong place.'

Monica, being less confrontational, asks the man if she can help, and the man asks if there are any brochures for America or England. Monica points to the rack at the brochures facing out with pictures of São Paulo, Rio de Janeiro, Buenos Aires, searching herself, and then and along a lower shelf, aha, Las Vegas, San Francisco, New York, and there it is, London. 'Where are you thinking in England,' she asks, and realizes she can't think of anywhere other than London. London, England, even though she has relatives who live in Manchester. She can't remember booking anyone a trip to anywhere other than America, North and South, in a long time. She tries to chat but it isn't easy this morning: to be honest everyone figures out their own arrangements these days (she's talking nonsense because she just can't focus). Everyone has a computer. She makes a grimace and the man smiles. After the smile he steps forward as if they are a little more intimate.

'London? OK? That's what you wanted?'

He gives a dismissive blink, a slight head shake, and asks if she speaks English. Monica answers in English.

'I do. A little.'

'You are Monica Cristobari?'

And here she realizes her mistake. There is no holiday. There are no plans. The man, like many others, has sought her out and now he will tell her why, they always do.

'Did you recognize them? The brothers? Did you remember them?'

Monica raises her hand to her head, unconscious of the movement. Elisa flies at the man as he speaks.

'My name is Doctor Arturo Lanzetti. I live at via Capasso 29. I have seen them before. I recognize them.' The man, walking backwards now, is repelled from the shop by Elisa with a loud *Out, out, out.* Monica, stunned, moves as if she is swimming. Before Elisa has the man expelled, the door closed, the lock secured, the bolt drawn, Monica has her jacket over her arm and speaks as if this is rational – she thinks she should be getting home if that's all right. And Elisa guides her to the back of the shop, insists that she sits down, swears at the man, tells Monica she should wait a moment, let him leave and she will call her a taxi.

'You shouldn't have come in today.'

Elisa returns to the window to check the street, but can't see the man because the market is busy. Monica shakes her head. 'It isn't going to stop, is it? It's never going to stop.'

The man stands on the opposite kerb until Elisa makes a show of calling the police, her phone held up dramatically, to demonstrate her intention. Once the police do arrive, purely coincidentally, the man disappears.

Elisa turns the blinds to direct the light from the street and close the view. A distraction? Is that what they need right now? Some noise? A distraction? The radio?

'He won't be back.'

Early afternoon, on a bright day, most days, the gold lettering on the opposite shop window shines across the floor, and slips slowly across the linoleum to the foot of Monica's desk. Monica would slip off one shoe and slide her foot into the path. Today she stands at the edge, mind blanking on ideas on how she can excuse herself and leave.

Elisa bins the newspaper, unread. 'I'm not in the mood for news.' No interest today in reading about the film or the actors – which out of respect has stopped production, or at least filming in town.

'It's – honestly. I'm OK.' Monica watches Elisa rearrange the draw-strings for the blinds: her blouse untucks from her skirt. 'It's just,' she shakes her head, still can't think of anything to say. 'Rude. The point shouldn't need making.'

This is how things are these days, the women agree, without any real thought, any conscience. Someone has an idea about something and they just go ahead and do exactly whatever they please.

Elisa always agrees with Monica, even when she disagrees, you're right, she'll say, then pick a word and stick with it. Most days Monica finds this funny, endearing even. Some days, though, it would be nice if this didn't have to happen.

'You're right. There's no respect for privacy. That's really the prob-lem. That's honestly what this is about. If we're being honest about this, they didn't have to do it here at all. The film. And they've chosen the actual places. Honestly. The palazzo. Ercolano,' she hesitates, man-ages not to say the station, the abduction and it is still only an abduction, because no body has been found, the boy, carted away from the piazza, has disappeared. 'Can you imagine?'

Monica hums her disagreement. 'Can we not do this today?' Her computer fades into sleep mode. On screen a man swimming, a shot taken underwater looking up, spars of sunlight radiating about him.

That afternoon, while changing into her swimming costume, Monica feels a cold pulse pass across her lower back. She has stuck with her regular routine. Insisted upon it. She checks herself in the mirror and remembers a rash she discovered that morning. Not a rash, so much – nothing more in fact than a small area of dry skin, but it has now divided into two patches on either side of her spine. Monica prefers to keep out of the sun, and exercises in an enclosed pool. Her skin is snowy white. She seldom sits under direct sunlight.

Troubled by the rash she decides not to swim. There are chemicals in the water, she tells herself, which will aggravate the condition. Monica believes that this discomfort is caused by stress. *It would be strange if it didn't happen.* It's impossible to avoid the news about the film, or news about the boy, who was taken, they suggest, as a stand-in for the girl they didn't take two years ago. A fascination now with Yee Jan Lee, a boy, who by rights should not have looked so pretty. It's impossible to avoid the storm growing around the conviction of Marek Krawiec, who was right all along. It appears. An appeal is lodged. So who are these men, these brothers? And why would they come to the city to kill one boy then grab another? She isn't sure she understands. Uneasy with her part in this, she finds herself featured in reports in the *Cronache* and the *Corriere* as 'the witness', or 'the sole witness' to the first killing, and while her name has not become generally known, it's no secret that 'the sole witness' works for a travel agency located close by the Centro Direzionale. Her clients, her friends, her family all know the story and are all alarmed by the weekend's developments. *People being picked off the streets.* Truth is she's thoroughly sick of it.

By example: when Monica returns home her cousin Davide asks if it would make sense for her to take some kind of a holiday until everything blows over.

Monica, preparing the evening meal, her hands wet, pauses long enough to ask why she should have to stop her work and head off to some place – if it was even possible – where they hadn't heard of this case?

'Maybe China,' she says, 'or India? Or some place where people don't read?'

Davide insists that he's serious.

'And I go, and then the film comes out and there's a big fuss in the newspapers and all over the television. I leave again and then I come back. Then it's released on DVD – there's more fuss, I leave and I come back. And then it goes on cable, then RaiUno. And on and on.' She draws her hands out of the bowl, wet ring-less fingers. 'And then . . . perhaps someone will write a book about making a film about a story that is taken from this book which is taken from a real-life story that was copied from a story in a book. You know? Or maybe there will be a video game? Something they can play in the arcades? And then later they can remake the film, or make the film of the video game? Or maybe there will be some other imagined crime that these men can act on and make real?'

Davide visibly weakens under this reasoning – in his defence he's trying to suggest something practical.

'There isn't any escape, Davide. There isn't an ending. It doesn't just stop because we are tired of it.'

Despite herself Monica is becoming increasingly preoccupied by the three minutes or less in which she witnessed the young man at the train station. And this is two years ago now, two whole years. The man had sorted through his bags with little hurry, unaware of the people about him, as if he had somewhere to go, somewhere to be. Two years ago she become frozen by the event, caught in endless possibilities, so that the event itself became completely unreal, a fiction. What if he had not paused? What if he had taken a moment longer? What if she had spoken to him? Would the sequence of events that brought him to the small basement room in a dirty palazzo on via Capasso have played out differently? To add to this she wrestles with the uncertainty of what has recently occurred. Like everyone else she entertains alternative possibilities: perhaps the boy isn't dead, perhaps this is just like the book, an elaborate scam?

These ideas set fire to her skin. The rash won't quieten.

She calls a specialist recommended by her sister-in-law and makes an appointment.

THURSDAY

Monica takes the morning off work and turns up early at the special-ist's office in Portici. The rash hasn't improved. Dr Novi carefully checks her back and asks after her diet and sleeping pattern. He washes his hands after the inspection and says that this is minor, although he is certain that it must irritate her, it's unlikely to be caused by the chlorinated water. More likely than not the condition is caused by stress (and this is something she didn't know?), although it was always possible that they were using different chemicals, or more chemicals than they should. He cannot be certain. He will provide a prescription for a salve, and suggests that if she wishes to continue her exercise that she swims instead in salt water where she will benefit from both the ions and the iodine, but failing that, there's a mineral pool in Lucrino, a small distance from the city. It is, he said, a far second best, because it might be better if she does not swim at all.

Monica sits on the doctor's raised bed, dissatisfied with the exam-ination. She'd mentioned swimming only because this was easier than explaining about the cause of her stress. She can't be certain about his recommendation either. Can she or can't she swim? It isn't clear. Swim-ming offers her the one pure moment when she does not have to answer to her family, or to work. While she swims, in that brief thirty-five minutes each day, she is completely alone, and the isolation that the activity brings is a welcome and rare pleasure.

Immediately out of the office Monica takes the metro to Cavalleggeri d'Aosta, and in the heat and bustle her clothes irritate the skin, and send a small charge, a pulse around her back. She tries to scratch her wrist instead of her back but finds this useless.

The pool is new, less than a year old, and managed by a university. Monica changes in a private booth, conscious that her costume is old, and that chlorine is beginning to rot the stitching. The pool itself is steel, of even depth, and encased in glass, one side looks out to a bright view of a honey-coloured cliff, the lip of a crater, the other to a parking lot, and in the distance, the other side of the crater.

Monica is joined at the poolside by a young man. Like Monica the man has with him a towel, which he sets on the slate side away from the pool, and goggles, the straps wrapped about his hand. She watches as the man walks to the head of the pool and chooses the centre lane, and she considers quickly who she would be able to keep pace with, and picks the lane beside the young man.

On her first few laps she finds herself swimming faster than her usual pace. Her stroke, although clean, is usually underpowered, but once she is comfortable she begins to move with economy and feels the motion to be smooth and direct, and for twenty minutes she swims without a break, aware of the young man in the lane beside her. As Monica swims freestyle, the young man swims breaststroke, and they fall into an easy rhythm, swimming at points side by side. When she stops, the man continues, and she watches him set the pace for the lane with a powerful, simple stroke – as his hands dive forward his head ducks down and his shoulders follow in a sequence that is direct and uncomplicated. Unlike the other swimmers he causes little disturbance in the water, no splashing, and no hurry, just a smooth and considered series of movements. When she starts again, she finds herself falling into the same rhythm and is mindful to contain her stroke and make the movement as direct and uncomplicated as she can. Hand slightly cupped, she breaks the water, thrusts her arm full length, then folds it under her in a long swift swipe, and finds with this simple adaptation that she moves quicker, further, faster.

At the end of his swim the young man stands at the end of the lane. Tall and gangly, he has none of the poise and grace out that he commands when he is in the water.

Monica returns to the changing rooms exhilarated, not only by the swim but by the coincidence of swimming beside the young man. It is only when she sits to take off her costume that her mood changes and she remembers the boy at the station, and an unreasonable notion strikes her that if one man she had noticed disappeared, it could possibly happen again. As soon as the thought occurs she dismisses it. There was no killing, she tells herself. No such thing.

FRIDAY

Monica returns to the pool at the same time. As she walks into the building she's surprised to see the young man ahead of her, smartly dressed with a small backpack. He leans forward a little as he walks. She guesses that he has come directly from work, and wonders if the people he works with understand how exceptionally graceful he is in the water. Out of the water there's nothing exceptional about him, but when he swims everything about him seems in tune and in place. She stands beside him to pay for her ticket, neither smiles nor acknowledges the other, and the previous day's anxiety is remembered but not felt. The man has returned, of course he has returned. Nevertheless, if she hadn't seen him, his absence would have troubled her.

And so she swims beside the man again, each keeping pace, that one or the other sometimes breaks, and she finds this silent company comforting and imagines that a familiarity is growing between them. While she fights to keep pace she begins to recognize when her own stroke becomes similarly economical and pure. In just two sessions her stroke is beginning to change, she is becoming long, more decisive with her reach, so that the motion is unconsciously fluid. Afterward, she wonders if the man deliberately keeps pace with her, he made no attempt to force any other kind of contact between them. Out of the water they are strangers, in the water they are companions, and their bodies move at the same pace. She can feel his company as soon as she slips into the water. She is familiar now with the set of his mouth as he comes up for air, his quick efficient gasp, the hunch of his shoulders as he lunges forward, and the speed with which he pulls deep into the water.

This is, she understands, a distraction. The more preoccupied she becomes with the swimmer, the less she needs to think about the student at the station, about the boy at the piazza.

SATURDAY

On the Saturday, the swimmer does not appear, it shouldn't surprise her, but she finds it impossible to swim, and sits at the poolside waiting. That night her anxieties return in a full and wide-eyed sleepless distraction. She sits upright in bed, her back irritating, the nerve ends prickle, sharp and sensitive. The heat of the room and the oily stink of traffic catch in the night air, familiar to her as the station that morning two years ago. She sees it time and time again, the train door, the boy crouched beside his bags with his back to her, the shirt as it was on his back, and the shirt as it was, bloodied and cut. Why hadn't she delayed him? Why hadn't she spoken to him?

On the news the boy's parents, Mr and Dr Lee, who move like people who do not trust themselves, whose bodies might at any point fail them, who look torn by grief and unknowing. They beg for the release of their son. Dr Lee speaks in Italian, explains how much her son loves the city. Speaks in the present tense to keep him alive.

Monica watches the news. The footage of the vigil. The candles as a map or a sea, all comfort taken from the image. They show the brothers, a still of their faces which gives nothing away. A politician explains that Krawiec is to be released but banned from the country. She does not know how they can do this. These brothers, the politician struggles for adequate words, come to our city to feed on us, not once, but twice, like wolves. There are calls again for information regarding Mizuki Katsura, the thinking now is that the killers have taken her absence, her disappearance, the belief that she was killed to be instruction and script on the abduction of the boy. She must come forward. How then did they find the first American? Was this an accident? Did they choose him the moment she passed by, or had the decision already been made, the boy as good as dead?

She sits at the edge of her bed, her back needling. The room is close, the air sticky, and she tries to calm herself by thinking of the swimmer instead of the student at the station. But the substitution of one man for another will not work. The man in the pool and the youth at the station, while not similar, were also too similar, and the sound of the traffic, the scooters, the taxis, the night bustle of the city, while not like the sounds of the station, were not unlike the sounds of the station. The familiarity, the associations were uncanny and close.

She thinks of opposites, of things that are not there and memories that will not trouble her. Instead of heat, she thinks of snow. Instead of the city, she imagines herself above it, safely distant, alone on the mountain. Her immediate memory is of her first close view of snow. She was five when her father drove her to the volcano and presented it to her as if it were of his own making. It was winter, the first day of the year, and she remembers the long and steep road along the flanks of the mountain, and her excitement at how strange it was to be looking back at the city rather than out at the mountain. The inner cone sheltered by the separate shattered ridge of Monte Somma, and between the two peaks ran a long and lower field of rucked and fluid lines of stone capped and softened with snow. The trees, so thin and precarious on the steep lip, appeared sparse and burned, black against a thin white drift, and it is with this thought, the notion of a field of blankness, of coldness, of everything alien to the physical heat currently pressing down upon her, that she is able to slowly shut the chatter out her mind. And to this place she brings the swimmer, and the two of them sit, silent, side by side, overlooking a plain snowbound void.

There was no killing. There were no brothers. The city does not exist.

THE HIT

THE FIRST SUTLER

1.1

The trouble starts as soon as they arrive. The flight to Damascus is delayed for an unspecified reason, which means another three hours with Udo.

Rike thinks they should leave him at the airport but doubts that Henning would approve. It doesn't help that they are early. Udo wants to know if the trouble with the flight is a regular problem, or something more ominous. *Damascus*, he says, fretting the word. *Damascus*. He suggests a drive around the salt flats or into Larnaca, when Henning receives a call.

Henning dips his head to listen, one hand at his hip he strikes a pose of concentrated irritation. The call is bad news, and he looks to Udo. 'We have identification,' he says. 'Papers on the train.'

Henning wants Udo to explain how an intelligent man can somehow disappear from inside a sealed train, moving at, what, sixty, seventy, eighty kilometres an hour, with doors which do not open, with windows which do not lower, to be found in pieces on the tracks? How is this possible? How does a man who has evaded capture for so long find himself caught between the Napoli–Roma Express and the Milano Eurostar? How?

In any case, he doesn't believe that this is Stephen Sutler on the train tracks in Rome, any more than he believes Sutler was sighted in Grenoble, or that the man currently in hospital in Damascus is Sutler. Whatever identification they've found on the train will prove false.

Udo isn't happy to be challenged. He isn't happy to be talking about this in Rike's presence. He begins to explain they don't yet know what happened in Rome, and anyway, this isn't their business. If he's honest he doesn't see why they should be responsible for the man in Damascus. He's serious. 'This isn't our concern.' Leave it to the Americans. Leave it to the British.

Henning holds out his hands, insulted.

'This is your best advice?'

'The police. The appropriate *British* authorities. Let them work this out.'

*

789

They view the salt lake from the car. The land slopes toward the sea then flattens in a perfect line to a field of white. Rike squints to take it in. There are stories of resurrections, visions, transpositions. Cities have been seen in the shimmering light, ships traversing or hovering above the plain. The salt is blindingly bright and moisture rises from the bed in waves which obliterate the horizon. While they have time, Udo doesn't want to visit the shrine.

Henning asks Rike where else she wanted to go. Some mosque, right, a sepulchre or mausoleum? Could Rike explain to Udo about the sepulchre? Udo says he's heard about it. Umm Haram? Hala Tekke? That building across the salt flat surrounded by palms. The only feature in an otherwise blank terrain.

None of them know for certain.

There's some other place she's thinking of in town.

'I know,' Udo says. 'I know. I know what you're going to say.'

Henning wants to make a point and won't be robbed of the opportunity.

In town Rike visits the tomb on her own. Henning and Udo stay with the car and talk business. It's exactly what you'd hope for. Something and nothing. Steps down to a chamber and an open tomb. A ceiling so low you have to bow. A row of censers. Stone and dust. The absent body of a saint. She isn't sure how to behave in such a place, even on her own.

When she returns to the street Henning and Udo are leaning against the car, smoking and sulking.

'Tell him,' he says, 'who was buried here.'

'I know.'

Rike opens the car door, sits inside, winds down the window and tells Udo that this is Lazarus's tomb, although the lid is shattered and the tomb is empty.

Udo holds up his hands, it's the same gesture Henning uses. He rolls his eyes. 'I know.'

Henning stands upright and the car adjusts.

'We bring him here.'

'We don't bring him here.'

Henning turns to Rike. 'Tell him why he's here. Tell him about Lazarus.'

'He isn't here. It's empty.'

'But tell him. And tell him why he came here.'

'He had to escape. He fled and came to Cyprus. This is where he died.'

'We bring him here.'

Udo indulges Henning's idea, although it's clear that he doesn't agree. 'Why?'

'Because he's in our care. Because we can keep him safe.'

Udo straightens his suit jacket. He hates stories, he says, especially stories like this.

'We bring him here,' Henning turns to Udo, 'to Cyprus, and we see who comes after him.'

'This isn't thought through. It's undigested. It looks like a solution, but it isn't.'

'We bring him here.'

'We do no such thing.' This is Udo's final word.

On their way home, Henning stops to show Rike the view. Behind him a single peak rises from a flat plain. On top of this peak sits a monastery. She's seen the image in postcards, the blocked walls bridging boulders and outcrops. Without a bare blue summer sky it isn't as impressive as expected. Henning sucks on an ice-pop. One hand on his hip again, but this time he isn't annoyed. He asks Rike not to tell her sister about the man on the train. Not one word. Isa doesn't need to know, and she isn't to mention it. OK? Agreed? He tucks his tie into his pocket and leans forward so the lolly won't drip onto his shirt. His lips are stained red and he laughs. He stands in front of a sign that says *no photographs – military installation* and asks Rike to take a photo. 'Send it to Isa,' he says, 'tell her we'll be back in an hour.' They will stop by work first.

Rike holds the phone to Henning's ear as he drives because his fingers are sticky, and the headset hasn't worked since he dropped it. Udo is stuck in the departure lounge and there's a rumour that this will be the last civilian flight into Damascus. He's thinking they should go back to their original plan. He wants Henning to join him, not immediately, but in a couple of days. There will be military flights from the British base at Akrotiri.

Henning disagrees with almost everything he's hearing. He shakes his head.

'How? Why? It makes no sense. Train doors do not open. They just don't. Not while it's moving. Even in Italy.' Pause. 'No. Why would he?' Pause. 'I don't know. I don't see how that's possible.' Henning will soon become a father. His imminent fatherhood has made him particular, exact. He's a little insufferable.

He begins to drive faster, indicates that Rike needs to keep the phone to his ear. 'These aren't the questions I'd be asking. I'd question how he got from inside a sealed train to outside.' Then, finally, more emphatically. 'It isn't Sutler. It can't be. It has to be someone else. Sutler doesn't exist . . . And Grenoble,' he asks, 'before you go. What's the news from Grenoble?' Henning listens then agrees to make the call himself.

The problem, he explains to Rike, is that we have three Sutlers and a level of unimaginable incompetence, in Iraq, in Turkey, in Malta, in Italy. At every turn. The first, in Rome, was caught between two trains and ripped to pieces. This Sutler, to demonstrate the confusion, doesn't match any earlier description of Sutler. The second was a man sighted in Grenoble who has since disappeared. The third is a man found wandering in the Syrian desert, currently in hospital in Damascus.

'The thing is,' he says. 'We have three Sutlers, when we shouldn't have one.' Sutler, he is convinced, *does not exist.*

'I'll have to go to Damascus,' he says. 'I can see this happening. It could be for a while.'

Henning seldom talks about his work, and today, while speaking with Udo about Sutler, she sensed something she couldn't place. Regret?

'Make sure Isa doesn't get into trouble. Keep an eye on her? Make sure she doesn't do too much. Make sure she keeps her appointments. Keep her out of trouble, and above all, keep her calm. If I go,' he says. 'If. I'll be back before the birth.'

This, Rike guesses, was the point of today's trip. Not to deliver his superior to the airport, not to help choose a gift, but to gain an assurance. Isa needs to take things easy.

1.2

The first report – that Stephen Sutler has been killed in Italy, struck by a train – sounds implausible. Gibson struggles to confirm the information. He calls Parson but gets no reply. He calls two journalists at the IP, then a friend at the Home Office. Finally he calls Paul Geezler, former Advisor to a Division Chief at HOSCO, now Director of CON-PORT, thinking this is good news, which makes discussing what he needs to discuss a little easier.

'This is what we know,' he says. 'It isn't much. I suppose there's some way to identify him, otherwise, why would this be announced?'

While it's frustrating not to have Parson's word on this, Gibson feels some vindication. Parson wasn't wrong: Sutler is in southern Italy, and has been, more than likely, for all this time.

Geezler isn't so sure. Why is this man believed to be Sutler? It seems a spurious attribution? What are the facts?

Gibson repeats what he's heard. Nothing is confirmed. It's still a rumour. As soon as he has details, he'll let him know. He looks at the river as he speaks, at the long span of Blackfriars Bridge. He asks about the reconstruction, the dissolution of HOSCO and its re-emergence as CONPORT. He asks if Geezler has seen the *Financial Times*. 'There's nothing but admiration,' he says, 'everyone is sounding confident.'

Geezler confides that he would like the whole thing over. He's taken a company which is now the byword for corruption, divided its business into separate zones, and parsed out the responsibilities. He isn't saying there shouldn't be some accounting, someone held responsible, especially the authors of this disaster, Sutler, Howell, the men at Camp Liberty, but it needs to end. As soon as the hearing is done, they can all move on.

'Look, Paul . . .' Gibson is grateful that Geezler has introduced the subject. On the river a barge works against the current. 'They've called me in. They want me at the hearing.' Gibson shifts his weight and balance to keep the barge in the centre of vision. 'I've already spoken with them. I'm guessing they want me to repeat everything at the actual hearing. I have nothing new.' Gibson refers to his notes laid across his desk. 'April. Twentieth. I don't quite know what they're after.'

Geezler says this is anyone's guess. He wonders why Gibson has been asked to appear in person, when others have submitted testimonies and are not being called, and others will appear in prepared video statements. He sounds impatient. 'HOSCO is over. It's history. What's left of the military contracts are now handled by CONPORT. They should be happy that this, at least, has been salvaged. Everybody is tired of all the bad news. We need to be moving forward,' he says. 'I have to be honest. If the man in Rome turns out to be Sutler, it won't be a bad thing.'

Gibson agrees.

The windows are dusty. He shuts his right eye and the barge loses distinction. He wonders if this is new or something he hasn't noticed before. His left eye has always been weaker. At some point the body offers only disappointment.

1.3

Rike finds the cat flopped over the kerb, impossibly soft with a long black tail tracing the edge of the paving. A hard sun cooks a vegetable stink off the road. The cat has been shot and much of its head is lost to the dust, the blood can't be distinguished at a distance from the fur (an oily black) so the animal's shape shifts from something familiar and toy-like – tail, legs, a handsome skinny body, a luxuriant pelt – to something approximate, a spill or a smattering. The cat, in contradiction to its pose and silky fur, isn't soft at all but stiff, and this is what makes her feel sorry – how she knows something is wrong, because even from a distance the head doesn't make sense.

Rike can't remember the name her sister gave it, but is certain that this is the one Isa singled out because of his skinny grace and how he seemed simultaneously wild but familiar enough with people. These cats are distinctive: thin and long and built for speed and stealth with small and narrow heads.

She crouches beside the animal, doesn't want to touch it but finds it hard not to reach out, at least to run a finger over its paw. The previous night she'd felt the same urge, as the cat, startlingly black, materialized from the night and crept toward the food. People round here, would they kill a domestic animal for sport? Superstition? Fun? Henning talks about rivalries and vendettas between the families who fled the north and were assigned houses, decades ago, in town or in the villages, and the families who still live in the small row-on-row blockhouses of what was once a simple refugee camp but is now referred to as a *settlement*, a *township*. Even now, the people in the settlement don't properly belong in town or out of town, and there are second, third, and fourth generations who have no direct memory of their exodus, who insist that Famagusta, Kyrenia, North Nicosia are home when those houses have accepted new owners, long-since established. Killing a cat would be a way to keep trouble bubbling, to remind someone that this is not their home.

Rike also feels displaced, albeit in a lesser, trivial, way. They were supposed to be in Damascus (*they* being Rike, her sister, her sister's husband, and soon-to-arrive baby). Her sister's child was to be born in Syria, they dearly wanted this, but no, the majority of the German consulate and their families have been evacuated. Most have been sent home, some to Turkey: a few, who need to monitor the remaining interests of German nationals in Syria, have been relocated to Cyprus. While Henning works in Nicosia, Isa has chosen accommodation in Limassol, a good forty-five minutes away and closer to a hospital. So the child's birthplace will be Cyprus, and Cyprus feels like nowhere. A holiday island, a place to play – and Rike pines for the break she isn't going to have, the one the two sisters planned, *their time*, before everything changes with the baby.

Rike speaks with Henning about the cat when he calls in the morning. She makes sure she's the first to answer, because it's possible he's arranged to have the cats removed as he doesn't like his wife's habit of feeding the strays and can't understand her sentimentality.

'I'm pretty sure it's one of her favourites. Black. A little wild. She's given them names.' Arabic names, names of districts, streets, and markets.

Between them they agree not to tell Isa. The move, their own exodus, has been disruptive enough.

Too lazy to pick up, Isa takes her calls on speakerphone. Rike shouts, *It's Henning*, and leaves for her room because she doesn't like to hear their arguments, every detail cutting through the apartment, which is much too large, hollow and temporary. Today Henning holds his ground.

'You're not doing them any favours. You're prolonging the inevitable.' Henning makes no secret of the fact that he doesn't want Isa feeding these creatures. 'You shouldn't be near them. They have scabies, this is why they are bald, fleas, and ticks, and god-knows-what. You should think about what you're doing.' He hopes to be home soon. Udo is coming round to his idea.

Rike can hear Henning's exasperation. Doubt roils in his classic pauses (Henning is known for his pauses). He can make you feel stupid, he can posit doubt – all with the briefest pause. When Isa hangs up she ambles back to Rike's room, hand on her belly, a slow wading walk. 'They give them training: How to Manipulate People.' She makes bunny-ear quotations with her fingers, then, walking away, casually drops the complaint. 'You know where he's staying? He's staying in the Hyatt. Where we were engaged. The Hyatt. *Some covert operation.*' While Henning is not a spy, there is, nevertheless, some truth to the fact that the intelligence community prefer the Hyatt, Henning would confirm this. The Hyatt, it's a standing joke among the staffers, is always the last refuge in a coup.

Rike has to agree about the cats. It might not sound rational, but who knows if there's rabies on the island, or if a cat scratch could open some improbable complication in the last trimester. She knows you can get lockjaw, or that allergy where you grow hard buboes in your neck or armpits. Jesus. Cats aren't as friendly as they appear: fur, teeth, instinct, selfishness and cunning. Essentially they're just big rats. Unlike Henning, Rike can't speak about her fears without sounding ridiculous. Henning is always certain. Not one gram of doubt or self-consciousness. Everything about the man announces confidence, the silences and withdrawals, his assured authority. And he is back in Syria, secretly, to help identify a man found in the desert. A man in a coma. A man hooked to drips and machines. A man they are pumping back to life so they can transport him to Cyprus. A man everyone has been looking for: *Stephen Lawrence Sutler*. Sutler Number Three.

Rike follows the news about Rome on the internet. The man who died was seen running along the tracks before he was hit. There are rumours, and rumours about rumours. There are photographs of men standing on railway sidings, an aqueduct beside them, captions explaining that the evidence was spread over two hundred metres. The men are wearing sunglasses and they look down, about, concentrated on their task.

Isa spoons cat food into one of five bowls, her face set in a grimace. The sisters play a game: how did the man get to the desert? Sutler Number Three.

'Dumped.'
'Bad business . . .'
'Drugs.'

'. . . ran out of fuel. Walked in the wrong direction.'
'Asked a Russian for directions.'
'Punishment. A quarrel. Bad love.'
'Stag night.'
'Outcast. Because people hate him.'

Three books sit in a line across the counter, Isa is undecided on which thriller she wants to read. She tells Rike that she can't work out her mood this morning, and Rike knows well enough not to pester her. It's important to match the right book to the right mood. Isa is wearing one of her brother's T-shirts: 'Show Me Your Junk', which she claims not to understand. Her favourite reads 'It Isn't Going to Suck Itself'. Henning dislikes the T-shirt almost as much as he despises her brother. 'It's a point of fact,' Isa likes to say, which only makes him shake his head. She's not to be seen within a hundred kilometres of anyone from the embassy wearing those T-shirts. 'I'll take it off,' she agrees, 'before I answer the door.' Isa studied psychology before switching to the diplomatic service (two reasons why she will always finish an argument). She reminds Henning that there are more present worries, for example: the apartment is owned by a Russian company. *Russian*. She found this out today. Karnezis Property is owned by Palakov International. Andrei Palakov is a self-styled community investor and *biznizman*. What percentage of their rent, she wonders, is going to fund the trouble they've so recently fled?

On Rike's first evening Henning had warned her that there were bars she shouldn't frequent, a casino, a good number of the nightclubs and hotels, all owned by a Russian consortium, little more than a mini-Mafia, and she should avoid them – not because they are corrupt, and not because of the known drug-trafficking, but because of the 'current tension'. *The situation*. She should do nothing to embarrass him. Does she understand? It's just about OK to shop in the Russian market, and maybe, if she has to, there's the hair salon and nail bar, but where possible she shouldn't patronize Russian businesses. *Just to be sure*. Isa spoke with Rike afterward and said that she should do whatever she likes, within reason, and isn't it amazing how seriously Henning takes himself. *Mini-Mafia*? *Situation*? Seriously? 'Just don't bring a Russian home, OK?'

Isa has her own reservations about Russians, since, in their first week, a cargo ship loaded with arms for the Syrian government weathered a storm in Cypriot waters. Customs wouldn't check it, she said.

Wouldn't go near. Imagine that happening anywhere else. Isa has a theory about Cyprus. How everything is falling apart because it bene-fits Europe and Russia to allow the country to ruin itself. It's all about minerals. It's all about untapped off-shore gas. She has other ideas about Syria, about situations which involve direct conflict.

Isa retrieves another can of cat food from the cupboard and asks Rike if she can guess what they're calling the man they found in the desert. She pauses, a beat. 'Mr Crispy.'

She holds up the can to read the label, 'What do you think is in this?' Reads Greek then English. 'It says chicken. I don't think it's chicken. I think they mean pony. Or dog. That's why they like it so much.' She sets the bowls side by side on the patio and waves her arm for balance. She hasn't forgiven Henning for the Hyatt. 'He'll be swimming laps. Like he needs to.' She reaches out for her sister to help her up. 'Still, I'm glad you're here.' She strains on the words as she rises. 'If people knew half the stuff about pregnancy that I know now, nobody would bother.' Isa collects bad birthing stories. Not stories where sad and terrible events occur, but stories of indignity, people fouling themselves, assaulting husbands and partners, slapping midwives. Women addled by seda-tives, convinced they're giving birth to a monkey or a piece of fruit. Not stories, so much, as tools to mortify Henning. Given the circum-stances, Rike finds this a little distasteful.

Once upright Isa tells Rike that they need to talk, her voice becom-ing darker. The older sister about to set her right.

'I've been thinking. I know Henning wants you to look after me. I know. But you can't spend the whole time stuck in the house with me. It will drive you crazy and it will drive me crazy. You can't do nothing.' And then the news. 'I think I've found you a job.'

Rike watches her sister pick one of the books from the counter. On the cover a graphic of a man in a coffin buried alive. Black and red and angular. Two weeks, that's as long as Isa could manage before chang-ing the terms of Rike's stay.

In the garden the cats stir from their hiding places, little divots scratched in the dust beneath the fig trees. Their paths avoid the lemons fallen either side which mould and soften and send out a sharp soapy tang. A familiar movement of cats emerging then stretching, one leg, two legs, a yawn, and tails, if they have them, curling back and shivering. They each do this and the women watch with pleasure. Among them a black cat moves silkily along the wall. Wary, but loose.

There must have been two, Rike tells herself, unless, of course, it's the same cat claiming its other lives.

1.4

The news about Parson comes directly from the police.

Gibson doesn't understand why it's taken so long to inform them. He asks: when did this become clear? When was this certain? Sutler's death has caused a frenzy of calls, work, and bother, and in one short statement the news is refigured into an uncomprehendable shape. It was Parson.

He asks the question again. Are they certain?

The answer is simple. The material they found on the train, the papers found in a bag, mentioned Sutler. These were Parson's notes.

It doesn't make sense. Parson running along a train track? He can't imagine the man running. A man like Parson doesn't run. He tells this to the police. He asks if they are absolutely certain.

They need to know more about Parson. Was he working for Gibson & Baker or HOSCO?

'He was working for us. We assess claims for HOSCO – we used to. Parson was in Iraq when Stephen Sutler disappeared. HOSCO wanted someone immediately on the job and Parson was available.' Gibson closes his eyes when he speaks. Partly to think, but also because he doesn't want to look at either of the policemen. He explains: Stephen Lawrence Sutler stole a great deal of money. He was managing a project for HOSCO in Iraq, and he disappeared. The investigation has exposed a good amount of, let's not call it *illegal*, exactly, but *non-standard* activity in HOSCO's dealings with the military and with US funding sources. As a result the company has collapsed, or rather, it has been dissolved, and there's a great deal of interest in finding the man responsible.

The men know this. They want to see Parson's reports. He did make reports?

Gibson asks for his secretary, Margaret. He apologizes first and asks that she join him. Poised in the door, arm extended, he waits for her to set aside her work. In the outer office the staff stop working, the room quietens, and attention focuses on Gibson's door as Margaret approaches.

Margaret is asked to sit. The door is closed, and the information is repeated. She struggles to understand. This must be, she says, a terrible mistake. Surely? He was here before Christmas. After his wife came out of hospital. We were talking last week.

She turns to Gibson and asks, almost in a whisper, if someone has contacted Laura. His wife, she says. Wasn't she also with him? She's only recently out of hospital.

Gibson waits until the afternoon to call Geezler, and still does not understand the news as he repeats it.

Geezler, who has been aggravated by Parson's comings and goings, is respectful, perhaps contrite. Like everyone else he is confused by the circumstances.

'He was on the tracks?'

Gibson says he doesn't understand it either.

'Tracks?'

He has no further information.

Geezler wants to extend condolences to Parson's wife, but he doesn't want to intrude. If there's anything he can do Gibson should let him know. Any expense. Any way in which he might be able to help. Perhaps he doesn't need to mention his involvement, in which case Gibson could act as mediator. Gibson agrees. This isn't the time to be talking about HOSCO. Geezler's offer is sensitive to the situation.

'Do they have any idea why he was on the tracks?'

Gibson is at a loss. There is only one idea. Parson was in Europe to find a man called Sutler. It isn't unreasonable to imagine that Sutler is involved, perhaps responsible.

'But they have no information?'

'There's nothing.'

Geezler asks Parson to keep him informed. If anything happens, any news, or development. For the newspapers this is a sensational turnaround. Sutler dead. Sutler alive. Neither Gibson nor Geezler are prepared for the complications this causes.

Geezler closes repeating his offer of assistance.

Gibson thinks of his office as a lung. It faces the river, and he recognizes the traffic, the barges, tugs, tour boats, riverboats and ferries. At night, as the South Bank lights up, the room, he thinks, seems poised in expectation, as if holding its breath. He has thought this for many years, and in the evenings he seldom fails to appreciate the view: the shift in colour as the day falls, and how the quality of this light changes through the year. He's sure he would have mentioned this to Parson. Was it Parson who'd said you can't look at the river without thinking of fires and spitfires, pageants, floods, but what you actually see, dressed in industrial greys, are the mounting blocks in which hundreds and thousands of people labour, eat, sleep, live. When you look at the river you think of events, he'd said. Not people.

There was a whale once which swam right outside his office.

Margaret, inconsolable, had hidden in the office, blind with tears, hands to her face as if ashamed of her distress.

1.5

The job will last for seven weeks. Rike can teach English because there isn't any call for German or Italian. The pay is good enough for her to accept without thinking it over, but she wants to pass the idea by her sister and give the matter a little discussion anyway. You don't want to appear too grateful. Teaching English isn't much fun, she finds the language practical, bare, obvious. English is the language of bureaucrats and pedants. Rike had expected a negotiation, something more like an interview, but the woman faces her with the decision made and an expression that won't broker refusal. They talk through the noise of jets taking off, thundering over them – the British base is less than a kilometre away, and these jets come howling over the salt lake with a splintering sound, low enough to vibrate the paper on the table, to shake glasses. Rike smiles through the noise. The woman smiles back. The jets are heading to the Lebanon, to Syria. There is talk of bombing government compounds, ports, barracks, signal stations, power stations, installations, of going to town on the place just like they did with Libya, but there's no real commitment yet. Rike keeps the smile but feels the weight of these fighters over her, and wonders if this time they have the right permissions. Locally, everybody understands the threat: if the British *take action* in Syria and on the Russian ports, the Russians will *take action* in Cyprus and on the British bases. Tit-for-tat. They haven't said as much, no one is that explicit, but the security level is high, and there are soldiers in bunkers with green smudged on their faces, and these bunkers line the orchards and the roads from Akrotiri to Limassol (east), from Akrotiri to Episkopi (west), from Episkopi to the signals base in the foothills of the Troodos mountains (north). She tells herself that she shouldn't be here, that none of this should be happening, and having grown up in the wake of the cold war this feels, anyway, like a punch on an old bruise. Instead she smiles, promises to bring in her passport, guarantees that the recommendations from the German consulate will come through by the end of the day, and that she'll be happy to teach Intermediate English to Cypriot nationals who have been cleared to work at a British military base. Perfect, isn't it? She's still smiling when she leaves.

Rike returns through the old city, follows a wall which curves alongside the road, no pavement here, a dangerous corner crowned with jasmine in full flower. The scent – one of her favourites – dry and sweet, isn't so much a scent as a sensation of space opening in the back of her head. This corner isn't a place to pause. The jasmine is a bad distraction. Supposing a car came round that curve – you wouldn't see it. You wouldn't stand a chance. There wouldn't be anything you could do. You couldn't step aside because there isn't a pavement. She thinks like this all of the time. Things that might go wrong. Like Henning, she worries about her sister's pregnancy, and conjures up scenarios for a miscarriage in order to dispel the possibility. Falls, faints, dizzy spells, bumpy car rides, blood disorders, food poisoning, organ failure, a stroke, some kind of a prolapse, sepsis, various or multiple and synchronous allergic reactions, cat-scratch lock-jaw, some kind of massive muscle spasm, heat exhaustion; and lately more extreme situations which might once have seemed impossible: a bullet, a bomb, an assassin – one of those British or Russian missiles, a shot in the head when she's feeding the cats. In addition she imagines scenarios in which her sister might be crushed: stampeding crowds, falling masonry, some kind of large rogue animal, a tsunami, a blast, an avalanche, the ground opening up to a sink hole or a lava flow – because *you never know.*

Since seeing the black cat she hasn't given one thought to the shooting, convinced that it was the result of some local unpleasantness. In the news there are more important items: patchy home footage of the uprising in Homs. Chaotic and sketchy. Mobile footage of civilians skittering in terror, running in a crouch, people taking a stand, one at a time. Long grey roads stippled with chunks of concrete. People lined on sidewalks watching tiny acts of defiance and courage, as if receiving instruction. Isa weeps every time: covers her face and sobs. As soon as the TV is switched on she seeks out the news and has to watch, then cries because it makes her wretched.

The road behind the complex is too narrow for cars, so narrow that when the company come to clean the communal pool the van must be parked on the main road and the hoses extended all the way to the compound and heaved over the wall. It's a job the men accomplish with great effort. They lug, they haul, they brace like men in a tug-of-war. They slowly take off their shirts to make the job easier. A thin and empty street, nothing more than a rat's tail, with the compound wall running on one side and the chain-link fence of a new development on the other. The development behind the fence is vacant, in the afternoons small powdery dust devils whip through the site and raise twists of sand and dry grass. This, a sign announces, will be a world-class hotel, *The Meridian Hiat*. She wonders if there is a lawsuit over the name: Hyatt, Hiat. It's a little close. Perhaps this is why building work appears to have stopped? All that stands so far is a shell, poured floor and pillars, the Hiroshima-like framework of a cupola. Midday and the sun falls directly down: in the street another dead cat, ginger, fur faintly striped, shot in the head. In the centre of the street, dry now from the sun, lies a sack of dry cat food slit open.

Rike kneels beside the cat. Appalled. A fresh kill, the head pulpy, wet and repugnant. It doesn't bear thinking about that someone would lay out food, then wait. She reports these shootings to the number Henning left with her. *Because this is starting to look like a warning*.

In the evening Rike prepares her lessons in the garden. Isa sits half in, half out of the apartment, her feet aligned to a rutted edge of sunlight. Already halfway through her book her thumbs stroke the unread pages.

Feet up, Rike stretches under the fragrant lemon tree with Isa's computer on her lap, a certain pleasure at how familiar this is: holidays camping in Bavaria or at Punta Sabbione on the Venetian lagoon were always alike. Isa, book in hand, lounged across a chair, slack and happy, reading with a kind of fury. Sometimes a book a day. Rike, on the other hand, even now, takes her time and prefers to become immersed, her chair set in the same place, a coffee and iced water to hand, early to mid-morning, so orderly that her sister calls her autistic. Isa and Mattaus read thrillers. Rike reads *subjects*, as if revising for an exam, ideas tested first through fiction.

This is almost the holiday they planned, and two weeks into a ten-week stay, Rike already feels time melting, just going. It's hard to stick in the moment, to fix at one point. Seven weeks' teaching, one final week to recoup, then on to Hamburg to her brother's apartment, everything already sent ahead, luggage and bedding.

Done with her preparation Rike checks her email and finds a message from the language school withdrawing the offer of employment. For one day she has enjoyed the idea that she will be a teacher, even if the job is temporary, even if she has to teach English. She has decided on the exercises she will use for her first lesson, and the examples she will show in case the class are too timid – and now there's an email taking the job away. Surprised at her disappointment Rike calls to her sister.

'What is it?'

'It's from the school. I don't have permission. The British won't let me onto their base. Security.'

'Wouldn't they know that before they hired you?'

'You'd think so.'

'You have a contract, don't you?' Isa reads as she talks. 'You did sign a contract?' Isa looks up, a finger marking her place. 'Seriously? You didn't sign anything?'

'It's all word of mouth.'

'Anyway, why do you have to teach on the base? They wouldn't hold language classes on a military base. They have offices, don't they? Get them to change venues? Surely none of the students will have clearance?'

Isa's clarity on this, on any issue, is irritating.

'I don't know. It doesn't matter. Now they want me to teach one-on-one.' Rike reads from the screen. 'Private lessons.'

'Private?'

'Conversation.'

'That's good?'

'Apparently.'

'And the money?'

'More for an advanced class.'

'There you go, then.' Isa closes her book and awkwardly draws herself upright. 'I don't know why you complain so much.'

Easily stung, Rike resents having to explain herself. 'They want me to go to his apartment. It says that he wants to practise his conversation. There won't be any exams. I get more money for exams.'

'For how long?'

'One month.'

'Why don't you have Henning look into it? I'm sure he can arrange whatever you need to get onto the British base. Then you can do both. Classes and private one-on-one.'

Rike's frown remains fixed. 'This was supposed to be a holiday.'

'You don't need to be looking after me. And anyway it's money.' Isa leans into the garden, serious now, touching a subject Rike doesn't want to discuss. 'And money is a good thing. Remember?' She turns as the doorbell chimes, first puzzled, then remembering.

Isa is in a bad mood. Her day started with a broken washing-machine. One month in the apartment and already equipment is beginning to fail. The owner / owner's son / first or second cousin (nobody can quite figure out the dynamic) is a handsome boy who studied in New York. Isa doesn't trust him the way she would trust an ugly boy. Rike watches him walk about the kitchen. Cocky. Self-assured. He's comfortable with women asking him to check out things which actually don't need checking out. Sadly the washing machine is legitimate, and the boy, who misuses American phrases all the time, stands back from the machine and mumbles, 'Shit the bed.'

Isa, enraged, hands on hips, belly round and protruding, asks him what, exactly, does he mean by this?

Rike sucks in her breath. 'It's a phrase,' she explains. 'He means it's broken.'

'Even so.'

Shade from the lemon tree sheds a map across the patio. Rike looks up at the canopy, picks out the angled pockets of blue sky and wonders if the boy is responsible for shooting the cats.

1.6

Three Sutlers: one walking into the path of a train, another into a desert. It's hard to fathom. How is it possible that a man is found walking through a desert, alone, with no water and no food, ninety-two kilometres from where he was last seen (by a witness at a gas station), and thirty-seven kilometres from the most rudimentary habitation? For Rike the answer is pragmatic. It's best not to think of *how*, as in, *How would you manage such a thing*, but, *why. Why would anyone do that?*

She thinks of this event as an unfortunate coincidence, a collision of bad choice and bad luck. Imagine this: you hire or buy a car which is barely serviceable. You plan to drive it a long distance trusting that as it's managed to convey you so far already, there's no reason to worry, and anyway, you're driving at night when it's not so hot, and however remote the route you're assured that the vehicle will double as shelter if something should happen. She can see this, it isn't hard to imagine – so the first splutter, that hint of failure, isn't exactly a surprise, but neither is it such a terrible moment. It might test your patience, and you might start to wonder what the problem is, pause and ask yourself if you should continue, or if you should make some attempt to return.

There have been other people travelling this route, not so many in recent hours, true. In fact, the only vehicle you've noticed recently is one of those black sedans the Arabs are fond of, with black windows, impenetrable, which drive at a speed, and while they overtake with plenty of room, your vehicle still shudders as they pass – a reminder, as if you need it, of your vehicle's inferiority.

You marvel at the night sky. How clear it is and how those stars are so much more complex out here, and there are times when this spangled black makes you feel part of something, connected, dot-to-dot. There are times, looking up, when you feel infinitely insignificant, the sheer number of stars obliterates your uniqueness.

When it happens, it happens with brutal speed. Perhaps it's your fault because you see something in the road. A rogue camel, maybe something more exotic – some fantastic creature poised as it crosses, yellow eyes flashing as you veer off the road and pick up some brush which lodges under the vehicle. Or maybe something more banal, which comes as a change in tone. The car just doesn't sound right. Or a vibration shivers through the steering wheel before a loss of power. You are, goddammit, slowing down.

Or maybe a woman in a gaberdine comes staggering out from the roadside, hands aflap, shoeless but on the run. Her sobs run over the radio as you drive toward trouble.

1.7

There are two witnesses. The first, a clerk for Trenitalia, saw Parson at the station in Naples, and can confirm he took an express to Rome. The second witness, a construction worker, saw Parson running along the track until the train obscured his view. He heard the second train but couldn't see it. It wasn't until he caught the news that he understood what he'd seen.

The man was running like he was being chased.

Gibson gives the news to Geezler. 'I can't see him running. Parson never hurried. I can't see it.'

And what of Sutler?

Gibson doesn't know. There's so much here that is unknown. The newspapers are speculating that Sutler is responsible. Perhaps there was a confrontation? He doesn't know. It would not be like Parson to confront someone. But you never know. Unless other witnesses come forward no one is likely to find out. When this settles he will ask for Parson's papers which are currently with the Italian police.

Geezler isn't happy. Parson was tracking Sutler, those papers belong to them. They should be retrieved.

'Send someone,' he says. 'Tidy this up. Find out what he knew and see if Sutler is responsible.'

Gibson doesn't mention the expense of hiring a PR firm. How insensitive the calls and enquiries have become. The accusative tone that follows any mention of Sutler, HOSCO, Gibson & Baker. There is a photograph of Parson in the lobby set on a flimsy easel, under which staff have begun to leave flowers. On their website is an announcement: *It is with deep regret . . .*

1.8

Isa stands at the counter, the *Cyprus Mail* open in front of her. She recognizes the name, she says. Parson. It's unusual. It means priest, no? She recognizes the name because early last summer Henning had to go to Istanbul to sort out some business with a photographer. She's heard the name before. Henning met him.

What she doesn't understand is why this man called Parson, who was supposed to be looking for Sutler, came to be confused with the man he was looking for? Odd, no? And what a way to go? Hit by two trains. Can you imagine?

Rike reads the article over her sister's shoulder. *Geezler. HOSCO.* These names are also familiar.

Isa shrugs. It's all confusing, she says, and a little strange. Henning isn't exactly forthcoming with the detail. He won't be happy.

Henning calls at nine. Rike is on the couch and Isa is preparing for bed, apologizing for her lack of energy. Rike answers and Henning asks if Isa is about. When Rike says she'll get her, ready to open the call to speakerphone, Henning tells her to wait a moment.

It's Rike he wants to speak to.

'Steer her away from the news,' he says.

'She's going to bed.'

'But in the next couple of days.'

Rike asks if this has anything to do with the man in Rome. 'She already knows.'

Henning groans, this is the last thing he needs. Once Isa gets her nose into this she won't leave him alone. There won't be an end to it.

'She says you knew him.'

'Who?'

'Parson. She said you met him last year in Istanbul. She remembered the name.'

'Just keep her off the subject,' Henning asks.

THE FIRST LESSON

2.1

Rike follows a small map she's printed from the internet and counts down the house numbers. The apartment, one of a row of new developments, is set on the outskirts of Limassol, close to the hospital: a twenty-five-minute walk in the full heat of the day.

The air tastes of gasoline. On every landing she finds a sign posted in English and Greek: *No littering, no loitering, no deliveries, Karnezis Management*. This is the same company that manages Isa's complex.

Rike's thoughts catch on how strange it is, a little risky, to arrive unaccompanied at the apartment of a man you haven't met. But now, exchanging greetings at his door, those doubts are gone, and anyway, he works for the UN. There, inside, a white jacket folded over a folding chair with the blue insignia stitched to the upper sleeve.

She imagines that he recognizes her; that in the slight eye-narrowing is the tiniest trace of familiarity. Perhaps she reminds him of someone? It's hard to tell as the reaction is so fleeting. For her part she doesn't recognize him. She knows few men of his age so he isn't familiar on any level.

Tomas Berens steps aside, and speaking in German invites her in. 'A bird,' he says, 'just now. I had a bird fly into my room.'

Rike looks up at the high ceiling in the hallway. 'A bird?'

'Very nervous. It came into the room.'

A thin face. Hard grey eyes. A clean jawline. A small head with a boxy nose: cut features, compact, definitively Nordic. Tomas Berens's complexion is a little bloodless, arms and face pale and smooth as a shoreline stone, and while he isn't handsome he is at least interesting. In Cyprus such a look is distinctive as brown eyes, dark skin, dark hair are the norm. Nevertheless, in his white shirt and khaki trousers the man is a type – in Europe or America you might see any number of men like him buzzing about offices, banks, and airports. If she found Tomas Berens on a late afternoon at a table in any one of the smarter restaurants she would single him out and dream up some story for him. His manner is curiously formal, as he shakes her hand he almost gives a small bow. At least, there's a pause, a hesitation where this gesture might be offered. There's a prideful leanness to him despite his age (he must be forty, forty-five?). Tomas Berens clearly looks after himself.

They face each other in an otherwise empty room. The balcony door, wedged open, allows in a light breeze and the noise and smell of the traffic, a pinched view that leads eventually out to the sea. She speaks first in German, a language they share, and tells him from now on, as agreed, they will speak in English throughout the session.

'OK,' she says. 'Let's start. I would like you to tell me a story.' A variation of the usual: where are you from / what do you do / tell me something about yourself / why do you want to learn English? These facts will come later. She wants to start with a story. Rike carefully pronounces each word so he can understand, and makes a gesture indicating that it is his turn to speak.

'A story?'

Over his shoulder, trapped between buildings in a bright slit of sky hangs the silhouette of a passenger plane. It glides sideways across the gap toward his ear. Noise cooks in the street below them: men, always men, bullish and loud, car horns, a bevy of sirens as ambulances approach the hospital.

Tomas takes a moment to think. He coughs, he turns his head slightly. 'A story?'

Rike nods.

The sun slides along the aircraft's white belly as it veers away.

'OK.' He coughs again, then straightens his back, decided. 'My neighbour takes photographs for weddings and wedding parties. He comes from a small village. He is friendly.' His voice is supple and intimate; his English is a little unpractised. 'There is a scar on his hand.' Tomas says 'scar' in German and holds up his right hand to draw a crescent that runs from his thumb to his wrist. 'Because, one year ago, he killed a dog. The dog is a very big, a crazy dog, and it comes from the square and attacks a smaller dog.' He looks at Rike to clarify his thoughts. 'The big dog kills the smaller dog in a square out-side the church. He is waiting in his car before a wedding, and he sees this. And the dog, this big dog, looks like it now wants to attack a boy outside the church, a little boy. So he goes to it, he runs to it, and he takes the dog by the neck, like this.' Tomas holds up his arms. His hands start out of his shirt cuffs and grip at nothing. He looks up, thinking, then switches to German. 'He lifts it up by its neck and he kills it.'

Rike nods and asks him to speak in English, only English. She will help with the words.

'He strangles the dog. Does that make sense? With his hands. But the dog has only killed a rat. It wasn't going to attack the boy. It belongs to the boy. The boy is its owner. You understand?'

Rike smiles at this, which is intended to be polite, but shows that she's a little nervous. The truth is she's a little alarmed by the size of his hands. Tomas Berens has large hands, heavy and rubbery, and these hands, once noticed, distract her.

Tomas gives a concentrated nod. He asks if she would like to hear more stories and Rike indicates that he should continue. 'Tell me another story about your neighbour.'

'Another story?' Tomas switches back to English. 'My neighbour isn't lucky. Last week he was in a car accident. He's OK, but he cannot drive his car for work.'

They nod, slowly, in unison.

'He and his wife are unhappy. They fight every day. In the morning they argue about work. In the evening they argue about money. They are loud and the building is,' he struggles for a word, '*loud.*' He shrugs, matter of fact. 'Everyone can hear. All of us.' To prove his point the sounds of running water and the chatter of a TV echo from the stairwell in competition with the noise from the street.

'What is your neighbour's name?'

Tomas says he has no idea, then, quickly remembering, says: *Christos.*

Immediately out of the apartment Rike hurries downstairs. She will remember many details about this meeting: the adhesive light, the empty room, his clothes, his winter-pale skin, the aircraft, long gone, and the martins skimming level with the window and wheeling out over the flat roofs and how their sharp calls sound of alarm. As she crosses the landing below Tomas's floor she catches sight of Christos's name on a small plaque under a doorbell. The name has been scratched over. She switches her phone back from silent and checks her messages. On the last landing she passes a woman with a young boy, they both have the same round unhappy faces. The woman fans herself with one hand and shepherds the child ahead and tells him to mind his business. While the mother is slight, the boy is fat. His elbows are scabbed, rough with some skin complaint.

Her sister won't be home for another hour, but Rike heads back in any case and walks under the palms that line the front of the hospital.

The city is busy with men. Boys jostle a football across the road and workmen unload flat-packed stalls and awnings onto the sidewalk. They watch her out of habit, not because she is pretty or because they desire her, but because this is what men do.

2.2

Rike calls the school and asks to speak with Rosaria. Tomas Berens, she reports, already speaks English. In fact his English is very good.

Rosaria is a little dismissive. She reminds Rike to bring in her passport. The contract is ready to be signed and there are a few details about the programme she'd like to explain. She asks Rike how the first lesson went, and if she is happy.

'He's out of practice.' Rike makes sure there is a pinch of doubt in her voice. 'But he's a serious student.' She doesn't want to admit that she's out of her depth. Besides, it's too early to give a proper assessment. In a few days, once they are less nervous with each other, she'll have a better idea. She tries not to sound perfunctory, and anyway, Rosaria is only asking because they have nothing else to discuss.

'Did he mention why he's taking the lessons?' It's hard to make this question sound casual. 'Did he give any particular reason?'

The smallest hesitation makes Rosaria sound cunning. 'Practice. He said he wants to practise. Ask him. Have him tell you.'

'I was just wondering, because he seems so advanced already.'

'Well, he specifically asked for you.'

The idea makes Rike laugh. This, she is certain, is a polite invention. After she has hung up Rike sits with the phone in her lap and scans the yard hoping to spy a cat.

Rike holds on to the idea of the man in her head. The third Sutler. Mr Crispy. She's walked him from his car into the desert. Had him loose and alone for two days, in which he's almost driven himself insane with fears over what might happen: a realization that things don't always work out for the best, that there will come a time when he just runs out of luck. Soon, irrevocable events will occur, prompted by thirst, hunger, heat, and exhaustion, his decisions will no longer be sound, but even so, he wavers between desperation and hope.

He begins to make bargains because he believes that if he changes in some way he will survive this crisis. He can live a simpler life. He can be kinder, certainly this is manageable. Still walking, he becomes giddy with a sense of hope, joyful now, because he is descending, and he feels certain of an arrival.

Rike sits at the kitchen table with her sister, she doesn't know which is worse, the threat of rats or the growing stink. Uncollected trash sits in the adjoining alley and the stench fills the garden.

Isa has bought a gift for Henning. She doesn't know what it is precisely – some kind of ceremonial staff. It's African, so it will go with his other pieces. The staff is smooth, polished, ebony, she thinks. 'I did like it,' she says, her expression now undecided. Isa shrugs. 'I've been thinking. There needs to be some *adjusting* in this household.' Isa runs her hand over her belly. Most of her conversation is about the coming baby or her appetite. 'This needs to be a girl.'

Rike attends to the coffee. Isa signals that she doesn't want one.

'A boy wouldn't be so bad.'

'No.' Isa is absolute. 'I don't want to be around more men. Henning is enough.'

'You're fretting.' Rike stirs sugar into her coffee mindful that her sister doesn't appreciate being told what she is like. 'I can't stop looking at you.'

'I know. I'm so fat.'

Round is the word that occurs to Rike. Her sister, who has always been angular, is decidedly round. She wants to say something like: *You suit a little weight*. This at least would not be a lie, and it would be appropriate payback for the times her sister has told her that very same fact. Instead, she says, vaguely, that Isa looks gorgeous.

'Don't. I'm too heavy.' Isa changes her mind and takes a taste from her sister's cup, anything more will start off her stomach. She tuts and shakes her head and takes a second sip, a third sip, and gives a small hum of pleasure. 'Don't even ask what I've eaten today.'

A car horn sounds immediately outside. Isa pays no attention and picks absent-mindedly at the washed grapes. 'I still haven't unpacked everything. I keep thinking we'll be going back soon so what's the point.' She shakes the thought away. 'God. So? How did it go today? How was your man?'

Rike settles, stretches her legs: her turn to become pensive. 'His English isn't bad. He's out of practice, and beyond that it's . . .' She pauses. *Advanced* isn't the word she wants. 'Good. I guess. I don't know. He can express himself. I don't know what he wants. I've asked him to prepare a report on his neighbours.'

'Is he interesting?'

'He has a nice voice. I like his voice.'

'Is he handsome?'

Rike shakes her head, brisk and decisive. 'No, he's not handsome.'

'Shame. Why his neighbours?'

'He told me a story about one of his neighbours. He said his neighbour strangled a dog that belonged to a boy. He thought it was going to attack the boy.'

Isa, laughing, points a segment of apple at her sister. 'No. Wait. Don't tell me. With his bare hands? Outside a mosque after prayers?'

'A church. You know this?'

'Of course. It's a famous story. It isn't true.'

Rike doesn't understand.

'It's one of those stories. You must know it? The men come out of the mosque after evening prayers, and a mad dog runs into the group. And right in front of them, right in at the steps to the mosque, it kills another dog, or a small dog, or a cat. Whatever it is it rips it to pieces, then it goes for one of the people in the crowd, but one of the men catches the dog, and before anyone can stop him he strangles it or kicks it or beats it to death with a stick. And then, too late, he sees it wasn't a small dog or a cat that it had killed at all, but a very, very large rat. The mother of all rats. And the boy it was going to attack is the owner of the dog.'

'He said his neighbour told him this. Christos. He has a scar on his hand.'

'It's a story. It isn't true. How could it be? Dogs are different here, people generally don't keep pets in the Middle East, they have livestock.'

'Cyprus is Greece.'

'Cyprus is in the Middle East. Greek-*ish*, at least this part.'

'But the scar?'

'What about it?' Isa shrugs.

Rike begins to clear the table. She rubs at sticky fingerprints with the heel of her fist. An orange stain imprinted on the Formica top. 'Then the story doesn't make sense. If people don't keep dogs, why does the boy have a dog?'

'You're brooding.'

'I'm not brooding. I knew it wasn't true. I asked him for a story.'

'Yes, you are. You're disappointed. You feel deceived. Maybe he didn't know it was a story? Or maybe he's a little more interesting than you think? Anyway, you've missed the point. The story isn't about the dog, it's about the man who kills the dog. It's a story about how you shouldn't interfere. It's a story about the Turks. It's basically a little piece of cultural stereotyping.'

Rike stops at the sink, mouth compressed, disappointed but she doesn't know why. Alongside this runs the irritation of Isa knowing better, of how, after less than a month, she has some kind of insight already. 'I'm not sure what he wants. I don't think he knows either. That's probably the problem, he's just taking language lessons because he can.'

Rising slowly, Isa dusts off her hands. 'If he's paying, does it matter? You need the money. Just let him talk.'

Outside a helicopter cuts over the building with a deep percussive shudder, loud enough to momentarily erase every other sound. This could be the coastguard, she doesn't know for sure, but makes the assumption that every vehicle is a military craft heading for the hospital at Akrotiri. She crowds the sky with possible stories.

She dreams about the man: she's in a supermarket and Tomas Berens is fucking her from behind, only it isn't fucking, or maybe it is, in any case his hands, stupidly huge, firmly grasp her hips, and she's jolting so much can't keep her shopping in her arms. This isn't Rike's kind of dream – sex, shopping – and she knows this, even while it's happening. It's like she's channelling her sister, who is having the most extraordinary dreams these days. At some point she gives up resisting the idea, and there's fruit bouncing out of her hands, a pair of limes rolling across a linoleum floor, it's more like a bumpy car ride than sex, and her mind is solidly on her shopping, on fruits spilling from her hands, until a sudden blossom of heat spreads through her. She wakes herself laughing, but also embarrassed because she never has dreams like this, never so explicit, and is relieved to find that she is alone in the apartment, the screen doors open, the same path of sunlight on her and the cat, that sleek black cat sleeping under the fig tree, paws twitching, is sharing the same dream.

2.3

Geezler understands. 'I do. I know what I'm asking.' If it wasn't for the hearing, he wouldn't trouble him, but the fact is he wants Gibson to retrieve Parson's notes. He wants him to speak with Parson's wife, Laura. 'Find out what was going on.' He wants to give Parson an opportunity to be proven right. It isn't only what's on paper, but what was in the man's head. If Parson thought that Sutler was in southern Italy, then his notes will explain more, but Gibson will need to show some intuition because Parson wasn't playing straight with them. All that time following Sutler, and not one sighting. So what was he doing?

'I want to be wrong.'

Gibson thinks intuition belongs to the young. He knows his mind. What he doesn't have is impulse, or a pressing need to enquire. He finds himself in Rome, walking through customs, pushing a suitcase with its own wheels on a trolley, because dragging it annoys him, and because he feels that what he's doing is crossing some line. This is beginning to spoil his idea of Rome.

The driver, of course, is waiting outside in the car. There is no apology for the delay, but the man is polite, even deferential, as he lifts Gibson's case, sets it into the boot, opens the door for him.

Rome is the city he visited with his wife for three, or was it four trips. Each unassociated with business. The first a kind of honeymoon, six months or so after their marriage when they could get away: the city still holds the same sense of possibility for him. A notion that something could start here, and whatever it was, that something would be good. Even on their final visit, not quite their last attempt to reconcile, but certainly late in their decline, the city still managed to offer some freshness, a hint of their first visit. And he had felt grateful for this reprieve.

The driver offers his condolences and asks if Parson was a friend. Gibson looks at the city as they drive and realizes he knows nothing about the neighbourhoods, couldn't even name them, that all he knows of Rome is perhaps a few streets based around the centre. He watches the bustle of scooters and cars, how they stop and start, and the sky slipping into twilight as the buildings on either side light up, their tops in silhouette and a sense that they are stacked, strata after strata. It's easier to say employee. He would not have called Parson a friend although he knew him for seven years. This number is a weight.

There's a witness who says he saw him being chased. Another who can place him at the station. Dental records and details from Parson's wife confirm a positive identification.

He stands in his room bereft. His luggage beside the bed. Everything in order. There is a private garden behind the hotel, he remembers there was once a tennis court and a bar. Imagining himself in Rome he'd pictured himself doing business, holding necessary conversations and making arrangements, a calm centre in this small, shaded garden: the busier streets within earshot, the pips and shouts and holler of traffic. The reality doesn't have such polish, a sign in the lobby announces that the garden is closed, and while the room is comfortable, it is also precisely how he remembers it. There's nothing new, and while this familiarity should be comforting, he feels only exhausted. It's possibly a mistake coming here. He has to speak with Laura, find out her arrangements, her wishes, and ensure that he does, absolutely, everything he can for her. He thinks he should exhaust himself, and when they meet he will be able to remain composed. He isn't sure that she likes him, an issue he has never worried over before. Isn't he the person who sent Parson away? Didn't he insist he take the work? And doesn't that make him responsible?

He wakes in the night, the covers a little heavy on his legs, which means that he wakes lying in the same position with the idea that he hasn't slept at all. The television is on, the sound muted, tuned to a news channel, an image of an earthquake. It takes a moment to register that this is Syria, a city razed. This is no earthquake.

The driver, he can't remember his name or rank, had asked how long he'd known Parson, and this question strikes Gibson as meaningful. Did Parson know the person who chased him? Imagine that you have this answer first. *He knew him well. He did not know him. He met him that morning. The man (it has to be a man) was casually familiar.*

Then you would learn a great deal about the incident, its motives, its commission.

On the television people stand beside the rubble of houses and shops, as if this is ordinary. When people protest and cry to camera there is a theatre about it, a language which looks assumed, as if, moments before, moments after, they might be holding ordinary arguments and conversations, but the camera demands they strike themselves, they weep, they raise their hands skyward. Grief, he thinks, makes for an intolerably amateur display, crude and dulling. Foreign.

He misses Parson. Misses knowing the man is out there. Believes that something is wrong now with the shape of the world.

THE SECOND LESSON

3.1

The next morning Rike returns to Tomas's apartment. In the hallway she finds four large rolls of white insulation, taller than her, wrapped in plastic with labels in Greek. On her way to Tomas's apartment she again notices Christos's name on the list of occupants at the main entrance, then at his door, in English first, then Greek, both crossed through. The scratches aren't recent. She's deliberately thinking about details, like the sign, to distance herself from the dream.

It's possible, this scratching out, that Christos has annoyed someone.

The previous evening she spoke with Henning and attempted to pry a little more from him about the man in hospital: Sutler Number Three. Henning, having fended off Isa's questions about Parson, refused to give details, but did admit to a small triumph. Udo has conceded. Sutler Number Three, Mr Crispy, will be brought to Cyprus. She is not to talk about this, understand? And neither is Isa. The decision, he thinks, has more to do with expense than security.

The sisters feed their curiosity through internet searches: *Sutler*, *HOSCO*, *Iraq Conspiracy*, *Sutler One*, *Two*, *Three*, tapped in to furnish the smallest details, and finally, *Parson*, who they feel some connection to because Henning has met the man, interviewed him, discussed details about Sutler which he will not divulge. Speculation on Parson's death includes the involvement of the Neapolitan Camorra. Isa prefers this theory, and pictures the man's chaotic run from a band of armed thugs. His stumbling across railroad ties. She loves the idea that the Mafia might be involved, however improbable.

Rike takes the steps to Tomas's apartment preoccupied. What they do know: Sutler is British, he worked in Iraq as a contractor with an American company called HOSCO, he has absconded with anything between forty-five and fifty-three million dollars. No small change. She thinks of him trudging through the desert with sacks of cash, and losing, on each day, one sack after another. The man is like a bug, a tiny thing wheeling massive balls of cash across the desert. The man sheds money as he walks, it flies from him, stripped by the wind.

A million dollars in twenty-dollar notes weighs about twenty kilos.

*

823

Tomas's door stands open in anticipation. Tomas, in the kitchen, answers her knock with a greeting and a question – would she like coffee or water? He has cold still water but no ice. He hasn't eaten; he's running late himself. He bends over in the kitchen so she can see only his haunch through the doorway as he searches through his fridge. *It's like he knows.* For a forty-year-old he's in very good shape. When he straightens, he stretches. This is her weakness: necks, backs, shoulders, forearms. The equine shapes these muscles define. She prefers lean to strong: a racehorse rather than a bear.

Rike waits at the door, makes small talk about the packets left out in the hall (insulation, no?) and for the first time she takes a proper account of the room; the loose water-stained parquet floor which makes the whole room feel unsteady; bare white walls bruised with grey scuffs. A window overlooks a small playground, and opposite, behind her, double doors lead to a balcony which overlooks the street. A sad room, if rooms can be sad, weighted by the absence of furniture and the fact that month after month new people live here.

Set ready by Tomas's chair: a notebook, a newspaper, a dictionary.

'No birds today?'

'Yesterday,' he says in German. 'Today we have snow in the hall. Snow, in bags, fake snow, polystyrene, in bags as big as this.' He gestures up to his chest, then shrugs. 'I have my homework. Here.' He points to the window overlooking the back of the apartments, and they stand side by side and look out.

The building describes a hard U. Tomas's apartment is almost dead centre. The two wings of the complex, east and west, curve on either side; between them lies a small, bare playground. The flagstones have been recently hosed and swept. This view feels English to her despite the row of stumpy palms (in Peckham every estate had a play park with swings, a slide, and sometimes a roundabout, and how these parks became the territory for thugs not children). Rike looks at the wings, at the parallel lines of balconies and windows. Most of the shutters are closed, but where they are open it's impossible not to invent stories of these lives. Once again there are the sounds of people, dishes chipping together, a radio, nothing as loud as the previous day. A man in swimming trunks vacuums his apartment. There's a rhythm in his dips and sweeps, even in the way he pauses to smoke.

'I was reading about Syria this morning. Again, the news is very bad.'

Rike hasn't heard the news today. Most of what she knows comes via the internet or her sister. Neither is reliable.

'It's hard to know what's happening.'

Tomas sips his coffee, his elbow on the window ledge so that the cup and saucer are held over the drop. Below, on the flagstones, a cat.

'The Arabs. They should do something. They wait, and what for?'

Tomas Berens is making conversation and it would be polite to respond. Rike can't quite formulate her thoughts. She can't think of Syria without thinking of her sister, and then there's the report Isa read out loud two nights ago about how the unrest was nothing more than war-by-proxy. This isn't Egypt or Libya, this isn't about *freedom*, not with Russia, China, Iran stuck in the mix. She doesn't like to think of Syria as a place where something is enacted, where moves are made, but she isn't naive enough to think that this is new, it's impossible to think of a small country which doesn't have associations with bigger, more ambitious neighbours. She can't figure out the sides. Exactly who are the rebels the government are suppressing? Rike can't make small talk because she doesn't know what she thinks, so she asks instead to hear about Tomas's neighbours. Even this isn't simple. Her self-awareness has created tension. It's strange to stand next to a man you have dreamed about, as if, by dreaming, some line has been crossed.

'We should speak only in English? Yes?'

Once again Rike speaks slowly, aware that Tomas is watching her mouth. This is normal, students watch the shape of her mouth, how the lips stretch or curl to a word, to notice where the tongue is placed: visible or not. Not so normal were the three men she taught in London last summer who looked only at her breasts, expectant, not with lust, so much, as hunger, so she couldn't look at them without thinking of them as being parched or starved. Her one discomfort with teaching is the sense that she's being sapped dry, although, she admits it's slightly nonsensical to think of knowledge as nourishment. It's not uncommon, Isa tells her, for teachers to imagine that their students are obsessed with them. It isn't that Rike actively considers these ideas as she stands beside Tomas, or even believes them, but they come at her as a package, one thought tied to another, bound by habit and connections. Isa's ideas are crafted to be wicked, ridiculous, and sticky. Nevertheless, those grey Nordic eyes as they coolly watch her mouth are a little unsettling.

'Show me where they live and tell me their location. You under-stand?' She points to the apartment where the man has finished his cleaning. The blinds are still open but the room is now vacant. 'Tell me where these people are. Describe their location. Inside? Outside? Behind? Beneath? *On top*. Tell me where they live.' The dream sits with her as a residue. Everything she says today brims with innuendo. Rike focuses her attention on Tomas's right hand, *and such big hands*. She hopes that Tomas doesn't sense what passes through her mind.

Tomas nods, sets down his cup, then points to the windows to his right: east wing, one floor below. 'Christos the driver and his wife live on the third floor.' He points now at the west wing: a window with open shutters, where pale blue curtains, thin as a nightdress, drop over the sill. 'Below. One floor,' he points directly down, 'is the Kozmatikos family. The mother is a speech therapist. Sometimes you hear the stu-dents. Peh-peh-peh. Treh-treh-treh.' He trills the 'r'. 'It must be the school holiday because her son is always home. Maybe he is sick. I often see her son at the window,' and again in German. 'I spoke with her husband yesterday. I don't remember his first name. He works as a pharmacist. The Kozmatikos family have lived here for a long time. It's close to the hospital and easy for work. He inherited his apartment from his father. I think that's what he said.'

Rike asks that he speak in English.

'Before, there were fourteen children here, but now there are only three. He says that Limassol isn't so friendly now, it's bigger, and there are many people who come for their holidays. Many businessmen also, and many Russians.' He points at the opposite building. 'Most of the rooms on this side are bedrooms and bathrooms. On the front are the sitting rooms.'

They return to the room, then Tomas draws Rike to the balcony and points to the street and the opposite building, the last before the hos-pital.

'A judge lives there. He lives on the top floor with his wife. In the evening you can see it's one long room. The apartment is modern. You see, with the black and white painting? He wears a suit and house shoes. You would not know he is a judge. His wife is an elegant woman. Christos says that the judge has a house at the coast near Larnaca and another in the Troodos mountains. This is where he stays when the court is in session.'

Tomas quickly checks his notebook.

'I sit here in the morning with my coffee. This is my routine. Every morning I watch the judge's driver. His car is parked in the same place and the man stands in the same place, like this.' Tomas folds his arms in demonstration. 'According to Christos he is a police officer. He is always calm and relaxed. His expression is always the same. He notices everything.'

Tomas looks up from his notes and smiles his first proper smile.

'The doctor's son ran away – the Kozmatikos boy. This morning, the mother accused the supervisor of leaving the main door open. The boy is seven or eight and he's always dressed in his football clothes. He was gone for four hours. He isn't allowed out of the building on his own. Along the street there is a café which is managed by two brothers, then a news-stand which sells comics and books. There is a man who watches the parking spaces on both sides of the street. He never speaks with the judge's driver, who is often waiting in the street. During the day the street appears respectable, but at night there are women on the corner. They sit on mopeds. I'm not certain they are all women.'

Tomas checks the notebook again to ensure he has said everything.

'Every morning I make a coffee and I come to the window. Christos is always the first to leave, sometimes he returns just before eight. He parks in front of the building and waits for his wife.'

When Tomas looks up from his notebook Rike congratulates him.

Sunlight, reflected from the glass doors, slips from the balcony into the room in a widening block to capture her shoes and calves; the edges vibrate and heat prickles her skin. She hasn't seen the driver. He isn't there now. None of the characters Tomas has described are about.

Satisfied with his presentation, Tomas adds, 'I didn't explain yesterday that Christos drives a taxi.'

'I thought he was a photographer?'

'This is his hobby for a little extra money. For work he takes people to the airport at Paphos and Larnaca. Christos and his wife fight every moment they are together. In the morning they argue about work. In the evening they argue about money.'

'This morning, I woke to hear him shouting that everything that is happening is her fault.'

Rike waits until Tomas has finished. There isn't much to say. Perhaps talking in a group would be good for him. She could ask about sessions at the school. 'Conversation would help,' she says. 'Try using the simple past tense. Tell me more about Christos. Have you seen him today?'

'I saw Christos this morning. But we didn't speak because he is in a bad mood. He had an accident so he cannot drive.'

Rike asks Tomas to describe Christos's accident in detail. Taxi, stop-lights, bus. He's lucky to be alive. The minibus is a write-off, and as the taxi driver was *unofficial* and therefore *uninsured* this is going to cost an unbearable amount of money. Now he considers himself unlucky. He can't work without his vehicle, which leaves him at home with too much time on his hands.

Tomas shrugs, matter of fact.

Pleased, Rike leans forward, her elbows on her knees, her hands clasped. 'Now,' she demands, 'let's practise conversation. OK. I will ask you questions and you will answer me. Tell me about your parents.'

Tomas asks blankly why she is interested in his parents.

Rike isn't sure how to answer. 'I want to hear you talk. You can say anything. Tell me specific events. Something you remember? Your parents. Where are they from?' She smiles in encouragement.

'They are from Norway. And your parents?' Tomas asks.

'My father was an academic.' She answers, deliberately, in the simple past tense. 'He taught at the university in Freiburg. My mother was Italian and she was a student at the university at the same time. She was a little younger. Tell me, did you grow up in Norway? What is your first memory of Norway as a child.'

'My first memory?'

'Something from the past.'

Tomas looks up, reflecting, his chin set out.

'A birthday? A holiday?'

'My birthday is in the summer. I don't remember anything special.'

'A party, then. Describe a party.'

'I don't remember a party.'

To counter Tomas's resistance Rike offers her own example. 'My sister is five years older than me. When she was eleven we had a birthday party for her. We lived in an apartment – in Freiburg – and I don't remember why, but I wasn't happy about this party. I don't think I did this deliberately – my sister would probably tell this differently – but I remember standing beside a table, there were other children, and there was a cake, but I had a glass, a beaker, and I must have been drinking juice, and somehow I bit off the lip of the glass. I remember it coming off.' She gestures holding a glass to her mouth and biting.

'And what happened?'

'My parents were busy, but when my mother noticed she became very worried. She took the glass from me, and I remember very clearly that she thought that the missing piece from the glass was in my mouth. But it wasn't. I remember it breaking off, but I don't remember anything else about the glass. My mother became very upset, and it was the end of the party because they had to take me to hospital to make sure I hadn't swallowed the glass.'

'And did they find it?'

'I don't think so. I don't know. I hadn't swallowed it, and I had no cuts. So they thought that I'd done this deliberately for attention. We didn't have any more parties after that.'

'Is this true?'

A little surprised Rike says yes, the story is true, of course. 'And you?'

'Me?'

'Do you have any brothers or sisters?'

Arms folded, Tomas gives a firm no.

'And now, in Norway, where do you live?'

'I don't spend much time there.' Tomas shifts uncomfortably in his seat.

'Tell me about your school.'

Of all questions, this seems the most innocuous, but his reaction, how he moves his weight from his left side to his right, unfolds his arms, tucks his hands away, and looks, she has to admit, a little irritated.

Tomas compresses his mouth, appears to be thinking. He shifts back into his original position. 'I left school early.'

Rike isn't sure why the conversation has become so tense. 'If I'm asking things you'd rather not answer, please change the subject. Speak about anything you like – or ask me questions.'

'You have one sister?'

'One sister and one brother.'

'And where does your brother live?'

'He lives in Hamburg.'

'You are the youngest?'

'Then my brother, and my sister is the oldest. Yes. In fact I'm here for my sister. She is about to have a child.' She stops herself from saying *first*, a noticeable hesitation. 'Which is why I am here.'

'When is your sister having the baby?'

'Soon, in eighteen days.'

'Why is she here?'

'She worked until recently for the diplomatic corps.'

'And her husband?'

'The same. At the moment he works for the German consulate in Nicosia. He was working in Damascus but they were evacuated. He has had to go back because there is a man in hospital.'

Tomas doesn't appear to understand.

'There is a man in hospital in Syria, in a serious condition. It's complicated because they don't know who he is.' She makes a gesture implying movement. Picking up an object and placing it somewhere else.

'And your brother is helping him?'

'It's part of his work – when people are in trouble, if they're in hospital, if they have an accident, they lose their money and passport, or if there's trouble or a problem back home with their family. He travels all around the Middle East helping people. German people.'

'Your brother?'

Rike gives a small corrective laugh. 'No. Sorry. My brother-in-law.'

'How long were you in England?'

This question surprises her, and she asks why he's asked.

'You have a slight English accent. You are German, though?'

Rike nods again. She doesn't think of herself having an accent, and finds the comment interesting. She wonders how many Scandinavians there are in Limassol, and what it would take to bring a man from Norway to Cyprus – if this situation is usual or unusual. When she asks why he wants to practise his English the man smiles.

'How will you use your English?'

His smile broadens. 'To be honest,' he says, 'it's about keeping active.' He taps his head and Rike completely understands. After all it is a muscle, they agree.

'How long are you here?'

'It depends, six or seven weeks.'

'And then you go to London?'

'No. I'll go back to Germany. To my brother's apartment in Hamburg.'

'You have work?'

'I'm not sure what I'll do. I haven't decided.'

'But you won't stay here?'

Something about the suggestion makes her laugh. While she hasn't considered remaining in Cyprus, it could be a possibility.

'It depends on what happens. My sister and her husband will return to Damascus. Unless things become worse. I don't know what they will do if that happens. The consulate won't keep them here indefinitely. Henning has said as much. If this looks like a permanent situation they will withdraw the staff and have them return to Germany. Some will be reassigned to Turkey, but Henning, almost certainly, will be recalled to Berlin.'

'And you would you go with them?'

'No. I'm only here while she has the baby. Do you know Germany?'

Tomas nods. 'Berlin. Frankfurt. I don't know Hamburg.'

'And what were you doing there?'

'The same work I'll be doing here. I don't have any brothers or sisters, and no parents.' Tomas finishes the thought in German. 'Just me.'

The air in the room appears to have thinned, become delicate, without a clear reason. Every conversation, she understands, is a kind of currency, or at least an expenditure, but this discussion, being so scattershot, is uncertain, and Rike isn't sure what is being brokered. She breathes carefully unsure how she should proceed. It is his decision to exchange personal details or not. This happens, she tells herself. Everyone has history, and not everyone is comfortable sharing.

3.2

At the end of the hour, Rike writes down what she has asked, with the growing sense that Tomas is impatient for the lesson to end. He stands up and takes the paper when she offers it, then accompanies her to the door.

'I have a meeting now,' he explains, 'I should go.'

He has, she thinks, an exceptionally disarming smile. They talk as he accompanies her to the door. 'Cyprus must be a disappointment after London?'

'London?'

'Yesterday you told me that you lived in London.'

'I worked for a charity for a short while, freelance to start with.' She can't help but make a face. 'But that was for a very short time.'

'You didn't like the work, or you were unhappy?'

Rike is taken aback by the question. 'It wasn't home. And it didn't feel like it would ever become home. Anyway, I'm here now.' Rike reaches to her shoulder and realizes that she has left her bag. Tomas returns to the room to fetch it for her.

'Thank you. I'm always doing that.' Rike closes the bag and shucks it over her arm. 'And you?' she asks. 'Why Cyprus?'

Tomas leans into the doorframe. 'It's a long story. It's possible I'll be reassigned to Cyprus. I came to see if I like it.'

'And do you?'

'I don't know yet. I'll let you know. Careful as you go down,' he warns. 'There might be pieces of glass.' He pauses, clicks his finger to prompt himself, his hand attempts to shape a word. 'This morning the Kozmatikos boy smashed his mother's ornaments. Little figures. Figurines? He lined them up and dropped them over the steps.'

They both look at the landing. The floor, swept clean, shows no sign of the morning's tantrum.

'I think this is why he ran away.'

'You saw this?'

'I saw a little. It was deliberate. He put them on the steps and pushed them over, one at a time. He wanted to make her angry.'

'And then he ran away?'

Tomas nods, and she notices the faint trace of a smile.

'Is he back?'

'Yes. Now she isn't shouting.' Tomas shrugs, and now they both smile.

No sign on the door, no sound, no bustle or trouble. Safe enough to assume that the boy is home.

'It's strange,' she says, 'how ordinary you take everything to be, but when you look there are a lot of unordinary things.' Rike isn't sure she's making herself clear. 'Like pets. You don't see people with too many pets here. Not as many as in Germany. There aren't many dogs, so much.'

Tomas folds his arms and says that there is a lot to be said for this.

'You don't like dogs?'

'They don't like me.'

*

Tomas has agreed to meet the rental agent immediately after the lesson. The man comes up to find Rike and Tomas on the landing. The three of them walk down the stairs to the courtyard. The agent is brash and short and Rike talks with him as they come down the stairs. The man seems misproportioned, with small fat hands, a thick neck, and plump body unbalanced by a broad head, and oddest of all, a puff of thinning grey hair with a purplish tinge. The man walks in a stiff side-to-side sway, a little out of breath; keys hang from a chain fastened to his belt. He wears a pair of sunglasses which give him a suspicious air. Rike takes the stairs one at a time and grips the rail.

The windows overlooking the playground are shuttered and as they walk the agent describes the basement. Most of the space is open, although there are some smaller rentable units. These units are good for storage and safe. No one ever goes down there. The agent speaks in a voice which sounds bored and exhausted. The main area is used by a designer.

Rike's ears are suddenly itchy. A roll-down shutter protects the basement door. Before they open it, Rike makes her excuse. She has promised to meet her sister.

3.3

The sisters wait in the corridor on a flat-backed bench, school-like, or hospital-like, which is exactly where they are, in a hospital. Isa comments on their surroundings: the benches, long slats of lacquered wood, orange and sticky, run the length of the wall. The walls are painted marine blue to eye level (when seated) and run minty-green above. Isa can't see the logic, except the blue being gloss is wipeable, easy to clean.

'You think I don't know.'

Distracted by the nurses Rike doesn't hear her sister's comment. Nurses hurry down the corridor.

'It's strange seeing everyone here.'

'The nurses?'

'No. People like him.' Isa nods to the end of the corridor where the doors stand open to show two suited men; one leans forward as if to listen, the other, taller and bald, leans back with his arms folded. Rike can't quite see but thinks that the bald man is Udo.

'Ordinarily you wouldn't see them talking.'

Rike asks why. They talk about anything except for the reason they are at the hospital. The reason why Isa requires so many check-ups.

'He doesn't approve. The one with his arms folded got rid of his wife about a year ago. After twenty years of marriage he sent her home. The rumour is that he was having an affair, but he hasn't been seen with anyone. The other one, Udo, is Henning's section boss, and they can't stand each other. Henning is hoping he'll leave, but they won't offer him another post.' Isa yawns and rubs her stomach. 'He can't stand him.'

Rike takes another look, but Udo is out of sight.

'Back in Damascus you'd never see those two in the same room. Now you see them together the whole time. It's just how it is. Crisis makes for strange bedfellows.' Isa yawns harder, like the first yawn was a warm-up. This time she shows her teeth before she covers her mouth. 'Creepy. Creeps.'

'How long will this take?'

'I don't know. It could take ages. They're going to weigh me. It's insulting. They give me a paper gown, make me take off my clothes and have me stand on a scale. Then they'll take blood, because they always take blood. They weigh, they measure, then they take blood.'

Isa's eye follows the nurse as she returns; her dress zipping between her thighs, her soft shoes making no sound on the red tiled floor.

'Do British women deliberately try to look like that?'

Rike follows her sister's gaze, but can't see the problem.

'They don't care about themselves. Look. There isn't any dignity. Look at those shoulders. See how she walks. Like a cow heading to a barn. I hate these places. I know about the cats, by the way.'

Rike looks to her sister. Eye-to-eye.

'Of course I know.'

'The cats?'

'The cats. The cats. I spoke with Henning this morning.'

'He told you?'

'I made him.'

The sisters look to each other for some kind of measurement or assurance.

'Why didn't you say anything?'

'I didn't want to upset you.'

'I'm not upset. Honestly. This is the last thing to worry about. I'm not going to cry over a neighbour who's taken a dislike to three cats.'

'Two.' Rike can't judge if Isa is sincere. Sometimes there's no way of reading her.

'It doesn't matter. This is Cyprus, the problems here aren't on the same scale. Anyway, I'm more worried about Henning. He never talks. He's probably more upset than me, and I wouldn't know. Everything that's left from his family is in Damascus, everything from Henning's father, and we don't know what will happen.' Isa pauses because she's upsetting herself. 'What worries me is that we've only known each other in Damascus. It's our city. It's where we met. It's where we married.'

'He seems all right. It's you he's worried about.'

'This is how he copes. His job is about managing, so he worries about me instead.'

'Of course he worries.'

Isa draws her thumb under her eyes. 'I'm just angry.' At this her voice begins to wobble. 'It's so pathetic.'

Rike smiles at this and slips her hand along the bench to rest under her sister's thigh.

'The Heiztlermann's horses. Can you imagine? She must be going out of her mind.' Isa clears her throat. 'Oh. I heard from Mattaus this morning.'

Rike nods. Mattaus. Perfect. This is not what she needs right now. 'Why didn't you tell me earlier?'

Isa shrugs. 'I'm telling you now. He said he wants to visit. He wants to bring a new man he's met.' Isa is uncomfortable. 'You know what he's like.'

'But what about Franco?'

'There is no Franco. They've broken up.'

'When did this happen?' Rike feels herself tighten up, contract.

'I don't know the details. You know Mattaus. Everything has to change when he gets bored. He's met someone else. Franco is still in their apartment. You know how it goes, someone will come along and he'll go with them, then disappear until it's all over. I think he doesn't like to tell you these things because you can be judgemental.'

'And you aren't?'

'Look, you know how he is. Anyway, he says he's in love. He's an architect.'

The sisters roll their eyes in unison.

'Poor Franco. Did he say anything about him?'

'Only that he refuses to leave the apartment. I don't think it's quite the story you imagine.'

'And Henning? Have you spoken with Henning about this?'

Isa sharply dismisses the idea. 'Oh god no. Can you imagine? Anyway, I've told Mattaus he can't stay with us. He can sleep on the beach.'

Rike sits alone in a marine-blue and minty-green corridor while Isa speaks with the consultant, and wonders what Tomas Berens might be doing. She'd like to tell her sister about the dream, but knows she wouldn't hear the last of it if she did. Mattaus is an unwelcome interruption. A bad thought.

She finds the market, she's come here once before with Isa and Henning.

The market is held every day except Sunday. On weekdays the small avenues between the stalls are especially crowded, and in the morning it can take a while to walk from one end to the other. In the afternoon the market is almost empty. The building has a temporary feel, with windows along the roof, fine wood shavings on the concrete floor, and a line of counters – raised chopping blocks and white marble table tops on which the meat is dressed and displayed. Along one side is a row of upright ancient freezers, their doors scuffed and dented.

While she is squeamish, she's inured to the displays of cut meat, the hooks stuck through shins and tendons, the cold iron-like stink of blood. Once in a while there's a sight which makes her cringe, retreat a little – a hoof on a severed limb, a peeled goat's head, eyeballs and teeth and no skin, slippy layers of pink veins and white fat. Never mind the flies, the small clots of blood, the cloths used to wipe the knives and cutting boards, the butchers' hands. All men. There are only men here.

The man in Rome. The first Sutler flung into the path of a train. Luggage on the train. Man off, strewn between tracks. Although, no, this isn't quite the case, in the papers now it isn't Sutler who died, but Parson, the man who was following him, which means that Sutler is potentially responsible: a thief and a murderer.

She hasn't come here for death either. She just wants to see something *actual*. The slaughtered and prepared meat is exactly what it is, flesh, it isn't a metaphor for anything.

THE HIT

It's here that she reconsiders Mr Crispy, Sutler Number Three. Her story is wrong-headed. She has romanticized him, sure, and played with the idea that he unwittingly entered a situation. This is a foolish idea. The man isn't *accidentally* in the desert, he hasn't wandered off. Not at all. This is *flight*. Sutler is a force, propelling itself forward, a determined energy that wills itself to life. This is why he has survived.

Here he is, disguised, wearing Arab dress, concealed already, in some kind of public transport, a rough bus in which people hang heads and arms out of windows, women and children sleep, and an undignified scrum of people bundle together, half-conscious, dozy with the heat. In an attempt to destroy evidence the man was caught in an explosion (she's heard this from Henning, and read it herself online). He could be bandaged, seriously wounded. Nobody knows the extent of the damage. He could be fingerless, deeply disfigured. He could be numb and witless. Maybe this damage is what makes them so certain that this third Sutler is the real Sutler?

Sutler's problem isn't money, it's his new-found notoriety. He can't go back, can't even think about it. He can only move forward.

This figure isn't devastated by the sun but transformed. The burns are part of a process in which he becomes new. The sun fashions Sutler into a new man. Mr Crispy is no accident, he's the best option from a limited set of choices. Nothing will remain of the old Sutler. Ears, nose, mouth, the skin off his feet and hands are scorched from him. According to Isa they will slice skin from his back to rebuild his face.

Walking through the market, Rike can believe in this transfiguration. It isn't something that anyone would plan. But the situation is useable. A man this determined could make it work for him. It's part of what he needs to do.

She can't find her keys. Typical. And can't believe her luck when she sees the door open, Isa home and complaining about the smell, a fan in the corridor blowing air into the apartment.

'I just needed some fresh air.'

'How did it go?'

'Twins.' Isa looks for a reaction which Rike won't give. 'Only kidding. Does it smell in here? I think it still smells. They've collected the trash, but the stink lingers.'

Rike checks the kitchen drawer and finds a second set of keys. She takes these and uses her body to block Isa's view. She'll have them re-cut. Henning, a stickler with keys, would make a big fuss if he knew.

'So what did they say? Seriously?'

'Nothing. I've put on a little more weight than I need – that's me, not the baby. But nothing. Really. Nothing.'

'Blood pressure?'

'Fine. Not great, but fine.'

'Did he say when?'

Isa smiles and nods, can't help herself. 'Same date. A little less, maybe. Maybe two days earlier. I have a feeling he's right.'

The sisters hug and hold on to each other.

Isa speaks with Henning on the phone, her voice low, but not low enough. It's possible that she's unaware that Rike has returned. For almost an hour Rike has been reading in the garden, and when Isa went for a shower she slipped out quickly to have a new set of keys cut in the corner shop.

It takes a moment for her to realize that she is the subject of the conversation.

'*That's the problem*. That's it right there. It's always the wrong person. At school she had this thing for an autistic boy. What was his name? It was like a project or something. Her project. I don't know. You know how she is. And then Franco. That whole thing.' Isa pauses, then interrupts. 'No, she had this whole thing for him, fell in love with him.' Another pause, and when she resumes speaking her voice has an unexpected sincerity. 'Because I worry for her.'

Rike returns to the garden, is tempted to make some noise – make a point. Under the tree, stretched out, head up with bright little eyes, is the black cat – long and lovely. Rike pockets the keys, looks at the cat, and while she should feel delight, she doesn't. She doesn't feel anything other than irritation about being the third party to a conversation about her private life. Rike takes her seat a little distracted by her lack of outrage. It doesn't mean anything. Isa always has to take things too far. All that nonsense about the autistic boy. And what was his name? Michael Something. Michael Koenig. Short, fat (didn't Isa always point that out?), Michael Koenig with his pudgy face which generated any quantity of stuff: noise primarily, but also snot, tears, spittle. A boy whose tantrums and violence were unparalleled, but who was also, often, peaceful, calming. The boy behaved without constraint. In every action, every response, Michael Koenig never lied, had zero cunning, and despite his moods she knew exactly where she stood with him. Unlike Isa, Michael never disappointed her, because she expected little from him. Other people, on the other hand, were infinitely disappointing. Had she loved him? Certainly, in whatever way you love someone when you are younger. Her desire to include him in every activity (she insisted that he be invited camping with them) bordered on mania. Isa just didn't like him. She probably felt replaced.

That Isa would still be resentful doesn't surprise her.

The nonsense about Franco is so outrageous she can't reason her way around it. And yet, isn't this typical? Doesn't Isa break every confidence between them, blab out everything they share, *because this is what Isa does*? And how ugly is it to take her concern and twist it in this way? She begins to feel some heat on the matter. Mattaus behaves like a shit toward Franco. For five years, perhaps longer, Franco is as good as family, so why shouldn't she be concerned for him when Mattaus behaves the way he does? This is typical of Isa, so busy with herself that she doesn't see the full picture. Isa doesn't know how Mattaus behaves with Franco, not in the same way as Rike – and yes, why not, she does feel protective of Franco. But how typical. Really. How typical of Isa to say such a thing.

It's possible that her overhearing the conversation wasn't accidental. In any case, it doesn't matter. Rike won't be provoked.

Isa comes into the garden with news.

The man from the desert is being brought to Cyprus. Today or tomorrow. This is now definite. Henning will have his way, and he'll return soon, although they don't know exactly when, and she doesn't know which hospital the man is being brought to: military or civil.

Rike says she knows, not about the hospital, but about the man. She spoke with Henning right after Udo gave his consent to the move.

'No,' Isa corrects her. 'You must have heard wrong. He's only just told me. This is probably why Udo was at the hospital today.' Isa sucks air between her teeth, considering. 'My guess is the military hospital at Akrotiri will have better facilities. And they'll want to keep him secure, don't you think?'

Rike agrees without showing interest. So Henning will be back soon? Good. This, at least, will make things easier.

3.4

In the morning the driver takes Gibson to Naples. Sullen after viewing the site of the incident, Gibson sits in the back seat and does not talk. The driver says that there are details which will need to be discussed, but this can wait for the moment. Rooms have been booked in Hotel Laurino on via dei Tribunali, and when they arrive, they find a man waiting for them in the lobby, knees together, arms crossed, unlikely to be a guest. He rises to shake the driver's hand and Gibson realizes that he has this wrong. The man isn't a driver but someone more senior. Gibson recalls the man introducing himself as Sandro, and giving a second name and rank he hadn't caught. The ranking and organization of the Italian police is confusing. There's the police, and then the carabinieri. He isn't sure how the duties are divided. And magistrates? In Italy the magistrate is part of the investigation.

Gibson offers his hand to the other man, who smiles but says nothing. If Gibson would like, Sandro says, he can go over some of the details for him, and explain the procedures. It might make the day a little easier. 'You will be seeing Laura Parson?' he asks. Given the circumstances she has been helpful, and remarkably courageous.

Sandro believes he has everything straight. He understands the reason for Parson's time in Italy. He understands the working relationships: how Parson worked for Gibson & Baker, and how HOSCO was their client. This he understands.

What is less clear is the reason why hotel rooms – in Palermo, Bari, Castellammare, and Naples – have been booked in Paul Geezler's name.

'I checked them,' he says, and found that nearly eighty per cent of the bookings were not used. 'A room was booked, but nobody stayed. In some cases the room was not paid for.'

Sandro has copies of the papers found on the train, if Gibson wouldn't mind. He lays the papers out across the glass coffee table. Gibson recognizes Parson's handwriting.

'These don't look like notes, wouldn't you say? The numbers here are telephone numbers for hotels. But these numbers are confirmation or reservation numbers for rooms.'

Does Gibson follow the implication? It isn't Sutler making the bookings under Geezler's name. It's Parson. Would he have any idea why?

Lost for an explanation, Gibson asks if Sandro has spoken with Laura about this.

The man says no. And this is another strange element. Why, when Parson is undertaking such demanding, and ultimately dangerous work, would he ask his wife to accompany him?

It hadn't seemed so unusual to Gibson. Because of his work Parson was separated from his wife for several months, the simple answer is that he wanted to be with her, and the job didn't seem dangerous at all.

The problem, Sandro agrees, probably isn't a problem. In most cases people's lives are messy and unfathomable, because we are guided by habits and superstitions, ways of behaving which are impenetrable, irrational.

When Sandro leaves, the other man, who has still not spoken, accompanies him.

Gibson catches his reflection in the long mirrors either side of the reception desk, and is surprised to appear less stern and weary than he feels. It is encouraging to hear that Parson has inconsistencies.

Sunlight rebounding off the traffic scores across the lobby in sharp bands. He decides to walk to Laura's hotel although he does not know Naples.

THE THIRD LESSON

4.1

The door to Tomas's apartment stands open in anticipation. Rike has had to hurry, and she makes it to the top of the stairs a little breathless. Tomas sits ready, his notebook open on his lap and a dictionary at his feet. He leans over the notebook and reads with a singular focus. Rike pauses at the door before knocking. It was wrong, she concedes, to call him *unhandsome*, or to say that he is *not handsome*. His face is masculine, angular, his mouth, full and slightly pronounced (in profile), has the same effect on her as his hands – a slight out-of-kilter difference in scale, so small in this instance it could easily be imagined.

She knows nothing about him, and realizes that Tomas has offered her no real information. In fact he's shown little interest in speaking with her about his life, in sharing details, or in impressing her. His one interest is in learning English, a language he already commands.

Rike knocks on the door, steps in, says hello. She takes the seat offered. Once again they chat in German before the session starts.

'You should have stayed yesterday. Downstairs, in the basement. You should have come. It was very strange.' The landlord, the janitor, a supervisor, perhaps even someone who has rented the basement, uses the space to store Christmas decorations.

Rike smiles and allows the conversation to settle her.

'There were reindeer and . . .' Tomas clicks his fingers because he can't remember, then does a dance, something like a dance, he turns about, waddles with his arms at his side. 'Penguins?' He pulls a face. 'Do they have an ass?'

Rike isn't sure what he's asking. 'An *S*? Penguins. Plural? I think so. Yes.'

It's endearing to see his enthusiasm. The first real evidence of warmth. Again Tomas offers Rike a drink. He has sparkling water this time, cold, if she would like. He brings the bottle and two glasses to the room.

'There are figures which move – you can see they have moving parts. You should take a look before you go today. I don't think anyone would mind.' Tomas smooths his hand over the notebook, flattening it. He gives an exaggerated frown. 'Did you see the police?'

'See?'

'The police?'

'No. I just arrived.'

'They were here just a little before you. The Kozmatikos boy is missing again. The mother is very upset. She was shouting. You didn't hear her? It was very bad.'

'She must be worried. How long has he been missing?'

'Since this morning.'

'Do you know why?'

'Why he runs away? I think it's something boys do at a certain age.'

Rike smiles and shucks off her shoulder-bag and pointing at the bottle says that she would like a glass of water, please.

'The news today from Syria is very bad. The government have destroyed two villages in the mountains above Damascus. Two journalists were wounded. They were housing the rebels so they just—' He makes a magician-like gesture that might mean something exploding or something disappearing.

Today she does not need to steer, and Tomas begins to speak in English without being asked.

'First, this morning, I took a walk. There are businesses on the side of the building. A café. The supervisor lives in an apartment opposite the speech therapist and the doctor. This morning she was arguing with the people outside as they were unloading a van. She is a midget.'

'He,' Rike makes the corrections, 'is a *dwarf*,' although this sounds wrong. The supervisor was short, she saw him herself. Calling him a dwarf is a little harsh. She reminds Tomas that today she would like him to speak in the simple past tense. She encourages him to stop reading from his notes. 'Try without them.' She gestures toward the book. 'Your notes are holding you back.'

Tomas disagrees. 'She? The supervisor is a woman.'

'But yesterday, we met the supervisor?'

'That was the agent.' Tomas continues. 'Christos is a nice man. But he is also a difficult man. This morning there is an argument between Christos and the judge's driver. The man in the street who waits – with his car. The judge's driver.' Tomas pauses to make sure that Rike has understood him.

'The argument was very quick, and very aggressive. Christos comes, came, as usual to the café. He was there five minutes and the driver arrives. He's never spoken to his man before and the driver speaks to him, he says, "Good morning," and asks for a coffee, and sits at the same table. Christos has no idea what to say. He sees the man every day but has no idea what to say to him. When the coffee arrives, the driver drinks his quickly, then he says to Christos, "*It always tastes better away from home.*"'

Rike asks Tomas to repeat the sentence to make sure she understands him.

Tomas speaks in German. '*It always tastes better away from home.* This is what he said. Unusual, no? A little strange. Christos thinks the man is somehow mocking him. He is telling him, he thinks, that he is with his wife.' And again in German, 'Christos believes the driver is having an affair with his wife.'

'Why would anyone think this?' Rike can't follow the logic. 'And after?'

'And after, Christos returns home and accuses his wife of having an affair. Which she denies, and naturally he doesn't believe her.' Tomas settles back. 'I can tell you the driver isn't having an affair because I've seen him with a young woman who comes to his car. Sometimes they drive away together. I think Christos has the wrong idea. He sees only what he wants to see.'

Rike moves the session along with a simple instruction. 'Today, like yesterday, we will ask and answer questions. I want lots of questions.'

Tomas nods and says that he will start. 'Have you heard from your brother-in-law?'

'He calls every morning.'

'From Syria?'

'Yes, from Syria.'

'And he is safe?'

'He is staying at a hotel. I think the hotel is very safe.'

'And the man he is looking after?'

'I think he is safe also. Now.'

'Is he very ill?'

'Yes, he is seriously ill.'

'And they don't know who he is?'

'They have an idea, which makes his recovery important.'

'Who do they think he is?'

'They think he is a contractor from Iraq. A man called Stephen Sutler.'

Tomas admits he's heard the name. He looks puzzled. 'There was news recently, I think?'

Rike nods and admits it's confusing. 'There are Sutlers everywhere. Henning doesn't see how it's possible.' She explains to Tomas how the man is supposed to have walked across the desert, from Iraq to Syria, and how he's responsible for millions in lost money, for absconding with reconstruction funds. The internet sings with ideas. There are fan sites, and sites which condemn him. Others see him as part of a global anti-capitalist struggle. While everyone argues over his identity, none, yet, know that he will shortly be brought to Cyprus.

Rike stops herself. 'I didn't say that. I'm not supposed to know.'

Tomas says it doesn't matter. He won't mention it to anyone. There isn't anyone he could tell. 'So I think the information is technically still a secret.'

Rike has embarrassed herself.

Tomas assures her. 'I didn't hear a thing.' Information like this will pass around quickly. Too many people are involved. She shouldn't worry.

'Henning is sceptical. One man can't be responsible for such a thing.' Once you know the name, she says, you'll find it everywhere. Henning met the man who was killed by a train in Rome. He met him in Istanbul. So Henning is involved in all of this, tangentially of course.

Tomas isn't to say a word. He must promise. Not one word.

Once the lesson is complete Rike again has the feeling that Tomas would like her to leave as quickly as possible.

His vocabulary, she says, is exemplary. Today he has managed to switch between tenses and had no difficulty expressing complex and conditional ideas. In three sessions he has become infinitely more confident. In fact – if she's honest – she's not entirely sure why he needs these lessons.

Tomas smiles at the question and says that he's mostly interested in conversation.

Rike, uncertain that he has completely understood her, states carefully, 'It would help if you could tell me what you want from these sessions. Rosaria said that you asked for me directly?'

Tomas shakes his head. 'No. I asked for a new teacher. I think she misunderstood me.' He opens his hands, a little apologetic. 'My problem isn't vocabulary, but practice. Conversation.'

And there it is, a simple misunderstanding. The answer is disappointing. Rike sits a little forward and asks if she can look at his notebook. She senses Tomas's reluctance, but he hands over the small notebook. She finds the pages he was referring to, the notes on his neighbours are almost word for word what he has told her. The discussion is anticipated, studied, rehearsed. Aware that she is being watched she tries not to react and becomes unconfident about her expression. Her face is a little flushed. 'See. What you are doing is good, but I'm not sure what you want from me exactly?'

'I want you to correct what I'm saying.'

Rike holds the pages open.

'You're managing this by yourself. Is there something specific you want me to help with?'

'I need to practise speaking.'

She closes the book and hands it back. Still unclear. 'But you speak very well. Very little of what you say needs to be corrected. What you need is practice with a variety of people so you can gain confidence, pick up small details, colloquialisms.' Rike points to the balcony. 'Everything you're asking for you'd get from an advanced class, from being around native speakers. I'm very happy with the sessions,' she says, 'I only want to be sure that you are as well.'

Tomas shakes his head and becomes silent.

Rike apologizes, she can't read his response, not sure what the issue is she picks up her bag and says that she should go, and maybe he should think about what he wants.

Tomas walks with her to the door. 'Unless I have something specific to do, something I can't avoid, I don't go out,' he says.

His expression, flat, matter of fact, surprises her, and she realizes that this is the crux of the matter.

'You don't go out?'

'Unless there is something specific I have to do.'

Can't or *don't* – there are different intentions behind these words. She wants to know how he manages the café, how he speaks with Christos?

'I don't like to go out.' Tomas closes his eyes for a moment.

Rike suddenly understands that what she had taken for a holiday isn't a holiday at all, but some kind of recuperation. Now embarrassed, she bows her head and apologizes. 'I'm sorry. You don't need to explain anything.'

Tomas opens his hands. The gesture is genuine, intimate. 'I have to decide the kind of work I want to do. I have to decide if I should continue or if I should change. And if I decide to change then I need to think about what that change might be.' Tomas folds his arms, his face up and expression open. 'I know that what I'm doing right now doesn't work. But I don't know anything else.' The man straightens up. 'Most of what I do, I do because I have to. Not because I choose to. And if you do that for long enough then you get to an age where you think there isn't anything else you can do. I have to give this a lot of thought. I'm thinking seriously that this is the right time to make a change.'

'How can you decide if you can't go out?'

'It isn't that I can't go out. I choose not to. I need a reason. Something to do.'

'If I set you an assignment, to go to a museum for example?'

'Then I would go.' If this is what she wants, Tomas agrees, he'll do this. 'I had another story for you today. I meant to tell you about what happened here. They had something happen here a couple of years ago. An incident which involves the basement.'

They agree to take this up later. Rike wants to go, and is happy to leave now the subject has changed. This is an easier place to stop.

4.2

Rike walks back to the apartment with two things on her mind: cats and Tomas Berens. Cats because she has to walk along the small street beside the hotel development, and Tomas because she wants to challenge him, or help him, but has no idea for the moment how she might achieve this. The sun is pleasantly warm. She walks through the narrow street, a little ashamed of her clumsiness during the session. Tomas, in his way, has let her know that he is managing some kind of problem – who knows what – and she's trying hard not to think of him as someone damaged or vulnerable.

Rike checks the road to make sure there are no dead cats, and finds, happily, no cat, but a new bag of cat food. Again, the bag is slit open. She picks it up, thinking this is another plan to lure cats out into the open, and comes into the apartment through the back entrance, and notices a smell, which could, just might be, jasmine.

Isa stands at the kitchen counter. Legs braced slightly apart. In front of her a spread of oranges. Rike's job is to keep her busy until Henning returns. *And for god's sake keep her away from the television. Don't let her watch the news.*

'The fruit. It's exceptional here.' Isa rolls an orange across the counter to Rike. 'Seriously, you should try one. I've already had three. They go right through me.' She quickly shifts topic. 'You noticed how no one speaks about the other Sutler? Number two? The middle man?'

Rike says she hasn't thought about it much. 'When is he back?'

Out of habit Isa looks at the clock although this question involves days not hours. 'Henning? The day after tomorrow. He thinks. Once everything is ready.'

'So he isn't here? The man from the hospital?'

'Mr Crispy?' Isa shrugs. 'Not yet. Henning said that he was stable, and everything's ready. As long as he can survive the flight, they can bring him over.' Isa brushes back her hair, a thought catching as something remembered. 'You know not to say anything.'

'Who would I speak to?' Rike shakes her head as she peels the orange.

Isa describes how the man is kept cool, how he has to be spritzed with water and kept in a sterile environment. Seriously disgusting. Chunks of him are flaking off. 'Mr Hamburger.' She takes an orange segment even before it is fully peeled, then reaches behind her for a stool, for somewhere to sit. 'No one's managed to speak with him yet. *No lips* – I'm joking. I don't know that. But the hospital have kept him sedated and he does need to have all of these operations now. They keep him in a tent in a room, no one sees him but doctors and nurses. She tuts playfully. 'Henning is hopeful that no one knows about Cyprus. Once he's here the situation *will be contained*.' Isa deepens her voice at the last phrase. 'Absurd. Anyway. That's what he said. Something like that? Sometimes I can't believe people actually talk like this. Can you imagine a room full of these people? How pompous they are. It isn't the real world. They have no knowledge of it. No understanding. They still believe in spies and Russia. Everything is back like it was in the seventies. Iron curtain. Walls. Poison pellets, suits and guns. The good old days.'

'And Henning.'

'He's loving it.' Isa bites through half a segment, catches the juice before it runs to her chin. 'He's in his element. Don't they taste amazing?' They look to each other in agreement. 'You know what they've called this whole operation?'

Rike shakes her head.

'Guess.'

Rike takes the last piece. Her sister's eyes follow her hand to her mouth.

'Go on. Guess.'

'I don't know.'

'But guess. You'll never guess.'

Again, Rike shakes her head.

'Operation Lazarus. Lazarus. Honestly. Lazarus. Someone gets paid to come up with these ideas.'

They walk into the garden, and it strikes Rike that the space seems more intimate in the softer afternoon light than at any other time: a small walled arbour with orange trees, branches heavy with fruit. A deep mottled shade just broad enough for the two of them. A dry heat hits her shoulders as soon as she steps onto the patio.

'Do me a favour and pick some more.' Isa points at the branches. 'They fruit so much they break their own branches. You wouldn't think anything would do that, would you?'

Rike agrees, it does seem strange. She walks behind the fig tree, careful where she's treading to avoid the cats or any cat mess. Except there are none. Not one cat. 'There's something about the sun here,' she says. 'It just doesn't feel Mediterranean.'

She reaches into tree, holds the branch as she plucks the fruit, and aims to keep her voice uninflected as she asks her sister if she has seen any of the cats.

Isa holds one hand to her forehead, the other on her hip. 'You know what? I haven't. There's food here as well. Do you think something's happened?'

They look to each other, disturbed by the possibility.

'I'll go look.'

'No.' Isa waves her hand. 'You know what? Don't. It's better not to know. If we think about this too much it will become something upsetting.' And then, decisive, 'Let's go out instead.'

Rike tucks three oranges into the cleft of her arm. She can smell the cats, cat urine and rotting lemons, and makes her way cautiously back to the path.

4.3

Within the hour Rike sits with her sister in the quadrangle in front of the Palestinian café. In the square behind them students begin to gather. Isa doesn't quite understand why Rike has become so agitated. Rike doesn't quite understand herself. The conversation with Tomas has changed in her mind, and mulling through the bare facts the causal tone of the conversation has become lost to the single idea that Tomas is learning English because he doesn't know what he wants. The man, in a word, is lost.

'So he tells you stories about his neighbours? If you ask me it sounds boring.'

Rike shakes her head and sinks forward. That isn't it. Not quite. 'He does everything I ask, and that's the problem. Everything is practised. Everything he says. He keeps a notebook and he writes everything down, word for word.'

Isa shrugs. 'Surely that's what you want a student to do?'

'But *everything*. He writes out the conversations. The sessions are one long monologue.'

'And you correct him?'

'There's nothing to correct. Tiny, tiny, small things, *maybe*. But he writes himself a script.' She shakes her head. 'I asked him why he's taking the lessons, and what he wants from them, from me. I told him that everything he needs he could find in an advanced class with other students. But he said that he doesn't like to go out.'

'He doesn't like going out?' Confused, Isa shakes her head. 'I don't follow. He's uncomfortable going out? Or he doesn't like speaking English in front of other people?'

'He said he doesn't go out – he avoids going out. He gets his food downstairs at the café. Otherwise he stays in, he watches people from his balcony early in the morning, then works on what he wants to say until the lesson.'

'I don't get it. What's he doing in Cyprus?'

Rike shifts uneasily in her seat. 'He works for the UN.'

'But where? What does he do?'

Rike shrugs. 'That's the other thing. I don't think this is a holiday exactly. He's learning a language because he's taking time off work.'

'But what's he doing here? And what's the problem?'

Rike looks to Isa with an expression meaning *take this seriously*.

'So, why is he taking time off work?'

'Stress.'

'Stress?'

'Stress. I think it's stress.'

'He's suffering from stress?' Isa pulls a face and turns away, actively uninterested.

'What's wrong with that?'

'Nothing's wrong with it. People have trouble with work all the time. But stress? It's a little unimaginative. Why would you learn a language if you're stressed? If you're stressed you take a holiday, you get away from everything.'

'Maybe he doesn't have a choice?'

'It still doesn't make sense.'

'Maybe,' Rike breathes in to summon patience, 'he doesn't know how to relax? Maybe that's why he's so stressed?'

'Seriously? Rike, everybody knows how to relax. Men especially.'

Rike gives a small groan of frustration.

Isa looks hard at her sister. 'I'm just asking questions. Is he comfortable when he's talking with you?'

'Why?'

'I'm just asking. I'm making conversation.'

'He can be funny. He notices things. He has a good eye. He's sympathetic. He isn't like most men, he doesn't have an instant opinion on everything.'

'So he isn't shy?'

'Not especially, after three lessons he seems very confident. And he talks with his neighbours.'

Isa nods. 'But he's been here for a month already so maybe he feels they are familiar.'

'Are you going to tell me he's crazy and that I shouldn't be alone with him?'

'No. I don't understand really why he's here? You said he works for the UN?'

Now Rike has doubts. 'He said he isn't sure he wants to do this kind of work now.'

'Maybe it isn't *stress* per se, maybe it's *anxiety*, and maybe he wants to work on this. People tend to develop coping mechanisms for anxiety. With stress people shut down. Perhaps this is why he's having lessons, so that for at least part of the day he's forced to socialize.' Isa looks out across the road, caught on a thought.

'What?'

'Nothing.'

'You're frowning. Why?'

'It's nothing.'

'But nothing about what?'

'Seriously, nothing. I'm just wondering how you got him to talk so much?'

'It's a language lesson. You *talk*.'

'But yesterday I asked about the lesson and how he was and you knew nothing. Today you know everything. Why is he talking so much about this? In one day?'

'I asked him why he was learning English and it all came out.' Rike is suddenly upset. Frustrated, she leans forward and covers her face. She shakes her head, a little surprised at her reaction. 'I don't know why it's so complicated. I don't understand why anyone would learn a language they are already fluent in, and I don't understand why they would stay only in one room. And I feel stupid because I should know what to do.' Rike wipes her eyes and sits back in her chair. 'That's it,' she says, sweeping her hands out. 'I will never make a good teacher.'

'I don't understand why you're upset. It sounds like you're helping him. It's not going to help if you're getting upset.'

'Because it shouldn't be so difficult. It should be easy. And straight-forward. And simple.'

'But you're the best person he could be working with.' Isa says this as an inarguable fact. 'I'm serious. He needs to talk with someone he can trust. You did a good thing challenging him today. Now he has to consider the next step. Isn't this more interesting than a boring lan-guage lesson? Anyway.' Isa pushes forward her glass. 'You can probably really help him. You know what's good for anxiety? Sex.'

Isa laughs and Rike laughs with her.

'I gave him an assignment. He said he would go out if I gave him a reason.'

'I'm serious. Tell him you're going to teach him something French. You both need it. See. You can help each other.'

Rike draws her hands in a line and closes the subject. She asks Isa if she is going to eat.

'I was sick this morning. Twice. I told you this? Then yoghurt, then I ate those oranges. So now I have an acid stomach.'

In front of the café runs a low and cropped hibiscus bush behind which a photographer poses a young couple. The woman straddles a parked motorbike, the man stands beside her with an idiot grin, like a man who can't believe his luck. The photographer arranges the woman's hair over her shoulder. The pictures are for an album that will show how and where the couple met, a picture book of recreated memories.

Isa scowls at the couple. 'She's so out of his league. Look at that hair.'

They return to the apartment by taxi. Isa sober, Rike a little woozy on beer. Rike drops her purse getting out of the cab, then her keys in the lobby and laughs as she tries to pick them up.

'Are you expecting a delivery or something?'

Isa says no and asks her to hurry.

'There's something in the hallway.' Rike finds the key and manages to open the door with Isa giggling beside her telling her to hurry. 'It's Henning.'

Isa rushes through as soon as the door is open. 'Henning? Henning!' She hurries to the front room in quick short steps. 'Oh, oh, oh. Rike, go see where he is.' Then slips into the bathroom without closing the door.

Rike comes slowly into the apartment, feeling happy – because she likes Henning, and because her sister has missed her husband so much – but also a little excluded, because this is not her reunion, and her time with her sister is now effectively over.

'Where is he?' Isa calls from the bathroom. 'Henning?'

Rike walks through the apartment but can't find him. His bags are in the hallway, but the man is not in the apartment. And now, confusingly, she feels disappointed at having to explain this to Isa. On the table, in a large vase, stands a bouquet of roses. Small pink heads. The colour and the quantity are extravagant. The pink buzzes against the white walls.

The situation resolves quickly. As Isa comes out of the bathroom, adjusting her clothes, Henning comes to the front door, a shopping bag in one hand, hooked on one finger. Isa is upon him before he can close the door. Arms up then locked about his neck.

Henning stoops to receive his wife's embrace. They rock together, eyes, at first, closed. And then, because this is looking to become drawn out, he opens his eyes, sees Rike and offers her the shopping bag – the same finger that is holding the bag wiggles to call her forward. As Rike takes the bag Henning gives her a smile, a wink, then wraps both arms about his wife.

Rike doesn't know what to do with herself. It's awkward, the two of them in the hallway holding tight, so she walks into the garden and startles the black cat. While she dearly loves her brother-in-law, his return, unannounced, points out that she has no one who will return to her.

If Henning is here, then so is the man from the desert. Mr Crispy. Sutler Number Three.

The cat scampers then freezes at the wall, mid-stride, ready to disappear. Rike holds herself still, and the woman and cat eye each other, the cat won't look her in the eyes, and then suddenly, after a moment shoots up the wall, its tail flicks as it disappears.

4.4

Gibson waits in the lobby of Laura's hotel on via Miano, opposite the Parco di Capodimonte. The walk has left him hot, and he is sweating through his shirt. While it is a bright day, the sun holds little heat.

Instead of Laura another woman comes down the stairs, and explains, with an apology, that Laura is sleeping. She introduces herself as Sarah. 'I know everything,' she says. 'I can answer any questions you might have.' Gibson doesn't catch if she is a friend or someone from the family. She asks if Gibson would prefer to walk or find somewhere else to go. Gibson looks about the lobby. He has no idea where they should go. Hasn't considered the mechanics of the day in any way.

Sarah walks ahead to the door, then pauses. The papers Gibson asked for, she's left them in the room.

'The day he left,' she explains, 'Laura moved hotels. They agreed to stay near the park.' She points to the city to their right. 'There's an observatory. He liked the view. You can see the Albergo di Poveri, the Duomo, Vesuvius. Capri, I think. When she arrived he brought her here. Made the taxi drive by and wait.' Sarah steers Gibson across the road. 'The park,' she says.

They walk through the gates, kept lawns lousy with dogs spill out from the museum. 'It's probably easier if I describe everything. I think that's easier. If I show you his papers you'll think less of him. You'll find out anyway. You'll need to consider what you want do with this. With what I'm going to tell you.' They come to an avenue, trees on either side with mast-like trunks. They agree it's surprising in such a crowded city to have such a vast and private park.

'It was all invented. Almost all. Most of what he told you. He was never close to finding Sutler. Not in Turkey, and not in Malta. The truth is he didn't want to return to Iraq. So when Sutler came up it was his opportunity to leave. I don't think he knew that at the time. The longer he spent chasing Sutler the less he wanted to return to Iraq. He just wanted to come home. That's all he wanted.' She pauses, waits for a troupe of motley dogs to pass in front of them. Abandoned by their owners, these dogs become wild, she says. They run about the park and nobody stops them.

'At some point he realized that no one was interested in finding Sutler. Not really. They wanted Sutler to disappear, especially HOSCO. They wanted the whole thing to die down. So he started booking hotels under Paul Geezler's name, as if he was Sutler, as if he had a point to make. I think that's all it was. Making enough noise to keep up interest, to keep the story alive, and as long as the story was alive he wouldn't have to return to Iraq.'

Their pace slows to a standstill halfway down the avenue. At one end a gate, at the other a stone statue of Hercules: the paved road runs straight in a soft descent.

'He knew it wouldn't last. When he heard Sutler was in Malta he followed him there. Then he invented a route from Sicily across the southern mainland. After Laura's surgery she joined him as soon as she was able. She didn't have much to do with it, she would have, but he spent all of his time creating a false trail. He said you have to invent the whole story, but only give out small pieces to make it credible. I think he enjoyed this. He had Sutler stay in Puglia for a while, so he hired a car, drove down, worked everything out – where he'd stay, what he might do from day to day. I think he sometimes pretended to be him – to leave evidence.'

Through a break in the trees Gibson can see another avenue, and beyond that an open field. Sarah clears her throat. She asks if Gibson has followed her so far. 'In the last three weeks there have been changes. Laura wanted him to return to England with her. He thought someone was following him. He was convinced. He thought it was Paul Geezler, or that he was somehow behind it. Laura didn't believe him.

But there was an occasion when they went to the museum and they both felt that they were being followed. There's one exhibit for which you need a separate ticket. They bought tickets but didn't go inside. You could see people going in from the stairwell. So they waited. There was one man. He went into the exhibition but came out, so it was obvious that he wasn't interested. The thing is, Laura is certain that she's seen him before. There's a café on via Toledo close by the hotel. I don't know the name.'

Gibson asks if she can describe the man.

'Laura took a photograph. I have it on my phone if you want it. I sent it to the police, I can send it to you.'

When they return to the hotel, Gibson accompanies Sarah to the room. She asks him to wait and holds the door as she enters so that he can't see inside the room. He hears voices, a small conversation, and when Sarah returns she slips out, and offers Gibson a selection of papers. 'Here,' she says. 'Here you go. Laura will email you the photo.' She closes the door and walks down the corridor with him to the lift. The carpet absorbs their footfalls. Sarah sees Gibson to the lobby. 'She doesn't want to see you again. I can't imagine any situation in which you would need to be in contact.'

Gibson can't think of a response. Instead he nods, as if this is deserved.

The walk back to the centre is downhill and he walks with the sun in his face. By the time he reaches the historic centre his back and knees ache and he is ready to sit down. This information, Parson's deception, his suspicions about Geezler, Laura's instruction to stay away, are too large to take in. He stops at a café on via Mezzocannone but finds nowhere to sit, the small room overtaken by students from the Orientale. Out of sorts he leans against the counter, surrounded by the buzz of Italian. It was a job, a simple job. If Parson disliked Iraq so much why wasn't this discussed? He knows the answer even as he asks the question. He would have fired him, or otherwise obliged him, because no one else would do the work.

4.5

Henning prepares to cook steaks out on the patio. A master with the grill he sets the fire, heaps the charcoal and waits for it to burn red and the flames to die down. He walks about the living room a little lost himself, the tongs in his hand, and clicks them together in time to the music he's playing – soft American rock. All of this time together Rike and Isa have not played any music, and the apartment feels different. Not only because of Henning and because there is something undeniably *Henning* about his presence, but because he has brought with him dominant habits which make noise, break concentration, demand attention. Henning is a pacer, a cogitator. He'll circle the living room, absorbed, for any length of time, appearing to chew over one thought, and then without doubting that someone will pay attention he'll ask a question or make a statement.

'You know Udo? You know what he said today? He said, and this is after an entire day with us, an entire department, waiting on the result of a piece of work he was supposed to do, that it didn't matter if he did or didn't do it.' Henning looks to Isa. Isa looks to Henning, she lowers the magazine she's almost reading. His expression is mock disbelief.

'Tell me. What was this thing he didn't do?'

'He said it didn't matter. When, in fact, this is key to everything we have been working on.'

'Is this about Sutler?'

'I'm being deliberately non-specific.'

'Which one? One? Two? Or three?'

'I remain unspecific on this subject.'

'But the general area?'

'The general area would be about security.'

'Then it has to be number three. And did it matter, this thing he didn't do?'

'You're missing the point.' Henning clacks the tongs. 'As it happens. It didn't matter.'

'So he was right? I don't see the problem. So I take it he's here?'

'Last night.'

'You were here last night?'

'They flew him in yesterday, before midnight.'

'So you were here at yesterday. You would have been here. You would have come with him.' Isa purses her mouth, threatening a shift in mood.

'We have three units watching this man. Can you imagine the cost? Do you know what he calls him? Udo. Did I tell you what he calls this mystery man?' Henning steers the conversation to safer ground.

'Mr Crispy?'

'No, that's our name. Kraiz came up with that.'

Isa closes the magazine, folds it over her knee. 'I'm not going to guess.'

'You're not interested.'

'No, tell me.'

'But you aren't listening.'

'My magazine is closed. I'm listening.'

'He calls him burger-head.'

'Burger-head?'

'Mr Tartare. Because of his face.' Henning gestures at his face with the tongs.

'You tell me this before we eat?'

'He's going to need a new face. His nose. Gone. They have to make new eyelids. It looks like he's been in a fire. And this is just from being in the sun for so long. He smells like he's been cooked. The doctors have a name for this . . .'

'And we're having steak tonight?'

'You like steak.'

'I do like steak. But I don't like stories about men who look like steak. Tell me a nicer story. Tell Rike the horror. Tell me happy things.'

Chastised, Henning points the tongs at her stomach. 'You have to eat.'

'So you were here last night and you didn't call?'

Rike, fingers in ears to signal her dislike of such stories, tells Henning she seriously doesn't want to hear anything graphic about this man. How he looks. How he suffers. Not one word. It's bad enough thinking about the man on the train.

'They take skin in strips from your back. Like bacon.' Henning clacks the tongs after his wife.

The fire, ready for the meat, is spread across the pan. Rike catches Henning's eye as he places the grate on top of the grill, and again he gives her a smile and a wink. This is his thank you. This is his appreciation. Meat. Gin. Conversation.

Isa wants to know when he has to return to Nicosia, what the plan is? She speaks to Rike in an aside. They have to make decisions because they are running out of time. 'It's getting close now.' She runs her hand slowly round her stomach. 'I don't think he's really thought it through.'

'So why don't you ask him?'

'I don't want to spoil things. Not on the first night.'

Rike watches Henning through the glass and Henning smiles back with a small salute-like nod. Everything has changed, in one day. The grill is outside. The cats are gone. But more than this the house has slipped from being theirs to being his. She remembers now how simply Henning manages to take over, and how little he appreciates this.

At the dining table they sit with a full bowl of salad, artichoke hearts, roasted peppers, the steaks, the frikadelle and bratwurst Kraiz brought from Frankfurt. Isa wears a pink T-shirt with an American flag and the slogan: 'Never Fuck a Republican', which Henning, for the moment, ignores.

No one has asked about Damascus. The bowls and plates end up within Henning's reach. He takes food from his plate, picks up a steak from another, prongs a tomato from the salad, chewing all the time, eating without pause, feasting.

'So Udo—'

'Not again.' Isa sets down her knife and fork in real irritation.

'No, this is different.'

'Now I have it back in my head.'

'No, this is another story. Udo says that Rudi has another woman.'

'And you are all how old?'

'Rudi is fifty-seven.'

Isa explains to Rike that Rudi and Udo were the men they saw in the hospital. The disagreeable-looking man was Rudi.

'You saw him? Here? In Limassol?'

'At the hospital. Before my last appointment.'

Henning raises his eyebrows as if this is something he didn't know.

'Why the face?'

'What face?'

'You're making a face.'

Henning holds a sausage close to his lips. 'Because he shouldn't be here. He has work in Nicosia. This has nothing to do with him.'

'We're talking Sutler again? Mr Three. So why was Rudi here?'

'Because he works with Iraq. His field is the entire Middle East. Because he becomes involved in things which shouldn't concern him, and when he does everything becomes difficult.' Henning sets the sausage on the plate. 'Things with the British are complicated. They really want this man. They aren't sure he's the person they think he is, but want him, and if they take responsibility for him they'll give him to the Americans.' Henning looks at Isa. 'Anyway I was explaining about Rudi. He has a Cypriot girlfriend.'

'And this means . . .'

'And this means he won't go home. He'll stay. And if he stays then we stay – until this is over. He won't go back to Berlin. So we won't go back to Berlin.'

'I don't see how this works?'

'As long as Rudi stays in love, we stay in Cyprus.'

The fear held by Isa and Henning is that a return to Berlin would mean reassignment. If they can't return to Damascus, then they might be deployed elsewhere. The spectre of a single posting, of Henning unaccompanied in Iraq or Afghanistan, again raises its head.

'And how long has he being seeing this *person*?'

'Udo says it's been going on for a while now. She also worked in Damascus.'

'The public service,' Isa grimly shakes her head, 'is run by deviants and schoolboys.' She picks up her cutlery. 'So we stay as long as he stays.'

'Unless everything resolves beforehand.'

'But this won't happen. It's never going back to what it was. It's not going to happen. I don't think it's anywhere near started yet.'

Henning pauses as if thinking, he looks at Rike, places his fork at the side of his plate and rises from the table without fuss.

'Udo is ugly.' Isa nods at her plate. 'I mean, how long has he been snooping on Rudi? It's not right. He's like one of those blackmailers. Like in the movies. Ugly inside and out.'

Henning, out of the room now, disagrees.

'I don't think he was snooping.'

'He's spreading rumours.'

'Udo's job is to make sure we're fit for purpose.'

'And what does that mean?'

'That we can work. That we do nothing foolish.'

Rike watches Henning in the hall, he unzips his bag, opens the top and unfolds his clothes, searching.

'Of course. But to pry.' Isa looks square at her sister. 'Don't you think it's sneaky? Maybe it's not? Maybe it's just me?'

Henning returns to the table with a package in his hand which he offers to Isa. 'I was back at the apartment.'

Isa looks up, mouth slightly open, enough to show her surprise. 'You went back?'

'I made sure everything is safe.'

Isa looks down at her hands, then opens the package, carefully unfolding the paper.

'I didn't know what to bring. I didn't have much time. I made sure that everything was put away, that the shutters were closed. I asked Etta to keep an eye on everything.'

'They're still there?'

'They're still there, and everything is all right. He's keeping an eye open. Everything is OK.'

Isa sets the package on the table. A framed photograph of Isa and Rike's grandparents, separate portraits in the same frame. Isa wipes her eyes, and softly touches the frame. She reaches for Henning's hand and holds it, silent for the moment.

'I brought a suitcase also. There were clothes in the basket which you wanted to bring. I didn't have much time to look for anything else. I just checked the apartment and made sure that everything was OK.'

It surprises Rike that Henning is so hesitant. Worried perhaps that this subject should be completely avoided, and concerned that he has returned with the wrong things. Isa, apologizing, sets the photograph face down on the table and leaves for her room. 'It's too much,' she says, a quick gasp for breath. 'I'm sorry. It's just too much right now.'

With Isa and Henning in bed Rike finds herself confined to her room. It isn't that she has to stay in the room, but their goodnight was an agreement that the day was over, and while she had felt tired, she isn't sure that she can sleep now.

Rike lies on top of her bed, fully clothed. A window runs alongside the bed, starting at her knees and ending at her chest. She can't see why the bed is placed here, right beside the window so that lying down, if she keeps the blind up, anyone in the garden can see her. All she can see is the white wall that makes up one of the sides of the garden, and the edge of a fig tree with its big, deep green, hand-like leaves.

The doors and windows are open to draw in the evening breeze, but the air in the room is still. The rooms are too broad and too empty. She decides to set Tomas assignments. Museums, outings, cultural events organized by the school, she will ask him to eat with her. They will go to the café where she will encourage him to speak, to interact, to open his world a little more every day.

She watches part of a movie on her computer and picks up twenty minutes into the film. She lies on her side, earplugs in, but can't settle, just isn't tired. There are no emails, nothing to reply to, no messages to send, so when she opens the browser she types in *Damascus* and checks the news-streams.

There's nothing here either, nothing more than conjecture.

She types in *Sutler* and again finds a long list of sites, some reports from papers, Grenoble, an entry in Wikipedia, his name connected on every hit with a business, HOSCO, now failing because of the contested sum the man has embezzled from them: thirty, fifty, sixty million. Speculation on Parson now focuses, implausibly, on the Mafia, and how, in pursuing Sutler, Parson had exposed himself to dangerous elements. While there is no mention of Sutler Number Three, ideas about Sutler Number Two are rife. The man, positively identified in Grenoble, is connected to crime syndicates in Marseilles. In a separate strand, a car delivery service in Westphalia is accused of providing cover for him. Each strand, hydra-like, generates new heads. With that much money what would you do? It's no surprise that Henning, the British, and the Americans are interested in him.

She takes a shower before bed. She binds her hair and pins it back, and watches her reflection in the hallway mirror – and notices a message on her phone. The message is from her brother. Leaving a new local number he asks her to call as soon as possible.

She calls Mattaus and is surprised when he picks up. Her brother keeps the conversation smooth, away from trouble. She catches up with his news. He's told her all of this, hasn't he? Surely? When did they last speak?

Rike asks after Franco. She's sorry, she says, to hear of his breakup.

Mattaus dismisses the comment. It's history. Ancient.

'And who is the new man?'

She doesn't like her brother's voice. Sour and lazy, deception nests in his slow and calculated intonation. He sounds younger than he is, and smarter. It's hard to see how men like him, unfathomable. The kind of men they are, journalists, architects, doctors, teachers, all of them affable, clever, handsome. A type. They trust him. They adore him. They even find him funny. And his treatment of them leaves them startled and wounded. Mattaus's sexual history is a field of debris from which he alone walks free.

Rike checks herself in the mirror. She taps the glass with her fingernail. She is nearly thirty, it will be her birthday in under a month.

'When are you arriving?' she asks, making sure there is no measure of welcome in her voice.

'We're already here,' he answers, smug and precise.

Her brother is here already, ready to interfere in any plans she has with Isa, ready to take over – because this is what he does.

'So when do we get to see you?'

Mattaus gives a vague response. He'll speak with Isa, speak with his friend. He says *friend* deliberately – the man won't be given a name – to keep everything in its compartment. But yes, hasn't he already explained all of this? They flew in to Paphos, what, four, five days ago. Oh god, he can't remember, was it last week already or longer? He asks the question to some third party and waits for a response. Must have been. He asks her not to tell Isa just yet. 'We're hoping to spend a couple of days on the beach, and take it easy before we bring in any family. No offence, but it's nice to have time to ourselves.'

No offence taken, she assures him. Take all the time you need. She won't whisper a word.

Rike can't wait to tell Isa, to see how it feels to be on the other side of Mattaus's manipulations for a change. She can't wait either to see Henning's reaction. It would be worth bursting into their room right now to share the news. *Guess what? He's here already.* Henning would explode. Only she won't do this. Would never go that far. Besides, Isa has probably had the same conversation with Mattaus. *Don't tell Rike. You know how she is. We just want a couple of days to ourselves.* The only person she can be certain to be left out of Mattaus's complex machinations is Henning. It's almost worth the trouble.

She wants to ask him more about Franco. Not only because she would like some information, but because she wants to remind him of the damage he's caused. She would appreciate some acknowledgement, a reference to the man he's shared his life with for the past five years and dropped for a new, doubtlessly younger flash, *an architect* no less. She can imagine the scene too easily, Mattaus telling Franco, and probably not face to face.

In the night a helicopter cuts over the house, the sound wavers, bounces so she can't determine the direction of travel, if it's coming from the British base or heading toward it.

4.6

A fire alarm at the hotel sends Gibson out to the street halfway through the call.

Geezler isn't happy at the news, and becomes irritated at the confusion as Gibson moves about to secure a better signal.

'It's nonsense—' that Geezler would have Parson followed. 'It doesn't make sense—' why Parson would invent any of this. The pure aimlessness of his travels, his *ambling*. To what end would Parson fabricate lies about Sutler? Why would he take advantage of HOSCO, of Geezler, when there is no obvious profit from it?

'I don't see why she would lie.'

'She's lost her husband. She wants to sow doubt.' It is, Geezler suggests, an accentuated part of the process. 'She's angry at us all.'

Gibson does not explain that he didn't speak directly with Laura.

He stands separate from the staff, who lean against the blue shutters of the enoteca opposite the hotel, and smoke and look a little intense, like arsonists. There is no fire, he's assured. The manager, a lean man, unshaven, appears disappointed with the news. The guests bustle out with a little more urgency, wait for a break in the traffic to cross, and stand together at the steps of the church, Purgatorio ad Arco. Some take photographs of the front of the hotel and the long and narrow strip of via Tribunale, of scooters bouncing and skidding across the black street slabs, a few sit at the steps. All of them rub their hands, one at a time, over the four bronze skulls mounted on bollards in front of the church.

Gibson walks to via Mezzocannone, returns to the café where there are fewer students, a place to sit. He sets out the papers and reads each of the hotel bookings to Geezler: the phone numbers, the dates, the reference numbers. He looks up at the long grey wall opposite. The university. 'These are all in your name. There's no doubt that this is Parson's work.'

Geezler is less happy, but somehow not surprised, with the news about the man following Parson and his wife. 'It can't be true. These are paranoid fantasies. Of someone who –' the connection falters '– desperate. I fail to see the logic.' It is absurd.

'She has a photo of the man. She recognizes him from other occasions.'

The line becomes silent.

'I said she has—'

Geezler asks him to send the photograph. Can it be emailed? He asks Gibson to describe the man.

'Well,' Gibson tries to recall the image, 'the picture shows very little. Something of a staircase and there is a man in a doorway. It's very clear.'

The stairway might be marble, there is a suggestion that it is vast and grand. A curved wall. A doorway in which a figure hesitates, his right hand raised. On a small screen the image appears deceptively clear. This is a European male. Light skinned. Light hair, shorn but not shaven. An angular face, with strong features, Gibson thinks, with a new or trimmed beard which emphasizes his mouth.

Enlarged, the image shows nothing new, and what appears distinct begins to lose definition. The most striking element is that the man knows he has been caught. His eyes look directly at the camera.

THE FOURTH LESSON

5.1

Rike sleeps late. She wakes with one clear thought, an ambition: today the lesson will be outside. It doesn't matter where, but outside, away from the apartment. She isn't interested in hearing news about his neighbours, has no desire to know Christos's thoughts or experiences with his wife. She does not want to hear about the Kozmatikos boy or know what kind of trouble he has brought down upon himself. No. Today they will walk through the city, and maybe have a drink at one of the terraces overlooking the bay. Today they will take in Limassol and they will discuss what they find, whatever they happen upon.

She finds Henning in the kitchen in his shorts. He walks through the apartment without a shirt, an electric razor in hand. The buzz maps his walk. Rike watches from the garden, her feet up on the small side wall. It's like he's checking his territory, she thinks. He's taking stock.

'So no more cats?'

'I haven't seen them today. There's one black one left. That's all I've seen.'

'I thought the black one was dead?' Henning leans against the door. Rike hasn't noticed before how the kitchen and the front room are linked by a continuous line of windows which should all open up. Henning hangs about like he has something to say.

'What?'

'Nothing?'

'No, what is it?'

Henning turns back to the apartment but doesn't yet go inside. 'Isa said you're teaching?'

'Yes, there's a school in Limassol.'

'She said you were teaching a man in his house?'

'I go to his apartment.'

Henning frowns.

'It's safe. It's all organized through the school.'

'For how long?'

'Seven weeks.'

'And you like it?'

Rike takes a sip from her coffee and slowly agrees. 'Yes, I like it enough. Why did you come back early?'

Henning rubs his hand over his cheek and chin to check his shave. 'Everything's done.'

'With the man from the desert?'

'Yes, everything is settled.'

'You still think he isn't Sutler?'

Henning isn't pleased to hear the name. 'I doubt it.'

'But you aren't sure?'

Henning runs his tongue inside his cheek. 'Do you know what a sutler is? It's a person or a company which provides for the military. This is a man, who works for a trans-national company which provides for the American military, and his name is the name of the service he provides. And because no one takes so much money from these people so easily, not without someone knowing. It doesn't happen.' Henning points the shaver at the cat-food bowls.

'But someone thinks that it's him?'

'Someone, yes. Some people.'

Henning points again to the cat bowls and asks if Rike can pick them up. 'We'll have rats.'

'She won't listen to me.'

'You think I'll have more luck?'

'You could ask for anything right now.'

'I'd better ask then. It won't last long.'

She thinks Henning disapproves of her teaching. The idea, one he approved, was that Rike would spend time with Isa while Henning was away. If she's teaching, she isn't providing company.

Rike walks to the school offices on the Limassol waterfront. She delivers her passport and waits while it is copied. The language teachers are all women. Rosaria, the woman who hired her, is friendly and formal in equal measure, certainly less blank than the first time they met and the times they have spoken on the phone. As she waits the door buzzer sounds intermittently. There is an expectant atmosphere, a little nervousness among the students as they gather in the common room. It wouldn't be so bad teaching here. English, German, Italian. In the afternoons, between classes, she could swim.

Rosaria points out the library. It's nothing more than a stacked shelf in each room of DVDs, CDs, course books, and other books – novels and poetry – which seem so random they were possibly left by students. Greek in one room. Spanish in another. Italian in another. English in two rooms. Rike is welcome to borrow the books as she pleases, and she should tell her student about the facility. Rosaria presses a brochure into Rike's hand.

'Make sure he knows about these. There are trips, half-day trips to the museum, to Curium, to other archaeological sites, and a meal. Then full-day trips to Paphos, which take in a stop at Aphrodite's Beach. He's welcome to come.' She points out that these are *extras*, run in association with the school. Rike would also be welcome on these trips and her ticket would come at a reduced price.

As the bell sounds Rosaria turns to the door. She hesitates. 'He really hasn't told you about himself?'

It seems to Rike that this question is reflexive. Rosaria asks Rike to walk with her. 'Has he said anything?'

'Only that he isn't working.'

'He was on a day course with us, but he only stayed for the morning. When we were in touch with him he explained that he would be more comfortable taking the lessons at home. I met with him to discuss what he might need, and that's when he asked for you.'

'Did he say what the problem was?'

'Oh yes. He was assaulted.' Rosaria looks meaningfully at Rike – who isn't sure about what she's implying.

'Assaulted?' This word sounds different when applied to a man.

'Hospitalized.' Rosaria nods and adds in a low voice. 'What I'm telling you is confidential.'

In the office Rosaria looks in the small filing cabinet and takes a moment to locate the file.

She passes a handwritten note to Rike. It simply states that he regrets that he's unable to attend meetings or events with groups of people because of a continuing health issue, and would the school extend his apologies to the teacher.

Rosaria compresses her lips, an air about her: there is more information she cannot possibly share.

'How do you know what happened?'

'I spoke with him for a long time. He had a family,' she says. 'He was attacked at work. The injuries were serious. I'm telling you so you won't be surprised. It's probably best to let him raise the subject.'

Rike can't imagine a situation in which Tomas would offer such information. She just can't see it.

5.2

Immediately before the session Rike takes her lunch at the café opposite Tomas's apartment.

The café is smaller and busier than she imagined, and a queue gathers at the back where a man serves from a counter of cooked meats and vegetables. The café is little more than a corridor with two high tables, six stools, and a banquette which reaches across the width of the café. Stacked beside a door stand crates of soft drinks. No more than six or eight people could eat at one time. Most, she's happy to see, take their food out in paper-wrapped packages. Rike chooses white fish and capers and sits facing the wall and a poster of the Last Supper with local politicians and film stars replacing the disciples. Beside her two men share a plate of bread and olives.

One man stoops over the bowl and complains as he eats. His companion tears bread and shakes his head in agreement as if they are considering something of great weight, something hard to comprehend. The first man continues and gestures with the bread. For one moment Rike catches the man's eye, but his thoughts are elsewhere and he looks through her.

Tomas is remote, she has to admit, and when he smiles it's generally in response, as if he's copying something he's unable to freely volunteer. He had a family. *Had*. It isn't hard to understand everything about Tomas Berens in the light of a catastrophic incident: he doesn't socialize, and he's distant, uninvolved. The man is remote, unmoored. The apartment shows almost no evidence of habitation yet he lives there and rarely leaves it. The kitchen, what she has seen of it, is almost bare – he can't eat there, he almost certainly doesn't cook. Tomas Berens has a story. She stops herself from imagining fires, car accidents, devastating incidents, domestic in nature. She can't picture him being assaulted, or see how this has led to the loss of his family. *A family* means more than a wife. One child or two. Easy to imagine, Tomas with wife and child, a house somewhere, a home, a life with work, associations, club memberships, schools, habits she can only imagine. She furnishes him with such a life, which makes his current situation an intolerable void.

Up on the fourth floor Rike is hopeful that they can take the lesson outside. She doesn't want Tomas Berens to become a collection of facts: a man managing the consequences of a serious assault, a man who has lost his family, a man adrift. As she comes up the final flight she struggles to set these thoughts aside.

Two folding chairs face each other. Beside Tomas's chair are set out his notebook, a dictionary, and a small tin of biscuits. The balcony doors are open, and the sun reflects off the opposite building to throw a general light into the room.

Tomas holds a ticket. 'It's a ticket for the Cultural Centre.'

The museum is close. She knows it, of course?

He turns the ticket over and reads both sides.

'It's still valid.' He offers it to her. 'It's a pass so it's valid for two days.'

Rike asks what is currently showing. 'Paintings of churches and beaches?'

'Some. They aren't so bad. But it's worth going. There's another show upstairs.' The artists are French, he thinks, with a German name. He isn't clear on the details. In any case it's a group, he can't remember the name, and you can participate in the piece, if you like, you can take part in it. He turns the ticket over again. No, the name isn't on it.

She doesn't go to galleries much – a small confession – in fact she isn't much interested in art.

'I liked it,' he smiles. 'Probably for the wrong reasons.'

Rike asks for an example.

Tomas insists. 'Take the ticket. They have a booth, and you can record what you want, and they add it to the piece. I know it sounds strange. Go and see it. Tell me what you think.'

Tomas sets the ticket on her knee.

'Practise asking me questions.'

Tomas looks down at his hands, folds them together. There are specks of white paint on the backs of his hands and forearms. 'What is the news from your brother-in-law?'

'He's home.' Rike nods and smiles.

'So the man in the hospital no longer needs him?'

'I think he's stable. They are keeping him in a coma to help him recover.'

'Is it true that he walked across the desert?'

Rike isn't sure. It doesn't sound feasible. 'I don't know. They found him in the desert. A team from Tübingen. Archaeologists from the university. He is very sick and dehydrated and he has sunburn.' She strokes her face, her arms, gestures at her throat. '*Serious* sunburn. It doesn't look good. His health. It's very bad. They want to move him, but they don't know if he will recover.'

'So they are waiting?'

'So they're waiting. And trying to find out who he really is.'

'This is your brother-in-law's work?'

'Yes, this is what Henning has to find out.' She changes the subject. 'You have paint on your hands.'

'I was helping Christos in the basement.'

Rike is pleased to hear this. 'Have you decided to come to Cyprus?'

'Not exactly. But I'm here, and doing nothing. I might as well help. If I do decide, then I will need space for storage. I haven't thought this through properly.'

Rike doesn't understand, and Tomas admits it isn't exactly logical. 'It's something to do. And it might be useful. If I make up my mind it will make everything easier.'

Rike admits that this makes sense. 'And perhaps this is one way to make the decision?'

Perhaps, he agrees, perhaps. 'I haven't told you the story about the basement.'

Rike opens her hands in invitation.

'It isn't pleasant.' Tomas wipes the side of his nose. 'Christos told me. There are rooms in the basement for storage. Sometimes they rent them out. Some are used by the residents. Four years ago two men rented one of them, and when they left they found evidence of a crime.'

'Evidence?'

'It's hard to explain. But the room was lined with plastic, and sorry, it's a little disgusting,' he looks apologetically to Rike, 'but the room was full of blood, and other things. Clothes, I think. But they didn't find a body.'

Rike does not know what to say. 'When was this?'

'I'm not sure. It can't have been so long ago because Christos was living here, also the doctor.'

'And the two men?'

'Disappeared. They have no idea who did it, or who they killed. They think that these men picked up someone from the port, but they don't know. No one was ever reported missing.'

'But it was a murder? How do they know?'

'It isn't pleasant. There was blood in the room. A lot of blood, and a tongue found outside, in a plastic bag with clothes.'

Rike sits forward with her elbows on her knees. The chairs are a little small and there is no other way to sit. He's right, she says, the story, it isn't so pleasant. She doesn't know what else to say.

5.3

Sandro waits in the hotel lobby, legs crossed, he sits crooked in the seat with one arm across the shoulder. A studied look. Practised and conscious.

Gibson wants Sandro to invite him home, to extract him from the misery of shower caps, hand soaps, white towels, suitcases with wheels, double beds and hotel rooms which cannot be filled. He wants to meet the man's wife. See how he behaves with his children. Their house will be an apartment in a palazzo, dark, chaotic, intimate, overloaded, with scents of home cooking, washing. A place noisy with neighbours, cats, dogs, children: both a pleasure and an irritation. He wants to be absorbed. He wants a stranger to be uncommonly friendly.

Sandro, unshaven, wears a suit, and again has a sloping, apologetic smile. He was in court this morning at the Centro Direzionale, close by the prison. 'Another world.' On some other occasion Gibson might like to visit? It is like an office and a church, he says. He asks about the man in Laura's photograph. Gibson has seen this, yes?

'I assume you checked the hotels?'

'We have.'

'And nothing?'

'And nothing.' The man runs his finger under his mouth, pinches his chin as if in thought. 'If you have the time, you might try Hotel Sette on via Toledo.' Sandro sits back, assumes his original position, one leg hitched across another, an arm stretched across the chair-back. 'Sometimes people aren't so willing to talk with the police. It's nothing personal, but there are habits, ways in which things are done.'

'They won't talk to me.'

'You underestimate yourself. Information is more available to you as an ordinary man. Go see what they say. Give them a story so they are involved.'

He finds Hotel Sette on the third floor on via Toledo opposite the Café Roma. He buys coffee after coffee, short espressos, which have no effect and taste charred. He watches the hotel doorway, the shops beneath: a clothing store with a single a white window, brightly lit, a manikin with purple earmuffs dressed in yellow hot pants (isn't that what they're called?). To the right a patisserie, dark and old-fashioned, wood and glass. Customers leave with wrapped packages.

Gibson isn't sure what day this is, he thinks to ask the barista, but doesn't want to appear foolish. There is no movement in the hotel. The windows, three floors of them, all open with blinds pulled up, but nothing to see, except ceilings, the top corners of rooms. Small, he guesses, and plain.

He has no idea who he's looking for. Less idea about what to do with the information. He thinks to order another coffee, his fourth, but notices that his hand is shaking. He finds the photo on his phone. It takes a while to remember the sequence (unlock, swipe to the third screen, select the camera . . .). With the image on view, he props the phone upright on the counter, turns it to the barista, and attempts to explain.

'This man. He was here perhaps? Did he come to the café? He was staying in the hotel opposite.'

The man leans in to the phone and squints, then shakes his head.

'I'm looking for my daughter.'

The barista, now attentive, picks up the phone and shows it to the woman behind the counter who gives a long, considered nod.

'Sure,' he says. 'He was here. I remember him. Not so long ago.' He speaks in Italian to the woman and they appear to disagree. He points to Gibson, to the hotel, to the entrance. 'This is where he was staying. He was in that room. One, two, three windows.' He points to the third floor, the window immediately above the clothes shop. He knows the room he says, because the man would watch the street all day.

Gibson isn't sure who to contact first: Sandro or Geezler.

5.4

The museum isn't on her way, and Rike arrives with half a mind not to go inside, but the building is dressed with bright banners, and there's no reason not to now she has walked there and has a free ticket. Besides, any kind of art, pictures of beaches even, pretty domed churches, would be a pleasant change of subject after stories of blood and stories of severed tongues.

She passes quickly through the lobby, seeking the room on the upper floor, but has to ask directions.

The guard points to a poster, right in front of her, with the letters *MFP* and underneath *Mannfunktionprojekt*: 'I want / I wish: One Year of Trouble'. The letters, in a smart unadorned script, promise some style.

The exhibit, on the top floor, is very simple. The grey walls have a brick-red script printed with *I want I wish I want I wish I want I wish I want I wish* in a solid block, so insistent that 'I' looks only to be a separation between 'want' and 'wish'. So emphatic that the words become a simple command.

Centred above the text a smart neon sign announces: *One Year of Trouble*. Headphones hang by their cords, upside down in a grid, in eight rows of eight. Voices pipe gently into the space announcing dates, a different voice for each day. The days slur one into another. *November the twenty-first. November twenty-second, November twenty-third, nineteen eighty-one.* Men's voices, women's voices, most speaking in English. Not all of the headphones play in sync, on one set, in the centre, other voices are superimposed, giving dates and explanations: *June seven, nineteen ninety-four, my father passed away. June eighth is the anniversary of my divorce. June ninth, I failed my final exams. June tenth, two thousand and nine, I had an unsuccessful operation on my lower spine.* She listens on, November, December, January, the days run chronologically through random years, and on February twelfth she recognizes his voice. Tomas Berens. Short, but distinctive. A date with no explanation.

Surprised to hear Tomas's voice, Rike instinctively turns about, checks the entrance, checks the corners, not expecting him to be in the room, but out of self-consciousness, as if she has been caught prying. She waits, listens to the year count back to February twelfth, many of the dates are missing, the cycle is incomplete. His voice repeats. She's less certain the second time.

In the corner of the room is a small booth. In a statement the artists ask that you record a date, and if you like, a short reason.

She stands on tiptoe when she records her message. Most of the days record deaths, which makes her reluctant to add another. *October twenty-fifth, two thousand and seven. To the memory of Tobias Georg Bastian.* One ear to the headphone, the other poised at the microphone.

As soon as she is finished she feels her voice recede, become indistinct, one among many messages, and then she worries that her sister might hear this, or Henning. But the idea no longer belongs to her, and she feels a detachment, as if, in some small way, she has somehow shed the date and its associations. The machine beeps once, and Rike is offered the choice to save or delete the message.

She chooses delete. This is not her information to tell.

Rike returns to the apartment clear about her decision not to save the message, but still feels part of the piece. Neither Isa nor Henning would want to hear the message, and she is not sure that she would care to share the information with Tomas. There is too much of an imbalance. Tomas knows basic facts about her – opinions and trivia – the bones of the past five years, but Rike knows little about Tomas.

Isa wants to know if Rike has gone through any of Henning's papers. At first it's a clear question, without blame. The papers were on the table. Did she look at them? Rike says she didn't, of course she didn't. She asks what papers Isa is talking about, there was nothing on the table this morning, nor last night, as far as she can remember, except his briefcase.

'That's what I'm talking about. The papers were in his briefcase.'

Now Rike is alarmed. Isa should know she wouldn't go through Henning's papers, and she would certainly never search through his briefcase.

Isa folds her arms. It doesn't make sense then. 'He has information about Parson. He was sent some photographs.'

Rike doesn't quite see what she's being asked. 'And are they missing?'

'No. But they were in two envelopes. Separate. Now they are

together. Someone has been looking through his papers, because they are in a completely different order. Photos of the train. Photos of the body. They were in sealed envelopes. They were opened and mixed together.'

Although this has nothing to do with her, Rike still feels responsible.

5.5

At the Banco di Napoli Gibson draws out the maximum three hundred euro from his personal account. He tries his other cards, debit and credit, struggles to remember the numbers, and is pleased to be able to draw out, in total, a further nine hundred euro. He tries his business cards, but has to go into the bank as these cards are refused. Here they tell him that the sum he wishes to withdraw would take ten days to transfer.

Twelve hundred euro is as much as he can muster.

He stuffs the money into his inside jacket pocket, then returns to the entrance to Hotel Sette.

The passageway leads to a courtyard, then a larger staircase and a caged elevator. The steps are long and sloped, easy to ascend. At the third floor the signs for the hotel with arrows indicating the front of the building are hand-printed and curl from the walls.

The woman behind the counter wears large glasses and appears startled. She doesn't speak English, and when Gibson talks to her she blinks.

'There is a man,' he says, 'who stayed here. In this room.' Gibson points to the room beside reception. 'This one. At the front.'

The woman blinks at him.

'English?' he asks. '*Inglese? Parla Inglese? Trova un persona che parla Inglese?*'

This doesn't help. It isn't even schoolboy Italian. 'I need to speak with someone. It is important.'

A man comes out from an office. A simple beaded curtain divides the rooms. A beaded curtain. A man in a string vest with thick slicked-back hair. So familiar it's a little laughable.

The man politely asks if he can help.

'I need information about one of your guests.'

The man folds his arms. 'What is the name?'

'The man was staying in this room. I think he was staying in this room. I know that it was this hotel.'

The man says he can't help unless Gibson has a name and tells him what he needs.

Gibson gives the woman a cautious glance and lowers his voice. 'It's a little *delicate.*' And here he takes out the money. 'I need to give him this. I need an address.'

The man, now confused, looks hard at the money.

Gibson leans forward and lowers voice a little more. 'I have a daughter. You understand. A daughter who is interested in this man.'

The man looks from the money to Gibson with equal incredulity. 'I wish to give him something so that he will leave my daughter alone. You understand?' Gibson allows his finger to divide the money in half. 'I need some information, I need his name and I need an address. I want to make sure he isn't coming back.' He begins to wish he'd kept with the original idea, that his daughter had disappeared.

The man shakes his head. There wasn't anyone here, not in this room, within the last month, and not with any woman.

'My daughter is fifteen years old.' Gibson sets half of the money on the counter. He keeps his voice flat and cold. 'Fifteen. Do you see the problem? She is fifteen. I need a name and an address. I know you keep these details. He left eight days ago.'

The man steps back behind the counter and speaks quickly to the woman as he searches through a drawer. She looks up, swipes the man's hands away then searches through the drawer herself and brings out a register. She places the register on the counter, over the money.

THE FIFTH LESSON

6.1

Rike suggests that they take a walk. If they follow the street it will lead them to the bay. There are the wine factories on one side and the town on the other, the road is the dividing line between a light industrial zone and a living quarter. Today they will walk and talk.

Tomas, naturally, isn't keen. And while he doesn't refuse, he asks if this is a good idea. It's hard to think out there: the sun, the noise, the distraction.

No books, she insists. No notebooks, no prepared speeches, no pocket dictionaries. 'We shall speak today about what we find in front of us. Today you will demonstrate a mix of tenses, you aren't to worry about your vocabulary, you aren't to worry about being perfectly correct. Today you are to walk with me and speak about things you have not prepared.'

Tomas's reaction is stern. He'd much rather not, if she didn't mind.

'Believe me, you'll find out that you know more than you realize. It won't be so hard. I'll help you.'

Tomas nods, and searches in his pockets for his keys.

In the stairwell, as he locks the door and tests to make sure it is shut, he asks about the museum. Did she go? Did she see that piece. The artists are German?

'They are here, you know,' he says in English. 'The artists are in Limassol, and they're making new work for the internet. I heard them interviewed on BFPS.' He has a flyer, he says, something he picked up when he left the museum. He hasn't yet checked to see what this work is, but now that he's seen one piece by them – and here he falters a little – in fact *participated* in the piece, he's curious to see other works. Not that he really understands them. But he's curious.

Rike admits she's also curious. Having participated in the piece it would be interesting to see what else they've done. Yes, she's curious.

'And you did take part?' he asks.

'I did.'

'You recorded something?'

'I did.'

'Can I ask what it was?'

Rike comes down the stairs ahead of Tomas. 'It's a little complicated. I chose a date, but I didn't save it because it isn't my story. My sister lost a child before he was born.' Even now, the bluntness of the fact hurts. Something so horribly complex, so easily described. 'I left the date and name, but chose not to save it.'

She walks ahead to avoid his reaction, and is relieved when he doesn't respond. It takes a great effort not to explain further, to allow the fact to sit.

'And now,' he asks, 'you said she is going to have another child?'

They are further along already, Rike explains, and doctors, Henning, everyone, are prepared this time, and yes, everything is going very well. She is too superstitious to say more.

'And your brother, he comes here as well?'

This, Rike explains, is a whole other issue. 'When I first lived in London I lived with my brother and his partner. A man called Franco.' For three months Rike lived with her brother and witnessed what she can only call wilful cruelty. 'He's a bully. He knows how to get inside people.' This is the simple fact. 'The trouble is, Franco couldn't see it. He just let it happen, and it was like watching someone fall, who doesn't put out their hands or make an attempt to save themselves.' And here is the complication. The more hopeless Franco appeared, the more the situation mattered to her.

Tomas is quiet. For a moment she thinks that she is over-explaining herself.

They come to the entrance, stand side by side. It is an infinite relief when Tomas simply nods.

'He's here. In Cyprus, and I just don't want to be involved. I don't want to be part of it.' The words embarrass her, but the facts are plain. 'Right now. I would be happy if he just disappeared.'

They step into the street and a small but noticeable change overcomes Tomas. His discomfort is clear in how he shies away, walks close to the wall, seems in every way keen not to be seen or to take part in the outside world.

Rike's confession emboldens her and she asks Tomas about his message. 'It was your voice? February twelfth?'

'I thought about speaking in Norwegian.' He looks sideways, a little sly, 'but I think they want messages that can be understood, no? In the end I also decided not to record a reason.'

Tomas looks ahead, wipes his hand across his mouth. 'Did the school tell you anything? I spoke with the woman who runs it.'

Rike automatically answers no.

'I was monitoring security and I caught a team of men stealing from a depot.' He holds up his arms to describe the assault. 'The thing is I remember very little. But they came at me with iron bars.'

Shocked, Rike stops walking. She's sorry, she says. This is none of her business. She's really sorry.

Tomas dismisses the apology. 'It's a fact. Yes? Something that happened.'

'I'm so sorry.'

'I was unlucky. I was in the wrong place. I didn't have to be there. But I saw them, and they came after me. I have no memory of this.' He holds his hand first over his forehead, slightly to the right. 'I was hit here, one time, at the front, and also on my chest, my arms. But the damage was worst for my head. This happened in the depot, but I was found at the security post, which is across a large car park. But I have no memory of this, of what happened, or how I got there. After, of course, everything was different.'

Rike can't think of anything to say except how sorry she is. And isn't this a lesson about caution, about how she needs to plan to keep them clean and clear of personal revelation – because this is none of her business.

Tomas points across the road. 'I'm not much in the mood for walking. We should sit perhaps?'

Rike agrees, and follows as Tomas leads her across the road to a café.

They sit side by side with their coffees and face the street, both uncomfortable with the silence. Occasionally Rike feels an obligation to restart the conversation, but the impetus isn't there. Tomas looks down at his cup and Rike apologizes and says they can forget about today.

'I can make it up another time. I didn't mean to ask about personal things.'

Tomas straightens his back. 'I was painting the room today, in the basement. Christos came to see me. I asked him about what happened.'

'Did you find anything?'

'Nothing. Christos said these people were clever. They rented a room for a month. They had someone prepare it for them. They used it once, only for one weekend. They picked up the first person they met. There was no meaning to it. No intention. Except they wanted to do this horrendous thing.'

Tomas turns the spoon over on his saucer, And without fuss he begins to set the salt, pepper, the sauce pots in order on the table.

The air, stale with coffee from the café and the fruited malt from the wineries and breweries closes over them, and the room yaws open to the street with a long overhanging hood, so that the café might be a cave.

'They rebuilt my skull. See. On this side.' His hand traces an area from his temple to the crown.

The conversation falls into shadow, stops, and Rike wants desperately to open this into something new. She changes the subject, tells him about Sutler. Thinking that this subject is a remedy, strange enough to distract him.

'He's here. The man from the desert.'

The shift works, and she's pleased with his reaction. It's water to a dry plant the way he stirs and listens, becomes present.

'They flew him to the hospital at Akrotiri, but I don't think he's staying there because the burns unit is in Limassol.' She points left, indicates the hospital no more than two hundred metres away. *You know about this?* The hospital, she explains, has a burns unit. The British use the hospital for soldiers from Iraq, from Afghanistan, who have – it's impossible to imagine – wounds you wouldn't believe. The unit is world-leading for the treatment of burns, and it's here, in Cyprus, right here, just up the street. So this man has been flown in, wrapped up – Rike combines details picked from Henning and pure invention. It isn't that she wants to lie, she wants him distracted, she wants Tomas thinking about details, procedures, impossible tit-tats of information. 'What they do is wrap you in this plastic film to stop the oxygen reaching the burn, it stops the air and bacteria from entering the wounds. They wash you in a saline solution, and they cover you in this *wrapper* and in these creams, and then lower your body temperature with these silver blankets. They keep you cold so the body slowly recovers, and this is what stops the scarring, the cold, the slow healing, and as with all burns the only problem they have to be particular about is infection, because these super-bacteria are resistant to all forms of antibiotic. Henning has seen this, she says, he's sat with the man, observed him, and while the facilities look crude, he can assure you they have developed advanced techniques in treating skin and burns and lesions, and they've learned all of this through treating soldiers. They sent a group of doctors from here to Damascus to bring him back. They want this man to live.

Information pours from her. The British have insisted on bringing him here because Britain, Germany, the US are squabbling over who should take responsibility for this man. 'They all believe he is the man from Iraq. Stephen Sutler.' She isn't sure if she has mentioned this, but Henning has other attachments to the case. Last summer he met Parson, the man they were calling Sutler Number One. He met the man and advised him, according to Isa the meeting didn't go well, and Henning advised the man that this was all – as far as he could see – a scam. That no company could be so cavalier or clueless, not with that amount of money. Parson shouldn't be searching Turkey for Sutler, he should be examining HOSCO, the correspondence, the emails, calls, and contracts. The man is a construction, a front to disguise more serious misbehaviour.

Tomas isn't to say a word. He must promise not to say one word.

6.2

The police arrive in two vans. They line the street, blue-black uniforms, batons, sky blue helmets and clear shields, then swarm the entrance to the hotel. The whole business is settled in a matter of minutes. One section of the street is closed, and a group of tourists are caught inside the patisserie and instructed to remain inside while the men go swiftly about their business. *Their appointed rounds.* Gibson watches from the café but once the police are inside little can be seen. At the upper windows he catches the backs of the police, and against expectation there is little shouting. Noise instead, a hammering, comes from a building site, out of view. People are hauled out of the hotel, the woman with the glasses, the man in the singlet among them, and divided, male from female, then taken to one of the waiting vans.

In the café, once the police are gone, the two baristas and the counter clerk eye him suspiciously and say nothing.

6.3

Later in the afternoon the three of them drive from Limassol to Akrotiri. Henning has business on the British base. There are people to speak with, discussions to be held. Advances to be stopped. Yesterday the British brought in lawyers. We bring doctors, he says, the British bring lawyers and PR.

The drive alongside the salt lake, a flat plain of sand and salt, a white crusted line furred pink along a soft horizon. The colour is miraculous, iridescent, just a line, bright and wild with specks of black and white to signal other kinds of birds, then a rich blue sky.

'The flamingos come every year. They've started coming earlier. They come from Africa, or on their way, and stay for the spring. I don't think they breed here, I don't know. And I don't know where they're from.'

Isa sits quietly at the front. One hand on her lap, the other supporting her hat against the wind. She braces against the bumps in the road but doesn't complain. This lake is different than the lake at Larnaca, and the road sweeps round as if to contain it. The sea borders the salt flat on two sides, so that Akrotiri rises almost as a separate island. There isn't the same sense of scope. As the road curves alongside the lake, a building rises in the background, a block that elsewhere would look like a housing complex.

'That's the military hospital.'

'That's where we're going?'

'That's where I'm going. You're going to the beach club.'

Isa complains that Rike is *making that face* again. 'Sometimes you have this strained expression like you don't want to be here, or you're expecting something bad, like the entire room is going to laugh at you.'

If it were deliberate, Rike replies, then she'd stop, but she doesn't even know she's doing it.

'Like now. Right now.'

This is Isa, picking at the stitching until she's left with a lap-full of patches and threads.

Henning drives to the hospital then lets Rike out of the back seat to drive. He stands in the sunlight beside the car, sweat already marking his shirt in dark curves.

Isa looks to the front of the hospital, blocked stone columns, long white windows, metal instead of wood. A serious building: the stone, the glass, the sensible design.

'Is this where he is?' Isa asks, her voice deliberately conspiratorial although there's no one about to overhear them.

Rike watches for his reaction, but he keeps his face straight, ignores the question and leans into the car to kiss his wife.

'Keep those passes with you, and keep that badge in the car so it can be seen. Take the road we came in on to the end and you'll find the bay and the beaches. I'll meet you at the boathouse at four.'

Rike drives carefully and quite a bit slower than Henning. She follows the road to a small shopping centre, a NAAFI, a cinema, a plaza for parking: open, low buildings built in the same stone as the hospital, neat and old-fashioned.

'Not many people. Have you noticed how clean it is?' Isa asks Rike if anything is wrong. 'You're quiet today. Quieter than usual, even for you.'

Rike says it's nothing.

'You weren't quiet this morning. I heard you chatting with Henning. How did the lesson go? How is your Nordic man?'

Rike can't help but grimace.

'Are you still making him spy on his neighbours?'

The road curves by a group of houses set back from the road with dry gardens, sparse bushes and long low walls. Deep concrete storm drains run either side of the road.

'You'll like what he was talking about today.'

'What about it?'

'There was a murder.' The word is too ridiculous spoken out in the sunlight, stupidly implausible. She can't quite believe it, but doesn't know what it would take to make it such an event credible. Falling buildings, burning planes, deserts on fire, more plausible because of the scale. 'They never found the victim.'

'When was this? Who?'

'I don't know. I think it was some time ago. They never found who did it, and they never found a body.'

'Here? Are you serious?'

'Very serious.'

'When did this happen?'

'I'm not sure? A while ago. Two men rented a room, they had it specially prepared. When they left it was covered in blood.'

Isa pulls a face. 'How fantastic.'

'It just doesn't seem possible.'

'You think these things don't happen?'

'I've never heard anything like this before.'

'Why? It's just a matter of density, of where you live. It isn't so uncommon. People kill each other all of the time.'

'I don't know. I just think it's sad.'

'And how did you get to talk about this? It's not your usual discussion during language school?' Isa asks almost with admiration.

'I was asking for details about his family. I think he wanted to avoid the subject.'

'Well, well done.'

Rike gives her sister a small angry glance.

'And did he talk?'

'Just about the room.'

'He didn't start talking about himself?'

'A little. He told me he was assaulted. He was in hospital. He was attacked.'

Isa nods as if this is not uncommon.

'Now he's talking about it, he probably won't shut up.'

'You think?'

'That tends to be the case. Uncork something like that and you won't be able to shift the discussion to anything else.'

'Oh, god.'

This is perfect, exactly what she wants, a daily rehashing of today's discussion. An endless speculative loop of loss. 'Thanks,' Rike says flatly.

'What for?'

'For getting me this job. Thanks. Thanks a whole lot.'

'So this is the cause of his stress? You're going to have to take him.'

'Oh god. Isa.'

'I'm serious. Ride it out of him. Distract him. Men can only think of one thing at a time.'

'I'm his teacher.'

'Oh, like this has never happened. You're both adults. Give him back his money if it troubles you.'

'It's not going to happen.'

'You haven't said you *don't* want it to happen. The idea doesn't horrify you.'

'It's always the same with you. Why is everything about sex.'

'Because everything is about sex. But I'm right aren't I? Would you?'

'Would I what?'

'I'm being serious. Would you? You like him? You must like him, and he must like you if he's telling you all this information.' Isa whispers conspiratorially. 'He's confiding in you. He trusts you.'

Rike rolls her eyes.

'I'm serious, if he's telling you about his deep emotional scars then he trusts you. Just don't do what you usually do and turn him into a friend.' Isa won't drop the subject. 'Is he handsome?'

'No. You already asked.'

'But you like him?'

Rike points out the sea. She parks the vehicle and they walk in silence across the sand. Rike lays the towels side by side and wonders if Isa will be able to sit down and get back up.

'Is he muscular?'

'Who?'

'Your Norwegian. They're outdoorsy, those Nords. I bet he's muscular.'

'He keeps himself fit.'

'Fit? Sounds old.'

'Not so much. But he keeps himself in shape.'

'So, you've been checking him out. Eyeing him up between his conjugations? I like them muscular, not too much. Henning could use some muscles.'

'You're complaining already?'

'I'm just stating a fact. Henning is in need of some muscle.' Isa kneels on the towel. 'So if Henning and your Norwegian were in a fight who do you think would win?'

'Tomas.'

'He has a name!' Isa clasps her hands heavenward. 'Is he smooth or hairy?'

'I don't know, I think smooth?' Rike takes the question semi-seriously. 'He has a little hair on his arms. But I think he's smooth.'

'Take the opportunity, Rike, I'm serious. Just don't screw it up.'

Isa settles onto her elbows and looks out at the bay, middle distance, with a wince at some subterranean movement, the child unsettled inside her. Sometimes Rike finds her sister unbearable.

Rike checks her computer for messages. She checks for messages from her brother.

Isa asks if Rike has spoken with Mattaus yet.

'I'm trying to find out what his plans are. Is Franco still in the apartment?'

'I think that's what he said. He – obviously – wasn't saying much. It isn't as black and white as you think.'

'Good.' Rike resists the urge to defend Franco.

'Listen.' Isa's voice remains flat, rational. It is the voice she uses when she needs to explain something that might, in any other circumstances, be unreasonable. 'About Mattaus. Has he said anything about the man he's seeing? What has he told you?'

'Nothing.'

'The man he's seeing has paid for a house somewhere, he's rented a villa, but I don't think he's staying there. The villa is in Larnaca, but I think he works in Limassol.'

Rike doesn't understand. 'The apartment is shared with Franco and Mattaus. They both bought it?'

'I'm talking about where he is now. He's living in a villa.'

'Where?' Rike settles in the seat, turns to see her sister. 'He's here on holiday, no?'

Neither of them know where Mattaus is exactly.

'Look.' Isa is hesitant. 'There's no good way to say this. But why is he living in a villa that another man is paying for? I mean. What does that make him?'

Isa pauses again, she has warmed a plate of pastries and the air tastes of hot butter.

'Who pays for somewhere they don't live?'

'What are you thinking?'

Isa is uncharacteristically slow in coming to the point.

'What are you trying to say?'

'I think Mattaus' new boyfriend must be married.'

Rike laughs. The idea that her brother is seeing a married man is neither shocking nor a surprise. 'It's possible, but Mattaus would have said.'

'Would he?'

'Of course. It's another man on his team. We would know. You'd have it on a T-shirt already.'

'What if he didn't know? Or what if he was lying to us?'

'But why would he lie?'

'That's what Henning says, but usually he tells us everything, every last detail. We only have what Mattaus says. There's nothing else to go on, no other information.'

Rike laughs at the absurdity. 'I don't understand why you're so worried?'

'Because it's strange. Even for Mattaus. And it's strange that he would lie to us or keep something hidden and that's what I think he's doing.'

Rike shuts the computer and says that there's no reason to doubt him. 'All you ever have is what someone tells you. That's normal. That's what we do.'

'But I think he's lying.'

For Rike the problem isn't *why* her brother would lie to them, but why he would share with them the details of his life. Unlike Isa she isn't so certain that they are the kind of family who share confidences.

6.4

Rike wakes in the early pre-dawn to a heavy rainfall, her mind too active to return to sleep. It's a clean awakening, right out of sleep, and if this hadn't happened most nights since her arrival she'd think that there was a reason for this, some disturbance, some problem, something to fret over.

She checks her emails and finds a message marked MFP with a link to a website. It doesn't make sense that work like this would be happening in Cyprus, and not New York or Berlin, although some of their events, when she checks them online, have occurred in similarly offbeat places: an airport lounge at Kuala Lumpur, a lakeside beach on Fraser Island, a castle courtyard in northern Italy.

Three videos are already online. One at Kolossi, right by the castle, no more than five kilometres away. The man wears a mask, not a mask so much as part of a costume, a fake panda head, round and black and white, with crosses for eyes as if it might be blinking, or maybe even dead. The man is wearing shorts, slightly baggy and blue, with a white cord. Shirtless, his body seems American to her: thick, broadshouldered, a man who works out perhaps, or works out but doesn't particularly watch his weight. In this first video, the man picks up a stone from one side of the path, in front of the entrance to the castle, carries it to the other side of the path then stands back, in position, right in the centre of the path and faces the camera.

The man with the panda head takes his time. He looks to the stone, to the camera, to the place where the stone was, then, with some deliberation he looks at a third spot. Having identified this new place the man returns to the stone, picks it up and moves the stone to the new, third place. The stone, not small by any means, is white and doesn't come from the castle, but looks to have been brought from a beach, being smooth and almost perfectly round. And the way he holds it, with both hands, she can see it isn't light. When he returns to the centre of the path he looks with great care at four places. The place where he has now set the stone, the place where the stone was last, at the place where the stone was originally set, and finally, the camera.

She doesn't know why this is funny. His gesture? The minimal movement of his head, or perhaps the anticipation? *That you know exactly what he will do?* Is this what delights her, what she finds so pleasing?

The video continues.

The man, after looking, regards the two places where the stone has been set and where it now lies, then identifies a fourth spot – and so he moves the stone to this place, a little further from view, almost out of frame. Once again he returns to the centre of the path, and again he regards the place where the stone now lies, and the three places where the stone has previously been set.

On the fourth move the man sets the stone out of the range of view. He does this seven times, always returning to the path to stand dead centre and look to each of the places he has set the stone. The castle behind him, a square stone block, the sky behind that a simple blue, in the distance the handsome spindles of a row of cypress trees, a slight wind bothering them, but nothing else within the frame: the man, the path, the castle, the trees and the sky. The man is now sweating, and she can see why he isn't wearing a shirt.

She insists that Henning and Isa watch the video, plays it for them on Isa's laptop, and at first, like her, they find it hard to be interested, but after the second move, once there's a pattern established, they both look puzzled, and remain curious and quiet while they watch the entire clip.

Isa takes the laptop to watch the video again.

'I never get this stuff,' she said, 'I don't understand why it's so compelling. What is this?' Light from the screen illuminates her face. There is a memory here that Rike can't place.

'Does anybody know who they are? Why the head?' Henning chews as he speaks.

Rike doesn't know. They have a Facebook page, they call themselves *Mannfunktionprojekt* or *MFP* for short, and this, she guesses, maybe means that they're German. There's a date on the website to show when another piece will go online.

The video is puzzling: the man picking up stones and placing them elsewhere achieves nothing, however deliberate the action. On TV the characters speak to you, the radio plays songs overstuffed with meaning. This, similarly, feels directed. It's a pointless activity with no result. That's what she sees, and what troubles her is that by looking directly into the camera the panda-headed man appears to know it too. And he knows that you know. That, day to day, most of what you do is pointless. Aren't you ever going to figure that out?

The rain stops abruptly at eight o'clock. Rike walks without purpose and finds herself on Tomas's street, outside his apartment. She's much more interested in the hospital and the idea that Sutler Number Three lies inside in some private room with security guards. A lot of people are working hard to keep him safe and alive. She hurries across the street to the café conscious that if Tomas sees her she'll have to explain herself – although, would that really be so bad? An hour's longer meandering through the shuttered streets of the main town than she'd intended means that she's missed the preparations for the day – and isn't Saturday always a day in which a routine is followed: families go shopping, provisions are bought, obligations are fulfilled. Time is spent with the people you live with, the people you love. Isn't this what Saturday means?

As she steps into the café Rike is treated to a quick view of Tomas on his balcony. Tomas, four flights up, comes out, the morning's first coffee in his hand, and gives the street a quick overview. Nothing in particular to be discovered, nothing to observe.

The day has long-started and Rike has missed the judge's walk, missed seeing also how he dries the dog's paws on his handkerchief before he returns to his apartment, how he pets and spoils the dog with treats from his jacket pocket. The street is wet and the air smells of rain, vehicles drum by occasionally, faster than they should. One ambulance, and two police cars. People walk with open umbrellas as balconies and awnings funnel down the last of the rain. To the east the sun strikes the glass front of the judge's apartment to throw spars of light onto the opposite wall – and in these bright patches she can see where the plaster wasn't always painted magenta, underneath appears a faint ghost of decoration. Inside the apartment, a man, the judge, sorts through sheaves of paper stacked along a table. He walks to the window to stand in the sunlight, the papers held high as he reads. A woman cleans in the kitchen behind him. Light bounces through to illuminate pans and book spines and bleach colour from the walls. Down in the darker street a waiter takes coffee to a car and squats beside the driver to talk. As she sips her coffee she imagines the driver peeling back the foil cap, sweetening, stirring, then looking out at the same street. He pauses for a moment, anticipating the taste. That, right there, is the story of the morning.

Behind her, on the radio, is news of a massacre in Syria. Thirty-four civilians killed, among the number are men queuing for temporary work, and thirteen children, all of them deliberately sought out and shot. Here, in Limassol, there are reports of a hotel fire, suspicions suggested, but not spoken outright. Bad things are happening everywhere and they must be announced.

The waiter brings a second coffee, and because it's quiet she allows herself to be caught in a conversation.

The water speaks excellent English, some German. He asks where she's from and when she says Hamburg, he's suddenly enthusiastic. His favourite place is Berlin. The Funkturm. The Political Sector, not so new now. He wants to study architecture, and Berlin is his preferred choice if he can get a place and a scholarship.

Rike asks about the café, and he answers, less interested, that it's been here forever, although they've only run it for, what was it, four years now? He can't remember. And no, the owner is an English woman who used to be a nurse.

'There are some characters here. On this street. The judge.'

The boy asks her to repeat what she's just said.

Rike answers in German. 'A judge. With the dog, a small dog. On the top floor?'

The waiter shakes his head. There's no judge.

'His driver?'

Again, the man doesn't know what she's talking about. 'Does she like Berlin? All of the buildings? It's a nice place.'

A nice place, she agrees, a little put out that he hasn't understood.

Rike receives a call from Isa as she returns to the apartment. Isa asks where she is and Rike explains that she couldn't sleep so took an early walk. Is everything all right?

'I've just spoken with Mattaus.' Isa sounds weary. 'He's coming for dinner tonight with his new friend?' Isa's voice is strained and it's clear that this isn't the reason for the call. Rike says she could be back in five minutes, is there anything she needs to pick up?

Isa takes in a long breath. 'Mattaus was asking questions about the apartment in Hamburg.'

'What did he want to know?'

'His plans have changed.'

'About the apartment?'

'Yes. It looks like Franco is being difficult.'

'Why hasn't he called me directly?'

'I don't know.'

The reason for the call becomes blindingly obvious. 'I can't stay there, can I?'

Isa begins to explain that she understands how inconvenient this all is, but understandable.

'It isn't his. It's Franco's, they bought it together. It's their place. I've had everything shipped there already. I've paid to have everything delivered.'

Isa heaves out a breath. 'That's not the point, is it? The problem here is that Mattaus and Franco have broken up, and Mattaus needs his place back.' Isa pauses. 'Look. We can arrange for someone to pick up all of your things. It can all go in storage. You don't have to go back.'

'And what am I supposed to do now? Where am I supposed to live?'

Rike stops at the entrance to the apartment.

'I'm not happy.'

'He wants you to think about it before tonight.'

'Think about what? If I can't stay there then there's nothing to *think* about except what I'm supposed to do with my belongings and where I'm going to live.'

'Then think about that.'

'I could have stayed in London. Do you know how much this has cost me?'

'He said he was sorry.'

'Then he can call me, he knows my number. He can tell me just how sorry he is.'

'Maybe he didn't call because he knew you'd react like this. I don't understand why you are so hostile to him. This is his business. His life, his apartment. Why do you have these expectations of him?'

'I should have known that you'd take his side.'

Isa complains that this isn't about taking sides. If Mattaus is starting a new relationship then he needs to resolve the details from his old one, in his own time, in his own way. The apartment is one of those elements. Surely she can understand?

Rike's shoes scuff on the steps. 'Isa, this is too much, it really is.' She comes quickly to the door fixing a hair clasp as she walks and decides that this isn't where she wants to be. If Mattaus is coming tonight with his new *friend*, there will be arrangements to make, a whole day of preparation, which, given how things usually work out, will fall on Rike, not Isa.

6.5

Sandro arranges to meet Gibson at a small restaurant close to the street market and the Montesanto station. The restaurant is reached through a long tiled corridor, barrels of fat obstruct the entrance. Inside, the tables and chairs are mismatched. Knives and forks and paper napkins sit centre-table in open cans. Gibson finds Sandro already seated. He explains there is no menu, if Gibson tells him what he likes he can order.

'You speak Italian?'

Gibson apologizes, no. 'I learned French and Italian at school. I was passably good. But my wife had a command of languages. It makes you lazy. It takes from you what you know.'

Gibson hopes his story will prompt information from Sandro. He holds to this notion of Sandro as a family man, pure Italian, realizing that such assumptions cannot be made, not these days. Sandro asks if Gibson really has a daughter.

'That was ingenious.' His smile is genuine. 'You are a natural. But why did you have the money? The story would have worked without the money.'

Gibson doesn't know. 'I wanted leverage. I thought a lot of money would make me look serious.'

'I'm not sure that he believed you, but it's interesting that he went along with it. I must remember this. It isn't the story at all, but the conviction with which it is delivered. The money is something else, a distraction. Maybe this is part of it?'

Flattered, Gibson says he isn't so sure.

'You understand that we needed to make a gesture. Twenty policemen make everything look serious in the way that we need to look serious. We speak with people, they tell us nothing. We go back and make a little noise, and maybe next time they will be more helpful.' Sandro broadens his smile. 'I doubt it, but this is the tactic we like to use. Force has no meaning unless you deliver once in a while. You cannot always hold up your hand in warning. Sometimes it is necessary to strike. We have a little information because of it. Some of it is useful.' Sandro speaks about the man in the singlet, the woman with the glasses. 'They admitted they had made a mistake earlier when speaking with me, and that there was indeed a man staying with them, who was there for ten days, and who caused them no disturbance while he stayed. The Hotel Sette does not keep precise records, as they should, but they recognize the man in the picture and say that he was German. I would question this a little, but they were certain that he was German.'

A waitress approaches the table and Sandro speaks with her.

'Do you like hot food? Spices?'

Gibson says that he would rather have something plainer, a cutlet if they have it, and Sandro nods, and places the order. The woman listens but writes nothing down.

'So, I think this is all we will discover. I think they have told us what they know. They spoke with the man but have no idea where he was going. He left the same day as the incident in Rome. He paid the night before and took his bags early in the morning. There was nothing in the room. In fact, it looked like he had not slept there, but sat at the window. There is no record of him arriving at the Stazione Centrale, he is not on any of the video we have collected. Which does not mean, of course, that he was not there.'

While they wait for the food Gibson calls Geezler. This needs to be explained. Geezler has the photograph, but does not know about the search of the hotel.

Gibson lays out the situation. Parson, it appears, was being followed, and while they have not yet linked this man to his death, the possibility is looking strong.

'The police think that we have as much information as we are going to find. They can make the photograph public, but it seems counterproductive at this point. I'm not sure. If nothing else is discovered they are going to have to use it.'

In his exasperation Geezler says that *this wasn't supposed to happen*. Parson was hired to find Stephen Sutler. Instead, what do they have? They have a situation which is increasingly hard to control. Worse. They now have information, so destabilizing, it cannot possibly go forward to the hearing. Gibson himself should not attend because this *evidence*, this photograph, this coincidence, cannot be presented at this point as it will cause much too much disruption. Does Parson understand what is at stake? HOSCO, apparently dissolved, survives as a network of companies, a new constellation of associated concerns which orbit the new company CONPORT. Who knows, in future years these elements might coalesce, conjoin. This future is now in doubt. If these rumours increase about the old company and gather any more pace, any kind of survival, for CONPORT, for Geezler, for Gibson & Baker is in jeopardy. *I only have control because I have cut out the problem and appear to have established order.* Everything will be lost. The implications are vast. Unthread this and we undermine our very presence in the Middle East, how every company manages itself on foreign soil. *Does he understand?*

The waitress hurries past him, runs across the street to the market and returns with a single raw pork chop on a plate. Gibson looks at the bustle. There is an intelligence at work here. He watches the crowd and considers how its movements are constrained. The produce, water-filled buckets of clams, sardines, he isn't sure what kinds of fish, the plates of squid and tubs of octopus, and either side the vegetable stalls, are set out in blocks of colour, organized mounds of tomatoes, bundles of greens, onions, garlic, peppers, everything classified by size and kind. Superimposed on this is the disorder of the crowd, who come and go, return, haggle, argue, pinch, taste, converse and pay. There are two elements, the seller and the buyer, which appear hectic, but are contained and controlled by two basic principles: the need to sell and the need to buy. In this regard, it isn't hectic at all.

When he returns to the restaurant Gibson asks Sandro what he knows about HOSCO. Supposing Parson was right – entertain the idea – but if he was right, and the man who chased him across the tracks, the man who is responsible for his death, was commissioned by HOSCO. Supposing. What would happen next?

Sandro sets his elbows on the table. 'It's interesting. Do we assume the man who was after Parson wasn't Stephen Sutler?'

'Laura's photograph doesn't match the picture we have of Sutler. We have the one photograph from an ID and it looks nothing like this man.'

'Then we imagine that this is something different. He was not finding the man he was sent to find. Instead the issue becomes more complex, because he helps to make it complex.'

Gibson can't quite organize the thought. 'Think of what is supposed to happen. The design. What was intended. Not about what has happened.'

Sandro asks him what he means.

'I was speaking with Paul Geezler, and he is frustrated because this can't be controlled. Parson. Sutler. It is too chaotic now. There is too much attention. And it continues to make damage.' Gibson wants to distil recent events to their essential intentions, to reduce everything back to what was supposed to happen. 'Parson was supposed to find Sutler. Not finding Sutler becomes a problem, because Sutler is still active. He is still getting attention. Making noise. Making more noise perhaps. If you eliminate Parson, then you eliminate Sutler. Because if no one is searching for Stephen Sutler, then he is no longer a matter of attention. So what would be the next step?' Gibson looks up. 'Or is this all over?'

Sandro laughs softly. 'The method is not impressive. But the result is interesting. If we no longer have these people looking for Sutler, then, as far as everyone is concerned, we no longer have Sutler to worry about. I can see this. It makes sense.'

'So is it over?'

Sandro gives the smallest head shake. 'If there is someone making sure that Sutler is not discovered, then anyone who is involved is – I suppose – a threat.' He looks quizzically at Gibson, the thought taking shape. 'This means Paul Geezler,' he softly clears his throat. 'And it also means you.'

SUPPER WITH MATTAUS

7.1

Mattaus and his *friend* are due to arrive at seven-thirty. Rike arranges the table setting and tries not to work herself into a bother. Henning, unfazed, cleans the cutlery and glasses that Rike has set out.

Once the table is prepared Isa comes out of the main bedroom, and, stroking back her hair, asks if it wouldn't be better to take the table outside for a change. It is *nice*, after all.

'We eat outside every night,' Henning argues without much fight.

'It's only Mattaus. You know what he's like, inside is best, once he starts laughing the neighbours will complain.'

Isa gives Rike a glance, a warning shot not to start. 'Be nice.'

'I'm always nice.'

'I can't believe we don't know his name.'

Henning moves away from the sisters, then stands in the kitchen, bowls lined before him: one ready for the pasta, another for the sauce, another for the salad. Isa might have planned the evening but it's Rike who has to cook. Rike fries the last of the pancetta. Isa, she notices, walks with a more pronounced waddle. Her hand tucked into the small of her back. Really working the pregnancy.

'She's laying it on a bit thick,' Henning whispers.

Rike shrugs, Isa catches the expression.

'You are going to be nice, you two?'

Both Rike and Henning give innocent smiles.

'I'm always nice.'

'No you aren't. You make comments, you snipe at him until there's an argument. I don't want any of that this time. Just leave him alone.'

Rike brings the salad to the table. Henning tells Isa that someone is at the door, and simultaneously the doorbell rings. Isa hurries to answer and Rike returns to the kitchen area.

'I don't snipe. Do I?' she asks Henning.

Henning gives a *don't-ask-me* shrug and turns away. 'Let her have her evening.'

'He's my brother as well.'

'Just let it go the way she wants.'

Rike gives a small nod of agreement. Things always go how Isa wants. At the door, Mattaus stands on his own, arms up in welcome, Isa making excuses for him already, and in the same breath apologizing for the apartment. At least he's remembered to bring wine.

'Oh, he couldn't come? Give me that. You shouldn't have. We're not long out of boxes, not everything is in the right place. We've no idea how long we're staying so we haven't settled.' She returns to the lounge, a little red-faced and flustered, Mattaus behind her, looking, Rike has to admit, fresh, a little thinner, in good shape.

'You've been on the beach.' Isa strokes her brother's shoulder.

Mattaus looks about the apartment. Both Rike and Henning make their way to him. Henning awkwardly shakes his hand then guides him to one of the two soft chairs and asks what he would like to drink. Mattaus asks for red wine, although he's brought white, and keeps looking around the room, his eye a little critical.

'You left everything in Damascus? I wanted to visit you there.'

'When we get back.' Isa hands him his wine. 'Who knows when that might be.'

'But everything's in the house? You had to leave it all?'

'Everything. We had no choice. I was given three days to get everything together, and we were limited on what we could bring. It's still hard to believe.'

'But you look good.' Mattaus points his glass at his sister's stomach.

'I look like shit.'

'You look good.' Mattaus walks to Rike with his arms open. He apologizes about the apartment. 'You know how it is. I wish it didn't work out this way. Give me a kiss, teacher.'

Rike allows him to hug her but puts no enthusiasm into it. Understanding the rejection, Mattaus lets her go.

'So tell me. Who is this man? What is his name?'

'He's an architect.'

'We know.'

'There isn't much to say.'

'Older? Younger? Dark hair, light hair, what?'

'He's a little older.'

'What's a little?'

'Oh, a little.'

'And where's he from?'

'Cyprus.'

'He's a Cypriot?'

'No, he works in Cyprus.'

'Why are you being so mysterious? What's his name? When can we meet him?'

'He would have come tonight, but he has work, and this is all new, more or less, neither of us want to jinx it, you know.'

More or less. Rike sees a story here.

Rike stands away from the table, her arms folded. She unfolds her arms, works to find a happier expression before her sister notices and comments.

Isa asks how hungry he is. Rike has cooked his favourite, she says. Pasta. Mattaus automatically pats his stomach and while he says he's looking forward to it, he also mentions that he's trying not to put on any more weight.

'There's nothing on you,' Isa coos.

They eat at the table, inside. Everything in place. Rike opposite her brother, Isa seated beside him. Henning opens more wine and keeps himself distant, the bottle placed as a barrier between brother and brother-in-law.

The subject turns to Rike's teaching, this man, another unknown, dropped into the conversation (she thinks a little meanly) by Isa, announced as *her Norwegian*.

'So what are you teaching? English?'

'I am.'

'Anything else?' Mattaus winks at Henning. Henning, to his credit, doesn't respond.

Rike also doesn't trouble herself with such a weak parry.

'Is he cute?'

'He's a student.'

'But how hot is he? What's his name? Maybe I know him.' Mattaus and Isa share a smile. This is Mattaus, pure and simple, each person an opportunity, actual or potential, every man measured by his availability.

'Tomas Berens. He's Norwegian. And yes, he is your type.'

Mattaus raises his eyebrows. 'My type?'

'Male. Breathing.'

'Berens. Seriously?'

'Seriously.'

'A literary man?'

Rike shakes her head. 'He works for the UN.'

'Apparently,' Isa interrupts, 'he's a little damaged.'

Mattaus immediately perks up.

Isa begins the story about the assault. Rike looks to Henning. Deeply interested in the salad, he doesn't take part.

'I told you that in confidence.'

'Oh, come on.' Isa gives a little snort.

'You can't tell her *anything*,' Mattaus laughs, 'you know that.'

'Tell him about the murder. Tell him the story he told you.'

'There isn't a story.' Again Rike looks to Henning.

'Tell me. Tell me, tell me. I demand.'

Rike keeps her explanation blunt and to the point. 'Two or three years ago they found evidence of a murder in the basement of his building.'

'Evidence?'

'Blood. Blood and some clothes. The room was covered in plastic.'

Mattaus's head jots back a fraction. 'Hang on. *I know this.*' For one moment he looks puzzled, then a smile spreads across his face. 'Wait. I remember. I've seen this. It's from a film. It's a movie.' He uses the American word, deliberately. 'Oh my god. It's a *movie.*'

Rike feels a familiar weight. Doesn't it always go like this? Mattaus and Isa on one side, Henning disengaged, then Rike, distant, on the opposite bank. *Everything I say becomes about them.*

Isa holds the salad spoon in one hand and picks from the bowl with the other. 'Wait? What? Again? He's done this before.'

Mattaus's eyes brighten with delight. 'It's a film. It's the plot of a film. *And you believed him?*'

Rike's voice is small, swallowed by Mattaus's laughter. 'It's not funny. It's not funny at all.'

'It's definitely a film. Wait. Oh, God. I can't remember. OK. Did they find his tongue in a bag?'

Rike rises from the table, takes Henning's plate, looks to the kitchen. The bowls set out for pasta, for sauce, the water already boiling. What she feels is shame, why can't she just let go enough to join in? Play with Mattaus's absurd idea, to push it further along.

Isa is trying to remember if she's seen this film. It does sound familiar now he mentions it. Only, no? She looks up, confused. 'I'm sure I've read it. Ages ago. God. I can't remember anything these days. I read a book I'd finished about three weeks ago. Didn't remember until I got to the end.'

This, to Mattaus, is endlessly funny.

Henning straightens his napkin, cringes at the peal of laughter, but won't engage, won't even look at Isa. He seems, instead, to be somewhere else entirely.

'So Rike, tell me. Rike, listen,' Mattaus shouts across the room, 'what else has he told you? Come on. Share.'

Rike sets the plates in the sink. She lines the bowls equidistant from each other. Looks for the salt to add to the boiling water. She's already taken the packet of fresh pasta out of the fridge so that it won't cool the water down too much.

'Rike. Come on. What else has he told you?'

The pasta will take three minutes once the water has boiled. On the packet it says five minutes, but three is long enough given the time it takes to drain, pour into a bowl, and be kept piping hot with the sauce.

'What did he do last Christmas, Rike? Was he a caretaker in a hotel? Was he writing his novel with his wife and child? *Red rum, red rum.*'

It takes Isa a moment to get the reference, once she does she gives a hard and mean laugh.

'Oh, I'm in trouble!' Mattaus roars. 'She's ignoring me.'

Rike prefers to put the whole cloves of roasted garlic into the sauce, although the recipe calls for you to mash them in, so that the flavour carries throughout the sauce, but she likes it better this way.

'Better watch out!'

Rike tips the pasta into the water and watches it settle, the water froths and quietens.

Mattaus moves along, answers a question from Isa that Rike does not catch, and begins to recount his week, how they spend only the mornings and early afternoons together because business keeps his friend away, he isn't even sure what this business was, decorating is a broad field, who knows, maybe he works as an international spy?

'You said he was an architect.' Isa looks a little puzzled. 'He works at night?'

'Interiors. Interior architecture. Remodelling? I don't know.'

'What's his name?' Rike turns from the pot of pasta. 'You haven't told us.'

'His name?' Mattaus looks unaccountably blank.

'He has a name. You won't tell us. What's his name?'

Mattaus scoffs, but Henning and Isa are quiet and interested, and look to him with an encouraging *come on.*

His name, and here comes the blow, is Lexi.

Olexei.

Henning stiffens, sucks energy right out of the air to galvanize himself, say, politely, 'Sorry?' as if he hasn't heard.

Olexei.

Russian.

The name sparks for Rike. *He's fucking a Russian.* How could this get any better? Best of all, Isa can't figure out her reaction and flutters from the bemused *oh?* of the recently slapped to the confusion of someone who being cursed in a foreign language understands the intent but not the specifics.

Olexei?

Henning folds his napkin. Leans forward, incredulous.

Mattaus has ditched Franco for a Russian. A Russian decorator, for christsakes.

Rike turns off the heat, leaves the pasta in the water.

This can only get better.

Mattaus tries to move things along by talking about the sincerity of the relationship.

'He doesn't believe in taking things fast.'

This information, Rike is certain, wasn't supposed to slip out. She doesn't understand why he didn't just make up a name: *Markus, Stefan, Tomas.* Something generic. After the revelation prompted by the name, and with no hope offered that Lexi might be, say, a stage name, a nom de plume, a whimsical nickname or some family foible – as in, all the firstborn Kieserholzen males are named Olexei, nobody knows why. No. Genius that he is, Mattaus gives the man's real name. The facts confirm the problem: Olexei comes from a place once known as Gorki, known now as Nizhny, or Nizhny Novgorod, Russia's fifth largest city, which makes him definitively Russian. He couldn't be more Russian.

'So?'

The possibility that Mattaus doesn't quite understand the infringement, or his predicament, isn't an option. The man grasps for something, explains, falteringly: 'We're taking it easy at the moment. We're both out of relationships, and because we're both, you know, neither of us is new at this, and we really want to give it a chance, a better chance by not rushing.'

'Rushing?' Isa can't fathom the idea.

'We're taking this slowly, you know.' Mattaus has to clear his throat, and in a feeble voice admits, 'We just want to give this the best chance possible.'

Isa pushes her chair back and says she's getting some water. Rike waits a beat then says, 'There's water on the table.'

'I want fresh water.'

Mattaus and Henning face each other. Henning stares with unblinking force.

Isa runs the tap. There's cold water in the fridge, bottled water, which Rike takes out. They stand with their backs to the table.

'Ice. There's ice.' Isa points without looking up from the sink. 'I said, I want ice.'

There is, to Rike's surprise, real disappointment in her sister's face. 'He's thrown over Franco for a man who won't even fuck?'

'A Russian?' Rike likes the sound of the word. *Russian.* Loves the idea that this time she isn't the source of this heavy disappointment. No, Mattaus has surpassed her. Whatever happens next he is always going to hold the prize.

Rike opens the bottle, pours the water into a carafe, Isa repeats, irritated, 'There's ice, get some ice,' but Rike pours the water without regard.

'You know he's – it's probably not deliberate.'

'You don't know.' Isa's voice begins to rise. 'This isn't about *appearances*. This isn't about some *inconvenience*. There's a situation here and he's sitting at our table with no idea about what's coming out of his mouth and who he is speaking with.'

Things at the table aren't going well. Henning is pressing Mattaus for details. Who is this man? How did they meet? Does he have any idea about the kind of work Henning does? Has he any conception of how ridiculous this will make him appear if the news gets out?

Mattaus is dumbfounded, and gabbles for breath. He pours out their history. They met at a nightclub, the Nightingale. No, not the one in Limassol – all right, yes it was. And it hasn't been very long.

'I knew this would happen. It's none of your business.' He struggles to justify himself.

'That isn't how this works.' Henning stubs his forefinger on the table.

Isa turns from the sink. Mouth open. A thought taking shape. 'If this isn't about fucking then what is it about?'

Mattaus now looks slapped and he half stands.

'It's all about fucking with you. So if that isn't happening, what is it about? Drugs? It is isn't it? You met him at a club.'

The clarity of this idea strikes them all with its rightness, and opens up yet more consequences.

Rike watches in wonderment as the evening flowers in front of her.

'He's not an architect or a decorator. He works for one of the clubs. He works for the Nightingale.'

Henning gives a small whimper. This isn't possible, he picks up his napkin, drops it for effect (not a great effect, it's all he has to hand).

Mattaus stands up and says he's going.

'No. I don't think so. You're not going.'

Mattaus freezes.

'You aren't going anywhere. I need to know exactly what you're doing. Is she right? Are you doing drugs?'

Mattaus won't answer.

'Tell me who he is, this Olexei?'

Again, no answer.

'Are you going to the Nightingale? Are you going to the clubs? Are you associating with the Russians who own those clubs?'

Mattaus won't answer, instead he looks to Rike for some kind of rescue.

Rike doesn't move a muscle.

Henning rises from his seat and now he's shouting. 'Do you know anything about these people? Do you know who you are associating with? Have you got any fucking idea about what you're doing? About the effect of what you are doing and what it means to me – to us?'

Whatever satisfaction Rike was enjoying is wiped away by her understanding that this actually is an issue. Henning, who has never shouted, not to her knowledge, who holds his silences as his key weapon, is now exceptionally angry, his face red, his throat swollen, his voice bristling with effort. This is not a small misstep. Mattaus has seriously fucked up.

'How long have you been here?'

Mattaus scrambles for excuses, but can't minimize the trouble he's causing, the truth, obviously, is the only route. 'I've been back and forth.'

'Back and forth?' Isa doesn't understand. 'For how long?'

'Since March.' He closes his eyes. 'February. No. Yes. Early February.'

'You were here before we arrived? I don't understand. Why you didn't tell us?'

'Franco kicked me out. January. At the end of January. I came here for a break. I've been back and forward.'

Henning, seated again, has his head in his hands. 'These people are like the Mafia. Do you know what you are involved with? Do you know what they do?'

'It's not like that.' For a moment it looks like Mattaus might start to laugh.

'Drugs. Prostitution. He says it's not like that? Tell me, Mattaus, tell me what it's like. Tell me something I don't know about these people. You've made friends with the people who run the nightclubs on this island and you're going to tell me that you all hold hands and go out for pizza, you get a movie when the mood takes you? You sit and you talk about your favourite films? You talk about spa treatments? These people are thugs, Mattaus. They are involved in people-trafficking, in drugs. And you have a boyfriend you're taking things easy with? On what planet is this possible, Mattaus?' Henning shakes his head, can't stop his exasperation. 'What did you think would happen tonight? Why did you come? Why now? What point did you want to make?' A small realization comes to him. 'Or is there something else? You have something else to say, Mattaus? You have some other reason for coming here?'

'No.'

'You always have a reason. For everything you do there's a reason – what is it now?'

'No.'

'I need to know where you're staying. You can't see these people any more.'

When Mattaus starts to protest Henning holds up his hand. 'You've done enough,' he says.

Rike clears the dishes, throws out the pasta and pours the sauce into a container. Isa sits on her own, the light from the kitchen dresses the room with long shadows.

'I've never seen him like that.'

'Henning.'

'I think Mattaus knew what was going to happen. I think he came here knowing what to expect.'

Rike doubts that Mattaus had thought this through. The man reacts to situations when and as they occur, why would he ever think ahead?

With the meal cleared away Rike warms two glasses of milk and sits with her sister.

'What will Henning do?'

'He'll find out about the boyfriend. It might not be that bad.' Isa draws her hand across her brow. 'Who am I kidding? He's been with these people, partying, taking drugs. He doesn't care who they are. This Olexei sounds like a new arrival, but it looks like he's spent months with a whole group. It isn't good.'

'And Mattaus?'

'He can't stay. The embassy will want him to leave.'

'And Henning?'

'It's just the wrong time for all of this. Anything that potentially compromises him, anything that looks out of order, makes his work more difficult. If Udo gets any word of this then it's over. We'll be returned to Germany. It will all be over. There will be no possibility of returning to Damascus.'

Rike cups the glass in her hands and nods. 'Do you think he has a problem?'

'With drugs?' Isa shakes her head. 'He's such a fucking tourist.' Isa picks up her drink. 'How old is he now? Thirty-one? Thirty-two? Time is running out for him and he knows it. He can't behave like this.'

'I feel sorry for Franco.'

'Franco was no angel. He knew what he was getting.'

A silence falls between them. Isa exhausted but unwilling to go to bed.

Living with Mattaus and Franco, close to the end of her stay, Rike had woken with the sound of them returning from a club. Two in the morning, then three. Someone in the kitchen, and she had come out to find Franco leaning against the cabinets, arms folded. The door to their bedroom closed. And then the painful realization that they had met someone at the club and brought them home. It was difficult to understand the set-up, but Franco wasn't pleased. Until this point they had lived formal lives with each other, but now, on the understanding that she was leaving, she sensed that they were returning to a different life, to old and established routines.

When she left, it was Franco, not Mattaus, who said that he would miss her.

The evening, being so exceptionally strange, has left Rike with the sense that she's permeable. She sits in the chair, legs tucked under her, the glass of milk in her hand, and senses the night air and the distance between herself and her sister, the glass, the small square garden outside, and the wall, aware that beyond this is a void. The apartment could be floating, it could be free. They could be in this box and be anywhere in the world, even above it.

7.2

At three in the morning Rike wakes again. There's little point in attempting to sleep. She slips into the lounge and checks her email. Included is a message from *Mannfunktionprojekt*.

She retrieves a pass code for the final piece in an email titled 'with love'. The date – the beginning of the month – means that this was not actually the final piece, but the second. When she enters the site she's prompted to fill in her name, her age, her email address, and generate a password. A small warning comes up: This Contains Adult Material.

Enter / Return to Site. Rike clicks *Enter*.

Members / Guests. She clicks *Members* and is prompted to enter her password.

The entire screen becomes black.

'With Someone You Love' comes up as a title, and then underneath a second title: 'With Someone You Do Not Love'. Both are options which can be clicked.

Isa comes out of the bedroom an hour later.

'He can't sleep either,' she says. 'So I can't sleep. What are you watching?' Isa leans over the couch as Rike automatically covers the screen, expecting Isa to become angry.

'It's art.'

'Art?' Isa peels back her sister's hand. 'You're watching porn? Of all nights? Now I have to worry about you?' She comes around the couch and sits beside her sister.

'It's art.'

'So move your hand away.'

'I'm not Mattaus.'

'Let's not go there.'

'It's that group. You liked the last one. It's another video, a series of videos.'

Isa picks the computer from Rike's lap. She clicks to restart the movie. After a moment she moves the laptop so they can both see the screen. 'You dirty girl,' then clicking through the options asks Rike which one she wants to watch: with love, or without?

Isa becomes serious once they have watched both films.

'It's interesting. I mean I don't know if it's art, but it's interesting. You think at some level it's all the same. Fucking, I mean. It's just fucking after all.'

Rike rolls her eyes. That's something Mattaus would say.

'Not exactly what you'd call *hot* though, is it?'

'I don't think it's supposed to be.'

'You know if Henning was ever with anyone else, I think the only way I could make it through would be to think that whoever he was with, it wouldn't be the same, it would be something different. That when he's with me it's more, I don't know, *intended*. I don't know. Men say it doesn't mean anything, you know, when they mess up. That's the standard line.'

'It's not the same.'

Isa gives a short laugh. 'You know. It kind of *is*. I mean that's where it gets to. Once or twice maybe it's something special, but you have these habits, you know. You spend all of your time thinking about it when it doesn't happen, and then, when it does, it's a function. Like having a good shit, I mean how many different ways can you have a good shit? I'm being serious.'

The sisters sit in silence.

'You think we're the only animal that cares about this?' Isa points to the yard. 'You think those cats care? You think other animals watch each other go at it and it does something for them?'

'Like cat-porn.'

Isa turns to Rike and they both laugh, and try to keep quiet to not disturb Henning, but laughing hard.

'So when did you last do it?'

'You're asking me?'

'Of course I'm asking.'

Rike gives a short involuntary eyes-closed shrug.

'Really? That long?'

'What? No. It's not been that long.'

'So this year. We're talking this year? You've had sex this year? Who with?'

'I'm not telling you. We're not discussing this.'

'I bet you haven't. You like those farm boys, that's your problem.'

'I don't like farm boys. You like farm boys.'

'I do. Very much. But so do you. You never go for them though. You always end up with the complicated ones. The spoiled ones. The ones who are too shy, who need written permission, notes from their mothers. That's your whole problem, you don't go for what you want.'

Rike considers returning to bed. 'This isn't fair. You don't know what it's like. You're married now. It's all different.'

'It's true though. Look at them. There was that French boy.'

'Don't.'

'And he really liked you. I still don't understand what your problem was. See. I know you like him. I'm talking about Tomas.'

'I don't like him.'

'Yes. You do. I can tell.'

'I don't. I'm his teacher.'

'You keep saying that like it's a problem. You're adults. And men always like teachers. Teachers and librarians. Ask Henning.'

'I don't like him. I don't know him. He doesn't have the first idea about me.'

'I bet he sits close. I bet he leans forward and asks you questions. I bet he whispers so you have to get close. He's asked you to his house. See. It's not like you're in a classroom. You're already in the vicinity.'

Rike didn't understand. 'Of what?'

'Of his bedroom. God, you really are hopeless.' Isa shakes her head with genuine frustration. 'I'm joking. I'm having fun. God forbid you'd let yourself have any fun. Ever.'

'I know how to have fun.'

Isa stops talking for a moment, then screws up her mouth. 'You know, with Mattaus, I can't believe he's been here longer than we have. All this time. I know what he's like. But it's just hurtful that he does this. He has no idea. I mean we love him. But he does this to us. All the fucking time.'

Hearing a noise in the hallway both Rike and Isa turn to see Henning fully dressed.

'What's the matter?' Isa asks, her voice still quiet. 'Did we disturb you?'

'I have to go. I've had a call. The man in the hospital. There are problems with security.'

Isa struggles to her feet. When she kisses him goodbye she cradles his face in her hands and whispers, *Poor baby, we really are too much for you.* An apology, Rike thinks, not unjustified, for her family.

The clock counts down to zero, white numbers on a black field. Rike sits up in bed with the laptop. Once the numbers stop a title fuzzes into view: first, *Mannfunktionprojekt*, then after, *MFP – 02:06*. The image, two fields of blue, a landscape, one a flat bright blue, the other slightly mottled, a darker blue. The resolution isn't so clear and the image speckles, fizzes, falls into digitized squares, especially in the lower, darker segment. And what is this? Nothing, a kind of landscape she supposes, and then slowly, steadily, it becomes clearer and draws into focus. She's looking at the sea and the sky, and as the image becomes focused she can tell that this is a shoreline. Rike watches, intrigued, expectant, and then finally impatient, because it seems that nothing will happen. She realizes also that she's holding her breath, and just at the moment she lets it out something begins to rise from the sea.

At first she thinks that this is a gold-coloured ball. But then realizes it's the head, the panda head from the first video, except it's not black and white, but gilded, and the sun reflects from it, not sharply, but with a soft touch, as the sun in the late afternoon when the harshness has burned out. It makes her laugh. This gold static head rising from the surface, perfectly round with two semi-circular ears. Then slowly, so slowly the man emerges from the water, semi-naked as before, wearing the same shorts, his arms, as ever, at his side. As she watches she began to find the image hostile, and can't quite figure why this is so: because the man is almost naked? Because his figure is presented face-on, but the head is disguised, which seems thug-like, no different from a youth wearing a hood? Because it's controlled, confrontational: this time he doesn't look away, the head doesn't turn, but insists and stares, black double Xs for eyes as if it/he might be dead. By the time the man can be seen, full-figured, the sky behind him has turned mauve, then violet, and she realizes that this has been shot over a long period of time, and that the man has spent many hours slowly emerging from the sea while behind him the day slowly falls into night. As it becomes dark she watches the body, the head, slowly diminish, become indistinct and dissolve into the night – a small regret at the disappearance. This is, she's certain, an enigmatic farewell.

Just before the light is completely gone the man spells out a sentence, shaping the letters with his hands. The gestures are repeated until, being so dark, there is nothing more to see.

WHATDIDYOUDOTODAY

At the end of the video the small inset square becomes black, and GPS coordinates fade in.

She clicks on the coordinates and finds a link to the beach. The birthplace of Aphrodite. How lovely, how perfect. These men, she thinks, have a gentle disposition.

. . . WHATDIDYOUDOTODAY

. . . that counts?

. . . that carries meaning?

. . . that made the day worthwhile?

. . . what will you do tomorrow?

THE BOOK

8.1

She catches him first in a reflection as she walks to Tomas's. Monday midday. A boy hurrying across a road, looking to the traffic as he crosses. In the same reflection she's walking as if contained, all held in, like it embarrasses her to take up space. The boy looks Russian, or what she takes to be Russian. Blond, short hair, not what she'd call stocky exactly, but thick, too young to be called toned, and perhaps the real giveaway, a loud short-sleeve shirt, not quite Hawaiian, and skimpy shorts. He's wearing an expensive pair of sunglasses. One nice thing. Isn't that what Mattaus would say. It doesn't matter what else you wear, but one nice thing, something select, expensive, to define you.

He catches her at the door. One foot on the step, her hand on the glass. He speaks to her in German.

'Excuse me. Rike Falsen?'

She stops, her hand flat to the glass door. In five minutes she needs to be teaching.

'Rike?'

'Yes?'

'I want to give you this.' He offers her a book, a hardback, slim and new. Rike won't accept it. There's no solid reason behind this, perhaps because he's used her name and she knows that she does not know him and this seems to be some kind of a scam. Once made, the decision cements itself.

He lets the book brush her arm, by accident. This handing-over constitutes some kind of contract. If she takes the book it will mean something. Although, as yet, she has no idea what this might be, but clearly he wants her to take it.

'This is for you.'

'I'm sorry?'

It isn't the strangeness of being approached by a person you do not know, or being addressed in your home language, but the boy's insistence.

'Do I know you?'

The boy is polite. 'I know your brother.'

'Is he here?'

'No. But he wants me to give you this.'

The subject has changed now.

'When did you see him?'

'He gave me this to give to you. Here. The book is for you.'

'Is he here now?'

'Please, take the book.' The boy holds it out and again she refuses to accept. This time her hands go behind her back, and she looks at him with a fastness that shows determination. It's just not going to happen.

'Tell him he needs to get in touch with either me or my sister. His sister. He's caused enough trouble. If he wants me to have the book then he can give it to me himself.'

The boy swears to himself. It's too much. 'I'm not passing on any messages. The book is for you.'

He could throw the book down, he could place it somewhere – on her head, on her shoulder, where she would have to take hold of it. He could push it against her breasts so she might automatically raise her hands in some kind of outrage. Instead he places it at her feet, literally leans it against her right foot.

Rike stubbornly refuses to move.

'I'm not taking it. Tell him what I said.' And then she's gone, pushed through the door and gone. The book is tipped now against the step.

Rike couldn't care less. She has no idea what her brother is up to, nor who this boy is to him, or why he would pass on a book. The whole thing is irritating. It's a book, and who cares about a book? To be honest, if Mattaus wants her to have it, then he should deliver it himself. After Saturday night she has no tolerance for his nonsense.

The boy walks up the street, disappointed, and it occurs to her that not accepting the book might appear petty.

Rike hurries up the stairs to Tomas's apartment.

He's ready for her after the lesson when she comes out of the building. Rike looks quickly up and down the street as if she might be ready for him also. As soon as she passes by the café he steps forward, strides, in pace, right behind her.

'Take the book.'

She turns to face him, rolls her eyes. 'You again.'

'Take the book.'

'No.'

'Take it.'

'No.'

'Take it. Take it. Take it. Take it.'

She doesn't respond. In fact, she's not even bothered by him. She isn't threatened at all.

'Take the book. Take the book. Take the book.'

A man steps off the pavement in advance and watches them pass. They both notice him.

'It's her book. She won't take it.' Then to Rike, 'Take the book.' Still walking. 'I have nothing else to do today.'

'Did you tell him?'

The boy hurries to walk beside her now, no break in pace.

'Who?'

Rike stops. 'Mattaus. Did you tell him?'

'I'm not a messenger.'

'What's your name?'

'My name? Sol.'

'Well, listen, Sol. When you next talk to my brother, tell him we need to talk. It's the only way I can get in touch with him.' She shunts her bag higher on her shoulder. 'He isn't answering his messages. You're going to have to tell him.'

'No.'

'Good luck with the book then.'

'If I tell him you'll take the book?'

'I'm not bargaining.'

Now frustrated he stops. 'Fuck you. Fuck the book.'

'Read it yourself,' she says, in a taunt that sounds childish, so he gives up and lets her go.

As she walks away it occurs to her that he might throw the book at her, hard.

8.2

Gibson waits in the lobby for Sandro. While he waits he reads through the *Herald Tribune* and sees an article about Paul Geezler. *Embattled CONPORT Head Goes Missing.*

The news from London confirms his fears. Geezler was spending the weekend in New Mexico. His car has been found outside a motel, with his wallet, his briefcase in plain view on the backseat. The driver's door was left wide open. A heavy rain. Papers stuck to the motel forecourt. His passport under the car. Money in the glove compartment. Undisturbed.

Sandro organizes a room in Posillipo. He brings a small suitcase with a change of clothes. Gibson unpacks the case and lays the items across the bed. He has not worn shorts in thirty years.

'Nobody knows you are here. I arranged this myself. There are no records. You are booked on a flight to London. This is secure.' Sandro sits on the opposite bed. 'We will have a man with you here. He does not know your name, he does not know your business. As far as you are concerned you are on holiday. This is a vacation.' He hands Gibson a pair of sunglasses. 'The secret to disappearing is to stay where you are.'

8.3

Rike eats at the café alone. And there, once again, the Russian. She isn't surprised to see him.

Three times in one day.

Rike, determined not to show her irritation, makes no response when he sits at her table. He places the book on his lap, believing this to be a more diplomatic approach. As he settles in his chair, she leans back and folds her arms.

'Did you speak with him?'

Sol shakes his head as if scolded.

'I know him from the club. He comes to the Nightingale with one of the managers.'

'In Limassol?' She says this with great irritation.

'He's with Lexi. We have two clubs, in Limassol and Larnaca. Lexi runs the club in Larnaca. It's always best to leave Lexi alone.'

'What do you mean?'

'Your brother is with the club manager in Larnaca. You understand? He wants me to give you this book. He said I should make sure you have it. That's all.' He sets the book on the table. 'That's what I've been asked to do. You can take it, do what you want. You can throw it away. My job is to make sure you have it in your hands.'

'You've read it?' There's an element of disbelief she can't manage to hide. 'How do you know him?'

'I don't know your brother. I know Lexi. I'm at the club, most nights.'

'You work there?'

'I'm here until the summer. The man who runs the club in Limassol is a family friend. I'm staying at the Miramar just up the road.'

They nod simultaneously.

'Why won't you take the book?'

Rike looks down at the table.

'Why not?'

Rike turns her chair askance to the table. Her eyes flutter closed for a moment. 'Because.' And then she stops herself. 'It's not your problem.'

'Actually. It is my problem if you don't take it.'

'I don't know why I don't take it, and I don't know why I don't want to read it. I don't know why my brother would be wasting his time on something so petty when he's in a great deal of trouble.'

'Trouble?'

'He shouldn't be at that club. He shouldn't be with the people he's seeing.'

She means *him*, she means *the Russians*, and he immediately understands. 'It's a club. There are plenty of clubs in Cyprus. It's one of the reasons people come here.'

'No. They come here for what the clubs bring with them. For what happens in the clubs.'

'It's probably not what you think.'

'It probably isn't.' Rike smiles for the first time. 'You're probably right. I'm making assumptions.'

'I still don't understand the book.'

'It's – family. It's how we are. Do you have brothers or sisters?'

'No.'

'It isn't complicated.' Rike isn't sure how much she wants to explain, but begins to explain in any case. 'There are three of us in our family, and one person can't have something without the other two spoiling it. That's what the book is about. The older we get the more childish it becomes.' Rike runs her finger along the tabletop. 'I'm not going to read it. You can tell him that. If you see him.'

'You're not curious?'

'Not at all.'

'It's just some story about a murder.' Sol looks out at the street. 'Two brothers take a basement room, they pick up someone from the station and kill him. If you like thrillers it's a good story. It's true.' He watches the traffic come left to right. 'It's not like he even solves it.'

Rike struggles to her feet. How typical is this? Mattaus, determined to insert himself where he isn't wanted, has dug out one book, out of millions of books, with a familiar sounding plot. It's pathetic. That's what it is. Pathetic. Flustered, she goes through her pockets, then stops to look at the boy. 'Did he tell you to say this?'

'I don't know your brother. He comes to the club, but I don't know him.'

'Liar.'

Her exit is messy. She bumps into a chair, walking, blind almost, extra-clumsy, humiliated. It doesn't make sense that Mattaus would work so hard at this, unless, of course, he blames Rike for the farce on Saturday night.

Rike returns to the apartment and finds the book on the hallway table, with a note in Isa's handwriting. 'You have a fan! This was delivered for you today.'

She walks to the kitchen, opens the trash and is ready to drop the book without a thought, but decides against it. Fine. This is now evidence. Maybe Isa will see just how much of a bully her brother is, how pathetic and petty.

Even so. It's hard not to be a little curious.

THE THIRD SUTLER

9.1

He doesn't know what's happening, the road stretches ahead of him, grey and rubbery: the desert on either side a flat stony pitch, with heat rising in waves so the land appears furred. Whitby loves this, thinks of it as a TV landscape, something known, pre-encountered. The Americans he hires work in chinos and brown boots, white or blue shirts, regardless of their status or duty. Whitby, nicknamed *English*, has his own style: a lightweight suit, which he sweats through. He spends his life in an office or a 4x4, subject to air-conditioning.

The problem is this: he needs core samples for a road project financed three years ago. The road doesn't exist, but the samples should already be in boxes, logged and housed in the company stores, proof of work done. And now he's having to collect these samples himself, three years after the fact because people are getting sticky about these details. Once he has the samples he'll have to drive back and make sure they are stored where they would have been stored, should the project actually have gone ahead. He calls these projects *gophers*, as in, go-for-the-money (don't-deliver-the-project).

He's on the phone as he drives. 'My concern,' he says, 'is that we undertook the work we were required to undertake but this appears not to have been logged.' Silence. 'I was looking at them this morning. Those samples are in the store.' The person he is speaking with contradicts him, and goes against the grain of the conversation. Whitby invites him to check tomorrow morning.

'The road? I wouldn't know about the road. That's out of my *scope*. It's not my problem. I was contracted to undertake a geological assessment, and I've completed the work that was requested.' It's a bald-faced lie. He knows it, the person he's speaking with knows it. HOSCO published the pre-solicitation (PS), then the specific General Procurement Notice (GPN). MasterWork-Roadways (MW-R) submitted the successful Statement of Work (SOW), and subcontracted Whitby Earth Science Services (WESS) to undertake the surveys. That's fact. After this the whole idea becomes *abstract*. WESS didn't complete the survey, because MW-R didn't intend to build the highway, because not one person in Iraq would actually ever need to drive along the

933

entire border with Saudi and Syria. 'Let's make that clear,' he says. 'Not. One. Person.'

Whitby catches his in-caution. You can't speak like this on a sat-phone. It's not wise. Signals bounce off the ether, travel for millennia. NASA will capture it in echoes, crawlers on Mars will forward the information to god knows who, because who knows when this is coming back at you? You have to shut your mouth these days.

Against his better judgement he has to spell it out. 'I know how this works. OK? I know. When I worked for you we built bypasses around towns that weren't much more than encampments, bridges over dry wadis, turns in roads that didn't need turns.' He needs to be emphatic. 'You're forgetting. I. Know.'

He decides he can't hear the caller, the signal, he says, it's just not there. Nope, can't hear you. Then cancels the call. It's a small joy to imagine that frustration. The situation doesn't need managing, not in its entirety. He just needs to look after his own part.

Whitby drives with the satisfaction of another man's frustration chasing after him. He likes the idea that the burn of this conversation is making someone ache. He's had the last word. As if to confirm this finality the signal for the satphone properly dies.

And the road. On the surface it looks the same now as it did when he started. Yellow to white plates of broken stone. Something that looks like a raw landscaped lot. Running under the surface it's a whole other story. He can take core samples here, where the schist breaks through. In one or two miles the road curls as close as it's going to get to the Syrian border. You could take samples at any point along here because there's just the right concentration of fossil matter and silicates and gypsum, and say they came from anywhere along the entire length.

He has to get out of his car. He has a core-sampler with him. Needs to pick a spot that's going to provide him with enough material. He slams the door and hears it automatically lock. Which isn't right.

This is the first thing that goes wrong.

The keys won't work. That's great. The key is a hard plastic button. Something about it makes him think of Sweden. The pure design of it. A black button the size of a thumb print. A man's thumb print. You press this button and the car unlocks, the engine starts, the vehicle adjusts to the driver, seats move, lower, lengthen. Air flows and temperatures alter. You can set the audio for your listening pleasure. He likes Caruso to greet him. 'Una Furtiva Lagrima'. He hears the music and he's in the movie. The keys won't work and the door won't open.

Fantastic.

He's in the desert, thirty-something miles from the Syrian border. His vehicle has locked him out, and it's playing Caruso. He has to listen to it, because you have to. The way the music steps, a little up, a little down. You know exactly where it's heading. That tender baritone and the knowledge that singing this, his final aria, caused his throat to bleed. Caruso dead at forty-eight at the Hotel Vesuvio, beloved Naples. And here, in the desert, with the ground undulating in the white heat, it just makes perfect sense. His car has locked him out, and now it's humming to itself.

He stands in the desert. Gives the car a look of hate, turns a whole 360, and lets out a sigh as the aria starts up a third time. No choice but to smash a window.

The thing is, and now he remembers, any damage and the vehicle goes into 'alert'. The system locks down, the alarm sounds, a signal is sent across the world, supposing a signal can be sent. Only, wasn't that removed? The man he bought the vehicle from had made some adjustments because he didn't want to be tracked by some CIA car dealership.

It comes to him piece by piece. Locked out. Car in lockdown. No power to the phone. By his calculation he's sixty miles from the nearest garage. From what he remembers the closest village is actually across the border in Syria. It won't come to that. Not yet. All you do is wait. The goddamned thing will reset itself. The alarm will have to stop sometime soon. Just leave it alone and the codes automatically reset.

He waits an hour. Sits on the road with his knees up, and his suit jacket hitched over his head. With his fingers in his ears. It's unnerving just how bleak it is, and how can there be flies out here when there is no other living creature? He sits on the tarmac with his back against the car and hides from the sun. The car, while it provides shade, becomes much too hot. For all of the expense, those self-adjusting seats, the assisted steering, the brakes, the interface between computer and vehicle – it's nothing more than a heat-attracting can.

THOMAS BERENS

10.1

While in Naples Berens tells this story about William Tecumseh Sherman to Paul Geezler as distraction and example: the great general, in an early posting, was sent to Florida, and for almost a year he spent much of his time fishing in the company of a Sergeant Ashlock. This sergeant was sent to accompany a man on a court martial, and when he returned he brought with him a young wife. The breakers that day were rougher than usual, and while the first boat crossed the bar without trouble, the others, including Ashlock's, were overturned. Ashlock's wife had made the first safe trip, and stood on the shoreline with her sister and watched as the other boats fell into trouble. A nice day but a rough sea. The boats, caught in the surf, were quickly swamped and broken, and the men set upon by sharks. The next morning Sherman had the unpleasant task of walking the surf-line to identify the washed-up pieces of bodies, and the later duty of confirming the sergeant's death to his young wife. It's a small event in a larger life, but in writing it, Sherman expresses regret. As if this need not have happened.

Berens likes to imagine what it would be like to meet the general, say before the Civil War, on his way to an earlier campaign, travelling around Cape Horn, on the long voyage from East to West America prior to the Panama Canal. It would be interesting to meet the man, before he knew himself who he was. He'd like to meet Grant as well. Although he'd choose a later period, days before his death, when he'd given up eating, and worked to complete his manuscript for no less a publisher than Mark Twain. Berens would sit on the porch and watch the great man labour over words during his final days. This is what he'd like to see. Sherman before the conflict, and Grant long after.

Aside from this desire, Berens finds Sherman's Ashlock tale instructive: at any given time you don't know what's coming at you. You really don't. Ashlock single. Ashlock married. Ashlock in pieces along the shore. After the fact there is a certainty to this progression. Before, there's only unknowing. Berens uses this story as a stall when he doesn't want to give an immediate response, when he wants an idea to penetrate.

The entire endeavour is compromised right at the start. Berens sees the woman raise her hand, and only as she is lowering her hand does he notice that she is holding a mobile phone, and understand that she has probably taken a photograph of him. He gives no reaction, but passes through the hallway back into the museum. He deliberately does not turn about to watch Laura Parson and her husband as they come back down the stairs and make their way to the entrance to leave.

10.2

Berens waits on Piazza Municipio for Parson to come out of his hotel. When he does, he immediately calls Geezler. It's just as he thought, he says, Parson has been booking into hotels under Geezler's name, which means, in all likelihood, after all these months, Parson has been stringing them along: Sutler isn't in Italy. Probably never was.

The next evening Paul Geezler calls with a new instruction. He's had a discussion with Parson, and Parson is convinced that Stephen Sutler is now heading to Rome. The discussion, he says, wasn't entirely agreeable. Parson is attached to the hunt in a way Geezler doesn't like. Berens needs to re-check the hotel bookings. According to Parson, Sutler is still making hotel bookings in Geezler's name. It's confusing.

Geezler calls Tomas in the morning to discuss his concerns about the man in Grenoble. The man the newspapers are calling *Sutler Number Two*. He isn't comfortable with the silence surrounding this story, which gives this version some credibility.

Tomas, who has already spent the better half of a week in Grenoble, is less convinced, and he persuades Geezler not to send him back. Berens's bed is little more than a thin mat. As he talks he sits half up on his elbows and changes the phone from hand to hand – then finally sits upright, resenting that he is more awake than he cares to be.

'It's a whole other matter,' he says, 'with its own complications.' A missing boy, a frantic mother, a pair of incompetent New York PIs who believe their own small drama intersects something more dynamic. 'I found nothing. They're using this story to make their own newsworthy.'

THE HIT

Tomas talks Geezler down.

'These new Sutlers aren't a problem. We need more than three. Let them proliferate. This is about density. Three Sutlers keep the attention on you. Thirty Sutlers is the start of a craze. It's something else completely, and everyone will forget about the first Sutler. Right?'

Geezler isn't buying the idea. It's nearly April, he says. He wants them gone before the hearing.

Berens walks to the port. After waiting the day in his hotel for Geezler's call it's his first opportunity to see the city. He stands on the pier and watches the ferries turn at the mouth of the harbour, and something about their motion, which at first seems random, begins to make sense. Each of these boats is either departing or arriving, which means there's a hierarchy and an order to who can dock first and where. By watching you can figure this out. Behind him the hills of the old city are crowned with forts and palaces, all handsomely familiar. But it's the ferries for Procida, Ischia, Capri, and the brightening shoreline that hold his attention.

There's less logic in his movement. Geezler wants something done about Parson. Parson seems always to be at Sutler's heels, but never in step.

Tomas Berens watches Parson with his wife. The man assists the woman out of the taxi, leads her off the road to the sidewalk and kisses her goodbye at the concourse fronting the Stazione Centrale. She doesn't see her husband to the platform – she has other business in town – and walks away, a rooted walk in flip-flops, her thoughts on the crowd, her path a slight curve toward the doors, passing the ticket machines to avoid the beggars, to the glass front, the broad plaza, into the day.

In the week Berens has spent in Naples he's come to admire Parson, although he doesn't fully understand – nor in fact does he need to – the reason why the man has been booking hotel rooms under the name 'Paul Geezler'.

At the station bookstore he contacts Geezler, tells the man that everything is in place, does he want him to go ahead? The man answers yes. Berens has the feeling he's with someone.

'Yes,' he says, 'I'm happy for you to go ahead with this.'

Berens starts to give details and Geezler interrupts.

'That's nice,' he says, 'but I don't need to know.'

Berens buys a book by Finn Cullman. The name, he thinks, is a mix of Scandinavian and North American.

10.3

Berens has three calls from an unregistered number. When he finally answers Geezler asks if he's free to talk. Is this convenient? An edge to his voice suggests he has no choice. It isn't unexpected.

'I'm alone. I should tell you it wasn't ideal.'

'Ideal?' Geezler's voice is clipped. 'The news I'm watching is telling me that Stephen Sutler was hit by two trains in Rome.' Geezler pauses to take in breath. 'I'm seeing this on CNN, CBS, on NBC, on Fox. The probability of this is, what, next to impossible, given that you were recently in Rome?' He wants to know what is happening. 'This is Parson. This news is about Parson.' He doesn't wait for confirmation. 'I know in my bones that this is Parson.'

'The situation wasn't ideal.'

Geezler cautions him not to give details. 'Why do they think that this is Sutler?'

Berens doesn't know. Parson's luggage was on one of the trains. Sooner or later they are going to work it out.

Geezler isn't happy. It isn't ideal to have one Sutler obliterated by two trains with less than a month left before the hearings. And once they realize that this is Parson, interest is going to redouble. 'Was this,' he asks, 'in any shape or form *an accident*?'

'There was a problem.'

'The arrangement is that they disappear. Without remark. Unobtrusive. I'm thinking accidents. Stepping off pavements, stairs. Falling. Drowning. Vanishing. These are better options. This is preferable.' The key to success is discretion. Berens needs to understand that the death of Parson prefaced with him running across railway tracks is the opposite of discrete. In death, Parson is sensationally more troublesome than he was in life.

Geezler wants his assurance. 'The others, can we agree, will be undertaken without drama?'

Berens does not reply.

'Can we agree?' Geezler demands an answer.

10.4

Geezler contacts Berens and instructs him not to go to Damascus. The whole situation with Parson has become so hot he can't run the risk of another mess.

Berens asks Geezler to clarify what he's saying. They have less than a month. He can go to Damascus and end this in one night. He needs to leave for Damascus before they stop civilian flights. Parson was a mistake, he admits, there wasn't anything he could do. The situation couldn't be controlled. It isn't going to happen again. There's no need to act rashly.

Geezler won't have any of it. Berens needs to lie low. He needs to reconsider. It isn't good, he says. This isn't good.

Geezler calls back an hour later. He's reconsidered and now wants Berens to go to Cyprus. The diplomatic corps for Britain, Germany, the US and France have temporarily moved essential services to Cyprus. Others have decamped to Turkey. Berens should base himself in Cyprus, wait this out. He is to take no action without Geezler's explicit authority. What happened in Rome cannot be repeated. Observation. Preparation. When the situation is clearer, and the opportunity is right, Geezler will move him to Damascus.

Within this plan is a small provision, a possibility. If the diplomats are in Cyprus then it is possible that Sutler will also be relocated.

The upcoming hearing means that any noise is unwelcome. Any more trouble like Parson and they are sunk. Any number of Sutlers running random about Europe and the Middle East is *bad news*, but they cannot act rashly. Berens should consider himself constrained until further notice. Go to Cyprus. Find information. *Take no action without my word.*

It's only when Berens looks at the map that he begins to understand Geezler's concern. To this point Sutler has somehow traversed the entire length of Iraq, exiting into Turkey, along a heavily monitored border. It's barely feasible. Given that Parson has lied about Sutler's movements from Malta to Italy, it's likely that he lied about his movements in Turkey. Two journalists, Heida and Grüner, saw Sutler twice in Turkey, which again seems increasingly implausible, and something Parson might have over-emphasized.

Berens studies the map. He calculates the timings and distances. It's all possible. But just not that likely.

What would he do?

The question is impossible to answer. He can't place Sutler, has a limited idea of the man. He walks through what he knows: the man has embezzled a vast amount of money, and realizing he has been discovered he attempts to destroy the records held in a government office. This, naturally, goes wrong, which exacerbates the problem. Now he has to run. He wouldn't have entered such a situation without a plan, without any number of plans and preparations. Perhaps he had vehicles ready? Perhaps he had other people helping him?

The choice is limited. Sutler can't remain in the country. He can't get to the Kurdish north without hitting Baghdad and without passing through checkpoints. And east, toward Iran, would be out of the question. South to Kuwait presents itself as the most viable possibility, but almost as risky as heading north, given the concentration of American troops and contractors now based at the border.

Only when he inspects the map, and finds a fine thread, a small road running parallel to the Saudi border, does Berens see another option. If this was planned. If this was prepared, then this route would be the most secure. Take the border road, drive alongside Saudi until you reach Syria. From here, to an inexperienced eye, the desert might offer the better option, in theory, at least, you could travel from village to village. On paper this looks possible. Syria, given the current chaos, is an attractive proposition, once there Sutler would have richer choices.

Berens understands Geezler's anxiety. *Sutler Number Three* is beginning to look like their man.

In Cyprus he finds a room in Nicosia and awaits instruction. There are decisions to make. Choices. Geezler needs to be attentive. Berens spends the first week reading. Hires himself a car and drives through the Troodos range. He follows the Green Line as it cuts along ridges and mountain valleys, divides villages. He visits churches and disused asbestos mines, spends one day speaking only German, another speaking English. He spends his evenings at the bars and clubs in Paphos, Limassol, Larnaca. He meets a woman called Carla Strozer and learns that the Germans are the people he should pay attention to, in particular the office of Udo Kellman, and his go-to man, Henning Bastian.

If you look hard enough at any system, at some point it is going to reveal its patterns, habits, and operations.

Berens waits outside the offices for Carla Strozer. He follows her home to her apartment block, waits, and when she comes out, changed from office drab into more comfortable white slacks and a purple top, he again follows her, this time into the old city.

She takes a seat outside a café, takes out her cigarettes and looks about. Tomas reintroduces himself and sits at her table before she invites him.

'The bar,' she smiles. 'The other night. I remember you.'

He asks if he can buy her a drink, and Carla, looking over her shoulder, says that there's a better place across the square, beside the cathedral. As she stands he draws out her chair and sets his hand in the small of her back.

The woman freezes. 'Just so you know,' her voice is cold, 'I have no interest in you.'

She's more interested in the drinks. He buys mojitos, margaritas, and the conversation quickly becomes more fluid. Her steers the discussion to work, pries out details. She'd mentioned Udo Kellman and his work in Damascus?

'It's so interesting.' She leans in, picks up her glass. 'Damascus. You should go when it settles down.' She doesn't like the division she works for, and is hopeful that she can transfer from Rudi's to Udo's section as soon as they return to Damascus. 'It's no secret,' she confides, 'the tensions between Rudi and Udo,' she holds her hand high to indicate an upper level, 'and between Udo and Henning and Kraiz.' She lowers her hand. 'When it collapses, that's when I move in.'

'Why would it collapse?'

'They have a situation. A disagreement. Let's just say that someone has been a little too ambitious.' She leans forward again to whisper. 'He's making all of these arrangements for a transfer before the decision is made. The cost is outrageous. Do you know how much security it will take to monitor a hospital? Can you imagine the expense?'

Berens says he has no idea.

'The last thing they want is the British involved, so where does he make the arrangements?' Carla leans back for emphasis, then mouths. 'Only Limassol. Limassol is practically Britain with their little bases nearby. Akrotiri and Episkopi.' Carla combs her hair behind her ears.

'If they want a burns unit they should take him home. Berlin,' she nods, 'or one of the university hospitals. He's using this man to build his career.'

'Udo?'

'God no. Henning. Henning Bastian.'

'And when will this happen?'

Carla scrunches up her nose. 'Oh, who knows? Udo's going over in a couple of days. And anyway, the man might not even survive.'

'Henning?'

'No.' She laughs, gives a little scoff. 'You're funny. You are a very funny man.'

Berens realizes he's in the wrong city. He spends an hour talking with Geezler explaining the details. Henning Bastian is planning to transfer the patient, Sutler Number Three, to Cyprus. To Limassol. Geezler is pleased. This is looking much more manageable.

'Only information,' he counsels. 'Do nothing without my instruction.'

LIMASSOL

11.1

Tomas follows Rike and the supervisor down the stairs. The supervisor is so small that with Rike behind him, and Tomas behind her, he can see only the man's arms swinging as he scurries down the steps. Rike, a talker when she's nervous, keeps the little man occupied. So the supervisor pays her more attention. Which is exactly the point.

She's gone before they look at the room. Changed her mind. There isn't much to see in any case, the back end of an oblong bunker packed with crates of Keo beer, and what look to be promotional decorations: two sooty and gruff polar bears, an animatronic reindeer, and penguins in different poses (some realistic, some cartoonish with scarves and hats and skates), and what look like rolls of thick white cotton that will stand in for fields of snow – this is what he can see from the door. The rest of the space, about eight by eight metres, has been hastily cleared. The landlord guarantees that whatever is stored here can be removed. The door, with a damaged lock, has to be wedged open because the handle is missing from the inside. The landlord also promises to have that fixed. 'You get stuck in here without a key,' he says with a little snicker, 'and you won't be getting out.' The man responsible for all of this used to work for Keo breweries, he's now working across the road for the hospital if Tomas wants to have a word with him.

Tomas says he isn't worried. He has no intention of being associated with the hospital in any way. Although he needs to know more details, even now, he doesn't want any kind of connection that maps him here, now.

The hotel, a bare structure, is nothing more than a series of cast concrete platforms, with heavy pillars, an iron framework and almost no walls – the floors stand open, and look something like a high-rise car park. The second storey provides the most sheltered vantage point, but the best view is from the rooftop under the cupola. It's not unpleasant to lie on the concrete and feel the draught running over his back.

From the cupola level he can see into the living room, the kitchen beyond – it's all one open space, more or less, divided by a small banquette. To the right of the living room lies Rike's room, after that the bathroom with its small frosted window. Her sister's bedroom is on the far side, which he can't see. From the cupola, if he stands up – if it's night – he can see into the garden, but not much of it. If Rike and her sister sit outside, then he has a great view. But the compound wall, the fig tree beside the bathroom, and a larger lemon tree block the remaining view.

He watches them in the evening. Sits with binoculars trained on the apartment. Rike cooks and Isa watches. The way they move when they speak shows them to be wary. Isa is more open. Rike, in everything she does, appears tight and controlled.

11.2

The days are long and unpleasant. It takes longer than he likes to prepare for the lessons. He regrets his choice of source material, the Finn Cullman book isn't popular, but from what he's found on the internet, a film based on the story had a limited release in Europe to art-house cinemas. Committed, he works out a timeline, collects the information into manageable blocks. He thinks of this as a kind of architecture. Each project is a purpose-built structure for one-time use. It's a pity that no one will ever know. Although this *unknown-ness* is part of his craft.

Very little of what he uncovers is useful – there's no way of knowing this when he starts. He works standing up, papers spread across the counter and stove top.

When he comes across useable material he tears the pages out of the book, writes notes, then sets the notes and pages in order. It doesn't need to take as long as it does.

This is the only time Tomas wants to smoke. He stands in the kitchen, stooped over papers. A coffee in his left hand, his right hand unoccupied, shifting paper for the sake of it. Even after four years he still misses smoking. To make sure he tells a story the same way he's told it before, he practises speaking out loud. Gives the same detail. Doesn't deviate. Never improvises.

There's a nice duplication in today's story, which he could use straight, but has an idea that it could be fashioned more appropriately. It's a simple anecdote: while researching his book on the murders in

Naples, the author hired an assistant. The assistant, a university student, sets up meetings ahead of the visit, and is generally helpful. Once the author arrives things don't go so cosily. There isn't any chemistry and the men don't particularly like each other. One night the author receives a call telling him that the assistant has been kidnapped. For some reason the author is suspicious, the calls aren't necessarily credible. When the author returns to his hotel he discovers the whole thing was set up as a run-around to get him out of the room so he can be robbed. Everything is gone. He doesn't see or hear of the assistant again. Rather than return home, the writer, robbed and dejected, starts the project over. Right from scratch.

The story has potential use, but the details aren't distinct enough. Sometimes that's just how it goes.

Everything now depends on plausibility. Circumstances have meant some *stretching*, which he doesn't like. As Rike is new to Cyprus it's unlikely that she can check in too much detail, and right now there's simply no reason for her to doubt him. He's lucky, if she knew more people it wouldn't work. If she asked the neighbours she'd learn enough to invalidate much of what he's told her. At some point, he knows, Rike is going to do some homework. She'll get online. She'll check out the neighbours. She'll pick out one detail and discover the source. Having used the story about the murder already, it's starting to sound absurd. When it drops, when the idea collapses, it will thunder down. He's hopeful that this won't happen immediately.

He doesn't have to do it this way. He knows. He could get to the same place quicker with cruder means, or by simply being patient. This is, after all, what he does – *almost nothing*. Stick to the room, assess what is happening, move incrementally. Baby steps.

Tomas calls Geezler to let him know that he is in place. He needs a decision.

This isn't going the way he wants. Hasn't from the start. There's a low-lying discomfort at how everything has steadily become unworkable.

He doesn't tell Geezler about the stories, about Rike, or about the basement. Geezler doesn't need to be concerned. What he needs from Geezler is a decision. *Which one does he go for first?*

He waits for the call: 10am, 2pm, 6pm, the usual times, but there's no word.

*

He works on another approach. A backup. The basement is easy to pre-pare. He buys expanding foam and fills the ducts and the inside of the air vent. The vinegar stink of the chemical as it expands gives him a headache and he's obliged to return to the stairs, to open the door and allow a draught.

Down in the basement again, he has to unpack the crates to reach the furthest vent. The only air that could come in to the room now would be through the door, and that, when he closes it from the out-side, appears tight.

He doesn't know how long it would take to exhaust the room of oxygen, and doubts that this would be possible. But it would become hot and intensely uncomfortable, enough to discourage action, enough to make the subject weary, weak. The room is deep enough that any noise would be contained.

Berens re-attaches a pulley system to the door, a counterweight which automatically slams it closed. He oils the hinges and uses foam to fill the hole left by the inside handle. While working on these final touches, he secures two pieces of wood as a wedge to ensure that the door will not close and he will not become trapped.

11.3

Rike insists on taking the lesson outside. He loses confidence while talking about the assault, a story he wishes he hadn't used. She com-plains about her brother, tells a pitiful story about her sister, and repeats what he already knows about the man in Damascus. Bastian returned two days ago, and the patient was airlifted yesterday. Rike isn't clear about which hospital they've brought him to: Limassol or Akrotiri.

While he's patient, Tomas is also ready to exploit chance and possi-bility. Discussions with Rike which might feed into the structure. Having something work to plan is preferable, but the tedium of it means he often entertains other notions. A well-considered idea is like an object suspended, which can be re-approached, improved on each consideration. This is the best way he has of explaining the satisfac-tions of his work. It's all about craft.

If he's honest she isn't exactly forthcoming. She knows precious little about Sutler, and Bastian, now he's back from Syria, sounds even more reticent on the subject. He's getting a limited return for all of his work.

And still no word from Geezler.

Tomas returns to the basement for a final check. He brings with him a pack of six large water bottles, and leaves them inside the door. He isn't sure about the noise now. He remembers a scene from a film (this has bothered him all night), where a man, father to two very pretty girls, who is planning to bury someone alive, asks his daughters to scream. They are in a forest. Remote. It's fun, he tells them. It's a game. The daughters shriek and holler loud enough to test, to make sure that, whatever the noise, however loud, he can be confident no one is going to hear it. They do this without knowing what is being asked of them.

As the café is across the street, Tomas thinks it's worth testing. He'll have to play the role of the daughters himself – if this doesn't work, then he'll need to find another method. If someone comes to find out what the noise is about then he won't be able to use the basement. The risk is larger, now he's faced with it, than he'd first realized. It's getting too late to make mistakes.

He's surprised by how uncomfortable it is to walk into the room, it's airless, and he immediately begins to sweat. His brow, his back. It's incredibly close. The chemical smell from the previous day has cured, and is replaced with a musty stink. Strong. Cold concrete. Mould.

He bangs a stick against the wall. Timid at first, and then with force. Then shouting: *Hey, hey, hey, hey*. He can't do this for very long as he quickly becomes dizzy.

He shouts. His voice breaks with the heat, yodels and cracks. He tries again, but just can't grab the air. It isn't impossible, but he doubts that he could sustain it.

This doesn't take long. He cleans up after himself, leaves, and then returns, takes out the light bulb and throws it behind the stack of decorations. Once the door is shut it will not open from inside.

With the room soundproofed, Tomas leaves a message for Geezler then waits for a call. He needs a decision. When Geezler doesn't call, he goes to the wasteland behind Rike's apartment, and takes with him a pair of binoculars and a water bottle.

Tomas returns to the hotel and sits behind the concrete columns in the lower section until the sun falls behind the brewery. Boys play in the street and while he can't see them he can hear them. The boys settle into their game, and the soft punch of the ball, their shouts and hollers carry across the scruff.

He watches a taxi arrive at the front of the apartment. A man pays, sees the cab off, stands outside to smoke. He paces in front of the entrance, ducks to read the names, takes a long draw from his cigarette and backs away, clearly nervous.

Inside, Rike stands with her back to the living area. She works at the counter beside the sink, preparing what looks to be a salad. Picks what she needs from the fridge. Even in this she's hesitant. Her hand hovers uncertain in front of the shelves. Isa doesn't appear to be doing much of any purpose. Rike's industry appears to irritate her and she picks at details, points at things in the living room, demanding attention. The few houseplants are inspected, a coffee table is pushed square. For a moment she looks directly out, straightens up and draws her top straight, checks her reflection in the long glass doors.

He can't see the man for the moment. He paces at the corner, so that Tomas's view is obscured. And when Tomas looks back to the living room Isa has also gone. Rike, now on her own, checks the kitchen drawers, finds the cutlery, counts out the settings, checks the place mats. She leaves these together on the counter, clearly busy. She looks into the apartment. Appears to be talking as she settles her hair behind her ears. Tomas draws the focus to her face, steadies the lens. Is that anger? Is she irritated? She appears to give in, becomes suddenly active, walks round the island and begins to set the table. Once she is done Isa returns, her purple top changed for an orange one with a wide collar, slightly clownish. She points at the table, then further to the garden, and makes wafting gestures. Rike stands with her hands on her hips. She nods and shrugs, her expression watchful but guarded, again, he thinks, irritated.

Henning comes out, dressed in a sports top with short sleeves and old-mannish long trousers. Both Rike and Henning face each other and wait. Neither appears to be talking.

The man, back outside the apartment, walks directly to the door, ducks at the console and presumably presses the apartment bell. Inside Isa immediately turns.

The greetings are stilted. This must be the brother, *Mattaus*, it has to be. Tomas steadies the binoculars and focuses closer. The man's anxiety translates into sudden gestures. Rike barely moves when she kisses him, does not return his hug. Henning shakes hands and almost immediately turns away, and while it becomes evident that he's offering Mattaus a drink, it's clear that Mattaus is all at sea.

The sound of an ambulance passes through the city, close but unseen.

There is a resemblance: Rike, Isa, Mattaus. The brow line, their dark eyes and dark hair. Long, angular faces.

There are two sets of gestures in the apartment, easily distinguished. The awkward stillness of Rike and Henning, and the more expressive gestures of Mattaus and Isa. These couples pair up at the dining table, Rike with her back to the window. She sits with one hand at her side. Tomas again focuses in. Sometimes she tucks her hand under the seat, other times she runs her fingernails along the wood rail. Isa's hands hover just above the table, are animated; she describes shapes, is unresting, draws designs in the air as she speaks. Mattaus's hands flutter busy about his face. Touching his nose, wiping the back of his neck, animated also, but evidently demonstrating his anxiety. Henning is the only one who does not move. He watches, as if from a distance.

There is a moment when they all seem to lean in, as if to listen, their bodies tighten. Mattaus laughing, Isa laughing, and Rike shortly on her feet in the kitchen.

At the kitchen Rike's movements become autonomic. Mattaus remains excitable. Isa laughs, head forward, head back. And then a sudden change.

Tomas, so focused on his subject, realizes that he can no longer hear the children playing football. Darker now, there's no light in the building site, the street behind the apartments is also unlit, and the sky striates into two parallel purple bands, each quickly darkening. He lies on the concrete absorbing the radiant heat, widens his legs so his feet can rest flatter. He thinks himself out of the picture, less solid than air. A rising wind picks up heat and feathers through the empty and open building.

Inside the apartment an argument gathers force. New boundaries are drawn. Rike and Isa at the sink, Henning and Mattaus at the table. Combative in his gestures, Henning can't keep still, his legs jigger under the table. He balls up the napkin in his fist, releases it, aggressively shakes his head with tight and emphatic movement. Isa, in contrast to her husband, has become less animated, stands as if stuffed. Rike, who is facing Tomas, is similarly transformed, appears to suppress a smile, not pleasure so much as disbelief. All of this a bright oblong in the first floor of a darkening block. Other windows are lit up, two or three with closed shutters, no one out on their balconies.

Mattaus shunts back his chair, arms on either side. This motion sparks Tomas into action. If he's not quick enough he'll lose Mattaus. Tomas stands, secure in the darkness, tugs off the short-sleeved shirt he's been wearing inside out, shakes off the dirt and slaps his trousers. He hides the binoculars behind the column, these he can return for later, then, his eye on the apartment, he carefully and quickly picks his way through the open stairs to the ground. Once on the scrubland he begins to sprint, shirt in his hand, until he reaches the fence. Tomas ducks quickly through, the route picked out, anticipated from many such visits. At the street he runs to the compound wall, jumps carefully up, hands on top of the wall, and draws himself to the top where he settles on his forearms.

Inside, through the branches and leaves of the lemon tree, he can see everyone except Henning. Rike, Isa, and Mattaus are standing, Mattaus makes his way to the door by himself.

Tomas lowers himself, then re-dresses. He dusts his trousers again, tucks in his shirt, holds back before the corner, poised to walk.

Mattaus comes out of the lobby alone and at a pace, hands rooting through his pockets as he heads down the street. The night air thick about them. Mattaus walks under the street lights to the chipper quarrel of cicadas.

Tomas looks first to the lobby to make sure no one is following with last hesitant pleas or final words. Mattaus is truly alone, and he walks fast, agitated, stops to dig through his pockets and draw out a phone, a pack of cigarettes. The man immediately lights up, attempts a call, but evidently has no answer or no signal.

The two men walk into town, there being little or no traffic until they are down at the waterfront. Mattaus holds his head back and huffs out smoke. Taxis line under the stumpy city walls, and Mattaus walks into the traffic with little caution.

He follows Mattaus along the seafront, his walk now a little more relaxed, and Tomas dithers deliberately, slipping into stalls, hangs back, side-steps tourists, hears languages: Greek, English, Russian, the signage for restaurant in three-tiers, hand-painted and sometimes neon. *Happy Hour. Two-for-One. Keo. Local Wines. Kleftico. BBQ. Fish*

& *Chips*. Ahead of him Rike's brother speaking agitated into his mobile.

They walk to the bay hotels, to the start of the resorts. At the Sovereign Tomas finally stops, and enters a club: Nightingale 1.

The Nightingale 1 is part of the Sovereign Resort complex. The club, a three storey bunker, overlooks the bay. The Sovereign Hotel has its back to the land, and during the day causes a long shadow to sweep the beach, from right to left. For the most part, the beach is obscured. There's a joke that the hotel was built the wrong way round: the steep side facing the water, the sloped side facing the land, but Tomas thinks this isn't the case. It can't be. The pool, for example, being to the side of the hotel, takes the sun almost the whole day through, and this only works because the back is sloped. The rooms and balconies on the seaward side take the shade.

He watches Mattaus and can't understand why the man stays, given how he's ignored by the people he sits with, except one man, the manager, who buzzes about him briefly, then disappears for a good hour. These people, younger, excitable, a nervous edge to them with their sudden enthusiasms and keen bodies, they shout, bicker, go to the toilet cubicles to take drugs because this is the place for such activities, and come out energized and glassy-eyed. This group is watched over by the club's security. As far as he can tell the club is divided into zones. This, anyway, is how it appears to be monitored. Across the club there are other such areas, although the patrons would not know it. There's a certain balance to the excesses here. One boy, Russian, dressed in sports gear, sits at the bar, and keeps a cool eye on the room. Disengaged, but observant.

Tomas finds it hard to watch, even at this distance, and remain uninvolved. His interest at this point is on how he's going to approach Mattaus. Speaking to him directly would be unwise, although he will already be recorded on the club's cameras. Impatient to do something, he understands that tonight might not provide the right opportunity.

A possibility opens later in the evening, when it becomes clear to Tomas that the manager, Mattaus's friend, is robbing the club blind.

Drinks bought at the bar pass through the register, but drinks bought from the waiting staff are unregistered, cash in hand. Money paid at the door is kept in a cash box. The arrangement appears deliberately slack, and only the manager, who collects the takings in a black sack, can have any idea what the takings are at any point, on any given night. The opportunity for the man to help himself is evident. In Tomas's experience, when such a possibility exists, there's usually a taker. He watches with particular interest. The manager comes by almost every sixty to eighty minutes, and counts out the money, makes a note in a small pad, then binds the cash with the note in a rubber band, which he drops into a pouch. It's laughable. He does this without any security. No one oversees his accounting, no one offers him protection.

To test the diligence of the guards, Tomas follows the man through the club from bar to bar, up and down between the levels, and then it happens. As they walk down the stairs Tomas witnesses, to his great satisfaction, the manager reach into the pouch and help himself. So lazy, so incautious; he doesn't even look around him. None of the guards is concerned that the manager is alone while he collects the money. At the top bar he ties a knot in the neck of the bag, then comes back down the staircase to return to his office. The only person distantly aware of Tomas's movements is the boy at the bar.

Before he leaves Tomas steals Mattaus's phone. This is ridiculously easy, a technical move, but not so sophisticated. The man doesn't see him. Tomas keeps to the dark side of the stairs, comes at him from the curve. Mattaus doesn't feel a hand slip into his pocket – and if he did feel something, this sleight of hand, in this kind of club, the gesture would translate as a small intimacy. As it stands, Tomas keeps this nice and tidy. No error involved. Mattaus knows only that a man nudged by him on the stairs, and bumped shoulders.

They leave before the club closes, Mattaus and the manager. Tomas follows after them, but outside, the manager has a car waiting, and Tomas returns to the club and sits at the bar.

The club is still busy, and while the clientele is mixed, the younger ones look worse for wear, except one, the boy in sports gear, who, like Tomas, appears to be watching.

It doesn't take much to get the boy to talk, and Tomas learns that the manager of Nightingale 1, Kolya, runs a private game of poker. Anyone he likes the look of can play as a guest. Kolya likes to win, for many reasons, not least of all for the money, this is his one vice, the single benefit he allows himself with his work, and so the cards are stacked, and once he has their money the guest is escorted out of the club, invariably to a cash machine or a hotel to empty their safety deposit. The boy, Sol, enjoys the drama. It's impossible to tire of that frustration, the inevitability of failure, the sheer breathlessness of their losses.

Sol goes to the toilets, and when he comes back he's a little wired and won't answer his phone. When Tomas asks who is calling he says *Lexi*, with clear dislike. Right now he's supposed to be with Lexi, he should be in Larnaca, but Lexi, who runs Nightingale 2, is such a bore. Sol is working hard to avoid him. He doesn't understand why the others tolerate the man and take him so seriously. Lexi runs the club in Larnaca, and Kolya runs the club in Limassol, there are other duties divided between them. Lexi manages the money, more or less, and Kolya manages the stocks and staff. Which makes them equal. Kolya is certainly more the figure you'd imagine for a nightclub manager: big, brusque, tattoos running fist to fist, while Lexi looks like he should be running a boutique. If there is a hierarchy his worry is that Lexi is possibly the man in control.

Tomas understands that the manager he was watching was Lexi.

The boy won't drop the subject. It's the way people listen to Lexi, give him attention, the way they really seem to like him that gets under his skin, and he doesn't know why. Lexi is a waste of space: the man is so tedious atoms unwind around him, tire of life, cohesion, basic physical principles, everything *undoes*, gives up, DNA unravels, brains melt, entire species evaporate, the universe dissolves.

The people who come to the club, Sol has to admit, aren't so pretty, and charging a higher entrance fee has done nothing to improve the clientele. The talent is seriously lacking. His own compatriots aren't much to go by. Entrance at least requires footwear, shorts or a skirt, some kind of top, but every night they turn away boys in fancy dress or shirtless, stag parties, hen parties, girls in thongs, and one time, a girl in sandals and gold makeup, nothing else. The police in both towns are regular visitors, known by their first names. Kolya has a talent for looking after them. Kolya is a hulking Cossack, hairy shoulders, broad and solid, the man is both architectural and animal, which makes him what? Some kind of a machine. Vast and bald. Sol admits that Kolya looks after him, makes sure he keeps out of trouble. Kolya knows Sol's father, *they've worked together*, which either enhances or complicates their association, although this link is deliberately under-discussed.

Sol's monologue runs freestyle, but returns to Lexi, his pet hate. Tomas wants to know why the manager of the club at Larnaca is here in the evening in Limassol, instead of watching over his own business.

Sol doesn't know the answer, but that's exactly what he's talking about. 'Like there's a specific way everything has to be done.'

The people who know him (namely Kolya, Matti, Max) know not to ask Sol about boarding school, but Lexi won't leave it alone. It's as if Sol's schooling in England, in the US, in Switzerland, is what makes him interesting, when in fact, everybody knows, the school you go to is just about how much money your parents are prepared to spend. Sol's dislike is long established. It isn't that Lexi likes him, not in that way. Sol doesn't have to worry about that. Lexi goes with the dancers, the boys, the 'go-go's', as a consequence Lexi's year, so far, has been a series of sulks and pointless crushes, except now he's met this *Fritz*, this German and everything's hunky-dory. Sol isn't judgemental, he really doesn't mind people like Lexi. That isn't his problem. His problem is that the man doesn't *partake* in the way everyone else partakes in substances and pleasure, and nothing dampens a buzz more than a superior *govno* constantly giving you the disapproving eye. And so what if Lexi really runs the place? You know, it's not like Sol is looking for a career. All he wants, until he starts university, is some major distraction.

Sol asks if Tomas would like a drink. Tomas says he has an idea. He'd like to play cards with the manager. What was his name? Kolya?

Sol looks at him, a little astonished. 'You can't win.'

'Perhaps. I'd like to figure out how he does it.'

The boy appears to understand but doesn't move.

'I'm serious. Go see if he's interested.'

'You'll lose.'

Tomas shrugs. 'I'll lose,' he says, 'but I'll learn how he does it.'

Kolya agrees to a game. He sends over drinks, then sits with him. Sol sits separately and watches as Kolya and Tomas become acquainted. The small booths at the back of the club are intimate enough, under-lit against the cavernous dance floor, but the sound bounces, is so enhanced, so deep and penetrating, that every conversation is busy with head ducking, repetition, gestures.

He follows Sol and Kolya through the club to the lower office. They each walk in pace to the beat. Once Sol notices this he breaks his stride. Kolya holds the office door open and asks why Sol is smiling.

Lit by a line of fluorescent light, the office is small and cluttered with equipment, buckets, and crates, and the smell reminds Tomas of boiled cabbage. He gives small answers to Kolya's questions but clearly wants the game to start. When it does start, he loses every hand.

Kolya asks Sol to accompany Berens to the ATM. As they walk they make small talk.

He asks Tomas if he learned anything.

'How he does it?'

Tomas nods, thoughtfully. 'Possibly. I have an idea.'

'And you don't mind?'

'Mind?'

'Losing?'

Kolya has no respect for losers, not in the club, and not out of it. Sol holds the same ideas. 'We own this island. They don't even know how much. They have no idea. They like this,' he can't think of the word, '*half-ness*. They like to be known only for their disagreement. Everyone in this country is an amateur.'

The national debt is a subject of deep distaste to Kolya and Sol alike. Both value business and business ethics, and deeply mistrust the idea of compounded debt. That an entire nation would impoverish itself without knowing what it is doing is pathetic. A kind of death. It's worse that they accept help, and seem happy to be weak. He calls them zombies. Undead. It isn't that Europe is corrupt, so much, as weak and slothful. Yes, sloth. This is the nature of their greed. There have been demonstrations, which makes Sol suck in breath between his teeth. Water cannon. Rubber bullets. Hoses. When people lose their houses they will properly understand their folly.

Tomas takes the money from the machine, counts it into Sol's hand. He tells him to be careful walking back. Sol thinks this is funny, how some men speak to him as if he were still a boy.

11.4

On the Monday Rike comes to the apartment early, deliberately, she says, because she wants to try out a new café. Her sister has rated the mozzarella as *unsurpassable*. It's the real thing, proper buffalo mozzarella. Isa is an authority, and now she is pregnant she's not allowed to eat cheese with any kind of live culture. In this café they keep the mozzarella in a clear plastic barrel filled with briny-looking milt (it actually looks like breast milk). According to Isa this is the freshest mozzarella outside of Italy. If you want it any fresher you'd have to lay under a buffalo's teat.

She looks tired. Tomas asks her how she is, says that she doesn't look her usual self, and gives a good smile, as if it might matter to him that she is out of sorts.

'My brother,' Rike delivers the news without emphasis, 'came over on Saturday.' She rubs her face, runs her hand alongside her nose. It's an ungracious gesture, a range of expression he hasn't seen from her before. 'It was awful. Just awful.'

'What happened?'

'I can't describe it. Just, *horrible*. And my sister. I couldn't believe it was happening. When he left he was really angry. We don't know where he is.' Rike grimaces. 'This is just like him. He makes a mess of everything then disappears, and leaves everyone else to clear up. When I first arrived, Henning warned me about things I shouldn't do while I was in Cyprus. His work is sensitive. If things even look wrong he could be sent back to Germany and they would never return to Syria. It's a huge pressure for him. Even Isa takes this seriously. On some level it just doesn't register with Mattaus. He just doesn't care how much it matters to other people.'

Mattaus has always been selfish. That's his problem. But nobody sees this. Everybody *likes* him. (She just can't believe this. How does it happen?) Everybody sees what he wants them to see. He manipulates people and they just don't get it. He attracts the nicest men, and it always ends badly. Always.

Tomas agrees. She's probably right. But this is family, right? Don't sisters always disapprove?

'I didn't even know he was in Cyprus.' Rike shrugs. 'We'll not hear from him, and then one day, out of the blue, he'll show up, expecting everything to be forgiven. He'll make a joke out of it. A story. *Remember that time . . .*'

'And for your brother-in-law, has he made much trouble?'

'I really don't know. Henning takes it all pretty seriously. It'll probably blow over, but Henning is the kind of man who'd feel obliged to tell someone about it. And that would be very unwise. It's just a bad situation. Mattaus said he recognized your name?'

'It's common. Berens. Not so rare.'

Rike shakes her head. That wasn't it, he *recognized* the name. *Placed it.*

'Sometimes it's a first name. But in German it's a shortened version of "baron" which means "freeman". In Norwegian it's a little different and it means "bear", wild bear.'

The question or statement about her brother is lost, and if she even thinks about it now, which he doubts, she'll imagine that the subject is closed.

Rike starts the lesson and the idea of going somewhere else is passed over. 'Today,' she says, 'we talk about aspirations. What I would like, what I hope for. What I would want to see.' These are, she says, conditional clauses. Tough to master, and she would like to see him demonstrate them.

This is almost too easy now. Tomas uses the example, Finn Cullman in Naples. It's satisfying to find a use for it.

'I've always wanted to write,' he says, 'not fiction but real stories. What has happened to other people. This is what I like to read. I've taken it seriously and once I hired a researcher, but he took advantage of me. It didn't go so well.'

Rike nods as she listens.

'I think it would be good to write about something current. I don't know, but it is interesting to me, the stories you have been telling me about this man they found in the desert. It is always more interesting when these stories are true, no?'

Rike agrees. It is much more interesting.

'I mean you have to wonder who he really is, and why he walked so far. What would make someone do that. I think that would be interesting. To nervier people who are involved. To investigate. I don't know. Maybe even help.' He stops short of making a more direct appeal and turns the conversation to another subject.

By the end of the session Rike is looking pleased. 'Tomorrow,' she says, 'we should try that mozzarella.'

'Tomorrow,' Tomas answers, 'the weather is supposed to stay nice. We should do something different.'

He isn't sure just what to suggest, but one more opportunity to learn something from her, to take her close to the military base to prompt more information on Sutler. 'There is a beach you know. Lady's Mile. You like to swim?'

Rike, suddenly coy, says that she likes to swim very much. Tomorrow, then, it is agreed, a picnic, a swim, at Lady's Mile beach.

After the lesson Tomas watches Rike walk up the street. This is wasting time. He should be more direct. Even with the suggestion posed today he can't guarantee that she will return with any information. He looks out toward the hospital and waits for a call from Geezler, knowing instinctively that there is little time to waste. Tomas has everything he needs. From this point he needs to work decisively, with intent.

Geezler has unsettling news from Italy. 'They have a photograph of you. Parson's wife took a photograph and she has passed it on to the police. If they make this public, it's a possible problem. The picture is clear, it looks like you. Even in Cyprus I think you'll have a difficult time explaining this.'

They discuss their options. Information from Rike has been limited. It isn't working as expected. Geezler decides: stop wasting time on the sister, use the brother. Mattaus. Tonight.

11.5

Tomas isn't properly dressed for a night out. He unbuttons the top two shirt buttons, untucks the tail, smooths his hair. At the Bank of Cyprus, he draws out cash then heads to the club. By the time he arrives Mattaus will be settled with the same group as before. Lexi will be roaming, collecting money. At some early hour they will return to Larnaca. He does not doubt that their evenings follow the same pattern.

Tomas walks with one hand in his pocket, more self-conscious than usual, given the possibility that he could be recognized and associated with Parson's death. The air, sweet with grilled meats from the roadside restaurants, reminds him that he hasn't eaten. It's easy to forget those details. The harbour lights darken at the kerb, so the sea is hidden but present as a faint, over-ripe stink of fish, or fish waste.

When he arrives at the club he finds Mattaus and Lexi on the sidewalk ready to leave. Mattaus, highly animated, aggravated, in conversation with Lexi. Lexi's face is long, his jaw sharpened by a slight overbite. He appears sulkier than before and weary. He holds his hand out to halt a car, his car, and takes the keys without a word. Tomas has as good as lost them.

He searches through the club for Kolya. As he comes up the stairs Tomas can feel the music pulse in his chest. Blood-red walls, heat, and a synthetic heartbeat, is that what makes these places so familiar? Kolya isn't about, instead he finds the boy, Sol, and lets him know that he wants to speak with Kolya. Can he set this up? He can do that, right?

The boy looks surprised. If it's about the card game, the money, it would be better for Tomas to leave everything alone. Just forget it.

'This is about something else. I think he'll want to hear this.'

Sol pauses, still doubtful, but Tomas assures him this is for Kolya's benefit.

'Someone is stealing from the club.' Tomas makes a gesture like he isn't bothered either way, and the boy slips away.

Sol returns immediately with Kolya, who invites Tomas to a booth. Tonight the man wears a white singlet which shows a tattoo on either shoulder: the talons of a beast mounting his back, the nails piercing the skin.

He asks Tomas if he would like a drink. Tomas immediately asks after Lexi. 'The manager from the other club. The man who deals with the money.'

Kolya has a scar on his neck, a small, smooth puncture. He asks why they are talking about Lexi. The men lean toward each other to be heard over the music.

'How much do you think you're losing each night?' Tomas's voice is strained. 'How much do you think he's taking? You think he takes from both clubs? Or maybe just yours?'

Kolya coughs into his hand and asks what Tomas is talking about.

'The other manager, who collects the money. Do you have any idea how much he's taking?'

Tomas can't help but stretch his neck, twist his head from side to side. He waits for the music to change so that he does not need to shout. 'I'm here for the German, the man he brings here. I can tell you how he's doing this. But I want the German. I want to know where his friend is staying.'

'What is your interest in this?'

'It's separate. This is something different. I need to know where he is staying.'

Kolya folds his arms. 'So how? How is this happening?'

Tomas rubs his face, takes his time to answer. 'It's simple. He collects the money himself. How long is he here before he goes to the other club? Two hours? Three. So he collects the takings every hour, two or three times a night. You have no record of what is coming in, except what you collect yourself at the end.'

Kolya begins to smile and it occurs to Tomas that he is making a mistake. It's entirely possible that he hasn't witnessed a theft at all, but something which can be otherwise explained. It's possible that the theft is of no consequence, both managers appear to run a little rene-gade: Lexi's thievery, Kolya's gambling.

'This is nothing.'

'He takes the money on the stairwell, between levels. There are no cameras on the second stairwell.' Tomas explains that the system isn't clever, it's snatch and grab, essentially, so simple you'd only know it was happening if you saw it with your own eyes. Perhaps he has this wrong, he admits. It's possible.

He wants information on the German. He wants a guarantee, if he's right, that Kolya won't act on this information tonight.

Berens returns to his apartment, showers and changes. He picks up his car and drives to Larnaca, then further, following Kolya's directions beyond the airport toward the cape. The air here is swampy, damp from the sea. On high tide the land floods, and the road sparkles with sea salt. Another salt flat, considerably larger than the one at Akrotiri, runs alongside the road and beyond this a small village built on a flood plain, on what was once a malarial swamp. He follows Kolya's map with ease, because there isn't much to it, three right turns in the entire drive. The final section has no street lights. He continues along the road which dips down and levels out at the edge of the salt flats. The road continues straight. Tomas dims his headlights and drives toward an area of palm trees, a grove which shelters a single building, and when he comes to the bungalow Lexi has recently hired he finds the gates closed, the lights off, no sign of the car. No one at home.

He takes his time. He drives the car further down the track, not hidden, but out of view.

It's simple luck that the bedroom shutters are raised enough to allow air into the room. The grille covering the lower pane is loosely fixed to the wall and comes away with little persuasion. This is basi-cally an invitation.

Tomas slides into the room and slips feet first onto the bed. He sets himself carefully down and turns on the bedroom light. There's little sign of intimacy in the room. The bed is unmade. There are clothes scattered to one side. Two pillows lie lengthwise down the centre, and it appears that only one person has slept here. At the end of the bed, side by side, are one small holdall and three large suitcases. Inside the holdall he finds a set of freshly laundered clothes and a wash-bag which contains condoms, hair gel, small samples of aftershave. Lexi is leaving. The drawers and closets are empty. Tomas lifts the valance and looks under the bed. There is nothing to be found in the entire room. No indication either of where he might be going.

Disappointed, Tomas opens the bathroom door and discovers, inside, sat on its hind legs, a dog. A svelte black Dobermann.

But of course, a dog.

Tomas does not move.

The dog does not move. Neither does it growl.

They are, it appears, locked together: Tomas standing by the door, the dog seated beside the shower. Across the floor lie scattered scraps of the shower mat the dog has ripped to pieces.

Tomas remains absolutely still, his hand on the door handle, then, slowly he starts to retreat. The dog dips its head and growls, a small overture, but a growl. An introduction to trouble. He can't shut the door. At any movement, his best guess, the dog will lunge, and he will need to jump back and pull the door closed. It's doubtful that he can manage this. The Dobermann sits the same distance from Tomas as Tomas stands from the bedroom. The odds aren't great.

The dog breaks the impasse.

First, it urinates in a half squat. A broadening puddle on the tiled floor. A pool which joins, dot to dot, the scraps of torn matting, and takes an unnecessary amount of time. The dog looks at him as it pisses. Eye to eye. Intentional.

Second, it yawns, and shows, even in the slice of light spilling from the bedroom, a strong set of teeth.

Third, it stands up, walks by Tomas, and sits square in front of the bedroom door.

The dog looks from the door to Tomas to the door. It's a slow series of movements, brimming with expectation.

Tomas returns to the bedroom. One step at a time. He keeps his movements controlled, limited only to what is necessary. He steadies his breath. He creeps back to the window, and begins to sneak wide of the bed and the dog.

As soon as Tomas approaches the bed, the dog begins to growl.

It isn't much of a threat: a guttural roll. Almost sub-sonic. A warning.

The dog makes no complaint when he approaches the bedroom

door, and when he opens it the dog trots through. The house is silent except for the dog's claws on the tiles. Then, right in the hall, right before the doormat, the Dobermann again positions herself so that she can watch him while she squats and takes a long slow piss. The same in the living room. The same in the kitchen. In each room the dog silently demands entrance, and then urinates. Copiously.

Finally Tomas takes a seat in the sitting room, on a white couch. The room, even in the darkness, is too *mannered*. White carpets, white furnishings, white walls, white paintings flecked with texture, a mania for white.

The dog sits up alert. Ears pricked. Watching him. Watching the exits.

A car turns into the driveway. On the side table is a heavy onyx lighter. He waits for the key to turn in the lock. The lighter handsomely fits his grip, his fingers comfortably span the stone. Hungry, his stomach tightens and growls. For a moment the dog turns to look at him. Then back to the door. Tomas flexes his hands, then stretches his arms to his shoulders. He takes deep breaths, sits forward. Ready.

First the dog – *make your intentions clear, define your terms* – second, the thief, Olexei.

The lights come on in the hall, and he hears Lexi's exasperation, swearing, in Russian, from the door. It's clear he's alone. Mattaus is not with him. Tomas listens. There are two conversations. The greeting, in Russian, to the dog, and a conversation on the phone, in English. The dog, now sat in the doorway between the sitting room and the hall, is delicately focused, poised. A picture.

Tomas listens as Lexi speaks. Is he inside? Or is he still at the door?

'No. I've said. I'm done. That's what I'll tell them – *pause* – You're getting shit from your family. I'm taking shit every day. At some point you just have to stop and consider if it's worth it – *pause* – If they won't let me – *pause* – What do you mean if they won't let me. They don't have a choice – *pause* – With Kolya? What about him? – *pause* – I'll just tell him. This is how it is. I don't want to do this any more – *pause* – You need to replace your phone. No. I'll bring you one. No. You don't need to. Forget it. I'll give you one.' There's more frustration. 'I come home and she's shit all over the place. I shut her in the bathroom, in the en suite, and she manages to get out. The house is full of – *pause* – You can imagine.' (He's still only in the hall.) 'I can't stand it. It smells so bad in here. Something has to happen. I don't know. I don't want to think about it, but I think I have to do something. Maybe she's senile. Maybe? I don't know – *pause* – Later, then. Yes. An hour. It's so late I don't think so – *pause* – OK, in an hour. Truss.'

When Lexi comes into the sitting room he turns the light on, then stops, just freezes when he sees Tomas.

Tomas fixes Lexi, a dry welcome, not unexpected. Lexi slips his phone into his pocket and looks for a moment like he might run.

Lexi speaks in Russian. His voice quiet. He sets a bag at his feet. Slowly, as if repressing the urge to react, to give himself away. His hand grips and ungrasps.

'Speak to me in English.' Tomas invites Lexi to sit down. Lexi holds a second bag in his hands. Tomas holds out his hand and Lexi crosses the room and passes him the bag, then sinks slowly onto the opposite couch.

Has he ever met anyone so malleable?

Inside the bag is a good deal of money. The notes bound together again with rubber bands. The night's takings from the club, which should, Tomas guesses, be secure in a safe. Tomas resists making comments. He looks into the bag, indifferent, then sets the bag aside. Money makes sense to Tomas in situations where it's lacking, where people are struggling, and where the gaining of it has meaning. That's why it's called *currency*. But here, in a smart house, expensively furnished, in Cyprus no less, he finds it squalid. He can empathize with most situations and predicaments, understands all other cardinal sins, except greed. Greed he finds intolerable, ugly.

'Kolya?'

'I said speak to me in English.'

Lexi swallows before making himself clear. His voice comes sticky and particular. 'Kolya sent you?'

Tomas shakes his head.

Lexi, already crestfallen, slumps lower in his seat. 'Lev.' This is a statement, not a question.

Tomas can't help but smile. On one hand the situation is writing itself. On the other it's much more complex than he would like it.

'Lev.'

Tomas picks a thread out of his mouth. A dog hair, short and coarse.

Lexi looks at the wet patch in the middle of the carpet – in outline, not unlike Alaska – then back to Tomas.

They remain looking at each other, Lexi weighted with sorrow.

'I can call someone? There is someone I would like to speak to.'

Tomas shakes his head and Lexi gently nods.

'I can get you the money. You want to know where the money is?'

'This is no longer about the money.'

Again Lexi nods.

'Please.' His voice now grainy and small. 'I would like to call some-one. He is expecting me.' Lexi draws deep, uneven breaths in an attempt to hold his dignity. The man shivers, and can't steady the vibration breaking his words. 'I would like to explain to him. I don't think he will understand.'

Tomas again shakes his head.

Lexi looks at him directly. 'He has nothing to do with this. Please. He has nothing to do with this. You have me. Take the money. Please.'

The dog, without regard to either of them, patters behind Lexi's couch, looks to Tomas, squats and pees again.

'What's wrong with your dog?'

'The dog?'

Tomas has to repeat the question, as the question, clearly, is off-script. 'The dog. The dog.'

Lexi's brow unfurrows slightly, perhaps hopeful. 'She has diabetes.'

'What's her name?'

'Her name?'

'Don't ask me. I'm asking you. What is the name of your dog?'

'Mishka.'

Tomas sits forward, his elbows on his knees. 'I want you to kill your dog. Take a knife from the kitchen and kill your dog. I want you to put this animal out of its misery.'

Lexi is struck with grief. His expression slips register, becomes honest, mouth slightly open, his brow creased, sorrowful and pained. He rises, ageing right before Tomas's eyes, he shakes, appears unstable, turns to go to the kitchen, but isn't able to take the steps, to move his feet. The man can't stand completely upright, can't straighten himself. It's also clear that Lexi is so terrified that he will do whatever Tomas demands, perhaps with the hope that whatever happens to him, what-ever Tomas has in mind, it will be swift and decent.

Tomas now actively dislikes him. A man should always have dignity. He regrets the direction this has taken.

The walk to the kitchen takes a long time. It's probably not a good idea to tell him to get a knife. But Lexi isn't thinking, is in some animal state where he'll do whatever Tomas tells him. Tomas lets him walk to the kitchen, and when the man doesn't come right out he follows after.

Lexi stands over the counter with a steak knife to his ribs, testing, finding a proper space between them. The man is shaking so badly he can't hold the knife steady. Tomas picks a cup up from the counter. He knows these situations, knows exactly what to do. Push the event off-kilter.

'Tea?' he says, holding the cup at eye level.

To Lexi, this is nonsense. Exactly as it should be.

Tomas punches him in the temple with the cup, and Lexi's head hits the kitchen cupboard. Tomas punches again, left hook, without the cup, left temple, to knock him out. He isn't sure that Lexi is unconscious, but the knife is free. One blow, blunt and certain, and Lexi won't be the same person when he wakes.

Tomas picks up the knife and tells himself that enough is enough.

The Russian wakes and finds himself laid out on the couch, a wet towel wrapped about his head, and Tomas sat at the edge of the opposite couch with a cup of tea. Tomas has had a shower. His hair is neatly combed. The dog is missing.

'Where were you going?' Tomas points the cup to the bedroom. 'The suitcases. Where did you think you'd go?'

Lexi attempts to sit upright, fails, appears to be looking for his dog.

'Where's the German?'

'He doesn't know anything.'

'Concentrate on the question.' Tomas speaks very slowly, and hopes he didn't hit Lexi too hard. 'Where is Mattaus Falsen? I want to know where he is.'

Lexi's head jolts on hearing Mattaus's name. 'Limassol. He's staying in Limassol.'

'Now you're lying to me.'

'He's in Limassol. I took him back to his hotel before I came here.'

'In Limassol?'

Lexi nods.

'Which hotel?'

The man refuses to answer, looks fearfully at Tomas but refuses to answer.

'Tell me the hotel and room number.'

'The Miramar. Room 709.'

'When did you intend to see him next?'

'Tonight. I go back to the club before they close.'

'What time is he expecting you?'

'Four,' Lexi stutters, 'four or five.'

'And were you both intending to leave?'

Again, Lexi nods. 'He thinks this is a holiday.'

'Here's what we're going to do. We're going back to Limassol.'

Lexi gives a cautious nod. His eyes intent on Tomas.

'Good.' Tomas sets the cup down and stands up. 'I have to tell you, this is against my better judgement.'

As Tomas turns the car to the road another dog starts up a bark. A cold yip, sharp in a humid night. Glassy. At this moment it becomes clear to Tomas how problematic this is – the dog, Lexi, have compromised his preparations. It isn't unfixable, but it isn't clean. His decision to stay in the house, on the expectation that Mattaus and Lexi would return together, was, in hindsight, a poor choice. While this is messy, Tomas thinks he can find a satisfactory result. Neither strategy, Rike, Mattaus, is working.

It's possible that he hit Lexi too hard. The man can't focus. Worries about his dog. Can't speak without a stutter, and Tomas hates to hear a stutter. Lexi operates within a bubble in which much of what is spoken is misheard, and Tomas wishes there was a simpler resolve. This idea is too complex. This is what happens when he works ad hoc. He shouldn't be driving at this hour. He shouldn't be wasting time, because this might possibly be a terrible waste of time.

Lexi has trouble giving directions to the hotel. The Miramar is the hotel the Russians use. They party there. They chase the prissy British tourists out. They shock the Scandinavians with their appetites and disregard to civil decency. They misbehave. Mattaus is housed there, licking wounds after a family misunderstanding. Mattaus has no idea how bad his night is about to become. Lexi has an inkling.

Tomas parks in front of the hotel and coaches Lexi in what he will do. He goes through the lobby, he takes the lift. He waits outside the lift for Tomas. He does not go to the room until Tomas arrives. Lexi seems to have it straight. Appears to be composed. It isn't complicated.

Lexi produces a card key from his wallet.

Tomas takes the card key, and tells Lexi he'll meet him outside the elevator on the seventh floor. He doesn't intend to leave Lexi out of his sight for very long, but he doesn't want to be seen entering the hotel.

Tomas comes into the hotel from the pool, finds the stairs and makes his way to the seventh floor without any kind of challenge. Even so, he arrives before Lexi. When the lift doors open Lexi looks different, as if he's used to this level of threat, acclimatized now, dulled. The man complains that he's dizzy. Feels a little sick. He's distracted with it and doesn't want to focus, drifts when Tomas draws his attention to the room.

The room is empty. Mattaus is nowhere: the bed is still made, undisturbed. There's no sign that the room has been used.

Tomas sits Lexi on the bed. 'Where is he? You said he would be here.'

Lexi swears he has no idea, shakes his head. The man speaks to himself in Russian.

Tomas holds Lexi's head between both hands. 'Where is Mattaus Falsen?'

Lexi complains that his head hurts, he needs fresh air. He asks Tomas to open the door. He needs air.

'Where is he?' Tomas shakes Lexi, tries to make him focus. 'Is he in this hotel?'

Lexi nods and then shakes his head. The man won't look him in the eye.

Tomas asks him what he's done.

Tomas goes to the balcony and opens up the curtain, the door and the screen.

'What have you done?'

He feels some admiration now. Lexi is fighting back in some small way.

'Is someone coming?'

Lexi complains that he can't breathe.

'Why did it take you so long to get to the room?'

Lexi doesn't answer.

'He doesn't use this room, does he?'

Lexi softly nods.

'And have you called him and warned him?'

Again, Lexi nods.

'Do you know where he is at all?'

Lexi mutters a reply. Tomas asks him to repeat himself.

'I told him to go. I don't know where he will be.'

Tomas beckons Lexi forward and asks again what he has done.

Lexi looks partly over his shoulder at the open balcony door. The pool.

'You're not leaving this room,' Tomas whispers in his ear, the tone is final, and Lexi's face sets back in the same expression he'd had when he'd first set eyes on Tomas.

Pushed or jumped, it doesn't matter. Lexi falls without noise. No shouting. Face out, perhaps in hope. Pitched forward. Arms wheeling. A long way from the pool. The impact is a compact sound, final enough to be only exactly what it is. A body hitting concrete. It doesn't bring the chaos Tomas expected. And he thinks that this wrong, that such an incident should bring no attention seems a little obscene.

If Mattaus is on the run, Tomas admits that he'd probably not find him.

He takes out Mattaus's phone. Carefully wipes it, then drops it onto the floor. He nudges it under the bed, just far enough. This now, is far from the shape and dimension he had determined.

He sits in the car, watches the police arrive, the ambulance. Satisfied with what he's done with the phone (an uncannily smart idea), he asks himself if this could have played out any differently. Although Lexi misunderstood who Tomas was, he read the situation, understood the result, and Tomas wonders if this couldn't have been different, and how Mattaus will hear about this. The news, the discovery of his telephone, will make a world of trouble for him – which should certainly make him run.

Today, he remembers, he has arranged to go swimming. Tomas and Rike are taking a picnic to Lady's Mile.

11.6

They meet on the sea front. Rike has a backpack with a swimming costume, a swimming cap, and a towel. She's ready for everything, she says. Tomas is in his hire car which stinks now of carpet cleaner. He unwinds the windows because the smell bothers him, already his throat feels thick and the heat threatens a headache. Like he isn't tired enough anyway. The bay's long swoop can be seen from the front. You can literally see where you're going. He points this out to Rike as she ducks into the car. Something about her, as always, comes across as fresh and welcoming, if a little pathetic. Rike lumbers the backpack onto the back seat and explains she's packed a towel and the costume, of course, but also some treats, out of habit, ginger beer, and mentioning it she turns a little red, her cheeks gain colour – because this is childish, or it's something she did when she was a child? He can't decide. She has suntan lotion, factor 50 if they need it, although how strong is the sun anyway at this time of year? She has rum in a small bottle. She has wipes. She has insect repellent, although, apart from wasps, there really isn't much to worry about. She didn't tell her sister, she explains, just said she was going on her own to the beach at Amathus. She'd only have ideas if she knew, and Isa's humour can be fierce. She doesn't know, really, how aggressive she appears to other people sometimes.

They were here the other day, but on the other side of the perimeter, so to speak, on the British base, and one man had caught an octopus, told them also there were moray eels, a ray of some kind. The man's face had shone as he described the sighting, one week before. A ray with a wingspan of say, one metre, one and a half, mottled brown and black, and white underneath. It moved, the man said, only the tips of its wings. Funny word that, giving a creature wings under water.

There were also pottery shards to collect, and he'd brought them up. Pieces of amphora, most of them pinkish and curved and softened by their time underwater, some encrusted with white snail-like trails. A few pieces displayed how antique they were, the mouths of the jars, the double handles. Ships taken in storms? Perhaps even run aground. The island ends in a stub, and from that stub runs a sharp shelf, so that the sea bed drops from two metres to seven.

They drive out of Limassol, by the castle keep at Kolossi, the air a kind of blanket, folds of heat. After the castle, the refugee camp, bunkers in long rows, then suddenly lines of trees, behind them citrus orchards. Rike closes her eyes, and Tomas watches, and wonders if anyone has ever been so relaxed about him. If this was so he couldn't remember. Rike holds her arm out to the breeze and suggests that they stop. When they came by here the other day they'd passed a shop, all on its own, which sold fruit and souvenirs. There were baskets out front, hanging from the awning, and she'd liked the look of it but they hadn't time to stop.

At the next crossroads they come to the store.

The line of trees remind him of New Hampshire – it's a little unguarded he realizes to give an actual location. Remote, you know, completely out in the woods, and he was cycling along a path and felt something above him, a bird, right at the tree tops overtaking then flying just ahead, broad wing span, bigger than his outstretched arms. This bird, this hawk or something – are hawks even that large? – but there at some height, ahead, following the same path.

'I heard it.' He locks the car doors once they are out. 'I could hear it when I was working, but this one time I could see it.'

Rike, ahead of him, smiling also.

They buy baskets and fill them with oranges and grapefruit. Rike decides that these will be gifts for people in her building. She hasn't met them yet and feels that it is about time to say hello, see who everyone is.

'I've decided not to worry,' she announces, walking between the bins of fruit. The grapes look good, tight bunches, sweet, fat, still a little dusty. 'I'm not going to worry about Mattaus. He's big enough to look after himself. I'm not responsible. I'm not going to worry about what happens after the summer.' She leans forward. 'I've even been thinking I might stay. I could find a place of my own and I could teach. I don't think it's what I want to do, but it will buy me time until I can decide.'

Heading south now they cut through the groves and the orchards. Of a sudden they give way, the treeline stops, the groves stop, and give abruptly to a savage white plate. They both squint at the salt flats. The fierce brightness sparks about them, the sky peeled a flat burnished blue, an impossible colour. Tomas pushes back his sunglasses, takes the soft curve of the road, which somehow seems to be a kind of expression, a leaning glide, and Rike smiles without reserve. This is, she says, incredible.

'Isn't this something?' she asks him, sincere and insistent. 'Really something to see.'

The sea lies on either side of the salt flat; a drying lake with a fine furred pink line. Rike explains about the flamingos, repeats Henning's facts, which again are questions about the birds and how surprising it is that of all places they should end up here.

The heat draws a wind off the gulf, and as they drive Rike is grateful for the cooler air.

*

On the beach she lugs the backpack in both arms insisting that Tomas doesn't need to help. She kneels as she unpacks it, happy with the job. The sand is fine, with no wind to disturb it. Tomas looks about but there's no shade. While it's warm, there isn't any real heat to the sun. A loose line of people sit and face the sea. Some stand at the shoreline, hands on hips, and look out at a bare horizon.

The first thing she finds in the backpack is a book, a thin hardback without a cover. She holds it up and says that Isa must have slipped it in. 'I deliberately didn't pack it.' After a quick search she finds only the food and drinks she had packed herself.

He watches her read. Is too tired to think it through. It never occurs to him, although he notices how her head gives a small jolt – nothing more than a pulse, a beat, a kind of double-take. She sits more upright, turns the pages, looks through, flicks ahead, and at each page seems more confused.

He asks *what is it*, and she answers *nothing*. She doesn't, and this is noticeable, look up. Not once.

And then he realizes. She's reading Finn Cullman's book.

The change in mood is significant. He can't quite describe the difference, but he can read the register – she scowls hard at the paper. It's the same day, no doubt about it, the same blue sky front and back, the same stretch of sea, calm and placid. The same flat plate of white land, of sand a good mile or so on either side. But Rike has hardened.

He never imagined that he would be present when it happened.

When he swims she doesn't join him. She tilts her book and looks up, appears to examine him.

Ten metres out and he can still stand with the water level at his chest. He tastes salt, remembers how pleasurable it is to swim in the sea, and how surprising it is to be so buoyant. It's a good temperature, a good colour. Rike, back on the beach, knees raised, together, book slanted down, head up and looking out, her expression still one of concern.

Tomas turns away from the land, swims at a steady pace directly out, with Limassol on his left, the beach immediately behind him. He wants to know exactly what is disturbing her, *which element gave him away?* He can't understand her stillness. He draws thirty strokes in one burst, but still, when he stops, finds the sea no deeper, only Rike is smaller. He bounces on his toes and looks up. It isn't Rike he's looking at. In fact, there isn't anyone directly in front of him.

He steadies himself in the water, allows his legs to fall back and floats on his stomach facing the land, a slight strain to keep his head upright, consciously drawing in breath. She isn't on the beach, not directly in front of him.

Tomas takes a few strokes back, he keeps the pace deliberately slow. How, here, and at this point, could anything go wrong?

She isn't in the water either. Looking away, toward the military base, he doesn't see her. But further down the beach, where the umbrellas start, he thinks he sees her, but isn't entirely sure. There's a girl, what looks to be a girl, further up, speaking with a family, and yes, she appears to have a backpack.

He swims back now, faster, but not hurried. He walks out at a stride. His clothes are still folded beside his towel, and where Rike sat are the contents of the backpack, set carefully aside.

With his towel over his shoulder he walks toward the umbrellas. The first group, two adults, two children, appear to be in a hurry. A woman with big sunglasses, a canary-yellow swimming costume, pink shoulders and thighs, glowers in Tomas's direction as she walks away. Rike steps quickly over the sand, *not* looking at him. The woman, Rike, and two boys make a slightly chaotic path to the line of cars parked on the shoulder of the beach.

As Tomas draws nearer they break into a run, in response he starts to jog. The mother opens the doors, and throws her bags into the trunk. They have left their umbrella tilted in the sand. Tomas reaches it, nothing but sand and footprints.

When he reaches the car the woman is pushing her children inside and telling them to hurry.

'She doesn't want to speak with you. You better stay where you are.'

Rike, in the back seat, sits with her head bent forward, a penitent, a doubter, her hair covering her face. She isn't dressed either, is still in her swimsuit, he can see her shoulders. She won't look up.

'I'm serious. You don't come any closer!'

Tomas stands in front of the car.

'Rike? Rike?'

'Just keep where you are.' The woman holds the driver's door open, as if this is an adequate shield.

'Rike. Can you get out of the car?' Tomas steadies his voice to sound reasoned, in control, as if this is something that has happened to them before. As if this is some kind of episode. 'I need to take her home.' He smiles at the woman, a wan and patient smile. A man who has suffered because his girlfriend, his wife, his sister is irrational. And now a softer, cajoling, 'Rike, are you coming with me?'

'I said, stay where you are.'

'Rike?' Tomas slaps his hands to his side, draws his towel from his shoulder. As he walks to the side of the car, Rike instinctively turns away.

The woman, now seated, starts the motor and as she reverses, clumsy and unsteady, he can see an element of panic. Tomas can touch the car. He tries to open the door, but the car is moving, the door is locked. The two children, one in the back seat beside Rike, the other in the front, both look at him, both uncertain of what is happening. As the car lurches forward and begins to pick up pace, Rike looks at him, a long and low look, a face so sucked of joy that as he runs after the car, he's certain that she has discovered that everything he has told her is a lie. Everything is stolen. This realization, right at this moment, must be blossoming within her. Who is Tomas Berens? She has to be thinking this. Why has he done this?

He watches the car round the salt lake. Small and silver, shimmering. He starts running as it joins the road and heads toward the green bank of cypresses, almost gone. Of all the scenarios he's worked through, none were this complicated. Tomas looks to the town. This wasn't supposed to happen until after he'd left.

A man walks into a desert. He walks for four days, maybe five if he carries or comes across water. He's found by an archaeological team. The man is unrecognizable. He looks like scabbed raw meat. His head, his hands and arms alive with flies.

He isn't dead, which is somehow more shocking. And he resists being helped. They haul him into a jeep. No one wants to sit beside him. And the man, who has made no movement, makes it clear that he wants to get out of his clothes. The skin on his chest and back is a sore crimson, but not broken, not erupted, unlike the fully exposed skin. Under his pants, right at the buckle, there's a line where the red immediately cools, and the body becomes human again and can't be compared to meat, or a crust, or something infernal.

The archaeologists aren't naive, and they understand how suffering doesn't compare to anything else. It is exactly what this is: a person reduced to animal function.

11.7

Rike asks to be brought into town. Once away from the beach she's embarrassed about her reaction. The woman, Sarah, says that she will take her home, or to a police station. She advises Rike to talk to the police.

'That man was harassing you, and you should report it.' She senses Rike's reticence. 'Look, it was you today, and you got away. The next one might not be so lucky.'

Rike agrees, feels a little shame over the story she'd told to the woman. *That man is bothering me. He won't leave me alone.* Given the circumstances she's not happy about lying, but how else to explain this?

She promises that she will speak with someone. Promises. But insists on being let out as soon as they reach Limassol waterfront.

Rike waves goodbye to the children then hurries from the car, slips down a pedestrian street busy with tourist trade, the tables of carved wood goods, T-shirts, place mats, bangles, and finds a café where she can look again at the book – because this is crazy, this hasn't happened. Somehow she has this all wrong. She sits in the café and marks up passages with a pencil. At each page the discoveries are familiar and deeply unsettling. Rike sits with the book and reads. She doesn't like to have the book in her hands, doesn't like to read, line for line, the stories Berens has passed as his own. It helps that the book isn't very good. She can justifiably dislike it on these grounds. It's an effort to sit with it, a conscious effort.

It doesn't take much to find the material. The discoveries are so immediate she begins to think there's something a little dumb about the whole thing. It's just plagiarism, that's all this is. Petty theft.

Not clever. Not at all.

She returns to find the apartment empty and a note from Henning with a mobile number she doesn't recognize. The note is simple. *Isa is in hospital. It isn't serious. It is a precaution.* She calls the mobile number and speaks with Henning.

'How serious is this?'

'It's nothing. They're just being careful.' He's with Isa right now and she's laughing. He probably shouldn't be on his mobile.

Rike says she'll come directly to the hospital.

Henning tells her not to worry. 'They have her on a stretcher,' he says. 'She's behaving as if she's lying on a sunbed. This is just a precaution. It really isn't that serious.'

Rike asks what the problem is.

'She had a little bleeding. It's nothing serious.'

They've heard news about Mattaus. He'll speak with her when he gets back.

Rike can hear the medics telling Isa to breathe slowly.

'I'm coming,' she says. 'I'll be there as soon as I can.'

Henning doesn't discourage her, and asks if she could bring Isa's overnight bag. It looks like they'll want to keep her in overnight.

Rike takes a taxi. Grateful for a little time to digest what's happening. Baby. Mattaus. Tomas. And while she's spared an excruciating discussion with her sister (what did I tell you about the man? What did I say? The minute I heard the story about the dog, *I knew*), she's mortified by the possibility that the situation, with an unborn child, has shifted into territory none of them want to revisit. While she's recently felt secure in the fact that she's hit bedrock, that things couldn't get worse, she's beginning to realize that this isn't the case. Things can always get worse. Even now the situation is unstable, worse could be about to happen. She concentrates on the immediate moment and focuses on arriving at the hospital. She sits in the front passenger seat and ignores the driver as he tries to be polite.

'Nothing serious', the hospital advises. Henning comes out of Isa's cubicle. It's what they call *spotting*, he says, scratching his head. Which both is and isn't unusual at this point depending on who you speak with. It's only a problem if it doesn't stop. To be on the safe side they want to keep her under observation. It's a little unexpected but they've told him not to worry. He doesn't know what any of this means. Doesn't know either how long they will keep her. He's never heard of *spotting* before, nor how long it might continue? An hour? A day? Until the baby is born? He's called Udo, because Udo wants to speak with him about Mattaus, and because Udo needs to know what is happening. If Rike could do him a favour and keep Udo busy, just for the moment. The information from the doctors can only be described as random.

Hands clasped, Rike makes a deal that she will suffer any kind of indignity just as long as the baby is OK. Just this one thing. I'll never ask for anything else.

Henning summarizes for Rike. She needs to catch up. 'Mattaus has disappeared.' He drops facts. Is clumsy with them. Her brother's name rings with accusation. As if he's the cause of this trouble with Isa.

'Rike. There has been an accident. Last night a man fell from a balcony at the Miramar.' He allows Rike to digest the information. 'OK? The man who fell was Mattaus's boyfriend. They found Mattaus's phone in the same room. They've only just traced it.'

Rike isn't sure how to take this. She wants to know what happened to Mattaus's boyfriend.

'You brought that book?' Henning asks, as if this is insensitive. Another connection to Mattaus they just don't need. Rike holds it up as if she intends to read it out loud or swear an oath. 'The man fell seven floors. He hit the poolside.'

Rike looks at the book and says, 'Oh.'

Rike isn't allowed to speak with Isa, every time she approaches the booth curtains are drawn and she is asked to wait. After an hour Isa is moved to a private room with brisk efficient fuss. Nurses surround the trolley and Rike can't see her sister, just bare feet, just hair. If she could see Isa she would know how serious this is. *It's just a little spotting. She needs a little rest.* Unconvincing platitudes and little theories. A little bed rest at the worst of times. Rike repeats her deal: let the baby be OK. If anything bad needs to happen, let it happen to me.

She starts to add clauses when Udo arrives. Anything can happen as long as the baby *and Isa* are OK. OK means no complications. OK means everything returns to how it was *pre*-spotting. Assuming that everything was OK then, and this isn't the result of some condition, of some other trouble. If she thinks about it Rike isn't sure what *OK* means. Baby. Isa. Mattaus. Lexi. None of these people are OK. Tomas Berens, most certainly, is not OK.

Udo confronts Henning, Rike can't prevent him. He wants to know more about Mattaus's dealings with the Russians. Rike is asked to move away; instead she sits down close by. She can't believe he would challenge Henning at this time, in this place. The conversation is taken to a corner. Once Udo stops haranguing, almost shouting, with bad and tight gestures, they both become silent and appear to sulk. Udo recaps the information. Fills in the blanks.

'Were they a couple?'

'I think so. They haven't known each other long.'

'How long is *not long*?'

Henning looks to Rike for support and they both agree that *not long* possibly means two months, maybe even a little longer. They barter dates, slowly admit to the facts as they understand them. Is this really the right time? Rike wants to take the man aside, push him down some stairs.

Udo makes a show about counting the weeks. Fingers out.

Henning crosses his arms and clenches his fists. 'It's not that long.'

How could this be worse for Henning? A pregnancy – so close to the due date – concluding with *spotting*, an errant brother-in-law, and now a manager who wields immeasurable influence over his future. Henning doesn't deserve to be cornered like this. Add Tomas to this mess. Tomas is a falling piano, a random surprise from the sky. Just when you need it.

'And how long have you known?'

'Saturday. He came to dinner and told us, and since then he hasn't been in touch. Look. I can't think about this now.'

The men stand with their arms folded, mouths pursed. Rike sits and faces the corridor, waits for news about Isa. Hasn't she expected this? Wasn't this, more or less, what she fretted about? And while she couldn't have anticipated the accompanying troubles (Mattaus. Tomas. Lexi), didn't she always know something would go wrong? Udo, though, there's no accounting for Udo's lack of timing and tact.

She knows enough not to say anything. Not even a hint.

Instead they wait for news, with an occasional expression from Udo. 'You don't tell me this – I had no idea? I find out now?'

Henning, summoned by a doctor, leaves Rike with Udo. As he walks away the doctor talks. If the baby is in distress they will induce. The situation isn't so serious, he advises (an arm now on Henning's shoulder), he just wants Henning to understand the possibilities. To be prepared to make choices. These aren't little things any more.

Udo wants to talk. Rike can't think about an unborn child in distress. Can't imagine what this really means. She doesn't like the organized quiet of the waiting room. She doesn't like the word *spotting*. Instead it's easier to focus on Udo.

Rike opens the conversation by saying she hopes Henning returns soon with news – and adds: 'So what happened with – what was his name?' She can't look at the man. 'What happened with the Russian? How did he fall?'

Udo answers so slowly he blinks between words. 'We don't properly know.'

This isn't unusual. Udo explains. Drunk guests (Brits, almost always), convinced by the proximity of the pool to their balcony, take the plunge and commit themselves either to death or a lifetime of feeding tubes and bed baths. There's actually a procedure for closing off the pool and drawing the blinds in the bar and reception every time this happens, it's that frequent.

Udo draws an expression which implies that this a little tiresome. It's happened a good number of times. It isn't unusual.

'So it's not exactly *suspicious*, then?'

Udo again makes the same broad-mouthed shrug that says this is of interest, he supposes, but little concern. 'If your brother hadn't disappeared, then this would all be dealt with. It would be over. It's the *connection* we have to worry about.'

'I don't know what that means?'

'It means we have to find him.'

'It won't be hard. He's no criminal. He'll be clueless.' Rike tucks her hands under her thighs. It isn't that she doesn't trust herself, but the idea that she would like to slap Udo – not particularly hard – is growing louder in volume. 'Is he in serious trouble?'

'He ran away from an incident, which is a criminal offence. Yes, it's serious. Until we know what happened more clearly it's very serious.'

'But, is it? Technically, you don't know if he's run away or not. You only know his phone was in the room.'

'We need to speak with him.' Udo can't help but sneer. It isn't that this is idiocy, this sneer suggests, just pedantic conjecture. He attempts to be polite. 'You're teaching? Henning said.'

'I was,' she gives a deliberate, insincere smile, 'but I'm going to quit. My student has been lying to me.' She likes saying this to him, just to open up the spite. She's quitting because it's all too complicated. She's had enough. Lying is such a masculine weakness. It didn't work out with Tomas Berens, so she isn't going to make any effort.

'Lying?' Udo wipes a finger across his upper lip. He isn't particularly listening.

She holds out the book. 'Telling me stories from this book. Like they were his stories.'

'Good stories?'

'Lies.'

'When did you last see your brother?'

'The same time as Henning. The same meal.' Rike wants to explain about the book, she'd like to speak with someone about Tomas (not Henning, certainly not Isa) without automatically sparking an argument. It might help to work through what has happened. 'Mattaus gave me this book.'

'Sorry?'

'Mattaus. He said he recognized the name of the man I'm teaching. And then he arranged for someone to give me this book. Yesterday, so I think he must still be in Cyprus.'

Udo makes a droll double-take. 'You didn't see him – but he gave you the book?'

'He had someone deliver it to me. A boy. Russian. I think a friend of his . . .' She can't figure out the word, not *partner*, not *boyfriend*. How close an association did Mattaus have with Lexi? 'I was so angry I wouldn't take it from him. So the boy delivered it to Isa. He took it to the apartment.'

'The club manager? The man who fell?'

'No. A boy. A young boy. He said he had to deliver the book right into my hands.'

Udo wants to see the book. Now he wants to hear the story. 'So Mattaus knows this man?'

'Who? My student? I doubt that he knows him. He said he recognized the name.'

She tells him what has happened. Gives short details: the jealous Christos, the doctor, the doctor's son. The speech-therapist mother. This is what she's found so far. Borrowings, situations, and histories. At first, as an overall idea, it doesn't sound unusual. She set assignments for the man and he stole the material and used it as his own. These are the facts. What's really so terrible? But that he achieved this in such a bare-faced way starts to sound unhinged. He didn't even bother to invent anything, he just changed the location.

'That's what I don't understand. I think he expected me to find out.'

With unexpected insight, Udo hits another problem. *Did he believe these stories? Did he believe what he was telling her?*

The answer is yes. It has to be. But even so, the basic act is wrong – because stories are good, aren't they? Stories are how we connect. Evolution isn't seriously about thumbs but about how we use language – that's what raises us above dumb animals, right? Language? There's something Rike just isn't getting. While every other student wants to connect, Tomas wanted to misconnect. Deceive.

Rike understands that everything is beginning to sound rehearsed.

Udo flicks through the pages, cocks his head when he finds an underlined passage. 'He said that, about the coffee? *It always tastes better*?' He holds his finger to the page.

'Word for word.' And again, she asks herself, why? To what end? 'There's probably more. I can't bear to read it.'

'And what did Henning say?'

'He's had enough going on, don't you think?'

Udo, out of niceness, she can't think of another reason, asks if she wants him to check this out.

'I can talk with him. Find out what's going on.'

'Oh god no. I don't want to cause trouble.' Does he think she's asking for help? The situation offers unending possibilities for humiliation. 'I just want to forget this. Honestly.'

'Grooming,' he says. 'He was grooming you.' Then looking up. 'It's a technique the Stasi used. If you can't intimidate someone, if it's not possible or appropriate, then you befriend them. You give information which isn't yours, so they know nothing about you.'

Now he thinks she's stupid. 'I know plenty about him.' Rike doesn't like how defensive she's sounding.

'You take a story from somewhere else and use it as your own. This way you give a consistent idea, something formed. It's harder to detect if you are lying. It's a quick way to gain someone's confidence when you want information.'

This is ridiculous. 'What do I know?'

'What did you talk about?'

'We talked about his neighbours. The other people who lived in his building.'

'That's what he talked about. But what did you talk about?'

'I taught him English.'

Udo waves his hand as if this is probably nothing. He'll visit Tomas Berens. See for himself. 'I'll take Henning. We'll go see this man.'

She asks him not to take Henning, the whole thing has been embarrassing enough. The idea makes her cringe, sending her brother-in-law, in whatever capacity, to check up on a man who has cheated on his homework (if that's even what you'd call it) just feels juvenile. She can't think of any aspect of this event which hasn't been grindingly humiliating. He hasn't broken any law, and there isn't any requirement that a student should tell the truth to their tutor. If she thinks about it, the idea that students always tell the truth is a little ridiculous. How many times has she listened, kept herself attentive to the turgid details of an unremarkable life: where people come from, their families, their schools, their childhoods; thousands of unremarkable facts traded as confidences, which seldom hold interest or meaning? Tomas Berens took stories out in the public domain. Stuff to be used. *Grooming?* To what purpose?

She wants to know why. Didn't he lay the ground first with those banalities, all of that detail about his neighbours? Didn't he soften her up first?

Udo takes the book and says that he will read it first.

With Isa in hospital the apartment is much too empty. She hankers for Isa's company, finds the hospital visits unsatisfactory. Yearns to see the black cat, even briefly, but there's nothing in the garden except fallen fruit, a few scattered lemons.

She takes a phone call from Henning, who hands her over to Udo.

They want to know if Berens made any threats.

'Threats?'

'Did he say anything which sounded inappropriate? Anything at all?'

'He just spoke about the people in the apartments. Then about his assault. All of those stories from the book.'

There's an inordinate number of drugs in his apartment. Did she know anything about this?

'Drugs?'

'Medication. Anti-depressants. Anti-psychotics.'

She knows nothing about this.

Did he say anything about the man in hospital? The man from Syria?

Rike rests her hand on her heart and feels it thumping. She has to think before she answers, not because she doesn't know the answer, but because the answer will be complex. If she says *yes*, then she is admitting to being indiscreet. And hasn't she already caused Henning enough trouble? Isn't her family bothersome enough?

'Did he mention the man in the hospital?'

She says yes.

Udo is quiet and she has to ask why this matters.

'I'd better come and speak with you.'

'What does he say?'

'He isn't here.'

11.8

She finds the boy poolside at the Del Mare not the Miramar. Sunlight bounces off the pool, so bright she shies away. Sol stretches across a lounger, wears his sunglasses, and a pair of briefs – a posing pouch – with a picture of a kitten on the front. The kitten is cute, nestled in a ball, big saucer eyes, just adorable, and ridiculous ears. She can't see why a young man would want to wear something so absurd, so girlish. He turns again to find a comfortable position, and she can see, printed across the seat in a pretty italic script, the words 'kitty kat'.

She watches him for a short while. With earphones and a small player he likes to stand over the pool and look out at the sea. There's a ring of winsome mothers in the shallow end who are less shy about staring at him than their daughters. But he looks bored, and she imagines it can't be much fun sitting in the sun, with the pool, the interested mothers, the distant daughters, the uppity staff, and the very pissed-off pool boy (who isn't getting any attention while Sol takes the boards). What he needs is company, other boys, it's wrong to see a young man so isolated.

She decides to speak to him. The honest truth is that she isn't entirely sure what to ask him, but has a notion that he can help resolve some of the confusion. Perhaps she means to apologize?

The boy returns to his lounger and lies back. Rike, with her bag over her shoulder, comes tentatively forward and clears her throat.

'I don't mean to interrupt.'

She isn't prepared for his reaction. The boy is alarmed to see her, and he immediately sits up on his elbows.

Rike gestures to the sunbed beside him and she sits side on. The straps on her shoulder bag stroke down her legs as the bag softens at her feet.

'I need to speak with my brother.'

Sol shuffles up, and searches for a towel, a little too naked perhaps for a conversation about brothers.

'I can't speak with you.'

Surprised by his reaction, Rike repeats her question. She just wants to know where her brother is.

'I can't help you.'

'He hasn't been in touch. I just need to speak with him.'

The boy looks hard at her for a moment. 'We shouldn't be talking.'

Rike asks why. 'He's my brother. I need to speak with him. You might know where he is?'

'You seriously haven't heard?'

'I told you he hasn't been in touch.'

Sol shakes his head and she thinks he looks frightened. 'No one knows where he is. He's disappeared.'

'I'm sorry about the manager. Lexi.'

The boy looks away.

'I really don't think Mattaus had anything to do with it. I think it was an accident.'

Sol now looks very confused. Rike thinks he has more to say. She looks to the pool, notes the pattern where water has splashed along the stone side. She asks why he isn't in the Miramar, and Sol automatically looks up at the rising ranks of balconies.

'The book.' Rike changes the subject. 'I looked at the book.' She holds her hand to her chest, then to her brows. 'I really need to know where Mattaus is. It would help to know when you last saw him. Nobody knows where he is.'

Kolya's arrival isn't best timed. Sol sees him from across the pool. The man strides out from the shadow of the lobby, shorts on, sandals going clap, clap, clap, looking mean and nasty with his newly shaved head (the skin whiter on his head than his face and neck), a monster tattoo of a dragon clambers up his back, she sees this as he twists about to make his way through the tables and chairs, one claw stuck into his belly, another to his thigh, two others dug into his shoulder. The tail coils around his leg – the claws look like they puncture his skin. It's a crazy tattoo, the thing is scrambling over his body. Compared to the crudity of the blue-black scribbles on his arms, this is fine art.

Kolya clocks onto Rike immediately. His head twists inquisitively as he changes direction and speed as if he's expecting her to make a dash.

'Just pretend you're from the hotel.'

Rike doesn't hear him.

'The hotel. Just pretend. You're a guest.'

As Kolya rounds the near corner of the pool he's suddenly all smiles, all charm and delight.

'Hey.' Sol stands up. 'I was just heading in.' He directs this to Kolya, then turning to Rike says he hopes she has a nice stay, perhaps they can talk tomorrow?

'Sure.' Rike holds up her hand, like she might wave. 'Tomorrow.'

Kolya wraps his arm about Sol's shoulder. 'You call those shorts? You walk about in public like this?' He tells the boy to go inside, hands him a key and then speaks to him in Russian. Sol indicates Rike, a small hand gesture, and Kolya asks Rike directly why she is bothering the boy. He knows nothing, and given what has happened, he doesn't want the boy involved. 'We cannot talk with you. We can't help.'

Rike says she's sorry, but she doesn't understand what this is about.

And here Sol steps forward. 'He called me. Before he fell. He asked me to tell your brother that he should run. That he was in trouble. That someone was after him.'

Kolya holds up his hand and tells Sol to be quiet. Rike should go.

'Why?' she asks the boy directly.

'I don't know.'

'Where was he?'

'He was staying here. He's gone now. He left as soon as I spoke with him. I don't know where he's gone.'

Kolya again instructs the boy to be quiet.

'He needs to tell this to the police.'

Kolya says no. The boy is not involved. Whatever trouble her brother is in, Sol has nothing to do with. 'He can't help you.'

11.9

Udo comes to the apartment on his own. Henning, he says, is with the manager and the boy from the nightclub but they aren't getting any information. The boy won't even confirm what he told Rike earlier. He wants to speak about the other matter, Tomas Berens. He'd like to go through everything Berens has told her, everything she might have said to him. Anything that might seem particularly odd to her now. Udo tells her: *You are the stories you tell, whatever their basis in fact or experience.* It's who you are. This sounds like Isa, truthful and banal. Once she can understand Tomas Berens, she can let him go.

What did she tell him? 'Are there any discussions which stand out? Things which at the time were peculiar?'

Rike honestly can't remember. In hindsight she just feels stupid about everything. The story about the assault is perhaps the most ridiculous element.

'What did he tell you?' Udo insists on detail.

It's hard to remember specific conversations, all of that stuff about his neighbours.

Udo is definite. 'What did you talk about? Try to remember.'

He needs to explain, she asks, how this matters. 'What difference will it make?'

Udo holds his breath, as if he needs to say something, but wants to spare her. 'We have nothing except for the stories. His apartment is close to the hospital. Henning thinks this is relevant. It could be a coincidence, but I doubt it.'

This isn't so bad, she thinks. Surely? This can be explained. And what about the medication?

'He won't explain what he's doing here.' The medication the man was supposed to be taking is unbelievable. She should have seen it. The quantity. The bathroom had every anti-psychotic you could imagine. All suppressants of one form or another. The man isn't well.

'It's all attributable.' Udo is insistent. It will all come from some-where. He won't be completely making it up because that takes time and creativity he just doesn't have.' The books are his source. Perhaps, on some level, he wants you to know how clever he is. He wants the shape of this deception to be discovered. He wants to be acknowl-edged.

Udo lays out the possibilities. 'This is what we think we know. The man is suffering some kind of breakdown. It's possible he's here because he's fixated on the man they discovered in the desert.' He asks again, 'Is there anything he's said which makes either or both of these seem likely? Is there anything you might have said which could have encouraged him?'

Rike stands at the window and looks for a while to the patio. She should shower, freshen up, put this aside and take a break. He wasn't well. Didn't he admit to that?

'There's no record of a family, the Berens, in Bergen.'

'So where is he? Is he dangerous?'

'I doubt it.' Udo doesn't think the man is dangerous, just delusional.

Rike lets the water fall hard on her scalp, turns under it, twists the head so that the stream becomes sharper and more focused. The pressure penetrates, at least preoccupies her so she can focus only on the water, the heat. She doesn't want to think of Tomas, and cannot believe that he is disturbed in any way.

When Rike and Henning visit they find Isa sat up in bed, flowers on the table, flowers beside the bedside. Isa asks Rike if it's too funereal. 'I mean, seriously, look.'

Rike holds back at the door, and Isa asks why she's looking at her like that. She can't bear how kind they've become. Everyone is being overly nice.

'Hen.' Isa purses her hands, as if in prayer. 'Would you give us a moment?'

Isa is seldom this serious. Henning holds up his hands in surrender. 'Let me know when you're done.'

'I'll let you know.'

Rike asks what's wrong. Isa gathers papers from the side unit. 'The boy who came to fix the washing machine—'

'Shit-the-bed?'

'Right. Little Mr Shit-the-bed. They think he's the one shooting the cats.'

'They know? Or they think?'

Isa closes her eyes and softly rubs her eyelids. 'That's not what I wanted to talk about.'

Here it comes.

'Henning and I. Actually, it doesn't have anything to do with Henning. I think. Not right now. But after the baby comes. I think you should start thinking about leaving Cyprus. This isn't what it sounds like. I just don't think you should stay here. I don't think it's healthy. I think you should make a new start. We can still keep looking for Mattaus. We aren't giving up. You can still be involved.' She reaches for Rike's hand. 'Rike. I'm worried about you. I don't think it's healthy to stay here.'

Rike sits back and folds her arms.

'Do you hate me?'

'I don't hate you.'

'But you don't like me much right now?' Isa shifts her weight awkwardly in the bed. 'I know what you're thinking. You're thinking that nobody wants you to be happy. That everything is working against you. I just want you to have a fresh start.' Isa pauses and purses her lips. 'He's sick. I don't think you can blame him either. He's a clever man who is also very sick. He's a fantasist who thinks he's more powerful than he is. This is all about power. He finds stuff in the real world and insinuates himself into it. Telling stories to make himself into something that he isn't. We all do it. We all tell stories to make ourselves look better.'

Rike looks at the books and papers spread out across the bed.

'Let it go.'

She finds her brother, or thinks this is her brother, online, in a video posted by *MFP*, a short piece, 'Hotel, Hotel', in which different couples repeatedly check in under the same name. The quality is poor, the pixels vibrate so that the image shudders, drops colour. Light fuzzes unevenly across the faces, stretches them into blades, and behind there's one man at a table – right beside the reception. It's the hunch, the way he leans on a table, the whole forearm flat to the table top so he's leaning in, that makes her think *Mattaus* even before she properly reads the image: a reception, a receptionist, a couple, a table behind. First – a man whose face, whose body language, might or might not be her brother's. The scene changes, flickers to another foyer, and again, the same scene replaying, the same four couples, with a title in the right-hand corner which names the hotel and place. Hotel Mons, Troodos. The Ziggurat, Limassol. Hotel 5, Ayia Napa. Hotel Montparnasse, Nicosia. Four couples check in, one after another, under the same name.

Henning and Isa haven't spoken to her about Mattaus. While they talk about Lexi's accident and the associated dangers of 'a certain kind of lifestyle', Mattaus, as a subject of discussion, is studiously avoided. Officially, Mattaus Falsen remains a *person of interest*. His flight, they assume, is one of panic. Rike senses that she has always misread her brother. Always looked for trouble, and regarded him with mistrust.

How could it happen? One minute someone is right there, the next,

they've tipped over a low balcony. No one heard it. To Rike the sudden-
ness, in how she imagines this, is profoundly saddening. Poor Mattaus.
Poor, poor Mattaus. This will haunt him. This will eat him alive.

Rike replays the clip from the beginning. It seems more degraded
the second time, holds just enough information to show a hunched
figure at a table. Those shoulders, the outline of the head. He would
wear a jacket, it's exactly what he would do, even though the brightness of the images shows how hot it must be. He's in Troodos, she
thinks. She hopes. He's up in the mountains, and when he's ready, he'll
do what he always does. He'll show up and face whatever is coming to
him.

Henning brings Rike a glass of wine to her bedroom. She closes the
computer. Isn't ready to talk about this.

'Stay as long as you like.' Henning bows down as he sets the glass
beside her. There's no hurry. Once Henning is gone Rike returns to the
computer, looks again at the clip and finds herself frustrated at how
long it takes to reboot. She watches again, then again, this man who
might be her brother. The figure is no clearer, and she is sometimes
certain, at other times she cringes away from certainty.

The fact is she sees him frequently. Elements of him. Out in the
street these small sightings, familiar as a scent.

RIKE

12.1

Rike calls her sister on her mobile. Isa has news. It was an accident, she says, a slip where the nurse said *she.* 'We have to be careful,' it started, 'if *she* is in distress . . .'

'It's a girl,' she says, 'I knew it. I'm going to have a daughter.'

While the issue doesn't matter to Rike she's moved to hear the news, because the event is now inevitable, impending.

Isa asks if she's still there.

'I'm here.'

'It's happening.' She's at that point where they need to make a decision. Her blood pressure hasn't levelled, the child is in distress. They want to induce, and if this fails to draw on labour there will be a caesarean. The doctors have carefully explained the risks. 'It's because of last time,' she says. Everything otherwise is in good shape. Ordinarily they wouldn't worry. Except for last time.

Isa isn't frightened over what might go wrong. 'I could never say this to Henning, but what frightens me is what happens when everything works out? What if she is fine? What happens then? What if she hates me? What if we don't get along? What if she is hateful? Wicked?'

'You love her.' Rike answers. Her phone beeps, the power is low. She promises to visit Isa in an hour. Nothing will happen before then.

'We have a name.'

'Tell me when I'm there.'

Rike returns to Tomas's building in the early afternoon. The decision, she knows, is foolish, but she wants to see the building, perhaps even the apartment.

The balcony doors are open, but there's no sign otherwise that anyone is inside.

The name Christos on the brass tag, scratched through because he doesn't live there, and hasn't lived there for two years. Tomas picked the name up, dressed it with someone else's story, and delivered it to her, almost verbatim. His notebooks show word for word preparation.

The door is open and she walks in, cautious. The room is different. Busier, unkempt. One suitcase, open, clothes strewn across the floor, still no furniture. She's surprised not to find a bed, just a thin rubber mat, a sheet, a pillow and a blanket. The kitchen door stands open to show a similar chaos. What once appeared simple and well kept now appears squalid.

Back in the stairwell she hurries down the stairs, at the entrance she notices that the door to the basement is open. Tomas had spoken about the basement, this was the most absurd story of all, more bizarre than the story about his assault. Two brothers. A bloody room. And hadn't he said that he was helping Christos, the man who hasn't lived here for two years?

She comes down the stairs and into a corridor with a low ceiling. To her right, just ahead, she can see an open door. She regrets the decision to look as soon as she acts on it. Looking sets her on a certain path.

Inside the room, Tomas Berens lies on a cot. A strip of light falls from the corridor over his forehead. His hair is dyed dark, freshly cut. His face appears rounder, less distinguished – it could be someone else, and she thinks to apologize for her interruption before realizing that this is Tomas.

He doesn't appear surprised. He sits up, as if tired, and asks if she is with anyone else.

Rike says no, and can't understand why she's being polite.

'I can imagine that you're confused.' His voice has a transatlantic undertone. His body also, in its basic movements, appears confident, he's lost that tight Scandinavian reserve. At least this is how she reads it.

Rike can't help but step into the room. 'What are you doing?'

Tomas has cleared the stored promotion and advertising material – a heap of plastic penguins, stuffed plastic bags – to the back wall. The room is unbearably hot and smells of sweat, spiced and sour. 'What is this?'

Berens rises, and comes slowly forward. He looks to Rike, the cot, the water. Steps into the corridor and then closes the door.

Hands up Rike traces the sides of the door searching for a handle and finds nothing. The darkness is absolute, unbroken. There's no sound other than her breathing, her heartbeat, the pressure increasing in her ears.

She beats at the door, shouts, struggles for breath and sits down, dizzy.

*

She wakes to find Tomas over her, and immediately recoils. The light is unbearably bright. He has brought ice, he says. This will help. She has been sweating, her hair is matted to her forehead, her clothes twisted so that she can't move comfortably. As she rolls from her stomach to her back her head throbs, her tongue feels thick in her mouth. She can't quite make sense of what he's saying.

There are things which make no sense to her, memories from a long time back. A woman changing out of her bathing costume on a beach, and the way she holds the string of the costume aside with a little disbelief. This is what? Punta Sabbione, nineteen-what? Another, more specific, climbing worn steps to a belfry. It's Köln cathedral, and the wall opens suddenly to a view of the square. The market below, the slabbed court. Her father had reached out to secure her, but held his hand flat, as if to push. A shocking thing, to stand so close to an edge, to have your father's hand thrust forward, as if to shove. And did she properly trust him after that?

Tomas beside her: Rike shielding her eyes, trying nevertheless to calculate the distance between Tomas and the door. Her legs are so heavy there's no point making the attempt. She tells herself not to sleep. Next time. However long, she needs to be ready.

The door makes a suck as it closes and in a matter of minutes the heat overwhelms her.

When she wakes she reaches out, finds the metal bowl, and the ice melted but the water still cold, which could be three hours, perhaps. She can't judge. Holds her wrist to her face to see if she can tell the time. The darkness is so complete, so thorough her arm could be a kilometre from her face, or centimetres. As long as she is lying on the cot she has an instrument to place herself in the space.

Her body reacts badly to the heat, she feels sick, her head aches. She attempts to rationalize these sensations, and fights against a rising squabble of panic and fear.

The room has been prepared. A bed. Water. But no commode. She can't judge if this is deliberate or opportunistic. Would he have brought her here if she hadn't come? Does he intend this to be short, as in hours, or long, as in days? Is this some kind of punishment?

When he returns she will tell him that she is diabetic. That there are certain requirements, problems, details he hasn't accounted for. She will not ask why this is happening.

12.2

It's a whole different thing being inside the house after observing it from outside, from the shell of the hotel. For one thing it's smaller, and what seemed to be clean and ordered is actually battered. This is rented accommodation, other people have lived here, and they remain in some way, through scuffs on the walls and scratches on the floor. There is a history of use.

He's not keen on how everything is placed. The sofa faces the garden, cuts the room in half. It's uncaring in the way things don't fit. It isn't lived in. It isn't accommodating either for Tomas – chairs block the exits.

Neither is it personable. Two photographs mounted in the same frame are the only personal element. Relatives, he supposes, people from another century who have a vague wash of history, a little startled awe in their slightly open mouths, their black eyes.

Isa is still in hospital.

Tomas collects towels from the house. Two tea towels, a striped beach towel, a small blanket with an Air France logo. He places these aside with a roll of duct tape. Under the kitchen sink he finds a black bin bag and two clear plastic shopping bags.

When Henning returns he makes no attempt to sound an alarm. He sits where he is told, and hands Tomas his phone without comment. Tomas explains that Henning shouldn't waste time thinking over what he needs to do.

'Rike is safe. I need information about the man in hospital. Do you know who he is?'

Henning remains composed, dignified.

'I want to know who he is. Is he Sutler?'

'No.'

'You're certain.'

'I'm certain.'

Tomas nods in agreement.

'Who is he?'

'We don't know.'

Tomas leans forward with his elbows on his knees. 'Who do you think he is?'

Henning shakes his head. 'I don't know who he is.'

'How certain are you he isn't Sutler?'

'Absolutely certain. He's Caucasian, between forty-five and fifty. He might be too old to be Sutler. He has had a procedure on his upper inner arm to remove a tattoo. There is no mention of Sutler having a tattoo. Within the past month he has had replacement fillings in his front teeth and a front crown, this would have happened while Sutler was already in Iraq.' Henning's voice thins and dries. He pauses to wet his lips, looks to the window. Calculating. 'We're almost certain that he has lived in Europe. He meets the profile of most contractors. There is trafficking along the Syrian border. It is possible he is involved, which would explain why no one has come forward. Why are you here? Where is Rike?'

Tomas ignores the questions. He can see Henning thinking, can trace the calculations. Henning understands the economy of their discussion: the values, the costs, exactly what is at stake.

'What do you need to release her?'

Tomas again refuses to answer.

'Why are you interested in Stephen Sutler?'

Tomas allows a small pause. 'What did you discuss with Parson when you met him in Istanbul?'

'It doesn't matter.'

'What did you talk about?'

'It's pointless now. It's redundant. It doesn't matter.' Henning closes his eyes and runs a hand hard across his forehead. 'The man we have in hospital won't live. He has an infection we can't control, and respiratory problems. He isn't responding to the drugs. It no longer matters who he is. None of this matters any more.'

'What did you discuss?'

'I told him that Sutler was a fiction. It was my belief that HOSCO invented Sutler, they either invented him, or they used someone. Sutler is a scapegoat.' Henning clears his throat. 'None of this matters. Paul Geezler, the man who reorganized HOSCO in the Middle East, is missing. No one has any idea where he is. He was in New Mexico. He is missing. No one has heard from him. Whatever this was about, it's over. Sutler is gone. Geezler is gone. Parson is dead. The company is now refigured as something else. It's all redundant. Whatever point this had – it doesn't matter any more.'

Tomas takes the African staff from the coffee table and strikes Henning with a horizontal swipe. The force runs through his wrist, so that the staff rebounds, almost bounces free from his grip. The first blow is intentionally savage. There is no backward step, no going back. After the first blow Tomas is committed. He swoops the staff overhand and draws it down, this time on Henning, knocked to the floor, hands either side, not in defence, but ready to push himself upright.

Tomas washes his hands at the sink. Douses water over the back of his neck. Does not look at the mess in the room behind him. The pathway from the bed to the hall. His knuckles are cut, he has no idea how this has happened, and does not want to clean the staff nor the room but understands this to be necessary.

12.3

Rike wakes to the smallest slice of light coming through the doorframe, and then the door opens with a blinding wall of light. She shields her eyes with her arms, attempts to stand but finds this impossible. He strikes once: hits the side of her head and her raised right forearm. He is on her immediately. Rike, stunned, lies immobile. Plastic is pulled over her head, and tape binds the bag about her throat. He does this three times, then drops her and leaves.

In the darkness Rike struggles to upright herself. She bites and struggles with the plastic, pokes a hole so she can breathe, then loses herself to panic until she is weak and breathless.

This isn't happening.

She wants to understand how this started, to unthread a sequence and understand the origin, because everything has a start, a place where what is happening is set in motion. She can take it back to Parson at the trackside, running, hectic, perhaps hopeful in those last moments of escape, steps ahead of the train, perhaps in panic with the knowledge that he cannot possibly outrun what is coming. Or earlier, to Henning and Parson in Istanbul with no notion of what lies ahead. Earlier still, to Sutler in his multiple guises, proto-Sutler, the first Sutler arriving in Iraq as a contractor. Is this the start? A man eager for a contract to work in the desert, or does she need to go back further to the company who hired the man, accepted his bid, or further still, should she consider the military who required that company for operational support, food, weapons, shelter, because without them they cannot function? Is this the proper start, here with these men, these boys, who have trained specifically for this kind of endeavour, but who would otherwise never have left their country if it wasn't for a year or so of threats, of provocations, of governments shouldering into each other? Does she take it back to here? Or further? Back to those buildings? Back to those planes? Back to that city and that early workday morning? Does she need to retreat this far? If this far then why not further, because what she is finding is that there is no single starting point, only multiple threads which appear to bind because of distance, but only ever run parallel?

At every point, how clear this seems to her, there appears to have been a choice, and most often the choice that has been exercised is a choice to do harm.

She knows this is too simple. As she understands that what is happening isn't history. Not in any way which matters.

Either: one of us, or both of us.

He will come back. She is certain. The door closes fast by itself. She will wait by the door, and when he returns he will come into the room and she will shut the door, even if she has to remain inside, because there needs to be an end.

Acknowledgements

With gratitude to:
Kris Doyle, Paul Baggaley, Tony Peake,
Lynne Tillman, Anne Bentley, Jeff Black, Travis Garth,
Chris Rose, Nathalie de Sant Phalle, Eva Orner,
Luke Kennard, Cristiana Ligouri.

Video & audio:
Elsa Braekkan Payne, Drew Conrad, Sugi Ganeshananthan,
Bill Goldstein, Nam Le, Oliver Mason, Mary Medlin,
Adam Sims, Sian Thomas.

These books were generously supported by fellowships from
the Corporation of Yaddo, Saratoga Springs, NY, and
The MacDowell Colony, Peterborough, NH,
and with grants from
the Arts Council, England, and
the Arts & Humanities Research Council, UK.

About the Author

RICHARD HOUSE is a writer, artist, filmmaker, and teacher. He is the author of two short dark novels, *Bruiser* and *Uninvited*, published by Ira Silverberg in the Serpent's Tail High Risk series. He is a member of the Chicago-based collaborative Haha, whose work has appeared at the New Museum, New York; the Museum of Contemporary Art, Chicago; and the Venice Biennale. He teaches at the University of Birmingham, and is the editor of *Fatboy Review*, a digital literary magazine.